THE MATRIARCH MESSIAH

MAXIME TRENCAVEL

Copyright © 2025 by Tail of the Bird Books
All rights reserved.
978-0-9993350-5-5 Ebook
978-0-9993350-6-2 Paperback

Library of Congress Control Number: 2024927276
Edition 1.1.0.0
Published by Tail of the Bird Books, Larchmont
https://www.tailofthebird.com/

Please visit our website for behind-the-scenes background, historical comments, and more.

À la mémoire de ma défunte mère.
Puisse-t-elle avoir atteint la paix de la lumière bleue.

❧

In memory of my late mother.
May she have reached the peace of the blue light.

PREFACE

I completed the manuscript for *The Matriarch Messiah* in 2018, which went through developmental and copy editing throughout 2019. However, as I was incorporating recommendations from the copy editor, the world plunged into unprecedented chaos. The greatest global pandemic since the Spanish Flu. Millions upon millions of deaths, followed by years of social and political upheaval around the world. The near final manuscript sat in cloud drive for nearly five years untouched. Therefore, this story, created in 2018, set five years in the future, 2023, reflects the geopolitical realities of seven years before the publication of this sequel to *The Matriarch Matrix*.

After the tragedies of October 2023 and the resulting suffering, I struggled with whether to publish this epic tale out of concerns for potential misunderstandings from readers regarding my respect and intentions toward different cultures and faiths portrayed in this sequel. The story introduces a new pivotal character named Rachel, an Israeli Torah historian and archaeologist who plays a crucial role in solving the mythical elements of this sequel. The story juxtaposes her culture and faith with those of Zara, the devout Islamic Kurdish protagonist from *The Matriarch Matrix*, and a minor Palestinian character. In 2018 and 2019, Jewish and Muslim beta readers provided feedback that both cultures and religions were treated respectfully and with dignity. I hope that in 2025 and beyond, readers will find the same.

The premise of this story revolves around two devout women of seemingly different faiths, cultures, and family pressures—Zara and Rachel—who must overcome their disparities and come together to save humanity. Both follow a matriarchal lineage that believes in an ancient prophecy about a cavern of blue light: "*Women would return to save humanity, bringing peace from the blue light. But to return, one must overcome one's fear of death. Two women will fight so that one will die. For only in the death of life as one knows it can one be in the light.*"

Other characters in *The Matriarch Messiah* also face clashes of culture, religious beliefs, and family expectations on their quest to help find the cavern of blue light. And just like our protagonists, they too must confront their inner demons and learn to trust one another for the world to be saved. Their journey serves as a reminder that we must all strive away from dark, destructive stereotypes and strive toward mutual understanding to achieve peaceful coexistence.

Similar to *The Matriarch Matrix*, this story also features a parallel storyline about pre-Neolithic ancients whose chapters serve as parables to explain the origins of customs, faiths, and disharmonies in our modern world. The premise is that ancient societies' oral traditions, spanning tens of thousands of years, form the basis of many of our current beliefs. The story's ancient barbarities mirror the documented atrocities faced by the Kurds, like Zara and her family, over the past decades and beyond, highlighting "humanity's unchanging dark nature.

I hope readers will embrace the wisdom spoken by one of the pivotal ancient characters from 9525 BCE, Illyana:

"For a better future, we must let go of hate and violence from the past."

May this book inspire us all to strive toward a peaceful future in a world that is rapidly heading in the opposite direction.

PART I

Be wary of the reindeer warrior giants, for when they arrive, you must flee. Follow the vision and words of the black object as you seek safety in your new land.
The object you might see in your sleep, you might hear. But only as man and woman. The object can destroy. The object can save. But only as man and woman together may you guide the salvation of others.

Nanshe, the great matriarch, 9600 BCE

PROLOGUE

Theirs not to reason why,
Theirs but to do and die.
Into the valley of Death…

—Alfred, Lord Tennyson

German-Occupied Crimea
1944 CE

Irony is a poem handed to us by a dark god. So his mother has told him every day since her husband, his father, left for the Eastern Front, where millions of German soldiers have died already.

Irony was why his mother told him that. As he was her only child, she had to tell him what her grandmother had said to tell only her granddaughter.

Irony was why Nikolas was born male—a gender not endowed with the verbal abstraction to make sense of what his mother has told him to memorize. "Someday, her daughter would return. Two women will fight for the light. One must die. For only in the death of life can one be in the chamber of the blue light." Nevertheless, she said that these legendary phrases might one day save his life.

Two months after turning sixteen, Nikolas Gollinger mulled over his mother's last words to him before he took the train from Austria to Odessa, then a boat to Sevastopol, to join his father, Professor Gollinger, and the German paranormal research unit he'd voluntarily joined.

Now, as the Russian troops close in on the last Germans defending this odd peninsula jutting into the Black Sea, the lanky blond Nikolas waits in an oak grove near the hidden mouth of a cave for the return of the stout, black-haired Kemel Ghurdzi, a native from the local Jewish community, the Crimean Krymchaks. The distinct smells of gunpowder and blood waft through the air around them.

Like Nikolas, Ghurdzi suffers dreams of an ancient torment. Like Nikolas, Ghurdzi's male lineage has passed along an oral tradition of an ancient mystery. And like Nikolas, Ghurdzi has been taught by his father that life is, first and foremost, a chance to solve the mystery.

The oral tradition passed down from dream-afflicted father to dream-afflicted son talks of an ancient star falling to Earth, enslaving giants of the north, the bright star in the Cygnus constellation, and a black object that will save the world—but only if the destined man and woman find the object together.

Every Gollinger man dedicates his life to solving the mystery of the all-powerful black object. And thus, Ghurdzi pleaded, part of the mystery could be solved if he could enter this cavern before the Russians retook Crimea: the reason why Nikolas now waits for this Crimean Krymchak outside these secret caverns hidden in an ancient forest where he once took Ghurdzi's wife.

A half hour passes as Nikolas paces back and forth, wearing a new trail into the ground before he lets out a juicy curse in German, one his mother would not approve of. He had brought Gurdzhi's wife here, helping her flee the Russians, when she warned no man should enter. At risk he dies here by Russian bullets or dies inside, he enters the cavern to find Ghurdzi, to find the truth of the mystery. Minutes into the cavern, Nikolas's torchlight illuminates ancient skeletons. All male, from the tilt of the pelvic bones. All signs that men were not to survive the trip into this cave, just as Ghurdzi's wife said. His breathing slows as he notes these bones belong to men over three meters tall; Nikolas's first hard proof of the ancient oral traditions.

The narrowing sandstone-lined cavern shakes with thunderous booms, dropping bits of sand onto his head. Nikolas waffles between going back outside and descending further to get Ghurdzi. Why did he say he had special permission to enter when all other men died? More booms rock the cavern. But the skeletons, evidence of the giants of the legend, compel him to brave death to find out the truth.

One would think the air would be only stale. Perhaps with a tinge of the dank, dark smell of death, given these skeletons. But from further down the passageway comes a different smell. Like the air after it rains. Like the first morning of spring after a long, cold winter. It is the smell of life, and it calls him to descend further.

His nose plays tricks on him, then his eyes do the same. A blue glint? Or is he going blind in these endless passageways? He turns off his lamp, and a tiny glint of blue shimmers from another symbol on the wall. A bull's head. Didn't Dr. Murometz, the Russian physician working with his father, wear a pendant with a similar bull's head?

Blue. The color of the light in that chamber his mother described. He must keep going. For his mother. For every Gollinger who has tried to solve the legend.

He descends further, and his torch illuminates another engraving on the wall. The tail of the bird star, the brightest star in the Cygnus constellation, same as the legend says. He takes out paper and pencil and traces the inscription, written in a language no longer known. A dozen more twists and turns, or was that three dozen? Nikolas is lost as he comes back full circle to the tail of the bird star on the wall. Ghurdzi better still be alive, or Nikolas's mother's last words to him were truly the last.

In the distance, he hears a woman's faint voice. She says Ghurdzi's wife must spread the word to her daughters. Must tell the woman's side of the story. That he must sacrifice all so that these teachings can be passed to their children. Ghurdzi's voice says, "I believe in the light. I believe in you. I will not fail you. She will return to you. She will. But you must trust what I ask."

A bright blue flash blinds Nikolas. Before his eyes fully recover, Ghurdzi emerges, skin crispy and burnt, shirt off, wrapped around something glowing blue. The Jewish Krymchak says they must protect this blue stone at all costs.

Hanging from his neck is a pendant built around a small black stone, one of a pair Ghurdzi's wife brought out of these caverns when Nikolas stopped here with her, helping her escape the impending Russian onslaught.

Nikolas asks who he was talking with. Ghurdzi says the same who gave his wife the essence of the sacred-gene-activating vaccine Dr. Murometz injected them all with three months ago.

Emerging from the darkness comes an elder woman in a long beige robe that covers her body, neck to ankles, head covered by a pure white headscarf. She ignores Ghurdzi, addressing only Nikolas, who is holding the injured Krymchak. "Men are forbidden in here. Why should I spare you the fate of your friend who dared intrude upon our sanctuary?"

As Ghurdzi's oozing burns begin to seep onto Nikolas's clothing, the young Austrian's mind races. Knowing he has only moments to save his life or become one of those male skeletons, he blurts out, "Because my mother sent me to say that one day, the daughter would return here. That only in the death of life as one knows it can one be in the chamber of the blue light."

Glancing at him, she puts her hand on his forehead. A blue aura emanates from the juncture, a color Nikolas prays is not the beginning of scorching pain.

She says, "Your mother is wise. You must leave and raise children with a woman of purity like us. Teach your descendants as well as your mother did you. For one of them will help the right woman return to the chamber of the blue light. You will know which one. Tell no one but your child, their child, and only after they have known the truest love of their other half."

Thankful for his mother's wisdom, thankful for his life, Nikolas now faces too many twists and turns to remember as Ghurdzi describes how to leave the cave. When finally they emerge back onto the main trail, they find the SS outside with machine guns pointed at Ghurdzi.

Dr. Murometz has his hands up as the SS commander says he is a traitorous spy playing doctor among the German ranks. Nikolas's father, Professor Gollinger, stands behind the SS soldiers in a German Ahnenerbe uniform, his machine gun aimed at Dr. Murometz as well.

The SS commander says to Ghurdzi, "Hand over what is in your hands.

It belongs only to the Aryan race. We have been searching for the past year for this holy stone from Orion. As described in the logbooks of a Russian researcher which we confiscated from Dr. Murometz, it transmits the cosmic energy Herr Himmler has long searched for."

With a look of resignation, the destined-to-be-executed Jewish Crimean freedom fighter tosses the blue aura stone to the ground. The SS commander picks it up, inspects it, and then drops it, his hands crisped. Howling curses in German, the red-faced SS commander shoots Ghurdzi. Once, twice, thrice in the chest as Nikolas cries out, "No, no! He is innocent."

An artillery shell explodes nearby, and dirt pellets and rocks shower them. While the SS soldiers are distracted, using their hands to protect their heads, Professor Gollinger guns them down, an act of betrayal if the SS command finds out he killed them to save a Russian.

Nikolas kneels to Ghurdzi, hearing his dying words. "My given first name is Ya'akov. Only my wife knows that. Take this stone pendant and return it to my Ariella. Only the destined man and woman can reenter the grotto in the cavern. Only with these can they both navigate the pathway through the caverns."

No time for Nikolas to mourn the dead, as Russian soldiers are heard. Dr. Murometz says, "They will not like Austrians any better than Germans. You must flee or be captured."

Nikolas cries out, "But how are we going to hide the blue stone from the Russians?"

With a smile, Dr. Murometz says to the professor, "You can run away and live, or die with this rock of no significance."

The Russian doctor takes Professor Gollinger's gun, shakes his hand, and says, "May God bless our children and our grandchildren with the genetics to finish this."

Paralyzed, Nikolas wants to tell this doctor what he heard in the caverns, but his father grabs his hand to flee into the forest.

The Russian soldiers enter the grove from the woods, astonished to find this physician scientist with a smoking submachine gun surrounded by a dozen dead SS soldiers. The senior officer says, "You will be a hero of the

Motherland. Stalin will reward you handsomely."

Around the doctor's neck, an in-field medal for the Defense of the Caucasus is hung. It dangles next to another pendant. A bull's head.

CHAPTER 1

O my Lord, the stars glitter
and the eyes of men are closed.
Kings have locked their doors
and each lover is alone with his love.
Here, I am alone with you.

—Rabi'a al-Adawiyya,
eighth-century Persian philosopher and mystic

Skyline Boulevard above Silicon Valley, California
7:15 a.m. GMT-8, January 2, 2023

She never realized it would be this long. She never, never thought she would be holding his, his…his thing. Yes, she has seen one before. But it enchanted her. It called to her, as it seemed to purr in her two hands.

This moment is exactly what he has been waiting for since they first touched. And finally, here she is with him. Outdoors in his redwood forests, amidst his mountains. He referred to a game children play. I'll show you mine if you show me yours.

Zara squeezes his dearest thing gently so and says, "Like a ripe banana with a brownish tinge and little reddish spots."

As the two gaze down at the seven-inch-long banana slug wiggling in

Zara's hands, wisps of drifting white fluffy fog float by, swarming the majestic redwood giants in the grove they have found by this mountain crest drive overlooking the San Francisco Bay.

Peter had been such a dear. Zara had mentioned how much she missed the mountains of her childhood in Duhok Province in Iraq. And so, he suggested they spend time in the mountains of his childhood. It was time for her to know what drove his fondness for these yellow creatures.

As Peter draws his fingers lightly across his beloved banana slug, they land upon Zara's fingers. And her finger purrs as much as the slug does.

Six months ago, she was about to leave Peter at his grandfather Nikolas's grave. She had completed the mission her "Sasha" Murometz had coerced her into—the search for the black object of the ancient matriarch. As she was leaving the cemetery, Peter surprised her as he went back to pray at his grandfather Pappy's grave.

The man-boy, who'd believed in aliens over God when she had met him, found solace in praying. Not because his mother told him to do so. Not because she would have wanted him to do so. But because he had an inner calling. At that moment, she had thought maybe, just maybe, he would be different from any other man who had sought her love.

As Peter touches her banana slug earrings, Zara responds by rubbing her scarred cheek against his hand, wondering if he truly is the one her late great-grandmother said he was. A drop of dew from the giant redwood above them lands on her nose. She puts her nose upon his to wipe the drop, followed by a light, affectionate peck on his lips.

"This means so much to me," whispers Peter in her ear. "You being here with me so early in the morning—the most likely time to catch banana slugs slithering out to bathe in the mists. Most women wouldn't dream of doing this."

Another dewdrop forms on the brow of Zara's dark plum headscarf from the dampness of the passing fog drifts. She passes the wiggling object of Peter's second fascination back to him so she can brush the dew off her headscarf before it lands in the eye of Peter's first fascination. Her.

"So, am I to assume an outing into the cold damp woods before sunrise is not your typical first date?" muses Zara.

"First date, huh? We are so far beyond first date, aren't we? Only the women who count in my life come here," asserts Peter as he puts his treasured yellow friend back onto the forest floor matted with fern leaves and redwood twigs and needles.

"My father took my mother, my sister, and me up here on family outings," says Peter. "I fell in love with these denizens of the Pacific coastal forests. They are so peaceful. They hurt no one."

Glancing toward the road, Peter looked at the broad trunks of the surrounding redwoods. "Except if someone hits them as they cross the road. No one would be driving so fast out here at this time of morning."

But her eyes do not gaze upon that road. They do not disrupt the deepest mutual intimacy he has shared—his beloved banana slugs in his most sacred place on Earth. In this regard, she realizes he is like her, as she has a sacred place on her mountain back at her childhood home. A flattop rock next to the twisting trail where her beloved father would take her hiking. The place where she found her greatest peace. That is, until she met Peter.

Her grandmother Roza said peace comes from tolerance. The root of tolerance is mutual understanding. His communing in these woods with his yellow mollusk friends is his source of deep mysticism. No different from her Roza's father's Sufi twirling dance. Both ways to understand Xwedê's world and be closer to Her.

Hence why she made the long journey from the Anatolian Kurdish State to California many times since his pappy's funeral—the culmination of their two-month mission together searching for the mythical black object of his family's legends. There is more to this man than his odd demeanor would portray. His composure, his placid eyes gazing in unity with nature remind her so much of her father on her mountain back home. Perhaps he really is a man seeking the Divine. Like her. Like what her mother had with her father. *We shall see*, she thinks.

Her serene moment is interrupted as Peter challenges, "So, I showed you mine." He brushes a dewdrop from her nose as they make eye contact again. "Time for you to show me yours."

Having grown up on the other side of the world, both geographically and culturally, from this man who now asks her to show him something most intimate of her inner being, Zara purses her lips, unsure what he is truly seeking in her. Their several-month relationship has already transcended the physical, the emotional, the limits of what she has had with previous boyfriends. What could he have not already seen in her given their ancient ability to spiritually bond?

She tugs on her headscarf more tightly to her head. Shelter from the cold fog? Shielding her most intimate thoughts from this man? Or simply an instinctive subconscious action?

She turns her back to him, facing the redwoods. The negative-ion-charged Pacific air passes so quietly as it flows through these monolithic beings. Ones who have seen a millennium pass. Ones whose family has seen the passage of time since the ancients. Seen the mysteries of the ancients. Like the mystery she and Peter saw because of their genetic descendancy from the ancient matriarch Nanshe's family. Through their solving the mystery of Nanshe's words passed from generation to generation.

The words that Peter's pappy, Nikolas, had made him memorize. The words that her Sasha knew would lead to an ancient monolith, the black object. Known to the rest of the world as Alexander Murometz, her malevolent Sasha had built the world's most powerful and politically invasive private enterprise so he would have access to the resources needed to find this object. The black object that spawned Zara's prophecies; this stone could destroy the world. And this silly man in front of her outfoxed, outargued, outwitted the most politically manipulative man in the world, her Sasha, to prevent Turkey, the US, China, and Russia from starting a world war.

Another dewdrop hits her nose. But this time, she does not wipe it off as it mingles with the drops from her eyes while she searches inside for the strength to remember that which remains unresolved in her life, with her family, with her destiny. Is he really the one? Should she reveal what should only be revealed to the one man who will bring her to her destiny?

A purse of her lips and she finally says, "Sara, my great-grandmother, she was our link to the wisdom of generations of spiritually inspired women before her."

Still facing away from Peter, she says, "Sara liked you. She saw something in you when she first met you at that first dinner at her ancestral house when we were staging for our mission to retrieve the object."

Turning back to him, she says, "Sara said to my grandmother Roza, her daughter, that you harbor the same light her husband, a Sufi imam, my great-grandfather, had within him when they first met."

She points to his eyes. Blue ones which naturally go with his once-blond and now-sandy-brown hair. Sara said the light is blue. The light we should seek is blue. The world thinks the light is white. But the one we seek, we yearn for, we die for, is blue. She so feared dying before she could find the blue light. For in the blue light, we shall return, she said.

Peter, who knows so much trivia because he is an editor of all sorts of topics, papers, and books, is speechless until he finally mutters, "Blue? Where did that come from? I'm not getting the connection to the mystery of the ancient matriarch we solved."

"As you had with your grandfather, your pappy, who entrusted you with an ancient family oral tradition, passed from mouth to mouth, from generation to generation, as far back in time as that temple, the world's oldest temple, which our follies led to be destroyed, so there is a line of similar wisdom passed down in my family line. But through the women. Mother to daughter and to granddaughter."

She sucks in her cheeks, then continues. "I had always thought the wisdom originally came from Rabi'a al-Adawiyya, the saintly woman whose beliefs inspired the Sufi faith. A woman who dedicated her life to the love of God, of Xwedê. The woman who, since I stopped working as Sasha's mercenary, I have strived to emulate. But after meeting you, meeting Jean-Paul, whose research says these oral traditions come from an age twelve thousand ago, I can only wonder if I should tell you of the other side of the story that they missed."

Eyes cast aside for a moment, she says, "That ancient pendant hanging from Jean-Paul's neck next to his crucifix, portraying a woman praying to God who had a worm next to her, is thousands of years old. When Jean-Paul stated that worm was in fact an image of your beloved banana slug, he shook my spiritual paradigms. The ancient text next to the carving said in proto-Greek, 'And she hears the voice of God.' This ancient woman with two halves of an apple standing next to a spotted banana slug became my clear sign from Xwedê to unite with my other half so I could speak with God."

Alone in this ancient grove, she pecks his lips and says, "Who would have thought that a pendant would foretell a five-thousand-year-old prophecy of our relationship?"

A peck on her forehead back, and Peter says, "Imagine if you hadn't realized our meeting had been prophesied? You wouldn't have bonded with me in the ways of the ancient matriarch. We wouldn't have found the black object, which gave you the ability to hear the voice. Her. Who you believe is Xwedê. All because of an image of my friends here. My banana slugs."

Her eyes close as she thanks the voice for guiding her openness to ultimately allow the spiritual intimacies with him she would never otherwise have permitted. Intimacies that conflicted with her traditions of modesty. Same as she chose to wear a headscarf out of respect for her family's traditions, her modesty, she chose celibacy as her path forward. That is, before meeting Peter.

She exhales long and deeply and turns to face her other half now. She unbuttons the top of her jacket and then the top of her shirt, spying Peter's eyes glued to her shirt top as she pipes back, "Showing you 'mine' does not mean that."

With a light scoff, he smiles and retorts, "That coming from a woman who sleeps with me every night we have been together. For the months since we found that our bonding accessed the powers of that black object that empowered you to talk with Her."

He runs his finger lightly along her long earlobe and adds, "And how many men do you know who could go through the intimacies of the night next to you, under the bedsheets with you, and not look or touch?"

She moves closer to him. Pecks his lips lightly. "You do look, you do touch the nakedness of my bared soul, as I do yours. This intimacy, far more revealing than physical intimacy, is our gift for touching the object and from the genetics that the ancient matriarch left for us."

Head canted slightly down, she gives him a playful, lascivious smile. "If you must see my chest, you can look now."

Out from under her shirt, she pulls out a slim gold chain with a pendant.

An ancient stone emblem. A circle atop a crescent. "My mother thought you the man the prophecies spoke of, and she first entrusted this family heirloom to you. A secret they had not even shared with me. And to my surprise, you fulfilled their expectations. And mine, by giving this back to me."

She rubs the pendant, kisses it, then puts it up to his lips. "After the blast that destroyed the object and knocked you out, I left you in that hospital in Rome only because my great-grandmother Sara was near death. I made it back only hours before she left us. She could no longer speak. In her hands, she held a parchment I was to have, or so she told my mother. Mama said her last words before she lost the ability to speak were that I must carry on with what this parchment said. I took her hands in mine and cried and cried."

Turning away from him again, she adds, "I do not know why I keep coming back. We are so different. Night and day. Dogs and cats. Goats and sheep."

With a quick flip back toward the impetuous Peter, she adds, "But I have no one else to turn to. I do not understand what my great-grandmother has asked me to do. From the visions we had when we touched in that special way near the object, you and I are like the reincarnations of the ancient matriarch and her husband. Sasha, Mei, and Jean-Paul all said we are the two people on Earth who have DNA most closely resembling the ancient matriarch and her husband. In that, you are like my husband. The one my Sara said I should turn to. The one whose dreams, whose visions could shed light on what I need to do."

He makes a fist and lightly taps her chest below her neck. "That is more of a tease than pretending to strip off your shirt. But I'll take it. I'm your ancient husband who will wait at your side, will support you, and will be there when you are ready for someone more than a husband-like brother."

Tapping the tip of her nose again, he then reaches for their gear on the ground and pulls out her prayer mat.

Tucking her family's pendant safely under her shirt, she glances at her MoxWrap around her wrist, the never-needs-charging, nearly cost-free device that provides 12G data from anywhere in the world where a satellite connection can be made. It's the omni device that propelled MoxWorld Holdings into the dominant global digital platform company.

Zara says, "I almost forgot. Sunrise. You know I appreciate your respect for my traditions, my faith." She pulls her headscarf again around her neck and loosens her jacket so she can supplicate in prayer.

Handing her a gallon jug of spring water, Peter says, "For your purification."

Following her faith's wudu ritual, she washes three times each her hands, then mouth, nostrils, face, lower arms, head, ears, and feet in that specific order.

After she finishes reciting the du'as, a specific invocation, Peter points across to the road. "That way is Mecca, no?" He kneels, clearing a place among the redwood twigs and fern leaves matting the forest floor to place her prayer mat.

She watches as his hands gently move along his beloved slug friends who dine on the forest flora. She now feels it, understands it. His serenity in his grove. His deep meditation here. Not on the mollusks, but his deep connection to something more transcendent. She was right at the cemetery. He is a man of prayer. But a prayer of his own derivation. He does not wear his faith on the outside.

Zara loosens her jacket a bit to bend in prayer. "Peter, you do not have to pray with me to show your respect for me." She glances around at the banana slugs moving through the leaves. "I see in here your place of worship. You pray in your own way. And I respect that."

Patting the place on the mat next to him, Peter replies, "I do so because I want to. You said to me you wanted to follow the path of Rabi'a al-Adawiyya, the saintly woman whose beliefs inspired the Sufi faith. What she is to you, I hope you will be to me. The saintly woman who helps me come closer to submission to God. To Xwedê. Only you can hear Her voice. And I will follow what you hear Her say."

With one eyebrow dipping down, she asks, "And you do this because She is an alien? When we met, you believed that aliens created all religions."

His head down in submission, he meekly replies, "By definition, She is not from this earthly domain. But since you and I have joined spiritually, I know now that She is not ET or Spock or other media manifestations of aliens."

And with that attestation, they pray together. Man and woman as the prophecy of the ancient originators had foretold.

CHAPTER 2

Knowing your own darkness is the best method for dealing with the darknesses of other people.

—Carl Jung

Skyline Boulevard above Silicon Valley, California
7:35 a.m. GMT-8, January 2, 2023

Prayer completed, Zara rises to roll up her mat. She rubs her foot through her boot as Peter intently stares. "Still find my feet arousing, do you?" she says, staring back.

"You'll never let me live that down. The first time you caught me staring at your feet on the plane ride to Kurdistan to find Alexander's object. You didn't seem to mind so much after you found out what a wicked foot massage I can give."

"Now is not the time or place for one, but my feet. I have spent years in military boots fighting Saddam with the Peshmerga, then Assad, and then the Daesh with the YPJ," laments Zara. "I do not understand why they hurt now. These boots you bought me are the exact size I used to wear. My feet must have grown soft."

A tender moment, literally for her feet and figuratively for their relationship. Her vulnerabilities exposed, and yet she still feels safe. A feeling of safety with a male she only ever truly experienced with her father and brother.

Her eyes scanned the misty redwood tops as she inhaled deeply, a sense of calm washing over her. But as she turned to face him, her gaze was met with his expectant eyes. She struggled to find the words, torn between the confidence she had promised and what her heart was telling her.

"What you professed earlier, it was more than I could have hoped for," she finally spoke, trying to find the right balance between honesty and respect for tradition.

His eyes glance down at his slithering slugs. "Your grandmother Roza always said I needed to give you space to grow into the saintly woman you were meant to be. I didn't want to push you about your great-grandmother Sara's last words. I know it's something you need to share on your own terms."

She took another deep breath, her eyes too lingering on his cherished yellow mollusks. "Sara would have thought your professed love and submission for Her words were a sign for me to tell you more about the parchment. It's something that has been passed down through the women in my family, but I trust you enough to share it with you. I have no one else to turn to for help."

A single tear rolled down her cheek, a mix of emotions causing it to fall. He gently brushed it away before taking her hand in his.

"In her final moments, I rubbed my tears on her hand and she miraculously spoke. 'Seek the light. Blue light. She awaits you.'"

He held her in a warm embrace, one that reminded her of her father's and made her feel safe and loved. "What did the parchment say?" he whispers in her ear.

She looked down, a sad smile forming on her lips. "I don't know for sure. Sara waited decades before showing it to my great-grandfather, who said it was an ancient form of pre-Kurdish."

"Why haven't you asked Jean-Paul? With his expertise in ancient languages and biblical archaeology, he should have been able to decipher it."

"It's something that was only meant to be shared between a woman and her husband if absolutely necessary, after years of marriage and children," she explains.

He let out a small snort. "And I'm assuming you're sharing it with me now because I qualify for that 'H' word? Your mother certainly thinks so. Just say the word and we can move on to the next phase of our relationship."

She playfully punched him in the chest. "You should be grateful that I come back as often as I do. You know I cannot be rushed, especially not anymore."

The intimacy of the moment was broken by loud noises, like crunching and snapping, followed by a woman's screams from the nearby road. The runner in Peter comes out as he springs up as if he were in the Olympic hundred-meter dash, racing to the road to aid those in need. But when he gets there, he screams, "Oh my God. The poor slugs."

By the time Zara catches up to him, her ancient genetic husband is helping a cyclist, a Lycra-fleece-clad woman, off the ground. Her carbon fiber bike is shattered in many places. A couple meters up the road, she sees Peter's friends, or what is left of them, smeared across the road. This woman hit and slid through a herd of banana slugs trying to slither across the daunting damp descent.

A curdling scream from the other direction. The type of cry she heard all too many times in the battlefields of Iraq and Syria. Three meters downhill, another cyclist, a man in a bright yellow Lycra jacket with a torn left sleeve, shrieks in torturous pain. The type of scream she heard when one of her soldiers took a bullet to the abdomen. The type of scream her Ezidi cousin, Rona, let out as the Daesh, who had held them as slaves, mercilessly violated both of them.

The woman trying to untangle herself from her trashed bike tells Peter to help her fiancé first. Zara hears tires at high-speed coming around the corner from them. As the lights of the oncoming car come into view, Peter, like the rabbit caught in the headlights, bolts up. Faster than Zara has ever seen him move, he dashes in front of the oncoming car, shielding the screaming rider on the ground, waving his jacket as a signal flag.

The charging red Mini Cooper suddenly slides diagonally across the road, smashing into the grey steel railings meant to prevent vehicles from rolling down the mountain toward the San Francisco Bay.

Zara yells to Peter, "Check the driver of the car. I have the screaming guy covered." Her in-field combat medical training comes into play as she determines the wailing guy has dislocated his shoulder and likely has a broken wrist along with a good deal of road rash lacerations.

Peter assists the Mini Cooper driver out of his mangled motorcar. He is okay, but furious at the situation as he taps his MoxWrap for road service. Peter returns to help the woman cyclist. He scans around at the sadness. At least half a dozen banana slugs were killed because two cyclists were joyriding down a mountain road at a time when it was not safe. For man or slug.

Zara says, "This man will be okay, but needs medical attention. I called 911, but it will be more than an hour for emergency medical help to reach our location because of some sort of traffic congestion this morning. His injuries do not warrant an airlift out."

After determining the woman has only road rash—and a snapped three-hundred-dollar handlebar, a shattered two-thousand-dollar carbon wheel, and a smashed seven-thousand-dollar bike frame—Peter asks, "What were you two doing racing down this road at this hour?"

The woman cyclist taps her MoxWrap. Up comes a 3-D projection of a contest for fastest time down this mountain road, only good until 7:45 a.m. The prize? Free trip for two to the Tour de France. She says, "My Harold wanted to win this so bad, so we planned our equipment perfectly for the fastest descending speed just after sunrise."

His arm around the woman, Peter brings the black-fleece-clad woman down the road over to Zara and the injured man. Zara says, "I can reset this shoulder. I did this several times in the battle for Kobanî."

The man's panicked eyes are alight, and his fiancée cries, "We have to get my Harold to an urgent care facility sooner than the ambulance can. If you could kindly give us a lift in your MoxMover, we can make our appointment with our wedding planner, and then the church at noon. The whole family is coming into town tonight. Harold has to be ready."

Shaking her head so ever slightly, Zara contrasts this woman's dilemma with those of her people she fought for. She battled Saddam, Assad, and the Daesh for Kurdish freedom. And now, this woman's wedding plans are more important than anything else in the world. Such is love. Or at least, life in love.

Zara and Peter help them into their MoxMover. Between them, their bikes, and Peter's gear, there is only room for either Peter or Zara. She offers to stay up here as she calls for another MoxMover. There is one only minutes away that can pick her up. She is acutely aware that Peter also needs to be back in the city to prepare for his special day tomorrow. The launch of his first book, his first creation.

She pecks Peter's forehead and says, "I will see you later at your mother's house. Take care."

And off Peter goes with the killers of his beloved slugs. It is a great person who helps those who mercilessly murder the ones they love most.

Standing with her prayer rug, Zara tightens her jacket as the damp fog chills her, her adrenaline rush subsiding. She rubs her pendant through her shirt. Did she do the right thing by opening up to Peter? He is not her husband. He may never be her husband. The tradition said the words were only for women. Only shared with their lifelong mate, their forever husband, if absolutely necessary. Is being her ancient genetic match enough to be her husband? Oh, what did she do? Does she really feel that way about Peter?

The answers to her questions, the urgent reason she came out to see Peter this time, become clear again as she scans her MoxWrap. The headlines all speak of a mad search for meteorites by the world's powers, potentially leading to flash point conflicts across the globe.

What she did not tell Peter was what the voice said to her. The voice of Her, who said that, now that the black object had been found, Zara must find the cavern of the blue light to save her people. To save all people. And only Peter could help her find it.

As the MoxMover she called for arrives, its gull wing door opens, and his face appears. "My little Zara. I thought you would never call for me."

Sasha.

CHAPTER 3

I love God: I have no time left in which to hate the devil.

—Rabi'a al-Adawiyya,
eighth-century Persian philosopher and mystic

Skyline Boulevard above Silicon Valley, California
8:20 a.m. GMT-8, January 2, 2023

She could not say he was the last man she wanted to see at this moment, but he was near the top of the list. At nearly two-and-a-half meters tall, shy the length of her hand, a veritable giant, he fills the back seat of the MoxMover. Around his neck hangs his precious ancient bullhead pendant. She sneers as the monstrous man smiles. His straight white hair frames his modestly wrinkled long face with long earlobes.

"You?" she exclaims. "I told you I never wanted to see you face-to-face ever again. Not in this lifetime, nor any others, if this ancient matriarch DNA and past lives affliction Peter and I share means we will be two other people in another thousand years."

Zara taps her MoxWrap, refusing to engage this man's dark, dark eyes. A reflection of his heart, his soul, his power. Fury burns in her eyes as she spits out the words, "Go away and bother someone else. I will get another MoxMover. I am sure the world's most corrupt power broker, the head slave master of

MoxWorld Holdings, has many better things to attend to than chat with a humble Kurdish woman seeking everything that he is not."

Her protestation is met with a malicious sneer befitting the magnate monster she has just described. And the great Alexander Murometz replies, "I am quite certain, my dear little Zara, there are not, nor will there ever be, any other MoxMovers that will come here to pick you up. It is me or several hours of a bloodletting, blistering hike in those boots of yours. My sources say your feet have become softer in all the wrong places."

This man not only has no respect for data privacy laws, he has no respect for any laws, since he thinks he is above it all. Zara stamps her feet out of frustration and the deep desire to find a more comfortable position for her tender spots. Still refusing to engage him eye to eye, she focuses on her MoxWrap, tapping away as she replies, "Then I will have Peter come back and pick me up. Now go somewhere else to bother someone more interesting than me. Someone who might not care that you are the devil incarnate."

With another malicious snort, the monstrous magnate grins and says back, "Yes. The devil incarnate who has looked after you all your life. Such a great evil man am I that I paid for your father's freedom from Saddam's torture prison. Twice even. A malevolently great devil who sponsored your theology and economics education with the Jesuits at Georgetown and your international business education at Moscow's National Research University."

"Yes, you, the monster who sent a naïve young woman to chase what she thought was love at Georgetown and Moscow, only to find you wanted her to compromise those men for your own devious purposes."

Hand to chin, Alexander says, "Ah, now I am a monster. But one who spent several months bribing all his corrupt connections to find out where the Daesh soldiers had hidden you. Who arranged for you to be rescued from those sex slavers who violated, tormented, and tortured you and your cousins for nearly a year, and who helped you find redemption in killing all those involved. Freedom is never given, but taken, and it took a grand taker like me to free you and your father."

No longer facing him, with her stiffened back toward the MoxMover door, Zara answers, "You have played the guilt card for long enough. I repaid my debt to you four years ago when I left your service. And my family is clear of any obligation as well. How many lives did I end working for your personal security team? They are now spirits who haunt my nights. Did they deserve to be assassinated only because they were in your way? I told you four years ago—I told you when you kidnapped me last spring, coercing me to join with Peter to find the black object—I am no longer that woman of hate, vengeance, and violence. I seek only to be a simple, humble Sufi like the saintly Rab'ia of Basra, who dedicated her life to be in the love of Xwedê. In the love of God."

"May I remind you, my dear," says the giant, "one can never repay one's debt to one's mother—in my case, your parental other."

"You may be a nephew of Sara, my great-grandmother, but you are not my parent," insists Zara.

The mists of fog have morphed into a fine drizzle. Zara's headscarf is matted and clinging tightly to her face. Dripping like a wet sheep in the rain, she tries in vain to wring part of her scarf dry.

A sneeze and the malicious magnate says, "My dear little Zara. My child. My dearest. Please come inside and be dry. I have your favorite style of headscarf in here. The finest lamb's wool from the Kurdish region of the former Iraq where you grew up. Why torture yourself when I am here to pamper you as my precious princess?"

Looking into the white skies that spawned the drizzle pummeling her eyes, she wonders why the heavens have not been favorable to her this morning. Soaked, Zara concedes and begins to enter the MoxMover. She hesitates, and then points to the man with the munched Mini Cooper. "We should help him."

"No, my dear. I do not help such diminutive plebes who think to deceive their loved ones without a world-changing reason. No, I do not think that man wants anyone to know he was up here. You see, there is a chalet nearby, where he spent the night with someone he should not have." Alexander taps on his MoxWrap and a virtual screen appears. "He is already working on his alibi on his MoxWrap, as we speak."

Zara snorts. Another example of her Sasha's disrespect for individual privacy. She folds her arms across her damp chest and gazes out upon the carnage across the glistening road, smeared with the dead cousins of Sammy the Slug.

She turns back to sneer at Sasha, only to be met by the glint in his eye. She exclaims, "You monster. You arranged this massacre. The trip to that big French bicycle race. You arranged for it to be offered on their Mox devices, did you not? You timed this accident to happen. You arranged for that man to have his affair up here and you likely made him rush out just at this moment to cause this accident. You made that traffic jam stalling the ambulance. Why? Why nearly kill everyone in sight to get to me?"

"My dear Zara, you would do well not to rant so madly to others. They might wrongly conclude your psychiatric impairments you suffered in that year of torture of all things venereal have come back. Those psychological afflictions my medical experts tried to patch up, have they relapsed? Be careful, someone might think you were still suffering severe paranoid schizophrenia."

Her buttons pushed—no, insensitively smushed—she lets out a quick exhale through her nose, closes her eyes, and slowly inhales. Exactly the remedy one of those medical experts instructed.

That man. He knows exactly how to disarm and defeat the strongest psyche. And hers. Strong on the outside, but devastated on the inside. Well, an inner psyche on the mend since she met Peter.

Her face dripping, her eyebrows set to fierce, her eyes play chicken with his. Then the image comes back to her. They saw him one time, Peter and she, when they bonded near the object.

She breaks the eyeball chicken match. "You," she yells with finger pointed. "We saw your face on one of those monstrous giants who violated the women of the matriarch's family, who enslaved their men in deadly labor camps. You are one of them. No wonder you are such a misogynistic sadist. No better than all those who have tortured, imprisoned, and violated the Kurds for centuries."

"Tsk, tsk, tsk," utters the giant man, letting out another sneeze, then rubbing his nose. "The kettle calling the crucible black. When was the last time you looked at yourself? Because I am naturally gifted with height, out of prejudice, out of fear, out of intolerance, you call me a monstrous giant. Look at yourself."

Poor Zara. She straightens her back and gazes away from this man as she stands defiantly outside the MoxMover. Yes, she is of the same size as a pro woman basketball player. But she is still shorter than her accuser.

The nerve of that man, turning her accusation against her. Dripping and shivering in the cold, damp mountain breeze, Zara stomps her feet again. Legend tells stories of the saintly Rab'ia making a carpet fly. If only she could do the same and fly back home to her sunny warm mountain, to her spot where she shared peace with her father. Whoever coined the term "sunny" California certainly did not live on this mountain overlooking San Francisco.

Surrender is her only remaining choice. She gives the black MoxMover a once-over. Nodules along the length of the roof, along the front hood over the lights, and along the rear bumpers. "I take it this is not your grandfather's MoxMover."

"No, my dear, it is my presidential security model. I have loaned several to the US president. This is one of his West Coast fleet. My latest security technology equips it. It can defend and defeat air, armor, and commando attacks. Is that not right, Moxy?"

A firm female voice responds, "Yes. I am tasked with keeping you safe, Mr. Murometz. Would you like me to scan Ms. Khatum for weapons?"

He dismisses Moxy's request with a hand wave as Zara enters the advanced AI-guided self-driving vehicle. Solar-powered, using no fossil fuels, requiring no recharging, emitting no greenhouse gasses. Satellite-guided using information gathered from surrounding vehicles' onboard navigation systems along with occupants' and nearby pedestrians' Mox devices. Light years beyond competitors' ill-fated attempts to develop self-driving cars.

A blare of horns and flashing lights causes her to dive into the back seat, almost landing on the monstrous man. His brows pointed into a V formation, his eyes as dark as obsidian disks, her Sasha helps her sit upright as he commands, "Moxy, chase that attacker and take out his tires."

The MoxMover rockets from standstill to sixty miles per hour in one point four seconds, stabilizing at ten feet from the offending pickup truck's bumper. A blue beam emanates from the front nodules, and the pickup's rear tires explode. The doomed truck goes into a tailspin on the slick road, crashing into the aged trunk of a redwood.

As the MoxMover speeds innocently off, Zara screams, "We must stop and make sure the passengers are okay."

Alexander smiles as if he had the best meal a man could have and stares forward, saying simply, "Moxy, please take us to Peter's mother's house."

"But the pickup's passengers…we must make sure they get medical care," pleads a frantic Zara. "Moxy, turn around and call for paramedics."

The Moxy voice politely responds, "My protocols do not include your command. Mr. Murometz, would you wish to include Ms. Khatum in my command protocols?"

"No, Moxy. Not until she regains her rational sense. She must understand that anyone who endangers my dearest Zara will be subject to counterattack by my forces. No one endangers my family without lethal repercussions."

Zara curls down into the farthest corner of the back seat, away from this madman, her eyes beading down into tiny ruble-sized pupils. "You are not family, Sasha. You are plain mean. I pray you treat Peter better than you do me."

Towel in hand, Alexander says, "Here, my dear. Dry yourself off. Remember when you dived off my yacht and swam back to the Crimean coast? You suffered from pneumonia for weeks."

A snarl, a pause, then she grabs the towel he hands her, removes her headscarf, and dries her straight dark brown hair, rubbing her long earlobes in the warmth of the towel. If one squinted, one could imagine Sasha qualified as mahram—someone she could remove her headscarf in front of. Given the situation, Zara gives him the unorthodox benefit of the doubt. She hides her face in the towel, shaking her head at this morning's turn of events.

The man to whom she had loaned her soul after he saved her from the Daesh brushes her cheek with the black lamb's wool scarf with red and gold embroidery.

Bracing herself with her hands as the MoxMover blasts through the hairpin turns down Highway 92, Zara peers at him. "Do not think you can bribe me with the memory of my grandmother's scarf, which I lost in London when those Islamophobic boys tried to violate me. I have not forgiven you for abducting me after Ramadan last spring, forcing me to compromise my vow not to bear arms again so you could recover the two halves of the precious black monolithic object you said were the root of Peter's family's ancient legend." She grabs the utterly silky-soft scarf from him. "And I have not forgotten either how you tried to kill us last June on that pier jutting into the ominous Black Sea."

Head atilt, eyes asquint, and with a stifled sneeze, the monstrous man replies, "Nor have I forgotten how I saved the world by reuniting the two halves of the legendary black object, which evaporated back to the heavens whence they first came."

He nestles back into his seat with lips pouted. "And then the massive electromagnetic pulse emitted by the objects shut down all the modern military hardware deployed from southern Russia all the way down to Palestine. The hotspots of the world neutralized." He turns to Zara and asks, "And who, by chance equipped those military forces, made them addicted to those modern AI tech advances? I stopped the third world war from happening. I am the hero everyone should worship."

"Hero? Right," protests Zara. "You arranged for all those countries to be in the same spot at the same time, armed with all your advanced AI tech they bought at premium pricing. And you arranged for them to be purely mad at each other. Enough to nuke each other." She turns to glare out the back window. "Just like you made victims of Peter's poor simple, innocent, God-worshipping banana slugs. You, the hero who everyone knows is the villain."

With a dismissive puff of air through his thin, mean lips, the giant man says, "Speaking of my dear boy, have I not done for Peter what I have always done for you? Taken care of his deepest wishes? Once he has taken care of those two self-indulgent cyclists, Peter should be heading to his appointment with MoxWorld's finest public relation specialist, who will prep him for his first novel's book signing event. MoxMedia's newest company, MoxReads, selected his book and eleven others for its debut. I think he has already forgiven me for having pointed his own gun at his head and pulling the trigger."

"Forgive you? Not me," says Zara. "You shot me seven times in the chest. If not for two layers of body armor, I would not be here. And then you tried to shoot Peter."

The monstrous magnate touches scars around his hands and adds, "Forgiveness. Something we both need to do more of. And I have magnanimously forgiven Peter for handing me that gun primed to backfire in my hands and face. Perhaps you should be like him. Forgive this old man, as you would forgive an errant father. For this old man needs you more than ever. I need someone who I can trust explicitly."

Yet again, he has hit another one of her buttons with devilish precision. She exhales prominently. Something about this man brings out the worst in her. Ever since she kissed his cheek after he awaited with the medevac team receiving the MoxWorld commando team that extracted her from those Daesh slavers, he had claimed his deemed right to her in all ways possible, training her to be his most effective, and MoxWorld's most soulless, black ops specialist. But she is no longer that fragile, broken girl. She is in command of her body, her mind, and particularly her soul. Now and forever.

"A father," protests Zara. "You could only hope to be one percent of my father. He loved me for who I am. Not like you, who only pretend to love me when you need me to do dirty deeds. You are still manipulating us. What is your endgame in toying with Peter's heart? His secret desire to be an author after a decade editing others' words? Know that I hate you for what you do to the innocent. Your evil surpasses that of Saddam, Assad, the Daesh. All of whom I fought in the name of our people's freedom."

She turns to him, finger pointed between his darkened, obsidian disk eyes. "If you do anything that brings harm to Peter, I will inflict upon you what you strong-armed me into doing to so many others."

His response? Not what she expected. With an ear-to-ear grin, he takes her pointed finger and pets her hand. "That passion. That fervor. I am so proud of my girl. You embody the age-old saying—if you love someone, you will do anything for them."

She is taken aback by his remark. Did Sara not say this came from an ancient ancestor? How did he find out about it? However he did, he continues to find buttons within her she never knew about.

"You really do love my boy, Peter. Your passions reveal your true self," posits Alexander.

She shivers with a deep breath, her head quivering back and forth, buttons being smashed again and again. What are lies and what are truths coming from the world's most manipulative master?

He places her palm on his chest as he states, "I seek deliverance. I am destined for deliverance. And only you can bring me deliverance. The 'you' who Peter will help bring to her fullest being, your real essence. But only if you commit to him. As a woman. And he your husband. She who wants pearls has to dive into the sea."

Zara takes her hand back, revolted that he keeps using traditional Kurdish sayings to seduce her will. Her body is hers, as is her soul. She again protests, "Peter is not your son. No more than I am your daughter. You may think so, as you have tried to buy your way into the graces of my family. You may be my grandmother's second cousin. You may have the same ancient matriarch DNA that Peter and I share. But you are not my relative. You are not family."

That smugness returns as he points to her MoxWrap. "My dear. Am I not family? Look."

Gasp is all she can do as her eyes lock onto the image on her MoxWrap, flying back and forth as she tries to formulate words for what is in her mind. "How? How? This is my family's secret."

A sinister snort from her tall tormentor. "Yes, I know. You were sworn to secrecy. You could only tell your husband about it. And yet, you told Peter. What does that say about how you really feel about him?"

He makes an obscene gesture with his right index finger penetrating a tunnel formed by his left fingers, at which she narrows her eyes at him. He says, "You only need to consummate your love for each other tonight and you can fulfill what you have already signaled to your ancestors by your mere act of confiding in him."

She turns away from him, tightening her thighs together, her head still quivering.

"Look at your MoxWrap again," says the manipulative magnate. "My gift to you, my dearest."

A bigger gasp, and Zara replies, "But my great-grandfather said this was an unknown dead language, possibly spoken by those who preceded the Kurds. How did you translate it?"

With her lightning-fast reflexes, she turns and slaps his face, producing a thunderous sound. "You stole this. You and your microdrones. Shame on you."

Her hardest open-palm strike, and he only smiles even bigger. "So impetuous. I do love you so. You are so much like me when I was your age. Maybe you should come back to MoxWorld. You could run it one day."

"In your dreams," she scoffs. "I plan to quit the post you created for me as MoxWorld's Head of Turkish-Kurdish relations. I naïvely imagined our world's problems would be solved if your empire injected capital into the region. Now, they no longer fight with bullets. They fight with verbal abuse and threats. And me caught in between. I want to become like Rabi'a and devote myself to the love of Xwedê. Me, my lambs, and my mountains back home."

Her eyes back on her MoxWrap, reading the translations, she says, "Oh my. The black object was only a stepping stone to something far more ominous."

"My dear, I used Father Jean-Paul and his access to the Vatican's vast historical records to solve the Gollinger family's oral tradition in order to find the black object. What he did not have access to was why I needed the object to get to the true end goal. My father raised me to find the source of the blue light. That black object was only a means to activate yours and Peter's dormant genes for what is coming. You and he must procreate. Your child will allow you to find the blue light."

Ignoring him, Zara reexamines the photo of the document the translation is based upon. "This is not the parchment Sara left for me. This is someone's transcribed copy."

The giant innocently turns aside. "Well, as they say, I persuaded someone, someone very lovely, to hand-write me a copy." He turns back to her. "Somewhat forcefully persuaded, if you must know."

She scoffs again. "I put nothing beneath you." She continues to study the translation. "This describes the pathway to Xwedê. This is how I can be with Her."

Still with all smugness, he adds, "And the pathway to my deliverance.

Which, by the way, can only be made by you. And only if you are bearing the child of Peter."

Zara crosses her legs, turning away from him again, and stares out the window at the Crystal Springs Reservoir as the MoxMover takes a side road back to Peter's mother's home. She turns back to him, legs still pointed to the door, and says, "There lies the beginning of several nonnegotiable problems. First, my body is mine. Not yours. Not anyone else's. Second, I cannot bear children. Those Daesh savages' torture methods made sure of that. These scars on the outside of my body pale compared to what they did to the inside." She lays her hands atop her lower abdomen.

"I am fully aware of your medical report. Tell me, did not Mary's mother Saint Anne have a miraculous pregnancy? The Immaculate Conception. The objects have made you and Peter two unique beings. People of miracles."

What is it about Peter that makes her unable to commit to lifelong bonding? This thought has haunted her for the many months since they first found a higher-order love together. But this is not the time nor the place to resolve this question, so she redirects. "Then there is the incompleteness of this parchment's text. It says what exists, but not how we find it."

"You forget, my dear. My father and Peter's great-grandfather and grandfather worked together during World War II in Crimea. My father never knew the exact location of the caverns. But Peter's grandfather, Nikolas, did not take the secrets of the caverns in Crimea to his grave. He left Peter his diaries, coded to protect them from the wrong eyes. I have had MoxWorld's best cryptologists working on the answer, but the code is something that only Peter knows. But you know him. He has no idea of what lies within him."

Zara smiles as she pictures the innocent ignorance Peter emits every waking minute of his life.

"My little Zara, with your love—not just the spiritual love that you two share but your intimate, physical love—you and only you can empower him to crack the code."

Her buttons smashed again. She stomps her feet on the floorboard. "Oh, do not play that game again. You told me the last time I had to have sex with Peter to solve the mystery of the matriarch to find the object. You lied. Peter, he's genuine. He could have taken advantage of the situation for his own lascivious pleasure, but he respected me and found that the secret for the two of us to transcend is not sexual, but spiritual."

The giant puts his chin in his hand, nostrils flared. That V in the eyebrows returns. His eyes bear down into hers. His obsidian circles are fully darkened. "Very well, then," he states. "We play hardball. Moxy, get the president of Russia."

MoxWorld's vastly superior AI answer to the eighth-generation versions of the other digital giants' virtual assistants, Moxy replies, "Would you like his secure line this time?"

"No, I want my private direct line to him."

And the two larger-than-average human beings stare at each other in détente for a minute until Moxy says, "I have the president for you."

"Sasha, my friend. What is so urgent that you must interrupt my cabinet meeting with your ultra-private line?" says the president in Russian.

Grinning away, Alexander responds in Russian, "You flatter me by calling me a friend. Our last call, you called me something much viler. I know you would have me executed if you could find a way to replace how I pump up your economy. That and the security of all those votes I get swayed your way, inside and outside Russia."

The line is momentarily silent apart from the president's breathing. And then he speaks. "You must want something very gravely to extort me so early in the conversation. Did I not invade the Ukraine for you and your hunt for mythical pyramids? What more can you demand?"

"Yes, no pyramids this time. I want the city of Siirt in the Anatolian Kurdish State nuked within the hour."

Siirt is her home. Zara gasps as she searches the MoxMover interior for an off button, or at least a weapon she could use to stop this monster. If she could have been born one of those fashionistas like Mei, she would have eight-centimeter-long stiletto pump spikes to puncture his neck. There is no way she can do anything with these boots other than stomp on his monstrous, ocean-liner-like feet.

Before she can raise her right booted foot, the Russian president replies, "But, Sasha, the ramifications of a nuclear attack so close to Turkey must be considered.

Even though they are barely a NATO nation, thanks to your interference, those Americans will make objections, threats, and worse, sanctions."

Alexander lets loose a giant-sized scoff. "No worries, my comrade, my next call will be to the President of the United States, who also has a laundry list of a guilt card with me."

A sigh over the line, and the president replies, "Very well, Sasha. But the price this time will be more than just guaranteeing the next election for me. I have a few other countries' elections I would like guaranteed as well."

That giant grin back again, Alexander replies, "Very well yourself. Let me know which countries' elections you want fixed, but more importantly, when your nuclear forces will launch their attack."

The line goes silent and Moxy asks, "Mr. Murometz, would you like me to dial the American president on your private line?"

Before he can answer, Zara stomps on his feet, which only seems to cause her patron giant more pleasure. "You cannot destroy my home, my grandmother, my mother. They are your relatives too."

"Ah, good," replies Alexander with the smirk of smirks. "The truth comes out. I am family after all."

She stomps on his feet even harder. "You are just plain evil. And you must stop that attack. It is not right."

"My dear Zara, that is called negotiation leverage. You studied how to do this in your business master's program in Moscow. The fate of your home and your family is in your capable hands. Have a child with Peter so you can access the blue light for your own good. And of course, my good. Or have your family, friends, and neighbors vaporized. Very simple."

Now she beats on him with her fists as she screams, "This is pure insanity. You cannot ask that a city be destroyed just to force a poor Kurdish woman to submit her body, her womb, to your will. You cannot."

"You misjudge me," he says, no longer smiling. "I have done so before and will do so again. Now that the black object has activated the dormant genes in you and Peter, this quest to solve the legend of the blue light supersedes any other principle, moral, or concern. Moxy, how long until Moscow will be able to launch their nuclear assets?"

Moxy replies, "Fourteen minutes. Would you like me to get the US president for you now?"

Head into her hands, Zara cries out, "You cannot do this. Human life is too sacred for you to destroy just so you can own my body. Did you not hear me? My womb can no longer bear a child. I have been left barren by the will of Xwedê. My punishment for abandoning Her to chase those men in the military. Something I will always atone for."

She kneels at his feet and gazes up to meet his blackened eyes, emotionlessly focused on her, a flattened line between his thin lips, his head nodding ever so slightly. And then he leans down to kiss her forehead. "My child, you do have the best wishes for mankind in your heart. Your soul is no longer the darkened place it once was. The first of many changes your exposure to the object will bring upon you. You are ready for what is to come."

Moxy interrupts this precious moment, asking, "Twelve minutes until Russian cruise missiles are deployed. Do you still wish me to dial the American president?"

Alexander smiles at Zara kneeling subserviently at his feet. A sneeze, a rub of the nose, and he gathers the black lamb's wool headscarf and delicately wraps it around her head and neck, then says, "Moxy, end the nuclear attack demo program."

Face ashen, mouth agape, Zara quietly says, "You mean, that was a trick?"

"My virtual reality systems are superb, are they not? Even the Russian cabinet would not have been able to discern that was not their president. Even better, nor would the best voice recognition software of any country be able to determine that th was not their commander-in-chief. Soon, I will be able to have him sitting in here with us and you would not know the difference."

Zara gets up and sits away from him again. "You are evil. Pure evil. Hell is not hot enough for the likes of you."

"Compliments will get you everywhere with me. But only your compliments," he says with a face that beams as if 'he's had the world's finest meal.

He turns his head to gaze outside and adds, "If the threat of nuclear war sparked such terror in your soul, then you need to help me, help yourself find the cavern of the blue light. And if the world takes a turn for the worse and is on the edge of nuclear war, then you and Peter must bring another black object to be bonded with the source of that blue light."

"Oh no, you will not get me to chase another black object," she retorts.

"When that missile of utter devastation is falling on your beloved people, you will reconsider. I watch our Father Jean-Paul's secret search for another black object. And Mei also has another search that should elucidate its location. You, my dear, you must work on your relationship with Peter."

Her head turns, facing the other window. A long stream of air is released from the depths of her lungs through her nose as she pushes her head into the window, nodding.

"So, I take it we have a deal. You will let Peter father your child," asserts Alexander.

Face scrunched up into something hideous, she protests, "You have not heard me. It is not possible."

"My dear Zara, you please me you do not say you do not love him. Only that a physical impediment prevents you from loving him in that way."

Zara glances down, mulling the profoundness of his insinuations. The second time during this car ride he has caught her.

"My little Zara. If not with you, Peter is going to have to be a parent with some other woman with the right genetics. Only a woman with the matriarch's DNA who is with child can access the blue light. If not you, who? He must be that woman's child's father."

Glancing out the window again, she sees only stands of coastal pine trees. The MoxMover has parked in an isolated area away from the highway. And what she has never imagined would happen has. His hand is firmly placed upon her upper thigh.

"What do you think you are doing?" she yells as she tries to remove his monstrous hand from her.

As she tries to put his hand into a painful wristlock with no success, he scoffs. Her eyes are open wide, painfully wide. His face only reflects signs of pleasure, not pain, at her woeful attempt to deter his advance. Her chest caves with pressure, as if crushed by one of Saddam's tanks used to squash prisoners' heads in the Anfal Campaign.

Pins and needles prickle throughout her face, and in her head, logic triumphs over brute force. She says, "Why would you have saved me from the Daesh if this is what you wanted to do to me all along?"

Taking his hand back, he scoffs again. "My dear. If I wanted to have you in that way, I would have done so years ago. But for reasons we cannot discuss now, you are the one woman in the entire world I cannot touch in that way. Every other woman exists for my pleasure. But you? You are truly special. I need you with me in a different way."

Her head shakes ever so slightly side to side, eyelids still open to their extreme limit. But after a deep exhale, she says, "Then why the touch? Why are we parked where no one can rescue me?"

His hand approaches her again. She grabs it, ready to fight in vain for her dignity, for her honor. But he clasps his fingers lightly around hers and says, "I need you to be with me in the way you say you do with Peter. That way in which you can see the ancients."

"I did not think you believed in how Peter and I bond."

Head tilted down at her, he peers out the top edge of his eyelids and sneers. "Don't think I haven't bonded with my share of women who have the ancients' genes. Passionately—pleasurably so, at that. But with you, I cannot do so in the way other gene-afflicted women have learned to receive love from me."

"Why do you need to bond with me in that way?" she asks as she pushes her back well into the door on her side of the MoxMover, pulling her headscarf tighter around her face and neck with her free hand.

Pushing her fingers up against his, both palms pressed together, he says, "It is not I who needs to bond with you in that way, but you to me. For only if you do will you understand your path to fulfill your great-grandmother Sara's wishes."

A silent pause, their hands still laced together, and she feels perspiration build where her palm is pressed against his. She remembers how Peter ingeniously figured out that physical sex was not the only way he could bond with her. She takes his fingers and wets them with her palm, then moistens his index and middle fingers with her lips and tongue. Likewise, she puts her fingers up to his lips for him to lick.

Her wetted finger upon his temple and his upon hers, she says, "Close your eyes and focus on my breathing."

And then it happens.

Not the harmony, beauty, and bliss of bonding with Peter, but clouds—angry black ones. Swirling, twisting, and shouting. The type one sees out the plane window when flying through a thunderstorm.

Through the storm, through the haze, the image of a woman comes forth. Like her, but not her. Scared like her, backed into a corner with a giant staring at her.

Darkness. They are in a mud hut. Spears and bow and arrow hang from the wall. A blanket made of animal hide covers her. It is the time of the ancients. And the giant gets up, which sends the poor scared woman scrabbling to pull her meager blanket tighter against her.

Eyes wide open again, Zara screams. "I can't. I can't—I've seen too much pain like hers. I can't watch this."

Giving her the comfort of physical space, the modern-day giant, her Sasha, leans back against his side of the MoxMover.

"My dearest Zara. I too have seen this same vision with another who bonded with me, in the correct way as said by the ancients. Intensely, passionately so. That woman you see and that giant have something to do with the blue light you are to seek. You must understand her life if you are to solve the mystery of the blue light. And from that woman, you will find for me my path, what I must complete."

Shivering. Not from the cold, but from having lived a moment of an ancient originator's life. Not Nanshe, whose name Peter had called Zara in one of their bonding sessions, but someone like Nanshe.

Zara finally replies, "I cannot. I cannot be with Peter like you ask. I cannot bear his child."

The strained expression on his giant face eases, while his fierce gaze softens. He gently caresses her knee and soothingly speaks, "It must be painful for you knowing that the Daesh destroyed that part of your womanhood with such brutality. May your tormented soul find solace that MoxWorld medical genetics continues to advance. What we could not heal back then may become possible soon. Your 'cannot' may soon turn into 'can'."

Teary eyes droop down, fixed upon the floor as creases span across her forehead. She ponders, *Could I ever? Is 'cannot' because they destroyed my womb and all that leads to it? Or is it simply that Peter and I are cat and dog—complete opposites rather than the perfect halves of an apple, as the ancients' prophecy claimed?*

Silence as the MoxMover begins to move again. Twenty minutes of no words spoken, only Zara staring at her boots, which suffocate her aching feet. Finally, the MoxMover stops in front of Samantha Gollinger's house, the childhood world of her son Peter and daughter Michaela, and where Zara and Peter are staying while MoxWorld retrofits Peter's new condo with the latest security systems.

The monstrous man breaks the silence. "Peter's mother would want you as her daughter-in-law. You have been here a dozen times since meeting her. You know this is your new family as well as I do."

"Again, you are wrong," protests Zara. "I only want to follow the path of Rabi'a. She was and I am celibate by choice, and only in love with Xwedê."

Shaking his head, he replies, "If not you, Zara, then if you want to find God, if you want to fulfill Sara's dying request, you must help Peter find the woman who can make our destiny possible. Read for me what the translation of your great-grandmother's parchment says. I want to know you know this by heart."

Zara gazes at her MoxWrap and says, "With her miraculous child within, she met Her."

Shaking his head, the giant interrupts. "It says Him."

Undeterred, Zara continues, "Only with child could she have found Her. The blue light. The final point. The only point. The end and the beginning. And she who has been with the light knows that only another like her bearing a child can free her to be with the light. The blue light. The child of her child will one day return with a miraculous child and the cycle continues. So is the love of our God."

"Good," he replies. "You understand well what you must do. There are those who seek to betray me within MoxWorld, like the mole you killed on the last mission. You and Peter, I trust. I need you to remember this day for what is about to come."

Torn, Zara leaves the MoxMover, unsure whether to be angry, afraid, or in awe. Two steps to the house, she turns back and leans into the MoxMover to kiss the giant's cheek.

"That is for translating my great-grandmother Sara's parchment. She would have wanted to give you that kiss. That is the last affection you are to see from me."

CHAPTER 4

And also Maacah, King Asa's mother, he deposed from being the queen because she had made a frightful image of Asherah.

II Chronicles 15:16, Tanakh

Jerusalem, Israel
5:30 p.m. GMT+3, January 3, 2023

"Come on, Rach. A little lip rouge never hurt anyone," says the MoxWrap projection of a Chinese woman who has impeccably applied plum red lips complementing her plum eyeshadow and blood rose metallic designs interwoven into her black hair, which is equally impeccably styled in a smooth bun with braids that frame her oval face.

"Mei, I am not here to get a fashion lesson. I will never be one of your MoxFashion models. And I am certainly not going to be anyone's *frecha*. A bimbo," says an Israeli woman dressed in a thick cotton beige t-shirt and khaki pants. Dark brown hair up in a sloppy bun with random dangling strands framing her au natural face covered with nothing but the sporadic white residue of a zinc-based sunblock and the specks of granite flakes. In the middle of a fresh excavation of ancient tombs, she stands about one-hundred seventy-five centimeters high, taller than average for an Israeli woman, and has the fit muscularity that accompanies one who digs dirt for a living.

"Sometimes being a wee bit more feminine will get you much further than begging me to get Mr. Murometz to call in favors with your government," asserts Mei as her lips mock-kiss at Rachel. "What a woman archaeologist has to do to get ahead. Isn't that what you always say?"

Yimach shmo. May his name be erased. These words have been ingrained in the Israeli professor's head. More so recently by her father. And Mei is asking her to sleep with the enemy. What is she to do?

"Unlike you, a history professor moonlighting as MoxFashion's head, part-timing as MoxBiogenetics' deputy director, I am but a mere sometime Torah history professor who, if lucky, gets to play biblical archaeologist," says Rachel. "The only feminine fashion I learned is how to apply desert camouflage when I was conscripted into my Israel Defense Force tour of duty. The only fashion I get to see now is the rotted robes of the dead. Besides, shouldn't my knowledge of femininity in ancient religions be the basis of judgment rather than my physical femininity?

A little femininity, huh? Rachel pulls down her hastily made bun into a braided ponytail, poses for Mei, and then stops. Something about Mei's face is different. What is it? "Mei, did you use something different today? Trying out a new foundation, or what?"

"Honey, I have no idea what you are talking about," says Mei, giving that coy look she gives when she wants you to focus somewhere else.

Glancing at Mei's visage from the corner of her eye, Rachel gets it. But how do you tell your friend delicately that she's a bit puffier? And so, Rachel whispers, "Mei, you're expecting. Aren't you?"

"Shhhh, Rach. Not so loud. My mother is in the next room."

"You mean, you haven't told her? How many weeks?"

Mei bites her lips, sighs, and replies, "You mean, how many months."

Mouth wide open again, Rachel exclaims, "No, Mei. You hid your pregnancy for all this time? Why? Who is the father?"

A frown on the beautiful oval Asian face as Mei's eyes search for the right words. "It's a rather delicate situation. It has to do with that last mission I did for Alexander."

Her head tilted down, frowning as well, Rachel says, "You mean that man you had to seduce for him? Don't tell me you didn't use protection."

Biting her lip, Mei continues to frown. "Worse, Rach. That man is in a near-committed relationship with another friend of mine. That's why it has to be a secret. If this gets out, it will break them up. They are such an endearing couple, too, destined for greater things."

Shaking her head, not judgementally but in complete dismay, Rachel says, "If she is a good friend, then you need to tell her and him. If they really love each other, they will understand. Love will prevail. Isn't that what you always told me?"

After a violent shake of her head from side to side and then a pause, Mei finally says, "Yes, I told you that. But I wanted to ease your troubled conscience and heart when you mentioned amicably ending our more-than-friends relationship.

Another pause, but this time from Rachel. Head pointed down, she says, "My single-focused love for finding Asherah would have destroyed any long-term prospects with you or anyone else."

Eyes down and then up, Mei peers into Rachel's eyes. "Hey, we're good. Aren't we?"

Irises dilated, Rachel replies, "Yes, we are good. And still friends. And a friend would tell you to talk with your mother about something like this."

"It's complicated. Very complicated," laments Mei.

As Mei continues to shake her head, Rachel says, "Mei, you trust my judgment. I wouldn't steer you wrong. Promise me you will talk with your friend. What is her name?"

Her head still quivering, Mei says, "Her name is Zara. And she is not one you should upset with bad news. Even Alexander trembles under his devious exterior when she is at her fiercest."

"Don't tell me you are afraid of her?" Rachel admonishes. "Promise me you will tell her within the next day. Seriously."

Now Mei's face is glacier-cold frozen. Petrified. *Who is this woman who scares her so much?* Rachel wonders. She must be the modern incarnation of Lilith, the Babylonian demon of the night.

With her best "trust me" face, Rachel says, "My safta raba once taught me that if you love someone, you will do anything for them. If you love your friend Zara, you need to tell her."

Mei nods up and down slightly. Reluctantly.

"Your boss, he knows?" asks Rachel.

Her almond-shaped eyes glance down for a second. Pointing to her wrist, she replies, "Alexander knew the same time I did from the MoxWrap biological sensors."

A reflective moment between them as the sounds of commuter traffic on Hebron Road echo off the stone blocks of the tomb entrance Rachel uncovered after two weeks of a highly surgical dig. Alone, she stood in the park across from the Jerusalem House of Quality Cultural Center, for she had been stripped of graduate student assistants by the university. Her MoxLight lanterns line the excavation site as the twinkling of twilight envelops the skies.

It is no coincidence that this dig is near the site of Ketef Hinnom, next to the cultural center. For in the tombs at Ketef, two scrolls were uncovered with the oldest texts matching the same verses in the Torah. While one of the Israeli journalists said these were proof that the Books of Moses existed in the time of the First Temple, the biblical archaeology community approached these scrolls with more caution. What Professor Rachel Capsali has searched for might show otherwise. Perhaps something the established religious and political communities would want to keep quiet, as they have done for thousands of years.

Scanning the inside of the tomb, Rachel says, "I called because I needed your help. Not with my fashion sense, but with your access to MoxWorld tech. I have been poking around here for days now. I found one tomb entrance, five bodies of what appears a family, but not a scroll, an inscription, or an amulet. Only a tablet with a bird-shaped constellation and a pendant with a circle and crescent insignia."

That gets Mei's attention, and she puts up a 3-D diagram of an ancient T-shaped pillar. "You mean, like the one on top of this?"

Rachel makes the hand gestures to enlarge and zoom in and studies the image. "Kind of. Where is this one from?"

With a big grin spreading out her lips like a mini banana-shaped plum,

Mei says, "Honey, sit down. I wouldn't want you to get a concussion as you faint."

Finding a stone ledge to sit upon, Rachel says, "Okay, there's not far to fall from here. Why all the drama?"

"9000 BCE. Now that is dramatic," says Mei. "It comes from the one of two oldest temples in the world. This pillar is from Göbekli Tepe at the border of Turkey, Anatolian Kurdish State, and New Kurdistan."

As she searches her MoxWrap, Rachel says, "Isn't this the site bombed about six months ago during the war between Turkey, the Kurds, Russia, and the US? Wasn't it completely destroyed?"

Pursing her plum lips, Mei nods. "Don't mention that to Father Sobiros, our friend Jean-Paul. He still ruminates over its destruction, feeling somewhat responsible."

"Well, he should ruminate on sending me on this wild goose chase and ruining the park here," says Rachel, reading her MoxWrap. "Wait a minute. It says here another temple site as old as Göbekli Tepe was also bombed just days later, Karahan Tepe. Why only those two sites?"

"A question that still weighs heavily on the minds of Jean-Paul and my boss, Mr. Murometz. Unknown parties bombed the sites, and then their assassins kidnapped Jean-Paul, only to be saved by Zara and that super sweet guy I told you about."

"Assassins?" says Rachel, now standing. "From where? You mean, the type from 1200 CE Syria or 1100 CE Persia?"

A minute glance to the side, then Mei says, "We never found out. None of our team knew them. Well, maybe one of them. A disgruntled MoxWorld employee, apparently."

Her hands rubbing her chin, Rachel says, "Then I take it we cannot compare the pendant I found with the engraving on the T-pillar in person."

"Send me a few 3-D scans of it and I'll run them against the data Jean-Paul collected on the one at Göbekli Tepe," says Mei.

As she performs a 360-scan of the tablet with her MoxWrap, Rachel spies the silhouette of someone in the parking lot loading their backpack. Maybe that is the graduate student assistant she had asked the university to authorize.

Finally. Help. With a renewed smile, she taps her MoxWrap and says, "I just sent the scans to you."

After inspecting the scans, Mei taps her MoxWrap, replying, "Okay, I sent your newest information to Jean-Paul. He's in with the Holy Pontiff on something hush-hush, but he said to move the cosmogenic nuclide and electron spin resonance signal enhancer unit five meters north of its current position."

"Seriously, Mei, what is a few meters difference going to make?" says Rachel as she grunts and lifts the thirty-five-kilogram black box out of the pit she dug and counts off five meters.

"Honey, I wouldn't complain too much," says Mei, wagging her finger at Rachel. "Not that I mind that it's near midnight here, but the satellite Mr. Murometz re-tasked for reading your signal is costing ten million shekels an hour. Let's see. How many days have you been digging?"

"I get it. I do. I am forever grateful to that boss of yours. And like most of the world, I fear for the indebtedness he will forever hold over my head. I have so many debts I've already paid for my family," says Rachel as she takes local readings on the new spot.

"You're lucky, Rach. Normally, he would have demanded at least a week on his private yacht with a fit woman like you," says Mei, feigning another kiss at her.

"Mei, the Shanghai University history professor who moonlights as the world's most powerful monster's pimp," teases Rachel as she continues to scan.

"Honey, you know I love you. But Mr. Murometz only loves one thing. And that is not found in your pants. It's in the oral tradition your great-grandmother passed along to you. What is her name again?"

"Ariella," says Rachel. "Ariella Perahya."

"Perahya?" questions Mei. "Didn't she have another name?"

"Good memory, Mei. Perahya was her maiden name. After the Nazis and their Russian spy murdered her first husband, she feared for her life and changed her name. The Nazis cannot pay enough to compensate for their inhumanity. Not even with their lives."

"Okay, Ms. Nazi Hunter, calm down. Let's stay to task here," says Mei.

"What's more important to Murometz and his satellite is your Ariella's oral tradition and not the nine Nazis you, your father, and your grandmother helped incarcerate."

"So, what's so special about some random legend?" says Rachel. "My safta raba Ariella said, 'She said one day Nearat and her daughter will return. Humanity will wane and wobble. And the woman who will save humanity will bring peace from the blue light. But to return, one must overcome one's fear of death. Two women will fight so that one will die. For only in the death of life as one knows it can she be in the light. Until then, Inanna awaits.'"

With a light chuckle, Mei combs through ground-penetrating radiation scans as she says, "Be thankful you only had to memorize seven sentences. That guy from California with the Kurdish woman had to memorize four times that much. His grandfather made him say it backwards, even. As random as your safta raba's saying may seem, it isn't to Murometz, and even Jean-Paul, who's aggregating oral traditions like yours with thousands of others he's collected, including those from the Vatican archives. They are far from random now."

Slowly walking in concentric circles from the black box MoxWorld loaned her, Rachel views the real-time scan images as she says, "I wish I could have met Mr. Murometz when you and Jean-Paul screened me. Not that I didn't relish our time together."

"Come on, Rach. You wouldn't wear that dress I made for you, much less the vamp shoes and makeup we designed," says Mei.

"I didn't mean to meet him in 'that' way," says Rachel as she runs her hand along her braids. "If I'm not worthy enough minus my lady bits, then he isn't worthy enough for my time, I say."

"I never said you had to wear those simply ravishing clothes for him," says Mei.

"Well, certainly it wasn't for Father Sobiros, I assumed. And you said Murometz was fascinated that my safta raba's words included a reference to a Sumerian goddess whose priestesses were known for prostitution. I only assumed he was hinting he wanted the same out of me, as all the rumors would suggest," jests Rachel. "Wait. Do you see what I see?"

"Hold on, Rach. I have an incoming call from the president of China."

As Mei brushes her dangling hair strands back behind her ears, Rachel attempts to get better scan images. What starts as a cordial chat in Mandarin turns into a bout of anxious words from her friend Mei.

Eyes shut tight, lines radiating across her once-perfect visage, Mei lets those strands of her hair drop again, covering her face. "Men. Especially men in power. They think you exist for…for…"

"For their pleasure, Mei?"

A long exhale through her flared nostrils and Mei says, "I wish. I know how to deliver that. He asks something more impossible than what you ask of Alexander's satellites. And if I can't produce this artifact, this meteorite the world powers are seeking, the president of my country says he will launch preemptive nuclear strikes against Russia and the US to prevent them from obtaining it first. I'm trying to get him to focus on the comet that fell in the 1400s. The great Ming dynasty admiral, Zheng He, searched for that comet off the coast of New Zealand. Its remains should still be scattered around the South Pacific, far from us here in Shanghai."

"You think he would take proof of women's equality instead?" jests Rachel as she sends her latest scans.

Her mouth scrunched up into her nose, Mei pounds on her MoxWrap. "Where is she? She's supposed to be in Xian at my excavation there. With the president willing to start global nuclear war for that artifact, I need Jia to keep searching the tombs in Xian even more."

"Maybe your friend Jia would rather examine a real archaeological find. Look at the scans, would you?"

Mei enhances the scans. "Yes. Seems like a wax seal maker like the royal seals found at the City of David, which dated to the time of the First Temple. And what is that next to it? About the shape of a tablet."

Her fingers pointed to a smaller object about six to seven centimeters in length and a centimeter and a half in width. "Can we get more definition than this?" asks Rachel.

"Oh, my Rach. Wearing that dress isn't going to be enough to pay back my boss. Amping up the satellite beam will cost a hundred million shekels a minute," says Mei. "Good thing you look simply yummy in your birthday suit. He'll like that."

"Oy, what a woman archaeologist has to do to get ahead. And keeping her clothes on is part of what she needs to do. Thank you, Mr. Murometz," says Rachel as she magnifies the image of the object. "Yes. It looks like a miniature statue of Asherah. Refocus on the tablet if you could."

"Well, you know, that is going to cost you an entire month never seeing the sun on his yacht," muses Mei as she resets the satellite.

As she manipulates the new 3-D image, Rachel replies, "A month with you on that yacht. I'd even consider a month with Jean-Paul. He treats women with respect. Imagine what archaeological finds we two could make in a month on that yacht with this satellite."

"You see what I see?" asks Mei. "We got what appears to be text. I'll send this into Jean-Paul's text enhancer."

"Paleo-Hebrew," says Rachel. "Same as the scrolls that were found across the street in Ketef Hinnom. That might date this text back to the tenth century BCE. The time of King David."

"Hold on, honey," says Mei. "Your ancestors wrote in Paleo-Hebrew from the tenth through fifth centuries BCE, according to Moxipedia. We can only get a partial read of that tablet, as it's sitting at an angle. Moving a satellite another centimeter to the left is well above my pay grade."

Rachel falls over onto her rump. She breathes rapidly through her nose. "Yeesh! Mei. This is it. This is what we thought would be here. It mentions Nitzevet. King David's mother."

"Now, now. We historians do not take leaps of logic," admonishes Mei. "Let's do this by the book. Let's excavate properly and let an expert team witness and validate the claims."

"By the book? Don't your wide scans show what I see?" asks Rachel as she spies, highlighted by the park lights, dark-dressed men in stereotypical dark glasses watching from seventy-five meters distance and from three different vantage points.

She blinks and squints. Did she just catch a silver flash from the tallest onlooker from the farthest location away? Is that a man or woman who stands next to this tall, white-haired one?

Breaking Rachel's pondering, Mei interjects, "Yes. And they're armed. Who knows you and why you're excavating there?"

Feigning a chuckle, Rachel quips, "Any man or agency who wants to protect male sovereignty in the Torah. I am very watched, lest the truth about Asherah be verified."

"Do you want me to call in a MoxSecurity team?" asks Mei. "We'd have to bring in the ones stationed at the MoxWorld Resort Jerusalem."

Just on the outer rim of the excavation area, Rachel spots a young Palestinian woman with a backpack wearing a black, long-sleeved top, loose blue jeans, and a pink headscarf. Certainly not the graduate student from the university she requested. Rachel's eyes follow her as she visits each of the dark-dressed men in their blackened sunglasses.

"Rach, I confirmed that the resort security team can be there in fifteen," says Mei. "Better safe than you know what."

Shaking her head, Rachel muses to herself. A pendant with an image that dates back to when humanity emerged from the Ice Age into the agricultural era. A possible royal seal. Ancient text that might date back to the time of King David, mentioning his mother. And a statuette of the banished wife of Yahweh, the goddess Asherah. Who wouldn't want to snuff her out?

As this Palestinian girl begins to head toward her, Rachel checks her daypack and says, "That won't be necessary, Mei. I have here what every woman archaeologist should carry."

Shovels, brushes, and a forty-caliber Jericho pistol.

CHAPTER 5

The Prophet said that women totally dominate men of intellect and possessors of hearts, but ignorant men dominate women, for they are shackled by the ferocity of animals.
—Jalāl ad-Dīn Muḥammad Rūmī, thirteenth-century Persian Sufi mystic

House that one day will become Çatalhöyük, Turkey
9539 BCE

She shivers in her corner of the room. Not because it is cold, for he has provided her blankets. Ones he has washed with each change of season. She shivers because of him. The reindeer warrior giant who co-led the attack on her village. Who must have killed her friends and relatives in that rampage. Who might have violated the girls in the village as mercilessly as these giants deem it their right, given to them by their gods, to do.

She is Tallia. The daughter of Sarpani, one of the twin daughters of the much-revered matriarch of their family—Nanshe. The woman who found the black object with her husband Orzu and her older brother Namu and his wife Zamana. The woman who, upon splitting the mysterious object into two halves, one for her and one for her older brother, began to hear the voice. A gift passed down to Nanshe's twin daughters, Sarpani and Zirbani, her aunt. A gift Tallia had passed down to her two daughters, Illyana and Perima. Both of whom, she concludes, are either dead or enslaved by the leviathan beasts who regard humans as animals for their perverse pleasure.

Her grandmother Nanshe said the voice they heard was that of the one true god that she and her husband's sister, the first Illyana, prayed to as they were held slaves of the unspeakable in the encampment of these brutal reindeer warrior giants from the lands toward the tail of the bird star. Yes, Tallia named her oldest daughter after her great-aunt, who taught Nanshe the meaning of a kind god, who taught her that death was better than life in venereal servitude, bearing children for these inhumane giants.

Her mother only knew Tallia's grandfather Orzu during her childhood, living on the border of the big black lake. He was a physically broken man, having battled the giants to save his family. As the voice had warned, a great flood came upon the other side of the lake and swept away the reindeer warrior giants. Namu, his family, and as many animals as they could save, floated somewhere else with their half of the object in a giant wooden structure built like a nut.

After her husband Orzu stood and fell defending her and her family, Nanshe collected her wounded husband, her children, her younger brother Narn, his wife Sama, and their half of the object into their fishing boat to flee the giants. Miraculously, the winds pushed their vessel to the other side of the big black lake while massive waves pounded, inundated, and buried the giants' land and their pyramids.

Tallia had learned to fight from her Aunt Ki, who slew a giant in that battle on the other side of the lake. Or so she thought. Ki told her the stories of how her father Orzu went to save his sister Illyana from the violative world where she had been enslaved. Every night, terrible dreams plagued Orzu because, as a teen during their second encounter with a reindeer giant, he had failed his sister, who pleaded with him to kill her rather than let her be taken for a life of incessant unthinkable acts, as had happened to their mother, Thara. Orzu had hesitated, and she had suffered a fate she considered worse than death.

Two cycles of the sun spent in guilt. Tens and tens of moon cycles of restless nights. Orzu planned and plotted how to rescue Illyana and to redeem himself to his sister. One day, he did come for her. But she wanted him to save her by killing her, for too much had happened for her to live with. But she asked him to take care of a younger woman with her, Nanshe. Orzu fulfilled both of his sister's wishes, redeeming his first failure, and he and Nanshe became man and woman.

The lore of Illyana, the reverence Orzu and Nanshe had for her, led Tallia to name her first daughter after her legendary great-aunt.

Had she listened to Ki more intently. Had she trained with her more intensely. Maybe her fight with the giants would not have been a losing fight. She had seen her Aunt Ki die trying to save her daughter Illyana from capture. But the giant staring at her from across the room grabbed her before she could see if her daughter had escaped.

She had fought him with all she had, but her spear had snapped in his hands. Her knife could barely penetrate his skin, though she bled him. And he still stripped her lower clothes off, ready to do the horrible things that these giants so loved.

But he did not. For reasons she still cannot fathom, he faked her violation. He killed several villagers on the way out as he carried her like a dead carcass out of the morass. And for many days on end, he carried her. Until he settled here, in a house of unknown value to her, but of value to him.

Several moon cycles have passed, or so she thinks, as she has not left this corner since he brought her here. She sits in fear. No longer the fear of the unspeakable things giants do, but the greater fear of the unknown, as he has not even tried to touch her. Instead, he brings food, water, and freshly washed clothes and gives her privacy so she can take her of her bodily needs.

What does he want from her? He does not look afraid of her. He does not have those eyes that bespeak physical lust. He says nothing. But then again, neither does she.

She has not heard the voice since coming here. She misses Her and her sister, her mother, her aunt, her daughters praying around the object. She has heard the voice on a number of occasions. She is all that her grandmother Nanshe had said. And Tallia pledged her obedience. If only the voice would tell her what to do now.

She cannot help thinking about the flightless birds they kept. They would feed them and feed them to puff them up, then slaughter them for festival dinners. Is he doing that to her? She has heard of the sordid orgies these giants hold with the women assaulted by hundreds of giants and their allies. They are no more than animals in service for alliance, building favors. Is that what he is doing? Getting her ready to build his empire?

She is no longer a young woman. She no longer has the skin and body that creates the physical crazes a younger woman can induce in men. She is a mother of adult children. She was a mother. She so wants to find out if her daughters are safe.

She closes her eyes again. For these several moon cycles, she has practiced what her grandmother Nanshe had taught. What Nanshe had learned from Illyana as they were imprisoned in servitude of the monstrous giants' perversions. To save your mind, to save your soul, picture yourself in a place of peace. A place of love. A place where God protects you. And that, she tries again.

Suddenly, he rises and approaches her, interrupting her thoughts. She tries to hide further in the corner, pulling her headscarf over her face, burying herself in her blanket so no flesh shows. It is time for her to become the pained play toy for this beast. She prays he kills her instead, as her great-aunt prayed her brother Orzu would do.

But he sits down on the floor directly in front of her.

After some tense moments staring at each other, he finally speaks. "Tell me about your grandmother Nanshe. About your great-uncle Narn and his wife Sama. About your mother and father."

Stunned, all she can utter is, "What?" Her tongue strains at the utterance, as she has not spoken out loud for so long.

As if reading her mind, he rises to get a cup of water and hands it to her. She rinses her mouth, moistening her tongue, lips, and vocal cords.

"You keep me captive for many moon cycles and all you have to say is about my family?" cries Tallia.

"They are my family too," he says sullenly.

Inside herself, a giant-sized "what?" erupts. Is the reason this giant kept her without ever taking his pleasures upon her because someone had cracked his oversized head?

"Do not insult my family," protests Tallia in the first defiance she has shown since he attacked her. "You and your kind killed and assaulted my family. And you dare to ask me about the slaughtered innocent?"

To her surprise, his eyes well up. Giants do not have feelings. Certainly not soft ones.

He gently replies, "If I could have been born differently, I can only wish that I had been. Life as a giant is about everyone chiding you because either you are not going to be good enough to be a giant or you are hideous and hated by humans. Did everyone hate you as you grew up?"

Starting to feel her inner moxie come back, she protests, "You mean, as much as I hate you for holding me captive against my will?"

"I have not kept you captive," he states, to her surprise. "You have always been free to leave this house."

That stops her. Did she assume for all this time he was holding her as his pleasure-slave-to-be? That is all these giants do with human women. Aunt Ki told her that the giants deemed it their right, given to them by the gods, to take human women as their slaves, to force them to service their every depraved need and to bear them child after child.

She asks, "How do you know the names of my family? I did not think names meant anything to you giants."

"And there is my proof. You dehumanize me, generalize me as one of an evil group. Anything and anyone who does not look like you, behave like you, they must be evil. That is all I have heard from humans since I was young."

The giant takes a cowering position in front of her. Is this a ruse, or is that true pain he is feeling? Giants are uncaring, self-serving, monstrous, self-centered haters of humans. Especially women.

As she takes a compact defensive position, waiting for his ruse to turn into her demise, his massive head pops up out of the sitting fetal cower. "My mother is Sama, your great-uncle's wife."

Tallia loosens her defensive ball posture. Her Aunt Ki told her a story about having to shoot an arrow at Tallia's great-uncle's feet when she taught

Tallia a lesson about the necessity for extreme accuracy, lest you maim someone by accident. What was that story about? A child that he accused his wife of bearing that was not his.

"You are her bastard child," she spits out. "You are not of my family. My blood."

His eyes retrieve a glimpse of that giant anger for a moment. Huge, obsidian disks fill his eyelids. A hurricane of an exhale, and his pupils soften. He says, "You wonder why reindeer giant warriors are so angry. Humans can be so callous. So insensitive. No wonder giants treat them like animals. Humans have no culture, no tolerance."

Before she can defend her species, her kind, herself, he says, "But my mother taught me to think better than that of humans, as she was human herself. When your grandmother and great-aunt fought the giants on the other side of the big black lake, one of the giants raped my mother. I am the result of her violation. You call me a bastard child. My father, at least who I thought was my father, the man who named me Nirra, said the same horrible things. He hated me. And yet my mother always loved me."

Why was this part of the story left out by her Aunt Ki? A much calmer Tallia asks, "Then why is it my Aunt Ki shot at her uncle Narn when your mother ran away with you?"

"My mother said your Aunt Ki stopped my father, who disowned me, from killing me. My mother had to flee to protect me. She loved Narn. She loved his family. She loved how Nanshe looked after her. It was not fair. She did nothing wrong."

This ferocious reindeer warrior giant is not at all what she imagined. She never imagined giants valued family. Maybe he is right that when you grow up hated, you hate the world back, and you strike out in vengeance.

"My mother tried to find somewhere safe for us to live. But village after village chased us out because of their fear-driven hatred for me. 'No giant can be good. Just look at how tall he is.' They judged me on sight. They have no openness or tolerance for those different than they."

And the eyes well up again, and giant tears are veritable floods that could choke the ordinary human. But Tallia takes the first brave step since she was attacked. She takes off her headscarf to wipe his tears.

"You are kinder than most humans. You are like my mother. You care. All I wanted is what my mother said Nanshe's family had. Respect and love. That is why, when I saw you were one of her descendants, I moved quickly to save you."

He holds up his hands in an open gesture. Tallia can see the slash mark scars.

"I know you must have thought the worst. I took your knife wounds as my punishment. But I had to fake physically taking my pleasure with you, so the other giants would let me take you as my prize. I had only hoped that you and I could have what Orzu and Nanshe had. What Namu and Zamana had."

He gets up and leaves her to her solitude as he cries in the opposite corner of the room. Tallia crawls back into her corner. Her little safe haven of the last several moon cycles. She stares into the nothingness, wondering what the voice would have told her to do.

Daybreak. She must have fallen asleep. Then she sees him. She goes back into her defensive ball cower, for he is standing over her holding a spear in one hand and bow and arrow quiver in the other.

He hands her the spear as he helps her stand. Her legs wobble; they have not supported her full weight often since her confinement here.

"You are free to go," he states. His eyes emote sincerity.

She catches herself, as she thought giants were not sincere. Perhaps he was right about the biases and stereotypes humans cast upon strangers.

He puts the bow and quiver in her hands and says, "You are free to shoot me if you so desire. I deserve whatever punishment you deem fit for my participation in the killings and assaults of your family and friends, the killing and abuse of women I have taken part in all these lands. Just because the other giants said I had to do so to be a giant in their midst does not justify my actions. Complicity deserves the same punishment. If I were truly brave, if I were truly a nephew of Nanshe, I would have said no."

She trained enough with Aunt Ki on her hunts for dinner that the bow naturally balances in her hand. An arrow slots into the bowstring as if by magic, and her eyes train down the length of the shaft to the arrowhead pointed in between his eyes. Not long ago, Ki trained her to have the pull strength to drive an arrow deep into a tree. Back then, she could have killed this giant. But not now, not in her weakened state.

But her eyes lock onto his. Tears stream down his cheeks. Was he serious when he said that all he wanted was a family like she had known? She slowly releases her pull on the bowstring. She cannot kill this giant today.

She sees on the table he prepared a sack for her. Provisions for survival in the forest. Taking the spear, bow, arrow quiver, and the sack, she leaves him without a word.

Hungry, she stalks a rabbit the way Aunt Ki taught her. As she arrows the animal cleanly in the head, she remembers the story of how her grandfather Orzu was so docile he could not even kill a rabbit. His failure to defend his sister Illyana led to her captivity of the worst type by the reindeer giants. And thus, Tallia paid great heed to Ki's words about always being on guard for attacks by giants.

But then, she remembers Grandmother Nanshe's words about being people of peace. Her words about how one should do whatever is necessary for the ones they love. And then other words are heard. Not from anyone around, as she scans in a circle with her bow and arrow drawn.

It is Her. The voice. But how? She is not near the object. Tallia responds, "Yes, I heard you repeat what my grandmother said about peace. I am a woman of peace."

Tallia drops her bow to her waist. "Yes. I know how to forgive. But how can I? Yes, I will forgive those who have confessed their wrongs and who seek peace through love."

She drops to the ground with a bloody, partially decapitated rabbit next to her. She has only heard the voice when praying next to the object with her mother Sarpani and her Aunt Zirbani. She never has heard the voice by herself. What should she do?

She gathers her belongings and turns back to the house of Nirra. Ten paces and she turns completely around. She must find her children.

Her legs are wobbly, her feet in pain as she has not walked so much in many moon cycles. It is dark. It is cold. And she is lost, as the clouds obscure the direction the stars would have provided. She tumbles on a large branch. Exhausted, she huddles near an enormous tree trunk, knees up to her chin.

The rustling of the leaves. The thuds of the heaviest feet. She bolts up with spear in hand. But she is taken off guard by two reindeer giants attacking her from both sides. She stands no chance. She searches her belt for the knife Nirra packed for her. Better she kills herself than be a toy for these giants. But they are too fast. Her arms trapped by one and her legs spread by the other. Her worst nightmare has become all too real.

Her eyes close as she prays to the voice for mercy, she feels warm fluid spill across her face. Her eyes open, and she sees the spear piercing through the chest of one of her assailants as the other one has let her loose. She rolls on the ground to get her bow and an arrow and shoots the other one.

Nirra has come and battles the other giant he speared. Barbarians fighting for who will enslave the woman.

She aims her arrow at them, unsure who to kill.

Nirra yells, "Tallia, run! Fast! I can only delay this one so long."

Instinctually, she turns to run. But she sees the second giant she shot rise up. She shoots him again. Between the eyes this time. One giant killed. Ki would be proud of her.

The other giant, severely wounded, flees the area. Nirra is covered in crimson fluid, groaning on the ground.

Tallia comes to her giant. Her savior, she thinks. She surveys his wounds. Nanshe taught her how to gather certain plants and make salves that heal. Quickly, she scours the nearby vegetation and prepares a balm.

As she tends to his open wounds with his head in her lap, he opens his eyes and meets hers. Never in her life would she have imagined such a look from a giant.

He asks, "Why did you not flee when I told you to?"

His eyes are like a child's eyes. Do giants experience innocence? She answers, "The voice told me to do otherwise."

"And what else did this voice tell you?" queries the fascinated Nirra.

"She said I should honor your atonement for past transgressions. I should show you forgiveness if you had been genuine."

"And was I genuine?" he asks.

"You came and saved me," states she with the first smile Nirra has seen since his mother took care of him. "But if I am to stay with you, we must be equals," she insists. "We must show the world that man and woman together are together as equals."

"My mother was more than an equal for Narn," says the friendly giant.

"If you really wish to honor Nanshe," states Tallia, "then you will help me create the world she spoke of. One where man and woman ruled together, created peace together, and fostered love between peoples of different tribes together. We will create a world of abundance so peace can reign."

He smiles back at her and says, "You ask a lot out of a little giant like me."

Tallia laughs. "My grandmother said, if you love someone, you will figure out how to make it happen."

CHAPTER 6

In true love you want your partner to be happy.
In false love you want your partner.

—Paulo Coelho

MoxWorld Auditorium
San Francisco, California
10:10 a.m. GMT-8, January 4, 2023

"The e-book is dead. And today, I have killed it."

Towering over the audience like the monstrous monarch he is, the giant man pauses to let the statement sink in. Billions remotely view the MoxMedia News coverage of this soon-to-be-historic launch, with thousands live in the auditorium and another several thousand present by hologram. MoxWorld emitters surround the auditorium, as do MoxSecurity nodules.

"Utter mass murder do I, Alexander Murometz, commit. Not only are e-books massacred today, but the print book joins them. Because everything you love about print books will now be in your tactile hands through the new MoxReads program."

With a wave of his hand over his MoxWrap, a hologram book appears. "Today and forever, the old way is the new way for you to interact, touch, feel your books. You can turn pages, flip pages, even feel each page. You can write, highlight, and take notes on any part of a page using ordinary pencils or pens. You can even rip pages out. Everything you can do with your print book, you can do here on your MoxWrap.

"But wait. I give to you the freedom to do what you cannot do with your print book. And that is size your book to any dimension you wish," Alexander asserts with glee as he giant-sizes his hologram book to a meter and a half tall, and the world can see it is his official autobiography.

Backstage, Peter watches the deafening applause in the auditorium. Something about the timing of the sound seemed odd. Was it real, or did Alexander's tech fake the first applause that led to the rest of the room joining in? Put nothing beneath that man.

He glances at his MoxWrap. Not for the time, as he is due to hit the stage in ten more minutes to talk about his new book, but to rewatch Zara's hologram message to him. She does love him, after all. He feels the warmth as she declares she is so proud of him and his achievement. And after the book signing, she has something to tell him about the long-awaited next phase of their relationship. He is so ready to play papa to her two lambs.

He peeks into the audience and makes eye contact with Zara and his mother standing in the VIP section. Surrounded by two dozen of Alexander's security goons, of course. That man is so paranoid. He equipped Peter's MoxWrap with a special feature. A virtual sonic punch. Like pepper spray on steroids. Enough to stun someone, and with Peter's sprint speed, he might be able to flee.

Alexander gave up on Peter learning to stand and fight after Peter tried to train with MoxWorld Security's lead martial arts instructor and did something terribly wrong. Bones will heal. Usually. But after that, no other instructor has offered to help poor Peter for fear of their skeletal integrity.

But he does not need to cower anymore. Zara's message has given him all the inner strength and motivation to do magic on this worldwide stage today. As Alexander's soliloquy runs long, Peter remembers how much that man likes to talk. Peter's secret weapon to beating the giant on that pier six months ago—tangle the leviathan up in words, much like how Peter got that martial arts instructor tangled in his lanky limbs.

"And today, those of you in the room, in person and virtually, will be able to meet and greet the twelve authors who wrote books specifically for the MoxReads program," exclaims Alexander. "These pioneers will be available to sign your personal copy of their books. Yes, that signature will be permanent. And you can sell your MoxRead copy of their book the same as you can sell a print book. All part of my commitment to the freedom of the world's economy, and so all of you can make a living reselling the precious treasure you have worked so hard to obtain. I delivered true net neutrality when all others denied you such. Your book will be yours to do with what you wish."

The master of ceremonies readies the authors to take the stage. A flock of butterflies tries to fly through Peter's stomach. He closes his eyes and hears Zara's words of confidence, of love, of a future commitment play in utter harmony through his mind, and the butterflies pass him by and fly into the belly of the author next to him.

From the VIP area, Zara watches as Peter takes the stage. His moment of glory. His moment in the light. When her best friend Peri first took command of a squad and led an attack on a Syrian loyalist position, Zara was so proud of her. What she feels for Peter now might be a hundred times that, for reasons she still cannot fathom.

The blue light laser show illuminating the smoke clouds emitted for Peter's entrance reminds Zara of the prophecy the voice spoke of this morning.

She had been rubbing the object fragment Peter has kept near his bed ever since their last mission to bring the black object to Alexander Murometz. Then it happened again this morning. "What?" she asked. "Yes, I have not forgotten you. But it has been such a long time since you last spoke. Yes, I have been obedient to your words. Yes, I will follow your words. But how can I bring your words to the world? I am but a humble woman."

Zara opened her eyes. Looked around Peter's room. Not to assure herself she was not imagining this voice, but to make sure Peter's mother was not watching this act of the divine.

"Yes, I believe you are good. No. How can you be evil? Everything you have said to us has only brought good into this world. Yes, I understand. I will not let anyone mislead me. I believe in you. Yes, I believe in the light. The truth of the light. I will not be misled by the light."

She loosened her scarf, having become flush. She could not be menopausal yet. She was still well under forty. Her heart beat like a racing thoroughbred, but she stayed focused on Her.

"I have failed you in that. I cannot love him in that way. I cannot let him love me in that way. No, of course I love you in that way." She paused and swallowed. "Yes, I am obedient to your wishes. What? There is another black object? Yes, I will tell Peter that we must find the second black object. I understand that he and I must be man and woman in the deepest sense in order to search for this object. Yes, I understand that the search for this black object will lead us to the blue light."

Pausing again, she answered, "Yes, I heard you. But I do not understand. Two women will enter but only one will return, the other sacrificing her life as she knows it. This sacrifice must happen to maintain the balance of existence. Yes, I am prepared to make the sacrifice. Is this the same sacrifice which that tormented woman faced in the vision I had with Sasha? What do you mean? Yes and no?"

She inhaled, swallowed, and then added, "And I will tell Peter how I feel about him. But let me tell him after his big book unveiling this afternoon. I would not want him to be distracted. Please, I beg of you. Let him find what he searches for in being an author. It is the first time he has had the courage to create."

Her man, her ancient mate, takes the stage, and much to Zara's surprise, the crowds erupt on fire with ecstatic pounding of their feet, as if Peter were a rock star. After his book signing, she will fulfill her promise to the voice. She will tell Peter how she truly feels about him. The voice did not care about cats and dogs. Only that she needed to be obedient. To die in the blue light.

As Peter talks about the inspiration for his mythical sci-fi adventure story, Zara's MoxWrap taps her wrist. The emergency signal that only a select few have been given. She looks to see who it is. Do they not know how important this moment is to her?

And then she sees who. Excusing herself with Samantha, she exits the VIP area to find somewhere she can talk. A minute later, near the empty concessions area filled with Alexander Murometz swag, she taps her MoxWrap and her friend Peri appears.

"Zara, I am so sorry to bother you at this moment. My best wishes for Peter's success. But the Turkish delegation has stormed out of the negotiations. They called the Kurds terrorists, saying the Kurds should have been eliminated long ago."

Zara glances to the side, feigning ignorance, and then replies, "They said the same two months ago. They are just posturing, trying to get the Kurds to flinch. As Sasha would say—negotiation leverage."

"This time, they have mobilized their military to take MoxWorld's new factories by force. They say joint management of these new factories is a farce," cries Peri, making a scrunched face back at her.

Zara smiles and calmly says, "The EM pulse neutralized all the Turks' advanced military equipment six months ago. They no longer have technical superiority over the Anatolian Kurds."

Peri shakes her head. "Zara, there is a new player out there. While you have been in California, a global rival of your Mr. Murometz re-equipped half a dozen Turkish battalions with new AI-guided light arms and weaponized mini-drones."

Mouth agape, Zara says, "Tell the Kurds not to engage. Peaceful discussions must be the way forward through these times."

"They need you back here," states Peri. "I know you do not want to hear this, but many think you are holy. That you have a direct line to Xwedê. They think you can save them all. Fueling these flames, this morning, MoxNews came short of calling you the next messiah."

Now it's Zara's turn to shake her head. "I cannot save them. I am only a simple Kurdish woman. But I know someone who can. Tell everyone to hold tight."

Zara taps her MoxWrap for a map of the auditorium. Blocked? Alexander's tight security measures in action. She runs into the auditorium and heads backstage, only to be blocked by three security guards the size of the state of Texas. She pleads with them, "I must see Alexander Murometz right now."

"No ma'am," says the front most of the three titans. "Your access code has been blocked for these author presentations. If you would like, we can get you in front of the line for your favorite author's book signing."

Stomping her feet again—this time, with very comfortable sandals on—Zara says, "Do you know who I am? Call Mr. Murometz. He will tell you."

The senior guard steps forward, tapping his MoxWrap and says, "It says here you are his daughter. But your credentials read Khatum."

"I am not his daughter," insists Zara. "That man is deplorable, putting that into his databanks."

"It says here to gain access to Mr. Murometz, his daughter needs only to say the secret pass phrase."

"What pass phrase? This is a vital emergency where lives are at stake," says Zara, her hands gesticulating all about as if she were Italian.

"Ma'am, it should be on your MoxWrap," politely states the gargantuan man whose appearance would suggest such ceremony impossible.

Madly tapping on her wrist device, she pauses and utters, "You are kidding me. I will not say that. That man is playing a joke."

The senior guard, without a smirk, says, "I do not believe Mr. Murometz has a sense of humor, ma'am."

She taps her foot in contemplation and then, with a huff, says, "I love you, and I will do anything for you."

The guard smiles and says, "Yes, ma'am. You may enter. I will signal to the security chief you are looking for your father."

"He is not my father," she decries as she runs past the guards.

Watching from behind the stage, Alexander has his smug-as-a-thug face as she approaches. "Why, my little Zara, I knew you thought of me as family."

"I do not appreciate your specious public stunt," replies Zara. "I need you to call the Turkish president and get his negotiation team back at the table. They have mobilized their troops to take your factories by force."

Hell has no fury greater than a giant enraged. Alexander's face rotates through a panoply of red and redder hues as he taps away on his MoxWrap.

Zara gently touches his arm. "Please, do not ask your Russian friend to nuke them. That is not the answer."

Lips forming an oblong rectangle with eyes set to dark, obsidian glare, Alexander points at his MoxWrap and says, "Did you know this? That they struck a deal with that NiQihs company for advanced AI weapons?"

She pulls back from him with her hands defensively in front of her. "No. I just found out."

He taps and taps away on the MoxWrap and says as he walks away, "You need to take care of what you promised to do with Peter after the author signing. Then, I will have my security jet waiting for you to take you back to the negotiation table. You need to neutralize their threats with your own threat of that sacred voice you hear."

Peter exits the stage with the eleven other authors, savoring his victory like a delicacy he hasn't ever tasted so sweetly before. He pauses a second as he sees her. The woman who will profess her final love to him after this event. The woman who will gladly convince his highly Catholic mother that a Kurdish wedding in Siirt would be as good as one in St. Mary's Cathedral in San Francisco.

Odd. She appears preoccupied. Maybe she is trying to find the words for her ultimate commitment. The sanctity of finally saying yes to lifelong love. With his new sense of courage inspired by her call, he wraps his arms around her, undeterred. The bear hug that normally brings peace to her fits of angst.

He pulls back a bit to see her face. Odd. Not the wonderfully warm visage she emotes after such a hug. "Wasn't I just wonderful up there?" he asks. "Without that call you made while I was prepping with the other authors, I couldn't have had that kind of confidence. My win is your win." And he hugs her again.

This time, she pulls back a little bit, one eyebrow slanted down over a squinted eye. "What call?" she asks.

"Since when did you become the jokester?" quips Peter. "The one where you told me how much you truly loved me and I said I do truly love you as well. The one where you said we would talk about our life together after the book signing."

Her eyes gaze to the side as her lips mouth airy words of nothing. Well, her response was not what he would have expected. Peter pushes her back, his hands firmly around her arms as if he wanted to control the situation as he stares into her eyes. "You remember that conversation, don't you?"

"That monster. He has developed an AI program that can imitate anyone to the minutest detail," states Zara, stomping both feet. "He tried to fool me with it when he picked me up yesterday."

Peter lets her go, head to the side, and says, "But it was you. Your choice of words. Your body language. The way you looked me in the eye. It was all you."

"I am so sorry, Peter, that Alexander has played this trick on you. He has no humanity. No compassion. No soul."

Now his eyebrows form a V as he asks, "But you would've said what his fake message had said. Wouldn't you have? He can't make up something that isn't based on reality. Can he?"

Her silence slices through him like an alien phaser beam. Scorched cauterized blood congeals on his chest as he softly says, "Alexander was just saying how you weren't seeing me only to get closer to the voice. That you weren't using me and our ancient genetic connection. And your call was perfectly timed, refuting all those rumors he wanted me to ignore. You would've said the same things, wouldn't you?"

Scorching silence. Zara has never been so tongue-tied since Peter first met her. Aggressively assertive. A powerfully independent woman of great command and strength. And some great being somewhere is playing a cosmic joke on him, replacing her with this woman who cannot even say how she feels.

Giving her the benefit of the doubt, Peter changes tack and asks, "But wasn't I fantastic up there? All those blue lights on me and the world watching. I didn't even stutter. I bet my mother is finally proud of her wayward son. Aren't you?"

Another unexpected move by her as she glances down. She would never lie to him. Not even stretch the truth to help ease the situation, for he is somehow different from all the others. "I am so sorry, Peter. I missed your presentation. I had to attend to an emergency back in Kurdistan."

Flushed rosy cheeks turn to dusty grey. All love drains from his face. All hope follows it as Peter says, "I can't believe you, Zara. This was the greatest moment in my life. What I have dreamed of, aspired to, finally made possible by a man whom you despise. Who maybe isn't so bad after all. Who maybe wasn't lying about those rumors."

He turns away from her. "I had only hoped that the woman I love, the one who transcended the closeness of any other woman in my life, could share such a moment with me. At least my mother saw me. At least she can be proud that I finally was a man today. What happened to your admiration of what I professed on the mountain top? You still don't see me as your man. Not that man who you want on that mountain of yours. All I wanted was respect. And today was my day to get that. But not from you, apparently. Nor from your voice."

"Peter, Peter. The voice. I heard Her again after many months. And she has a message for us. It has to do with another object and the blue light."

"The voice. The voice. The voice. You love me for the voice, Zara. I would have never imagined it would come to this. I honestly believed you cared for me. But then again, you and Sasha are alike. You manipulate the innocent for your own gain. Today, I am a man, and I will stand up for myself. Even to you."

"But I have been true to you. Everything we have been through together. You have been in my soul as I have been in yours. The object empowered us. I do care for you."

"But do you love me?" asks Peter with arms folded in front. "Love me enough to share what I've dreamed of the most?"

"The visions, the voice, the dreams," implores Zara. "We have shared all of these and seen the truth together. I am true with you."

"The truth. Maybe the voice is misleading you. Maybe Alexander is truer than your voice," states Peter. "Okay, maybe he did try to kill me back on that pier. But since then, my life has gotten better working for him."

Out from the side stage access, a woman in a MoxWorld uniform calls out, "Mr. Gollinger. The audience is waiting for you at your book signing station." She winks at him. "There are a lot of young women there waiting for you. Your book is a hit with the ladies."

Lips pouted, he turns to Zara and says, "Maybe my words have made a difference in their lives. I hoped I had done the same for you. Your happiness is all I wanted. I'm sorry you don't feel the same back."

As he walks off to his next destiny, Zara ponders her next action. Chase after him? Beg him to stay with her? But why? If she is to die in the blue light as the voice had said, is he not better off without her? How could She insist on her declaring her love for him when she must sacrifice her life? Maybe Sasha was right. She should leave him with someone better for him.

All she can think of is her great-grandmother's saying: if you love someone, you will do anything for them.

CHAPTER 7

At the touch of love, everyone becomes a poet.

—Plato

MoxWorld Auditorium
San Francisco, California
11:50 a.m. GMT-8, January 4, 2023

"All you had to do is say you made the call," says the giant owner of the new hit MoxReads program. "I knew you would be tongue-tied, so I expressed what I know you would have wanted to say.

"You should have seen how bent out of shape Peter was coming to the book signing area," her Sasha laments. "I had to give him a pep talk and then seek the source of his distraction: one very strong-minded, stubborn, not-so-humble Kurdish woman."

"How dare you make a fake me?" protests Zara. "You cannot have my body, so you concoct your own."

Her Sasha grins, replying, "And how dare you hurt my boy Peter? How dare you fake your affections for him for your own devious purposes?"

"That is not true," she protests, stamping her foot again.

"You are such a superb actress, my dear little Zara," smiles the leviathan man. "This foot-stomping thing is a new little trick you have devised. Or do your feet still smart from those boots?"

A strategic pause as the world's most manipulative master toys with his prey, who shakes with her arms crossed, her eyebrows intensely raised. And just as her mouth began to move, he interjects, "Or is your relationship with Peter becoming that serious that you act out your trepidations through your feet?"

"You make me so mad. That is what this foot stomping is about. No act. No reaction to my relationship with Peter. You have exceeded my tolerance for your manipulative, conniving puppetry."

So, so smug. Thug smug as he tosses a logic grenade back at her. "And who is conniving here? Why can you not speak your heart to my boy? What is truly in your heart?"

No foot stomp this time. Only a pause as she tries to articulate what she feels. Nothing. No words.

"So, I see now what you did with Peter to nearly ruin all of that wondrous manly confidence I spent the last six months building up in him. You know what he confided in me? He only wants to be the man you need in your life. A real man. Not the little boy you had been calling him."

Her fighting face comes back as she retorts, "Peter knows what is in my heart. When we bonded near the object. When we meditate together. There is nothing within me he has not seen or touched. All because of those ancient DNA segments you desperately wanted to have activated in us on our last mission."

"My dear, ask your mother if you will not believe me. Things left unsaid fester like a slow-growing cancer. Eating at you slowly until one day…" says her Sasha in a delicate tone of voice she has never heard from him since that moment when the commandos handed her over to the medevac team. "You may think he knows what you feel, but until you say it to his face, say it with all sincerity, he will not truly know. Ask your dear mother, Maryam, about unsaid things. She knows."

"I do not know what you speak of. My mother is nearly a saint. She has protected me, loved me, and helped me through my father's suicide."

He turns from her, his towering figure throwing an ominous shadow upon her. Looking into the air, he says, "A horse. My kingdom for a horse."

Turning back to her, eyes locked onto hers, he says, "Well, not a horse but a new pass phrase. My dear little Zara. My most special Zara. My kingdom is yours for a pass phrase. All you have to do is say out loud, 'Peter, I truly love you. With all my heart, I love you,' and you will have access to my entire empire. All the power and services that MoxWorld Holdings can offer. You will become the most powerful woman in the world simply by declaring what is really in your heart."

She turns her back to him. "You are a sick man."

"Remember, wood can only be split with a wedge that is cut from its own tree. But what matters is the menu on the table now," says Alexander. "And Peter is that menu."

Back in his face, she retorts, "Do not resort to old Kurdish sayings to sway me."

His serious face returns as he states, "In mere moments, you will lose him. I hope that is by choice. Because if not you, I will need to take irrevocable actions to ensure he is with a woman bearing his child when he guides us to the cavern of the blue light."

Tapping his foot, then his MoxWrap, he adds, "Time is not on our side. My backup to you will expire in several weeks. You need to be decisive and take the action needed to fulfill your Sara's last wishes or we both will lose."

He turns and leaves her, then pauses in his step and says, "I fixed your Turkish negotiation problem. I hope you appreciate my solution. Do not be so headstrong that you do not recognize who here you cannot trust. I have always come through for you. So has Peter. Everyone else? Suspect." Tapping his MoxWrap, he quickly trots off.

What is with her? Before she met Peter, she was so self-assured. So much on the path to being like Rabi'a. Is this monster finally telling the truth? She cannot commit to Peter because she is using him to be closer to Xwedê? She shudders at the thought that he is right as she walks over to Peter's book signing area.

That woman from MoxWorld did not exaggerate. His signing area is swamped with women. Of all types. Maybe she should have read his book.

What did he write that only double X chromosomers flock to it?

Using her VIP credentials to get in close to him, she catches his eye. She smiles at him, and he smiles back. Maybe what happened between them is a natural relationship thing. Peri said that she and her husband, a former Jesuit priest friend of Father Jean-Paul, had their first all-out fight two months after he quit the order to marry her. Their differences, in culture, in religion, in family-raising philosophies, came to a head. But Peri said that post-fight makeup sex made it all worthwhile. Well, that is not in the cards for the celibate Zara. But maybe they will have just as worthwhile makeup spiritual bonding tonight.

She watches as a young woman with her "hunting" clothes, tightly affixed and showing much without revealing it all, interacts with Peter. "Hi, I'm Candy. One of your advance reviewers. Oh, Mr. Gollinger, is it true what they say? That what an author writes reflects who they really are? What they really can do?"

Clearly trying not to stare at all the wrong places, Peter blushes and says, "Why, of course."

With a lascivious wink, the woman puffs her chest out as she says, "So, you're saying you're as virile as that French ex-priest in your book who finally gets that chaste Moroccan woman to relent?"

Peter's blush turns into a full-on beet flush as he stammers, "What?" At which the woman shows him passage after passage of the most sensuously explicit erotica.

He turns to Zara and mouths something to her agitatedly. Seeing she cannot hear over the crowd, he taps out a message on his MoxWrap, "I didn't write anything like that!"

And then another woman with a shorter than short, tiny, hide-nothing skirt in this advance reviewer line interjects, "But didn't the priest finally conclude it was really rough backdoor sex that opened up that virgin's psychic abilities?" She flips her skirt up and twerks at him and adds, "Didn't you write how only with the threat of her little pink hole being violated did the truth finally come out. The truth of the visions?"

Hands over his eyes, lips quivering at 1000 rpms, he mutters, "No, no.

That was not in the book I wrote. I swear. My mother raised me better than that."

Zara laughs. She surmises that the new book tech of Peter's idol, Mr. Alexander Murometz, must be modifying a novel to the taste of the individual reader the same as his MoxWrap devices modify their configurations based on a user's DNA. That is how devious that monster is. This way, he'd guarantee every book to be a best seller. He is truly the devil incarnate.

Laughing next to her is another woman, a couple centimeters shorter than the average-American-height Peter. Dishwater-blonde hair with purple tints. Her earlobes have huge circles in them with matching, purple-accented silver rings inset into the holes. She wears a T-shirt with a grey flying saucer under which is written, "I want to believe." Seeing how Zara also laughed, the purple-earholed one introduces herself and asks, "So, what ghastly things did your version of Peter's book say?"

Zara replies, "I am sorry. I am not here for the signing. Only to watch the circus." She gives the woman a once-over, clearly noticing the small logo on her cap. A yellow slug sitting Buddha style.

The woman extends her hand. "My name is Tamarah. Tamarah Goldberg. But Peter preferred to call me Tara, for short. Something about the 'ara' suffix attracted him. His girlfriend after me was named Ciara."

Feigning innocence for the second time this morning, Zara asks, "So, did you know Mr. Gollinger very long?"

"Yeah. We dated in college. We hit it off right away. You see, I'm an astrophysicist. Sophomore year, I was working on a paper using a physics theorem to demonstrate that alien life must exist. He fell in love with my theorem. Then me, I suppose."

Somewhat embarrassed to be talking with one of his old girlfriends, but also determined to understand what it is in Peter she fails to understand, Zara asks, "So he always was a believer in extraterrestrial existence."

"Yes. Obsessively so. It was his dad who brainwashed him. Some voodoo mumbo-jumbo about a rock that the aliens left," says Tara. "His mother is a devout Catholic and had Peter enrolled in a Jesuit university hoping they would talk sense into him. But in his freshman year, he debated a senior Jesuit priest on the existence of God, arguing that deities were only aliens who visited Earth, that angels are only extraterrestrial beings guiding our destiny. Right or wrong, Peter's logic was flawed, and the priest trounced him in a very public debate. That devastated the poor boy. He lost all respect and couldn't show his face on campus, so he transferred to the exact opposite place on Earth. Our beloved banana slug school in the redwoods."

His lifelong search for respect, ponders Zara. That explains why, during the search for the object, he debated Father Jean-Paul on theological concerns. That also explains why he was so hurt earlier today. If she could have truly been that humble Kurdish woman she portrays, she would have recognized his modest need for her demonstrated respect.

Tara continues, "I am so thrilled for him. Look at him basking in the attention for his book. He was a madman about verbal logic ever since transferring to UC Santa Cruz. He would never ever be defeated again by his own soft verbal logic."

Zara remembers how Peter's verbal logic tied up Alexander that day on the dock. Long enough for Jean-Paul's ex-military priest friends to neutralize Alexander's security forces.

"Sounds like you two had the perfect relationship. Like minds. Like cultures. Cats belong with cats," posits Zara, who notes they are both blond as she tucks an errant strand of her straight dark brown hair under her scarf. "If you do not mind me asking, was marriage not a possibility?"

Putting a stick of gum in between her molars, Tara says, "You'd think. But this old gal is too much of a quant jock. I couldn't show him the kind of respect he needed. I'm just a numbers girl. Equations and all that. He needed words. And Ciara, the ancient civilizations major, spoke that language. You know, if you love someone, you should do what is right for them. And mathematically, I did love him. But I could see Ciara was better for him. I was a dog and Peter a cat. Ciara was a cat. Cats should be with cats. So, I kind of pushed him her way."

Tara blows a bubble and pops it. "Hey. Don't get me wrong. I got a great boyfriend now. But even though it was more than a decade ago, I have to wonder what might have happened."

Another bubble pop and she adds, "You know, he loved me so much he studied Hebrew. He would have converted to Judaism even though his mother raised him Catholic. I couldn't let him do that. It wasn't him. I loved him too much. Hey, I gotta go meet someone. Nice chatting with you."

What else about Peter does she not know? ponders Zara as she scans the other women in waiting. And what other versions of poor Peter's story do these women think he wrote?

Another woman stands directly in her face, wearing a T-shirt featuring the previous US president with a giant X through his face. She gives Zara the once-over, head to toe, and says, "You know, you're safe here in the US. You can dress how you want to. Not how those men of your religion tell you. Women are free here. You can take the covering off your head."

Zara smiles at her, putting her hands around her headscarf and loosening it, only to re-affix it tighter. "That is so kind of you to think of my well-being. Thank you. But I dress as I do not because any man, nor any religion, forces me to. I do so because I respect myself. I do so, so that others will deal with me for who I am and not how my body appears."

The other woman replies, "Wow. That is a direct quote from that guy's book. I didn't think anyone thought that way."

Another woman is wearing a tight T-shirt with a deep V-cut, imprinted with:

- Bad choices
- Questionable choices about men
- Skimpy outfits
- Terrible hair

Although Zara grew up on the other side of the world, women must be the same everywhere, for she had scored 75% on this T-shirt. For sure, she never had a visible bad hair day, thanks to the headscarf she has always worn since she came of age to practice her family's tradition of modesty. Well, almost always.

But bad choices in men? Third time's a charm did not happen for her. Three times in a row, she made questionable choices in men. First that boy, Zengo, whom she followed into the Iraqi Kurd military, the Peshmerga, at the age of seventeen. She convinced herself they'd both enlisted to free the Kurds from Saddam's torturous rule, but she never conceded to herself that she was smitten in love.

Then, on the rebound from Zengo's battlefield infidelities, she fell for a very handsome, charming American civil advisor to the Peshmerga, Dan, for whom she wanted to bear a beautiful new family, only to find out he already had a lovely wife and children back in Washington, D.C.

Swearing never to give her love away again, never to hurt her heart again, she decided she would play with men as they did with her. And with Anatoly, a Russian Special Forces officer she met when she studied in Moscow, she played. Her charms and her body she dangled in front of him as a child would dangle a toy mouse before a cat. But this cat fell deeply in love with her. He almost died on a mission he undertook to show the true depth of his love for her. And she had to leave him, for deep inside, she wished no harm to anyone anymore.

But what sealed her fate, what she believed Xwedê willed as her punishment for her transgressions of her faith's codes of modesty, came from the skimpy dresses she and her Ezidi cousins wore that cataclysmic day when the Daesh overran their village and took them all as slaves in servitude of the unspeakable.

Her nose violently shivers as she inhales with that thought. If she could trade her life forever in penance, even once again as a slave, for the freedom of her cousins, she would in a microsecond. For they were always faithful to Xwedê, to their traditions. It was she who broke from Xwedê, who flaunted her body with those men. It was she who deserved the horrible fate that befell her cousins. Or so she had thought until she met Peter.

As Zara glances at the line in front of Peter, she notices another woman adorned with a headscarf waiting for his autograph. Perhaps Peter did capture Zara's family tradition accurately in his book. Perhaps Sasha had the good sense not to alter that part.

As she scans the line backed up all the way to the hall exit, she spies that woman with the dishwater hair with purple tinges, Tamarah, near a tall man. Same loftiness as Sasha, but a little leaner, dressed in black. His facial features are unusual. A racial mix. Maybe Central Asian? Maybe East Asian–Caucasian mix? He hands Peter's former girlfriend a sizable envelope, from which Tamarah distributes smaller packets to other women who had been in line to see Peter.

As the hairs on her neck try to poke straight into her headscarf, her nose crinkles. She focuses on another female standing next to the tall man, who leaves the hall after patting her on the shoulder. That woman—she is familiar. Who is she?

Pursing her lips, closing her eyes, her nose still crinkled, Zara racks her cerebral mass, searching for when she has seen that woman before. She taps away on her MoxWrap and her eyes pop open.

There lies her answer. In person, she is more attractive than Zara remembered. Are not medical research professors supposed to be dowdy and nerdy?

One hundred seventy-five centimeters. Perfect model height in black patent Jimmy Choos. Dark brown wavy hair done up in a beehive with a metallic design accent. Trademark of Peter's sister, who is studying fashion and material sciences at the Shanghai-Paris Fashion Institute. Peter spent many late nights with her, editing her last book to get it published two months ago before the final push on his own book. She looked like not a million, but ten million dollars. Her book contract must have been quite lucrative.

Dr. Beverly Fontaine, recently promoted after her book deal to an associate professor of psychiatry at UC–San Francisco medical school, spots Zara staring at her and waves the suspicious Kurd over. The doctor shakes Zara's fingers, trying to feign elegance. Something about the light roughness along the thumb edge of the doctor's index finger alerts the soldier in Zara. Maybe it has to do with some medical procedure.

"My dear. I was hoping to run into you again. You are more radiant than when we met at Peter's pappy's funeral. You, the woman who has captured my precious editor's heart," states Dr. Fontaine. Her face turns less than gracious as she says, "And I fear his soul too."

"Pardon me," utters Zara, not knowing what to make of this doctor or her involvement with all these other women seeking Peter's newfound author fame. "I am sorry. I need to attend to something urgent. Please excuse me?"

Zara offers, as she tries to slip by this medical inquisitor.

But before she can pass her, the doctor says, "You know Captain Luciano, don't you? He remembers you."

Does she lie and flee, or does she stand her ground? That part of Zara has not gone soft as she stops, stiffens, and answers, "Tony. From the US Ranger battalion that my Peshmerga unit assisted."

"Well, your Tony is under my care at the VA," says the doctor. "You didn't know, did you? I suppose that's how you treat your so-called friends. PTSD does strange things to a person. Especially those who have been shelled, bombed, or tortured. Some think they know God. They hear God. They want others to follow them because they're more important now after their stress event than anyone else. And Tony and I talk with God together as part of his therapy."

Zara's face softens. "I did not know Tony lived here. Back then, he was based in Texas. I would have visited him if I had known."

"And as his physician, I wouldn't have let you," replies Dr. Fontaine sternly. "But I care too much about him, and Peter as well, to have a woman who doesn't know how much her own untreated severe PTSD is hurting others. Look at what Peter wrote in his book. His main character is a woman who talks with a voice from heaven that no one else hears. How will my innocent editor, my naïve Peter, be hurt by such a woman's untreated delusions?"

"I am not delusional," protests Zara. "Peter knows that. He sees what I see."

"Here's your Tony, and then you try telling me that again," says the doctor as she taps the MoxWrap on her wrist. Up pops a hologram of Captain Luciano muttering his hallucinations, his God delusions, repeating that he knows what will save the world.

Shaking as if the temperature has dropped a hundred degrees centigrade, Zara takes one last look into this psychiatrist's uncaring eyes and flees for the nearest exit. She never thought anyone could pulverize her buttons worse than Sasha, but she was wrong.

CHAPTER 8

Don't be quick to quarrel otherwise you may be ashamed in the end.
Yeshayahu/Isaiah 3:13, Tanakh

Jerusalem, Israel
4:20 p.m. GMT+3, January 4, 2023

I have to give this to her, this stubborn Palestinian woman. She is as tenacious as I was at her age. Professor Capsali, she calls me. My name is Rachel. But let her call me a formal title. That will keep our distance.

Yesterday evening, she came into my excavation area just as the MoxWorld Security team arrived. After watching her conspiring with those suspicious men in dark shades, I asked the security team to escort her away somewhere. They had asked if I would like her to be taught a lesson for bothering me. That look on her face. It wasn't one of fear, but of someone standing defiant who has endured such lessons before. I couldn't be the cause of inflicting more trauma in her life, and she left unharmed.

Today, she did the same thing. Checked out the men watching me and then came down to my excavation. You would think my compassion yesterday was my downfall, but curiosity truly is. Why else would I spend my life digging in dirt and rubble to find out the truth? I wanted to know what this woman wanted of me, that she would risk another call to the MoxWorld Security team.

If not for the writing on her long-sleeved black top, I wouldn't have let her come near my newly discovered tomb. But how can I not empathize with the logo written in a shade of pink matching her headscarf: "Not Your Habibti." The #MeToo-generation Palestinian woman's way of saying "bug off" to any would-be sexual harasser.

My hand on my Jericho in my backpack, I let her approach. Her timing was uncanny. After almost another day excavating this second tomb, an hour ago I carefully extracted the tablet from the times of King David, the proof that his mother worshipped the goddess Asherah. I had just sent detailed scans for Mei and Father Jean-Paul when this young woman arrived.

Her eyes on my hand hidden in my pack, she says nothing. We stare at each other, my eyes on her backpack. What does she hide in there? But then I recognize the pattern of the weave. I have seen this before? Where? So, I ask.

"Nagla," says Massa to my question. "My grandmother who taught me my family's traditional weaving pattern—her name is Nagla."

"So, you crafted an entire backpack using that pattern?" I ask.

"I made this in grade school in an afternoon program. My Taata Nagla had been teaching me about our family traditions once I reached the age of accountability. She taught me about hijab, modesty, and other more personal aspects of the women in our family lineage. I dedicated my school project in honor of our family's traditions."

Putting my hand out to feel the weave on her family-inspired craftwork, I remember now and say, "I recall seeing a similar handicraft at a high school I guest-lectured at a while ago."

And this Palestinian woman finally smiles at me. "That was mine. I can never forget your lecture on how the Torah does indeed teach tolerance. You gave me hope that true peace could one day be possible. You must have given hundreds of talks. Why would you even remember that one?"

Is the fact that I have only spoken once to a mixed audience why I remember? Everywhere I have taught has always been to people of my faith. Except that one time when my aba, my father, asked me to do this one favor for his dear friend, the principal of that school. I am certainly not saying that to this stranger.

"That is so silly of me. You are a brilliant professor," she says, to which I nod. "Your mind must remember everything. I have followed your career ever since that day."

Seriously, I never knew I had a fan club. Most of my lecturers are so controversial that audiences mostly remember their outrage. What is the catch here? What is the con that's about to happen now that she's set me up?

"Professor, please, please, let me help you with your excavation. I only want to follow in your footsteps. Your university only accepts Jewish students. Admissions, and then human resources only saw my headscarf and not my dedication and desire to show the world the truth that archaeology can reveal."

No fair. She is citing words that I have used in talks about truth and digging dirt for glimpses of our past.

"Massa, why is my work so important to you? There's a plethora of archaeological projects in nondenominational universities both in and outside of Israel. Why my work?"

She bites her lip. What is she hiding? I'm being set up. I need to get out in the open and see who else might be coming. I begin to pull out my Jericho from my backpack and try to get by her. But then her hand reaches into her handmade backpack. She's a suicide bomber like the one who killed my saba seventeen years ago at the Rosh Ha'ir shawarma restaurant in Tel Aviv!

"Professor, please. Please. Why do you have a gun in my face?" she yells as I pull back the slide on my Jericho, loading a limb-shredding forty-caliber shell, my eleventh birthday gift from my aba, son of my assassinated saba.

"Hand out of that backpack. Slowly," I assert in my deepest authoritarian voice as I focus on steadying my hands. I cannot show weakness to a suicide bomber. Not in memory of my poor saba.

Her backpack held out on three fingers of her left hand toward me, she pulls on her pink headscarf, tears forming at the corners of her eyes. "You are no different than the rest of them. You see this around my head and assume I am a terrorist. I only wanted to answer your question as to why I had, until this moment, wanted to be like you. Follow in your footsteps."

Gun barrel aimed square between her eyes, I say, "Do you take me for a *fri'er*? Someone you can fool? Put it down slowly. Do not touch anything inside or outside your pack. Then we can talk."

As she slowly lowers her childhood handicraft project to the granite floor of the tomb, she says, "Why would an archaeology professor have such a big gun with her on an excavation in the middle of a city park? I thought only professors in the movies or in books do that."

With my Jericho, I signal for her to move away from that backpack. I have no idea how to defuse a bomb. Certainly, it was not a core topic in either rabbinical school nor my graduate work in Cambridge. "After that suicide bomber killed my saba, my father gave me this gun so he would not lose his only daughter as well."

Now fully with tears in her eyes, Massa says, "Then it is true. You are connected with Mossad. Here only to find evidence that connects East Jerusalem with the stories in the Torah. To promote the claim that Israel has always been in these lands, before the Palestinians. You are no different from all those other nationalistic Jewish archaeologists. Agents of the secret government Zionist institutions."

Now that hurts. I am different. In all the right ways. I lower my gun, the oddest sign of a father's love for his daughter, and reply, "And now you stereotype me back. Just because someone is Israeli does not mean they are Zionist or, for that matter, work for the Mossad. But if you had a close relative killed by a suicide bomber, you too would be wary of a stranger with a backpack."

Drying her tears with the backs of her hands, she retorts, "In 2004, my father's older brother was killed by Israeli troops in your Operation Rainbow. Just because he dressed like a Palestinian did not mean he was Hamas. His only mistake was to move into the Gaza Strip, thinking that finally, a Palestinian State was real."

A renewed stream of drops come from Massa's eyes and now another stream from her nostrils, soaking her pink headscarf. As mucousy film coats her mouth, Massa utters, "I had hoped you could overlook my headscarf, my culture, as my ancestor El did with Asefeh of Jerusalem. Their desire to find Asherah led them to overcome any differences between their nations. I thought that might be you and me."

Did she say Asherah? How did she know? A quick glance down, a deep breath in, and I put my Jerico back into my pack. My palms up in front of me for a second, I say, "Okay. No violence between us, right? You are okay. I am okay. Right?"

She nods. Out of my backpack I pull out a handkerchief, wiping her cheeks and below her nose. "Here, take it. Maybe I overreacted."

Blowing her nose into my handkerchief, she says, "My taata said after the Occupation, things changed and they lived in fear of moments just like this. Until now, I had no problems in Jerusalem. Only the one issue of getting to be an assistant in your university."

Occupation. That is what the Arabic population called their territorial losses in the Six-Day War. I am sensitive enough to know that much. I am not an occupier. My great-grandfather Kemel was murdered by true occupiers—which I have sworn to avenge.

Biting my lips again, I search for any rational reason for my behavior. She is truly an innocent soul. Have I lost it now, having found the proof I have spent the last eight years searching for? The justification for not completing my rabbinical studies? And then she drops the real bomb.

"The men in black suits watching you," she says while in full eye contact with me. "One pair is Israeli intelligence. So perhaps not all Israeli men in dark outfits with sunglasses are Mossad, but these two are not passive observers."

My eyes are wide open, my mouth agape. I blow a deep breath through my nose as I process that "bomb." I ask, "How do you know that?"

"Yesterday, when I first approached you, I spotted three surveillance teams intently focused on the excavation. I walked up to all three groups of the men watching you and pretended to be a simple Palestinian street vendor. Stereotypes can work to your benefit when you need them to. I overheard those Israeli agents reporting in on your activities, awaiting orders to intercede with your dig. They had big guns, like you have. The exact same type."

I hit my MoxWrap, texting Mei. "I need those MoxWorld Security goons to come back pronto. And not for the Palestinian girl this time." As I wait for Mei to answer, I ask, "And what about the other two? Israeli agents too?"

"No. One pair is Russian. Yesterday, the other pair was Asian or Central Asian. The tall man was a little odd. His grin let off a blinding silver glint from a tooth. His eyes were grey. Eerily so. And the other man, he appeared more East Asian, more androgynous, with a beauty mark. A mole next to his left lip. Today, there are two big Asian men instead. Maybe Central Asian."

Now, I quiver. What is about to happen? Now, I wish that her backpack had a bomb in it, so I could toss it at any of these agents of possible ill intent.

"Rach, those scans of the tablet are awesome," interrupts Mei on my MoxWrap. "Do you think Israel will mind if we borrow them for a couple months so Jean-Paul can examine them in more detail at the Vatican? I haven't been able to focus on your project enough. I'm still missing my lead excavator, Jia. Mademoiselle Tsong must have found the love of her life and run off, because only love is more important than stopping China from nuking the world."

"Mei, seriously, I need the MoxWorld Security team here again pronto. I have a new associate here who says that those men watching me are from three factions. Israeli, Russian, and Asian."

With a laugh, Mei says, "I assure you that the Chinese have no interest in Asherah. Russian? That must be the big man himself. You know, your Mr. Murometz you dearly want to meet. But your own government? Why should you be concerned?"

"I don't know. I just have a bad feeling here. Maybe it is just my jitters. I have worked so long to find this tablet."

"No worries, Rach. I'll dispatch two security teams this time. It's near rush hour there, so it may be over fifteen minutes. You think you're safe for that long? I'll also check to see if those two Russians are MoxWorld agents."

With a deep breath out, I answer, "Maybe it's nothing. But at least they can escort this tablet back with me to the university. I'll ping you when the security team gets here. Thanks."

"Hey. That issue we talked about yesterday," says Mei. "I'm trying to reach the guy to tell him about my condition first. Telling Zara first didn't make sense. But I will soon. Love you." And Mei blows me her signature kiss as she signs off.

Poor Massa. She stands there, unsure of what to say. Watching her eyes darting back and forth, I apologize. "I am so sorry that you had to listen to my friend's soap opera drama. I have very unusual friends."

"Professor, I guess I never thought of you as a human being like the rest of us. Facing the ordinary problems of love and life," says Massa.

I hold out my hand and say, "It's Rachel. Simply Rachel."

At first, unsure of what my hand means, she feebly grasps my hand back and shakes. "Thank you, Profess…Rachel."

Glancing down at her backpack, I ask, "What did you want to show me in there before I rudely put the barrel of a gun between your eyes?"

As she cautiously gets her pack, with her eyes fixed on mine all the time, she says, "Remember when I said my taata taught me how to be a faithful Muslim woman once I reached the age of accountability? Well, she also taught me about where the women in our family came from. And she gifted me this heirloom."

Unbelievable. It was a bomb in there—not the TNT type, but an archaeological bomb. My hands shake as I ask to hold it. I never, ever thought I would find a piece of it.

"My taata said this came from times when the Mongols visited the Mount of the House. Oh, you call it the Temple Mount," says Massa.

My finger runs along the entire surface of the statue fragment. Twenty centimeters by fifteen. I shudder as I ask the critical question. "Did your taata say what statue this came from?"

Her lips in a flat line, the young woman says, "You know how legends are often exaggerated." She pauses, shuffling a foot. "But she said this came from the legendary statue of Asherah, which stood underneath what you call the First Temple."

Silence.

She's waiting for me to speak. And me? Stunned. The first proof of Elohim. Because only the Divine could have had the two of us meet. Or was it Asherah who made this meeting happen?

"I had applied at your university to be an intern. An unpaid intern," she says, breaking the silence. "My taata made me promise to abide by hijab modesty as well as find the rest of this statue. El is the name of our ancient matriarch. With a Jewish woman, Asefeh, they overcame religious differences and found the statue under the Temple Mount. Perhaps you and I are the same. Different, but with similar interests."

Oh Asherah, give me the strength to be the objective archeologist. My safta raba Ariella said She told her that two women of opposing faiths would lead to Armageddon. The end of the world as we know it. And yet this young woman says that Asherah's great statue was uncovered by an ancient Jewish woman with a Muslim woman working in harmony.

As the sunlight diminishes with evening on the verge of arriving, I use my MoxWrap light to show this amazing young woman the tablet. "The text proves that the mother of King David authorized construction of the statue of Asherah for the First Temple. The same that your fragment came from."

Her eyes are as wide as mine had been seeing her fragment. I show her the palm-sized statuette I found as well. "This was also in this tomb. It must have been a prototype that the king had authorized the full statue from. See how this one segment is where your fragment likely came from?"

But she surprises me. Instead of awe at the tablet and statuette, Massa's head quickly twists around, scanning the edges of the park. "Profess…Rachel. Two pairs of the men dressed in black are no longer watching. Where are they?"

And before I can fully assess the situation, she tries to grab the tablet and my backpack. Thinking she is going to bolt with my find, I clasp the backpack and tablet against my chest.

"*Yalla*. Let's go. You must hide this tablet," Massa says. "They must have seen you showing it to me. Men do not want the world to know of her. Of Asherah. You know that."

The trained scientist of all things ancient in me says that putting the tablet in a backpack is tantamount to a sacrilegious act of the most egregious kind. And then, we hear it. The androgen-fueled deep voices several meters distant, telling us not to move.

But this impetuous young woman whispers to me as she glances low on my body, "Stuff that statuette into that intimate place they don't dare search."

Oh my. But I quickly do just that while she commits sacrilege, not so delicately stuffing the tablet into my backpack. As the two men are upon us, I try to help her not ruin the tablet, only to make things worse as my backpack goes into free fall toward the granite flooring.

Her reactions are faster than mine as she dives to blunt the impact of the backpack on the floor. But fate is so cruel to the innocent. My Jericho tumbles out of the pack that she tries to stuff it back into.

"Gun," yells one of the men.

Bang. Bang.

Oh, Asherah. Save our souls.

CHAPTER 9

*I can assure you that, given they exist, these flying saucers
are made by no power on this Earth.*

—US President Harry S. Truman

*MoxWorld Auditorium
San Francisco, California
1:40 p.m. GMT-8, January 4, 2023*

Wondering what Bev was doing with Zara, Peter excuses himself from his newfound fans and bolts to the exit door to stop Zara's escape.

Physically blocking her way with his body, his hands open out to the sides, he implores, "Zara, don't run. I was so callous before. I shouldn't have said any of those things. I was just adrenaline pumped. I know you love me in your own way. Stay. Please. We can have a quiet dinner, talking about how our conversation could have been much different."

"Oh, Peter. I do not wish to ruin your long-awaited moment of glory any more than I already have. I just. I just…"

Lightly kissing her forehead, Peter licks his fingers and gently rubs her temple. What his mother did to calm him down turned out to be the secret to their intimate spiritual bonding.

She closes her eyes and sighs. "I heard Her again yesterday. The first time since the ambush with Alexander six months ago."

Eyes slowly open and peer into his. Not the darkened ones she had with Sasha, but lighter brown tones with a hint of a blue edging. "What if I am delusional? What if she is only my imagination? My impaired imagination. What if what happened to me, what the Daesh did to me, made me so mentally unstable that I believe I hear God? Made me insist you believe I hear Xwedê?"

Before he can respond, she hugs him and adds, "Whatever happens now, know that I do love you. No matter what happens. Whatever I do is because I do love you."

She pushes back, looking at her MoxWrap. "I need to go. It is near Isha'a. I need to find somewhere private to pray."

"Let me pray with you," insists Peter. "It can be our first makeup prayer."

As much as his proposition compels something much deeper within her, she says, "Peter, you should stay here with your fans. It is your moment. You deserve it. I am so proud of you."

As if she had cast a magical spell upon him, he floats back to the book signing, repeating every word she has just said to him.

Peter marvels at the MoxMover taking him to his mother's home, where he and Zara will have the delight of making up. These MoxMovers have quickly displaced ride share services in most major metropolitan areas. Totally solar-powered, with zero carbon emissions. Oil prices continue to plummet as more and more cities worldwide beg to have MoxMovers.

How can these cars generate so much power through their matte black, solar-absorbing coating? And how can there be enough batteries in these vehicles no bigger than their gasoline counterparts to allow them to drive all night long? But then again, none of the Mox devices require recharging either, nor battery replacements.

Those companies who have tried to reverse engineer Alexander's tech are met with an amazing meltdown of the digital AI components when they try to delve into any Mox device. MoxWorld Holdings responds by banishing those offenders from ever buying, using, or dealing with any Mox device or company for life.

Peter's lips turn up, jawbone to jawbone, watching the MoxMedia News reporting how the MoxRead books are rapidly taking market share from former industry leaders. Alexander launched a thousand new books as the book signing took place. All major publishers have signed long-term contracts with more favorable terms than previous digital distributors. Forecasts say that by next summer, MoxReads will have the number one worldwide share. The great Alexander Murometz crushes another industry within months.

Amid one of the most devastating rainstorms, Peter is relieved to not be driving. The MoxMover's state-of-the-art navigation system expertly guides them through the relentless sheets of rain to clearer back roads which are nevertheless so dark and spooky, rain or not, thinks Peter as he closes his eyes, remembering when he showed Zara her first episode of the *X-Files*, his father's favorite show. She watched several other episodes with him, trying to understand what drove his alien preoccupation. She had to stop watching when, from blinding white lights from above, the aliens abducted that FBI woman, Scully, who became genetically altered as a result. Her mysterious pregnancy was hinted to be alien-derived.

Peter tried to settle her concerns about this fictional woman's abduction as Zara touched the bump on the back of her neck. The God Gene Cluster bump, which she and Peter both have. She had felt so much like Scully. A genetic mutant who hears the voice of Xwedê because of a radiation event that altered the ancient matriarch of the object. She hoped that would be the only similarity she will have to that fictional FBI agent. Peter told her to rest assured; it was just science fiction. Not a speck of reality in the story.

His eyes open to a darker subject on MoxMedia News. Worldwide panic has set in as governments all over continue an insane search for and confiscation of all meteorite materials from museums and private collections. Russia rains more missiles down on the Donetsk region of the Ukraine. Are they really trying to control the ancient, buried pyramids that Alexander hinted at?

He remembers Alexander's remark a while back about those other fools in the government intelligence operations who thought the devastating EM pulse emanating from the pier in Turkey six months ago came from a meteorite. Little did they know the true story. Hence the insanity of the race to find another such meteorite, where the winner will achieve world domination.

Last night, Russian and Chinese troops engaged in a five-hour firefight at a suspected meteorite site on the border of Inner Mongolia and Siberia. Twelve dead and several dozen seriously injured. Unconfirmed reports about agents of another country taking the meteorite while the two countries battled. The Chinese accuse the Russians of using fake news to distract the world from their theft of Chinese property.

Then the MoxMedia broadcast abruptly goes dark. The MoxMover stops moving. Peter asks, "Moxy, what's happening? Why did you stop?"

Silence. Peter begins to panic, trying to open the doors. Locked. He looks out the windows on all sides. The rain has mysteriously stopped. Dark roads with no one in sight.

And then, it happens. Exactly like the old TV show. A bright white light above. The hum of some hovering craft emitting that light.

He madly taps his MoxWrap, only to see that time has stopped. His mind flips out. *It's The X-Files happening live, right now, to me. It's the aliens who abducted Fox Mulder's sister. Who abducted Dana Scully and impregnated her. And they now want me. Help. Anyone.*

A deep male voice booms from above. "Why have you stopped looking?"

Speechless. What does one say to one's alien masters? Peter's mind races. "Sirs. I'm afraid you have the wrong person."

No sense of humor, these aliens, as the booming voices echoes. "You must find the second black object. Is that not what your pappy asked of you before he died?"

Okay, they didn't buy the wrong number trick. What happens when your alien overlords get upset with you? Better tell the truth. And he does. "I'm sorry, alien sirs. I've run plum out of ancient oral traditions. Did you try Father Jean-Paul? If you'd just trot on over to Rome, you can find him. He knows more ancient traditions that might lead to your second object."

Silence as the white light blindingly gets brighter and brighter.

And the voice says, "A dark-haired woman in need will call. You must go to her. Be with her in the way a man is meant to be with a woman."

A flash of intensely blinding white, and that is all Peter is to remember.

CHAPTER 10

Vengeance is mine; I will repay.

—Leo Tolstoy, *Anna Karenina*

Jerusalem, Israel
1:15 p.m. GMT+3, January 15, 2023

Rachel's was a rich family. That is, if riches were measured by moral conviction. But measured in shekels, they lived a meager life with modest living quarters and the simplest of meals. A simple focus dominated the mindset of her father, his wife's mother, her grandmother— bring those who wronged their family to justice. Even if that justice meant incurring debts, favors to be paid back.

Sitting on her desk at home is a NiQband. Not one that she ordered, a gift of sorts. Or, more accurately, the instrument bearing her IOU. For as she touches the NiQband, not even trying to activate it, it shows his face. The subcommander of the SS medical unit that performed inhuman, monstrous tests on innocent people of the Crimean town of her great-grandparents.

As did the Americans, the Russians harbored war criminals who had technological or scientific secrets that could leapfrog their country decades into the future. And this subcommander, who was party to the vivisection of her great-grandmother's aunts and uncles, hid behind the Soviet curtain of secrecy. Several name changes, several faces, and several hidden villas later, his location was offered to her by an intelligence unit that would later be merged with NiQihs. The price? A favor sometime down the road.

And that time is now. A meet point pre-programmed on the NiQband's map function. A "see once" code phrase. Cold War spy tech hiding within new-world digital tech.

Who are these people? This merger has taken the world by surprise. What do they want from her other than to collect on a debt unpaid? Her alone, down an obscure passage at the farthest end of Zedekiah's Cave just before closing, and she would find out.

Dressed in her excavation clothing with her Israeli archaeology society badge, she wanders through the caverns on the northern side of the Temple Mount known to the Frankish crusaders as Solomon's Quarries. A passageway normally locked to the public is unlocked. Ten paces down and there are two men. Shrinking violet she is not, but two men larger than her in a dark place where no one could hear her screams? She puts her hand into her shoulder bag and grasps her trusted Jericho.

Emerging from the shadows, two Asiatic hulks. Both more Central Asian than East Asian, as she determined from her ethnology training. The same two that rushed her and poor Massa at the tomb. The one with the fresh scar across his neck shot the innocent Palestinian woman, who had only tried in vain to hide the ill-fated tablet. As they tried to take the statue fragment as well, she grabbed it back and sliced that would-be murderer's throat.

The Israeli pair watching her and Massa in the park indeed turned out to be agents of an agency all too well known to her. Not Mossad, but the one that guarded ancient antiquities from would-be thieves. One recently acquired by NiQihs's intelligence arm with promises to the Israeli government that national treasures would be protected, as would religious interests. Thus, they took both the statue fragment and the tablet, thanking the two Asian men for their service in defending the treasures of Israel from the Palestinians. Defending the world from a woman god.

The taller of the two men steps toward her and asks, "Do you think the Ark is really buried down here?"

Nodding, she replies, "Only if you believe the Templars still roam the streets of Old Jerusalem."

The second man steps out to stand watch, leaving the two to discuss affairs. The taller NiQihs man says, "You are not wearing your gift."

Rachel releases her grip on her weapon of last resort and pulls the NiQband from her shoulder bag. "It is too big for a petite wrist like mine. So, I carry it in my bag."

"If it was a free MoxWrap, you would wear it," jests the man.

"And what would the makers of the NiQband want from an unknown archaeologist like me?" asks Rachel, always wanting to get to the point rapidly.

"Mr. Conrad, your previous contact man, indicated that you privileged him with certain information from your contacts in Israeli intelligence."

Nodding, Rachel says, "I do not work for any national agency. I may have been a contractor for one once, but nothing of national importance."

The truth, only her and her aba will ever know. Or so she promised him. And as she promised him, she adds, "But know I am fully capable of lethal actions. I mercilessly executed three Nazis whom we tracked down and trapped. *Yimach shmam.* May their names be erased."

She pulls out her Jericho and says in her deepest, manliest voice, "I have the will and ability to use this instrument of death on you if you do anything untoward to me. And if you had not helped poor Massa, you would be dead already."

If it were not for what these two did to save Massa, she would not have come here. The Israeli police had arrested Massa as a terrorist and withheld the best medical care for her debilitating wounds. NiQihs stepped in and helped the Israeli police understand the actual situation. The police released Massa, and Rachel called in yet another favor to get the poor woman transferred to the city's newest and best-equipped ICU unit. There, Massa lay in a coma, but at least she had a chance to live. Perhaps a paraplegic for life, but still alive.

"The affairs of your country do not interest the leaders of NiQihs at this time. Your friendship with a Jesuit priest and a Chinese fashion executive do," says the tall man.

"And why should the affairs of NiQihs interest this modest professor of ancient history?"

"Everything you have been raised to believe to be right, just, and fair is what NiQihs means to protect. It is the only institution that stands in the way of Alexander's total domination of world economies and politics. NiQihs represents free markets, free world trade, employment for those who once prospered in the days before MoxWorld Holdings."

Pulling her well-worn, dusty jacket open, she says, "And do I look like I prospered in the golden age of all things free market and free trade?"

"As Mr. Conrad had delivered the SS subcommander to you and your father, a feat that no other organization could match, I can offer to you the grandson of the man who let your great-grandfather walk into a hail of Nazi bullets. Our intelligence suggests he has mystical treasures that may interest you. Ones passed to him from his grandfather, which are rightfully yours."

Her hands akimbo, her eyes squinted, she replies, "Why on Earth would I want to execute the great-grandson of the man who murdered my saba raba? That's too many generations removed. Even vengeance has its limits."

The taller man smiles and says, "And why would anyone execute the son of the murderer of your saba raba? Stage it to look like a suicide. Very elegantly so. This family has treasures that rightfully belong to your family."

Staring into her eyes, he says, "You appear surprised. Perhaps your father will elucidate your family debt?"

She taps her foot, lips pursed, head bobbing. She will not sell her soul for these would-be murderers of poor Massa.

Then, the smaller of the two finally pipes in. "By getting close to this man, you will get access to the son of the true murderer of your saba raba. The one who stole the black Stones of Orion from your family. Alexander Murometz."

Even in the passage's darkness, the tall man can see how Rachel's eyes brighten as the words *yimach shmo* echo in her head. She vaguely recalls her family mentioning these mysterious Stones of Orion. But what does this have to do with her?

With a smile that reveals a gold-capped molar, the shorter man says, "Then we have an arrangement."

"What is my price?" asks Rachel, still pondering the significance of these stones. "Not that I thought NiQihs would be offering free NiQbands as MoxWorld does its MoxWraps."

"NiQbands do not track your private data and transactions, which cannot be said for MoxWorld's offerings. Nothing is free," says the tall man. "We ask that you stay close to your Jesuit and Chinese friends. We will let you know when we need information about them."

With a face devoid of affect, she stares at him, her head swaying side to side. "And that's it? All of this spy versus spy nonsense just for that?"

The taller man reaches into his pocket, at which Rachel raises her Jericho at him. "Go slow there. I use hollow points, which will eviscerate your chest at this range."

Out of his pocket comes a clear plastic tube whose cap also has a swab. "Here. Swab your cheeks and spit into this tube," he says.

"Why should I?"

"So we can verify that you are truly who you say you are."

A pause. A glare into this man's eyes, then at the tube. She swabs and spits.

Clasping his hands around the tube as she hands it back, he says, "A doctor will approach you in the not-so-distant future. At that time, your involvement with the man in question will be delineated."

He begins to leave the cavern but turns back to her. "Mr. Conrad said you pulled the trigger on two others. Cold-blooded kills. No remorse."

Eyes narrowed, she replies, "As they say in the craft, I can neither confirm nor deny that allegation."

"Your new target's blood maybe yours to take in the same way, but you are not to kill him until we have what we want from him and Murometz," he says. "And from you."

CHAPTER 11

The course of true love never did run smooth.

—William Shakespeare

VIP Ward, MoxMedical Total Care Unit
San Francisco, California
11:20 a.m. GMT-8, January 15, 2023

"If you love. If you truly love…," murmurs Peter as he thrashes about, pushing the limits to rolling and tossing in a hospital bed. Sheets are flung across the edges, covering the medical monitoring equipment. Pillows diagonally planted across his face and arms. Bed railings padded with his blanket.

Samantha restrains the nurse from re-initiating the coma, pointing to her MoxWrap description of the ancient affliction. Men of the ancient matriarch's lineage have highly disturbed sleep. MoxWorld experts told her that an ancient traumatic incident, or several incidents, are hard-coded into their genetic memory, and they relive these events each sleep cycle.

The nurse explained to Zara that Mr. Gollinger had been in a medically induced coma for several days, since the MoxWorld Security team found him lying in the redwood groves covered in banana slugs. They found his abandoned MoxMover late on the night of the MoxRead launch. Peter remained missing for several days, eluding all searches. This is the first sign of his consciousness returning as the medical staff begin to titrate down the level of barbiturates used to maintain his coma. Only a couple hours ago did Mr. Alexander Murometz let Peter's status be known to his family, Zara included in that definition.

Zara stands stiff-backed against the far wall, listening to Peter's mother's explanation of the dream affliction. For Samantha lived every night with a husband who suffered the same. From mother to daughter, a comforting method had been taught. Except Zara's mother, who had not taught her as she had eloped with Zengo. Mei tried to teach her, but Zara would not lower herself to such male pandering.

She exhales deeply through her nose, glancing away from Samantha. The past several days have rivaled the *dûjeh*, the hell, she suffered with those evil kidnappers. Rab'ia would never have been so self-involved as to have let that doctor unnerve her. The voice is real. As real as is Xwedê. As real as her feelings for Peter. And this time, when Peter awakens, she will not hesitate to let him know.

Or will she? She stares at him as she tucks in a strand of her dark brown hair under her yellow headscarf. His blonde mother strokes her son's darkening blond hair. Goats and sheep. Cats and dogs. She needs to be decisive when he awakens. And then Samantha turns to her.

"Zara, my dear," says Samantha. "You know what to do with these afflicted men. These doctors have gotten it wrong. He needs you in that way, not these horrible drugs. These nurses have mistaken his afflicted dreams for signs that the coma should continue." She signals for the nurse to leave the room. "We'll just make the room real private, and you can comfort him in the way our mothers taught us."

Samantha comes to the back of the room and places her fingers on the back of Zara's neck. Likewise, she places Zara's fingers on the same bump on her own neck. "We, the daughters of the afflicted—we are kin. And our mothers have taught us how to calm our husbands who are afflicted."

Zara has never discussed this topic with Peter's mother. Her Sasha had been convinced this comforting comprised passionate, intimate touching, culminating in sex. Somehow, the ancient traditions must have been altered by men along the thousands of years to suit their own proclivities.

Zara apprehensively watches Samantha draw the curtain on the private ward's hallway window before she exits. Alone with Peter, she sits next to him. The five senses algorithm activated their dormant ancient genes through smell, taste, feel, sound, and sight.

What she saw Mei do six months ago in front of them at MoxWorld EU Headquarters was soft porn, having Peter's face planted into her bare breasts. And then, the part of the algorithm lower down. To find the object, both Sasha in his blunt, direct way and even the priest in a more oblique way suggested Zara needed to do the same to access Peter's dreams, which would tell the location of the object.

Perhaps why she finds Peter so endearing. Why she has kept coming back is not what Sasha said. But Peter was the only non-mahram man who did not take advantage of her body. Because, at the moment she finally caved, at the moment they had to access Peter's dreams or lose the object to unknown enemies, she consented to mutual touching in that intimate manner. But Peter, he miraculously determined another method that did not compromise her ownership of her body, her modesty, her self-respect.

And so, she wet-kisses his forehead, and then gently rubs her saliva around in circles as her other hand rubs his hand. Normally, the transfer of their fluids activates the dormant ancient DNA. The pathway to a deeper peace, a profound paradise, should open in both of them. But now, nothing.

She licks her fingers and rubs his temples. Nothing.

And she wets his own index finger in his mouth and rubs her temple. Nothing.

He is dead. Living, but his soul is dead. That must be what is happening, cries Zara's inner voice. She says, "Peter, if you can hear me, do you remember what I said when we last parted? Did you hear me say that I love you? Did you understand how deeply so?"

Nothing. And Zara cries into his hands. The rivers of her body's wetness run down his arm, dampening his hospital gown. And she cannot stop. She has not cried so hysterically since her father hanged himself. A double victim of imprisonment in Saddam's torture camps, he lived out several years as a shell of a person. A soulless being. A walking coma.

If only. If only she had not only said she loved him, but also kissed him one last time. Her father, whom she so loved, if only she had said those words one last time before he killed himself. And with Peter, if only.

Samantha comes rushing in, asking, "Honey, what's wrong? Is Peter okay?"

"No. No. Nothing I do helps," cries Zara. "He does not respond to me."

Samantha looks over her ailing son. She looks at his gown draped still around his legs, points to his crotch, and says, "Honey, I don't know what your mother taught you, but mine said we do our magic to our afflicted husbands down there."

"Samantha," pleads Zara. "I did what Peter and I always do. I thought that would surely connect us."

Shaking her head, no longer with the friendly face, Samantha says, "The good book says I should not pass judgment. But he is my son. I thought he was your endeared man that you would do anything to save."

Suddenly, as if he heard that, Peter, soaked in her tears, turns over, arms flailing, knocking Zara aside. He drools and slurs, "Sss, Sss, Ssarah. You'll do anything for the one. Sss, Sssarah. I luff you."

All Zara can see now is blonde. The blonde tresses of Sarah, his ex-girlfriend he loved so much before he got roped into the last mission with Alexander. She looks up at Samantha. Flowing blonde hair. Sheep and goats. Dogs and cats. They do not mix. Why did the voice insist that they do?

She gets up to leave the room, but Samantha intercedes. Zara can do nothing but stare at her long golden tresses as she says, "I saw her picture. Sarah's. Long, flowing blonde hair like you, Peter, and Michaela. You told me she left him because she could not have a child with him." Zara holds her abdomen and says, "I am barren. I cannot have a child with Peter either."

Samantha gives her a motherly hug, patting her on the back. "Oh, honey. Modern medicine can fix that. Sarah had been treated in this medical center by that nice Mr. Murometz's best gene therapy specialists. I hear Peter and Michaela's friend Mei discovered a cure."

In tears, Zara excuses herself. She needs to use the ladies' room. A change of tampon, a little tissue for the eyes, Zara emerges from the toilet cabinet feeling less unbalanced, less guilt-ridden as she approaches the mirrored wall above the sinks. As she tucks many loose strands of her hair back under her headscarf, she stares at the unknown face looking back at her. Not the face of the woman who stoically led her soldiers to attack enemy positions. Nor the face of the woman who killed dozens upon dozens for Sasha and her tormentors.

What did Sasha say? Somehow, the exposure to the object is changing her? Are these the changes he spoke of? That she would become weaker and softer?

As she emerges from the ladies' room as freshened and strong as she could possibly muster given the strangest of occurrences in the past two weeks, the second-to-last person she wants to see today waits at Peter's ward door.

Today, her appearance is more doctor-like. White lab coat with "Dr. Fontaine" embroidered above the pocket. White silk blouse and a pleated black wool skirt cut just above her bare knees. Her skin impeccably tanned. Brown hair up in a tight bun. She stands about ten centimeters shorter than Zara, not wearing those pumps she sported at the book signing. In her hand is what looks like a clipboard. Something that doctors no longer carry in this digital age.

Hand in her pocket, the doctor pulls out a tissue. "It's okay. Crying is normal. It's healthy for someone who has endured the traumas that you have. It is not uncommon for PTSD patients to have spontaneous tears."

Zara takes the tissue, just in case another episode occurs. "Dr. Fontaine, what brings you to this hospital? I thought you practiced at the University of California Medical Center and the VA."

"Several months ago, I also took an adjunct position here. My late fiancé worked in talent management for MoxWorld USA and said they had a part-time need for someone with my expertise."

"I am so sorry for your loss, Doctor," laments Zara, feeling more empathy for this woman who has rattled her.

On the doctor's clipboard are photos and charts. Zara notes the absence of a Mox device, as today, the doctor wears the newest MoxWrap competitor from that NiQihs conglomeration, the NiQband. Likely a gift from her publishers. It must not be compatible with MoxMedical's systems.

The doctor shows her Peter's charts. A neurological scan shows highly abnormal chemical imbalances in his brain. There is microscopic evidence of needle marks in certain parts of his body. One would think he was a junkie back from a weeks-long doping extravaganza.

And then, before Zara can avert her eyes, the doctor fumbles through the papers and out pops a close-up photo of his manhood. Not that she hasn't seen one before—just not his.

"Excuse my clumsiness. But you have seen his member before. Peter must have been sexually engaged during his absence. Maybe even abused, if you look closely at these marks along the shaft and his scrotum," the doctor points out in a perfectly neutral clinical tone.

Zara abruptly swallows, gazing past the clipboard—an act that catches the doctor's attention.

"Oh, I am so sorry, my dear. I had thought you and Peter were intimate. Hadn't you seen his male organ before?" queries Dr. Fontaine.

Yes, she had felt it radiate heat on frosty nights as they slept together. On occasions when Peter rolled over into her, it poked her. Not on purpose. She knew he fought with how physically stimulated he became sleeping with her. But he respected her celibacy. He had more respect for her than to force himself on her.

Zara tugs her headscarf across her face closest to the full-sized photo. "No. I meant I am very modest about that subject."

The doctor nods and coldly states, "Very common in sexually tortured trauma survivors. But you didn't cry. Good."

Hiding the photo, the doctor adds, "What a pair you two will make. When we worked on my past two books, I tried to counsel him about his delusions of aliens ruling us all. But I traced his deep-seated belief to the suicide of his father, who taught him such folly. It was Peter who found his father with a gun blast through his mouth out the back of his brain. A traumatic sight." The doctor pauses, watching Zara's face intently.

Not a flinch on Zara's face. Only her blank stare. So, the doctor continues. "His mind has recreated past events, transforming those he cannot accept into ones that justify his current perception of reality. He clings to these alien extraterrestrial notions as his only means of hanging onto his sanity. Take that away from him and we might unravel him permanently. He looks up to you. If you disrespect him on this matter, you will ruin him forever."

Zara is once again left speechless as the doctor sorts her clipboard and says, "I get it now. You and he are so different. No wonder he hasn't been able to be intimate with you. Not like the frisky rabbit he was with all his other girlfriends. You, my dear, you are a turtle. You need your space and to go at your own speed. I completely understand. I'll check back later when my rounds are completed. Nice talking with you again."

Her tense back against the wall, eyes fixed staring up at the ceiling, Zara cries out for the voice to talk with her again. Her guidance. Her reassurance. Zara pleads inside, "I did what I promised you. I told him how I felt. Direct and simple. Please, let him recover. Please."

Buzz. The sounding of her MoxWrap breaks her pleas.

"Oh, honey," says Mei. "Your eyes are so red. Have you been crying? Why, babe? I'm sure Peter will recover from his coma. His brain just needs time to process whatever has happened."

"Like me. He needs to process me," replies Zara. "And how I failed to tell him exactly how much I loved him before he was abducted. All over a stupid spat."

"A lover's spat," says Mei with a canyon-wide grin. "You are so lucky to be so deeply in love. Only true lovers have issues like you two have had."

No consolation for the Kurdish woman, as she only stares at the sterile hospital floor. "I never forgave myself for not telling my father one last time how much I loved him. I was mad at him for no longer being the man who raised me, for being a shell. It was not his fault. Saddam's torturers did that to him. But I needed him so much. So, I did not tell him I loved him for days as I sulked. And then, he took his own life. Maybe because he could not bear the lack of my love."

Silence. Zara only nods her head from side to side. Mei's face is frozen. Mouth open. Eyebrows up. Ridges elevated on her forehead.

Turning her head to the side, biting her lips, Mei breaks the silence. "A dear friend of mine from Jerusalem said, 'if you love someone, you'll do anything for them.'"

Her turn to have her eyebrows pointed down toward her crinkling nose, Zara says, "Odd. Peter muttered something similar only moments ago. It is a similar saying to what my grandmother told me."

"Good. Then you will stay with Peter, no matter what. Tell him you love him while he's coming out of his coma. He can hear you. Right, no matter what?"

Nodding as her headscarf rubs her cheeks, Zara says, "Do you really believe Peter is better off with me in his life? The doctor he edits for told me we are bad for each other. Both traumatized in different ways. His upbringing Catholic. Mine Islamic. His family blond. Mine, dark brunette. He's Californian. I'm Kurdish. I am dog and he is cat. Maybe he should be with another cat. One who can bear his mother the grand-kittens she desperately desires."

This time, Mei stamps her feet. "Oh, honey, why did you have to say that? You're making what I need to tell you so much harder."

Eyes beading up as the top of her nose wrinkles and her nostrils open, she asks, "What is it? Sasha? Something has happened with Sasha? Or worse— Jean-Paul? I should have called him to tell him how important his friendship is to me."

A long breath out and Mei touches her MoxWrap to reveal a 3-D hologram of herself lifting her top to show her the slight bulge of a belly.

"Oh my, Mei. You are expecting," gasps Zara. "Oh, how wonderful. Congratulations. I am so happy for you."

Another pause as Mei does not answer back.

"But who is the father?" asks Zara, now glancing at Mei from the side of her tilted head.

Fingers as if in prayer around her nose, Mei says, "It's complicated. You need to see this." And Mei taps her MoxWrap.

Eyebrows up and mouth agape, Zara studies the genetic maps from Peter, Michaela, Mei, and the unborn baby. What seems like minutes pass, but it's only seconds before Zara asks, "How many months? Six?"

"You guessed it, babe. Six or so," affirms Mei.

"That would make conception when that monstrous Sasha forced you to have sex with Peter in front of us," says Zara with her hands squeezed upon both cheeks. "I mean, you did not have sex with him after that, did you?"

"No, honey. He was and is all yours," affirms Mei after a strategic pause. "I didn't want to tell you or Peter because I didn't want my child to come between you two. I love both of you dearly. You, Michaela, and Peter have become my closest friends after Jean-Paul."

Straightening out her tunic top and then her headscarf, Zara states, "A child needs a father. A child deserves a father. Oh, my life would have been so much better had my father been around. If only I had told him how much I loved him."

"Honey, you need to stay with Peter," says Mei. "I am prepared to parent this child without him. I would never forgive myself if you break up with Peter. You don't know how much I agonized over whether or not to tell you."

"You did the right thing," affirms Zara. "Just like Peter. Doing the right thing. Cats and cats."

"Cats? What are you talking about?" asks Mei with one eyebrow pointed upside down.

Before Zara can answer, Samantha calls out that Peter is trying to talk again.

"I need to go," says Zara.

"Promise me you won't do anything rash," begs Mei before Zara signs out of the call.

As Zara heads to the ward, Samantha meets her outside the door. "My dear. You need to be understanding toward my son. He loves you dearly. And I see in your eyes how much you love him back. You two will have a long, happy marriage together, raising beautiful children. There will be bumps and turns along the way, but your love will guide you through."

Her head tilted, Zara stares into Samantha's eyes, then peers down. The words of a mother looking out for her son's best interests—and the grandkids he will bring her.

As she enters the ward, she finds out why Samantha has said what she did. Peter's eyes are still fluttering. Still a bit garbled, Peter utters, "Aliens. Aliens abducted me."

When Zara tries to hug him, he pushes back, now with a glassy-eyed stare into her eyes, and yammers, "They did all sorts of nasty things to me."

He looks down at his partially covered, somewhat damp crotch. "Nothing is sacred to them."

Eyes back on Zara's, he says more coherently, "They said they were gods. They said so. God exists. They created Him. They are our God. And they want me to make babies for them. Lots of them."

Eyes aghast, all sorts of thoughts zing through Zara's brain. Did she just lose Peter to aliens? Did his brain let loose the truth? He is not the man of the Divine as she had hoped only weeks earlier in the redwood groves. They truly are cats and dogs of different faiths. Is it best for him that she loses him? For if you love someone, you will do anything for them. Mei is a better woman for him. One who is capable and willing to give to him everything he deserves. Cats with cats.

Zara, for whatever reason, cannot. She says to herself, to the voice, to Xwedê, "I love him so much, I will let him follow his better destiny. Who am I to stand between a man and his child? He deserves to have a family. That child deserves a father. And Mei seems like a good woman. One who is more of a cat than I. This is the sign from Her. I can follow in peace what She has asked of me. To die peacefully in the blue light knowing Peter will be happy raising children with Mei. This must be the backup plan Alexander alluded to earlier."

As she turns to leave the doorway, Peter calls out to her. "Zzzara. Ppplease. I need you. The vvvoice. She is one of them. An alien."

A pause as she closes her eyes and exhales. She pictures her mother and father worshipping Xwedê together. So many signals since the MoxBook launch say the same thing. Peter and she are not to be. She pictures herself with her father on the mountain. No one should tear a child away from their father. Not her. Not anyone.

Never turning back, Zara runs down the hallway, yelling into her MoxWrap, "Moxy, ready Sasha's armored jet. I am to fly home immediately."

Moxy answers, "Ms. Khatum, do you want me to get your luggage at Mrs. Gollinger's home?"

Zara clicks her heels. "No, Moxy. Get me home as fast as possible. Get me home where I belong. Moxy, there is no place like home. Dogs should be with dogs."

CHAPTER 12

Village at the site of Çatalhöyük, Turkey
9528 BCE

What is wrong with circular huts? That notion formed the first of many points of contention Tallia faced as she learned to live with a reformed reindeer warrior giant.

The great matriarch herself, her grandmother Nanshe, lived in a circular mud-and-stick hut. If Nirra really wanted to live the life of her family, to know the love of her family, then why not live like they did?

She surveys the square room of their hut they have lived in for more than ten cycles of the sun. After a week of debate, the words of her grandmother won. Peace comes from tolerance of differences. Tolerance comes from truly understanding the other party and appreciating their culture. Thus, one night, she listened to his logic without her interruptions. Square huts would allow a village to be built with all neighbors abutting each other. Like an extended family, this closeness would either create disharmony or promote peace. And in Tallia's mind, the search for peace overruled anything else. Or so said the great matriarch.

Even though she is the leader of the small village, her square room measured no larger than anyone else's. For equality ruled this settlement. Men, women, old, and young, all equals.

Grrrrr. Grrrr. Around her ankles, one of her little baby foxes circles around and around. "Looking for your next meal, are you?" she says. But these domesticated foxes are smarter than people. The infant fox searches for her love, manifested by her petting their head between their ears. No sooner than she does this, than the sibling comes running for an equal dose of love.

As part of Nirra's quest to be a normal human trapped in the body of a reindeer warrior giant, he remembered how his cousin Ki found baby foxes and domesticated them. He scoured for moon cycle after moon cycle to find abandoned baby foxes to give to her. And one day, he came back with the cutest babies. Tallia said, "We cannot keep wild predators. They are born to be ferocious."

Which Nirra countered with, "But you kept me. Was I not that ferocious once?"

Inside Tallia and Nirra's room, bullhead ornaments adorn the walls. Her concession to the lore of the giants, to her husband's past. Her way of saying, "I forgive what you did to so many others." In the words of her grandmother, one must look forward and not backward when it comes to bad things. Only by getting beyond violence can you see peace. Or so Tallia remembered her grandmother saying in a dream.

Forgiveness is a long, arduous path full of treacherous cliffs and precipitous climbs. In their early days together, Nirra sought atonement and needed to confess all his past atrocities, his past rapes of innocent women, his past killing of their menfolk. Tallia could not bear to hear these travesties and would run away until he promised not to share more of these living nightmares. But the memories haunted his dreams as the ghosts of those he irreparably violated, maimed, or murdered would parade by, taunting him.

When a giant tosses and turns in bed, it is nearly lethal for the person sleeping next to him. Out of desperation, Tallia tried one night to calm him using the five senses therapy Nanshe used on her dream-troubled husband, Orzu. A therapy all her afflicted female relatives then used upon their afflicted male partners. Smell me. See me. Hear me. Taste me. Feel me. Inevitably, this pattern led to passionate, very intimate sex. Was it the pattern of senses or simply the sex that calmed the afflicted? Certainly, for her giant husband, the latter did not hurt matters at all.

Tallia walks outside, where man and woman work in the fields together. Inside, man and woman work together, taking care of the children, the houses, the meals. A community of equals. Nirra has honored her wishes to create a world of equality. As people visited them, the word spread, and others came to live as equals.

Like her Aunt Ki, the women went on the hunt with men. The young girls learned to shoot with the young boys. Tallia remembers her grandmother telling a tale from her grandmother about a community just like this long, long ago, in the direction of the tail of the bird star.

She passes a circle of children learning to carve stone. The children of the village fulfill Nirra's wish to have children, for Tallia can no longer bear a child at her age. A little girl holds up a statue of the form feminine. She says it is Tallia, the mother goddess. Tallia is bemused that all the other children are carving the same. All with exaggerated bosoms, for, thankfully for her back, she is not of those anatomical proportions. Oddly enough, the bosoms are exposed, unlike those of the village women, who follow her style of dress, covered head to ankles and wrists. Women are equal with men and with each other, not to be judged solely by how they appear.

As new people joined the village, they brought with them their faith around the mother goddess. For all around, people have heard about Tallia's special relationship with the divine and assumed she represents the earthly embodiment of the mother goddess. One rambunctious boy carves a statue of her with two lions instead of her foxes. Why? Because he thought lions were more ferocious. Other boys liked the lions and carved their own statues of her with lions.

Knowing that many paths exist toward the same faith, Tallia tolerates their notions and continues to lead prayer five times a day for anyone who wishes to join her, for faith is not a concept one can force upon others. People must follow out of their own heart, their own desire, their own willingness to submit. But most perform prayer with her at least once or twice daily.

Many from outside villages come to attend her prayer sessions. They have heard about how the words she derives from her divine prayers have prophetic powers. They all wish to be blessed by these powers. In particular, to sustain the peace their villages have enjoyed since they have come to see her pray and to learn how to care for seeded plants to create bountiful harvests. The mother goddess.

In the past sun cycles, others have also come hoping she can heal them or their loved one. For Tallia studied under her grandmother how to heal. What broke her heart the most was a dying child whose mother begged Tallia to save her. As much as she wished she could, Tallia sadly said to the mother that this was beyond her ability. And yet, Tallia prayed many times with the ailing child, who inevitably died. No human can bring life into the dying or dead, she would say to the villagers. The villagers responded by saying she is the mother goddess and only the faithful can benefit from her magic. That mother had not been truly faithful.

She has over fifty cycles of the sun and has communed with the voice more times in the last ten cycles than she ever did in the first forty. In the late-afternoon prayer she performs alone, she hears the voice once again.

"Seek your daughter," says the voice. "She longs for her mother to bless her own children, your grandchildren. You must teach what you know from your grandmother to your grandchildren."

Confused, Tallia asks, "My daughter survived? Oh, thank you. Which of my daughters, and where can I find her?"

The voice replies, "Your husband will know."

CHAPTER 13

The dress of the body should not discredit the good of the soul.
—Saint Cyprian, third-century Bishop of Carthage

Çatalhöyük, Turkey
4:15 p.m. GMT+3, January 16, 2023

Fabulously elegant. The belle of the ball. The most gorgeous woman in town. For nearly eighteen years, she wore the habit of a Catholic Sister. She insisted on continuing in her order through the Christmas season. But on January 1, she revoked her vows. And here she stands in one of the greatest cities in Anatolian history in her fuchsia-accented cream dress. Neck, arms, and legs covered to the ankles. Cream-colored leather sandals around her feet, which have the hint of a clear coat on her nails.

The breeze dances with the wisps of her crimson hair peeking out from her baby-blue headscarf. Perhaps in her Sister days, nursing in Catholic hospitals and in-country medical missions, she would have quickly tucked her hair under cloth, but the priest she has loved almost as much she loved God stands in sight. And she knows how much her scarlet locks visibly challenge his celibate composure.

Freedom from her vows did not mean she let loose everything she believed in. She feels more comfortable dressing close to her habit, but with a greater freedom of color expression. Her headscarf features the metallic design of Peter's sister, who sent her a dozen different colors of such design for Christmas.

Seventeen years ago, she almost abandoned taking her permanent vows when she met a Jesuit brother also about to take his final vows as they were both on separate missions in the Philippines. Everything about him swept her off her feet. Literally, as he was so tall.

What Sister Magali loved most in Father Jean-Paul was his dedication to her love and her need to love God. They both went on to take their vows, but she stayed in contact with her dearest Brother, now a Father in service of the Holy Pontiff.

After nearly two decades, their unrequited love for each other came to a head when that wonderful Kurdish woman, Zara, made a deal with her reticent favorite Father—that Zara would tell Peter of her love if Jean-Paul would call Magali and do the same. What a perceptive woman to fathom through his outwardly placid exterior what boiled beneath. She will forever owe Zara.

In her hands lies a highly complex device measuring EM waves and other emissions beyond her medical education, as designed by Jean-Paul. Last spring, the units made by MoxWorld were large, chest-mounted monsters requiring massive back and abdominal musculature to use. These new ones marked "Property of the Vatican" are much smaller and lighter, weighing only three kilos. They link to a base station in the pickup truck they drove to this ancient Neolithic site. Çatalhöyük, a city of great importance to her dearest man, her dearest Father, who will be able to fully fulfill his love for her by the year's end if the Cardinals Council most expediently decides to allow priests to marry.

Her love for him transcends the material world, for his soul yearns for the Lord as does hers. But in this material world, she loves him so, as this city below their feet shows that in the earliest days of the agricultural revolution humanity practiced gender equality. Her dearest Jean-Paul had explained how medical forensics of the bones found here revealed that both genders took part in household and farming duties equally.

A series of beeps come from the device. Excited, Magali says, "*Cheri*, I found something." *Oui, oui.* They are both French. She from a village outside Grenoble, he from a village outside of Lourdes. In private, Jean-Paul would confide in her that as a child, he considered himself more Occitan than French, as that area bordering Spain once contained the country of Occitania. Land of the Cathars.

As he leans over her, viewing the device's readings, she pulls his arms around her. Snug as a slug she is, she thinks in her tribute to Peter's friends, as she snuggles between his muscular biceps, his perfectly formed pecs warming her back.

Coquettishly, she runs her cheek along the length of his upper right arm as she asks, "*La vérité, mon père.* Are you more interested in what this box says than what my heart emotes?"

Oh, how the French love such logic traps. Only second to their love of evading such traps as Jean-Paul replies, "If only I could capture your heart's sense of all things right, we would have found what we are looking for days ago."

Millimeter by millimeter, she will slowly get him to the altar. And conceivably, once married, more of what he showed her of his deepest desires during those days in the Philippines will once again come into the full light. But for today, she will take his modest compliment.

"*Chérie,* your feet are the epitome of heaven," says the priest. "They sense the earth. They sense the magnificence of the past. They have led you to the spot we have been long searching for."

That is about as much love as she is going to get out of him for now. And she pushes further into his arms, saying, "And so, we can celebrate now?"

And, yes, it is time for *le goûter,* an afternoon snack for the French. Magali sits her beloved down near the pickup and unpacks a Turkish sparkling wine and locally sourced goat cheese. Of course, the academic in Jean-Paul notes that this bottle is a rarity, as the Turkish government banned advertising and promotion of wines in 2015. A real hardship on local wineries.

A clink of glasses in toast of their find and without warning, without a sound, without permission, a hologram of Alexander Murometz intrudes on their intimate celebration.

"My, my. My dearest Sister Magali. Or is it now the lovely laity Mademoiselle Magali who appears to have made much progress in her seduction of that fabulously faithful Father?" says the giant man.

Before Jean-Paul can defend her, she says, "The good Lord looks over those who love and cherish all of His work, all of His creations. Even you, Mr. Murometz. For He must be the most patient waiting for your atonements. And perhaps He will provide love for you too. One day."

She clinks her glass again with Jean-Paul's and rises to leave, adding, "But until then, we would appreciate you keeping your jealousy of our love to yourself. If you please, I will take my leave and let you gentlemen take care of men's business."

"My, my, my. Is she not the Catholic version of my dear little Zara?" jests the giant.

Jean-Paul straightens his collar and replies, "Need I remind you that I no longer work for you? I no longer need to remain acquiescent to your transgressions upon the dignity of others. Nor should I have to remind you that my renewal of oaths includes the Jesuits' fourth vow of complete and utter obedience to the Holy Pontiff."

"Yes, your dear and close friend," says Alexander more seriously. "It has not escaped my attention the rapidity with which he reinstated you to the Pontifical Commission for Sacred Archaeology and offered you the chair of his super-secret working group on extraterrestrial affairs, which you accepted only on an interim basis. Why, my dear Father, were you a double agent all that time you worked for me? Zara always suspected you were."

A very measured blink, and the priest responds, "The only point you should consider is that my fidelity and loyalty lies only with the Pontiff and the Lord. You should not have to second-guess my reporting structure."

"Good Jean-Paul," asserts Alexander with an air of satisfaction, "then you are not operating as a double agent for that NiQihs Corporation."

A blank expression dominates the priest's visage, only infuriating the giant, who demands, "Oh, do not act dumb on this subject. I know you are high enough up that you have access to all the Vatican's counterintelligence data and operations."

Finally, a smile breaks upon Jean-Paul's face. "In all the years I have known you, I have never seen anyone get the great Alexander Murometz unnerved. Well, other than Zara."

The priest chuckles under his breath, and then adds, "So, why would the rapid acquisition of the four former digital giants of the 2000s, the companies your devious MoxWorld Holdings has put into peril, create such anxiety in you? Why would any government legally allow such a monopolistic move unless they were seeking retribution for your strong-arm tactics?"

Alexander scoffs, but the lines across his face bely a different story.

In a rare moment of less-than-Christian humility, the Father who had been verbally abused by this giant for years launches his final strike. "And who could have financed such a rapid set of mergers? And why would so many banks offer such favorable terms to allow them to challenge you? Perhaps all of your misdeeds have finally caught up with you."

In an equally rare moment of humility, the great Alexander almost cowers as he says, "Jean-Paul, I need to know who my friends are at this moment. No, it has not escaped my attention that no one government has enough financial resources to have affected these rapid mergers. Nor is the mystery of who is behind this NiQihs Corporation failing to drive my nightmares. No amount of five senses algorithm comforting by dozens upon dozens of afflicted women has eased my pains."

Jean-Paul's face mostly remains blank. Just a twinge of his eyebrows tilting down on the outside edges. Alexander tilts his head to the side, eyeing the good Father.

"So, who do you think is behind NiQihs? Maybe the Vatican?" taunts Alexander. "Why else would IHS be in the corporate name?"

The good Father blinks rapidly before saying, "And why did you interrupt me today?"

"Other than the fact that the world around you is falling rapidly into a world war?" says Alexander. "The US Pacific Fleet has been placed on DEFCON2 as carrier groups from the Third and Seventh Fleets have been ordered to intercept a Chinese carrier group heading toward a US undersea salvage operation off the New Zealand coast. My military analysts believe

Russia has mobilized attack submarines in the same South Pacific operating area. All because Mei planted the idea of the legendary comet among the Chinese, and someone or some party leaked it to the Americans and Russians. The world has gone crazy trying to find another black object. One that could create another so destructive EM pulse and great underwater earthquake as did the uniting of the two halves of the black object you, Peter, and Zara tried to avert. They are chasing every report of large meteorites to the point of armed conflict. Are you trying to find another one too for your Vatican?"

After a glance upwards to check for any circling drones, the astute Father answers, "If I were, would there not be commandos from several countries ready to descend upon me once I did? Perhaps you would have better luck if you asked Peter that question. That is, once your medical staff brings him out of the induced coma."

"Lucky for all of us my security team found him a couple of days ago," Alexander says. "He was near psychotic, mumbling all the horrid things the aliens did to him. It sounded more like an interrogation. I have spent a good number of hours trying to understand who would have faked an alien abduction in order to extract what that poor boy knows about our plans. To extract that precious white sticky genetic substance of an ancient. You do not believe it was aliens, do you? Or, as the acting chair of the Pope's alien welcoming committee, do you know something I should?"

Another smile on Jean-Paul's face as he blinks rapidly again. "Rumor has it that you kidnapped Peter. But for what perverse purpose is the question. The great Alexander Murometz has always been beyond the common man's thinking."

And that gets the wrinkles on the giant's face to subside as the bullhead pendant sways below his neck. "Did my little Zara spread those malicious rumors about me? I hope you know that I always regarded you as a friend," admits Alexander. "Without fail, you could always ease my mind. Must be that rigorous Jesuit logic training. I need a friend right now. Even before the supposed alien abduction, the situation with Peter and Zara had become very tenuous. I am afraid she has made a very unfortunate, rash choice."

"Magali had told me that Zara wanted to see her," says Jean-Paul. "She wanted Magali's advice on happiness and the celibate commitment. Perhaps you are correct that she is reconsidering her future."

The smug-as-a-thug air returns as Alexander proudly states, "In that event, my arrangement for the two of them to find their future happiness with two other lucky people is well founded. The endgame must not be endangered. Peter has his role. And my Zara has hers."

His eyebrows now pointed inward with a puzzled look, Jean-Paul ponders. "But you worked so diligently to bring them together. All our tests, your billions of euros in AI development, all pointed to their destiny as the genetic manifestation of the originating couple of the oral traditions. They are literally genetically made for each other."

The Father pauses, reflecting on his own statement. "Perhaps I answered my own question. The object was found, and the need for their pairing disappeared."

Lips pursed, eyes darkened, the giant man says, "They are rabbit and turtle. Only bound to go their natural separate ways. More important, if the object has been found, then why are you probing a Neolithic site with your new devices? What is it you hope to find? All of my resources say the second object is not there."

"And why do you think I would be searching for another object?" posits the priest.

"I propose to you, my friend, that our interests are aligned. We seek the same thing, though perhaps for different reasons. Perhaps the object fragment you just found below," says Alexander, peering into the priest's blinking eyes.

"Oh, don't act innocent, my dear priest. I do not want the fragment. Your Vatican archives can store it away. But when the final battle comes, you may need to use it," says Alexander. "As your friend, I would propose we work together. I have information that the Vatican surely does not."

Scrunched dry lips pulsate on the Father's face as he focuses on the leviathan's eyes. Not the dark obsidian disks when this giant is in command mode. Jean-Paul's head bobs back and forth for a few seconds. Then he replies, "Understand that if my vows are in danger of being compromised, I will act in the best faith of the Pontiff, the Church, and of God. As well, if I believe the Vatican is best served by any information I uncover, I will tell you after I inform my superiors. Such as the evidence I found of an object fragment at this site."

"Your research techniques are beyond reproach, my good Father. As a sign of good faith, I will restrain myself from sending an extraction team to take that fragment for myself. I believe you will find our task at hand is in the interest of your Church. I think we seek to find the same god," says Alexander, who taps away on his MoxWrap.

A moment later, Jean-Paul's MoxWrap sounds. He reads the message and nods.

Smiling, Alexander says, "And as you can read, your boss also agrees with me." With a huge grin, he adds, "Well, your boss for now. After you get married, I will have to confer with the former Sister Magali for permission."

A few more taps of the MoxWrap and Alexander adds, "I have given you access to all I have on why we originally searched for the black object. I have also given all we obtained from Peter of what those aliens wanted from him. I cannot help but believe the alien abduction is intricately linked to what you and I have a shared interest in finding."

Minutes pass as the good Father scans some of the information his former interim boss has provided. His left hand combs through his hair as he stretches his back. "If this is true, then all of my work missed an entire half of the story."

Father Jean-Paul peers into the sky, into the heavens, into where the tail of the bird star would be at night. "It is as if I have failed as a researcher of the Vatican archives, as a researcher of human history. I have seen unrelatable bits and pieces, only hints, of what you show here, but not the magnitude, the revelation of the entirety of the story."

With a quick puff of air through his giant nostrils, Alexander says, "Do not chastise yourself so. It is not your fault you and I bear only one X chromosome. Women through time have hidden their side of the story. And as you can see, they hid the best part."

Another minute of reflection and Jean-Paul's gaze returns to focus into Alexander's eyes. "Magali hinted to me that history might not be as I have studied. That only half the story had been told. History has been written and recorded mostly by men. What we believe to be true comes from the writing of men. And that there is a complete oral tradition passed in complete secrecy down the female lineage. Why has not Magali shared more of this with me?"

"My dear priest, you have not figured this one out yet?" quips Alexander. "Why, you must ask her to marry you, father many children with her, and perchance she might tell you what she knows, only if she thinks it absolutely necessary for her to fulfill her obligation to find the blue light."

Astonishment does little to explain the shapes and lines that transcend upon the bewildered priest's face. "It will take decades of sifting through the archives using this new lens to find any more than a hint of what you have uncovered."

"My dear faithful Father, celibacy has its price. Until now, you probably thought your sweet former Sister's advances signaled only the decades of pent-up sexual desire. Perhaps she is wooing you so that she can tell her husband this secret she is dying to share."

Strategically changing the subject to spare his mind the wear from the number of implications this giant has just planted, Jean-Paul asks, "If what you are sharing is true, then you need, we need, the second black object to be brought to this cavern of blue light to prevent the next war to end all wars."

"That is my altruistic purpose," says the monstrous man. "I have my own destiny to fulfill, which I need Peter and a highly afflicted woman bearing his child to help deliver."

"And what is to happen with Peter and Zara? I had thought you had nudged Zara to finally accept Peter as her partner. His mother, of course, has been in contact with me about performing the marriage ceremony."

Now the eyes darken, the edges of the mouth down turned. Alexander says, "I am afraid the book launch backfired on these plans. My headstrong Zara failed the test of true love: standing by the one you love. When we stopped Peter's induced coma, she failed her chance to show her love. I can't help but think NiQihs ran interference between the two. Nevertheless, I cannot risk our plans on something as fickle as love. I have arranged two other paths for them. Either they will complete their destinies along these paths or a miracle will happen."

"Our last miracle happened because of the bonding between Zara and Peter. I cannot fathom another miracle happening without their bonding unless you have a private direct line to the Lord himself."

The giant laughs. "Herself. If you want to get Zara and Magali's cooperation, you need to adjust your gender references, Priest. Your dear Magali may need to console my dear little Zara on matters of the celibate heart. You, my dear Father, will need to console her on being a prophetess. As we speak, a worldwide outcry has grown for the next messiah—a stubborn, headstrong Kurd we know. Perhaps MoxWorld News has played a role in driving demand for her connection to the Divine. The EM pulse and earthquake from the two object halves are being feared as harbingers of the impending end of the world. Maybe the world is in its final moments crying for the next messiah to save them?"

Shaking his head, Jean-Paul says, "Is there nothing left sacred to you? Is there nothing your power cannot corrupt?"

Then the serious visage returns. "Things have not gone well since I overextended my powers, taxed my organization in that last go around getting Peter and Zara together and reuniting the first black object halves. I fear that my inattention to other areas of my business have led to the formation of NiQihs, as well as possible double agents in my organization. I know that I can only truly trust you, Peter, Zara, and of course, Mei. From now on, only use the private coded line between us. I will use my highest security measures and will be invisible to the world and the organization for the amount of time needed to flush out the spies in my holding companies."

The giant signs out. And on cue, Magali wanders back. "That monster. The good book does little to describe the true depths of the devil. Do not trust a thing he just told you."

He kisses Magali on the forehead and posits, "The Cathars believed that the good book spoke of two gods—one of the light, and one of the dark. Perhaps the latter created Alexander and all he can do is serve the dark Him."

The edges of Magali's lips drop at his statement.

Her hero priest takes her hands into his and says, "But I am sure that the God of the light created you. And that She blessed you with wisdom from your grandmothers, your great-grandmothers. Wisdom they would want you to share with me."

She pulls back from him with her finger wagging at his chest. "Not so quick there, Father Fast-Hands. Many are the treasures a woman holds until the man marries her. Perhaps if you would put a little of the persuasive power you learned from that monstrous man to use with your friend, the Holy Pontiff, who needs to pressure the Cardinals' Council on marriage to ratify the proposal allowing priests to marry."

"Maybe a little blue light would shine clarity on our search?" Jean-Paul asks innocently.

"Ha ha. The only light we shall discuss until your ring finger is occupied is the white light of the Lord," replies Magali. "There is the light that is needed in the orphanages in these regions. That explosion your Alexander caused knocked out the power grids for hundreds of kilometers around here. I have visited so many orphanages in need of food, blankets, and fuel for their generators."

She takes his hands into hers. "There are so many adorable children in need of loving parents. We can adopt, you know. Imagine a dozen of the cutest love-starved little ones calling you Papa."

Eyebrows raised, the good Father is beyond speechless.

CHAPTER 14

He who is devoid of the power to forgive is devoid of the power to love. There is some good in the worst of us and some evil in the best of us. When we discover this, we are less prone to hate our enemies.

—Martin Luther King Jr.

St. George's Monastery, Fiolent Cape, Crimea
7:35 p.m. GMT+3, January 18, 2023

"Fabulously elegant," says the Russian military intelligence officer as he gazes south upon the moonlit Black Sea next to Zara.

"I have never heard that said about a body of water," muses Zara. "Or are you talking about this romantic twelve-hundred-year-old monastery you have decided to take me to before the negotiations meeting?"

Anatoly turns to her and gazes into her pupils. "Perhaps I meant your eyes."

A frown runs across her face, then a playful smile. "Thank you, Anatoly. It has been nearly an hour since you picked me up at the Kacha naval air base, and not one pass. You were giving me a complex that you no longer cared for me," replies Zara teasingly.

"I am afraid, my dear, that those days are over," says a resigned Anatoly. "You are perfectly safe in my presence."

A bigger smile and Zara asks, "And who is she? Is she worth your love, Anatoly? Is she kind and gentle to you? Not as controlling as me?"

He purses his lips, then turns his head away from her as he says, "Please forgive me for being so shallow. But her physical beauty caught me. She is even taller than you. And more domineering. I am her slave."

"Oh, you picked up another innocent student from the university again. Like you did me."

He puts his wrist with a distinctive reddish ring around it next to hers and simulates handcuffs. "It was love at first bondage. She worked at the armory where I sourced the assault rifles and body armor I brought for your battle with Aleksandr over that black monolith. If we only knew its power, we would have taken it ourselves."

Pointing out to a speck in the moon's reflection upon the waters, he says, "That is his yacht. We know you meet him out there. I thought at first you were his lover, which made you only that much more desirable to me. But then, one day, he met me face-to-face. He warned me that if my intentions were not honorable, he would have my testicles bronzed."

No flinch from Zara at such a thought. She watched the giant's pleasure yacht from this same spot only two weeks ago, after she had fled the ill-fated book signing. But she had to interrupt her attendance at this important military summit to be with Peter as he awoke from his coma.

But Anatoly shivers as he asks, "What is he doing out there? His team works out there day in, day out. We have a missile frigate stationed nearby at your Aleksandr's request. We watch his divers working from the yacht. He is searching for something out there. But we do not know if he is there or not. He has disappeared from the world's view since your silly American's book launch."

Zara stares out upon the waters she once dived into off his yacht after that monster killed his own son because she would not marry him. She swam back to shore not far from here. And that murdering megalomaniac had the nerve to ask for forgiveness.

She turns her head the other direction, trying to focus on something more rational. Like Father Jean-Paul. "Remember my Jesuit priest friend? He told me that out there, under the waves, are the untold archaeological treasures of a civilization that once lived by the shores of the freshwater lake that became the Black Sea. It was perhaps the flood of the Prophet Nuh that inundated these shores, wiping out their old world."

Looking along the cliff sides below the monastery, down to the rocky shore that bore the brunt of the tsunami created by the black object's explosion, she says, "If these rocks could talk, what mysteries and wonders would they share of the people who shaped our cultures through their stories?"

Turning back to Anatoly, she says, "And that is all that Alexander is focused upon. Solving those mysteries. I am sure that he is somewhere working toward that single-focused aim."

She reflexively jerks back as his hands touch her face near her eyes. Anatoly remarks, "Your eyes. They have this tint of blue."

His face right up to hers as she jerks back more, thinking he is going to kiss her. He says, "Yes, it is like a glow around your irises. That was not there when we drove across the Balaclava hills."

Relaxing her defensive stance, she takes his hands off her face into hers and says, "Thank you, my old friend. For a moment there, I thought you were going to give me that line you used to seduce me when I was studying in Moscow."

He takes her hands to his lips for the lightest of caresses and says, "What did that soulless oligarch do to you? Did he irradiate you with something? My little kroshka, if he harmed you, it is I who will bronze his testicles."

"That is so sweet of you," replies a soft-eyed Zara. "Almost as sweet as when you had that hotel laundry treat Dan Connelly's briefs with a hot pepper extract. You were always so jealous and protective."

His face drops with a thought. "I must not love my Irina as much as you, as I have not tortured her past lovers. She really is a kind woman when we are dressed."

She strokes his hand and replies, "Forgive me, Anatoly. I had not been kind to you. I hope your Irina will be much better than I was for you."

His face lights with a glimpse of the smile that one has when true love hits, but then, a more somber one.

"What is wrong?" asks Zara. "Is she not a kind woman? Let me talk with her and I will let her know what a great man you are."

"No, it is not her. It is who you will be meeting shortly."

With swaggering shoulders, Zara asserts, "The Turks? I know how to handle their negotiators."

"I'm afraid not."

"The Kurds?" asks a perplexed Zara. "What can my own people do to surprise me?"

Astonished. Simply astonished. Not that her best friend Peri's baby bump was so much bigger. Not that three paces from her stood Dan "Mr. Pepper Briefs" Connelly from the US State Department. But that another "he" from her past would be here with the Kurdish negotiation team. Is this what her Sasha meant when he said he "fixed" her Turkish negotiation problem?

They stood more than a thousand meters back into the mountain next to the rocky Black Sea coastline. Once a Cold War submarine base built to withstand nuclear attack, this facility had been converted after the fall of the Soviet Union into a war museum. But after the surprising, massive EM pulse that Alexander set off over six months ago, for strategic reasons, the Russians recommissioned this base, Anatoly explained on the final car ride down from the monastery.

But for what purpose? No submarines were to be seen in this base. Not even Zara's best smile could coax this information from her old friend.

What he did say was that this facility was fully secure from eavesdropping. From Aleksandr and from anyone else. No transmissions could be sent or received from any device, nor could any radiation of any wavelength penetrate the layers of sandstone, granite rock, concrete, copper, and lead shielding surrounding the base, which spanned over ten thousand square meters behind the cliffs of Crimea.

Anatoly had led her down into the complex through archways and hallways lined with light grey concrete bricks. Once it was fully lit up for tourists; now, only the lights needed to find the negotiations chamber shined.

The labyrinth of the base's multitude of darkened corridors had the makings of a horror film. A line of yellow-orange tube lights illuminated the pathway along the five-hundred-meter-long abandoned submarine canal like a procession of monks with candles in hand.

Dropping the latest literal bombshell news, he tells her the Chinese and Russians have both escalated the conflict on the Inner Mongolian and Siberian borders. Yesterday, the Chinese launched a tactical nuclear strike a dozen kilometers from a Siberian village to demonstrate their resolve to get the disputed meteorite back. They want the world to know their resolve in defending Chinese territory and property. The Russians responded last night with a less-than-precision strike, bombing several power plants in Northern Chinese cities with extensive collateral damage, killing hundreds of civilians in the process.

Was she so preoccupied with breaking up with Peter on the flight back from the United States that she missed these pivotal world events? She spent most of the flight crafting her breakup message to him. One that let him know that she loved him enough to let him start a family with the woman who was best for him. For cats should be with cats.

Or was it the delay in Sasha sending his armored jet to get her that threw off her normally attuned senses? And why is Anatoly telling her this news now?

She is soon to find out as they near the deepest reaches into the mountain, where the conference chamber lies. An arched ceiling around walls of grey sintered cement blocks holds back the weight of the mountain overhead. A large square formation of tables lies dead center. At the farthest end sit the Russians, with the moderator, Admiral Nikolay Orlov, the base commander. To his left, the Turkish delegation. To his right, the Kurdish delegation, including her best friend Peri… and "him."

At the end of the square closest to Zara sits the man who made her his unknowing paramour. Dan Connelly, who had an open seat next to him adjacent to another Westerner and a very calm and composed white-haired man with a mix of Caucasian and Asian features, but who must be very tall given his stature in his seat.

As Anatoly leaves her to join the Russian side of the room, Zara beelines it to the open seat next to Dan. Better next to a happily married man than to take the open seat next to Peri, which is also next to "him."

As the room quiets while all eyes are on her, Dan stands up to greet her with a light hug. Old friends. She politely greets the other two people. Mr. Ching, representative of the People's Republic of China, whose presence Zara finds odd given how the exchange of nuclear attacks and bombings happened yesterday. And then the other Westerner, who only introduces himself as a representative of NiQihs, the corporation soon to dispose of MoxWorld Holdings. What a snide remark, notes Zara. But then again, why should she care what happens to Sasha's business?

Oddly, the tall man remains seated. Dark glasses. Whitish hair. He does not even glance at Zara, only focused on his NiQihs device. He appears familiar. Maybe he is wearing padding to build out his profile, but was this the same man not with Dr. Fontaine at Peter's book signing? The one who handed out what appeared to be payoffs?

As she reaches for the seat next to Dan, the NiQihs man points to the open seat next to Peri and says that is her place.

Hand firmly on the chair back, she replies, "I am afraid you are mistaken. I am not here representing the Kurdish governments. I am the authorized representative of MoxWorld Holdings, whose factories are in dispute. I sit here."

The whitish haired man nods at the head of the Turkish delegation, who stands up. Tall and mighty. A half a head shorter than her Sasha. Likewise, she glares into his eyes, for he is no stranger to her. Retired Colonel Yamut led the attack in which her brother died trying to save the villagers. He glares back at Zara as he demands, "Lieutenant Khatum. Or is it former lieutenant of the terrorist YPJ-PKK outfit? Your seat is there with the other Kurds. No more foolish delays from you. People's lives are at stake. People's livelihoods are at stake. People's souls are at stake. Or is the so-called new prophetess not interested in our souls?"

Her foot firmly planted. Does this man intend to kill her where she stands as he did her unarmed brother? Ready to make her last stand here and now over this chair with this murderer, Zara spies the eyes of motherhood. Peri's eyes, begging her to sit down next to her. She glares one more time at the colonel, tucks her headscarf tighter around her neck, and sits next to Peri. And "him."

She leans over, feels the moving baby bulge, and whispers to her best friend, "Are you okay? You should not have come here with your baby so restless."

"My baby will be just fine if you do not start World War III over past crimes," Peri states quietly. "Remember, this time I cannot fight to save your life when you charge a well-fortified position like that across the room."

As the heated colonel continues to berate her, she feels the heat from "him." His shoulders only centimeters away from hers. Those oh-so-wide shoulders that cradled her so securely when he bear-hugged her. She flinches to break that train of thought.

She tries to focus instead on the colonel, but that scent. The one she would inhale when she was buried in his arms. Disarming as it was back then. Diminished not one iota. She watches the colonel flapping his lips, spitting at her as she tries not to look left into "his" face. The visage that cheated on her. She would rather be shamed in the room by this outlandish colonel than gaze into "his" eyes again. Those brown objects that seduced her innocent self into joining the Peshmerga the day after high school graduation.

Her eyes dare not close as the ranting colonel berates her deviance from true Islam, belittles her gender, and defiles the honor of her people. Because each time they do, his scent overwhelms the rest of her senses. Every fiber in her strained body yells to ask Peri to switch seats. But that would only exacerbate the colonel's tirade even more.

With beet-red cheeks and blood-orange throat, the exhausted colonel finally sits down. Zara slowly scans the room, making contact with every pair of eyes except those to her direct left. "Him."

She stands and feigns a word of wisdom, only to pause, ensuring everyone's attention. Then she says, "I ask of everyone their forgiveness of my tardiness and absence. I put the love of a near-death friend before the concerns of each of your nations. If the selfless love of a dying man is a sin, then I ask for atonement."

As the blank faces stare back at her, she knows she has their minds working. Her eyebrows tilt inwards, her forehead scrunching into hills and valleys, she makes eye contact with the colonel. But abruptly, she relaxes her gesture as she says, "I had hoped these would be secular discussions, which is also the wish of Mr. Murometz. But given that the question of my faith has been raised as a barrier to a peaceful solution, let us remember that the Prophet, peace be upon him, said, 'You do not do evil to those who do evil to you, but you deal with them with forgiveness and kindness.' And may Allah find forgiveness for both you and me, for we have not been at our best."

She begins to sit down, only to rise again. "And I forgive you, Colonel Yamut, for killing my brother. I hold no grudge that will prevent us from finding the most peaceful solution to your concerns. What matters is the menu on the table now, or so says the old Kurdish proverb."

A neutral poker face from the Turkish officer stares back at her as she begins to sit. But once again, she rises. "I beg forgiveness for one more issue. I was not born with external genitalia. For if I were a man, I would remember that the Prophet, may peace be upon him, also said that a good man treats women with honor."

Finally, she sits, her hands clasped on the table in front of her, eyes affixed upon those of the unflinching colonel. Behind the crimson table skirting, invisible to others, Peri kicks Zara. To which Zara whispers, "I love you too."

To her left, "his" body rustles at her comment, and he finally whispers, "And that is the Zara I once loved so much."

CHAPTER 15

That which is false troubles the heart, but truth brings joyous tranquility.
—Jalāl ad-Dīn Muḥammad Rūmī, thirteenth-century Persian Sufi mystic

Balaklava Bay, Crimea
9:10 p.m. GMT+3, January 18, 2023

From across the room, someone mutters *fahişe,* "whore" in Turkish. Zara attempts to rise in attack, but "his" hand holds her down as he rises to say, "I think we can all agree that was an inappropriate comment. Personal attacks based on gender bias will not help anyone's cause in this room. I would ask that our colleagues across the room remember that Ms. Khatum's selfless work in the last six months has led to over two billion Turkish lira, or four hundred million euros, of economic growth. Through her, over five hundred hospitals and clinics across Turkey and the Anatolian Kurdish State were re-equipped with the latest medical equipment to replace that damaged in the devastating EM pulse."

Pausing while scanning the room, he rests his hand upon her shoulder, the warmth surprisingly a relief for her tense muscles.

"Instead of vilifying this good woman, we should recognize her for her selfless deeds helping both the Turkish and Kurdish people. Maybe she is not a prophet. Maybe she is. But what I am sure of is that she is near a saint."

Zara's mouth hangs open. Perhaps not visibly to everyone else, but clearly, she did not expect that from "him"—Zengo, her first love. Without engaging his eyes, she pats his knee as he sits down.

Before the Turks can counter, Admiral Orlov refocuses the room on the last points of the negotiation. The Turkish delegation continues to claim one hundred percent ownership of the MoxWorld factories but has offered the Kurds twenty percent of net profits from the three proposed factories across Turkey and the Anatolian Kurdish State in exchange for thirty-three percent of the net profits of the two factories proposed in New Kurdistan. They also expect MoxWorld Holdings to re-equip their military for free, as they did the hospitals.

The two Kurds next to Zengo rustle with the proposition as they huddle, discussing their response. Zengo stands and gives a mature, dispassionate, very logical oration about how most of the sales of these factories will come from Kurdish customers and therefore the profits should proportionally benefit the two Kurdish nations.

And for the first time in nearly nineteen years, she looks upon his face. Lines across those high cheeks bespeak the years of war. Dark curly hair with that same trimmed mustache that tickled so much on their first kiss. Age has not diminished his stature nor the definition of his arm muscles. She momentarily remembers his six-pack from the hundred sit-ups a day they would do together. She shames herself for noticing his physical traits, for she is a humble woman looking only for the love of Xwedê. Or so she repeats several times.

Then comes the less-than-dispassionate retort from across the room, during which Zengo remains cool and collected. For several minutes, the dispute centers on the claim that someone must owe the entire profits to Turkey to fund the reconstruction of their country after the devastating EM pulse. After which, all eyes turn to MoxWorld's representative.

She straightens her tunic and her scarf, then rises, making eye contact all around the room, including the viscerally evoking ones to her left. She states, "Lest everyone in this room forget, their countries stood minutes from a world war less than seven months ago. The EM pulse generated by the stones found by Mr. Murometz was accidental, but it served to neutralize the machines of war. Many of your loved ones still live today because of this accident."

She pauses again to let her words sink in. "But Mr. Murometz is a generous man. He is prepared to offer to the country of Turkey the first MoxMover factory in the Asia Minor area. Regarding advanced, AI-guided weapons, Mr. Murometz will guarantee to match the lowest price offered to any other nation to Turkey." She looks around to the Russian admiral, and then to Dan, and then to Mr. Ching, the Chinese representative. "But as these countries know, he will not rearm them until they have agreed to new, unilateral peace terms."

The man from NiQihs grins and leans over to Mr. Ching, who nods in agreement. Then Mr. Ching stands. "Honorable Colonel, the People's Republic of China is prepared to show the inheritors of the Great Ottoman Empire the extreme generosity of the Chinese people. The kindly NiQihs Corporation has refitted our most advanced fighter, the Shenyang J-31N, with NiQihs's advanced AI technology, which they claim is vastly superior to the weakly shielded technology Mr. Murometz sold to the world powers at inflated, monopolistic prices. In addition, our Type 99N tank has been similarly modified and will outperform the Leopard 2 tanks you bought from the traitorous Germans, who turned on you as you tried to rid northern Syria of PKK terrorists."

The three Kurds to Zara's left stand up, ready to contest these remarks, but Zara holds her hand out, signaling for them to sit back down.

"You are indeed as wise as Mr. Murometz's fake news network has purported," says Mr. Ching. "But your master should know that any party desiring our advanced military weapons will need to heed the wishes of the People's Republic. And our country only asks of the great country of Turkey that they refuse all offers from the disingenuous MoxWorld empire. No factories. No weapons. And we will allow you to manufacture the Type 99N tank for all countries in this part of the world who wish to purchase them. You, of course, will get manufacturer's cost on all tanks that you order. We will also sell you the squadron of J-31N fighters that should land in Incrilek Air Base within the day."

The Russian admiral begins to yell into Anatoly's ear in machine-gun Russian, then remembers something and yells in Russian directly at Zara, who says back in perfect Russian to remain calm. Admiral Orlov calls for a strategic half-hour break. The delayed dinner awaits in the outer room.

Both Dan and Anatoly grab Zara, pulling her into the corner of an adjacent chamber as Admiral Orlov pulls Mr. Ching into another room. Anatoly begs of Zara to talk her Aleksandr into releasing his newest weapon upgrades. He will give up Irina and forever be Zara's love slave if she will do this one little favor for him—still so adorable when he begs. Zara resists his overture, repeating that she has no control over Mr. Murometz.

To divert the conversation, she jests with Dan about whether or not he would offer to leave his devoted wife as an inducement for her to ask the same of Mr. Murometz. But Dan glances down, only to say that his wife left him after he took Zara and the US vice president on Air Force Two to Mecca so she could perform the Hajj. At the edge of being choked up, he adds that his wife had been seeing someone for a few years already and his taking Zara on such a personal trip burst open their tottering marriage.

Zara begs his forgiveness for her insensitivity. So that is why, when Air Force Two broke down on the way to Mecca after Peter's grandfather's funeral, Dan had to fly back to the US.

Dan admits that the president personally asked him to attend this meeting because of their past relationship. He cannot beg as well as Anatoly, but he can appeal to her rational self. The one who cool-headedly helped them hunt down Jahsh, Kurdish traitors, during Operation Iraqi Freedom. Mr. Murometz must arm both the Americans and Russians equally to neutralize the threat of the new Chinese weapons.

"Please believe me," Zara pleads. "I do not have that kind of influence with Alexander. He is a man all of his own. I feel so bad for each of you that your governments asked of you the humiliating task of begging me based on our past relationships. But Alexander has cut off communication with me for reasons I cannot speak of. I am sure you will be more successful in trying to get him directly. Your presidents both have direct lines."

Silence reigns. The two of them, her former lovers, both trying to woo her for what she can do to prevent the destruction of humanity as they did years before, getting her to go undercover to terminate threats to their respective national interests. She peers at Colonel Yamut, the one who evoked for a moment within her Zara, the avenging angel. Or was that the devil of death? She avenged her brother's death at the highest level. But that Zara is gone. The new Zara only wishes for the peace of which the voice speaks. The peace that Xwedê wants.

As she wrestles with the realities of impending war and the theological wishes of the unseen Divine, she spies her first lover, her first love, talking with the man from NiQihs. Is he trying to get their technology for the Kurds?

Anatoly breaks her silence. "Admiral Orlov is issuing an ultimatum to Mr. Ching. A direct message from our president. If the Chinese arm countries near Mother Russia, we will take preemptive steps to eliminate their ability to manufacture these weapons."

Then Dan frowns. Not at Anatoly, but at the floor as he admits, "The US president is prepared to have the US carrier groups make preemptive strikes on the Chinese carrier group steaming into the South Pacific. They cannot take the chance that this unknown, advanced NiQihs technology will cost American lives."

He smirks at Anatoly, and then, with a blank stare, says to Zara, "After my wife publicly left me, the president now thinks me a James Bond and expects me to use any means available to persuade Mr. Murometz's representative into arming the US. The director of national intelligence told him you broke up with Peter. They assumed I had a chance at romancing you into a military contract."

Zara nods. A smile, though. "And here we are. Friends and lovers, one step away from the world's demise. And the two of you are the most honest with me since I have known you both. Your presidents should be ashamed of thinking my body and your bodies were theirs to command. My body is mine and is not for negotiation. But if I could, I would get you an audience with Alexander. I cannot. And I do not know who has the authority in his absence."

Dan pulls out a folded paper from his jacket. All of them checked in their MoxWraps at the security gate, so old-fashioned paper is the mode of the moment. "Apparently, you have the authority," he says as he hands the document to her.

Scanning the printout of a coded MoxWrap message from Alexander to the US president, Zara reads that one, Ms. Z. Khatum has been granted authorization to contract with any nation on his behalf for economic, military, and political affairs of the MoxWorld Holdings organization.

She stomps her feet. That man. The nerve of him. How can she in good conscience arm these two superpowers? How many people will die if she does? How many more will die if she does not?

She says, still staring at the paper, "He knew full well my vows and commitments to lead a nonviolent life. I hated him for making me break my vows in helping him find that black ob…meteorite. But hate is behind me now. I have forgiven him, and more importantly, myself. But how can I, in good faith, fuel an arms race?"

Eyes to the floor, Dan says, "You remember what MAD stands for? Mutually assured destruction. Our analysts believe this situation could rapidly spiral out of control and a global thermonuclear war could devastate all life."

As Zara's lips purse, Dan says, "Not that it matters, but you know my brother Jerome. You and I had Thanksgiving dinner with his family. He's commanding a missile cruiser in one of the carrier task forces steaming to intercept the Chinese fleet. This is now very personal."

Anatoly says, "Ha, that is nothing. My sister Svetlana, you remember her. You two would go shopping in Moscow for the best things to make for dinner. She is a nurse with the troops on the Inner Mongolian border."

She remembers them both. Very fondly so. How can she be a prophetess? How could anyone think she could guide the world? She cannot make this decision.

Miracles do exist, as she sees Peri waddling around, looking for that magic room of instantaneous peace. Pregnant women's bladders are so abused. She excuses herself as she runs to Peri's rescue.

"Oh Zara, I have to go really, really bad. Quick, help me find that ladies' room before I let loose the next flood," cries the pregnant Peri. "In another minute, they will be able to float their submarines back in here."

Madly looking around for a ladies' room sign in Russian, Zara says, "I am so sorry that I was away when your second trimester pop happened. I think it might be down that way."

As Zara has her arm around Peri's, helping her waddle along, Peri says, "And what a pop that was. I do not know how this child is going to get through my pelvis. But I know you were taking care of Peter, as you should."

"Well, that is a subject for history," says Zara.

"And I suppose those three historical subjects in that room back there returned into your life for academic reasons," jests Peri. "What did you do when you were with Peter to get Xwedê so annoyed at you to put all four of you in the same room together in the middle of a contentious, world-altering debate?"

"I think She is testing me. I said I wanted to be like Rabi'a. My great-grandmother said Rabi'a had many suitors. And yet she chose celibacy." Zara peers around, still looking for the room of the moment's dire need. "Xwedê must be testing me today as she did to her."

"Well, she is surely testing my bladder today," cries Peri as she waddles more concertedly. "That Russian officer said the ladies' room was seven halls down this way. Did we miss it? Oh, what was I thinking? A Cold War base. There were no women stationed here. So why would they have a ladies' room?"

"You must be having pregnancy brain already," jests Zara. "They made this place into a museum decades ago. Of course they made ladies' rooms. You probably misunderstood that officer's Russian."

Zara peers down a very long, dark hallway veering at a perpendicular to the submarine canal. She pulls Peri down the passageway.

"Zara, that sign. Does it not say this is a high-security area?" asks Peri tepidly. "The ladies' room is certainly not down here."

"Shh. You want to alert the guards?" admonishes Zara. "Come on, pudding brains. Did you forget how to pee in combat conditions? We peed all over the battlefields of Syria, and there were no ladies' rooms to be found."

Fifty paces down into the darkness, they stop and squat with Peri moaning the moans of all moans. "Oh, these men," laments Peri. "They have no pregnancy pity. They argued for two hours straight about nonsense before you arrived. I could not step out.”

As the two rise, arranging their clothing, Peri stares at Zara. “Is there something wrong with your eye?”

“You are not going to tell me they glow like Anatoly did,” says Zara. “You are not hitting on me, are you? Anatoly tried that line just before we got here.”

“No, seriously, turn your head back down to the passage entrance,” says Peri as she follows her friend's eyes. “They fluctuated.” She grabs Zara's hand and with her free hand, she feels along the walls as she goes deeper into the darkness.

Thirty paces more and Peri peers into Zara's eyes. “The glow. It is slightly steadier. It is faint, but I swear it is there.” She drags Zara further into the blackness, carefully feeling each invisible step in front of her.

“Peri, we do not have flashlights or our MoxWraps,” pleads Zara. “You might walk us into an empty submarine canal.”

Another hundred paces. They can see nothing, not even each other, except Peri's hand as she puts it in front of Zara's face. It catches the faintest of glows, and finally, Zara can see what all the fuss is about.

“You are radiating,” says Peri. “Are you going to make lightning strike again? Because if you are, pregnant ladies need to be excused. Your eyes did not do this down the hallway. There's something further in the corridor that is reacting with you. Let's go.”

“Are you kidding?” cries Zara. “We might fall into something worse than a submarine canal. And that, your mother would not forgive me for. Yes, she would forgive me for having you lead the attack on a Daesh position. But a silly tint in the eye?”

The argument is settled by flashlights and laser pointers coming from the entrance to the passageway. Two women out for a piss caught in a mass of waving red laser dots signaling one false move and they will be shredded into cheese.

Zara yells at the soldiers in Russian, “You are about to shoot two women who did a little wee-wee in the hallway and got lost. Look at your boots. You splashed through our piss.”

The soldiers look and gag, rubbing their boots on the floor.

CHAPTER 16

*If God causes you to suffer much, it is a sign that He has great designs for you,
and that He certainly intends to make you a saint.*

—Saint Ignatius of Loyola

*Dr. Fontaine's office, MoxMedical Total Care Unit
San Francisco, California
6:10 p.m. GMT-8, January 19, 2023*

"They have nothing on you, Sammy. Don't you worry," says Peter to the image of his alma mater's mascot on his cap lying in his lap. Samantha quickly gathered travel clothes for him, along with a mother's care package for her daughter Michaela. Of course, she packed his UC Santa Cruz cap and polo shirt, both emblazoned with Sammy.

Why the rush? A life tsunami pounded Peter's life two afternoons ago. His one true love, Zara, went storming off. And then that strangest of strange breakup messages from Zara, telling him to be the father he was destined to be. But after he coerced his mother into telling him exactly what he'd said during his deliriums, he understands why Zara would be angry with him. Calling God an alien creation probably didn't help. Especially as he recanted his belief in aliens on the mountain top. But saying that angels were only extraterrestrials sealed his fate.

Yesterday and this morning, he used all the MoxWorld resources he had access to, to contact Zara. Even Alexander said he could not get to that "headstrong Kurd," as he put it, advising Peter to move on, as another woman in need would be reaching out to him.

And indeed, not one but three women in need called him a few hours ago. First Mei, crying for his help as her excavation in Xian had found what she had been searching for. But to find the second object, only Peter's abilities could help her solve the puzzles in time before the worst would happen. Her personal jet is already over the Pacific, heading to get him. Then a follow-up call from Michaela, saying he needs to do her a big favor. A family crisis. Won't he do anything for his little sister? Follow Mei's lead. Please, Michaela begged.

The third woman? His best editing client called, only to find out he was set to fly out tonight to China. Dr. Beverly Fontaine insisted on talking with him before he left. So, as he sits in a typically bland, perfectly sterile hospital office, Peter regards the three diplomas hanging on the wall. Princeton undergraduate; Yale MD; Harvard PhD in neuropsychology. Where has he seen these schools before? Certainly not in her home, nor her office at Angel's Rest nursing home, both places where he has worked with her on her book and academic papers.

Did she display these here because that was the only way she could get hired by MoxWorld? That talent management guy seemed so biased against Sammy's school when Peter interviewed for a job with MoxWorld. His mother wanted him to go to one of those schools. In contrast, his sister went to Stanford and now Shanghai University.

He finally got that moment of respect on the worldwide stage with his book, though. Vindication for his alma mater. But that was short-lived once he found out that Alexander's editors had altered his book to match three dozen genres custom-tailored to the reader. Fake respect. Fake authorship. His one moment to show Zara he was someone she could be proud of. No wonder she left him.

His thoughts are interrupted by Dr. Bev's return to her office, where he sits in front of her desk. "Peter, your recovery is nothing short of miraculous.

Those MoxMedicine treatments are extraordinary. What we must chat about is our discussion about your father?" she asks as he stares at her diplomas.

"Which one of those discussions?" replies Peter. "The ones about how oppressive the search for a mythical stone was in his life?"

"In part," responds Bev, as she sits down behind her desk. "His perception that he failed his father in that search brought about his severe depression. Seeking respect is a core human desire. His suicide may have been driven by his belief that he failed to gain the respect of those he loved. Your pappy. Your mother. The same two people whose respect has driven most of your life's decisions."

Peter cannot look her in the eyes. Only at the warmly accepting eyes of Sammy on his cap. Maybe she's right. He went off on Zara at the book signing because he thought she had disrespected him. Maybe his subliminal desire for respect has driven all his girlfriends to leave him.

"You're even more vulnerable now, Peter," adds the doctor. "Your need to process what is happening to you kept you in that coma for several days. Leaving now for China and facing the kidnappers of your friend, I fear may crack you again. You'll do anything to get the respect of the next woman who woos you just as you did with Zara."

"Just as I did with you, Bev?" quips Peter.

"Well, that was different," answers the doctor as she shifts in her chair. "What you did for me reflected your professional desire to do your best at editing."

She comes out from behind to sit on the edge of the desk, facing Peter. She puts a finger under his chin as she says, "I am very worried about your mental frailty at this moment. You had a psychotic episode that so severely stressed your brain we needed to induce a coma. Your fervor about aliens has gone amok. I care about you as a friend. We are friends, aren't we?"

"Of course, Bev. You're probably my only friend at this moment," says Peter. "Everyone else is either using me or is mad at me for things I clearly don't understand."

His eyes momentarily pass by her prominent chest. Embarrassed, he crosses his legs and tries to refocus. And all he can think of is the aliens and those things they did to him he can't remember.

"Those tests you said they did on me," says Peter as he gazes down at his crotch. "Why did they want parts of my reproductive system? Is it true they're harvesting us for some diabolical scheme?"

"I said someone did those things," answers Bev. "I didn't say aliens. I've seen photos of prisoners of war who were tortured. Some sexually abused. Some had marks like you. And the psychological impact on them is why I urge you to take caution in your trip. Your judgment may be impaired. You may make bad decisions based on ideas or conclusions clouded by your aberrations."

She switches the crossing of her legs, the smooth silkiness of her perfectly tanned, waxed calves in clear view as she asks, "And you're sure that your Kurdish friend won't be on this trip with you?"

Peter, trying desperately to maintain a professional point of view on his pappy's doctor friend, his editing client, his only friend at this moment, answers, "No, I don't think she will be traveling with me anytime soon. Or ever. Why is that important?"

"I say this as your friend, who truly cares about you as I did your pappy," she states. "You don't have to hide it from me if you had a physically intimate relationship with her. I'm an adult. So are you. But as your friend, I worry that the two of you together may be problematic. She is suffering from posttraumatic stress delusions. The voice you say she hears mimics what happened to Joan of Arc. From her descriptions of the past, it seems she may have paranoid schizophrenia. Zara's visions may very well be psychotic episodes. Dangerous to both of you if you pander to these delusions. And in your state, you are so vulnerable."

"It's true, Bev. Our relationship is very platonic, even though we are as intimate as two people could ever be. Or we were. Maybe you're right about my confused state. She left me a message that's so confusing. She loves me, but then she sounded like I should partner with some other woman. I don't get it."

Bev hops off the desk and sits in the chair in front of Peter. "That is my point. In your posttraumatic condition, you will be confused at most things.

She is years after her traumatic event, and see how confusing she is to you? Promise me, Peter, as your trusted friend, that you'll call me if you ever run into a moment when you get confused. You need a friend, even a hug. I am your best gauge of what is real and what is not. I've spent more time with you than any other woman in the past year, as we worked so closely together on my projects. I know you for who you really are."

She puts her forehead to his as he puts his hands around the back of her neck. No bump. Or at least not much of one. Is it shallow of an afflicted guy to judge a woman by the size of her God Gene bump?

Peter pulls back from her, peering into her fully dilated brown eyes. "And if there is a god who is trying to speak with us, how would we know if it is true? Will the person who hears God always be labeled delusional or said to suffer from some other psychiatric disorder? Bev, do you believe God exists?"

Mimicking him, she places her fingers on the back of his neck. "You should know. You helped me write my last book on that subject. I believe we are hard-wired to believe in a supernatural being who guides us. The God Gene Complex is real. It is tissue we can dissect and measure."

She rubs the bump on the back of his neck. "You and Zara have very pronounced God Gene Complexes. You two are highly predisposed to believe—her in her voice, you in your aliens."

He rubs her anatomically minimal bump. "Bev, do you know if what happened in our past to create this God Gene Complex trait could happen again?"

Pulling back from him, she reflects and then replies, "Theoretically. Was it an abnormal radiation event that led some of our ancestors to develop this gene? Or was it the normal course of genetic variance? Did natural selection favor those who were prone to believing in supernatural forces? I don't know. I don't think anyone would know."

"But, Bev, if it did happen again, where would that take us? Where would humanity evolve to next? Is that why the aliens abducted me? Did I just have sex with one of them to breed the next round of human evolution?"

With a subtle laugh, she responds, "Don't get carried away with those notions. This is exactly what I said would happen in your state, that you might jump to conclusions too fast." She sits back up on the desk in front of him, her glimmering calves bouncing slightly up and down.

Oblivious to her actions, Peter asks, "But you ask about the intimacies between Zara and me. I haven't had sex since I broke up with my last girlfriend."

"You mean a virile, handsome young man like you is totally abstinent? It must be wrecking you, not enjoying what men your age seek most." Bev stretches her legs out in front of her, wiggling her feet in her open-toe pumps.

"Yes. Oh, I mean no. I'm not like that. I mean, I have desires as all guys do," says Peter as the bouncing pumps hypnotize him. Shaking his head, he adds, "I can't say it's been easy not asking Zara about sex. I have hormones. But I respect her wishes so much. Do you think I was so sex-starved I made it with an alien of my own volition?"

Smiling at him, Bev responds, "Maybe you just answered your questions about her message to you. Maybe she knows the same, and she loves you so much that she would rather you be with someone who can let you be unrestrained."

Letting him ponder that thought, the doctor goes to a cabinet and pulls out a dark wooden box with a MoxWorld Security clasp. Two inches by two inches and one inch high, with a note. She turns and shows these to Peter. "From your late pappy. He asked me to hold these until your relationship with Zara came to a conclusive moment. I believe her leaving you with that message meets those criteria. He stressed to me the importance of giving this to you just at that moment."

"I know I've said this a million times before, but I have to say it again. I owe you so much for taking care of my pappy those last few months at the Angel's Rest home. Without you, he would've been just another patient to be medicated. You made him feel alive even though death was coming."

"He was my most special patient, as you are my most special editor friend. Read his note," she says as she hands the folded paper and black box to him.

Peter unfolds the paper, which says:

My dear Peter, my boy. I am so happy that you finally found the object. You made a thousand generations of Gollingers proud. But never forget the oral tradition that you worked so hard to memorize. Remember your sister, who can even say it backward. It is the "key" to opening the future even after the object has been found. You will inevitably be part of the search for the second object. Inside this case is something I have held since my days researching the object with my father in Crimea during the war. I trust you will only open this when you are with a woman who will take care of your very special needs. You know, the ones that help alleviate the pain of our afflictions, our tempests of the nights, those dreams. For she may be the one destined to wear it with you.

Fondling the box, he asks, "Have you opened this? What's in here?"

"No, I haven't. Your pappy told me he put it in a lead-and-copper-lined box so no one could peek either. He keyed the clasp to your fingers."

As his fingers rub the box, the doctor puts her fingers upon his. He senses the warmth radiating from each of her digits, then from her palms as she rubs him more.

In a much sultrier voice than she has ever used with him before, she says, "Peter, you have been so consumed with chasing your family legend, you probably didn't even notice my growing affection for you. As I listened to your pappy's stories about your dedication, I fell more and more in love with you. I promised your pappy that I would take care of you. I am ready to be the woman your pappy just said you need in your life. In all the ways a man could ever desire."

Every fiber in his body goes rigid, some going totally cold and others verging on raging hot. A shiver runs down his spine as her hands fully enclose his. So soft, warm, gentle, and supple.

That soft voice says, "Your pappy told me all the comforting techniques his wife used to ease his pains, his agonies of the night, those dreams your family suffers. I can do everything she did for you. Wouldn't you like that?"

Afraid to make eye contact with her, Peter rubs his right thumb on the MoxSecurity clasp, then each of his right hand's fingers. Nothing. Pappy. He keyed both hands. So, the left thumb is swiped along with the other four fingers. Click. And Peter pulls out a small black stone pendant on a silver chain.

He holds it up and says, "This doesn't look like a gemstone. It kind of looks like the object stone, but not quite. It's different. There's a blue hue when you back-light it."

Smiling, he gives it to Bev. "Here, he would've wanted you to wear this."

She looks at it and gives it back. "No, he specifically said you were to wear it." She puts it around his neck and pets his special bump again, kisses his forehead, then asks, "And what about letting me be that woman your pappy wanted you to be with?"

He presses his lips tightly together and takes a deep breath in through his nose, then puts his fingers on her cheek and says, "Bev, I value our friendship. It isn't one I want to endanger. Not that you aren't incredibly beautiful and smart and successful, but you said it yourself. I'm in such a vulnerable state right now. And I need to rush off for my sister and friend. Can we revisit this discussion after I finish what's required of me there? Friends until then?"

She runs her finger lightly down from his Adam's apple all the way down to the top of his belt buckle, which only makes him shiver more, then turns away from him, putting her fingers to her tear ducts.

"You know I'm your friend," she says. "I will wait until you're ready."

"Thanks, Bev."

In her doctor voice, she asks, "Have you made any progress breaking the code of the digitally encoded MoxBox containing other documents he left for you?"

"Nothing. I even let my friend Jean-Paul try to break the code. I guess now that he works for the Vatican, he doesn't have access to the same resources that Alexander had. But I let Alexander's specialists try and they couldn't either."

His MoxWrap taps his wrist. Time to leave. He gets up, collecting the note and the box, and hugs Bev, saying thank you for everything.

She kisses his forehead very lightly. "Remember. We are friends." She lightly kisses his lips as she strokes his arm and nuzzles her very prominent, protruding chest upon him. "Maybe friends with benefits if you would let me."

Nonresponsive, Peter can only look at Pappy's note, wondering what is to become of him.

As he leaves her office, she watches him exit the facility intently. Sure that he is gone, she goes back to her desk and pulls out a NiQband and taps, "Failed at getting him to make a play on me. Go to back-up plan."

❧

"It's certainly still Mei's private luxury jet," Peter remarks to himself as he passes through the first two galleys out of four on this highly customized jet. He settles into her video conference room, situated just before her bedroom. There, a headshot video of Mei sweetly tells him to make himself at home. She still looks ravishingly the same. A little rounder in the cheeks, which makes Peter glad she isn't on that fashion-model-strict starvation diet anymore.

He knows exactly where everything is from the last time he rode on this plane, originally designed to hold 250 passengers, now refitted to accommodate one with special guests. He sits on one of two divans in this galley as he rubs his hand gently across its ultra-soft velvet surface.

Oh, what a trip that was last year. Alexander made her play the role of the stereotypical Hollywood Asian seductress. How rude of that man. To be demeaned in that way. Peter grew to understand how much more talented Mei was than what her fabricated image was meant to connote. But she played that role well. She flirted with him all the way from San Francisco to the MoxWorld EU Headquarters in Luxembourg. It was on this divan that she introduced him to the five senses algorithm she'd learned from Jean-Paul's research and perfected on hundreds of test subjects. He was so hormonally stimulated during that flight; he thought he was going to have a below-the-belly-button visceral accident.

He peers into her bedchamber and ponders what actually did happen that night he slept there. Alone when he went to sleep. When he awoke, she was in bed with him, having comforted him in the ways the wives of the dream-afflicted men used for centuries. Did they, or didn't they? She was too discreet to tell him. Just like with the aliens, he never knows if he's had sex when he's out asleep or otherwise knocked out.

Back in the dining galley, he heats the dinner she ordered for him. As he eats, he plays with unlocking the MoxBox that holds Pappy's documents. Not his fingerprints. Not his iris scan. Not his breath. What could it be?

He turns on MoxWorld News, which appears on screens around the galley. One of the main newscasters, Rhonda, is impeccably dressed as always. The face of MoxFashions. Her wardrobe, hairstyles, and makeup set new fashion trends only available through your Mox devices. She is truly a woman of the world. Part African. Part Asian. Part Eastern European. Part Persian. They say the mixing of different racial backgrounds enhances human beauty. She is the living proof.

This afternoon, Rhonda wears Michaela's special dress and hair designs. Since his sister accepted Mei's gracious offer to share the latter's luxury penthouse in Shanghai, Rhonda wears more and more of Michaela's work, which is then featured for purchase across the MoxWorld Fashion systems and network.

The news, though, is not as aesthetically pleasing. Late-breaking rumors of a secret meeting between Russia, China, and the US. Satellite evidence shows both the Russians and the Chinese are backing off the border of Siberia and Inner Mongolia. A European Commission-derived assessment report will be released tomorrow from Brussels. MoxWorld Analysts believe they will be showing digital evidence that an unknown third party to this dispute stole the meteorite in question. World powers have gone mad with this search for meteorites that contain the most powerful explosives ever known. Some scientists have speculated off the record that this extraterrestrial power can vaporize entire metropolitan areas.

However, none of these events have deterred the Chinese and US carrier groups from steaming toward each other. Analysts expect them to be within aircraft striking distance of each other tomorrow. The US underwater excavation team has been observed by satellite to have extracted something from the ocean floor. Is this another meteorite?

On the business front, the NiQihs Corporation has secured security system contracts from seven different midlevel countries, taking business away from MoxWorld. A statement from the CEO of NiQihs is played. A blurred image of a distinguished white-haired man with dark glasses is shown. Rhonda notes that Mr. Murometz was not available to make a statement. She assures the audience that MoxWorld News is the foremost news source and remains unchallenged by the upstart NiQihs news network.

Most upsetting was the next news piece. Around the Middle East, crowds are gathering in fear of more and more signs that Armageddon is coming. The face of Zara comes on screen, with Rhonda saying they are asking for the next messiah to save them from doom.

Oh, his Zara, he laments as he taps his MoxWrap to watch her last message one more time. Self-torture for sure.

"Do not try to find me, Peter," the image of Zara says. "For everything, there is a beginning, a middle, and end. And the end of one time is only the beginning of another. Or so said my great-grandmother. And your new beginning has come. There is a Kurdish saying—see with your mind; hear with your heart. Be open to the new woman in your life. I can only thank Xwedê you will have a wonderful life. I can live my life knowing you will be happy with your new family. Give her time as you did me. For patience is bitter, but it bears sweet fruit."

Entirely confused by her message, mystified at what brought on Bev's emotionally charged confessions of intimate affection, perplexed at his sister's cryptic plea to follow Mei's lead, and so tired he cannot fathom why Mei needed him so urgently, he goes to Mei's bedroom.

On the bedspread lies the silk pajamas she had custom-made for him, embroidered with the signature MoxWorld logo. Special fibers that last time wicked her pheromones straight into his skin. After brushing his teeth, he crawls into her bed. Head to pillow, he smells her pheromones again. Like last time, when she hadn't been able to change the bedding. She must have just used this plane recently. They make him remember how viscerally stirring she was, her scent genetically engineered to arouse him on that flight. Oh, it's only been a few days since he last saw Zara and he's already hormonally unfaithful. If only he were born a monk.

Trying to distract himself from the chemical bombardment, he closes his eyes and thinks about the first time he met Zara. She thought he was a Peeping Tom and clobbered him in the head. And then come the images of the dilemma Alexander put them in. Following the purported ways of the ancients, Alexander forced him into public sex with either Mei or Zara to determine who he should bond with, for passionate, intimate sex would unlock the images of the object in his dormant DNA and reveal its hidden location—or so Alexander insisted. To save Zara's honor, he and Mei faked sex in front of everyone. A trick that didn't work.

Tossing and turning, thinking about all his subsequent adventures with Zara, he finally falls asleep.

He awakens halfway off the bed, his face planted on the floor and his feet tangled in the sheets. As happened each time Zara went back to Kurdistan and he was alone, his terrible nights of fights, fits, and terror dreams came back. The curse of those men afflicted with the dormant genes of the ancients who found the object. Sleeping with Zara was like being near the object. His horrific dreams went away, and he would have normal, restful sleep. He already misses her in so many ways.

Making his way to the bathroom mirror, he sees a haggard face staring back. He recalls Pappy's laments about how, if he could only solve the mystery of the object, it would set their dreams right. And Pappy made him recite that ancient oral tradition several times each time they met. He tries to say it for old time's sake. Michaela would tease him because she could do it backward perfectly. Then he gets it.

He rushes to the dining galley to get the note Pappy wrote. *But never forget the oral tradition that you worked so hard to memorize. Remember your sister, who can even say it backward. It is the "key"…*

He searches his MoxWrap for Ma's digitized videos of their childhood. There. He found it. Into the digitally secured MoxBox, Peter plays the video segment of Michaela reciting the oral tradition backward, mocking him. Click. *Oh joy,* echoes in his brain from the victory.

From the box pops a hologram of his pappy on his deathbed. "I am so proud of my boy for remembering the legacy word for word, even after my death. In here lies my diary from when I was a teenager in Crimea with my father, seeking the truth of the tail of the bird star. Please do not judge me or your great-grandfather too harshly for what we had to do in the name of finding the truth. Finding the object was only part of the story. There is another truth that lies buried elsewhere. Part of that path lies in Crimea. But you must go first to Israel to take care of an old family debt. A promise I made to a newlywed who sacrificed his life to save his bride. You must help a woman return to a place their family will know how to find. At the time of making this message, your relationship with Zara was still unknown, as you said you hadn't seen her since the destruction of the object on that Turkish pier. If that is still the case now, you should know that this Israeli woman could be your perfect other half. That is, if the family is not too upset at what happened in the Crimea."

As Peter's eyes well up, Pappy holds up the pendant. "Peter, you must fulfill my promise and find Ghurdzi's family. Return this pendant."

He then shows a paper tracing of a symbol and characters. "This comes from where you need to rediscover in Crimea. The design must be the tail of the bird constellation, as told in our family legend. But I could not translate the rest of this. No known language or derivative. Maybe Ghurdzi left something with his wife that would help decode it."

As if by reflex, Peter isolates the characters with the tail of the bird design and sends them to Jean-Paul. Before he can reflect further, the good Father pings back his astonishment at the finding. For Peter has sent him potentially the first evidence of what written Proto-Indo-European language must have looked like.

Jean-Paul asks if Peter's family has examined this text; Peter has to think. Yes. His father had been studying whether or not written languages existed before the Proto-Indo-Europeans, but his work mysteriously disappeared before his suicide.

With his condolences on Peter's father's demise, Jean-Paul says he will mobilize Vatican experts and the computing power of MoxWorld to decipher this amazing find. Heretofore, experts thought Proto-Indo-European was a theoretical oral language.

Head down, Peter bites his lower lip as he reflects upon his father. May he finally be in peace.

As Mei's jet begins its approach to Shanghai, Peter finds a seat to strap in. Out the window, he sees the airport. The tomb of the first emperor of China with the life-sized terracotta warriors is the next stop after Mei boards. He wonders if Mei will let him be a tourist for an afternoon.

He hasn't seen Mei since the funeral. Is she so dazzling all the time, or will he see what she is really like when she lets her hair down at home? If his sister has outfitted her, she's sure to be wrapped in metallic designs.

As the plane taxis at Shanghai airport, he is stunned by the number of military aircraft and trucks in the area. Isn't this a civilian airport?

As the pilots open the plane door, Peter rises to greet Mei, who is in an oversized dress. Surprise. She's pregnant. Very pregnant. And she is followed by an older Chinese woman.

Before Mei can hug him, the older Chinese woman steps in and hugs him first. "Son-in-law. Thanks be to Goddess Jiang."

CHAPTER 17

This world of ours… must avoid becoming a community of dreadful fear and hate, and be, instead, a proud confederation of mutual trust and respect.
—Dwight D. Eisenhower

Balaklava Bay, Crimea
8:25 p.m. GMT+3, January 19, 2023

Another day of threats, intimidations, and Zara sitting shoulder to shoulder with *him*. His body heat emanated toward her so familiarly. That shoulder. The one she reset after he dislocated it. Her form of showing love. But it was his scent that killed her. Peri pulled her aside several times when Zara seemed distracted.

Having finished dinner, with each party having separate rooms, Colonel Yamut finishes conversing with Admiral Orlov, who asks everyone to take their seats. "We have an agreement not to take rash actions. Russia will not vaporize each of the Chinese factories making these NiQihs-armed weapons. China will not arm the Turks for thirty days until MoxWorld Holdings to all nations makes a complete, competitive bid. That is, subject to the issue not in scope here playing out in the South Pacific. I urge all parties to accelerate their deliberations to a date earlier than thirty days so we can head off a possible South Pacific flash point that would render our negotiations here moot."

Then he turns to Colonel Yamut, who promises nothing. They reserve the right to take the MoxWorld factories being built by force with conventional weapons anytime they deem it to be in their national interest.

And where does this leave the Kurds? Nowhere, but potentially with a chance for partial economic freedom from oil income dependency.

Peri stands for the first time with hands supporting the lower part of her protruding belly. "I cannot help but watch how the different parties in this room act as if they have the upper hand in this negotiation, which has mostly excluded the Kurds from discussions."

Zara grabs her arm, begging her to sit down, but Peri persists. "There are only two women here in these discussions, and one of them you should all heed much more than you have."

Peri stares at Anatoly as she says, "The woman to my left is closer to the Divine than any of you know—except you, Anatoly. You saw what I saw, did you not?"

Admiral Orlov leans over to converse with Anatoly and a minute later, he signals a guard over. Seconds later, that soldier shuts off all light in the facility, leaving the room pitch black—except for the faintest wavering hue of blue around Zara's irises.

"Gentlemen," says Peri, "what you are witnessing is not a special effect driven by MoxWorld technology. It is the sign of the divinity that exists within this woman. She is like an angel, here to moderate affairs here on Earth. And like an angel, she can hit any of you with lightning on command."

The lights come back on, with Colonel Yamut standing and yelling, "That is outrageous. How dare you compare this terrorist to the Prophet? We came here in good faith, not to be played like blind heathens."

Zara gets it. In Kurdish, her friend's name is fairy. A joke on those who do not know how clever and devious she can be. And this fairy has set the room up.

She stands next to her "fairy" friend, looking at the Russians, the NiQihs man, Mr. Ching, and then says, "All of you have intelligence that tracked my whereabouts during our mission for Mr. Murometz to find the black object."

Silent nods among the non-Turkish in the room. Putting her hand on

Zara's shoulder, Peri answers, "Then tell us, how many times did lightning strike in the places Zara traveled?"

Peri turns to Dan, asking point blank, "And did not your satellites pick up a lightning strike at the epicenter of the EM pulse?"

Another slight nod from the US State Department man, whose rock-hard face defines serious.

By putting the stake in the figurative, palpitating hearts of the vampires in the room, Peri concludes, "As each of you leave this negotiation, be warned. Lightning can strike twice if Xwedê wishes. Tonight, you act as if you should not fear what Alexander Murometz will do to you and your political leaders. Then leave tonight wondering if you should fear a higher authority as you ask yourself if this woman is mad, or if she has some connection to unknown forces. Perhaps Divine. Perhaps not. But either way, know that she will align with those who seek peace."

After a nudge from Anatoly, Admiral Orlov applauds. "I, for one, do not want to tempt lightning to strike a hundred and fifty meters below ground. That would be miraculous indeed. But perhaps we are closer to Hell than Heaven down here, so I would suggest that the parties here leave in peace and ask your leaders to keep peace for the next thirty days until the next meeting is held."

The meeting comes to an end. The tall man with whitish hair stands and approaches Zara, towering over her. No hand extended to shake. Only his eerie smile with that silvery glint.

Staring up at him hurts her neck the same as staring up at Sasha does. What does he want? Only to stare at her?

Finally, he speaks. "Ms. Khatum, that was quite a show there. You are quite an unorthodox negotiator. But impressive. My organization could benefit from your talents and latent potential."

With a quick snort out her nostrils, Zara asks, "And just what organization do you represent?"

He flashes an even eerier smile and states, "I head a global foundation whose benefactor tasked us with achieving worldwide peace. Unity of the most unprecedented kind. If you ever wish to leave Mr. Murometz, I would welcome your assistance in our endeavor to find the world the final peace it has sought for millennia."

Before Zara can reply, Peri interjects. "Sir, if she switches, can you ensure the safety of the Kurds?"

Another shade of that eerie smile glinting silver, and he says, "The Kurds and all people of this Earth will be safe. One world. One people. In harmony."

Elbowing Zara, Peri smiles and says back to this man, "Do not mind my friend's lack of enthusiasm at your proposal. She has this weird relationship with Mr. Murometz. Let us say she wants to join you; how does she contact you?"

That smile again. His fingers push down his dark glasses. His irises flash a silvery-grey color. "Ms. Khatum, all you have to do is tell your Mr. Murometz through your MoxWrap that you resign and I will find you."

With pursed lips, Zara backs up slowly, unsure what to make of this man and his intentions. She is stopped by stepping on Zengo's feet. She turns to find herself back in his arms, after a fashion. The arms of the love of her life when she was sixteen going on seventeen. The man she broke with her family's traditions and faith to engage in physical love before marriage. The first woman in her family to do so. The man who gave her chlamydia, as she was not enough for his unbridled lust. The man who has three false front teeth from her knuckles.

Head down with much humility, he says, "I want you to know I did not ask for this assignment. The New Kurdistan Parliament abruptly requested me only two nights ago, and I rushed to arrive only hours before you had."

"Because they knew you and I were close," replies Zara. "I heard this story before today. Seems like a common disorder with national leaders, thinking men can own my body."

Shoulders slumped with a bend in his neck as he tries to lower his head, Zengo adds, "Not that it will make up for the injustice that I did to you—nothing ever will—but I am sorry for what I did. I hope someday you can forgive me. At least for a month while we work out terms acceptable to our people and to the Turks. I will try not to do anything improper with you. Only show you the respect that a woman of your station has earned and deserved."

Is this Xwedê's test of her faith? Every man she has scorned has gotten down on his knees to ask for her forgiveness in a thirty-hour period.

What should she say? "Zengo, you impressed me with your poise and command of your Kurdish blood in that discussion. The years have treated you well, and Xwedê has blessed you with the wisdom that age brings."

At first a stunned face, but then a warm smile from her first love as he says back, "From you, that is as deep and sincere a compliment as I will ever receive in my life. I thank you for your forgiveness. At least for my actions today."

Zara signals to Peri. "Let us find the real ladies' room before the flight back."

As Zara waits outside the ladies' room, which is in the exact opposite direction from where Peri first headed yesterday, the man from NiQihs approaches.

"That was a nice trick you and your friend played back there," he says. "I would have broken out in laughter except for the satellite video of a lightning strike breaking up a team of assassins who kidnapped your priest friend. It was meant only for your Russian and American lovers' eyes, but someone on the black web intercepted it."

Zara's eyes dart back and forth as she tries to recall that incident. The mole in Alexander's organization was the head of US talent management—Mr. Harlan Chapwell the Third, who committed suicide through biting a cyanide capsule embedded in a molar so Zara could not extract from him who he was really working for. A graduate of Princeton, Yale, and Harvard. Oh, how Peter's whimsical love of his alma mater's banana slug enraged the pure Ivy Harlan.

She looks at Zengo. Taller than her, muscular, with poise and command in the most contentious moments with the Turks. Dark, curly hair like her father and her brother. So much the other side of the world from Peter. There was a reason she ran away with him. Dogs should be with dogs, and cats should be with cats. Peter is now with a beautiful Asian cat bearing his child. And when Zara dies to save the world, she will be at peace, knowing he is with a good woman who will take care of him.

The man from NiQihs snaps her out of her mental diversion. "Our intelligence suggests you and that editor from California know more about where another meteorite of power might be hiding. You are in danger as long as you try to protect Alexander Murometz. Call us. We can protect you and Mr. Gollinger from forces that can be more invisibly malevolent than you could possibly understand."

As he walks away, she reflects how he was the only man today other than that tall man with the silvery-grey eyes who did not beg for her favors or forgiveness—only making her offers of security.

"If only we could pee into a bottle like a man," laments Peri as she exits the formerly elusive ladies' room.

"Come on, Ms. Sloshy Bladder," says Zara. "I can fly you back to Siirt. I have Sasha's flying tank waiting for us. I had the flight crew secure some Kurdish snacks for us. And there is a ladies' room all reserved just for you. You just have to curl into a ball to get in there."

With angst written on her face, Peri looks over at Zengo. "The rest of the Kurds are flying out to the EU in Brussels, except for you know who there. I cannot leave him to travel alone. We were going to take a flight tomorrow morning. Sevastopol to Sochi City, and then our separate ways."

"You are kidding me. Him with us?" says Zara with her arms akimbo.

"What was it you said the Prophet said about forgiveness?" asks Peri not so innocently.

Zara scrunches one side of her face and sticks a little tongue out at her battle-hardened friend. "Okay, but he is not sitting on the same side of the plane as me. You are."

The best of friends waddle over to the solo Zengo. Peri explains how Zara has generously offered to take them both back to Siirt, where he can catch a flight back to Erbil.

Zara looks him over again. If only she could clip her nose. His scent is killing part of her. The part that has lain dormant for many years. If she didn't know better, she'd think something down there was getting moist. But that is impossible with what the Daesh did to her. She must be nervously perspiring.

Zengo turns to her. Eyes down, not making eye contact. "I do not wish to be an imposition. I make you so uncomfortable. I can see that. I do not wish to be a burden to you any more than is necessary."

She turns her head aside for a moment, scrunching her scarf around her upper chest, then looks back at him and says, "You can come with us. But do not even contemplate that anything will pass between us other than negotiation terms."

Black curly hair and all, his head still drooped, he quietly replies, "You have nothing to worry about, Zara Khatum. I have been made harmless to women. Xwedê punished me, for I am no longer a man."

He stares at his crotch as he says, "An IED in Mosul did away with my manhood as we fought the Daesh. I no longer can be physically intimate with a woman. My just deserts for what I did to you. How could any woman want me? Not even a saint of a woman would."

CHAPTER 18

There are only two types of women—goddesses and doormats.

—Pablo Picasso

Village outside of Siirt, Anatolian Kurdish State
9:10 a.m. GMT+3, January 20, 2023

"No, Peter. No. We cannot keep kissing," screams Zara, as she bats her hand into a soft wall of fluff. Her eyes crack a millimeter open to spy her two lambs taking turns licking her. What a night. Or what a short night, in the case of last night.

As her two surrogate children continue their salivary onslaught, she asks, "Breakfast time, you two?" She sits up in her bed, surrounded by memories of her childhood. *Mehhh, mehhh,* plead the lambs, wagging their tails while nuzzling her, to which she says, "Or are you two simply needing a little love this morning?"

She hugs them while she glances at her clock. She overslept. Or underslept, as the case may be, as they did not land in Siirt until 1:50 a.m. Their departure had been delayed by extraordinary traffic in and out of the Kacha naval air base, which was mobilizing for the impending war.

The last day passed like a dream. She rubs her eyes and shakes her head, unsure if it was a good one or a bad one. The meeting in Crimea went as she would have expected. The Turks thus far have never been content with any offer, always asking for more. She has always been very generous in her offers from MoxWorld, holding out the olive branch to them, but it is never enough.

What makes her head hurt the most is not the Turks, but that all three of her past lovers came to the same meeting with her. How arranged was that? If she did not know better, she would have thought Sasha secretly made that happen. But after the first coded messages she has exchanged with him since the book signing, she is nearly sure he is not behind this. Not with the news he broke with her about his mole search and NiQihs. Xwedê is testing her. She is sure of that.

Her babies are not so babyish in weight as she pushes them off her bed, tails wagging away. As she stands, they swirl around her calves, seeking something. A pet behind each of their ears and still no joy. That normally does it. But their innocent eyes peer at her. The same look "he" gave her.

Walking to her dresser, she says, "If you are looking for your friend Peter, he is not coming back. I feel for you two. I know how much you loved him. And he loved you two very much. And not because of your wool, but because of who you really are inside. But Xwedê's plan has called him away to take care of another woman and his own baby. You will have to live life only with me. Get over it and let us get to our new day on a new path."

But she goes straight to an old path. A family photo on her dresser. Her father and brother with their curly dark hair. She and her mother with their straight dark hair. And their happy home in the hills in what was then Duhok Province in Iraq, now part of New Kurdistan. How is she going to break the news to her mother? Her lambs are so young they will learn to live without him. But her mother became so attached to him. Roza, fortunately, will be more pragmatic and supportive of her finally being a non-distracted, celibate follower of Xwedê.

Her eyes fall again on her family from the time she treasured the most. When innocence still ruled her life. Maryam is tall like she has become, her brother Soran much shorter than she. Her father just slightly shorter than her mother. Growing up, she never paid attention to height. What is it that has left these unsettled feelings in her?

She wanders next door to see her mother. Empty room, but she spies the combs her mother keeps of Soran and father's hair. Zara takes a strand from each of their combs and one from her mother's brush. On her MoxPad+ she scans the hairs, then her own. She is just about to tap a note to Mei to analyze with the greatest of security discretion when—

"My pretty little Zara," says Maryam, making Zara jump. "You should have told me you awoke; I would have had your breakfast ready."

Zara turns to the mirror on her mother's dresser and brushes her hair with Maryam's brush. She asks, "Mama. I do not remember well your grandmother Sara's husband. I was too young when they killed him. Did he have straight hair like we do?"

Maryam comes to her daughter and helps her brush her hair, just as she did when Zara was little. "Yes, and so did my father. That is why Xwedê blessed both of us with such bountiful hair."

Zara turns to kiss Maryam's hand and asks, "And Papa's family, they were all curly?"

"Mostly. Why do you ask?" replies Maryam, who then puts her finger on her daughter's lip. "Let me guess. You are trying to imagine what type of hair your children with Peter will have."

She sighs, dourness filling in all the places on her face once filled with joy before her trip to California. Maryam quickly hugs her daughter, the kind of hug she gives her each time Zara came back from breaking up with a man she thought she loved. "It is all right. Cry on my shoulders," Maryam whispers to her precious first—and now last—child.

No tears. No sniffling. Zara merely hugs her mother back, affirming, "I love you, Mama."

Pushing back, pursing her lips, she stares at the floor, covered with a rug her mother wove in the old house in Iraq—a classic Persian rug. "We were not right for each other. I knew that when we first met. His abduction left his mind unrestrained and his true feelings came out. We do not have the same faith. You cannot have a lifelong partner with whom you do not share the same god. You simply cannot."

Peri knocks on the door, announcing her entry. The two lambs run to get attention from a new person, almost knocking her over. Dancing around the two giant fluff balls, Peri hugs Maryam and asks Zara how she is doing. The latter muter than a stone.

As Zara continues her morning pout, Peri says she looks like she needs time in her mountains. Maryam says they should go out together. She has chores to tend to and Roza is with Kilda, a woman she once babysat as a child. Her daughter Waja needs Roza's balms.

Up on the mountain, Zara's lambs are nearly exhausted, running after her torrid pace. In the distance is Peri's voice, pleading for "mercy on pregnant friends, please." Zara stops in a familiar place and waits several minutes for Peri to catch up.

"What is with you? I know my doctor says I should still get my exercise, but I do not think he meant a blistering run up a mountain." Several moments of panting by both Peri and the two lambs pass before Peri finds a curved rock to perch upon and the lambs sit on the ground at her feet.

"It is about him, is it not?" asks Peri, whose breath starts to return.

"No, I am through with Peter. I have moved on."

"You cannot fool me, Zara Khatum. Am I not your best friend who followed you through three campaigns in Syria? I know you. The plane ride back with Zengo. It is eating at you."

"The world is eating at me. Not Zengo. Not Peter. Not any man."

"Sit," commands Peri, patting the space next to her on the rock. After Zara settles in, Peri takes her hand and lays it on her belly. A kick. Then another. "My mother said I did the same thing in her belly. You know, I have changed the way I look at the world, carrying my child these months. The only thing that matters is my child. And my child's father. For happy parents mean happy children."

The smile that deserted Zara days ago finds its way back as she feels the kicks in her best friend's belly.

"I know you keep telling me you cannot bear a child," says Peri. "But you really need to get pregnant and experience this. Modern medicine is full of miracles. I am so sad my best friend in the world cannot share the joy that I have discovered."

As Zara shakes her head back and forth, she says, "I have my lambs. They are children enough for me."

Peri takes her hand off her belly and then squeezes it with all her might. "Do not do it, Zara."

Taking her hand back and massaging the blood back into her fingers, Zara says, "Do what?"

"I saw your face when you tried not to talk to Zengo the entire plane ride home. At first you ignored him, but then, as you strategized the next negotiations, that look came into your eyes."

"What look?" pleads Zara, who then turns her head away. "I was only tired. So much has happened in such a short time."

"Rebound is deadly. Especially with your first love," states Peri, pulling Zara's face back toward her.

Zara slaps Peri's hands away from her face. Undeterred, Peri places her hand on Zara's thigh, squeezing her nearly rock-hard muscles, and says, "You know, bridging culture and religion is challenging in a marriage. When Petrus found out he was going to be a father, a whole different side to him came out. The French part. The Catholic part. And what his world raised him to believe about child rearing clashed with what my parents taught me. We had the worst fights, and I thought for sure I would be a single mother."

She taps her foot on Zara's. "But then, the makeup sex made up for everything. Did you not enjoy yourself dancing at our wedding? And that Peter. He is so innocent. Despite the embarrassment most people would have felt, he kept fumbling our traditional Kurdish dances."

Zara tries to hide her smile and swallow her giggle. "If we had set him loose against the Daesh, he would have broken all of their toes."

Her lambs, refreshed now that their Zara's lovely face has returned, sit up and beg for attention. She picks up a stick and throws it. They chase it, fighting over which one has the right to bring it back to their mother Zara.

"Your lambs are acting more and more like dogs," remarks Peri as Zara gives her the retrieved stick.

"Here. Keep them busy," says Zara. "There's something I have to go check out. I will be back in fifteen minutes or less."

Zara wanders off to the ravine where she first found her two baby lambs. She crawls down to where they cried next to their dead mother, who is but a skeleton now. She pulls the remains of the wooden crate into different positions, looking for any markings. And there it is. No mistaking that logo. MoxWorld BioGenetics. Mei's special division. Why would Mei have been shipping an ewe with babies? Is this why her lambs act so unusual? That Sasha. It has to be something he made her do. She cannot be mad at Mei for not saying anything. Not now. Not with her baby coming.

As she climbs out of the ravine, she has no recourse but to find out why her lambs were there and what genetic modifications they represent. For she cannot call Mei now. Not so soon after her hair genetic analysis request.

Walking at a much more relaxed pace, perfect for her pregnant BFF, Zara asks, "What made you bring up the lightning strikes last night?"

Peri stops and mimics a supplication in front of her friend. "Fear. They needed to fear you. They certainly did not respect you. Neither does your big buddy Sasha, who has been pumping your prophethood on MoxWorld News."

Knocking the top of Peri's head to get her to quit the fake supplication, Zara answers, "Mind you, Rab'ia is quoted as saying 'true devotion is for itself: not to desire heaven nor to fear hell.' They should not have to fear a prophet to derive inspiration for their devotion to Xwedê."

Peri stands tall again and slaps Zara's back. "So. You admit you are the next prophetess."

"Only because you are my friend, do I not chastise you for indulging in that false notion. Like many Kurds, I understand you are not as devout as I. But let me be clear. There is only one Prophet. And I am not he."

"And who is it you talk with? Isn't he a she?" half teasingly replies Peri.

Zara comes to a complete stop, which has her two adopted children coming up to her looking for the stick she must be readying to throw for their pleasure. "Are people humoring me because they know of my past? My enslavement? Do they tolerate me out of pity?"

Peri gently bends down to get a stick and tosses it to amuse Zara's lambs. "Now you have really lost me. Where is this coming from?"

"You know I went through years of psychiatric therapy after Sasha rescued me from the Daesh torturers. Did I finally crack when Sasha sent me out with Peter and Jean-Paul? I mean, is this voice only a product of my head trying to sort out the pain and abuse they put me through? A psychiatrist in San Francisco warned me about what happened to an American Ranger I worked with in Iraq. He is delusional and talks to God all the time. Am I delusional? Even at moments?"

The lambs come scampering back, still fighting each other for the stick. Peri tugs the stick out of one of their iron-grip teeth and tosses it down the trail. She chuckles and replies, "You know you are delusional. Why else would you voluntarily ask us to charge fortified building after building? Delusions of grandeur that the Daesh would fall at your feet. And they did. So call me delusional with you."

Peri looks around and then finds a partly hidden spot. "Pregnant lady needing to pee again. You going to squat with me again like we did down that submarine channel? The expression on those soldiers' faces when you told them what they stomped through was so precious."

As they have for many years, they share one more personal and private thing. Best of friends. Zara says, "I wish you had a brother. I might marry him."

Another chuckle and Peri replies, "Well, I am spoken for, but if Petrus ever gets out of hand, I will let him know he has competition."

As they descend the mountain and enter Zara's village, they pass by Kilda's house. Not more than six months ago, Zara saved her daughter Waja from a forced marriage. Today, Kilda is in tears again, kneeling next to her daughter, who is badly wounded by the family of that man Waja fled from. An honor killing attempt. Waja will not see a doctor, as she will be reported for the crime of fleeing her abusive husband.

As Zara kneels next to Waja, whose skin is badly burned, she grimaces. Not because of Waja's husband's family attempt to make it look like suicide—self-immolation, covered in gasoline and lit by a match—but because Waja is in such great pain she cries out in horrible squeals like a piglet being tortured. The same sounds her cousins made as the Daesh tormented them.

The odor from Waja's oozing burns haunts Zara, lifting the dark curtain her brain put around her memories of the electrical frying the Daesh performed on her most delicate body parts.

Roza says her best treatments with traditional balms are not working. Waja will die from these burns. Roza asks Zara to stay with Waja while she and Kilda seek another nearby healer to get different balms.

As Waja squeals, Zara holds her hand gently. The forsaken daughter cries into Zara's hands. Waja mumbles she did not love that old man her father committed her to marry. She fled to be with her boyfriend, who she wanted to marry. But that boy she loved never emotionally recovered from her arranged marriage. His family asked him to marry a cousin who was pregnant without a husband. Out of honor, her beloved boyfriend left her to take care of his familial responsibilities. All is lost in her life.

Honor before love. A story so true to what Zara has asked of another. Take care of his family and leave her. And for the first time since leaving Peter, the ocean of tears she had been holding back for days breaks open, splattering all over this girl. She prays to the voice as she sheds tears. Shared pain. Shared tears. But the tears of Zara are like none other that has touched this girl.

When Roz and Kilda come back with a healer, Peri is playing with the lambs outside the house. Peri warns them to brace themselves for what they are about to witness.

Inside, Waja is sitting up. Still singed, but the oozing burn wounds sealed. She is no longer in pain and is laughing with Zara.

Kilda drops to her knees in front of Waja. She asks Zara, "How? How?"

More serene than she had been moments before on her mountain, Zara smiles and simply replies, "Xwedê smiled upon Waja today."

The healer runs down the street, yelling something about how the prophetess can cure the dead.

Peri comes up to her friend and says, "And I bet you thought your delusions created that cure. World, watch out for Zara the Prophetess."

Roza watches the results of this miracle with an earnest eye. She closes her eyes and says, "And the Great Mother Talliat's tears covered his wounds, and he became family again. Became one again."

CHAPTER 19

When I let go of what I am, I become what I might be.
—Lao Tzu, sixth-century BCE founder of Daoism

MoxWorld Resort Xian, China
7:30 p.m. GMT+8, January 21, 2023

She said beautiful. Simply beautiful. Or something like that, as Peter recalls what Mei said her name meant.

And beautiful she was as she sat in front of Peter on the opposite divan. Her disarming smile framed by crimson lip gloss. Her ears adorned with 18k banana slug earrings—her testament to his alma mater. Her long, flowing black hair cascading over her black gown—an amalgamation of classic Mei design and Michaela's metallic insert fabrication. Not as tight around her once-svelte body as it was when he last saw her. The looseness of her gown obfuscates her bump, but her calves and ankles definitely look swollen. No more three-and-a-half-inch stiletto pumps for her. Only flat black cotton shoes sized for fabulously fat feet.

He has been dying to ask her about her upcoming baby, but her mother, who sits next to Mei, dominates his senses. This must be what a horse for sale goes through. She's visually inspected his teeth, his muscles all over, his posture, then palpitated his neck "bump." Shy is not a word he would ever use to describe Mei, and he's certain she must have received that trait from her mother.

He did learn that her name was Ming, meaning "soul," and that Mei's name meant "beautiful flower," which she remarkably represented as she constantly shifted on her divan, trying to be comfortable. And Mei did have a last name, contrary to how she teased Peter when they first met. Mei Tang. As translated by Mei, her mother discussed the importance of the Tang family through the centuries. Equally so, she inquisited Peter on all of his family members—their dreams and their bumps. She said Michaela has become as a second daughter to her, and she is so proud to have her brother as her son-in-law.

Mei tries to rub her swollen feet. A task that requires acrobatics given the size of her belly. Ming signals Peter to get up and leads him next to Mei, pointing toward her feet.

"She wants you to do your magic on my feet," says Mei, acceding to her mother's demands and putting her feet into Peter's lap.

As Peter's fingers restore sanity to her belabored soles, he asks, "How did she know you like my foot massages?"

"Your sister is simply wicked," replies Mei. "She told her that is how you seduced me and, well, now I am pregnant."

"But, Mei, how?" says Peter, but she interrupts him, subtly pointing to her mother, who is watching them in microscopic detail. And she proceeds to moan and moan, in ways that make Peter blush and Ming smile.

MoxWorld Resort Xian's lobby displayed an impressive, full-scale model of the inside of the first emperor of China's tomb, as interpreted from MoxWorld's ultrasound and lidar data. Mei leaves Peter in the lobby VIP area while she and Ming debrief with her colleague Jia over some documents shared between them all.

Peter scans Jia. Tall, mostly slender, plainly dressed in a loose cotton black ensemble devoid of Mei or Michaela's signature MoxWorld fashion. A distinctive little mole just left of her lips. But his eyes fix on her naked wrist. No MoxWorld there either. Odd.

Debriefing done after Jia passes Mei a mysterious beige envelope, Ming goes to the MoxWorld VIP services for a chat. While they wait for Ming, Peter has to ask the question burning all the way here from the plane. "Why does your mother think we are married? Not that any man wouldn't want to be married to you."

Before she can answer, her mother is back with the bellman, their luggage, and MoxWrap access to their room. In the suite, Peter peers around. A two-bedroom affair. Modest, given Mei's tastes. One room has a queen, the other two twins. Perfect. He directs the bellman to put his luggage in the queen room and the Ting family luggage in the two-twin bedroom. Ming interrupts the bellman, signaling her daughter's luggage goes with his.

Peter stares at the size of the queen bed and glances back at Mei, then the bed. There's no way to be a gentleman in that bed. There's not enough width not to be all over her.

The bellman interrupts his ponderous dilemma, asking if that will be all. Peter taps his MoxWrap and gives him an exceptionally generous tip. He is so proud that his author income now allows him to reward others. He notices Ming giving him an approving smile.

Mei has a rapid-fire exchange with her mother in what Peter surmises is Shanghainese, as he knows they are not yammering in Mandarin or Cantonese—the most common dialects in San Francisco. Ming winks at Peter with a devious smile as she leaves the room.

"What was that about?" asks a bewildered Peter as he puts Mei's suitcase up on the luggage rack.

She smiles, dabbing his hand still on her luggage. "Thank you, Peter. You play the role perfectly."

"What role?" asks Peter as he clenches her hand. "And whose idea was it to put us into a queen? Aren't there kings in this ultra-posh Alexander resort?"

She squeezes his hand to release hers and pets it. "My dear Peter, you have to look at things the way my mother sees things. You have been away from me for a long time, and of course you would want to be in an intimate bed to ravish me all night long. She left for a long walk so we could indulge in reunion coupling. Just as that dirty-minded Alexander put in your book."

"I'm missing a few steps here," says Peter with anxiety lines forming across his blushing face. "You're as smart as you are beautiful. Go slower for me. Let's start with the baby, and then our marriage."

Arms akimbo and her head bobbing side to side, she says, "Isn't it obvious that I'm pregnant?"

He comes up to her, putting his hands on her shoulders, and says, "And I'm the father? I mean, not that I mind. But it's so sudden."

"Silly Peter. That's what I love about you so much. So silly," she says as she gets her MoxPad+ out. "See this? That's my genetic profile. Here's yours. And that's baby's."

A big breath in and Peter says, "Oh, Mei. I wish you'd have told me earlier. I would've come right away." He gently strokes her belly. "Of course I'll take care of our child with you. It's only right."

She turns away from him, keeping his hand on her baby bulge. "How could I tell you? You were deeply in love with Zara. I would've broken you two up. I am fully capable of raising my baby myself."

"And Michaela knows what you just showed me?"

"Yes. I couldn't hide it from her. She's your sister."

He looks to the side, still bewildered. Just as Bev said he would be. "But she's my sister. How could she not tell me?"

Turning back to him, she dabs the tip of his nose. "Because I cared about you and your love for Zara. I asked her not to."

"And your mother thinks I'm your husband. How did that happen?" asks Peter as he puts his things on the left side of the bed.

"No, no, Peter. I take that side. That's the wife's side," insists Mei.

"Really? There's a wife's side?"

"Or so says my mother. I'm right-handed, Peter. I can't fully take care of my husband on the left," says Mei as she makes a hand gesture which fetches a rose-pink tone to Peter's visage.

"Oh my. She pays attention to that level of detail?"

"Yes. For a couple of months, my mother went with my story of an immaculate conception like what happened to the Goddess Jiang. She was so proud my pregnancy proved we were direct descendants. But my father, a nonbeliever in Jiang, wouldn't buy the story and threatened to hunt down the man who did this to me. I couldn't hide the baby bump from the extended family for long, and then the pressure of traditions built up. An unwed, pregnant daughter who was too old for any man in China to marry. Patriarchy runs deep in my world. The shame on the family honor became too intense for him to bear."

"So, you told them we were married," says Peter.

She pulls back from him with her hand on his chest. "Don't get angry. Promise me? She's your sister, and she looks up to her big brother. Your respect for her is very important."

Eyes really wide open, he says, "Michaela told your parents we were married? I can't believe she'd do that."

"Yes, she cares about me and couldn't bear seeing me cave into the family pressure every night when I came home. She said I couldn't make our marriage public as we were both reporting to Mr. Murometz and it would be a worldwide scandal. Your sister restored my parents' honor.

Mei's MoxWrap taps her wrist. Glancing at the message, Mei gasps. "Oh, girl. You shouldn't do this. Some things are best left to the unknown."

The curiosity gene in Peter perks up. "Who is that? Is it Zara? Is she asking about me?"

Shaking her head, she replies, "No. She wants a favor from me that has absolutely nothing to do with you." She taps out two messages.

Looking up, she gazes upon Peter's face. Cheeks drooped. Edges of his mouth pointing in the wrong direction for a man supposedly reuniting with his beloved wife. "Peter, you must understand women. There is a point where we fully conclude we need to move on from a man. She has definitively moved on from you. I know Zara all too well. She's not the type to go backward and rekindle an old romance."

She unpacks the night's essentials, including a lacy black-and-red, barely there, maternity-sized babydoll nightie. He spies a discreet red MoxWorld logo along the lower hem. As she coquettishly holds it up, allowing the light to shine through the metallic-laced fabric, Peter's face flushes the same red color.

She says in her silkiest, slinkiest voice, "Playing my husband has its perks. Cheer up. Pretend you are on the rebound, madly in love with me. And make my mother happy that you are her long-awaited son-in-law."

Seriously curious what other exotic items hide in her suitcase, Peter asks, "Is this what you normally wear at night? Seems a bit chilly to me."

"No, silly," she replies. "My mother packed these."

Eyes wide open like his mouth, Peter finally asks, "Why did you wait until now to show your husband to your mother?"

"The hidden marriage story held up well, as Michaela told my mother that my business trips included my intimate joinings with my husband, her brother, who is another MoxWorld executive. That is, until I needed you to come here. I called Alexander a few days ago about the situation unfolding with my excavation here in Xian and he told me that Zara was going to leave you. He said there was no reason why you couldn't come and play the part of husband."

"He knows about the genetic match?" asks Peter.

"Of course he did. He knew the moment I ran the test. He knows everything that goes through the MoxWorld system," says Mei as she unpacks other underthings that make Peter blush more. "In fact, he said my pregnancy solved most of his issues. Whatever that meant. But he was going to send my jet to pick you up, whether I agreed or not."

He comes to her and rests his hands on hers. "And if he didn't force the issue, if your family didn't force the issue, would you want me here?"

She pets his hand back. "I love your sister and you so much. I'd still want you here. It's easier now that Zara has made her choice. I feel for you, Peter. But we would've had to face this situation in a matter of weeks, anyway."

Peter gazes at the two of them in the mirrors lining the walls. He reflects upon Bev's warning about his judgment in his condition. Then he remembers Zara's message about the woman who would come back into his life and how he needs to take care of their needs. For family is family. She must have known Mei was pregnant with his child. That was why she left. She wanted him to take care of his newly revealed family responsibilities.

He hugs her gently, unsure of how much pressure her bulging belly should receive. "I assure you, I was raised a responsible man, Mei. I'll do everything that's right. Good father. Good husband, if that's what you want."

Fingers now around the other bump. The one at the base of her neck. Almost as big as Zara's, but now's not the time to mention another woman's glandular size. He says, "The traditions of the ancients said that their descendants needed to make children with the right genetics who would someday find the object and solve its mysteries. Didn't we just do that? Is that why Alexander is so happy?"

She rubs the same bump on the back of his neck and replies, "That man is never satisfied. His preferred plan would have been you fathering a child with Zara and me raising my child. Then he would've had two genetically perfect children for whatever it is he thinks our destiny needs."

Peter lightly kisses her forehead, and then asks, "Boy or girl?"

She knocks her forehead against his, replying, "Now, don't you be like the patriarchal Chinese, wanting boys."

"I promise I'll love our child no matter what. And our love for each other will grow as our child does," he says as he lightly kisses her forehead again. "So, the whole thing you said about the excavation here in Xian was only a ruse to get me to rush out here?"

She pulls back from him, starting to choke up. "I am so, so sorry. I had said it was urgent to get you here. Even Michaela agreed with Alexander. You wouldn't have hopped on my plane right away otherwise."

His arms around her, pushing the next-to-nothing nightie down to the bed, he says, "We're friends. Of course, I'd come if you asked."

Her fingers, shiny red polish on her nails, run along his cheek. "You are such a dear. Just like your sister, who knows you too well. If I hadn't said it was urgent, you would have gone chasing Zara. You two need space. Chasing her would only make her run faster. Like Alexander, she knows how to disappear."

His head down, shaking from side to side, he sits on the bed. His eyes glance up to meet hers, then the nightie, which he takes into his hands. The fabric stretched out between his hands, he stares through it. His hands come together, clasped in front of his face, the nightie scrunched up, as lines emanate from his clenched eyes.

The bed sags next to him. The warmth of her thigh radiates onto his as her hand pats his outer thigh. "I need you. Like I needed you in Luxembourg."

His hand pats her thigh back as his eyes meet hers. He lays the nightie on her lap. "You mean, like what we did to make our baby?"

Her hands now patting his inner thigh, she says, "I need to access your dreams like we needed to do then."

Taking her getting-too-intimate fingers up to that place behind his neck, he says, "Zara and I figured out that a different kind of intimacy allows us to see my dreams."

She rubs that spot, the nexus of God Genes. "I tried it this way with Michaela. Nothing."

A bow of her head and she says, "I am simply not endowed in the same way Zara is." A quick glance at him from the side of her eye and she puts her palms in front of her eyes as long black strands of hair wave in front while her head bobs.

Arm around her, hand rubbing her extended belly, Peter says, "I guess I shouldn't be so shy about intimacy with the mother of my child." He lifts her head up. His lips to hers. A gentle brush. A pause with eyes closed. And then, the heads move into each other. Lips pressed to lips. Tip of a tongue meets its partner. But deeper? Both heads pull back.

"Somehow, it feels like we're cheating on other people," says Peter with two fingers on where their moistened lips just embraced.

Her eyes aside for a microsecond, then fingers meet his on her lips too. "Peter, we have to get over that feeling. We have to be adults about this. We must. Everything will fall apart if we don't."

His fingers now rubbing the black-and-red-trimmed nightie, the metallic threads the work of his sister, he nods his head. "I missed something here. If it's just helping your parents adjust to your new child, I'm all in. I'll do anything for the woman who has become my sister's BFF."

"It's more than that," says Mei as she stands and gets that mysterious beige envelope. Sitting back aside him, she flashes pictures of the excavation site.

Examining the photos carefully, Peter inquires, "Why are we looking at old-fashioned print photos in this digital age?"

Patting his leg, she replies, "My Jia is either very old-fashioned herself or she simply doesn't want our boss to see these."

Peter nods and asks, "Where is this? The tomb of a great emperor?"

"It was the tomb of the favored concubine of Emperor Qin Shi Huang, the first emperor of China," Mei says as she shows him photos from inside the tomb. "My mother recognized the writing on the wall. That is also why she is here. It says, 'From the west she came. With the voice she knew. With no father, her child was born to bring food to a great land. With the wisdom of the object of the great matriarch.' Ming is a follower of the Goddess Jiang like me. This inscription links Jiang to the great matriarch and the object. The second black object that Jean-Paul has been desperate to find before the great powers of the world take it for its destructive potential."

Then a familiar symbol flashes on the next photo, to which Peter bolts up. "It's the same one my grandfather made a tracing of in Crimea," exclaims Peter as he points to a tracing of the Cygnus constellation with the tail of the bird star, Deneb, highlighted.

Grabbing his wrist, she says, "There's one of these in Jerusalem too."

Her hands around his wrist suddenly feel so wonderful. Maybe the search for the second object is their path to be a couple, as it was for him and Zara? Perhaps he can finally have unrestrained, visceral bonding with a woman that he will grow to love. He has to, for he will be a good family man, just as he was raised to be.

"Jerusalem? Pappy's message said I must go to Israel to settle a family debt before I can solve the mystery of where the next object hides."

Mei scans images of Peter's document, saying, "I'm sending this to my associate in Jerusalem. She's an archaeological historian, like me. She has been on a similar search to ours throughout the Levant." Mei smiles at Peter. "I found her during the search for afflicted people. She has a bump like us."

A bump? Peter reflects upon what Pappy had said about his perfect other half in Israel. But he is to be a papa with Mei. He can't stray already from his new wife.

After tapping messages back and forth with someone, she then strokes his chest affectionately and says, "But I'm better at the five-sense algorithm than she is."

Taking her hand into his, he replies, "So, is that how I fathered our child? When you performed the algorithm on me on the plane ride to Luxembourg six months ago?"

She kisses his cheek. "You know better than to ask a woman that. A nice woman doesn't kiss and tell."

And that answer was so Mei, thinks Peter. Never answering delicate questions directly. Zara, on the other hand, would have blasted him, with no guessing needed. How fate has changed his destiny in a matter of days. Or is that now the Goddess Jiang who changed their destiny?

"I missed something here," ponders Peter. "Must be the jet lag. How does your Goddess Jiang help us find the second object?"

A light tap on her MoxPad+ and she says, "You see here? Our dear Father has perfected a much more sensitive detection system to spot where the black object has been over time. This map traces the history of the black object you, he, and Zara found. The longer it resides in one place, the stronger the signal. So, the starting point was up here in Crimea, and the ending point is where you three found it at Karahan Tepe in the Anatolian Kurdish State. These faint blips are where it might have resided when the originating matriarch's family moved it from Crimea."

Stroking his chin, Peter says, "How does Jean-Paul come up with this tech? I bet the Vatican has special connections that no one else has."

"Don't say aliens," admonishes Mei. "I heard that's how you drove you know who away."

His head down. Eyes closed. Finger wiping under his nose.

A deep breath and he taps his MoxWrap, showing it to Mei. "Aliens or not, you be the judge. I sent Jean-Paul the inscription my pappy found in that passage next to the tail of the bird diagram. He said it was written in a language that predates Proto-Indo-European. He thinks it says: *From the direction of the tail of the bird star they fell. The dark and the light. The doorway. The beginning and the ending. The ending which is the beginning. Separate, they are. But meant to be together. Death the doorway. Behind the backdoor lies the truth. Fear keeps us with the dark, separated. Man's truth lies toward the tail of the bird star, where she first came.*"

"Cryptic, isn't it?" says Mei. "Is the reference to 'she' the voice that Zara hears?"

"Hmm…I didn't think of it that way. But Zara's great-grandmother said something about the end only being the start of the beginning. And Zara keeps talking about her own death. Could it be her family legend comes from the people who were in this cavern?"

He scratches his chin, adding, "I think this also validates what Pappy's diary said about two types of stones that need to be brought back together—both alien in origin. I could never have shared that thought with Zara. Not the word *alien*. It cost me our relationship."

Her arm around him, she says, "I know you still feel for her. I could never have hoped you would love me as you did her. And I do not ask that of you. Only that you love my child."

His arm around her again, he squeezes. "I will learn to love you as I learned to love her. And I will always be there for 'our' child."

She pokes her head under his hanging head and gives him a peck. "You are every bit as wonderful as Michaela has said."

Before he can respond, she puts the MoxPad+ in front of him again. "These scans come from his tests of the new equipment. He found evidence that a black object may have resided in Çatalhöyük, Turkey, or at least part of it. Jean-Paul recently found an object fragment there. He believes ancestors of the great matriarch lived there. He asked me to develop a genetic method of tracing the point of origin of the great matriarch. But that was lost in a plane heading to Crimea, which mysteriously crashed somewhere in Turkey, now the Anatolian Kurdish State."

Touching the screen so ever lightly, Peter asks, "Do you think they were Zara's ancestors?"

She taps the back of his neck and says, "Yours too. And maybe mine." She points to the screen again. "These are his newest traces. You see the strong one in Crimea? That's where the first object started out. Jean-Paul thinks the two originated in the same place. Maybe even were part of the extraterrestrial body that landed here tens of thousands of years ago."

His eyes perked up, Peter points to a faint spot on the Western Turkey

Black Sea coastline. "That spot—that's very near where Alexander found the other half of the first object."

"Very astute. Jean-Paul conjectures that the second object half may have split up under the Black Sea. You can see here faint traces where another sizable black object must have traveled from the Black Sea. The tracings head throughout the Middle East, with some heading out to China."

Stroking his chin, Peter says, "And because the engraving in the concubine's tomb says the Goddess Jiang brought the wisdom of the object and great matriarch, you think she may have brought the big, blackened behemoth with her all the way across the Gobi Desert just to do what? Have dim sum in China?"

Whap.

"Ouch. You didn't have to slap me," he cries out.

"Do not disrespect my goddess any more than you would Zara's Xwedê or her voice."

"I'm sorry. I should be more culturally respectful," says Peter as he rubs his blood-reddened cheek.

Her delicate fingers displace his as she strokes his cheek. "I'm so sorry. I acted too rashly. It must be the pregnancy."

"Or something," says Peter with his fingers now intermingled with hers. "Something is seriously bothering you. The goddess finding is only part of the story here."

Clasping his fingers in hers, she says, "I am under enormous pressure, Peter. It's so emotionally distressing being here." Pausing with a side glance. "I misspoke. I mean, every day, the big guy, yours and my Alexander, calls. Then the president of China calls. They all want what I find."

Taking on a neutral visage, she takes his fingers to her lips for a light caress. "That is why I need you more than ever. We desperately need you to access my dreams."

His fingers clasp hers back. "I am here for you."

Rubbing his fingers, she says, "I don't want to sound crass, as you and Zara have just split up, but we have a timeline. A deadly urgent one. When I give birth, game over. I will not be able to access where we need to go. The big man will not be pleased."

He pats her belly. "You mean, the chamber of the blue light? Zara told me about the women's side of the legend. And Alexander told me we had to find the other black object to bring to the blue light. I get it. But I didn't know about the urgency to get there before our child is born."

"Only women of purity may enter," she says, patting his hand on her belly. "We believe that means me with my child."

Tapping her MoxWrap to show him the latest news, she says, "Alexander said that once you succeeded in accessing your grandfather's notes, we would be ready to search for the second object. Latest news this morning tells of the US and Chinese fleets firing missiles at each other, with the Russians waiting for their chance. We need to find this object as soon as we can, so Alexander can tell those countries' presidents to knock it off, as the second object is secure in his possession."

"Well, Pappy said something about another 'truth' buried in Crimea," replies Peter. "Here, let me show you the parts of his diary that I've been able to read so far."

CHAPTER 20

This is a war to end all wars.

—Woodrow Wilson, 1917

MoxWorld Resort, Xian, China
8:45 p.m. GMT+8, January 21, 2023

Finally, he is gaining the intimacy he desired with his new, unexpected "wife." Not that of the body, but of the soul. Of what really matters.

He would do anything for her, as he would for his sister. It is not only his duty as father of their child, but it is their duty to the save the world. He will help Mei stop the upcoming war. Find the object and bring it to the cavern of blue light. He connects the MoxBox with his pappy's diary document written in German to his MoxWrap for a translation.

Fall 1942.

It is my fourteenth year on this earth and the world is crumbling all around us. The German armies surrounded Sevastopol in October. The next month, Himmler put his Ahnenerbe unit on ready alert to mobilize into Ukraine. The Nazis created the Ahnenerbe to find ancient proof of the Germanic race's superiority. But Himmler added his belief in the occult to its mission.

Like all Gollinger men since anyone could remember, my father's life has been dedicated to finding a mysterious black object cited in a family legend passed mouth to mouth from father to son and so on. As soon as I was able to read and research, he put me to work combing literature for further clues to this mysterious stone.

In 1939, after Anschluss, the annexation of Austria by Germany, my father voluntarily joined the SS to be part of the Ahnenerbe. He told my mother and me he did not know which was the greater family shame—not solving the mystery of the object or wearing an SS uniform.

My father, once a full professor of history specializing in antiquities at the University of Innsbruck, cleverly convinced the head of the Ahnenerbe that his family legend would prove that the Germanic race descended from the most ancient race that founded Western civilization. Around the time of my birth, he had traced other versions of our family legend to the Greuthungi-Gothic tribes who lived in the lands north of the Black Sea around the third century AD.

During 1939, he studied the works of Herr Professor Franz Altheim, who, funded by the Ahnenerbe, studied supposed evidence in Persia of an unknown force that the drove the Roman conquests to find their Nordic/Germanic origins. In 1940, he took me on my first trip outside of Europe to go to Iraq, which was courting an alliance with Germany. There, I found an inscription in an obscure ruins wall near Nineveh referring to a special stone of great power.

Further research suggested this inscription came from the first century BC, when the Scythians—tall, horse-mounted warriors—ruled the lands from Eastern Europe across Central Asia all the way to the edges of China. My father concluded we needed to follow the Scythes to where they first learned of the object.

Thus, he volunteered to be in the first Ahnenerbe group to enter Ukraine in the winter of 1941–42. My mother and I feared the worst for him, as we heard the horror stories of our soldiers freezing to death on the Eastern Front.

Summer 1942.

By the end of June, the Russians fled Sevastopol, and Crimea is now part of Germany. My father sent for me to join him following the Einsatzkommando 11, part of Einsatzgruppe D, of the Fifth SS Panzer, as it moved across the Ukraine to Crimea while it exterminated local populations in their gas trucks, looking for something of deep interest in the indigenous population.

I arrived by train to Odessa and then traveled eastward by truck to catch up with them, only to find the SS gathering women out of businesses and houses. Some sort of screening was done, and those who did not pass were taken to the gas van. The others—I would find out later what was in store for them. Death would have been better than what the SS soldiers did. Or worse, what the SS doctors did.

In tears, I confronted my father, asking why they could not save these people. He could only cry with me, saying we could only hope to focus on solving our family oral tradition. Complicity is the price we must pay so that we could. The secret to the legend rests in Crimea.

As he worked in their makeshift laboratories outside of Sevastopol, he made me read the secret account of Alexander Barchenko and his 1920s expedition to the top of the Kola Peninsula to find the source of "polar voices." German intelligence said he found Shangri-La, a colony that spoke to the heavens. Evidence of this expedition is part of what the Ahnenerbe searched for.

Then, in 1926, Barchenko embarked on an expedition into Crimea, searching for a grail stone that transferred psychic energy at a distance, making contact with the cosmos. They called it the "Stone of Orion." Most of his notes are hidden somewhere in Crimea, which father assigned to me to find. Some of his notes made it to Berlin via the Masonic lodge Barchenko belonged to. Those notes reported sightings of mysterious flying objects and secret local stories of a superior race in hidden buildings buried in Crimea. Himmler wants to find that evidence that shows this superior race is the Aryan race. Hence the screening of the indigenous populations to find genetic clues, with the SS exterminating all the human evidence of their search.

We were co-stationed with the Institute for Military Scientific Research, an Ahnenerbe subunit. I cannot describe the horrors of the testing these SS doctors committed upon subjects for fear of never being able to forget these atrocities if I write them down. Which was worse? Being gassed outright or being subjected to live dissections for days on end?

Every other day, I begged my father to help these victims. But the professor could only shake his head in resignation. Complicity. That is what history will say of us. Not that we found the object. We were complicit because we did nothing to stop these crimes against humanity.

A month after I arrived here, my father saved a Russian medical scientist in his mid-to-late twenties, who was based in a research facility in Crimea that the SS took over. A man who knows the oral traditions. Who does not sleep well like us. Doctor Pavel "Pasha" Murometz, whose father Zoran was born in Turkey but fled when the Western powers reneged on their promise of a Kurdish nation. His mother was a Russian woman from a very powerful family who moved to Crimea.

Winter 1943.

Tonight, I could not sleep. Was it the curse of the dreams we could never remember, or did my mind not accept complicity as the only answer?

I wandered through the test victims' ward and spotted a man a little older than me flailing his arms and legs around in his sleep. I awakened the man, who told me an all-too-familiar story of a lifetime of debilitating nightmares.

The next day, I got my father to save Ghurdzi, who knows part of the oral traditions different from our family's version. Ghurdzi reveals that his pregnant bride got separated from him. With a pass my father gave me, I escorted his wife out of the waiting area for vivisection, her body containing whatever the Ahnenerbe is looking for.

Ghurdzi and his bride spoke little to us of their lives with the affliction. Only stories of how badly the Russians treated the local Crimeans. After hearing of Dr. Murometz's theories of an ancient genetic trait passed down from the originators of the ancient legends, Ghurdzi came back with a vaccine formula from an ancient culture that his wife had obtained from a secret source, one that she could only tell her husband about. After analyzing the formula, testing it on animals for safety, Dr. Murometz administered it to himself. A month later, he administered it to me, Ghurdzi, and his bride. The doctor claimed this vaccine would enhance the ancient genetic mechanisms within us. But for what purpose? He discreetly did not say.

Spring 1944.

The Russian troops have broken through German defenses on the Crimea. Ghurdzi begged us to save his wife, Ariella. I volunteered to take her to the southern coastline. She told me to first take her to St. George's Monastery at the Fiolent Cape. I got an old car for the scientists' use and took her a back way through the old oak forests.

Partway there, Ariella made me wait for hours while she took care of something that only a pregnant woman of "innocence" can. She came back and gave me part of a small black stone on a pendant to give Ghurdzi. The other half she kept. With this stone, he could find her after the war. At the old monastery overlooking the Black Sea, we were met by Tartar partisans who took her by boat to Turkey.

When I returned, Ghurdzi said he owed his life to me. I gave him the black stone pendant. He said it was a blackish meteorite fragment. It likely came from an ancient cave his Ariella's great-grandmother knew of. He told a story of an ancient race that built the cave to guard a secret only certain pregnant women could access. He said that to end the war to end all wars; we needed to bring the black object back to this cavern. And if the war going on now is not the war to end all wars, then when would that be? Could this be the object for which our family has spent countless generations searching?

May 1944.

I don't have the time to write what happened, but the Russians are here. We are fleeing for our lives. The worst has happened and poor Ghurdzi is left dead. May God forgive our complicity.

"That's exactly what I said," exclaims Mei. "To get back to that cave, I still need to be pregnant. My due date is in early March, Peter. We're counting down weeks right now."

Beeeeep. Beeeeep. Mei's MoxWatch alert goes off. She says, "My mother got into the elevator in the lobby. We're counting down minutes now."

Peter's eyes bulge out as she strips out of her gown. Lovely, matching plum lace bra and panties entwined with Michaela's metallic insert designs.

"Don't sit there and stare," quips Mei as she madly pounds some app on her MoxWrap. "Strip down and get sweaty with me. She'll be here soon."

"What, here? Right now?" says a confused Peter.

With one eyebrow down and a matching downturn of her lips on that side, Mei says, "There's nothing under your clothes that I haven't seen before or hasn't been snuggled intimately to my body. So, lose the clothes and make noises like you've been pumping me senseless since she left us here."

He takes off his polo shirt and begins to unbutton his pants when he asks, "But why do we need to be so noisy for your mother?"

"Because the guy in your book had nonstop sex for hours," she says as she pulls him under the bedcovers with her. "And Michaela told my mother she heard from your old girlfriends that this was true of you. That you do you-know-what like a rabbit."

The outer door to the suite opens, and Mei begins to moan even louder than she did when he massaged her feet on the plane. She pulls Peter onto the bed with her and whispers, "Come on, boy. You need to make all those noises you made in front of Alexander, Jean-Paul, and Zara when we did it in front of them."

As she continues to wildly moan, Peter says, "But we faked sex that time, didn't we?"

She puts his hand on her naked belly and whispers, "Don't be so sure that public display was all that fake. And if you don't start moaning with me, this time won't be fake for much longer either."

The empirical physical evidence—his growing, throbbing bulge—should have said everything. But Peter looks up from his hands on their child's belly bump into her eyes. "Mei, back in Luxembourg, you were so apprehensive about having sex with me as Alexander demanded. What changed?"

Her hands now on his across her baby bump, she answers in neutral affect, "Peter, I am a woman driven by means to an end. If sex is the needed means to a needed end, then so be it. But sex in public like that monster demanded? That's the same as making a porn video for the world to see. This is my body, for my purposes. Not for the lurid titillation of perverted Peeping Toms. Like our boss."

Eyes aside for a second, then back into hers, he asks, "Means to an end. Is this really for your mother? Or is it that you want to activate our God Gene Complex to find the object?"

Her hands lower to stroke his full, engorged bulge as she replies, "Why Peter, you know me. I want everything."

Taking her hands to his temple, in a soft tone, he replies, "But I told everyone that the five sense algorithm doesn't need to end down there to work."

Her hands go back down again as she says very firmly, "Honey, I'm not as well-endowed as Zara. Well, God-Gene-bump-wise. We need to do this like the ancients did for me to have the visions with you."

Eyes still affixed deeply into hers, he bluntly asks, "Did you do this with Alexander?"

At warp speed, her hands drop back across her belly bump. Her eyes break from his, pointing downward, her smile eviscerated. "I know that you will judge me. But that would be judging me out of appearances. Not for depth of the matter that was at hand."

His brows knit together in confusion, creating deep furrows on his forehead. His eyes widen slightly, darting from side to side. Then he asks, "I've come to know you. Everything you do is with purpose, with splendid planning, and with a definitive outcome in mind. What compelled you to finish the five-sense algorithm with Alexander with you compromising your sense of sexual self-integrity?"

With a whisper, she says, "Honey, you don't know how much pressure an afflicted woman is under to find the blue light. Only Zara, Rachel, and me have that chance, according to Jean-Paul's research and my genetic analyses. And without mating with the right afflicted male, it would be impossible to find the sanctuary of the blue light."

Tapping her MoxWrap again, she adds, "How do you think we knew to send you your first MoxWrap? That BS I told you on that Luxembourg flight about you being first identified by the simpler MoxPad you mysteriously got for free? I bonded with Alexander to have the visions of finding you. Only if I had sex with that giant could any of us find the blue light."

She understood everything from Peter's momentary pause and sidelong glance. The never indecisive Mei shakes her head while her hand whisks away any and all between them, leaving not a molecule of fabric. "If you won't make this convincing for my mother, do it for your sister, who wants us to find the blue light. She wants you to consummate our 'marriage' tonight for the happiness of all."

CHAPTER 21

When I started working on women's history about thirty years ago, the field did not exist. People didn't think that women had a history worth knowing.
—Gerda Lerner, twentieth-century historian and author

Judaic University of Jerusalem Satellite Campus
2:10 p.m. GMT+3, January 21, 2023

She glances around the room. A dark room. Not because of the oak-paneled walls. Not because it is a small room, as it is large enough to host a lecture of fifty students. But the topic at hand has darkened the minds of the less intellectually flexible around her.

She is not petite at one-hundred seventy-five centimeters, taller than average for an Israeli woman, but some of her male students tower above her, as do the Persian cypress trees outside the room's windows. The fresh, resinous, smoky cypress scent with a lingering sweet, balsamic undertone yields a soothing and refreshing ambience to the open-minded students sitting in a circle in front of her. But they also adorn the places of the dead, commonly placed in Muslim cemeteries. And for some students, the death of what they hold true hangs in the waiting.

This woman who has challenged the room wears a simple white blouse buttoned to the V in her clavicle, olive khakis, and black leather sandals.

Framed by her dark wavy hair tied in a ponytail, her green eyes peer into her students' wide-open pupils. Some faces are ashen, others reddened. One tall young man clenches his fists, pressing them into the small table attached to his academic chair.

Her students sitting in a circle came into Biblical Archaeology 462: Controversies in the Torah thinking they would enlighten their understanding of their faith. For Professor Capsali had an outstanding reputation for guest-lecturing the Torah in rabbinical schools throughout the world. But this time, she shocked the room with her question: "Was she, or wasn't she?" Yahweh's wife, that is.

Once, she was an esteemed professor of biblical archaeology at this prestigious university. Today, she is but a guest lecturer. As she waits for the first brave soul in the room to comment on her provocative question, she recalls how only two weeks ago, the academic dean forced her department head to terminate her tenured position after her adamant stance that the Israeli government must return the artifacts she had found so that the public could know the truth about Her. Artifacts that could change how all would view the history of the Torah. Only the exceptionally generous grant provided through that Jesuit priest who had once worked for that mad Russian sycophant saved her. The university agreed to allow her to finish the academic year on a guest basis only, and only with doctoral students.

A woman to her left timidly speaks. "Professor, I can totally relate to the hypothesis that men wrote the Torah, and as such, it is possible that parts of what we have been taught, important parts of our faith relating to women, may not be as all our ancestors intended."

Rising higher in her chair, this student says with a firmer voice, "But I cannot fathom how removing Asherah from the ancients' places of worship, from the Torah, was anything more than the faithful Israelites following Yahweh's instructions to destroy idolatry and disavow the polytheism of Canaanites and other enemies of his people."

Another man from the other side of the room gives her the thumbs-up and chimes in. "I agree with Deborah. I agree that the pottery shards from Kuntillet Ajrud, the inscription in the tombs of Khirbet el-Kom, clearly indicate that the people who lived there in the eighth century BCE used both Yahweh and Asherah in their blessings. And the same were found in similar shrines to Yahweh in Samaria, Jerusalem, and Teman. But this was all before the fall of the Kingdom of Judah in 600 BCE. The authors of Deuteronomy clearly edited the Torah to reflect how Yahweh did not protect his people because of their belief in other deities such as Asherah. It is only right that today we do not believe that Yahweh had a wife."

A purposeful and very audible sigh comes from Malka next to him, who glances away out the window. "Saul, that is so patriarchal of you. Do you really believe the authors of Deuteronomy, the exiled elites of Judah, truly wrote Yahweh as both genders? It sounds good in principle that those scribes in Babylon incorporated Asherah as part of our one true god. But the Torah reads really male to me."

And the woman in front of the circle finally smiles. Her face simple, without makeup. Her bushy, dark eyebrows tilt upward, sitting prominently over her green irises with a distinct bluish tinge. As she ties her wavy dark hair into a loose bun, Rachel Capsali nods in acceptance that her students are engaging in controversy. Her job half done.

Rachel walks in front of each of her students, surveying their eyes, their faces, their posture. Stopping to gaze upon the majestic cypresses lining the sidewalk of the campus building, she states, "You all are correct in your suppositions. You must ask yourself why Deuteronomy chapter thirty-three, verses two and three, reads: 'Yahweh came from Sinai and shone forth from his own Seir. He showed himself from Mount Paran. Yes, he came among the myriads of Qudhsu, at his right hand his own Asherah. Indeed, he loves the clans and all his holy ones on his left.'"

Half her students quickly thumb through their hologram Torahs projecting from their MoxWraps. One, who has several versions open in a grid in front of him, says, "Professor, I don't see that in most versions of the Torah."

Rachel simply smiles as she asks, "Which ones are the oldest versions?"

Avi, with over a dozen versions now in the air in front of him, says, "It's in the oldest two."

Looking into the air with her index finger tapping her chin, Rachel asks, "Why would they rewrite this blessing to exclude mention of Asherah?"

As the rest of the room thumbs through many versions of the Torah, Rachel stands in front of Deborah, asking, "Perhaps what happened in 721 BCE will answer that question. What do you think?"

With a damp forehead—not from the heat, as this room is air-conditioned—Deborah wipes her face with a delicate white lace handkerchief. "That's not fair, Professor. You taught that last year in Seminar 334," she says as she taps her MoxWrap to pop up a written notebook hologram. "Here it is. In 721 BCE, Samaria, the capital of the Northern Kingdom of Israel, fell to the Assyrians, leaving the Southern Kingdom alone to defend itself against invasion."

"Good," says Rachel with a nod and smile. She turns to Saul, who has been watching intently, and asks, "What happened six years later?"

Saul already has his class notes up in the air and with a grin says, "Six years later, Hezekiah becomes King of Judah and purges the lands of idolatry and cleanses and purifies the Temple. He did this because he believed the Northern Kingdom fell because they defied Yahweh in continuing to worship the ancient Canaan gods and goddesses."

"Excellent, Saul," affirms Rachel as she turns to a red-faced man, tall enough in his chair that his eyes are at Rachel's chin. She would not want a man this size, this mad at her, following her at night in the narrow alleys of the Old City. She backs up to yield distance and says, "Lemuel, did this mark the end of Asherah?"

His upper body weight leaning on his elbow, his lips pouted, his head emitting heat rivaling the sun, Lemuel responds, "She died the death she deserved in 701 BCE, when King Hezekiah defeated the Assyrian siege of Jerusalem."

"Hmm. Interesting color you have given her demise," remarks Rachel, looking at Lemuel with her head tilted and a flat-lined expression on her lips. "Anyone else? How did Hezekiah defeat the Assyrians?"

"The Torah says the angel of Yahweh descended one night and smoked one hundred eighty thousand Assyrians," pipes in Saul.

"*Nu*. Come on. That's smote, Saul, not smoked," ribs Bina seated two chairs away from him.

With a mischievous grin, Saul replies, "Well, if Yahweh killed them all with lightning bolts, it would be smoked."

"So, Bina, what is another explanation for what happened?" asks Rachel.

"Some historians think a plague struck the Assyrians, or cholera spread throughout their camp as Hezekiah restricted their access to clean water," replies Bina.

Rachel turns back to Lemuel. "And wouldn't a plague from heaven give Hezekiah the proof he needed to prove to the twenty-five thousand people hiding behind the walls of Jerusalem that Yahweh was willing to fight for them if they gave up idolatry? If they gave up Asherah?"

"Like I said, they wasted her like all idol worshippers and atheists should be," replies Lemuel.

Before Rachel could respond, Malka pipes in. "That's exactly what the patriarchal forefathers would want us to believe. They've brainwashed you, Lemuel. Ask the professor about the records she found in Nineveh last year."

Her cheeks rise up her face, with the edges of her lips following suit. Rachel responds, "You've been reading ahead again. Malka, why do you think those records are so important?"

"The siege of Jerusalem was recorded on clay prisms by the Assyrian king, Sennacherib, in 690 BCE," states Malka. "Three prisms were found buried below the Nineveh Palace and were uncovered in the 1800s and early 1900s. That is, until you and a Jesuit priest found a fourth."

Kicking Saul, Yosef scoffs, "No disrespect, Professor, but most Torah scholars have rebuked the authenticity of the prism you found."

"No disrespect taken, Yosef," Rachel calmly replies. "We are all scholars here, only out to find the truth. Why do these Torah scholars not accept this fourth prism?"

"First, it is dated at least ten or twenty years before the other prisms," states Yosef. "Second, it is in a form of Akkadian older than the other three. And third, the story is absurd. A magical stone. A royal priestess from the First Temple. The threat of lightning striking down the Assyrian army if they did not leave Judah. And the promise of fertility of their lands if they did leave. More like the mythical stories of Canaanites than a historical record."

Deborah and Malka roll their eyes at each other as the latter interjects, "*Nu.* Come on. Just like a guy to disrespect the words of a prophetess."

Rachel intercedes, saying, "Let's all show respect of each other. Yosef made a very well-formed argument, whether you agree or not."

"But he left out the part where it was the high priestess from the First Temple who said that Asherah spoke to her of making peace," adds Deborah. "That only through abundance will there be peace, and Asherah will provide that abundance for all if the Assyrians leave Judah. To prove Asherah was that powerful, she kneeled and prayed, and lightning struck the tents of the Assyrian leaders."

Yosef scoffs again. "Seriously? Do you believe that? There was a magic stone in the First Temple and the priestess heard Asherah talk? We might as well believe the Templars took the Ark of the Covenant to a church in Scotland."

Lemuel sits to the left of Yosef, his arms crossed and his face a purplish beet-red. His silence slices at Rachel, who acknowledges him with a nod. She taps her MoxWrap and a holographic projection of a clay prism appears. She says to the beet-red Lemuel, "You are the best here in Akkadian. Could you please read the line fifth from the bottom?"

Spitting at Rachel's feet, he barks, "No. I won't. This is *chilul hashem.* Blasphemy. Only befitting an atheist like yourself." His arms fold tighter.

Tapping her foot and letting his saliva spill off, Rachel clenches her fists, emitting cracks. She peers around the room and asks Yiska, "You are studying Akkadian. Would you help enlighten your classmates as to what this says?"

"*Gvir'ti,* I'm only in my second year studying Akkadian and Sumerian. But I'll try. It says…the priestess proclaimed there is but one God. One for Israel. The same for Assyria. And She is beautiful."

Deborah blurts out, "But how does that say that Asherah is Yahweh's wife?"

Yiska shakes her head. "It doesn't. The last line says that the priestess returned to Jerusalem and never came back. The Assyrian spies say she was executed by King Hezekiah."

Malka screams, "That proves men have always tried to suppress women. They could not tolerate that a singular god would be female, so they killed the messenger and thereby killed Asherah. Just like a king to crush anyone who threatens their personal connection to their version of Yahweh." She glares at Lemuel.

The room erupts with students arguing among themselves. Rachel smiles; she has done her job as a professor and stimulated deep thought, deep reflection on what is truth and what is faith.

Lemuel, now a deeper purple than mere beet red, says, "If this were true, why does this prism lay within the Vatican archives and not in Israel? You are nothing but an agent of the Catholics, attempting to discredit the Jewish faith. You and your Jesuit priest lover. The rumors are, you were fired from your tenured spot here because of sexual misconduct with representatives of MoxWorld."

Now turning red herself, Rachel slaps her hands in front of Lemuel, demanding, "And what did Deuteronomy chapter twenty-two verse nineteen say about false accusations of a woman?"

Malka laughs and says, "*Ashkara*—literally, Lemuel—you owe her father a hundred shekels. How could you stoop so low as to accuse her of a sordid affair so she could slander the Torah? Maybe she has a point. Are you so closed-minded that you cannot examine the evidence and debate it?"

The room erupts in debate again. Rachel claps her hands to silence the room. Deliberately not engaging Lemuel's glaring eyes, she states, "Sometimes, you will find in life you have to make deals to get access to what is not accessible. The Jesuit priest, for your information, is the most honorable man I have met. He would not offend a woman. Not even one who wanted his affections. He is a true man of Yahweh. His intentions and mine were the same. We needed to find out the truth of what happened in the Assyrian siege of Jerusalem. He had both the resources of the Vatican and the technology of MoxWorld Holdings. Only with both could we have determined a fourth prism might have existed."

She walks to the windows to the cypresses. The trees of the Middle Eastern cemetery. For the dead talk to archaeologists. They certainly did to her mother, her grandmother Ariella, and her great-grandmother Oksana. She turns back to her students and says, "If you want a career in archaeology, you will have to face what deals you are willing to make to find out the truth. You should consider a different profession if you are not willing to pay that price. I am still paying the price for helping the world know the truth about Asherah and what she did to shape our world."

The tall Lemuel turns away from her and mumbles, "Sheltered academic. You have no idea what deals and debts really are."

She glances his way, then, facing the other students again, and says, "You all should be proud of how engaged you became in debate today. Your assignment for next week is a five-thousand-word argument on this subject. The women will argue that the Deuteronomists were correct in removing most references to Asherah in the Torah. The men will speculate on how history might have been different if the Deuteronomists had left Asherah in the Torah as Yahweh's wife."

Lemuel slams his chair into the wall as he rises to leave. "*Dai!* Enough! I have had it with you, Professor. The university should have banned you entirely. I don't care that you were the top student in your rabbinical school's history. You have turned evil. You have left Yahweh. I have no other choice than to drop this seminar." He storms out of the room, slamming the door shut.

Undoing her bun and retying her hair into a loose ponytail, Rachel watches the fuming tall man storm away. Her head bobs back and forth a bit as she asks, "Does anyone else have objections to their assignment?"

The room is quiet as students pick up their affairs to leave. Saul approaches Rachel, who reflexively puts a foot back to brace for another attack. Not that she has not suffered the same from the academic community. He says in an even-tempered voice, "I don't necessarily agree with your hypotheses, but I do find you have a clear line of logic. I find it refreshing to examine the old with a new eye. Most of the time, you will confirm why the old ways are correct, which only makes you stronger. Thank you for challenging us."

Rachel suppresses what could have been a very audible sigh of relief as she nods her appreciation back to Saul. As he leaves the room, he turns and says, "You should have cited the Law Code of Hammurabi instead. If anyone brings an accusation of any crime before the elders and does not prove what he has charged, he shall, if it be a capital offense charged, be put to death. Serves Lemuel right for being such a pr—stick in the mud today."

Deborah snickers at Saul's remark as she approaches Rachel. "I have never strayed in my belief in Yahweh, in his unique position as my one true deity. But since I've taken your seminars, I have found I have a deeper appreciation for my faith. I understand how to examine new perspectives on religion, on my life, without fear of my world being turned upside down if I listen to the argument. Last semester, you told us that openness was essential for tolerance. And tolerance will lead to peace. I want to thank you for what you have done to empower us."

As Rachel gathers her things, a warmth emanates from her chest to her lips as they relax into an expression of deep satisfaction. On her MoxWrap, she sees an encoded message from Mei waiting. Should she thank the Jesuit priest Jean-Paul for introducing them to each other? Mei, who touched her in very intimate ways, called the process the five sense algorithm. Sleeping with the enemy is what Rachel called it at first. For many months. But it got her closer to Alexander Murometz. She became friends with that monstrous Russian's inner circle. From there, she could one day meet him face-to-face. Meet her destiny. Just as the prophecy her grandmother Ariella said her mother told would happen.

Until then, Mei Tang and Father Jean-Paul have been invaluable conduits to technology that have led to further discoveries in Israel. And deep inside, Rachel admires the archaeological prowess of both of them. In a different life, they could have been true friends. Maybe in the next one.

She reads Mei's message on her MoxWorld-issued device, which is security encrypted especially for communications with MoxWorld heads. "The sign of the circle and crescent from Göbekli Tepe also found in a tomb near Xian, China."

Mei asks her to keep an eye out for this symbol in her excavations near the ninth-century City of Solomon ruins near the south wall of the Temple Mount. Rachel taps back, asking if Murometz has convinced the Israeli government to release the seal, statue fragment, and tablet she found a few weeks ago. Mei responds that negotiations are in the works. There is an unknown competitive bidder. Expect a visit by a MoxWorld team shortly.

A bit flush thinking about her time with the MoxWorlders, she loosens her hair from its ponytail, fluffing it across her shoulders, and unbuttons her blouse. Just a bit.

As she leaves the satellite campus, a tan sedan pulls up. In a city full of MoxMovers, a gas-powered 1980s car can only mean one thing. A visit from the dean of the Biblical Archaeology Department, her boss, Rabbi Mizrahi.

CHAPTER 22

Before you embark on a journey of revenge, dig two graves.

—Confucius

Judaic University of Jerusalem Satellite Campus
3:25 p.m. GMT+3, January 21, 2023

Her back arched, her toes digging into the cement, her vocal cords readied for deeper octaves, she yells first. "Don't lecture me, Ya'akov. Lemuel is not cut out to objectively evaluate archaeological evidence. He is too wedded to the literalness of the Torah. Let me finish this semester before you fire me again. The other students think I'm helping them. Just ask."

Loose, relaxed, cool, the rabbi opens his hands to her and says, "Shalom to you too, my dear Rachel. Lemuel was a plant. You're losing your touch. You didn't spot him. You let him get to you."

Rachel's back straightens. Her feet flatten out across her sandals. Her mouth agape. "*Lo!* No! Plant? The university is spying on me? Are they trying to build a case to ban me from all higher education institutes?"

Rabbi Mizrahi simply smiles as he replies, "No, my dear. He's not the university's plant."

Her jaw drops. Her head nods as she says, "I stopped working for them. Why are they checking on me? I have done nothing against Israel."

Smiling away, the rabbi states, "No one in archaeology ever stops working for them. But he is not who you are thinking."

Turning away from him, she says, "Then 'they' sent you. This is not an academic discussion."

"Please, my dear. Let us continue our discussion in the car," asks the rabbi as he looks above. "We will be away from prying eyes and ears in there."

With a stare worthy of Lemuel, Rachel says, "Well, you tell them I will not do any more favors unless they release the royal seal and tablet I found. And that poor Palestinian's statue fragment needs to be given back to her as well."

Again, with the open arms, the rabbi says, "Your safta raba would be very pleased if you would join me in the car."

She pauses, reflecting upon his precise choice of words. In religion as in cultural heritage protection, every word counts. Once inside the car, Rachel crosses her arms, and then says, "Those pompous, misogynistic keepers of all things sacred in our country. They wouldn't have had to send you to persuade me to do their dirty work if they had promoted me. Instead, they promoted a lesser man."

"A man whom they trust will do what is in the best interest of Israel," replies the rabbi.

"Everything I did benefited Israel."

"And other interests as well," he replies, still wearing his smile. "You were too smart for that post. Loyalty is at times best for the less intellectually endowed."

"Endowed?" she cries out and points to her lap. "If I were endowed down there with something else, they would have promoted me, and they wouldn't have taken away my archaeological find. That would have proven that the mother of David ordered a statue of Asherah to be placed in the First Temple. Evidence that the grandmother of Solomon worshipped the goddess. Ya'akov, tell me these men are not so insecure the world cannot know the truth."

Still smiling, he answers, "And how would that change modern history? My dear, there are greater threats to our future than whether or not the Deuteronomists rewrote biblical history to favor men. There is a movement in the Muslim community around a new messiah figure. A devout Kurdish woman, Zara Khatum. Even the fringe elements in Judaism are paying attention to her, with MoxWorld News broadcasting her alleged miracles. Mossad has issued an alert if she visits any major religious center. If she performs such miracles at Mecca, or even here at the Temple Mount, they fear that there will be an uprising of those who share her same faith, supported by the Arab Confederation and Egypt. They fear she is a false messiah who will challenge Israel's sovereign right to these lands."

Wiggling in her seat, she asks, "And exactly how do I fit in with this messiah?"

"She is friends with the Jesuit priest and the professor from Shanghai University you have been working with. Through them, you can get in close to this Kurdish woman and ensure she does no harm to Israel's interests and our people. You can guide them away from our interests. Or if she is uncooperative, you know what you have to do."

"Why me?" she asks as she clasps her hands tightly. "They have better assets to quietly remove her."

"You have the most credibility on the world stage. You are our foremost expert on ancient goddesses. You can rebuke possible Murometz claims that she comes from an ancient lineage. Counter any claim that she represents the modern incarnation of Asherah."

Rachel purses her lips as he mentions her name. She stares out the front window as they pass by the olive garden of the Gethsemane on one side and the Golden Gate of Old Jerusalem on the other. She asks, "And if I refuse? Ya'akov, be honest. Maybe the world would be better off if we have a woman as messiah."

He pulls out a print photo. "This Kurd just left a man you want to get close to. This is the great-grandson of Herr Professor Gollinger, the man who killed your saba raba. Our sources indicate he may present a grave danger— to Israel, and more importantly, our family."

"As my safta raba would say, *yimach shmo*. May Gollinger's name be erased. But after so much time, why should we worry about a family whose male lineage has killed themselves or is near death?"

Another chuckle and Ya'akov replies, "Months after you were screened by

Murometz's eugenics program, his team found the great-grandson, Peter Gollinger, an editor in San Francisco. Since then, Gollinger has been like an adopted son to Alexander Murometz, who we believe will take possession of your saba raba's stolen mystical pendant."

He pulls out two more print photos. "And this is him praying with the Kurdish woman, Zara Khatum. This other one is an infrared of them intimately intertwined in bed together. It seems they have a close relationship. But he has not given her the other pendant. The latest intel says he is currently heading west from Xian, China, with your Shanghai professor friend, whom he has not given the pendant to either. Maybe he's playing them both and keeping the pendant for his own devious purposes."

Can lightning strike someone sitting inside a 1980s sedan? Because it does, jolting Rachel so traumatically she flinches in front of her boss. Did she just convince Mei to talk to this Kurdish woman and break up her relationship?

"What is wrong, Professor?" says the rabbi. "No longer game to repay your great-grandmother's debt?"

She shakes her head to snap out of it and lets out a less-than-complimentary sound from her neutral affect lips. "He's a Gollinger. They are complicit collaborators and cannot be trusted."

"Make no mistake about the gravity of this situation," says the rabbi. "Seventeen years ago, we had to orchestrate Peter Gollinger's father's suicide. He had discovered the key to an ancient language that the Nazis had been searching for in Crimea, which could be used to prove the manifest destiny of the Aryan race. If this discovery had been made public, it would be a rallying call for today's neo-Nazis to rise up and unite. Intelligence reports Peter Gollinger has rediscovered this ancient language. He may be as much a danger to Israel as the Kurdish woman."

Pursing her lips, she exclaims, "You staged that suicide?"

"I did what needed to be done, as you will need to do," he replies with flat affect.

"Perhaps this family has already paid the price for their ancestor's complicity," she says as she gazes at the floorboard.

Pursing his lips, he pulls out more photos. "Your professor friend looks very pregnant from these surveillance photos. An agent in Shanghai verified with Mei Tang's aunt that Gollinger is the father of the baby."

Another less-than-complimentary noise comes from Rachel as she reflects how Mei deserves better than to carry this descendant of a complicit conspirator's child. Even worse, a conspirator who cheated on that Kurdish woman.

Rabbi Ya'akov's smile returns as he says, "I knew you would see it my way. You always did. They gave you a green light to liquidate the Kurdish woman if needed. Gollinger might present you with the way to get to her. But he is not to be harmed unless you can ascertain his ancient language find is contained and you get the pendant back first."

"You know me all too well. If we really must pay our debt to them, I can be very discreet and quick, or I can make this Kurd's death prolonged and torturous."

"*Ken*. Good. That is exactly what I trained you to say," says the rabbi, his lips a flat line as a stern demeanor washes across his face. "What else do you say to anyone who asks?" says the rabbi.

"I executed coldly and ruthlessly three Nazi conspirators. *Yimach shmam*. May their names be erased," she says with equal frigidness. With her fingers toward the rabbi's forehead, she says, "Three taps through the face after letting them suffer with leg shots, then stomach shots. No mercy."

"Good," he affirms.

In a much softer tone, she asks, "Why must I keep saying this over and over again? Why must I keep playing a deep undercover Mossad agent?"

The rabbi pats her knee. "Because that and the Jericho I gave you are the only two things I am sure will protect you when I am not around. Someday, you will need the courage to pull that trigger. Without hesitation."

Rabbi Ya'akov reaches over to her blouse and buttons up the lower button, covering up not only her ample cleavage, but a gold pendant. "We've arrived at your safta raba's convalescent home. You should look like a proper *nina* for her."

Out of her backpack comes a long skirt to pull over her khaki pants and a scarf to cover her hair. As Rachel prepares to leave the car, he holds his hands out. "Rachel, no goodbye hug today?"

"No, Aba," she replies as she wraps the skirt around her pants. "Don't you remember? You fired me from my post at the university."

"Remember, what a father must do for his daughter is always based on his love for her. Even firing her for her own good," says her aba.

From his pocket, he takes out two small black leather boxes with leather straps, which he hands to her. "I remember my young daughter praying with these each morning. The father who loves her asks for her own good to do so again. For what is to come, my daughter would be better served if she did so again."

Taking the boxes, she says, "You took these away from me after I replaced the parchment inside with one from my safta raba."

"I did not think words from Asherah were appropriate for even my headstrong daughter for morning prayer," he replies.

Opening one of the tefillin, she examines the parchment. "You put the original text back in."

"*Ken, betach.* Yes, of course. These passages discuss the unity of Yahweh, the miracles He performed for us when He took us out of Egypt, and how He alone has the power and dominion to do whatever He wants in the physical and spiritual worlds."

Putting the parchment back into her old tefillin, she hands them back to her aba. "She. I stopped using these because she is She."

Taking the tefillin back, he folds his arms and stares forward. "I trust that my daughter will do what she needs to do with Khatum and Gollinger. More importantly, your mother is expecting you for Shabbat shortly. So don't spend all afternoon with Ariella."

She kisses his cheek goodbye and stares into the eyes of a loving father who says, "Remember, the tefillin concept embodies the Chabad Chassidic teachings that the intellect must control the emotions. For what is to happen, you cannot become 'instinct-emotion centered.' With or without the tefillin, you must strive for unity of mind and heart, intellect and emotion. A father can only protect his daughter so much. And what they will ask, please do not make me choose between you and them."

❧

Her ninety-fifth birthday was only a month away and all she could do was to remain silent as she stroked her granddaughter's hand. Rachel broke the news that she had found her husband's murderer's great-grandson. The crime that irrevocably destroyed her life would be avenged by his death, as Rachel promised her. All her safta raba said was *Gott im Himmel*, God in heaven, and for the next ten minutes silence.

Rachel rubs her oldest living relation's wrinkled hands, which clasp a fossilized wooden object. A six-centimeter-high statuette of Asherah, which Rachel had found with the seal and tablet of King David's mother, Nitzevet. A great woman whom her great-grandmother regards as her ancestor. A relic small enough that Rachel was able to hide it in a personal place where, if they tried to search, she would have had legal grounds to lethally counterattack them in self-defense. A relic that with the seal and tablet proved Queen Nitzevet commissioned a statue of Asherah for the Temple. But more importantly, a relic that meant everything to her great-grandmother and all of her female ancestors.

The nonagenarian raises Rachel's hand to her lips and lightly caresses it. "Nina. My child. It is not about killing. It is about life. It is about the light. She was so beautiful. She is why I could survive all the evil that happened to us in Crimea. *Shelo neda*. We should never know what I lived through. But She is why I could survive after they murdered my beloved Kemel."

"Safta Raba, I can only hope to have a dream of Asherah as you have. I will do anything to show the world her beauty, her truth."

The aged hands place the statuette into Rachel's hands. "Nina, I did not dream of her. I sat with her. I talked with her. I prayed with her. She blessed my daughter, your grandmother, in my womb. *Shulem. Zol zain shulem.* Peace. Let there be peace, she asked of me."

The aged woman quietly says, "Come closer, my dear." And as Rachel leans closer, she unbuttons her blouse a couple notches and pulls out the pendant. A gold triangle with a woman's head with flowing hair, exposed breasts, and a tree sprouting from a pubic triangle.

Her great-grandmother says, "This was my great-grandmother's. You said this came from an ancient city north of here. How old did you say?"

"It is identical to other images and pendants found in Ugarit at the coast along the southern border of Turkey and New Kurdistan. I dated it to 2000 BCE. Images of goddesses in this area and farther north date all the way back to 6000 BCE."

"And you said you believe this is Asherah," affirms the elder woman. "You remember what I have said."

"*Ken.* Yes, Safta Raba. History and religion may have been written by men, but the truth is spoken by women. I have been faithful to your words. So much so, I keep getting fired."

A smile slowly arises across the elder wrinkled face framed by white, wiry, curly hair. "And you remember what else I have said."

"*Ken*, Safta Raba. And I will follow her words that you have raised me with after I retake what they stole from Saba Raba Kemel. I did what you had to do to survive your escape from Crimea. Our return to the blue light means no modesty. Nothing on my body is more sacred than our mission. In time, I will have the chance to bring this Gollinger descendant to his knees in repentance for what they stole from your husband."

Her safta raba says, "I know your aba has raised you with the fervor to seek vengeance which I have hereto condoned—the family has condoned. That is what my son taught him. As I am close to passing from this world, She tells me you must moderate what they ask of you. The return to the blue light is all that matters."

Taking both Rachel's hands into hers, from under her beige nightgown she brings out a gold chain that holds a black stone pendant. She says to Rachel to remove it from her neck. Rachel holds it up, and it glistens with an aura of blue. The same as that which more intensely surrounds her irises. "*Nina,* your eyes match this pendant. The sign you are the destined one. Your pursuit of finding her, returning to her, must be first and foremost. And only with this can you find Asherah. Only with its other half that they must have stolen from Kemel will it lead you to Asherah. Others will talk of revenge, but you must ignore them and find the other half before you commit yourself to the ultimate step in finding Asherah."

Still focused on the aura of blue from this stone, Rachel asks, "How will I know whom my other half will be? There's so many out there. Most women will never know. How can I?

"My Kemel, his given first name is like your aba's. She said only someone who is true to your mission to return to her will know this," states her eldest matriarch. "But most important to remember, She said to me that a young woman of my descent will fight another who claims the prophesy of the blue light. Only one woman of innocence can be in the blue light. And someone else must die. I hear the stories of a Kurdish woman whom they claim is the next messiah. You know what you have to do. She is not to stop you from returning to the blue light. It is your destiny."

"I will, Safta Raba. I will."

"One more thing," says the elder woman as she pulls Rachel down to whisper in her ear and then taps her stomach.

"*Lo.* No, Safta Raba," says Rachel. "I have done what no woman should have to do to get this far. But that, *lo.*"

Her great-grandmother leans back into her pillow, tersely saying, "*Ach nu.* Enough. I ask you no more than I did. You must, my child, or you can never reach Asherah. Do not let the agenda of others get in the way of our end goal."

❧

Outside her great-grandmother's room, Rachel leans her back against the hallway wall, her hands atop her abdomen. Shaking. Her head nodding from side to side. She has been the most relentless female biblical scholar Israel has ever known. She was once the most loyal red herring of an agent for the Israel's finest religious archaeological protection agency. She has been the best great-granddaughter anyone could have. She has done all that has been asked of her in loyalty to all. Exactly how far she went to get close to the MoxWorld leadership is something she cannot tell her safta raba. But now this. From complicity to cohabitance. How could she ask that much more? What else will fall on her head today?

A doctor comes around the corner and Rachel straightens up to let the physician about her height and build pass by. But to her surprise, the doctor stops and peers into her great-grandmother's room. This woman in a white medical jacket clearly cut to show she is not a man turns to Rachel and says, "I can't imagine what she just asked of you. Or maybe I can."

"Excuse me?" replies Rachel, as she backs away. "Are you part of her medical team?" She scans the doctor. Awfully attractive for someone on staff. Odd red marks around the wrists. Perhaps those hospital ID bands had been put on too tightly the day before.

The doctor takes a step toward Rachel. "No. I'm on yours," she asserts as she presses the NiQihs band on her wrist. Rachel's thigh flinches as a device in her pants pocket flicks at her.

Rachel's face becomes stone cold. Her brows point inward, her pupils eye-of-a-needle thin. "You're the doctor they said would come to see me."

"There is so much I can do for you if you do the same for me," replies the physician. She shows a hologram of Rachel's much-sought-after ancient seal and tablet and Massa's statue fragment. "We have secured these from the Israeli government. They are at your disposition to research and publish findings. Our gesture of appreciation for your loyalty."

Without even the slightest glance at the hologram, Rachel fires back in her deep voice, "Why have they sent a doctor this time? Whose organs do you want to cut out now? I told your agents I do my wet work with a gun."

"I am no different from you. They killed someone I loved. I want them dead as much as you do." She opens up her clipboard to a photo.

Rachel glances at the photo, then straight back into the doctor's eyes. "So, you want to kill them by cutting off their testicles? Radical feminist, are you?"

"Don't get hissy with me," the doctor says as her face scrunches. "I made sacrifices just like you did to get into the MoxWorld inner circles. If you don't believe me…" The doctor punches her NiQihs device a couple times.

Rachel takes her NiQihs device out of her pocket and reads the sent document. A complete record of the tests Mei and Father Jean-Paul ran on her, including detailed accounts and indiscrete photos of her time with Mei. "How did you get this? They didn't even share this with me."

"You better read up on the God Gene Complex," says the doctor. "You can read my book just published by NiQihs. You'll find out why your Mei Tang found you to be an exemplary fit for what they were looking for. But her genetics and that of another were a miniscule better fit for their purposes. Or so they said."

Tapping her MoxWorld device, Rachel says, "Dr. Beverly Fontaine. Associate professor of medicine at the University of San Francisco and part-time medical director at the MoxMedical Total Care Unit."

Shaking her head, Dr. Fontaine says, "You are much slower than I was told you would be. Are you distracted? Man problems? Shake off it, lady. You'll need to be fully focused on this assignment, or you will be dead like my fiancé."

Fontaine points back to another photo and adds, "Dead like the team that botched this work. They failed to get from Gollinger the viable genetic material needed to create the child and mother who can access the serum we are tasked with finding. Testicular sperm extraction is not such a new technique. It should have worked."

Shaking her head, Dr. Fontaine adds, "We used intracytoplasmic sperm injection to fertilize eggs from another woman who has a pronounced God Gene Complex. Too late for the dead extraction team in California, we now think we needed ejaculate-based sperm to make the fertilization procedure work."

Rachel puts her hands back on her belly, but this time more protectively as she meekly asks, "And what do you want of me?"

To her surprise, the doctor puts up a hologram of Mei. "Despite our work to conceive the requisite child, we believe Murometz already has created a genetically correct child. The Chinese woman you are working with is carrying this child. We need to confirm that the father is Gollinger."

Shaking her head side to side, Rachel asks, "Why is a child from people with this God Gene Complex so important?"

"Eugenics, my dear," replies Dr. Fontaine. "The same as Murometz's father was performing in Crimea. They found an ancient legend that says only the descendants of an ancient matriarch can access some secret stone that will lead to a place we also want to find. In there, we will retrieve a serum that has been sought after for centuries. A serum you and I would like to have for ourselves. Women like us could change the world if we had this serum. We uncovered other information from Murometz, saying only a woman carrying a child with the same genetics of an ancient matriarch and her husband can access this place."

Her back against the wall again, Rachel stares at the ceiling. First her safta raba says she needs to be with child to fulfill the family destiny. Now this doctor is telling her the same. Asherah must be really mad at her to make the world swirl around so.

"So, you think this Gollinger man has the genetics needed to make that child," says Rachel, wringing her hands in front of her abdomen.

"Yes. Mr. Peter Gollinger. He is an odd character. I've gotten very close to him. Worked intimately late at night rubbing myself on him. I tried to seduce him to get live genetic material, but he is oddly resistant to both subtle and overt female overtures. He thinks he is love with this Kurdish woman."

"You mean Zara Khatum?"

"Yes, how do you know her?"

Rachel's eyes glance to one side and her nose twitches as she answers, "She is in the news, proclaimed as the next messiah."

"Yes," affirms the doctor. "We cannot determine if Murometz is hyping her as a distraction or has some other ulterior motive. He's been one to two steps ahead of us every time."

Tapping her fingers on her clipboard, Dr. Fontaine adds, "But finally, we are ahead of Murometz's team. We have a source within Murometz's team who found a lead in the tomb of a concubine of the first emperor of China. We convinced the Chinese government to block their access to the tomb."

"What did you find in the tomb?" asks Rachel, whose archaeological inquisitiveness kicks in.

"That is not for you to know at this time. Your job is to confirm that the Kurdish woman has not been impregnated and to determine if your ex-girlfriend Mei's child was fathered by Peter Gollinger. If not, then you need to extract live genetic material from Mr. Gollinger."

"How do you expect me to do that?" asks Rachel.

Beverly steps in close and unbuttons Rachel's blouse one notch further down and runs her finger along her cleavage. "You are as well-proportioned as I. At a distance, you and I could look like twins."

"My mother would have raised a twin sister with more respect than to touch a strange woman so intimately as you do now," replies Rachel.

With a lascivious smile, the doctor says, "You are no stranger to the touch of a woman. You can do the same to Gollinger. He will like your perky assets. The sight of them will activate his God Gene Complex."

Rachel takes the doctor's fingers out of her blouse and buttons up. Reddened in the face, she retorts, "Your people better be clear. My body is mine to decide what to do with. I sell neither my body nor my soul to anyone."

"But you would to get close enough to Murometz," says the doctor. "We know why you slept with the Chinese woman. And you will sleep with Gollinger just the same if that gets you the chance to kill Murometz."

Beverly shapes her fingers like a gun and points it at Rachel's temple. "If we get the serum we seek, you, the Chinese woman, or the Kurdish woman will carry Gollinger's baby, and you'll need to blow Alexander Murometz's brain out."

A siren blares in the distance. Rachel peers back into her safta raba's room through her window. The horizon begins its telltale orange hues. It is time. She promised her father she would make it on time. As she scans the hallway for the exit, she says, "Aren't you due somewhere?"

The doctor merely smiles, moves a step closer in, and replies, "I am where I am supposed to be. Waiting for your commitment to our cause."

"Obviously, you are not religious," says Rachel as she takes a scarf out of her backpack.

"No, my dear, I am not Jewish," replies the doctor, not flinching or moving.

"Well, as my favorite rabbi says, no one is perfect," quips Rachel as she pushes the doctor aside, heading for the exit.

Out of sight of everyone, she lets her shoulders slump. Fulfill her family's debt, their transgressions, recovering her saba raba Kemel's stolen pendant, stopping that Kurdish woman by deadly force if necessary. Do whatever is needed to find Asherah, including doing the unthinkable with a Gollinger. And fool all the MoxWorlders into letting her get close enough to kill Murometz. What a woman archaeologist has to do to stay in the game.

CHAPTER 23

Have wings that feared ever touched the sun?
I was born when all I once feared—
I could love.
—Rabi'a al-Adawiyya, eighth-century Persian philosopher and mystic

Luxury conference hotel, Zahko, Duhok Province, New Kurdistan
9:30 a.m. GMT+3, February 3, 2023

The honeymoon suite filled with rose petals—the age-old sign of fertility. How could he? Is this a sick practical joke?

Zara brushes aside the rose petals to make room for her luggage as she packs. Someone at MoxTravel booked this room of nuptial consummation for her. The big rose-red round bed. The valentine-red velvet curtains with matching chairs. And of course, the rose petals across the surfaces of the dresser and desk. All the hallmarks of a sick joke by her Sasha.

As she picks up the rose-red velvet chair cushions off the floor to place them back in their chairs, she reflects upon Zengo's offer to sleep on the floor. For they were last to arrive at the negotiation planning summit with delegates from all around the two Kurdish nations who filled the hotel. Zengo offered to sleep on the floor of another New Kurdistan delegate, but Zara could not do that to him. Not with his injured shoulder. His sacrifice saving her oh so long ago.

How so much different he is than Peter. He stood by her side as they arrived in Zahko before the conference, where the crowds chanted for their new messiah. She addressed them, encouraging them to demand peace from their local governments. She said women should seek higher education and develop the skills needed by the new economy. The advent of the solar-powered MoxMovers meant that all nations in the Middle East needed to find sources of revenue other than oil. A great woman, perhaps the oldest matriarch in Kurdish history, once said that creating abundance was the source of peace. They must work with the Arab Confederation, the recent union of the non-Kurdish parts of Syria and Iraq, as well as Turkey, to avoid confrontations over the rights to natural resources or Mr. Murometz's generous offers of education and factories.

Perhaps, the geopolitical economics in her presentation were too high-level for the crowd to grasp. Perhaps, all they wanted was a spiritual leader, as many chanted for her to bring forth lightning to strike down the evil ones who oppress the Kurds. As she momentarily gazed at her feet, wondering how she could make a breakthrough and help these people who understand more violence only begets more violence, five enormous men rushed the MoxWorld security team, with one breaking through.

Zengo threw himself in the way of one of these madmen, and after a long minute of punches, blocks, kicks, and eventually both falling to the ground, Zengo prevailed. The other man with a broken arm and Zengo with a dislocated shoulder. The latter did not want Zara to fuss over his shoulder, saying the local hospital could take care of him.

Like old times, Zara said he should not be a baby about it, as she had reset his shoulder before. During Iraqi Freedom, his unit had attacked a Ba'ath military post that she had provided inside reconnaissance information about. She had infiltrated the post, posing as a harlot. Zengo had burst into the Ba'ath's office just in time to save her from the post commander. In the course of the very physical battle in that room, disarming the commander and then his guards, who rushed to save him, Zengo's shoulder had become dislodged. Very grateful for her love's rescue of her, she had reset it.

Ironically, the same shoulder became dislocated in Zahko—not atypical as, once dislocated, a shoulder becomes more vulnerable. The same can be said for hearts. For as Zara stripped his shirt off to begin the in-field reset method they had been taught, her eyes could not escape how his chest and abdominal muscles glistened, just as they had nearly fifteen years ago. His body was perfect above the waist. Above where the IED removed his manhood. A flutter passed through her stomach. One that she dismissed as a conflict-induced adrenaline rush.

As she leaned in closer to reset the shoulder, his musky, masculine scent engulfed her senses. It was a mixture of sweat and leather, with a subtle hint of that same old cologne that made her heart race in their teenage embraces. She couldn't help but inhale deeply, lost in the intoxicating aroma that surrounded her. It was like being enveloped again in an all so familiar warm embrace, comforting yet exhilarating at the same time. The scent alone was enough to send shivers down her spine and make her body tingle with anticipation

Finally, after she had physically muscled his shoulder back into place, she collapsed against his chest. His arms instinctively wrapped around her, pulling her into a warm embrace that brought back memories of the early days of their love. She could feel the strength of his embrace, the familiar scent of his love, and the comforting beat of his heart against her own. This was the hug that had first captured her heart, the one that made her believe in forever with him. So, how could she throw him out of this hotel's most special, luxurious room?

With his shoulder needing to mend, she gave the enormous round bed to him and bedded down on the chair cushions on the floor for the three nights of the conference. At her instigation, as they went to sleep, they reminisced about the old days in their village outside Duhok, not far from here. They talked of the trials and tribulations of teenagers learning to be soldiers in the Peshmerga. And each conversation would end in Zengo begging her forgiveness for what he had done and her saying she had learned to forgive and had forgiven him.

The conference concluded this morning with a breakfast session to summarize the negotiation terms the two Kurdistans would place in front of Turkey well before the thirty-day deadline. Now, as Zengo bids farewell to the New Kurdistan delegates, Zara makes one last round in their honeymoon room. As she searches the room for that one thing one always leaves in a hotel, she lifts the delicate rose petals that the hotel staff had romantically scattered each day. As she brings them to her face, she can still smell the faint fragrance of the rose that he had given her on that fateful afternoon in Duhok, which changed her life forever. She closes her eyes and feels a wave of emotions wash over her as she slowly crushes the soft petals between her fingertips. The scent of the rose intensifies, filling her senses, before gradually dissipating into the air. With a heavy sigh, she lets the crushed petals slip from her hand and flutter delicately to the ground, their vibrant colors fading into muted tones. Memories flood back as she shakes her head in disbelief, wondering how something so beautiful could have ended in such heartache.

Her momentary relapse into the forbidden is broken by the sounding of her MoxWrap. Dr. Beverly Fontaine appears and says, "Oh, Zara, I am so glad I could finally catch up with you. You've been so hard to contact. I reviewed your psych evaluation and therapy notes from the team that treated you after your abduction. I am transferring them to you now."

Before Zara can object or say anything, the doctor continues. "It is so nice what you are doing to promote world peace. But please, you must listen to your interviews from one month after your rescue. You said the same as your Captain Luciano. Your delusions were much more apparent back then. You can see over the months how you grasped desperately at your faith in Xwedê as the way to save yourself."

Dr. Beverly allows Zara a couple of minutes to watch herself, at which Zara can only emote a blank face. The doctor smiles and says, "That woman you see, she will hurt thousands, maybe millions, if she keeps acting like a prophetess. The best answer right now is to find a stable relationship. A man who can help her find the resolution to move forward in her life and rediscover the joy she once experienced."

The doctor signs off and Zara leans her head into the room's door. Everything seems so right. For the last two weeks, the Turks and the Kurds appear to be responding to her guidance. And things with Zengo. What if she is delusional? She hurt Peter. Who else is she going to hurt?

Her eyes focus up, searching. "Now would be a good time to speak. Tell me you are my delusional mind trying to sort out its pain." Nothing. Only silence greets her.

Her MoxWrap sounds again with a message from Magali, asking if she is still coming down to Jean-Paul's newest excavation at the Nineveh Palace in Mosul.

Zara taps back: We are just leaving. It should be a little over two hours if traffic is not bad in Mosul.

Magali types back: We? Who are you coming with?

With her smile coming back, Zara types: Someone. You will see.

She hasn't driven a Humvee since the war with the Daesh. Zengo doesn't trust the MoxMovers, so they drive his relic from the US Army's days in Kurdistan. The blue laser active-armor MoxMover that MoxWorld Security assigned to Zara follows them on autopilot. Zara finds relief and refreshment in her act of kindness, insisting that Zengo not drive until his shoulder is mended.

As they near the Nineveh Palace, Zara slows the Humvee to look at the destroyed Mashki Gate. The Daesh who occupied Mosul destroyed many parts of the ancient palace, which they regarded as idolatry and against the words of the Prophet. Jean-Paul told her the Daesh destroyed a mosque containing the tomb of the Prophet Jonah within the palace walls, ransacked the Mosul museum, and destroyed centuries-old manuscripts in the city's main libraries. They dug tunnels underneath the palace grounds, searching for other treasures to sell.

She closes her eyes and asks of Xwedê how people can misinterpret Her words to mean death and destruction. What the Daesh did to Mosul did not differ from what they did to her. Tunneled her body and destroyed her soul. She takes a deep breath and glances over at Zengo. Maybe she should follow the doctor's advice. Rediscover the joy she once had in life.

Cars parked with the MoxWorld Security team on watch out, Zengo says to Zara he will stand watch with them. She spies Magali walking toward her from the area between the Ishtar Temple and the Khosr River, where Jean-Paul is talking with a woman about a head and a half shorter than he. Under the khaki dig clothes are glimpses of a very fit, very taunt body, very bosomy. About ten centimeters shorter than she.

Magali hugs Zara, and then notices her noticing the "other" woman. "Oh, let us not interrupt them," says Magali. "Shop talk. So boring."

"Who is she?" asks Zara, who fights a twinge of jealousy herself. She thought only she could engage the priest in the shop-talk, platonic way that this woman seems to do. Of course, he is a priest and would not notice what is under her khaki jacket. But there is something about this woman nine to ten centimeters shorter than herself that appears so familiar.

Tucking a stray strand of red hair back under her blue headscarf, the former Catholic Sister replies, "She is young and intelligent and has a raw beauty to her. Not a lick of makeup on her, and she is quite alluring." Magali puts her finger under Zara's chin, turning her head to view her profile. "Quite like you, my dear."

Magali turns Zara's head toward Zengo and asks, "And who is the hunk you have brought? Is he the one you wanted to talk with me about?"

Pursing her lips as her cheeks blush and her eyes glance away, Zara responds, "Oh, him? He is one of the lead delegates from New Kurdistan. We are working together on the Kurdish negotiation strategies with Turkey over the MoxWorld factories."

"Hmmm. Working together," says Magali. "And maybe a little play together, I hope."

Blushing a deeper shade of rose, Zara says, "Where is your mind, Magali? You were a Sister of the Lord only a few weeks ago."

Tilting her head, the former Sister says, "I can only wish for you to find the same love I hope to have for myself. We both have hunks of our own now."

"Please, please. We are simply old friends," says Zara, drawing her rose-pink headscarf a little tighter.

"As are the good Father and I," replies Magali as she leads Zara down to the new excavation area. Zara's attention is hyper-focused on this new woman and the stance of Jean-Paul. The same he took with her as they debated early on the mission to find the first object. She overhears this mysterious woman say, "I understand Isaiah chapter eight verse three says his wife was a prophetess. But there is no other mention of her in any version of the Torah, much less the Old Testament."

With the same calm exterior he exuded with Zara, the Jesuit priest replies, "Humor me, I do not mean to argue with your exceptional knowledge of the Torah. As the early Catholic Church opted not to include the Books of Isaiah and Jonah in their Old Testament, my studies of Isaiah are mostly limited to what later Catholic scholars opined."

Without missing a beat, the shorter woman dives back into her argument. "But what if Isaiah's wife was a prophetess of Asherah? What if Isaiah's wisdom was also influenced by what his wife had relayed to him? That happens in marriages, doesn't it?"

"But that is very speculative," replies the taller Jean-Paul.

"Then remind me. What does Isaiah chapter thirty-seven verse thirty say?" demands the woman.

Beating Jean-Paul to the punch, Zara responds, "And this shall be the sign unto thee: ye shall eat this year that which groweth of itself, and in the second year that which springeth of the same; and in the third year sow ye, and reap and plant vineyards, and eat the fruit thereof."

The woman gives Zara a stare devoid of emotion while Jean-Paul provides a modest smile and nods.

Smiling back at the priest, Zara adds, "It is said that an ancient matriarch once prophesied *God asks us to be people of peace. Find ways to have peace and harmony. Find ways to create bounty to share and create community.*"

Her back stiff and her eyes narrowed, the shorter woman gruffly demands, "And who are you?"

Before Zara can respond, Jean-Paul says, "Rachel, this is my dear friend Zara Khatum. Zara, this is Professor Capsali, an academic archaeology colleague of mine and Mei."

ৎ

Hands akimbo in her olive, drab khaki tunic, Rachel's narrowly focused eyes scan this tall and imposing friend of the priest. So, this is the infamous Zara Khatum. The so-called prophetess. The one safta raba Ariella warned about. While she initially emits an air connoting humility, this tall woman appears to be hiding something. Very Muslim, notes Rachel, as the woman in front of her sports a pink hijab covering a light blue tunic and loose black leggings. Is she hiding radical Islamic ideology or is she merely a zealot?

After this instantaneous threat assessment, thanks to her IDF training, Rachel brusquely asks, "How do you know Hebrew traditions?"

Her hands clasped in front of her, Zara meekly answers, "I am not an expert, as you must be. I spent only three semesters in a Jesuit college studying the Torah, Talmud, and Rabbinic doctrines."

Rachel slowly walks around Zara, examining each element of this woman as she asserts, "My great-grandmother also told me something akin to your great matriarch's saying. But there is more to it than what you said. Please tell us more."

Her eyes following this professor who circles her like a predator, Zara responds, "My great-grandmother said only women should know these sayings from the great matriarch. And only to be told to their husbands if absolutely necessary."

Rachel stops and tiptoes up to Zara, saying, "You can whisper it to me. Just between us women."

As Zara's eyes scan her face, Rachel focuses on emitting no emotion, no statement, no heart. Zara whispers in her ear, "God asks us to be people of peace. Find ways to have peace and harmony. Find ways to create bounty to share and create community. For those who are close to God, they can find peace with ease. But for those who are not close to God, they need to have abundance to find peace. For without abundance, there is want, need, jealousy, intolerance, all things that stand in the way of peace."

Pursing her lips, taking a deep breath, and nodding her head, Rachel replies, "That is very similar to what my safta raba told me. Does your family come from the Levant?"

"No, my family comes from the hill above the birthplace of the Prophet Ibrāhīm," says Zara, first staring down at Rachel and then nodding at Jean-Paul.

Rachel notes in the priest's eyes his signal for the Kurdish woman to back off as his head nods and his finger wags at her.

Totally focused only on her target, the reason she asked the priest to call this Kurdish woman to join their dig, Rachel smiles and retorts, "The Torah does not say where the Prophet Abraham was born. At my last read, neither does the Quran. Genesis only states his brother died in Ur of the Chaldeans, in the land of the Prophet Abraham's birth. So, you are from the Sumerian city of Ur?"

The tall Kurd's eyes darken, at which Jean-Paul continues to signal "no." Zara shows him no recognition as she glances to the side with her lips beginning to sag at each end. A second later she replies, "That is verse twenty-eight of chapter eleven of 'your' Torah. But Harran, where the Prophet Ibrāhīm worked, is only fifty kilometers from Sanliurfa, where we believe he was born."

"That is very interesting," says Rachel, with her lips pointing in the opposite direction from those of the tall woman. "A shrine commemorating his birth can be found ten miles outside of the believed location of Babylon in ancient Iraq."

Her hands no longer loosely clasped in front of her, but now pulled together in loose fists, Zara retorts at a louder amplitude, "Are you making a derision about the Prophet Mohammed? If you are, I would caution you that there are those in these regions who would not take well to such a comment. Especially from someone of your faith."

With an ear-to-ear grin, the professor from Jerusalem stands into the tall woman's fists, taking them into her hands as she says, "So, do you follow the words of the Prophet that prescribes killing Jews? Or are you the religious zealot who makes up new words that you hear from your god?"

Zara responds by stepping on Rachel's feet, pushing the latter's hands back into her chest. "The words of the Prophet from his days in Medina are ones of peace and tolerance. Even the Constitution of Medina was inclusive of those of the Jewish faith. No one I know believes obedience and submission to Allah means killing people of other faiths."

Rachel firmly pushes her closed hand into Zara's lower abdomen, palpitating for a telltale bulge as she retorts, "Do not the Islamic end of times

Hadiths say that Muslims will kill the Jews? All of this brought about by the arrival of Al-Masih ad-Dajjal, the false messiah. Are you that Dajjal?"

As Zara's hands encircle Rachel's wrist, an omen of something tragically terrible about to happen, Jean-Paul, the Vatican-trained diplomat, steps in and physically separates these two women who are about to bring about the end of the world themselves.

"Rachel, I can affirm that Zara is a woman of peace. She does not wish ill to any faith or people," says Jean-Paul. He turns to Zara and says, "And you, my dearest friend, Rachel is a professor like the Jesuit professors you trained under. She is just testing you as she does her students."

"I can appreciate that. I loved studying with the Jesuits," says Zara, whose eyes have darkened completely. Those black discs beam into the stormy green eyes of the shorter woman as Zara proclaims, "To be clear between us—I have never claimed to be a messiah. I have not taken action to assume that role. As a faithful Muslim, I have never killed an Israeli. I came close. He was complicit in my kidnapping by the Daesh. He helped traffic women enslaved by the Daesh. But he did no direct harm to me or my sisters, so I left him missing something he treasured."

Stepping toward Zara again, staring straight into those obsidian disc pupils, stiff as a steel girder, Rachel says in her lowest baritone voice, "Well, I only killed two Kurds. And executed in the most ruthless manner three Nazi conspirators and one who assaulted my great-grandmother as she was escaping the Nazis."

Acceding to Jean-Paul's wishes, Zara steps back. She takes a breath, then asks, "What is a religion professor doing killing Nazis?"

Also stepping back, Rachel retorts, "What is the next messiah doing killing anyone?"

A minute of staring at each other. No blinks. Jean-Paul braces himself in a strategic position, as if to throw both of them into wristlocks if needed.

The tense moment is broken by the sweet, angelic, French-accented voice of Magali. "Oh my, it's time for lunch. Let us have some of these amazing sandwiches and pastries I found in this utterly delightful bakery in Mosul. It is so good that the Kurds and Iraqis did not go to war over this lovely city.

There so many wonderful places to eat here."

The four break to share Magali's savory delights and mint tea as they sit on various blocks of granite.

"I am neither the next prophet nor the next messiah," quietly asserts Zara. "The Prophet is the last prophet, and I follow the words of the Prophet."

Rachel says in a satirical manner, "I am very happy to hear you say that. Because if you did not, I would caution you that there are those in these regions who would not take well to a nonbeliever of the Prophet. Especially from someone of your gender."

Giggling, Magali, in her sweet higher octave voice says, "We have a saying in France. *On est tous dans le même bain.* We are all in the same bath. And you two are definitely from the same tub."

Jean-Paul laughs, adding, "I think she means you two are cut from the same cloth."

As the stares persist, Magali again chimes in. "*On ne marie pas les poules avec les renards.* You cannot marry chickens with foxes."

Zara stops and reflects. Sheep and goats. Dogs and cats. Peter and Zara. Her eyes soften as she gazes down, the softer part of herself reemerging. Her eyes well up, and she turns to hide them. The sage Magali takes her away to talk.

"What is wrong?" asks Magali. "You looked so happy with your stud of an old friend."

Shaking her head, Zara laments, "What was I doing back there? Arguing with a woman I just met?"

"Was it jealousy of another woman taking your place as religious debater with my dearest Jean-Paul? Perchance it is Peter? You are simply hurting from breaking up," asserts Magali. "I saw so many novice Sisters who entered the convent after a breakup. You do silly things when you think you have lost love."

"Do you think I might be delusional? I mean, this voice I hear. No one else hears Her. No one I know who is sane has ever heard Her."

"History is full of saints who hear what you hear," replies Magali as she strokes Zara's hair under her pink headscarf. "You have been blessed as they have been. I could only hope that someday I can hear Her as well. You are only suffering what hundreds of saints before you have endured."

"Alexander accused me of using Peter so I could hear the voice. What if that was true? For the life of me, I ask myself why I could not love him back in the way he loved me," Zara says as she cries again.

Magali holds her close so she can cry into her shoulder. As the tears subside, she asks Zara, "When did you last hear Her?"

"In Peter's old room at his mother's house. I found his object fragment, and She talked to me."

"What did she say?"

"That I should tell Peter I love him," says Zara in between sniffles. "We needed to be together to find a second object with which we could find the blue light."

"Blue light? My grandmother told me something incomprehensible about a blue light. That we all go to the blue light. There is so much I want to share with Jean-Paul about what my mother and grandmother told me, but I cannot unless we are married and have children."

"My great-grandmother said the same to me," replies Zara, as she clears a tear from her eye.

"What about Mr. Kurdistan hunk up there?" asks Magali as she squeezes Zara's arm. "He looks like he wants to take care of you."

Her face flushing a rose-red tone and turning slightly away, Zara quietly says, "No. He's just a friend."

"*Seulement un ami*," says the Frenchwoman. "You know how many times I heard that from different Sisters who eventually left to marry? Your eyes say you feel otherwise."

"But the voice said I needed to be with Peter to find the blue light."

"Follow your heart. Blue light or not. Trust your heart. I did," says Magali. "I waited decades for Jean-Paul, and he finally came. Well, with your nudging. And I love teasing him so about lusting for other younger women. He blushes so easily!"

They both smile and hug like the sisters they have become.

☙

"Are you sure your instruments are correct?" laments Rachel. "We have been digging here for more than a week and have found nothing but a wall fragment at the other dig with what looked like graffiti from the time of the fall of the city. Possibly 612 BCE. That is too early for what we want."

Jean-Paul pauses and says, "Give me a brush."

He pulls out a female figurine from the debris. Bare-breasted, bare pubic region. He says, "Ishtar. Nineveh served as the center of Ishtar's worship."

"Ishtar is the oldest goddess written in stone from the Sumerian tablets in 2100 BCE," adds Rachel as she opens up her khaki tunic to cool herself. She looks up at Jean-Paul, who is staring down her top.

"Why, Priest! Are you ogling me? Is the thought of Ishtar and her stories of love, beauty, sex, and desire arousing you?"

"No, no. Forgive me. I had not before noticed the pendant you are wearing," says the humble Jean-Paul, averting his eyes.

She pulls the golden pendant out while buttoning up a little more to save the priest the embarrassment as he turns flush from her comment.

"This is from Ugarit or farther north? Possibly 3000 BCE or 4000 BCE?" asks Jean-Paul as he examines the artifact.

"It has been passed down through generations of my mother's maternal lineage. I thought it similar to other goddess pendants found in Ugarit. Might be 2000 BCE or so."

Jean-Paul unbuttons his tunic, revealing not only the hairs of his chest but a substantial amount of his pectoral definition. Rachel lets out a wolf whistle, which flushes the priest even more.

"I leave you two alone and Jean-Paul is already stripping down to impress his young lady friend," yells Magali. "Perhaps Zara and I should leave you two alone to find an ancient room somewhere."

Very flustered and turning red not only on his face but across his upper chest, Jean-Paul says, "No, no. *Cherie*, this is not what you might think."

Magali comes up to him and rubs his chest. "Then maybe you and I should get an ancient room together."

A snicker by Rachel and Zara, then a glance at each other. The first common act they have taken since they have met.

Magali reaches around the priest's bright red chest and pulls out her medallion hanging around his neck, the one she loaned him in their days in the Philippines. "Were you going to show this shapely lovely lady this? My mark on you. My surrogate wedding band you wear because you want to show the world you are mine. And the Lord's, of course."

More snickers from Rachel and Zara. The latter becomes more somber as she recalls how that medallion broke her coldness toward Peter. For it showed the ancients meant they were destined to meet. Destined to find Xwedê together. And they did. They fulfilled their destiny.

She looks around for Zengo. Could her new destiny lie with someone who is more akin to her. Dogs and dogs.

Rachel asks, "What does this say? It is proto-Greek, isn't it?"

Magali rubs it. "It has been in my family as long as anyone can remember. It says 'She hears the voice of God.' This is Zara. Or her ancient ancestor."

Jean-Paul says, "Rachel, the screening project you took part in, we were trying to find people with genetic encoding of an ancient group emanating from Crimea. We believe the originator of this group was a woman who left a legend. You scored exceptionally high. But from the start of the project, Alexander said Zara would have the genetic profile to beat. She matches the ancient matriarch's DNA profile the best."

Rachel looks at the Kurdish woman over and over again. Could it be true? She is a prophetess? Was her aba intimating that the Mossad or that other agency had just authorized a sanction on her head? Was this the same kind of religious-political assassination that King Hezekiah authorized? Killing the woman prophet to preserve the patriarchal control of religion?

Zara glances away and says, "That mission is over. There is no need for my DNA anymore."

Jean-Paul states, "Do not be so sure, Zara. We found object EM traces all over this area. The second object must have been brought here."

Magali says to Rachel, "Please, may I see what my beloved priest was staring down your shirt for?"

Now it is Rachel's turn to blush as she says, "It was my family's pendant. Please believe me. Jean-Paul has always been the finest of gentlemen with me."

Jean-Paul grimaces, averting his eyes to the left, then the right.

Zara gasps and says, "There is a banana slug on hers, too."

"What slug?" asks Rachel. "What is a banana slug?"

A reengaged Jean-Paul looks closer. "There, along the bottom border," he says, pointing with his finger.

"That's just an imperfection," retorts Rachel.

Jean-Paul shakes his head no. "This is a worm-like creature. See, the same on Magali's medallion."

Zara looks at the feminine statue they dug up. Peter found many of these at the site where they found the first object. She had dismissed them as Neolithic porn, but he said many looked like her body, at which she chastised him for thinking about her naked body. But he was right. And this one is also very close to what her breasts looked like before they mutilated her.

"Jean-Paul, this is like the ones we found at Karahan Tepe," says Zara.

He takes the statue, running his figure along its shape. Magali whispers to him in French, "My dear, wishing that was me, no?"

His fingers now shaking, they stop upon a slightly elongated bump at the statue's feet. He shows it to Magali, who says, "Oh my, there is that worm here too."

Rachel says, "Why would the Assyrians carve a slug on the statue of Ishtar, or Inanna as the Sumerians called her?"

"Inanna?" queries Zara. "Jean-Paul, that's the ancient woman's name Peter uttered when we were being tested by Alexander."

"It was Illyana," says Jean-Paul.

Zara closes her eyes and remembers the bonding sessions she and Peter had when they sat with the object. There was a woman being attacked by the giants. Her name was Illyana as well.

With a puzzled face, Rachel asks, "Are you trying to tell me the goddess Inanna is mixed up with this great matriarch myth you two have been chasing?"

"I think Illyana is related to the great matriarch," replies Zara.

"The worship of Inanna is a precursor to the worship of Asherah in the Levant," says Rachel. "Are you telling me you are talking with Asherah?"

Zara shakes her head. "I do not know. I believe she is Xwedê. But I am getting so confused. Maybe she is just my torn imagination. Maybe Jean-Paul and Peter have just been humoring me. Maybe everyone is humoring me."

While Magali takes Zara for another little walk, Rachel spies something. She takes the brushes and quickly walks thirty paces away. She brushes at a grey area on the wall of their dig, higher up than the area where they found the Ishtar statue, suggesting a later date in the palace grounds.

She waves Jean-Paul to come over, and the two of them gently extract several large clay fragments. As they lay them out, she asks, "700 BCE Akkadian? Another find from the time of King Sennacherib?"

He pulls out a black device from his sack and scans the clay, gently placing dust particles into a chamber. He shakes his head. "No, much older."

Rachel screams as she reads the tablets, "Jean-Paul. This is Genesis. From a date far older than the oldest versions of the Torah by the Priestly source. We think they wrote sections of Genesis in the sixth century BCE. Are you saying these tablets predate the Elohists, who wrote sections of the Torah in the eighth century BCE and possibly in the late ninth century BCE?"

"Based on this MoxWorld carbon-oxygen dating field kit, these could come from 950 to 1000 BCE. A hundred years before the Elohists," states the priest.

Rachel becomes giddy as a schoolgirl. A far cry from the woman who compared number of kills with Zara only moments earlier. "Jean-Paul, there's Ilu, the Akkadian word for God, for Elohim, for Yahweh. And there next to it is Ašratu, the Akkadian word for Asherah. She is there when Ilu is talking with…isn't that the Akkadian word for Abraham? Oh, what a time for me to get my Akkadian and Sumerian mixed up."

The good priest takes her arm and strokes it. "Calm down, Rachel. We have years to decode this correctly and put it into the right context."

"But Jean-Paul," she exclaims, "this is the oldest proof that Genesis included Asherah with Yahweh. Proof that the Priestly authors and the Yahweh authors rewrote the early Torah to exclude her."

"Jean-Paul, let go of that young woman's arm," asserts Magali. "Really, I walk away for two minutes, and what?"

The good priest drops the Israeli professor's arm and turns red again. Magali comes up to him and kisses his cheek. "I love teasing you so much. You blush so fast with me. I love your blush."

She turns to the clay tablet fragments and asks, "So, what is this new commotion about?"

Rachel, still giddy, says, "Here, Ašratu is talking with Abraham's wife. There is a sacred stone that she insists they take with them as they travel south."

Turning to Jean-Paul, Rachel asks, "Is this Zara's stone? Does this mean Abraham took the stone with them to Israel?"

Before the priest can answer, a man's voice cries out in Kurdish. Zara says, "Zengo is warning us three men are charging toward our location."

They look up out of the dig and spy three black-clad men twenty paces away. Zara says to Jean-Paul, "These are the same outfits of the assassins who tried to kill you at Harran." She grabs a shovel to defend themselves.

Zengo tackles one assassin, only to have his shoulder struck. He cries out in excruciating pain. Zara jumps out of the pit and clobbers another assassin's face, but is knocked down by the third assassin. Down on the ground, she is ready to fight from that position with her feet, but Zengo staggers over, positioning himself between her and the assassins.

Six loud pops in rapid succession ring out. Zara scans around. The assassins are all on the ground, screaming and holding their knees. Jean-Paul emerges from the excavation pit, his arms around Rachel, who stands in combat-shooting pose with a compact Jericho 941 in her hands, which are covered by the priest's hands. Forty-caliber rounds, Zara estimates. A size that should make it impossible for any surgeon to save those assassins' knees.

Zengo helps Zara get up with his good arm. Before she or he knows it, she kisses his cheek and then goes to the assassins. She crushes the hands of one of them with her foot, breaking the bones as she searches for evidence of who they work for. NiQihs devices.

The MoxWorld Security team arrives late, distracted by a diversionary intrusion. Zengo is on his MoxWrap talking with New Kurdistan national police, who are minutes away.

As the Kurdish national police escort away the assassins, Zara asks Rachel what she knows about these assassins.

Wiping gunpowder residue off her hands, Rachel replies, "How would I know?"

Zara says, "Cut the act. Any Israeli national with a compact Jericho who has executed Nazis must be Mossad-trained."

Arms akimbo, Rachel retorts, "You are like the rest of the world and stereotype us Israelis. Because my father sent me to the target range once a week since I was eleven does not mean I am an Israeli spy. I lived in a world where being invaded by Muslim countries or threatened by Islamic terrorists was a daily reality."

Zara approaches her, towering over her, and Rachel takes a classic Krav Maga stance. Zara holds her hand out, which Rachel cautiously takes. "Thank you for having that gun readily available."

Rachel reaches out to shake. "Friends?"

Zara glances down, shakes Rachel's hand, and then smiles, saying, "Of course."

Taking a deep breath to calm down the adrenaline rush, Zara tends to her old friend, who is cringing on the ground, holding that bad shoulder.

"You dislocated it again," says Zara, completing her triage. And before Zengo can say no, she resets it.

Howling in pain, the type of scream that Zara knows all too well, Zengo holds Zara tight with his uninjured arm in a series of squeezes as the pain throbs from his other shoulder.

"Oh, come on now, do not be such a baby about it," whispers Zara.

Whispering back, Zengo says, "Now I remember. You used to love tying my wrists up and inflicting a certain sensuous pain."

Hitting his other shoulder, she sits back and whispers, "As I recall it, you started that by tying my wrists up. Not the other way around."

Staring at her wrists and remembering the red marks, the burn marks, she says, "This is a subject we are not to talk about again. I will never be tied up again. By anyone. I will kill them first."

Back in the pit, Magali stares at the clay tablet fragments with the line between her lips curling up as high as the tip of her nose. She has her arm intertwined with the arm of her favorite Jesuit. "You know, my dear, you have what we came here for now. We have evidence even our Lord was allowed to be married. We can visit your friend, the Holy Pontiff, who now has the proof source for the Cardinals' Council on Marriage to ratify the stalled proposal allowing priests to marry."

Before they can kiss to seal the deal, Zara cries out, "No, it cannot be possible." She taps at her MoxWrap. "No, Xwedê. Please not him. Not him."

CHAPTER 24

The light shines in the darkness but the darkness has not understood it.

John 1:5, New Testament

MoxWorld Resort, Xian, China
7:30 p.m. GMT+8, February 3, 2023

"Oh, Zara will not like this," exclaims Mei, dressed only in a robe after her post-dinner shower. Sitting with Peter in the luxurious queen bed, she taps away on her MoxWrap.

Peter is massaging her feet, which have taken an ungodly beating over the past weeks. They had finally discovered a new series of antechambers outside the sealed tomb of the first emperor, where they viewed firsthand the engravings that spoke of the Goddess Jiang.

Unlike her normally discreet self, Mei berated her excavation lead, Jia, for not finding what they needed faster. The crinkles on her face grew so deep no amount of foundation or anti-aging cream could hide the turmoil within Mei. She could only bemoan each night how many fewer days remained until she could no longer enter the cavern of the blue light.

Yes, they had found many other interesting wall carvings. All photographed by Jia and express-mailed to Jean-Paul for further analysis. And each night they returned, playing the married couple for Ming. And maybe for each other.

In response to Mei's comment, Peter inquires, "What won't Zara like? The list of what she doesn't like is already quite long."

With her disarming smile and raised eyebrows, Mei responds in typical Mei fashion. "Oh, that's a Zara thing. Nothing we two should be bothered with. That is until she asks us to be bothered." She taps her MoxWrap, forwarding whatever she was examining onward.

As her finger scrolls down her MoxWrap, she lets out a yelp. "No. No means no. What is it with you guys? I told him no. Not yet. Patience. Don't threaten me," she says. The multitudes of mirrors that surround their bed mercilessly show the furrows and creases which have taken their toll on her delicate visage.

His fingers give one last pressure point push into her sole and then the pains across her face soothe. "Charm me," she says, "like you do. That's what he should do."

"Who?" asks Peter, using the warmth of his palms as he rubs her cheek muscles. Finally, the lips' edges lift, and her natural smoothness returns.

"The president of China," she replies. "But I need not bother you with affairs of this country."

His forehead against hers, his nose perched atop hers, his fingers upon that place behind her neck, he says, "Bother me. Isn't that what husbands are for? Listening intently to their wives?"

Finally, a sparkle emanates from her smile as she pecks his lips. "You have been the ideal husband. Or so says my mother."

With a tug on both of her smoothened cheeks, he says, "Now that you're your regular glowing self again, tell your dear husband about what ails you. Something's been haunting you. Possibly many things."

Turning away with a downward glance, pursing her lips, she lets out a long breath through her nose. She bites her lower lip and says, "The president of China is going to revoke our permit to further excavate the antechambers of the first emperor's tomb. Another party has promised him they will obtain the second black object that everyone is searching for. Alexander refuses to let me share what I know so far other than to Admiral Zheng. He's legendary for searching for the comet fragments. I had hoped to use that piece of China's illustrious history to keep our access to the tomb, as the president would want more advice from me, which would allow them to find the comet remnants before the Americans."

Peter clasps his fingers around his mouth, glances down, and says, "According to my pappy's diary, another black object will be required to prevent another great war. With the world powers on edge, we must find both the other black object and this cavern of blue light. We only have a little more than four weeks left before baby comes."

He turns to her hand on his crotch. "And that's why you must have been trying so hard to access my dreams. I wish I could remember my dreams."

Holding her feet up, she points down. "Finish what you were doing down there, and we'll try to access your dreams again."

As he reaches down for her wiggling toes, he says, "Are you sure that's all that's bothering you? Nothing else? Nothing about us?"

Her feet in his lap, she presses into his belly. "Rub me, husband. And there'll be nothing else that I'll have in mind."

She wiggles her toes as Peter's fingers dig into the ball of her foot. "Oh, Peter. You are such a magician. I get orgasms from my feet as well as all the other places you touch me." Her eyes close as she takes a deep inhale, followed by an exasperated breath out as her head drops.

Furrowing his brow, he purses his lips and shakes his head in contemplation. The question lingers in the air—have all of her orgasms been real, or fake? A man can never truly know, but according to his mother, a good man knows when their partner is not fully present in bed, their thoughts intertwined with someone else's soul. But who?

Mei leans forward on their bed and pats his hands. "The way you make me scream all night long makes my mother extremely pleased. You are fulfilling her expectation of a good husband." She pulls him close to her, opening her robe just enough to bare her upper chest, and kisses him, adding, "And my expectations of my lover."

Gently pulling back from her kiss, Peter gazes at his crotch. "Not that I don't love being with you, but…"

Pulling back at his puzzled face, she pets his thigh and asks, "But what?

You're feeling guilty about not having the sex you did with her, aren't you?"

He shakes his head with a dour face. "No. We never had sex. What they did to her, what horrible things they did—she can't have sex ever again."

A light rub of her hand by the area he is so concerned about, and she gets up, saying, "Don't be so sure about that. The same radiation from that first object affecting you now also exposed her. Why did you finally feel compelled to bed with me? Because I said Michaela wanted you to? Or something deeper changing in you?"

Scratching his head, Peter asks, "Are you sure I can't call Michaela? I'd feel a whole lot better if I heard from her that she's safe in Shanghai. With impending war, an American in China could be accused of being a spy. The police could take her."

A pat on his head and Mei stands up. Facing away from him, her eyes glance down, hidden from his view. She pulls her long, silky black hair into a loose ponytail, turns and says, "Didn't she text you she's involved in a highly secret and very vital design project? If you bother her, it might derail their progress."

"Even so, I'm her big brother. I'll always worry about her."

Another pause, and then she stands, grabbing her next-to-nothing nightie with metallic designs embedded around the neckline and heads to the three-room luxury bathroom the size of some people's studio apartments. She says, "Your sister is like you. She's committed to the mission at hand. Whatever it takes. If you love someone, you'll do anything for them. At least, that is what my mother said the Goddess Jiang taught. I'll be a few moments, as my nightly facial regiment awaits."

A few cat-stretches and Peter pops up the MoxMedia Evening News—China edition. The immaculately wardrobed Rhonda is on, dressed in another metallic design blouse compliments of Peter's sister. After discussing the ongoing conflict in the Ukraine, video footage shows an American destroyer on fire. Chinese marines are waving victory signs from nearby salvage vessels. Rhonda annotates China's president declaring victory over the imperialist Americans, who attempted to steal Chinese property from the floor of the South China Sea. Then, the US president is shown addressing

Congress. He calls for a declaration of war. Not a trade war. A shooting war, unless China both returns the US found material and pays reparations for destroying US property.

A deep inhale, and Peter switches off the news. Mei was not kidding about her concerns. China is not the best place for anyone to be at this moment, speaking of being irradiated. Nuclear bombs would certainly hurt more than being next to the black object. But that is not what is blocking him and Mei from bonding like he and Zara had done. From accessing the ancient dreams like Zara had done.

Pursing his lips, he bobs his head back and forth, staring into nothingness. His fingers hover over his MoxWrap, but hesitate. How can one little call disturb her work? He knows her. She's as strong and steady as Mom. As Zara, for that matter.

As discrete, stifled moans come from behind the bathroom door, his fingers hover over the call button and then curl back. Thrice again this happens as his shoulders squeeze together, as if he were Atlas holding up the world.

And finally, with a determined stroke, he calls, and she pops up. Still wrapping a burgundy towel around her lithe body, with a matching towel around her hair, she says, "Why, big bro. Imagine you calling now."

"Did I interrupt anything? I'm sorry, I can call back," says her brother, noting the rose glow on her upper chest below her neck. "I don't want to interfere with your important project."

"No, no one so important. When I saw it was you, I told them I would call back. You're my big brother. If you need to talk, it's the very least a little sister can do to take the call."

As she dries her hair, a more relaxed Peter says, "I didn't know you were an evening shower person. You always fought me for the shower every morning."

"And I beat you most every time, sleepyhead," admonishes his grinning sister.

"The little sister taking advantage of her dream-afflicted brother. You must be happy now that Ma isn't pressuring you anymore to make little Gollingers, now that big brother is a father," says Peter, intently watching his little sis.

Glancing down, Michaela stops drying her hair, taking the towel into her hands as she squeezes the fluffy fabric. "I'm thrilled, Peter. For Mei…and for you."

"What's wrong, sis? Terrified of all those diaper changes you'll get to do when you're babysitting your niece or nephew?" asks Peter. ""'Auntie Michaela. Why do my diapers have this metallic design wrapping?'"

Her lips indecisive between a downward pout and a half side scrunch, Michaela retorts, "Come on, Peter. You know my designs will work only with the post-adolescent physiology. Your big, bad, boastful buddy has phase two in the waiting, after the world continues to fall in love with Mei and my fashion designs. We have nearly ten percent market penetration into the first world's eighteen-plus female population."

Finger wagging, Peter admonishes, "Michaela, I know you too well. You're not alone there, are you?"

"Of course I'm alone here," she says as she pans around the bathroom into the adjoining bedroom.

"You get to have a luxurious king bed," replies Peter. "And I am snuggled cozily with Mei in this teeny queen bed."

Another grimace from Michaela.

"You're very much in love, aren't you?" asks Peter.

Glancing aside as she brushes her hair, she replies, "I don't know what you mean. I'm alone here, getting ready to read another MoxRead book."

Silence as Peter stares her down. But no joy, as she refuses to engage his eyes as he says, "I can only imagine how difficult this must be for you. It is for Mei. And whatever it is between you two, it is blocking Mei's ability to access my dreams."

Sniffles. A blow of the nose. And Michaela mumbles, "If she has to get more intense with you in that way…I am glad it will be with you."

Then he says, holding up his right forearm, "Sis, you know I'll always be there for you. When you're ready to talk more, I'm your shining knight who gets his arm broken when he defends your honor from nasty boys."

"I know. You're the best brother a girl could have," she replies as the drops emerge at the edges of her eyes.

Lips forming a pointed pout as the drops now wiggle their way down her cheek, she says through a congested throat, "Please, Peter. Do whatever she asks of you. I know you will. Do that for me. Please."

"You know I will. I love you, sis."

She sniffs and says, "I gotta go, bro. We'll talk more tomorrow. I love you. Bye."

Sympathy tears beg to be birthed from his eyes as Peter nods. As the emergent muffled sounds of Mei's shower moans permeate through the door, Peter's mind plots. For he is an exceptional editor. Well, not as perverse as the MoxRead editor that rewrote his first novel into a triple X exposé. He gets it. What that woman in the nothing skirt at the book signing said to him about the backdoor to finding the truth. The same as Pappy's ancient parchment translation: "Behind the backdoor lies the truth".

He has learned Mei's shower sequence to the second. And as she is drying off behind the closed bathroom door, Peter strips into his best version of the newlywed, skin-only nothingness. With time running out, he desperately needs her to drop her façade. He needs to scare her into showing her true feelings. And thus, Mei opens the door to a totally buff Peter, who pulls off the top of her robe, taking her into his arms with a wet and amorous lip-to-lip massage.

She pulls back and cries, "Peter, what has gotten into you?"

Turning her around, he shuffles her back-first toward the highly intimate, tiny bed. "I had a call with Michaela. I asked for her advice about what turns you on the most. I know women tell each other things they won't tell guys. I think what she told me is that we need to roughen up our passions, intensify it to get the five-sense algorithm to show you want you want to see. Zara is so discrete and private. Of course, she wouldn't have told you that what really drove our ability to vision the ancient matriarchs was a little vigorous backdoor action."

Mouth agape, her hands clutching the bottom of her robe as tightly as possible, her trembling legs back up into their minuscule bed. She is trapped. As she looks side to side for somewhere to go, she pushes back on his chest, trying to move away from his angry red, rock-hard member wanting to go where no man has gone before.

Peter stares into her eyes. The same terror as Michaela's that afternoon

Peter saved her from those boys who had her pants off. That afternoon his arm fractured while saving her. He backs off, pulling her lower robe open, exposing her lower body as his hands grab well up her inner thighs to the edges of her derriere.

She steps up to his chest and strokes it. "Peter, I don't know what she told you, but we should continue the normal five-sense algorithm and have our intimacies that way."

Carefully blocking any avenue to doors unwanted, but opening the top of her robe instead, Mei sits both of them down on their love nest and brings his head into her neck. Smell me. Then his lips to her lips. Taste me. His ear to her bare breast. Hear me. His face between her breasts. See me. And before she can finish the fifth sense, touch me.

Before she can finish the rest of the five-sense algorithm, Peter grabs her hand, bringing it straight to his engorged crotch. "You need to let me in somewhere where Zara did." He pushes her down onto their once love nest, now the centerpiece of their den of iniquity, with no chance of her covering doors that should not be opened.

Not the gentleness of the Peter she's known so far. But to her relief, he does not put her into a compromising position. Only that his head is clearly over hers. Eye to eye. His fingers move to feel her carotid artery.

"Why, Peter," she says, shivering. "What has come over you? The most gentle man I've ever been with."

Her eyes said it all. Not panicked. Not scared. Her eyes had become like Michaela's. Sad. Mournfully missing someone. Staring into her eyes, not the so confident, not so composed Mei, he has his answer to what the "truth" is. A frown passes over Peter's visage, then a smile. "You love her, don't you?"

"Who, my dear? I love you."

"I know you do. And I love you too," he says, letting her go. "My sister-in-law."

As she sits up, he helps her cover herself, and then arranges the bedsheets to better cover himself. She stares into the opposite wall mirror, behind which her mother sits. Likely with ear to the wall. "You don't know how much my family would reject me if I did not have a husband."

"I love my sister too," says Peter. "I get it. You two are essentially married with vows and everything. I'll make all the noises you need to make your mother think that you are a good wife."

"Thank you," says Mei as her muscles release the tension built up over their struggle. "I have not been honest with you. Why would you do this for me?"

"Because we both love my sister."

Into the side of her robe she cries and mumbles, "I've tried, Peter. Every night I've tried. It's not that you aren't a wonderfully compassionate lover, but I feel like I'm cheating on Michaela."

He wraps his arm around her and gives the family-guy hug. "I hope you know how hard this has been for me. No sex for a year and a half since Sarah, except for that one moment you and I had in Luxembourg performing what I had thought was fake sex in front of Alexander and company. Every cell in my body wants you in that visceral way, but I too would feel that you would be cheating on my sister. Maybe it's all for the better. I can go back to Zara and plead. By the way, we certainly never had sex. And not back there for sure."

With a sign of relief, she hugs him back. "I'm so sorry for you. She's gone back to her boyfriend of her teen years. From what she texted me, she sounds smitten again."

"I wish the best for her," laments Peter as he slumps.

Clasping her robe, Mei puts her arms around his back, pulls tightly, and pats. "You are the most wonderful man I have ever met. Your sister is so lucky to have you as her brother."

Patting Mei's back as well, Peter says into her ear, "Speaking of Michaela, answer her messages. She's likely frantic after my call with her. Tell her I know, and I won't talk to Ma until she does."

As Mei taps her MoxWrap, at first frantically and then more softly with her smile returning, Peter stands near the mirrored wall, putting his ear against it to listen for Mei's mother. He yells, "Mei! What are you trying to do to me? Do you want another baby that bad? Easy on my poor…"

Mei stifles her giggle as she texts Michaela.

"I bet she'll like that one as much as you did," whispers Peter.

Sitting back with Mei, he jests, "Ma will have to get over you having slept with both her children."

She lightly slaps his thigh. "She will rejoice that I carry a Gollinger baby. Her grandchild."

He lightly pets her baby bump. "And Alexander. He must be happy."

"He is nervous. We need to find out where that second object is before China and the US start nuking each other. And by doing so, we will find out how to get where he is burning to get to. And we have to do this before I give birth, or so he says. For the life of me, I don't know why my pregnancy is so important to his end goal. My mother says she knows but won't tell me until you make me have the right dream."

Peter gives her a light peck on the cheek as he continues rubbing her belly. "I will be a good father for our child. Or is that uncle? And you can rub me any way you want to get access to the right dream."

"You, my dear, are the perfect Chinese parent. You respect honor, duty, and family," says Mei, pecking his cheek back.

She scratches his head as she says, "I just cannot figure out why the five-sense algorithm didn't get you to access your dreams. I've done my best to end each session with full and complete, passionate sex, as the legend says. The answer we seek must be buried much deeper in the genetic encoding in your head."

Fingers to his temples, he replies, "I tried to tell you that Zara and I saw what we did through a different algorithm. It has nothing to do with sex. I think Alexander made that up for whatever perversities turn him on."

Mei smiles again. Not the disarming smile. More of a flat line with teeny uplifts at the ends. She turns to him and uncovers her breasts. "Okay, we do it your way."

Peter wraps her robe over her bared chest, saying, "It's about connection. A different type of intimacy."

He wet-kisses her forehead and rubs his saliva gently in circles. He asks her to do the same back to him. He runs his two index fingers along her lips, pushing up her smile, and then plays with her tongue. Sufficiently wetted, he rubs her temples and asks her to do the same to him. Eyes closed, they touch in a way she has never known.

She brings his head to hers and open-mouth kisses. Tongue on tongue. He pulls back, putting her fingers on his neck bump and his on hers. He whispers for her to focus on his breath and his on hers.

She mumbles, "It's beautiful. It is peace. It is harmony. It's a little fuzzy."

He whispers back, "Be patient, my beautiful flower, Mei. Although we are near matched perfectly, give it time."

After what seems like eternity floating in a place neither on Earth nor in heaven, there appears a young woman. Not Asian. Not quite Caucasian. Camels appear, walking in a line. Then men appear with more Caucasoid features.

The woman, perhaps no more than a teen, rides on the back of a camel while the men walk beside. She comes up to a man pounding on a camel that pulls a sled, atop which lies a black object. She scolds the man for mistreating the camel and says to be careful the animal does not bolt as all their futures depend on that cargo.

Peter whispers, "Pull back from this view."

As if they had become eagles, they see the landscape. Mountains with white caps. The caravan is off the silk road, proceeding into the mountains.

Peter's tongue dancing with hers, all the while they stroke each other's special bump.

View down again, they are with the woman who has descended from her camel. Like Mei, she is with child. The master of the man she scolded argues with her, saying she carries a bastard child and has no noble right to order his men around. Arms akimbo, eyes narrowed, nose scrunched, she asserts that whether or not her child's father is known, he will be important to the well-being of all.

The men laugh, saying she is but a tramp they tolerate, one who slept with a stranger for the right price. She retorts she stepped into a giant's footstep, that of their Divine Supreme himself. She was then and is still a virgin. And she now bears a child who may become a god.

They laugh again, this time slapping each other's backs. As they do, she kneels in prayer next to the black object. Their laugher subsides as she appears to be talking to herself. Yes, I believe in you. I believe in the child you have placed in me. A son? I understand. From abundance comes peace.

Her prayer is interrupted by the men fleeing. Screaming, the giants are on the horizon. As well as such a lithe person could do, this young woman tries to hurry along the confused camel, dragging the object further into the mountains, saying they must find a sacred cave.

At the mouth of a cave, the giants catch her and strike her camel dead. The leader dismounts, towering nearly twice her height. She cranes her neck to regard his face and spots the bull's head hanging from a chain around his neck.

He lifts her so her little feet are atop his monstrous feet. A laugh that echoes through the mountain. He says that she ran away. She is his property. And his child is not hers to run with.

Stomping on his feet, she asserts her body is not his to command. She is no one's property. And her child is hers, not his or anyone else's.

He snorts, shoving his bulging loincloth into her face, saying she enjoyed him as all women have.

She spits at that piece of cloth, saying that happened only in his dreams. The one true God has blessed her with a child.

Before the giant can grab her again to teach her the lesson that giants of the north mercilessly impose on human women, she dives into a prostrate position next to the object, praying.

The skies darken. The sun is removed from the heavens. And the booming sounds of thunder force the giants to cover their ears. A blinding light strikes one giant down. Then another. The leader cries out for all to leave this witch and flee.

As the rains fall, the young woman, still in prayer, says I understand. I will make the lands moist and fertile. My son will introduce the wisdom of my ancestors. How to grow food.

Peter taps on Mei's face as she comes out of the haze, back on top of their love nest. She opens up her robe to ventilate her flush chest as she pants. She gasps, "That was so much better than sex."

Before Peter can hug her, someone is banging on the door. Mei says to

Peter to put a robe on and find a weapon. As Peter covers himself, he arms himself with a wooden chair.

But the voice at the door is all too familiar, and as Mei opens it, Ming rushes in, barely covered in a robe, making a beeline straight for Peter. She points at his crotch, screaming something in Shanghainese as she strips open her robe.

Waving her arms around, Mei yells at her mother in a tone unbecoming of a daughter, repeating the words the Goddess Jiang-Yuan said many times. Ming closes up her robe and pats Peter on the head, saying something like "good husband" in Mandarin.

Putting the chair back in place, Peter asks, "What was that all about? I thought for sure your father was breaking down our door to avenge your family's honor by killing me."

"That's what we have been fighting about for days," says Mei. "She threatened she would do the proper five sense algorithm on you if I kept failing. That I was a worthless daughter for not being able to fulfill what my husband needed."

Mei comes to Peter, hand out to pull him up, and then lightly kisses him. "Just as your sister said you would, you came to my rescue."

Back eye to eye with Mei, he asks, "What did I do?"

"You made me have the Goddess Jiang vision," she replies as she lightly kisses his lips again. "You made me a woman tonight. In my family's eyes, in my mother's eyes, I have become a real woman of the family line coming from Jiang-Yuan."

Ming rises and hugs the two of them, compressing her daughter and son-in-law intimately together. She pats Peter's head and makes a slight bow to him before she leaves their room.

They both sit down again at the edge of their love nest bed as Peter says, "Run this by me again. The Goddess Jiang. Vision. And becoming a woman."

Mei scruffs his hair and pats his knee. "In my family's oral tradition, a girl becomes a woman the day her husband mates with her in such a way that the Goddess Jiang appears in front of her."

"That was the goddess we saw?" asks Peter. "How do you know?"

"They say she came from the west. She was not of Chinese blood. Some say she became the wife of the mythical Di Ku, the first king of the Shu Dynasty. Some think the Shus existed around 2000 BCE near the Qin Ling mountains north of Chengdu, the capital of Szechuan Province. But my research suggests she came much earlier into the Neolithic Dadiwan culture in the 5800 to 5400 BCE period. They inhabited lands in Gansu Province. This is one of the earliest sites showing domesticated animals and agriculture. Her son of a virgin birth became the legendary founder of agriculture in China."

"So where does that leave us?" asks Peter.

"It leaves us with a guide to where we need to search," answers Mei. "The mountainous peak in the vision is the Bogoda near the capital of Xinjiang Uyghur Province, Urumqi. The Uyghur are a Turkish group. That would make sense, as the ancient matriarch came from Anatolia, formerly in Turkey."

Peter runs his finger along her baby bump. "When I said, 'Where does that leave us?' I meant us. And Michaela."

She leans her head on his shoulder with her hand upon his atop her bigger bump. "It is too much for me to keep asking you to play my husband. But for now, I must ask that which is too much to ask." She kisses his cheek. "If I were to have a husband, you would be the best husband I could ever have."

He kisses her cheek back and spies the many messages awaiting her on her MoxWrap. "I will be your husband as long as you need me to. As long as Michaela needs me to. Speaking of her, she must be having a conniption waiting for you to respond to her pings."

She taps her MoxWrap and says, "No. No. I can't."

"Can't what?" asks Peter. "I will be by your side, no matter what."

"No. No. I just can't," she cries.

CHAPTER 25

Better never to have met you in my dream than to wake
and reach for hands that are not there.
—Otomo No Yakamochi, eighth-century Japanese poet

Karahan Tepe, Ancient Anatolia
9525 BCE

Three cycles have passed since she first heard the voice by herself. She had immediately cornered Nirra, demanding to know why he'd never told her he knew her daughters were alive. For a giant to cower when a human woman is on a rampage is a testament to the fury that a good mother will emote.

In his defense, he said he had heard rumors but could not verify them without leaving. More importantly, the journey to find them would likely have led to her kidnapping and violation by the marauding giants' raiding parties. He could not bear that happening to her. Her wrath tempered a bit, and she told him that was not for him to decide but hers, as it was her life, her body, and more importantly, her daughters.

Acting more like a scolded little boy than a monstrous, towering behemoth, Nirra begged her to allow him time to develop a plan to find and travel to her daughters. In the meantime, they owed the village they had created enough time to ensure they would be safe when they left.

What had started as several block homes adjoined is now a large complex of hundreds. Their spiritual leader, Tallia, has become the great mother goddess to the newcomers. More statuettes of her bare-breasted with her foxes turned into lions are made and traded with other villages. Her compromise to the voice is that she will act as the earth goddess, such that those believers would join in the community—one of gender equality. The result of her not bending to their wishes meant the opposite would happen—returning to faiths that promoted gender inequality and the inevitable strife.

As Nirra came back from scouting expeditions, he would tell her of the other towns where his former fellow giants ruled. Women enslaved to make children to tend to the fields. Without a strong central mother goddess, the non-giants can only be enslaved and women denigrated into baby making. Tallia has not forgiven her husband for hiding what he knew, but she tolerates him in his desire to hide his violative giant past.

Each day she prays five to six times. Each day, she practices the arts that her Aunt Ki taught her. Arrows, spears, and how to puncture the thick hide of a leviathan rudely. Until one day, she packs arrows and spears.

Nirra barely catches her before she disappears into the forests without him. Mother goddess she cannot be any longer when her daughters need her, she says. Nirra implores her to stay in their town for the sake of her life. She says she has waited three years since the voice spoke. She waits no longer.

What else can a giant do when a woman of such strength talks? Pack your bags and go with her.

Twenty days later, Tallia is near defeat. Her sandals ragged and torn. Her feet mostly blistered. She was kidnapped by a giant raiding party, only to be saved by a childhood giant friend of Nirra who told the other giants that she was a black witch. Violating her would make their most treasured member fall off. After she was safely ensconced in a cave to recover, Nirra caught up with the raiding party and thanked his friend, who in return warned Nirra that he had changed too much ever to come back to the giants.

Several days of rest and sandal cobbling and the indomitable Tallia starts out again. It takes more than a moon cycle of constantly hiding from reindeer giant marauding parties for Tallia to recognize the terrain.

She and her mother, Sarpani, and her Aunt Zirbani had visited villages around the great temple that her Aunt Ki and Uncle An had built for the great matriarch grandmother Nanshe. She and Nirra now cross near many of those villages. But as they furtively peek into some, all they see are the slave laborer human men and the sex slave human women. The reindeer warrior giants who came to destroy Nanshe's temple have destroyed humankind all around. Tallia muffles her cries as she ponders what must have happened to her daughters.

Having heard the old great temple of Nanshe has become the epicenter of the ungodly giants and their abominable denigrations of humans, they make a wide arc away from that site toward where fleeing humans said there existed a place that no giant dares go. Lightning will strike them dead. Tallia assures Nirra that she would not let lightning strike him. He scoffs, saying even she is not that powerful. But he will die if needed to get her to her daughters. And Nirra courageously takes her where no giant will go.

On a mountain range days across a large valley from the old temple lies a familiar sight. Large T pillars rise from the ground like the ones her Aunt Ki designed at the old temple, the site of the carnage of her family, the place of her first husband's death. Tallia falls to her knees in tears, for she is nearing home, or what looks like her old home.

She implores Nirra not to go further toward the temple. Not out of fear of the lightning strikes, but out of fear for what his presence will do to scatter the worshippers at this pristine temple. Kissing him up on her tippy toes with his knees bent down, she promises that nothing will undo her love for him. That the past several sun cycles have been some of the best of her life due to him. With tears, they part.

Fifteen cycles of the sun have passed since that tragic day at the First Temple. A hundred giants led by a giant named Arnada, who had been left for dead by Aunt Ki on the other side of the big lake, came for revenge. At his side, Nirra and his mother. Together, they slaughtered the worshippers of the temple and took select women as sex slaves. Tallia knew not if any of her relatives had survived, only that Aunt Ki died defending Tallia's daughter Illyana.

As she approaches the new temple, she marvels at the two T-shaped pillars dominating the center of the structure, rising up to the height of two tall men. A circular enclosure of smaller pillars and a stone wall form the edges of the area of worship. A few other smaller enclosures lie nearby.

As prescribed by her grandfather Orzu's oral traditions, the top of the T pillars point in the direction of the tail of the bird star. The direction of the land of the giants. The direction they are to flee from if attacked, which is how her family ended up on this side of the big black lake.

But what stops her dead in her stride is the sight of the most sacred of the sacred objects of worship. The black stone of the great matriarch Nanshe sits in the center of a main enclosure. Atop the black object, a woman in a red hooded robe stands addressing the worshippers. Could that be…? Tallia has been gone for so long she rubs her eyes to get a better look.

Dressed in a drab, olive-green cloak with a black headscarf, Tallia slowly approaches the black object. The red-robed woman stops her speech as all eyes turn to the stranger approaching the holy site.

A man in a beige robe helps the woman down off the black object as she stares at Tallia. A moment passes and the woman sprints toward Tallia. Mama. Mama. You are still alive.

The biggest hug a daughter could give her mother and Tallia is reunited with her daughter Illyana, now the priestess of the Second Temple. As if no one else existed, as if no place else existed, Illyana takes her mother straight to the black object. Tallia drops to her knees and cries. With her daughter and granddaughters, they pray at the object. The man in the beige robe quietly kneels next to Illyana and prays with them. The worshippers all take the cue and pray as well.

Joy. It is being with your family in sight of the object of your god. Or so thinks Tallia as she rises from her prayer. Taking her hand, Illyana leads her straight to a round hut several minutes away as she babbles about the pain and agony, wondering if all her family had died at the First Temple.

Out from the hut run three adorable children. Two girls and one boy. All crying out, Mama. Tallia hugs her grandchildren and listens to their babble about the little disagreements they have had while Mama led prayer.

Joy. It is knowing your child has raised a fabulous family themselves. Or so thinks Tallia as she delicately inquisites these lovely little ones as to what they have learned about their family, their traditions, and the god of Nanshe as they twirl about her chasing each other. For the mission of grandmother is to ensure the afflicted children know of the traditions, the voice, and to be ready to one day marry another afflicted person and raise a family. It is what Nanshe did with her.

Tallia and her daughter catch up while the children go to the huts next door to play. Illyana cries as she breaks the news that Tallia's mother, Sarpani, died only a few moon cycles ago. Sarpani would have wanted to see her daughter Tallia before her death. But she led a good life here helping the spiritual development of these villagers.

That man in beige has waited in the distance for all this time, making Tallia think about her poor Nirra alone and emotionally isolated somewhere away from the temple. Illyana waves the man over, and he looks into Tallia's eyes, asking if she remembers him.

Tallia peers into his eyes, regards the lines and shape of his face, then licks her fingers and rubs his temple. He is one of the afflicted. She says, you are a grandson of my Aunt Zirbani. Her eyes gaze down as the visions of the destruction of the First Temple replay with all the screaming and agony suffered by the innocent. She says, you were to be wed to my daughter. Tallia hugs him. For he is Nargel, and she is so happy he too survived the carnage. She says, you have beautiful children. He shakes his head, to which Illyana says, we will talk later.

The village throws a wonderful celebration feast in honor of her return. Tallia marvels at how well her daughter and mother have encultured a world of faith to Nanshe's god. But she keeps within her disdain for the elements of patriarchy that remain. The gender equality she and Nirra have created in their village stands unique. Thinking about Nirra, she excuses herself, taking some food with her. Sneaking out of the village, she finds her oversized loved one still hiding, watching the bonfires of the feast. She reminds him to know how much she loves him.

Over the next days, Tallia learns to be a mother again, as Illyana slowly lets loose her pains. Tallia's grandchildren were sired by Domzi, another grandson of Zirbani. In fact, that tragic day at the First Temple, Illyana was to choose a husband between Nargel and Domzi. The process, as per the village elders, included their baring their bodies to all as she performed Nanshe's comforting technique to each of them. The one who had the most lucid, most visionary dream would be her husband. And, as demanded by the elders, she was to mate with her choice in full view of the village so they would know her children came from this holy union. Tallia remembers fighting the elders on this obscenity of a rite and winning the concession that her daughter would be partially robed.

Illyana admits that, before the ceremony, she had a teenaged crush on Nargel. Her first love for nearly a full sun cycle, carried out in secret. Domzi knew this, and the two young men were jealous of each other. On that fateful day, Domzi heroically placed himself in the way of a giant ready to violate Illyana and was speared. Nargel had disappeared during the battle and was thought to have been killed.

It was Illyana's prayers at the object that led to the lightning storm, which caused panic among the giants who fled the temple. As her grandmother Sarpani led the recovery process for the village, as they collected survivors and the object, they searched for new, safe grounds to build another temple. Sarpani had taught Illyana how to heal Domzi's wounds. As the course of nature progressed between them, Illyana began to care about Domzi.

But a few moon cycles later, Nargel wandered into their new encampment. Those tinges of first love overwhelmed Illyana. As the old village elders had been killed, enslaved, or dispersed, she would be free to choose her husband without the ceremony for the time being. She and Nargel married.

Everything she had hoped for in marrying her first love happened as she had wished for a few moon cycles. Then he began to change. Or maybe she changed. His eyes furtively followed the bodies of other women. Not long after, his body followed his eyes. When confronted by Sarpani about his infidelity, Nargel broke down and recounted the torture and violations of his captivity by the giants. His mind had been sickened by them. He needed Illyana's help in healing him, as she did to Domzi.

As much as Illyana tried to heal him through Nanshe's comforting methods, the five-sense bonding, the darkness of Nargel's soul overwhelmed her. She herself could only recover from this darkness by prayer at the object. One day, Nargel fled the village, saying he loved Illyana too much to continue torturing her with his soul.

Tallia comforts her daughter as she finally is able to cry with her mother. Illyana shunned all men for sun cycles, but Domzi was always there. Helping out grandmother Sarpani in her spiritual leadership. Helping Illyana with her prayer sessions. Leading the feasts in honor of Sarpani's mother, Nanshe. One evening, as Domzi suffered the torturous nightmares the afflicted men suffer, Illyana came to his hut and comforted him. With Sarpani present as her witness, Domzi shared the prophetic vision. Tens of tens of tens of sun cycles of a matriarchal society worshipping the god of Nanshe at this temple. Abundance and peace in these lands. They married the next week.

Appreciative and supportive of her newly found daughter's plight, Tallia asks where Domzi is now. Silence as Illyana stares off into nothingness. She stoically says she only hopes that she could be as brave and sage as her namesake, Orzu's sister Illyana, who taught Nanshe, who discovered the one true god with Nanshe in their captivity, who sacrificed herself to allow Nanshe to escape slavery with Orzu. For it is as if she were cursed. First Nargel is taken by the giants, then Domzi.

Holding her daughter, whose youth had been ripped apart by the giants, who survived this long without a real mother, Tallia rocks Illyana back and forth in her arms.

Between secretly visiting Nirra as he hides from the villagers and watching her cursed daughter deliberate on Nargel, her daughter's first love back again only two moon cycles ago, Tallia finds her own solace in her prayers at the object seven to eight times a day.

Then, one day, she hears Her again. The voice tells her that Illyana will someday be a great leader in the same way Nanshe had been. But she needs her mother. Not only her support, but her direct and frank intervention.

Tallia acknowledges and pledges her obedience. She asks the voice about her other daughter. The voice says through her other daughter, Tallia will find the pathway to the voice. How? Tallia asks, but is met only with silence.

The next day, when coming back from meeting Nirra, she spies Nargel walking hand in hand with Illyana. As she watches their lips touch now, that dormant memory resurrects, their first kiss as teens. Tallia recalls her mother's advice about first love. For it is the time to learn about one's self, about one's dreams, and if you are blessed, about one's destiny.

But for the afflicted girl, first love may be first unrequited love as the spiritual needs of the many require them to mate only with the best-matched afflicted male. Perhaps love manifests itself differently to the afflicted.

That evening, she takes a walk with Illyana, asking a loving but pointed question about Illyana's feelings toward Nargel. No matter the words, Illyana's eyes tell all. She is smitten. First love's magic rekindled. In Tallia's words to Illyana, first love's pain only waits to return. You cannot go backward to regain what you lost. The past is only that. We all must go forward.

Tallia reveals her own secret. Her marriage to Nirra. Her great-uncle Narn's son. She tells her daughter of the new love she has found. Different than that of her first love—Illyana's father, killed in the carnage at the First Temple.

Then, the repressed anger is released. Illyana scolds her mother for sleeping with the enemy. For abandoning the spirit of her father. For debasing all human women by pandering her body to a reindeer giant. Enraged, Illyana storms off. Tallia can only find solace in the voice's message. With her help, her daughter will one day find spiritual maturity.

Several days pass, and Illyana humbly comes to her mother to apologize for her rashness. Love is like the potions that cause the crazies. She commits to praying her way back to sanity with her mother but knows she plans to marry Nargel when the time is right.

That evening, as Tallia sneaks out to see her poor lonely, beloved behemoth, Illyana furtively follows her. Tallia rejoices in the literally huge arms of her Nirra. As if she knew her daughter has followed her, Tallia calls for Illyana to come out from the shadows.

After an introduction, Illyana remains silent as her fingers trace all around the reindeer giant's body, save the part only her mother should touch. You appear as a giant, she says, but you are not a giant. Nirra says he was born a giant, lived as a giant, and will always be scorned and hated as a giant. Such is mankind that hatred is based on appearances.

To Tallia's surprise, her daughter hugs this strange man, saying she thanks him for saving her mother. She will honor him for all time for allowing her mother to be reunited with her daughter.

The next day, the temple goers are wary of Nirra, for he killed many of their family and ancestors. Illyana tells of the evils of the giants but of the voice's words to forgive. For a better future can only be made by letting go of the hate of the past, the violence of the past.

Nirra spends most of the days hiding in the hut provided to Tallia. The glares of the villagers are too much for his guilt about his past. One day, as he tries to sneak out to go hunting, Illyana stops him and asks for the village to gather. She stands up on the object while he stands next to her and performs the non-intimate elements of the five-sense bonding. She says, I know you are not with blood from Nanshe, but you are her family as much as I. With palm over his heart, she says, you are absolved of your guilt of your past of killing my cousins, aunts, and uncles. I forgive you. My mother forgives you. The voice says She forgives you. Go forward in peace, devoted husband of my mother.

From that day forward, Nirra becomes an accepted member of the village, albeit head and shoulders above them all.

For Illyana, her life since the destruction of the First Temple has never been better. Her mother back. Her first love back. And her stepfather, the reformed giant, has turned out to be an inspiring grandfather figure for her children, who love climbing his tree-tall body.

Paradise lost befalls Illyana the day her stepfather comes back into the village after a hunting expedition. Nirra returns with Nargel in one hand and a wounded, not-fully-grown young giant in the other. Not that she would doubt her mother's new husband, but the villagers who were on the hunt with him corroborate the heart-breaking story.

Nargel is a conspirator. A plant from the giants. They plotted how to remove the object and kill Illyana and her mother, which would allow the giants to safely come and steal the women they needed from this village.

As the villagers call for the execution of both prisoners, Illyana runs to her hut, followed by Tallia. Illyana pulls off her headscarf and cries in her mother's arms, asking her to rock her again. All she wanted was the warmth, love, and safety of her childhood.

Tallia drops her to the ground, towering over Illyana, saying it is your time to be the woman you are destined to be. You know the voice, as do I. You know the wisdom of Nanshe, as do I. You have the faith of these villagers. You think you need to separate your heart from your spirit. But what you need now is to merge them together, for only then will you guide your people as a great matriarch should.

Eyes as wide as the rabbit about to be shot with an arrow, Illyana can only glare at her mother, at one moment coldly staring but now occupied with selecting an appropriate headscarf. Standing up, at first limply, then with firmness, Illyana says, I am ready. Tallia affirms she knows her daughter has always been ready as she adorns Illyana's head with a royal-blue headscarf.

Head high and covered in Nanshe's tradition of modesty, Illyana comes out and prays with Tallia at the black object and then stands upon it. She proclaims, the voice says we should be people of forgiveness. What matters is what is here in the village now. On their tables. The past is something we cannot undo. Something we cannot go back to. I say we forgive these two and let them suffer the damnation of living in the past.

Reluctantly, the villagers accede to the wisdom of the great-granddaughter of the great matriarch. Nirra escorts Nargel out of the village, dragging the near-dead body of the young giant. Tallia can hear him say for better or worse he is not a descendant of the great matriarch and has no issue revisiting the past with these two.

A few moon cycles pass, with Nirra continuing to play big tree for his step-grandchildren to climb upon and Tallia praying many times a day with her daughter as she had done with her mother. This time, they hear the voice together, who reveals that the black object of Nanshe's brother Namu, Tallia's great-great-uncle, resides at another village where the giants are holding Tallia's other daughter, Perima, as a sex slave priestess. The voice warns of the dire outcomes for all humans if the giants are successful in creating an alternative culture around Perima.

Wasting not a second, Tallia gathers her spears and bow and arrows. Followed by Nirra, they set off to save Perima and discover the final destiny that awaits Tallia.

CHAPTER 26

There is always some madness in love.
But there is also always some reason in madness.
—Friedrich Nietzsche, nineteenth-century German philosopher

Village ruins in Duhok Governorate, New Kurdistan
5:30 p.m. GMT+3, February 3, 2023

She felt like a bottle of soda shaken mercilessly with each bump of the road, much less each fit of the tormented mind. The seams of her tunic felt ready to burst. It was as if she were ready to have an explosive vomiting moment. Not from car sickness. Certainly not from Zengo in the passenger seat. And for sure not from this contentious Israeli woman who Zengo was all too kind to allow to come with them. But from the information Mei had sent her, which compelled her to rush "home" as soon as possible.

Zara fully anticipated a continued verbal battle from Rachel during their drive, but remarkably, the Israeli professor remained quiet. Conceivably, she is more perceptive than Zara gave her credit for. Perhaps she could sense that a single off remark would send Zara into rage, vomiting all over the woman. Her consent to this professor friend of Jean-Paul tagging along did not revolve around the forty-caliber Jericho pistol she carried, but her proficiency in using that gun in close quarters against multiple hostile targets. Apparently, the

MoxWorld Security team had been distracted by an intruder Zengo had told them about and three assassins broke through the security perimeter. Even though Jean-Paul had to help her during her shoot with his arms around her and fingers also on the trigger, their security would be better with Rachel nearby.

Every time Zara peered at Rachel in the rear-view mirror, she saw the eyes of a falcon scanning her back. Zara could not fault this so-called professor. Zara used to do the same thing and shoot the same way in the days before she proclaimed that she would be only a woman of peace, seeking the love of Xwedê. After another quick scan of the Israeli's face, Zara concludes she is older than her. Perhaps with time, Rachel will learn the hard lessons Zara had. For do they not worship the same god?

The ninety-minute drive back to her childhood home could not have finished soon enough as the maelstrom within Zara neared the unbearable. Her village now stands mostly deserted after the last fight between the Iraqi government and the Kurds who lived throughout northern Iraq. Peace only came to these lands once the price of oil dropped precipitously in the spring of 2021, as the forever-battery Mox devices began to dominate households across the world. Syria and Iraq, along with most other oil-producing nations, fell into deep economic crises.

More importantly for the Kurds, the diminished value of the oil wells in both northern Syria and northern Iraq meant the southern parts of those nations had neither the will nor financial ability to keep suppressing the Kurdish independence movement. Hence the birth of the countries of New Kurdistan in the north and the Arab Confederation in the south.

Now, in the next town from hers, the mosque her parents would take her to still stands untouched by the battles for independence. Once parked in her village, Zara notices the Israeli's perceptiveness as she lets Zengo and Zara have private time. She and Zengo walk through the abandoned buildings. Grey concrete block walls with aluminum sheeting for roofs and dust-covered floors. Other than a few goats now living here in peace, there remains for Zara only the ghosts and memories. Seeing him again, something compels her to face her past. If only she knew why.

They pass by Zengo's family home, which they abandoned before the battles. Zengo recalls his brothers' and sister's antics and the exasperation of his parents. At first, Zara says to herself, do not go there, but the irrational overcomes her and she takes his hand as they climb up the hill behind his house. The clearing still exists. A bit overgrown, but this landmark of the moment she became a woman stands firm. Love's first kiss. The subtle tones of nectar mingled with honey. He tasted so sweet. How could this be against Xwedê's wishes, an innocent kiss, the teenaged Zara asked.

Her adult self, now gazing at this clearing, then peruses the man next to her. How could an innocent kiss here be against what Zara wants for herself? They can only be platonic friends, right? That flutter in her stomach returns. This time, she cannot be so dismissive.

Before Zengo can say a word, she plants her lips lightly upon his. So she imagined the nectar part of their first kiss, but it still felt good. After what feels like an eternity in the clouds of the heavens called the past, she pulls back to gaze into his eyes. For the eyes never lie, or so she bets. Wonderfully hazel dilated eyes meet hers.

He leans toward her hesitantly, as if waiting for her to make the first move. She looks down at his chest, remembering the hairs and hardened muscles that she saw during their first kiss. When she meets his gaze again, she nods slightly. Time seems to stand still as their lips slowly come together. Lower lips touch first, followed by a gentle dance of tongues that guides their upper lips to meet in a passionate union. They become lost in each other, as if no time has passed since that first moment they shared in this very clearing. Tongues intertwined, Zara takes his hands under her headscarf and guides them to expose her hair, her ears, her neck. His hands run across all that was once his domain with the electrifying touch she first experienced back then. Her hands run across his arms, his shoulders, his back. How could this not be right? He is so strong. He protected her from those assassins. What more could signal he is her destiny?

As if Xwedê heard her, his lips slowly move away from hers until the tips of their noses touch. Before she can say a thing, he puts his finger on her lips and takes her hand. And down to his old house they go, to none other than the prayer room. He signals the time on his MoxWrap. Isha prayer. She shakes her head, as she has kissed him. They are not clean.

A smile and he leads her to their spring-fed well, which still works. Wudu, the ritual purification, performed. Both of them washing together thrice each body part in the proper sequence. Together as man and woman. A point that does not go unnoticed by her. And they pray together. As he offers his hand to lift her from the floor, she asks herself again, is there a man who could love her only for her prayers, only for her love of Xwedê? Maybe it is him.

❧

As they walk back to her family's home, her tilted head rubs along his shoulder full of warm, meaty muscles. She mumbles, "Dogs love dogs."

"Excuse me?" he says back, kissing the top of her headscarf-less head.

She raises her head and kisses his lips. "Lambs love lambs."

"There has always been part of you that mystified me, Zara," he responds, his lips caressing the tip of her nose. "But that was the charm you captured my heart with."

He squeezes her hand as they walk and says, "It takes time for a man to learn what is right and what is clearly wrong. I suppose this awareness comes faster for women. I strayed. I paid the price. And you do not have to believe me, but time has taught me you were and still are the finest woman who Xwedê could entrust to carry forth the virtues he wants of his people."

"She," muses Zara. "And do not think you can talk your way back into my pants with words like those. Besides, neither of us is equipped to fulfill that desire." She squeezes his hand.

"If I were still equipped, could I have talked both of us into each other's pants again?" jests Zengo.

"No," says Zara emphatically as she squeezes his hand even harder. A few steps further, she gives him a light peck on the cheek. "That means 'no' in a nicer way."

He squeezes her hand back, saying, "In any way you would want, I am prepared to be at your side for as long as you want me. In prayer. In negotiations. In life. For life."

She elbows his rib. "Oh, you are just trying to sweet-talk your way into my pants again." She smiles and adds, "But keep talking. It is pleasing to my ears." And those flutters in her stomach become flutters in her heart.

The dark cloud called somber casts its shadow across her visage as they reach her family's home. For in those previous moments with Zengo, all of her woes vanished. But the cold hard reality sits in front of her. She stiffens, releasing Zengo's hand. He follows her into the house. She stands in the room where her father hung himself. She shivers and puts her face into her hands.

Letting her have a moment, Zengo waits before putting his arm around her. "He would have been proud of how his little Zara grew up to be one of the leaders of faith throughout Kurdistan and beyond. If I remember correctly, his side of the family were orthodox Muslims."

She sniffles and says, "His accepting my mother and her Sufi upbringing taught me the importance of tolerance and understanding. For in the end, we all worship the same god. Just in different ways."

As they pass by her little brother Soran's room, another shiver passes through her spine to her arms. She utters, "Cats and dogs."

"What is with the menagerie, Zara?" ponders Zengo.

"I thought we were alike, me and Soran," says Zara. "But in the end, we were no more than cats and dogs. Goats and sheep. Lions and foxes."

Then, in her room, he nudges her. "Remember what we did here when everyone was at the market?"

"Father Jean-Paul might call that 'original sin,'" jests Zara, as she pokes him. "But you assured me that your mouth did not constitute sex or breaching my modesty. Did you ever lie!"

She wanders to her parents' room. She was born in this room. She recalls her baby pictures and how her father's face beamed with pride as he held her in his arms. As if an electrical shock passes through her body, she goes rigid. Near rigor mortis. Her jaw convulses and she dry-heaves. Once. Twice. Three times as Zengo holds his arms around her frigid body.

She mumbles, "How could she do that? How?"

As she curls into a ball in the corner of her parents' room, Zengo encases her frozen body with the heat of his. She feels the warmth that her father had given her when she needed his love. She misses him so much. Her father, that is.

For what seems an hour, she continues to mumble, "How could she?" as she becomes catatonic.

She awakens to Zengo's hand petting her hair. "Are you better now, *ferîşteya min*, my angel?" he asks.

"I am so sorry. I do not know what came over me," says Zara in a weakened tone. "How long have we been here?"

"Not long," replies Zengo, straightening out her hair. "Perhaps a half hour. Your mind went somewhere else for fifteen minutes."

She gets up with a few wobbles, leaning on Zengo. She says, "I need to get out of here. Nothing good came from this place. Only misery befell my parents."

"Do you want to talk about it?" asks Zengo. "Sometimes, saying things out loud helps your pain."

She pets his arm. "You are too kind. But now is not the time. I need to go now to my spot up on the mountain. My head needs to take a break up there."

A few more moments as Zara's face contorts. From lost girl to the soldier that she once was with Zengo oh so long ago.

As they head toward Zengo's Humvee, Zara's MoxMover, and the MoxWorld Security team, Zara spies Rachel, who is deep in conversation with Alexander's head agent. As she nears, Rachel's falcon eyes scan Zara's bared head.

"Now we know you are not ultra-orthodox," comments Rachel.

Zengo hands Zara her pink scarf, but she says, "For going to my father's favorite spot, I would like to wear the black lamb's wool one with red-and-gold embroidery. Like the one Roza gave me. Could you be a dear and get it out of my luggage for me?"

Alone with the Israeli professor, Zara wastes no time in asking, "Did you get what you needed out of the MoxWorld Security team?"

At first, with her head tilted forward, glaring at Zara through the upper part of her eyes, Rachel pulls her ponytail to the front of her shoulder, brushing it. She cops a modest smile, saying, "The same as you are getting with your friend. What's a girl to do with a half dozen hyper-masculine, steroid-enhanced men? A little flirt here. A little nudge there."

Her favorite headscarf back in hand, Zara carefully wraps it around her head in the way Roza taught her nearly thirty years ago in that house she has just ran away from. She takes a deep breath, glares back at Rachel, and asks, "There. Are you more comfortable with my religious traditions? Or do I remind you of a favorite Palestinian terrorist you have blown away?"

A visceral jerk back by Rachel. Beading and squinting her eyes, she spits back, "You know nothing of the kindness Palestinians are capable of."

A nod at Zengo, as Zara knows he is no stranger to her tones of voice. On cue he says, "Perhaps you two should go along first. I will make sure the MoxWorld guys are all set and then bring the sleeping gear up. Rachel, am I correct that you want to join us up there? Or we can have Zara's MoxMover take you back to Nineveh instead."

With what looks like a bat of eyelids at him, Rachel says, "She is right. You are such a dear to be concerned about me. Jean-Paul had asked if I could make sure you two were secure here. Besides, I think your Zara would like words with me. So, we will have our little girls' talk on our hike up." She pulls her Jericho pistol out, pulls the slide back to chamber a round, and places it back into her bag. "There. We will be safe from any wild animals or wild men."

Heading to the trailhead, Zara shakes her head side to side. "The only beast you need to keep me safe from is the one who is carrying a loaded gun."

As they head up the trailhead out of sight of the others, Zara stops and faces Rachel. "So, why are you here? It cannot be that you want to spy on two desexed Kurds figuring out how to have a torrid affair at their childhood make-out spot."

Rachel stares at her momentarily, then takes the lead on the trail. Two hundred meters later, she stops and reaches into the brush beside the trail, pulling out a very hefty, stout stick and handing it to Zara. "There. You can defend yourself against me. Stick beats gun at this range."

The tall Kurdish woman twirls the makeshift short staff about with perfect precision. Her Filipino martial art teacher would be proud. That is Jean-Paul.

She then tosses the stick back into the brush. "For the record, I do not need a stick to beat your gun," she says as she lifts her tunic to show the bullet wounds.

Again, Rachel takes the lead going up the trail, saying, "Is that because you will call upon Xwedê to smite me with lightning?"

With her longer legs, Zara passes Rachel at accelerating speed, replying, "Is that what the prophets of the Book of Israel would do to nonbelievers? If so, then I am not a prophetess, if that is the question you are here to answer for the Mossad."

Now panting from the torrid pace set by this crazed Kurdish woman, Rachel comes alongside the near-trotting Zara and says, "First, there were all kinds of prophets. Some who smote their enemies with plagues or lightning from the heavens. Others who preached love and peace. Second, I do not work for the Mossad. They are afraid of me. As should you be. And third, if you had taken the time to research me on your MoxWrap instead of making out with your boyfriend there, you would have found I am one of the world's foremost experts on the goddess Asherah."

The tall one comes to a dead halt, catching Rachel off guard. Her head dripping, Rachel bends forward, catching her breath. She lifts her head and bemoans, "What is wrong with you? Don't prophetesses need to breathe as they are running?"

Arms akimbo, Zara wipes a tiny speck of moisture from her brow. "First, I never said I was a prophetess. Nor a messiah. That madman Murometz did that. And maybe a little bit from my grandmother. Second, I am of no value to any agency, country, or faith. I am but a simple, humble Kurdish woman wishing to follow in the footsteps of Rab'ia of Bashra. And third, I do not care about your goddess Asherah. If I am not mistaken, she represents the polytheism that the Prophet spoke out against."

The shorter Israeli woman stands right up to Zara. Her eyes at her chin. Looking up, she says, "If we were guys, we would have whipped our penises out by now, comparing whose was bigger and could piss farther. We could still do the latter. Would that make you happy?"

That got a laugh out of the tall Kurd. It was the exact kind of challenge

Peri would have fielded to fetch her out of a furious funk. She rubs her knuckles on Rachel's head and says, "You are okay. I misjudged you."

Taken aback for a moment, a smile spreads its way across Rachel's face, only to be stymied by the Kurdish woman's next comment. Zara hits Rachel's bag and says, "But if I did have a penis, mine would be bigger. You carry only a forty-caliber weapon. Back in the day, I carried fifty-caliber subsonic, armor-piercing rounds capable of cutting a man in half or eviscerating their chest."

"So, what does that make you? Russian FSB?" pipes back Rachel.

"As much as you are Mossad," says Zara as she lets out a deep lung laugh and slaps Rachel's upper back. The latter does the same, a deep laugh and slap of Zara's lower back. They begin to hike again, albeit at a more human pace.

Rachel says, "At the risk of you suddenly deciding to squat here on the spot and challenge me to a pissing contest, our mutual friend, Father Jean-Paul, led me to believe you might find Asherah of great interest."

A burst of a longer stride and Zara peers into Rachel's eyes to gauge her question. "And why would my favorite Jesuit priest say that?"

"He said you speak with a woman god. That your Xwedê speaks with a female voice."

Facing forward and picking up the tempo just a bit, Zara says, "Is that the same Jean-Paul who once told me that God speaks in the voice of the listener? In the language of the listener?"

"You saw what we uncovered in Nineveh," says Rachel. "Proof that my ancestors, maybe yours, worshipped Asherah alongside Yahweh. Humor me before you protest polytheism. What if God was a woman all along? And men rewrote history, rewrote religion, to make God a man."

Again, Zara comes to a full stop. This time, Rachel runs right into her back. "Ouch. You are bonier than you look," exclaims the Israeli professor.

"Really? And I thought you were making a pass at me, Professor," says a smiling Zara. "Did my Jesuit friend share with you the history of the ancient matriarch?"

"Only that I was not as good of a match as you and Mei."

"So, you know Mei as well."

"We continue to collaborate on archaeological finds in both our countries," says Rachel without a hint of anything on her face other than flat-lined lips as she tries to view Zara from different angles.

"What did she tell you about me?" asks Zara, also with flat-lined lips, trying to view Rachel at different angles.

"She never talked of you. Only some man named Peter."

With a slight jerk of her head, Zara glances away as Rachel's falcon eyes affix on her. At Zara's telltale silence, Rachel asks, "So, were you close to this Peter person?"

Back into hiking mode, Zara says, "We worked very closely together for a number of months. But that project is over. I have not seen him since. What did Mei say about him?"

"Not much. Only that he would win any you-know-what is bigger contest with any man she knows," says Rachel with a flat intonation.

Zara breaks her stride for two steps, then continues in her rhythmic march.

Doing her best to get in front of the Kurd, Rachel peers into her eyes, "What do you think? Is she right? You know, girl to girl."

Dead stop again. This time, Rachel trips, almost falling. With hand out to help Rachel regain her balance, Zara replies, "No, I do not know. But I do know that his favorite thing is seven inches long, with a yellow hue and little spots." She laughs as Rachel stares at her with one eyebrow pointed down.

Rachel takes the lead again, but Zara says, "Where are you going? We are here." She points to a large flattop rock two meters off the trail. Her hand patting the sitting surface of this stone, she says, "When Saddam bombed and gassed our village, my mother fled with me in her arms. She cried and cried as she waited on this stone for my father to come with the rest of the village. Hours passed and my mother thought the worst. He finally arrived with chemical burns and his clothing powdered in orange. His lungs were never the same, but he saved nearly half the village by staying behind and guiding them up to safety. As I grew up, I found the most peace here in this spot. He would take me here and teach me about nature, about life."

"You Kurds have had a hard time with persecution," says Rachel in a somber tone.

Zara turns to her, saying, "We Kurds are like the Jews had been. Thirty million people of the same culture without a geographic country. Persecuted by every country we lived in. Tortured, massacred, and raped by regime after regime. But finally, not long ago, we too finally got our countries. But like you, we must fight for our independence and safety every day."

Her lips pursed, head nodding in agreement, Rachel replies, "In that, we have a common bond."

Nodding back, Zara says, "You ask me if I am the messiah. If that means a savior for my people, then I am the messiah of the moment in my work accessing Murometz's economic growth engine for my people. If you are working for the welfare of Israel, then you are as much a messiah as I."

Wagging her finger at the tall woman, Rachel says, "You are very clever, turning me into the messiah and deflecting attention from yourself. I hope you and I never get into a race to see who will save the world first."

"Please excuse me," begs Zara, as she kneels. "I must pray here as I did with my father, my mother, and even my brother. I would invite you to join me, but I pray in the Muslim manner, if that offends you."

After a visit to wash at a nearby spring, Zara prostrates herself as Rachel also kneels in prayer. Her MoxWrap sounds and Rachel says, "Please excuse me. I need to take this urgent message."

CHAPTER 27

Listen! Clam up your mouth and be silent like an oyster shell,
for that tongue of yours is the enemy of the soul, my friend.
When the lips are silent, the heart has a hundred tongues.
—Jalāl ad-Dīn Muḥammad Rūmī, thirteenth-century Persian Sufi mystic

Zara's mountain in Duhok Governorate, New Kurdistan
7:00 p.m. GMT+3, February 3, 2023

Rachel walks further up the trail. Checking her MoxWrap, she reads Mei's message: Made a breakthrough. Your goddess theory may pan out. En route to new location. Heard from JP you also made a breakthrough @ Nineveh. Congrats.

Rachel sees Mei is live on her MoxWrap and texts: Also met your Kurdish friend. Special lady.

Mei: I sent her something important. How is she feeling?

Rachel: She's blue that you stole her boyfriend.

Mei: Who told you that? Zara would not.

Rachel: She said he is packing in his pants and you could not resist.

Mei: Are you getting jealous? I thought things were good between us.

Rachel: We are good. 😊 I didn't know you wanted a man so "long" in that way.

Mei: My mother would not want me talking of a man in that way. Let's say Mr. Peter Gollinger is honorable, duty-bound, family oriented, and average in all other dimensions.

Rachel: May Asherah bless your child. I am so happy for you.

Mei texts back a heart.

A short exhale and Rachel says, "What an archaeologist has to do to get other archaeologists to reveal all."

Taking the NiQihs device from her pocket, she texts: You were right. ZK had no sexual intimacy with him. No chance she bears his child. How do we handle PG?

Text back: A black outfit with a plunging neckline. Nature will take care of the rest.

Rachel: You are joking.

Text back: Doctors never joke about that. Especially female ones.

Rachel: Funny, that is the type of order a man would give.

Text back: One did. He is greater than all of us.

Shaking her head, Rachel says to herself, "What a woman archaeologist has to do to get the world to know the truth."

Reaching into her pocket again, she pulls out a third device and texts: Subject not a threat at the moment. Will advise if changes.

A long exhale and she says, "What a woman archaeologist has to do to get respect."

As she heads back, Rachel hears Zara talking to someone. She approaches in stealth mode, taking a hidden vantage point within earshot.

Sitting atop the stone where she would sit, listening to her father's interpretations of Hadiths, of the plight of the Kurds, of why he was so proud of his little daughter, Zara has her eyes closed as she says, "Not that I doubt you. I am and will also be obedient to your wishes. I am confused how such a good man as my father could have this happen to him. How such a good woman as my mother could do that to him. And what am I? Am I not who he thought I was?"

Wiping a tiny bit of moisture from the edges of her eyes, she says, "I will not cry. I have cried too much since you first spoke to me. I was not a crying baby, a crying girl, and certainly not now a crying woman. Not anymore."

A little rise in her cheeks appears to lift the edges of her lips as Zara replies, "Thank you. I can only hope to be what Rab'ia was to you. In this regard, I ask your patience."

Her head tilts as she asks, "But should I not go to her first? Why is he so important?"

Silence as Zara rocks back and forth. She slowly opens her eyes to gaze upon the horizon, biting, then licking her lips. "I am prepared to give up my life so he can reach his objective. I am subservient to your will." With that, Zara descends from the rock and begins to pray toward Mecca.

Still hidden, Rachel slowly and silently backs away. She takes her dark, hexagonal, palm-sized third device and texts: Situation changed. Subject dangerous. Suicidal martyr. Will advise if need backup.

Quietly and carefully, she takes her Jericho out of her bag, unloads the chambered bullet, releases the magazine, and inserts a different set of bullets. RIPs, or radically invasive projectiles, designed for maximum shock wave with organ-exploding, limb-shredding lethality. This Kurdish woman has survived gunshot wounds before and certainly now could be Israel's greatest danger. Rachel cannot allow her the chance to survive the first couple bullets. Closing her eyes, wrapping her shaking hands around the cold steel barrel, she prays for forgiveness and the strength, the courage, to do what she may have to do.

So in goes the RIP-filled magazine into the Jericho. She chambers the first round before she places the source of this prophetess's imminent demise back into her bag. Something more innocuous replaces the pistol, as Rachel undoes her ponytail and begins brushing her hair as she quietly heads back to Zara.

Still prostrate in prayer, Zara heard the teeniest clink of two pebbles sliding. Now, those same feet approach. She reaches for an oval rock to use as a projectile as she positions her head for maximum peripheral vision. As Rachel comes into view with something man-made and dark in hand, Zara rolls away in a fashion that makes her a poor target, as well as allowing her arm to exert maximum projectile launch velocity. With her keen combat senses still intact after all these years, she pulls the throw at the very last moment as she recognizes the black plastic handle belongs to a hairbrush and not a firearm.

Eyes open wide, Rachel drops the hairbrush as she catches the rock with both hands, as an American football wide receiver would a bullet pass. Once neutralized, Rachel drops the rock, simultaneously reaching into her bag.

Rolling on the ground while howling, Zara comes to a kneeling position and says, "You were almost as good as my little brother with this game we played here as kids. The literal translation from Kurdish is 'catch as catch can or be really bruised.'" Her eyes flick slightly to the side as she finishes the sentence.

Zara gets up and mimics how one catches a rock in motion and throws it back. She finishes with a smile and uplifted eyebrows back at Rachel, who slowly withdraws her hand from her backpack.

Before this odd conversation can go further, the footsteps and voice of Zengo come from lower down the trail. "Zara, it is your Zengo. Do not ambush me. I am friendly." Hearing this, Rachel relaxes, her shoulders dropping from rigid and tense to loosely ready.

"So, what have you two been doing to entertain yourselves while I made sure the MoxWorld guys did not get distracted this time?" asks Zengo as he puts down the sleeping bags he carried up from his car.

Zara says to Rachel, "There is one for you, unless you would rather go back to your nice warm hotel in Mosul. Of course, you are welcome to stay with us. I believe Jean-Paul was thoughtful enough to have packed some Kosher snacks for you as well."

Eyes still on Zengo, Rachel answers him. "We were just playing your cute game. What was that called again? Catch as catch can or be really hurt?"

As he rolls out the first floor pad, Zengo scrunches his nose. "Say what? Did Zara make that up?"

Coming over to help Zengo, Zara says, "Oh, that is a game you play with your little brother." She glances back at Rachel and adds, "You certainly would not play that with your boyfriend. If he misses a catch, a girl might not like what he could not do afterwards." She winks at Rachel.

A nonplussed visage stares back at Zara, who asks, "There is something you are seeking up here, is there not? Tell me. I will pray for you to be one with your deepest need."

Rachel's eyes gaze first into Zara's, then to the side. "That is so kind of you. But I will pray to Asherah myself."

Having rolled out the three pads and sleeping bags, Rachel excuses herself to take care of some girl things before settling down for the night.

∾

As they tuck into their separate but adjacent bags, Zara asked, "Was there anything wrong back there?"

With a whisper, he replies, "I talked with my personal contact on the Turkish negotiation committee and an old friend from before the Anatolian Kurdish State formed. He says the Turks will not settle with us only on financial terms. The MoxDefense package of advanced weapons must be part of the deal, or they will arm themselves with NiQihs weapons and take the factories by force."

"Why the hard stance?" asks Zara. "I thought they were good two days ago with my promise of terms given well before the thirty-day timeline."

"I guess we got too distracted with that Israeli professor's woman god. The scenario that Russian admiral warned of has played out," replies Zengo. "Remember the MoxDefense prototypes you got for your other boyfriends, the Russian and the American? Well, the Americans rushed them to the South China Seas, where they shot down China's NiQihs advanced AI missiles. And one of China's NiQihs equipped J-31N fighters was shot down by the new MoxDefense modified F-35 prototype."

"That's my Sasha. He never lies about being bigger, badder, and bolder than everyone else," muses Zara. She pauses, peering into his eyes. "My other boyfriends, huh? Is that jealously I hear?"

He pulls her hand into his. "I want to protect you. In ways that I failed to do when I was younger and too stupid to know better. They did not protect you. I know you do not need to be protected. But I want to be there, just in case. His eyes point down to his crotch. "You know, if I miss the catch, there is nothing down there to get damaged. We can play your little brother's game to your heart's content."

She laughs. How can nearly two decades pass and they lie at this very spot as if nothing has changed?

"Lambs love lambs," says Zengo. "I now get what you were saying. We share a similar past, similar families, similar faith, and similar adult hardships. We are both lambs. Let us grow into sheep together."

Her smile dissolves as her facial lines harden. "You are going to ask me to get the Kurds the same weapons. And all that will happen is not a negotiated peace, but both sides going down the path to another Turk versus Kurd war. How can I condone this?"

He strokes her face, as if trying to soften those lines. "Because you are the messiah. Our messiah. You will find a way for us to have peace. For the two Kurdistans to unite. For the Kurds in Iran to join us. Thirty million Kurds will have great-grandchildren living in a safe, peaceful, united Kurdistan who will thank the woman who became their messiah."

Her finger flicks his nose. "It is true. You really are only trying to get in my pants. Or at least into my sleeping bag."

As Rachel comes back, they say their goodnights. In the clear night sky that comes with being on a mountain, Zara stares at the stars. She sees the outline of the bird. The Cygnus constellation with the tail of the bird star shining most brightly, as stated in the legend of the husband of Nanshe. If only she could be as sage as that ancient matriarch.

The tail of the bird star. The legend of Peter. Zara's head turns, staring at Rachel's back, then over toward Zengo, and finally back at the stars as she wishes Peter has or will have found the love and family he deserves, as she has found now.

"Rachel, Rachel, you do not look well," says Zara, comforting the Israeli woman, who has just dry-heaved into the bushes.

"I'm okay. Thank you for your concern," replies Rachel right before she dry-heaves again.

Zara opens up the Israeli's blouse to help her inhale deeper breaths. The gold goddess pendant falls forward, followed by a Star of David pendant. Rachel tries to put them back atop her breasts, but the third time's a charm as she upheaves once more.

Now sitting on the ground, Zara holds Rachel in her arms, comforting her. Rachel reaches into her bag for a tube of analgesics, the handle of her Jericho clearly in view. Zara pets Rachel's hair, a sure remedy to calm the restless soul and stomach.

"I was sure one or more of those copper-tipped bullets would be giving me a headache this morning," jests Zara, still petting Rachel's hair. "How ironic that I did not wake up with a splitting headache, but you did," she says with a little hmmm in her breath.

Pink around the mouth and nose, Rachel says, "That is a very odd thing to say to someone who is wishing she was back in her bed in Jerusalem, two steps from the toilet."

"I figured after you saw me talking with Her you would either join me in communing with a female god or feel compelled to defend the Hebrew god. Or perhaps Mossad had given you the kill order," says a nonplussed Zara.

Rachel taps Zara in the belly. "Yeah, the Mossad signaled a green kill sign, same as the FSB said for you to act like you were Joan of Arc." They both let out a little laugh as Rachel scrunches down from the pain of the laugh.

"I did pray to Her that your Asherah helps you find what you were searching for," says Zara.

Rocking back and forth in Zara's arms, Rachel says, "Maybe, since you are a certified delusional person who talks to the divine, you won't berate me for my nightmares. The ones that left me hurting this morning."

"Tell me. They cannot be any stranger than what has happened to me in the last year," says Zara.

"You know the Prophet Jacob. Yaʿqūb in your book and Ya'akov in mine. I dreamed about when he slept on a stone and saw angels ascending and descending a ladder to heaven," says Rachel.

"You yearning to be one of those angels?" jests Zara.

"No. Seriously. Up the ladder where Yahweh and heaven should be was a blue light with a robed woman," says Rachel.

With a light scoff, Zara says, "I would not say that too loud around any mosque here. I did, and see what happened to me?"

"In rabbinical schools, I teach that Jacob's ladder is symbolic of the exiles the Jews will suffer before the coming of the true messiah," says Rachel.

"Yes, once again the Torah is only about the Jews and no one else," replies Zara.

Stiffening her back, but then curling with the pain, Rachel says, "Okay, just you and I—we will fight out the fight of all fights between the Muslims and Jews here and now." Laughing, then groaning, she elbows Zara.

With a laugh back, Zara says, "Well, let me get you your gun and you can blow out my uterus, as it is not doing me any good anymore." Both laughing, they lean against each other.

"Not to start a religious war with you, but my father's father was a mufti in Duhok," says Zara in a soft voice. "He taught me the ladder signified how creation will bring itself from its end to its beginning."

Rachel lets out a sigh of relief. "Bless your grandfather. I was sure you were going to tell me it was a parallel for your Prophet Mohammed and the Mi'raj, his journey to the Temple Mount and the Al-Aqsa Mosque. I was just waiting for you to claim Jerusalem for the Muslims."

"Who do you think I am?" says Zara with a huff. "I am Kurdish. Not Palestinian." She laughs, and then adds, "And you should be more afraid of us Kurds. Saladin captured Jerusalem in 1187 CE and he was a Kurd."

A laugh, then silence from Rachel with a contemplative face. "I've never dreamed of passages from the Torah. I mean, aside from the typical insomnia mulling over lectures or Rabbinic debates, I've never dreamed of a variation on the prophets until now."

Zara taps the poor distraught Israeli woman's hair at the base of her neck. She pauses a moment, feeling something there, and then massages Rachel's tense neck. "You know of the dreams that ail us, do you not? And you called me the prophetess. It is you, the Prophetess Yakova. Did I get the Hebrew feminine name right?"

Rubbing the Israeli professor lightly on the sacred spot, that God Gene Complex, Zara continues, "I had a dream. A mother and her daughter learning to forgive. Each other and a giant. Perhaps your Asherah is trying to show me what I have to do. And if so, she is wrong. Some things are not so easy to forgive."

An hour later, Zara shoulders the ailing Rachel down the mountain. In the back seat of Zengo's car, Rachel snuggles down to nap in the back seat as Zengo signals for Zara to talk in private.

Up comes the MoxMedia World News from his MoxWrap, with Sahir in a pure white suit with pink metallic pinstripes. Earlier this morning, Chinese submarines launched nuclear cruise missiles at the US carrier task forces. The attack critically damaged two US carriers, causing radiation exposure for thousands of sailors.

Only silence comes from Zara as she stares at scene after scene of soon-to-be-dead, crispy burnt sailors. As the US Senate Majority leader is shown lobbying for full nuclear war to be unleashed upon China, Zara's eyes narrow.

Turning her head to avoid seeing more carnage, she says, "I get it, Zengo. I will find a way to talk to Sasha. He has been missing for weeks now. But I am sure Mei knows how to get him. Some of the fashion models she dresses often are called upon for his perverse pleasures."

Zengo takes her hand and says, "Let me go with you. I can protect you better than his security team."

She smiles, stroking his hand, replying, "You forget, I trained his security team here.."

He kisses her forehead and says, "The protection I bring is much different from mere brawn and bullets."

Leaning her head into his shoulder for a moment and then back up, she says, "I know. I know. You should make sure Rachel makes it safely back to her dig with Jean-Paul." She turns to his car. "I should say goodbye to Sleeping Beauty there."

The color in Rachel's face has already begun its return, like the descending angels in her dream. She says to Zara, whose head pokes through the window, "You know, you lovebirds can get a room here. There are lots of empty ones."

"You should be so lucky that the woman said to be the messiah gets married and taken off the prophetess market," jests Zara.

The biblical archaeology professor lets out a little nasal snort. "You know that Xwedê had a wife. At least before 701 BCE."

"That is Yahweh who had a wife. Not Xwedê. For She does not need one," retorts Zara.

They both smile for a moment, with serious faces reemerging on both of them. Rachel stares at Zara as she tightens her headscarf around her neck—a distinct sign of what she is going to do.

Her eyes become black discs again, something Rachel is hyper-attentive to. Zara says, "When the time comes that you decide, or it is decided for you that you must shoot me, do not hesitate. I will not think less of you. I was prepared to die the last time around. I am ready to die this time around."

Zara closes her eyes for a moment. Open again, the obsidian discs are smaller. "I am comforted that I know who will see me to my end."

Without a blink, hiding her shaking hands below her legs, Rachel replies, "There will be no hesitation."

CHAPTER 28

The hottest love has the coldest end.

—Socrates

Yacht anchored ten kilometers off the Crimean Peninsula
6:30 p.m. GMT+3, February 8, 2023

Whap. Whap. Whap.

"Ow. That hurts," cries Zara.

The monster in front of her only grins at her attacks against his monstrous face. Minute after minute of on-again, off-again hand slaps against one cheek and then the other only leads to her own pain. In between each round, she agonizes over how much her hands hurt, and she stomps on his feet. No matter what she does, what pains her most is not released.

Her hands red as persimmons, she stomps with her women's euro size 39 boots on his men's euro size 60 shoes with no sign whatsoever she is hurting him as much as he has hurt her. She retreats with her back against the cabin wall.

"My dear little Zara," says the monstrous man, nodding to his lap. "Perhaps you should take the gun out from my desk and shoot me in an organ you do not think I need anymore. Perhaps that act will give you the cathartic moment you so desire. So much so you have asked me to come out of hiding to meet you."

Legs bent in front of her, she lets her back slide down against the wall until she is in a sitting position. "I know why you would have done this. Your perversions run in your blood, in your genes, originating in ancient times. But why would I believe you that my mother was complicit?" she bemoans. "I do not understand. How could she do this to her husband? She loved him as much as I did."

Her Sasha struggles to free himself, to no avail. Zara's ability to bind a prisoner into a chair is simply superb. He wiggles his nose and says, "My dear little Zara. I hope you did not neutralize my private guards. One would have thought they would have come to my rescue by now. You know that leaves us vulnerable if you did."

"You still have Moxy. I bet you rigged this room with hidden lethal lasers," says Zara.

The air in this cabin runs thick as Zara wipes her brow with her headscarf. But that is smugness that drips as her Sasha replies, "And then again, are you so presumptuous in believing I would let you eliminate my guards? And if that was so, why would I want you to be alone with me? Whatever happens, remember what I have said."

Her lips turn down at the edges, and her eyes darken as black as the sea outside. An upturn of his lips as he wiggles his nose and says, "I have this agonizing itch on the tip of my nose. Be a dear and help me scratch it."

"Good. Agonize away. At least I have caused you some pain," she retorts. She puts her head into her bent knees. "I used to say I am not your little Zara," she laments. "But I guess I was wrong. As I was about most things in my life."

His giant hands still struggling against the giant-sized plastic zip ties with which she secured him to his favorite antique Crimean oak chair, he says, "If you were any other woman, I would have had much pleasure from being tied up and beaten. But alas, blood is blood, and one does not say that about one's daughter, one's creation, one's finest gift to this earth."

"Fine. I feel safer already," says Zara, glaring at him. "Why? Why did she let you enter her? She is such a pious, loving woman."

"You said it yourself. She loved your father as much as you did. What was that my second cousin Roza would say? If you love someone, you will do anything for them, no? If it is any comfort, I allowed her to be fully robed through it all. Her modesty intact."

"You blackmailed her. You must have," shouts Zara, now standing. "She would not have betrayed her Nawdar, my beloved father, my real father. What did you have over her that she would commit a crime against her very self?"

"That sweet man Nawdar was born Kurdish, a culture that has the saying 'the male is born to be slaughtered,'" says Alexander. "You only recall the second time Saddam's regime imprisoned him. How do you think he got released? I got him out. Not only for our precious Maryam, your mother, but for their even more precious daughter."

She purses her lips now, gazing at the floor. "I suppose I should thank you. But somehow, I cannot find that within me given the situation."

"Your mother never told you about the first time Saddam's goons took him and tortured him because his brother was a Peshmerga officer. She begged her grandmother, Sara, my aunt, to introduce us, the distant relative who had sufficient financial resources to bribe the Saddam government."

Exhaling for nearly half a minute, she still stares down as she asks, "But why did you have to ask her to bed with you? And why did you not ask her about birth control?"

"Because she was my Peter," he says with utter neutrality. "As Peter is to you, she tested as having the best complementary genetics to mine. Our child would be the closest match to the original matriarch God ever created."

"Leave Xwedê out of this. She could not have been party to this travesty," says Zara. "You had a wife already. I would have thought you would have already picked your best match."

"My poor dear Lada. She had no idea," laments the giant man. "She thought she won a lottery when we dated. A simple, middle-class girl who tested surprisingly well in our early genetic screens. Our son Abram was a good match for the tail of the bird oral tradition originator's genetics. You and he would have had the near perfect baby. But not as perfect as the union of you and Peter."

Zara goes to his desk and searches the drawers. And there it is. She lifts it up and points it at his head. "Tell me why I should not pull the trigger."

No longer grinning, he replies, "Because you need me to get to what Sara asked of you. What you yourself want to find. Because she waits for both of us there."

"The drawing of the parchment Sara left for me. Maryam made that for you," states Zara.

"Yes. And she told me all the things an afflicted woman should only tell her husband. After you became familiar with Peter's nightly ails, did you not wonder why your father and brother did not suffer the dreams as much as Peter did?"

She puts the gun down on the desk and shakes her head. "That was the gun you used to kill Abram here on this yacht. I taint myself by touching it."

"There is so much you do not know, my little daughter. In the shadows where even my best intelligence system cannot find them lies a group who tails me, taunts me, tortures my paranoia. They followed up on everyone I have identified as a genetic possibility. Do you not understand? Your genetic material is more valuable to them than all the precious metal, gemstones, uranium, and oil in the world. But my idealistic son, he would not use the power of my empire to keep himself secure from these assailants. As our sayings go, the enemy of a father will never be friends of his son. They would have dissected him."

"So, when I said I would not marry him, you made sure his genetic material vanished. Is that it?" says Zara.

"As his wife, you would have protected him like you did Peter on the last mission," replies Alexander. "These other people created NiQihs while I was distracted with you and Peter. These other people would not stop where I stopped. They would take yours and Peter's genetic material and make the baby they need to end run me to the blue light. A thousand friends are too few, as the Kurds say. One enemy is one too many. One mole can take down our entire effort to get to the end goal. You and I, we must flush out the moles in our MoxWorld. Those underground demons who threaten your dearest Peter. Who would force him to give of himself."

"Like you did not force Maryam," scoffs Zara.

"She consented by choice."

"No. No. She would not do that."

"But she did. When I told her about what our child would represent, when I told her how all of what she learned from her great-grandmothers could come true, she consented," he says with no tonal inflection. "You of all people should know that it is not about the sex, the desire, the orgasmic. It is about creation. Your Peter understood that."

Her fingers run along the gun down on the desk. She then rubs her hands together, washing her fingers, then goes back to the wall she had been leaning against and knocks her head against it. From evil grain, no good seed can come, say her people. She is damned.

"My dearest little Zara. Did you have the dream of that woman again? The one in the square hut and her giant? Did she not forgive her giant? Didn't that forgiveness lead to her finding what she wanted to find? And why wouldn't a little forgiveness let you find what you seek most in life?"

Giving her several minutes to work out the implications of his prodding, Alexander waits until she nods again and finally says, "You must take over MoxWorld Holdings. I have several other holding companies I will still command, but I built MoxWorld with the sole focus of creating the resources necessary to find Her and the blue light cavern."

Her head knocking the wall a few more times, she turns and nods to him.

"Moxy," he calls out. "Make my daughter joint-tenant in MoxWorld Holdings. She will have equal power in ruling the empire. As the woman's oral traditional said, they would rule equally together as man and woman."

Moxy answers, "Joint-tenant status completed. Zara Khatum has complete access to all MoxWorld resources and archives. She has all access to Murometz-only data files and protocols."

She turns to face him, no joy in becoming the richest, most powerful woman in the world. "And where does that leave us with my mother?"

"My dearest, tell her you forgive her. She lives in shame over what we had to do to make you. She has always wanted to confess to you, but she could not find it in her. She needs that same cathartic moment you came here to find."

A big breath in and one out. Zara says, "And where does this leave us with the US, Russia, and China about to start a massive thermonuclear war? And my Kurdistan with the Turks?"

He smiles again. "Why, my dear, did you not know? You are the messiah. You are here to save the innocent, the weak, the good from the end of times. And now, you have all the tools to do so. Is that not right, Moxy?"

Moxy asks, "Ms. Khatum, would you like me to disarm the Chinese and the US?"

"Do not play with me with your fake protocols," snaps Zara.

Shaking his head, Alexander says, "That, my dear, is a genuine request. My—*our* defense network can neutralize any country's nuclear arsenal. It takes time, though, as the process is limited by the amount of electrical power I can harness. If we activated it right now, NiQihs would have enough time to analyze the pattern, then neutralize it. But if you and Peter can unite the black object and the source of the blue light, all wars will cease."

Before she can answer, a crack of wooden deck board echoes in the cabin. She puts her finger to her mouth to signal silence as she gets the gun from the desk. Leaning against the wall of the entrance to the cabin, she has the gun pointed to the doorway.

As the door slowly opens, she is ready to fire. But a voice says, "Zara, it is your Zengo. Do not ambush me. I am friendly."

Still ready to fire, Zara watches as his familiar body comes through the door. Without a word, she pulls him into the room. He is in a tight black outfit that hides nothing. Every line of muscle definition.

Checking the stairwell for anyone else, she goes upward to check as well. Returning, she loosens her grip on the gun that killed her half-brother. Still looking up the stairs, she asks Zengo, "How did you find me here?"

"Forgive me. I put a micro-tracker in your pack," he says with his eyes pointed in the same direction as his drooped shoulders. Eyes affixed on hers, he adds, "I only wanted to make sure you were safe, as I had promised I would do for you forever."

Still strapped in place, Alexander says, "Moxy. Initiate INTRBL with backup."

Nodules emitting blue flashes appear from the walls. Zara grabs Zengo, pulling him below the desk as she says, "Moxy. Cancel security protocols."

In the microsecond of his lips touching hers, her mind races between three rapidly moving thoughts. There is a bulge between his legs. It was not blown off. The Kurds do not have micro-tracker tech that could have evaded Sasha's security systems. This gun that killed Abram is about to be the gun Zara uses to kill her first love.

Before she can react, she feels the needle in her neck, and then the stinging contents rapidly dispersing. She tries to put him into a headlock and roll him into a choke hold, but laxity has already overcome her muscles. She slumps into his arms, no more ready to fight than a sack of lamb's wool.

In her remaining moments of consciousness, she looks up at another body in a tight black outfit. Wavy, dark-brown hair, nine centimeters shorter than herself, with clearly defined chesty mounds, around her wrists the telltale red signs of bondage play. Before Alexander can call Moxy again, this woman injects him.

Zengo lifts Zara's limp body onto the desk and then pulls the other woman into him, kissing her more feverishly than he ever did Zara. "Kidnapping makes me so horny," he says as he squeezes her ample protrusions.

The woman licks his lips up to the tip of his nose, then pushes him back, saying, "You should have your way with your little friend. Tie her up like you love to do, while I finish up with Murometz."

A pause as her lips pucker. "*Yimach shmo.* May his name be erased."

"You practiced that too well for this moment," says Zengo. "This was too easy. I heard she became wiser working for Murometz. She was as gullible to my love as she was back then. How could she believe I could love her again? A dead fish would be more exciting in bed than her. Not like you." He takes another needle and injects Zara again.

As she loses consciousness, all Zara can see is the wiggling seven inches of Peter's most favorite thing. All yellow with red spots. And then Peter's innocent eyes.

Dogs can love cats.

PART II

Great doubt will eventually lead to great awakening.

—Rabi'a al-Adawiyya,
eighth-century Persian philosopher and mystic

CHAPTER 29

When virtue and modesty enlighten her charms, the luster of a
beautiful woman is brighter than the stars of heaven,
and the influence of her power it is in vain to resist.
—Amenhotep IV, Egyptian Pharaoh

Bogoda Mountains of Xinjiang Province, China
11:30 p.m. GMT+7, February 8, 2023

"They all look so apprehensive," says Peter as he watches the local guides watching him. They have dismounted from one of two trucks that have ascended into the mountains 120 kilometers from the provincial capital city into the valley of Mei's dream. All around them are snow-covered peaks reaching four thousand plus meters toward the heavens. Or toward the aliens, muses Peter.

"Notice how the local population looks more Turkish than Chinese?" asks Mei, who finishes tapping away on her MoxWrap, her nose as crinkled as her forehead.

"And more Muslim as well," notes Peter.

"Like our friend Zara's Kurds, these people have been under Chinese rule on and off across the centuries. The Uyghurs, in particular, are seeking independence for their people, which is met with the same oppression as the Kurds faced."

"Is that why we hired a Uyghur guide group?" asks Peter, looking at the driver of their truck. A Caucasoid-looking mustached man with an octagonal white cap with intricate black designs and a grey-and-brown-plaid shirt covered by a forest-green vest.

Out of the other truck, Jia descends out of the front cab. The latter has the utmost attention of the men in her truck as she is dressed as Mei. A light olive, drab expedition jacket over a silk-cotton blend, form-enhancing blouse open enough for an eyeful of a peek.

The good husband he is, Peter does not glare at Mei's colleague, but at the tall man in the front seat of the other truck. An odd, white-haired man who gives commands to the Uyghur guides with glints of silver flashing as he speaks.

As Jia comes over to him, Peter's issue isn't trying not to peek as the other men do, but not focusing on her beauty mark. The little mole just left of her lips. She is so self-conscious about having to wear Mei's fashions he doesn't need to add to it by staring at her mark.

"Who is the big man in the front of your truck?" asks Peter.

"Him? He is the owner of the guide group," replies Jia.

"You seemed so chummy with him. Did you know him before this trip?"

Glancing down, she tries to close up her blouse, a design without buttons that might allow a modicum of modesty or discretion. A key Mei design. "He found my discussions of utmost interest," she says with a deadpan face.

Six large Uyghur men come over with Mei. Large planks, ropes, netting. They come prepared. But for what?

As he ponders, Jia says, "Your description of the black object requires that we have the strength and tools to lift it out of that canyon your dreams have described."

"Is that what you were discussing with that white-haired man?" asks Peter as he watches the guides leer at her attire.

Her hands trying in vain to close up her blouse, she replies, "I am not like Mei. Not in build nor in inclination. I cannot and will not persuade men of power in her manner. We need that man's help. Only he can save China from itself, as Mr. Murometz is apparently not willing to do. Or so says the beleaguered face of our Mei."

"When I find the black object, I will have saved China," says Peter, standing up straight, chest out. "And the rest of the world."

Taking his arm into hers, she lets her blouse open at the most opportune angle for his eyes. She says, "And may you succeed. Like Mei, my family has a legend of this chamber. If you were my husband, then I could tell you what we should find. I am counting on you to solve this legend. For you need to be with me to make the dream real."

Before he can ask her what legend, Mei takes Jia's arms away from Peter, placing them firmly under her arm. "He's spoken for, Jia. And he has a baby to take care of."

A few hours of arduous hiking pass, prolonged by Mei's need to stop to get her bloated feet massaged by her husband. And of course, the multiple nature breaks as their baby presses so tightly against her bladder. But Jia appreciates those breaks almost as much as Mei. And now, they rest in sight of an opening to a very narrow canyon, which Mei has signaled is the one.

Jia, having conferred with the lead Uyghur guide, comes back to say, "Our guide says the canyon is too narrow and dangerous for them with their equipment. If the legend is correct, then I suggest only Mei, Peter, and I go ahead through the canyon to scout it out. If we find the cavern you seek and the object is there, we can have the guides figure out how to get it out."

The three check their backpacks for the provisions they will need for at least a day's cave exploring. Jia escorts Mei and Peter, following the guide into the narrow canyon. What a great place for a Western film, muses Peter. Only room for one abreast through some of these rocks. A human evading giants would do well to go through this canyon.

A half hour later, Jia stops and peers into a two-meter-wide opening in the rocks. They have arrived, as the faintest of blue glimmers reflects from the dampness on the opening walls. She nods for everyone to enter. The smoothness of the cave's floor does not escape Peter's attention, nor does the narrowness. Perfect for the goddess Jiang to have dragged the object in here to hide from the giants' return.

Twenty-five or so paces into the cave, it opens up into a cavern with a distinct blue glow backlighting a blackened rock, which Jia points to. Peter pauses with one eye squinted and his nose twisted as he inspects the stone and lighting. It emits a blue aura. Odd.

"Mei, this isn't—" he tries to say.

"Oh, honey," Mei interrupts. "It's exactly what Jia's family legends said. The chamber of blue light that comes from the black object. We found it."

"But Pappy's diary," Peter exclaims.

Before he can finish, her swollen foot plants itself firmly onto his. With her disarming smile, she says, "Jia, we found it. Here's what our government has been searching for." Her eyes follow Jia like a night owl who spies a mouse as Jia peruses the rock. Mei adds, "I bet your grandmother told you of this place. Didn't she?"

Out of her backpack, Jia pulls out a pistol aimed at the two of them and says, "And I thank you both for making this possible. The man and woman who created the child that would allow the second woman access to the cavern of the blue light. And to think I got pregnant with that old, silver-toothed man's baby just so I could enter this cavern."

Guns always in his face. First in Manhattan when he had an editor job there. Then, when Alexander pointed a gun at his head in the battle for the first object. And now for this doomed expedition to find the second object. If only he could have learned from Alexander's martial arts instructor, he could show Mei and her mother what a superhero he was. But he is merely a keen-minded editor. One with a beta model MoxWrap, which he readies.

"And you, my dear Mei, we will take your baby. You'll get to live long enough to give birth," says Jia. "But as the legend says, one of us needs to die for the other to be in the blue light."

Mei responds, "And why would the Chinese government want my baby? Look at this guy next to me. He is not Han. The baby will not be pure Chinese."

Buttoning up her jacket with her free hand, Jia sneers. "Foolish woman. I had to bare my body in your silly fashions so I could find the legendary cavern of the blue light. No wonder Murometz is dead. His best people are fools and so viscerally petty. The Chinese have little to do with this operation. Only a brief part of their history matters here. The world is running from MoxWorld to NiQihs because they want the freedom to choose what they think

Murometz is denying them. Little do they know what NiQihs really is and how far our powers extend. But you, Mr. Gollinger, will never know. Only your extracted glands will live on in infamy."

As the NiQihs agent talked, Peter shuffled over several centimeters to get the correct angle on Jia. As she turns with the gun, aiming to kill Peter, he taps his MoxWrap. Jia's body jerks back once, then more violently again, and finally a third time, pounding her into the smooth, glistening cavern wall and sending her gun flying.

She slumps on the ground, her mouth closing, and Peter rushes forward and jams his fingers into the back of her mouth. He screams as she tries to chomp down. His fingers wrestle around in her oral orifice, and he pulls out a molar cap. And a capsule.

"You people can't fool me twice. That horrible Harlan Chapwell the Third got away with that cheesy cyanide-capsule-in-the-tooth gimmick. You're mine now," yells Peter, parading her molar cap and capsule in fist-punching victory rounds in the air.

Jia spits blood at Peter, saying, "So, what now? You sadistically violate me like the bad guys in your book did to that woman?"

He backs up, saying, "No. No, I'm not that kind of person."

Taking advantage of Peter's reaction, she tries to crawl away, seeking her gun. But the fast foot of Mei Tang tags her throat, pressing down on her airway. "He may not be that kind of person, but I might be. I have no pity on a woman who sells out her country. My China."

"Your China? You do not know," cries Jia. "The world is in perpetual crisis. We all will die shortly from a global thermonuclear war, and all you want is your self-serving MoxWorld to rule the Earth. We serve Him. The one who will once again rise up and reunite all the countries into one. The world will have order and peace. He is the true savior of us all."

"Who are you talking about?" asks Mei. "Most Chinese do not believe in a messiah. Are you a fanatic from one of the Abrahamic faiths?"

Jia wriggles her neck under Mei's bloated foot, trying to breathe. "We are ahead of you. You cannot get out of this cave with the sacred stone of the blue light. We will send another pregnant woman in here, and you will still die."

Mei waves to Peter to reach behind the rock. His eyes light up. Not from the blue light, but from what he sees. He reaches behind the rock and pulls up a self-powered blue light LED chip. A MoxWorld special that can illuminate for decades without recharging.

Her eyebrows at first rise well into her forehead, and then come crashing down into a nasty V as her nose scrunches. Jia says, "They will make a genetically perfect baby and beat you to the real chamber of the blue light. You fooled me, and my fate awaits me." Crunch goes her other molar, and before Peter can dive in to get the capsule out, a light pink foam spills out from the dead NiQihs agent's mouth.

"I'm sorry, Mei," says Peter. "I missed the chance to check her other molars. I guess I'll never make a good secret agent."

Mei helps him up and kisses him. Very deep and very wet. "You are my hero. You saved my life." She pats her belly. "And my child's life."

He pats her belly too. "Our child's life." Holding up the source of the blue light, he says, "So, this whole thing was a hoax? There is no chamber of the blue light? What about what my pappy's diary said?"

"We had to get the mole in MoxWorld to expose themself. Alexander has been in hiding, waiting for me to flush him or her out. And you killed her. You are the hero of MoxWorld."

"And your mother? The Uyghurs have her outside. If the Uyghurs are in with NiQihs, they won't take it well that their leader is dead," says Peter.

"Have faith in me. I'm more than a pretty face with an awesome pregnant body," teases Mei.

The edges of lips up toward his ears, he puts his palms around her ears and says, "And you said your natural talents rest under your dress. I say your true natural gift is between these ears."

Those words of honest praise said, Peter inspects the black object. "This is fake, isn't it?"

Getting her MoxPad+ out of her pack, she shows Peter scans of the black thing.

"You mean, it's real," exclaims Peter.

A snort of a laugh from the normally full-of-decorum Mei. "If the emissions can fool you, it will fool NiQihs or the Chinese."

"You mean you had a fake one fabricated? How ingenious."

"Well, credit our boss. The big guy. Alexander. Jean-Paul found a sizable black object fragment at his excavation at Çatalhöyük. Alexander had a secret MoxWorld tech team construct a black-object-like infrastructure around that fragment, and we discreetly fabricated this cavern shortly after you and I had the Goddess Jiang dream. He also let NiQihs hack a rigged version of his tracking software so they would think they could verify the object."

"So, what now?" ask Peter.

She runs her hands down her blouse. "Nothing that has to do with how fabulous I look all knocked up with our baby," she says with a smile. "Our fate is now in my mother's hands."

CHAPTER 30

*To have a great peace, the state must be united. The king does
what he must to fulfill his responsibilities as a king.*
—Qin Shi Huang, first emperor of China, second century BCE

*Bogoda Mountains of Xinjiang Province, China
5:30 a.m. GMT+7, February 9, 2023*

With Ming in the lead, following the legendary stories of the Goddess Jiang she had uncovered and studied since her school days, they traverse another narrow but rock-strewn path between rocky walls of these fabled mountains. Finally, another opening in these canyon walls.

Inside the cavern? No blue light. No black object. Only a series of sealed jars. Ming kneels, taking out tools from her backpack to open one up.

"How does she know what to do with antiquities?" asks Peter.

"Didn't you know?" says Mei. "She's a retired archaeology professor."

"Seriously?"

"Yes, seriously. How do you think I know so much about the subject?" replies Mei as she slowly kneels to help her mother.

Another half hour passes as they triage the jars like a nurse in an urban emergency ward. Taking photos of each step, they isolate a pile of wooden sticks preserved in one of the sealed jars. Mei explains to Peter that these were like mail in ancient China. As Mei reads them, she gasps.

"What?" asks Peter as Ming grabs the sticks to read for herself.

"The legend of the first emperor of China, Qin Shi Huang, ends with his search for the elixir of life. The secret to immortality. Legend has it he sent people all over the lands in search of this mythical cure. A thousand young people sailed east and founded Japan. He died of poisoning from the mercury pills his alchemists gave him as a longevity elixir. These sticks are the first records ever found saying he commissioned his most trusted agents to search for a magic black stone that would lead a pregnant prophetess to the source of immortality. But these other sticks speak of hidden riches to fund his most trusted agents, a secret society if needed, in the event of his premature death. That this magic stone would allow women the visions to make the elixir to bring Qin Shi Huang back from death."

"Qin Shi Huang," says Peter with his hand rubbing his mouth and chin. "Qin Shi. Qin Shi."

Before he can say more, Ming points madly at three more sticks. Mei gasps, then reads out loud, "The society of Qin Shi shall go forth and build the people's faith that one day he will return and reunite all the countries as he did in creating the Empire of China. Order and peace shall return to the world, who will have the immortal Qin Shi to protect them forever."

Reading his MoxWrap offline library, Peter says, "This guy was one badass dude. He makes Alexander look like a saint. He buried alive hundreds of scholars who criticized him. He burned all books so there would be no history before him. He's the one who buried thousands of workers under the Great Wall. Yes. He will come back to protect us by killing all of us who won't bow to him."

He gets a stick and asks, "Mei, could you write his name in the sand here?"

Mei writes out a bunch of Chinese characters. And Peter says, "No, no. The pinyin romanization version."

She scribbles: Q-I-N S-H-I H-U-A-N-G.

Peter takes the stick and scribbles: NIQ IHS GNAUH.

"NiQihs is his name spelled backwards," exclaims Peter.

After Mei explains to Ming, the latter smiles and rubs Peter's hair and kisses his cheek, whispering something in his ear. Ming laughs. Mei laughs as well, saying, "My mother said you may make another hundred babies with me. You make the family honorable and proud."

A distinct shrill breaks the profoundness of Peter's revelation.

"My MoxWrap worked only for a second, and then nothing," exclaims Peter as he stares at his wrist device.

"That's because NiQihs is blocking our signal. Might your MoxWrap had a hiccup," replies Mei, standing next to him.

Lines forming across his face. Nose flicking. Peter finishes staring at his MoxWrap with a nod.

Mei interrupts, "Hup, hup. We need to stay to task here."

"And what task is that?"

"Trust me. You will see."

Ming pulls on Mei's sleeve, pointing to a hole in the rocks. Slightly narrower than the ones around the fake object cavern. They enter the mouth of the cave, which is small enough that Peter needs to crouch. Certainly, a good place to keep the giants at bay, thinks Peter as his head scrapes solid rock.

Thirty paces in, they find a grotto. Using their MoxWraps as lanterns, they see the walls are full of drawings. Most describe people fleeing giants journeying across different lands. But the one that Peter drifts toward calls out "home" to him. The tail of the bird star nestled at the back of the Cygnus constellation. He says to everyone to shut off their MoxWrap lights. In the dark, a faint blue luminescence emanates from the tail of the bird star. He pulls out his black stone pendant, which emits a similar faint blue hue that grows stronger the closer he holds it to the star engraving.

Mei comes up behind Peter, putting her hands on his arms as she says into his ear, "She is calling you, isn't she?"

"It's as if part of me is supposed to be where the tail of the bird star leads," says Peter. "Does it feel like home to you too?"

She puts her hand on her upper belly. "Not really. The only thing I feel is my poor stomach. This child is pushing right up into it."

He turns around and puts his hand on her stomach, feeling the kick. "Soccer player, I hope."

As they both feel the movements, Peter asks, "Do you think Zara is safe?"

She squeezes his hand and replies, "Why are you asking that? Did you get an alert moments ago?"

"Both Alexander's MoxWrap and hers have been offline for weeks," says Peter, tapping his wrist device. "Funny, you know that 'hiccup' you thought happened to my MoxWrap? It was an emergency alert from Moxy. But I have to be in a MoxWorld Regional Headquarters to fully activate it. Do you have one of these?"

"No. That is odd that you got one and I didn't," says Mei.

Peter walks around the grotto with his hands out. "Do you feel that?"

"I'm pregnant, Peter. I feel all sorts of things I've never felt before," muses Mei.

Several minutes pass with Peter wandering about, bumping into everyone as the grotto is comfy for one or two max.

He glides his hands along the cave walls. Minutes later, he stops upon one rock. "Here," he says. "Does anyone have a digging tool?"

Ming reaches in her backpack and hands Peter a small pickaxe. A little chip, chip here, chip, chip, there, and Peter pulls out something all too familiar. He holds up the blackened fragment. Pitted dark stone, as if it sailed through an asteroid field. "Whoever was here, they had an object. This chunk is similar to the one I have back at home, but three times as large."

Ming points to engraved characters in a farther spot of the cavern. Mei searches her offline MoxWrap database and then says, "These characters come from a woman who accompanied Rabban Bar Sauma on his trip to find Jerusalem."

"Who's that?" asks Peter.

"Rabban was an emissary of Kublai Khan, grandson of Genghis Khan, and emperor of China in the twentieth century CE. While Marco Polo resided in China, Kublai Khan sent Rabban to explore the lands the Venetian spoke of. He and thirty others traveled by here along the silk road headed to Baghdad, Mosul, and into Syria. But wars there prevented them from reaching Jerusalem."

"What did Kublai Khan want in Jerusalem?" asks Peter.

Ming interrupts, pointing to another line of characters. Mei says, "A woman who heard a voice carved this inscription. She was a concubine of an important member of the imperial court who also suffered the dreams that revealed the location of the hidden cavern and the magical object within it, as well as the whereabouts of the tail of the bird star in Jerusalem.

Peter turns the object fragment around and around. "Do you think the whole second object came here, or only this piece?"

"Where is that circuitous head of yours going?" asks Mei.

"What if Kublai Khan heard of that elixir of life? Maybe from a concubine. Maybe this woman was his concubine. Maybe through Qin Shi's secret society?" asks Peter. "Could Rabban what's his name have been sent west to find the object and the source of the elixir of life? And that this woman would bring Qin Shi back to life?"

With a little snort, Mei says, "You found your calling as a fiction writer. That is wild thinking there." Rubbing circles around her blossoming baby bump, she continues, "Perhaps if we bond again, we can see what this woman was doing here and why they thought they should seek Jerusalem."

"Uh, the last time we tried to bond, we couldn't get that level of detail," says Peter.

"Are you saying my bump isn't as good as Zara's?" challenges Mei with eyes of ire.

Backing away from her, a timid Peter stutters as he says, "I would never compare two women's bumps as a measure of their worth."

He pats her neck bump, replying, "Perhaps with this larger object fragment, our pair bonding might have more of an effect than last time. Remember, Zara and I first bonded in the presence of a full-sized object." He rubs that special place on the back of her neck and says, "We need to get back to MoxWorld Shanghai Headquarters as soon as possible so I can see what this urgent alert is all about. Perhaps in the privacy of your jet on our way back to Shanghai, we can try to bond to determine the whereabouts of Zara and Alexander. Maybe it's not the size of the bump that matters but the mass of the object."

"Oh, you know how to charm an afflicted woman, don't you?" says Mei.

❧

Sitting face-to-face with Mei on the all so familiar bed of first intimacies in her MoxWorld jet, but this time with the object fragment between them, Peter adjusts her silk robe to show a little less skin. Mei gives him the evil eye and says, "My dress this morning showed more vivid details than this robe is showing." She opens up her robe again.

She pulls his hand into her robe, rubbing it along the full length of her upper torso. He pulls her head toward his and, with an open mouth, kisses her. Tongue on tongue, their wetness intermingles, the spiritual pheromones passing from one to the other. He takes her fingers, wet-kisses them, and places them on his temples. She does the same in return. In unison, their fingers circle each other's temples. Kissing again, they breathe deeply through their noses.

A deep peace comes to each of them. A warmth emanating from their temples, mouths, and down their necks into their chests and lower. The much lower part, Peter tries to suppress, with very little success. Mei moans with even more ecstasy than she did with his foot massages as she experiences the lower reaction. He whispers, "That's not what we're trying to do. Focus on your inner self. I'll focus on finding Zara."

Like a mist clearing to let the sunlight shine through, they see what appears to be a palace. Large arches line a walkway, with a woman dressed in a burgundy outer robe lined with gold lace flowers. A royal-blue headscarf waves in the breeze as she hurries in a near trot. As the vision becomes clearer, they can see her face. The mists come back, clouding the vision.

"That's not her," yells Peter, breaking their bond. "That's not Zara."

"That was the Great Mosque of Damascus," says Mei. "The citadel near the mosque was not in ruins. We must have seen someone of importance in ancient times. Peter, we need to go back."

"You saw the cloudiness. That's as good as the vision gets," says Peter.

She pauses as she stares up at the ceiling, then her hands roll down Peter's robe off his shoulders. "We have less than a week before our ploy is exposed. Michaela will understand. We tried it your way. Now, we try it my way."

CHAPTER 31

I am the punishment of God. If you had not committed great sins,
God would not have sent a punishment like me upon you.

—Genghis Khan

Damascus
January 10, 1300 CE

A long way from home. A long way from the land of her great-great-grandfather. A long way from the simple pleasures of riding her horses across the plains. She rises from her prayer, dressed in a burgundy outer gown with a delightful gold flower embroidery, which she got from a merchant who would give anything if her nephew spared their lives. For she has more respect for Allah than to enter the Great Mosque dressed in the horse warrior clothes in which she entered this half-deserted city.

Her royal-blue headscarf blows in the wind as she briskly walks along the outer corridors of the mosque. The screams of men on the way to either heaven or hell echo along the archways. So many have died already on the way here. Her grandfather razed Baghdad into dust, killing hundreds of thousands, if not a million people. Some say nearly nine out of ten people in Persia perished under her family's brutal massacres of the resistant towns and cities.

She prayed to Allah with her gratitude that this city surrendered to her nephew, Ghazan, the seventh ruler of the Ilkhanate, the western part of the Mongol empire. Instead of massacring the population, his men spend their days pillaging and plundering. As a woman, she finds a modicum of solace in the fact her people are civilized enough not to violate or kidnap women, unlike most other conquering armies.

Why the hurry? A messenger from her nephew said her favorite horse had been shot as they sieged the last remaining outpost of Syrian defiance—the Citadel of Damascus.

She arrives outside the mosque to see the siege artillery of the Mongols pummeling the citadel walls. The Chinese and Turkmen who operate these engines of war can carve a hole in a stone wall such that a camel could needle its way through.

She hears him. Crying into the wind. She runs over as much as her gown permits. Her hands around his head, she comforts him as much as one can to one who is nearing death. Neigh. Neigh. And then silence. Her favorite horse has died of a massive crossbow bolt wound through his abdomen, the most painful of ways to die.

Fire burning the edges of her eyelids, she looks up and yells, "Who rode my horse? Who got my horse killed?"

Soldiers a head taller than she cower as she scans each and every eye, searching for the inkling of guilt. A more moderate-sized man in a mail armor cloak and a cone-shaped metal helmet briskly walks over to save the men. As he reaches out to help her up, a bull's head medallion dangles forward from his chest armor.

"El, calm down. No one stole your horse," says Ghazan.

She points to the crossbow bolt, so large only a wall-mounted bow could have fired it, and says, "So my horse just fell on this arrow, which happened to be on the ground?"

Ghazan says, "The Supreme Judge of Damascus exaggerated when he said the city would surrender peacefully. These fools in the citadel have become more than a nuisance."

El Qutlugh Khatun, daughter of Abaqa Khan, the second ruler of the

Mongol Ilkhanate, waves a trepid soldier over. She disarms him of his crossbow and quiver. Walking thirty paces toward the citadel, she fires off seven bolts in less than a minute. Better than any man could in Damascus, Mongol or otherwise. Six men on the fortress wall near the mounted crossbow fall down, mortally wounded.

"Seven bolts. Six men dead. You wasted one," says Ghazan. "You are getting old and losing your touch."

She pulls out a curved dagger from under her coat and says, "Perhaps I should run up there and cut their heads off instead. Would that make you happier?"

"Why, yes. And you can parade their heads around hanging from the collar of your new horse as you did the head of the man who murdered your husband," jests Ghazan.

"Nephews should speak to their aunts with respect," chastises El. "Remember, my father ruled when you were born."

"You are only ten years my senior. Perhaps it is aunts who should speak with respect to their rulers," retorts Ghazan.

"Is that the respect that you learned by converting to the words of the Prophet, may God honor him and grant him peace?" says El.

"My people find greater respect for their leader now that he follows the one true God," says Ghazan.

"Odd. You converted five years ago to get the support of the people the traitor Nawruz ruled," says El. "You let him live, and look where that got him. You still had to execute him three years later."

Silence as the great ruler weighs his next words.

Not willing to afford him his silence, she says, "Deep inside, you still worship Tengri, the Mongol's Heavenly Father."

He instantly retorts, "No more than you still worship his wife Eje, the Earth Mother."

She pulls up her pendant, a circle and crescent design, and rubs it. "Before my half-brother became the Ilkhanate of these lands, he ruled Anatolia. He said one drunken evening a sorceress seduced him. She spoke of a voice she heard. This voice told the story of the family of the Prophet Nuh, who carried a holy stone with them as they settled into the lands that became Anatolia."

Her nephew stares with a puzzled face. She says, "You know, your debauched Uncle Gaykhatu, who foolishly tried to introduce paper money after he had spent all the riches in the treasury."

"Why should I believe a fairy tale from such a deranged man?" asks Ghazan.

"Because the tale is not from him but her," says El. "Gaykhatu had this sorceress woman sent down to teach me the ways of her kind." She touches behind her neck, adding, "We had more in common than a man's eyes could discern.

"Rumor has it our great-uncle Kublai Khan, emperor of China, sent an envoy to Jerusalem to find this magic, holy stone before he died," adds El. "You have worked hard to maintain good relations with his successor and the Golden Horde Mongols. Would it not be a grand gesture to have found this holy stone and present it to Kublai's successor?"

Another massive crossbow bolt pierces the ground ten paces from them. Nonplussed, Ghazan strokes his beard. "And this is why I keep you around. You are as smart as you are fierce."

She picks out four more bolts from the quiver and runs toward the citadel, firing in rapid succession. Four men fall from the wall. Walking back, she says, "You should have your catapults take out that mounted crossbow before more innocent horses die."

As her nephew signals to his catapults, she says, "Kublai's successor, Temür Khan, is a nice man. Rumor has it that an ancient Chinese secret society is funding his rule. If we are not careful, it will be the Chinese who rule the Mongols and not the other way around."

Ghazan stares at her, lips flattened. "As we speak here, the Chagatai Khanate that sits between us and China already sends long-range raiding parties as far as the Tigris River, well into our lands. We cannot afford to start a conflict with China as well."

Rubbing her nephew's arm, El says, "Did not my great-great-grandfather Genghis say, 'In the space of seven years, I have succeeded in accomplishing a great work uniting the whole world into one empire'? In the space of seventy years since, his empire has already fragmented among several feuding Khans."

His lips go from flat to a serious upside-down U.

She nods and adds, "What if this holy stone contains the power to unify the Mongol empire again? A way to expand through Europe and the Mediterranean? We would fulfill Genghis Khan's vision of one empire from sea to sea."

Ghazan scans around. His men, who are not part of the catapult teams, are lying against walls, tallying up the booty they have gained from plundering the city. "We do not stay here for long. We must take care of our horses first. Those Mamluk devils know our ways. They burn the pastures and fields before we arrive, knowing we can only fight for so long before we need to pasture our horses. In a month or two, I will need to take our forces back toward the Euphrates River and let our horses regain their strength for the final battle against Cairo."

She inspects the few bolts remaining in the quiver as she says, "Give me a dozen men dressed in Damascan clothing. We can scout Jerusalem and confirm the intelligence Hetoum II, King of Armenia, provided. I talked with his men. Jerusalem stands unprotected. The Mamluk have left the city for our taking. Only a hundred Frankish crusaders guard the Christian sites. You are friends with the Frankish barons. We can walk right in and take the holy stone."

"Damn tourist, that Hetoum. I send him with my troops to raid Cairo and he spends two weeks touring the Christian sites while my men die here," laments Ghazan.

The air pulses with the crash of one, then another massive stone pummeling the site of the mounted crossbow. Ghazan says, "Expert engineers from China direct my artillery. Having your holy stone will give me options. I am not saying I am giving it to Temür Khan or keeping it for myself. But a wise Khan has options. You may have a dozen of my scouts, one set of horses, and no soldiers. You have five weeks."

The evening moonrise highlights the skyline of Damascus. Still standing and not burning in flames, thanks to a generous conquering Mongol leader. Why did this leader come to Damascus and stop? A question that reigns in the mind of a solo horse rider exiting the city.

Just several months ago, Ghazan seized Aleppo and then routed troops from the Mamluk Al-Nasir Muhammad, sultan of Egypt, in the city of Homs. The Mamluk troops fled south to the safety of Egypt, leaving Damascus in the path of the Mongols.

Jerusalem lies a good six-day ride to the south. But this rider will only ride through half the night to a minor village that hopes the Mongols bypass them. Dismounting from the swift Mongolian horse, the helmeted, black-cloaked rider enters a small hut.

The rider removes her helmet and shakes her hair loose. It is El. The woman of the hut, wearing a dark red robe covering the first bulges of a baby, greets El.

El says, "Asefeh, you keep your shape well. Eight months has it been?"

"It would have been only seven and a half months had you not snuck us out of Damascus a week before the Mongols came," says Asefeh as she kisses El on both cheeks.

"Remember, I am Mongolian, not one of the Franks, who gut pregnant women," says El as she places her fingers behind Asefeh's neck. "But we are women of the dream-afflicted men."

Groans come from the only other room in this little hut. Asefeh says, "That is my husband. Since we fled Damascus, his dreams have gotten worse, if that is even possible. I had thought your last message said you would sneak into Damascus alone to meet me. It took us seven days to get to Damascus from Jerusalem. But before we knew it, the whole of the Mamluk army was fleeing, passing by the city, and half the city fled with them."

"I have intrigued my nephew," says El. "He gives me five weeks to determine the status of Jerusalem and ascertain whether the object of our matriarch resides there."

Asefeh nods. "I am sure it is buried below the Dome of the Rock, which sits above where our Second Temple lies."

"But you have not seen it yourself," asks El.

"Our order descended directly from Queen Nitzevet herself. The legends have passed from mother to daughter that our ancestors worshipped Yahweh's wife at the black stone of Abraham and Ya'akov. When King Hezekiah killed the Temple's high priestess, he buried the statue of Asherah along with the black stone under the temple. When King Herod rebuilt the temple, the black stone was found again, only to be buried again a hundred years later when the Romans burned down the Second Temple."

"I cannot have my nephew endanger the western front with the Chagatai Khanate ready to invade based on rumors. We must verify that this black stone exists. He is sending a dozen scouts with me. If we could remove it without calling in the soldiers, if we could be the most discreet, that would be the best outcome for all. More innocent people should not die because of this stone."

"I was born in Jerusalem near the Lions Gate. I know the tunnels under the Dome of the Rock," affirms Asefeh. "You are Muslim. I am Jewish. We share the same ancient prophets. It is said this is the rock that Ya'akov slept upon. We will experience the same visions he had as we get close to the stone."

"I hope you are right," says El. "The vision I fear is Jerusalem in flames because someone stupid resisted my nephew and his generals. Bringing the Mongols to Jerusalem is not in the best interest of God."

"Meet me in eight days at the Eastern Gates, called the Gates of Eternal Life by Muslims," says Asefeh. "We call them the Gates of Mercy, as they are the closest a Jew can get to the Second Temple grounds."

A thud comes from the other room, which has El drawing a curved dagger from under her cloak. "Please, please, it is only my husband fighting a mysterious foe in his dream. He keeps calling out, 'Illyana, Illyana.' These dreams haunted my father and his father."

"As they did my father, his father, and the uncle and father of my mother," says El.

"It is told by my grandmother that the secret priestess of Asherah at the time of Romans transcribed the words of Queen Nitzevet near the black stone," explains Asefeh.

"A prophetess from Anatolia taught me a legend," says El. "She said the great goddess proclaimed one day her daughter will return with unborn child.

And with her, a woman of great strength. One will die, as together, they will unlock the key to heaven. The key to death. And the key to the peace of the blue light."

"I heard part of the same from my grandmother," says Asefeh. "I bear that child, and you are the woman of great strength. Together, we must find this holy object. Soon. I am due within weeks."

The sound of approaching hoofbeats interrupts them. "Are you expecting anyone else?" asks El.

Asefeh shakes her head.

"Then I will lead them away from here. I will see you in eight days," says El as she dashes out to mount her horse.

El makes three rapid clicks of her tongue, and her horse begins to trot. Even though this is her third-in-line horse, he is well trained. Mongols go to war with six horses each, allowing them to rotate steeds as they cover up to a hundred kilometers per day.

She does a running mount and steers toward the oncoming riders, and then away. Two men on horseback immediately follow. She leads them on a chase, pulling away from them until she is sure she is their intended target. She then turns around and rides straight at them. Surprised, they pull up on their horses' reins to slow them down.

With their momentum gone, she turns around again and lets them chase. Classic Mongol tactics. Feign retreat, then attack. Around a knoll, she stops and waits. Just before they crest, she charges them, and with her shoulder, she knocks one of them off his horse. With a resounding thud, he falls heavily. The other rider in disarray, she turns and charges him, slashing the rider's reins with a dagger. With another turn and charge, she charges at the unknown rider, who now cannot control his horse. He dismounts before she gets there and prostrates himself in submission on the ground.

As Mamluks are known to be better close-in fighters than Mongols, she takes no chances. She jumps her horse over him and then turns to have her horse stomp the ground before the man with his front hooves.

Still prostrate on the ground before her, the frightened, beaten man says, "Please do not kill me. We are your messengers from His Highness. I bear his answer to your question. Sultan an-Nasir Muhammad would be honored to entertain your plea to have safe passage to Mecca and perform the Hajj. But the Sultan must know Her Highness's nephew's intentions for Jerusalem."

She has her horse stomp his hooves once again and says, "The Mongols will take Jerusalem by force if Mamluks come to defend it. If the town resists, we will make Jerusalem the next Baghdad. We only want to take non-Muslim treasures from the town. If you allow us safe passage in and out of Jerusalem, then I will tell my nephew to leave Damascus in three months."

Batter and bruised much more than anticipated, both riders try to regain their corporal composures and ride back to Mamluk territory, giving this fierce, unforgiving Mongol woman's demands to their sultan.

✍

El stares at the moon as she slowly rides back to Damascus, bathing in the joy that she will soon gain permission to go to Mecca. That smell. She stops and sniffs.

She sees them. All around her. Black-clad. Assassins? The Mongols crushed the Hashashin, the Syrian Assassins, over two decades ago. Perhaps she should not have been so headstrong about coming out here alone.

As she scans all directions for the best escape, she remembers the Mamluks employed a remnant group of assassins recently. If she had just agreed to help the Mamluks, why would they be trying to kill her now?

That scent. Where has she smelled this before? No time to ponder more. She dismounts and invites the assassins to come forward from around her. For she is El Qutlugh Khatun, daughter of Abaqa Khan. She has defeated ten mounted warriors while on foot.

But alas, with not a bow and quiver, not even a spear, but a meager knife, she must let something else prevail as six black-clad men with bows and quivers cautiously approach her.

Near enough they come, and she uses her deepest commanding voice. "You must know who I am. The daughter of one of the greatest Mongol Khans. My nephew would not take kindly to any ill fortune you may wish to bring to his favored aunt. You know we Mongols will hunt your people down and slaughter your villages, your cities, leaving no one alive. State your terms and let us be on with this."

The shortest of the men lowers his bow and steps forward. Off comes his black hood as she sees why the smell. These are not assassins. They are Chinese.

"You cannot hunt us down," says this man. "We are everywhere, and yet nowhere to be found."

Shaking her head, she replies, "No. You can be found. You are agents of Temür Khan, successor to Kublai Khan. I thought he and my nephew were at peace with each other."

A sneer and a scoff. "You have that backward. Perhaps the great Kublai Khan was but an agent of our society."

"And what society might this be?" asks a bewildered El, her hand still on the reins of her horse, ready to bolt at any opportunity.

"We have the same interests as you. The black stone in Jerusalem."

Unsure whether to feign ignorance or to play along with them, El decides to play the middle. "There are many black stones all over Jerusalem. Which specific one are you seeking?"

"It is said that Queen Nitzevet herself inscribed this black stone with the way to find an elixir our society wishes to find. You may keep the black stone. We only desire the elixir."

A scoff through her nose. Another one of these mystical magic potion hunts sponsored by some feudal lord. Humor them and move on, she thinks. "You are delaying me from my journey to Jerusalem, where I intend on sightseeing and shopping. If I find such a stone with directions to your elixir, I might consider a discussion with your society. But if you do not let me pass unharmed, I can never help you."

Out comes his knife, whose edge glistens in the moonlight. "We know you met with a pregnant Jewish woman. For only the purity of a woman with the right child can access the elixir. We will let you go. But if you fail to deliver, your friend will be the first we slice like a pig at a roast."

A snort through her nose. How dare he threaten her? Once she is armed again, this conversation will be very different. But for now, discretion is the best strategy. "How will I contact you if I do find information on your elixir?"

The man puts back on his black hood and says, "We will contact you."

Slowly remounting her horse, with eyes on each of the men's bows, she asks, "And how will I know the contact represents you?"

As the man backs up, waving to the other men to do the same, he says, "Nickiss. You will hear this. Nickiss."

CHAPTER 32

If I were to remain silent, I would be guilty of complicity.

—Albert Einstein

MoxWorld Jet en route to Shanghai
4:30 p.m. GMT+8, February 9, 2023

Deeply flushed. Her neck. Her upper chest. She lies in utter bliss, gazing upon the lofty ceiling as if she could see the constellations shining down upon her overheated bare body. "I don't care what you say. That was so much better than sex. So much better." Her head turns toward Peter, who is sitting in bed partially covered by pajamas, intensely focused on his MoxWrap.

"Is that like when a man has to smoke after sex?" Mei asks. "Because, if it is, you are destroying the ambience of what just happened."

Breaking his intense reading session, Peter turns to peer into Mei's eyes. "I told you that the secret to two afflicted people bonding is not physical sex. Alexander misled us. We should focus on what we saw in the dream of El and Asefeh."

Returning her gaze to the ceiling, she replies, "Now I understand why Zara says she's celibate. I would be too if I could have that afflicted person's bonding a few times a day. Do you think I can make it work between two afflicted women as well?"

Pausing again from his reading, he answers, "I don't know. I suppose it might. Unless the XX and XY chromosome pairing is needed to make the bond work correctly."

That smile she had when she first kissed another girl comes across her face. "Zara has a close girlfriend. Might it be she's the reason Zara couldn't commit to you? They were afflicted, ancient-gene-bonding day and night."

With a tiny snort, he says, "One, Peri doesn't have the God Gene bump. Two, Zara doesn't swing that way. She doesn't swing any which way. Only toward the love of Xwedê."

Her hand patting Peter's thigh, Mei retorts, "I think you underestimate her."

"You and she are very different," replies Peter. "You are much more visceral. She more spiritual."

Punching his thigh this time, she says, "That's only what she wants you to believe. That woman is as visceral as I am. As is your sister. Does Michaela know about this? I can't wait to try this bonding with her."

"She's my little sister. I certainly will not talk about her in such ways," says Peter, pulling his arms tighter to his side. "Seriously, we need to talk about the dream. NiQihs funded Kublai Khan's ascent to emperor of China. Those assassins who kidnapped Jean-Paul turned out to be agents of NiQihs, the same as your ex-friend Jia. This means NiQihs isn't a recent development but has existed for centuries, if not longer."

Pulling her robe around her now-cooled-off body, Mei sits up. "Actually, I was more interested in El and Asefeh's dynamic. A devout Muslim princess and a Jewish woman from Jerusalem. The parallels to two people I know are uncanny."

"So, you mean Zara and who else?"

"A biblical archaeology professor I'm in contact with from Jerusalem. In fact, she and Zara have met," she remarks with a giggle. "They hit it off like a match to a stick of dynamite, I'm told by poor Jean-Paul, who had to referee between them."

"You mean, like he did when Zara and I first met?" says Peter, this time his turn to chuckle.

Her MoxWrap emits an unmistakable shrieking sound. Bolting up straight, Mei reaches for her MoxWrap on the nightstand. Tap, tap. "Is this a repeat alert of the one you got at the caverns? Oh no."

"Oh no what? It's about Zara, isn't it?" asks Peter, bolting up straight as well.

"It's Alexander. He's been kidnapped or killed. This alert signifies his INTRBL protocol has been activated."

Fingers around his chin, Peter says, "You're kidding. INTRBL? In trouble? Seriously?"

"Even the big man has his sense of humor. Even when facing his own death," says Mei as she taps some more. "His senior leadership team has been trained on what to do in the event of this alert."

Her head drifts down as she scrolls through her MoxWrap messages. "Brace yourself, Peter. Bad news and bad news. No good news."

His hand in hers, he nods the affirmative.

"Bad news part one. The president of China has signaled that his deal with me is off. He has another source for the black object. That means NiQihs is working with China. They control whether or not the great powers will go to nuclear war."

Squeezing her hand, he says, "That's pretty bad. What could be worse?"

"Bad news part two. INTRBL protocol specifies that the heir apparent to Alexander is to take control of MoxWorld and its leadership team."

Releasing her hand, Peter says, "So, we're good. We just wait for the heir apparent. Who is that?"

Her bloodshot eyes peer into his. Her head tilts. "Our Zara."

Shoulders slumped. Flat-lined mouth. If he were a dog, his ears would be drooped and tail pointed to dûjeh, hell. "But if Alexander was killed or kidnapped, so too wouldn't have Zara?"

Arms around him, she squeezes. "She should have reached out to at least me and Jean-Paul. We're the two, other than you and Zara, that Alexander trusted most."

"If your dream is more prophetic than merely historical, it implies we need your Zara to work with my friend," says Mei, bowing her head with a long breath through her nose, her hand on his. "I am afraid we are in a terrible loop. We need Zara to work with my friend to find the black object. But we need the black object to get NiQihs to release her and Alexander."

Snuggling next to him, she takes his hands into hers again. "She is the love of your life, isn't she?"

"Wasn't she," laments Peter.

"She isn't dead."

"How do you know? Did she text you from the afterlife?"

Tapping his hand, she says, "Silly. We can bond again to understand what happened to her."

"My dreams. They only show us the far past. They can be dubious about what the future holds," he laments, head still drooping.

"What famous author once wrote, 'Our present has happened in the past from where our future appears. Our lesson learned from the voice of the object'?" asks Mei as she squeezes his hand.

"MoxWorld tech wrote that. Not me," he mutters.

Her delicate hands with those elegantly slender fingers warm his cheek. Lifting his head, she kisses him. "You are the greatest man I have ever met. Well, maybe equal to Jean-Paul, but greater than even Alexander."

His eyes meet hers, both with irises widened.

Her delicate fingers now under his chin, she says, "If I weren't so in love with your sister, I would be with you."

Tapping his bump behind his neck, she adds, "Jean-Paul said the dreams of the afflicted hold the truth of the path forward. Isn't that what your bonding with Zara did to show the pathway toward defeating Alexander last time? If our priest friend is correct, what you have hidden away back here tells of what we need to know in the past to change the world for the better in the future."

"You mean, El in the dream represents Zara and that she must still be alive?" says Peter, still peering into Mei's eyes.

"She's not dead until you let her die," she says. "Don't stop searching for her. She has to fulfill her destiny with my friend. That's what that dream was trying to tell us."

"You're more than visceral, Mei. My sister wouldn't be in a relationship with you if that were all you are," says Peter as he reaches for Pappy's diary. "I am happy she found you. As I am happy you are my friend. I'm happy you're my sister's…mate."

Snuggling tighter with him, she peers over his shoulder. "So, editor man, what were you so intently reading?"

"The dream got me to thinking about my pappy's diary. The last war time entry was dated August 1944. But in 1950, he adds more. I think your interpretation of the dream is right. We need to go to Jerusalem and not flounder about searching every crevice in Crimea. Your friend from Jerusalem will be essential to solving this mystery."

May 8, 1950

It is Elbe Day. The five-year anniversary of the beginning of the end of Nazi Germany, when the Russians met the Americans at the Elbe River. Who knew that peace would only bring on another kind of war—the one they call Cold?

Our escape from Crimea was our beginning of the end. At the train station in Odessa, my father received news that Himmler had told the Ahnenerbe command how his project in Crimea had been an abject failure. Germany had wasted thousands of valuable lives for naught. And that marked the beginning of the end of my father and his descent into the deepest of depressions.

What happened with Ariella, and then her husband, Ghurdzi, in that cavern of the blue light scared me almost as much as my mild-mannered father having gunned down in cold blood the SS squad he had worked with during our months in Crimea. Between his moodiness and my fear of who he had become, I barely said anything on the train ride home.

My mother saw the difference as well. As a mother does, she smothered me with love, food, and constant suggestions of available young women, as the war had depleted many marriageable men.

Nothing you can read or hear can prepare you for life in an occupied country. Germany had been occupied and split in half. My father said the

Americans would be better than the Russians. I asked would not that Russian, Dr. Murometz, have been able to protect us under Russian rule? As he looked at the Nuremberg tribunal hearings in the newspaper in front of him, he said not with what Murometz knew. The Russians would incarcerate him in some secret laboratory, never to be seen again. And within one or two more years, the Americans would put him on trial for his complicity in the atrocities the SS troops committed in Crimea.

On his desk were other articles about German scientists whom the Americans and Russians had whisked out of Germany. He said what he knows should not be shared with any of these governments, only with me and my descendants. He urged me to find and marry a woman whose father and uncles have the dreams and oral legends that we have. I should hide the pendant I retrieved from the cavern and speak to no one about what happened in that cavern. Not even my mother. Only if a woman with a pendant like mine comes into my life shall I speak of what I know.

I asked him if he was saying we must take these secrets to the grave. He said, only if I could not sire children who could solve the mystery of the black object. And then he shocked me. For the first time, he hinted that forces other than the Americans and Russians could be after our secrets. He found evidence in Crimea of their existence. He made me swear to kill myself rather than be captured by these forces' agents.

His depression only got worse. Several months later, the US Army police came and said he is not to leave the city. There would be hearings with him and others on their activities during the war. My mother found a psychiatrist from the US Army to come see my father. An odd man. From Central Asia, he said. Worked with US intelligence in China. He gave my father pills for his depression and other pills for his anxiety.

Before they could call him to the tribunal hearings, my father was found dead—having overdosed on those pills, we were told. Did he do what he told me to do? Commit suicide rather than have the secrets of the blue cave revealed? I will take the secret to my death if my children cannot solve the mystery.

The Russians surprised the world last year by detonating their first nuclear bomb. The worst is to come sooner than any of us imagined. I love my wife dearly. I can only hope our son will find the object and be able to find Ghurdzi's family in time, before America and Russia destroy each other and the rest of the world with them. For only when these two pendant stones are united can anyone ever hope to find their way back and stop the insanity.

"That Central Asian psychiatrist," cries out Peter. "He must have been a NiQihs agent. Pappy said that his father committed suicide rather than let the tribunal get the secrets we found. What if the NiQihs agent made it look like a suicide?"

Tapping away on her MoxWrap now, Mei says, "What is more important are the names Ariella and Ghurdzi. Her sabta raba's name is Ariella, isn't it?" She grasps Peter's hand, squeezing it. "My professor friend confirmed Ariella is her inspiration for her search for Asherah. Both your destiny and Zara's lie in Jerusalem. You need to find her."

CHAPTER 33

MoxWorld Health Center, Jerusalem
10:30 a.m. GMT+8, February 10, 2023

Guilt. She bears the guilt of hurting not all of Palestine. Only this one young woman lying in front of her who tried to save truth. A very politically, very religiously explosive truth. And all this young woman has to show for it is a healing wound where the bullet went through her throat, a plate in her head where another bullet grazed her brain, and a shattered spine where yet another bullet passed through her lower abdomen.

Paralyzed from the waist down. Unable to speak. Barely able to recognize her mother. And never able to bear the children that afflicted women are asked repeatedly to bear. Why shouldn't Rachel feel all the guilt that crushes down on her as if Yahweh had brought the whole Second Temple down upon her?

The very least she could do was to get her into the newest medical center, ironically run by the empire of the man whose father was party to her saba raba's murder. She thought about getting down on her knees with that doctor lady who works for NiQihs and beg for their help in rehabilitating Massa.

They could keep the tablet. Possibly, they could still let her have the statue fragment. Massa should keep that.

Although the Torah does not speak of the Devil, she is sure that between NiQihs and MoxWorld, she is to sell her soul to deeds forever dark, just as her family before her has. What a female archaeologist has to do to get rid of the burden of guilt. So, instead of NiQihs, she called Mei, asking if she could call in a favor with that monstrous boss of hers. Even if it meant she would spend a week on his private pleasure yacht.

But there is a God, and She blessed the world with Murometz's death in a tactical nuclear explosion. Rachel will be able to keep her clothes on after all, and she no longer needs to hunt him down to pay them back. And as a member of the executive board of MoxWorld, Mei could pull the strings necessary to get Massa placed in this ward indefinitely. Small consolations for the poor young woman's sacrifices.

As Rachel sits next to Massa, holding her hand, her mother, Amenah Kassis, stands by, showing a photo on her MoxWrap. It is the picture of their family house, which goes back at least ten generations. The guilt piles up more. The pressure of not only the Second Temple, but the First Temple as well, crushes Rachel.

"I am so sorry, Mrs. Kassis," pleads Rachel. "When the Israeli government convicts a terrorist, they raze that person's family home to the ground. I could not intervene fast enough to save yours. The best I could do was to get you those adjacent suites in the MoxWorld Resort as temporary housing."

"Oh, dear professor, you misunderstand," says Amenah. "I wanted you to see this picture."

Her eyes close as she searches for the courage to face another picture. Rachel's eyes open to gaze upon a photo of a new building being erected on the same spot. "But how? The policy normally means nothing is rebuilt on those lands, to serve as a message for other terrorists' families."

With the hint of the edges of her lips uprising, Amenah says, "The City of Jerusalem is rebuilding our home. The same architecture, but with updated amenities and NiQihs device access."

"But why?" ponders Rachel. "I am so happy for you, but I've not heard of such reparations before."

"As I understand, a certain rabbi, a department chairman at your university, pulled several strings to make this happen. He called me and said he loves his daughter and would do anything for her."

As if by magic, a few of those gigantic granite blocks from the Temple lift up off Rachel and she can breathe. Just a bit. "Mrs. Kassis, I swear to you and to Massa, I will do everything I can to help her recovery. Everything and anything," she says before rising to leave.

⚬⚬

Once again, she leans against the wall outside her Ariella's room on the other side of the complex. She has seen death before, but mostly of the Nazis her family caught who resisted. *Yimakh shemo.* May their names be erased.

She lived for her safta raba Ariella. For her visions of Asherah. For her words about the blue light. For finding the killers of her husband. And now, the aged woman lies in her bed in the palliative care ward, dying of a particularly aggressive pancreatic cancer, or so her doctor just told Rachel.

To have the woman to whom Rachel dedicated her life now ready to pass away has opened up a void within Rachel. A new void forming? Or one that has been there all along and simply not noticed?

And once again, in a delirious rant, her safta raba recalled the woman in the white robe. Her head covered in a grey headscarf. Her touch, which brought instantaneous inner peace. Her blessing of Ariella's unborn girl and how another woman's daughter will also return. And Rachel can find the same only if she carries the unborn child from her union with an afflicted man.

Had her great-grandfather said the same, Rachel would have said it was a man's thing to ask of a great-granddaughter. But it was Ariella.

She rubs the black stone pendant under her blouse. On top of everything else, she needs to get close enough to that Gollinger guy who two-timed that ornery Kurdish woman by siring a baby with her friend Mei. For his grandfather or Murometz's father stole the other half of this stone. The only way she will find her way to and inside the cavern of Ariella is to take it from him, dead or alive. But only after she is with child by a man she does not love.

Out of the corner of her eye, she follows the doctor at the end of the hallway, who has been clandestinely watching her. That woman again. What does she want now?

"My dear Rachel, you are as fond of your great-grandmother as Peter Gollinger was of his grandfather," says Dr. Fontaine.

"I fail to understand how my situation compares with that of the complicit, those who stand by as crimes against humanity are committed," replies Rachel. "Why are you haunting me? I delivered what you people wanted. I gave you intel on that Kurdish woman."

"Things went sideways," says the doctor. "Our agent in China killed by my dear Peter. I didn't think a violent bone existed in that man. And the afflicted woman we had impregnated went sideways. We will need a backup."

Dr. Fontaine reaches under Rachel's ponytail behind her neck and palpitates. "Murometz had considered you more than a strong possibility for their program."

"I am not your guinea pig," says Rachel, grabbing the doctor's hand away from that odd spot in the back of her neck. The same bump her mother has, her grandmother had, and that Ariella has.

"What if I could cure your great-grandmother's cancer? Would you consider our offer?" says Dr. Fontaine. She gives Rachel a soft cloth envelope from under her clipboard.

Peeking into the envelope, Rachel rolls her eyes. One that would hide nothing on her chest, as the doctor texted back to her that day on the Kurdish woman's mountain. She cannot imagine wearing this as she peers down at her chest. Didn't Catwoman in the Batman film series wear something stretchy like this? Well, something that covered her chest more than this?

She gives the doctor a once-over. Unlike any doctor Rachel knows, the doctor's white coat is fashionably cut to enhance her attributes. How can she entice this Gollinger man if the doctor could not?

"I find your taste in clothing a degrading reversion for women," says Rachel. "I find your offer offensive. I will be no one's *frecha*. Your bimbo, not. If you can cure my great-grandmother, then you should offer this outright without holding me hostage to a misplaced guilt."

"My dear Rachel, I understand you did not get that leadership position in our newly acquired intelligence security group because your loyalty to NiQihs' goals became suspect," says the doctor.

"And your loyalty? Why would you do what you do for them? What are they paying you?" says Rachel.

"What you really want deep inside. The security of your family, of the world. MoxWorld destroyed the mainstay digital companies of the 2000s as Murometz expanded worldwide, using massive profit losses to gain market share. A tactic only a private enterprise could employ without shareholder revolt. Many people lost their jobs. Many great companies disappeared. Many lost their retirement savings. Under the NiQihs, we all have a chance to save the free economy and our family and friends' retirement portfolios."

"The Canaanites resisted changing their ways of the past when the Israelis came," says Rachel, a bit tongue in cheek. "And look where that got them. Shouldn't we all learn from history?"

"My dear professor. I understand you were just on the other side of the complex in the ward of a certain Palestinian woman. One who would be able to bear children for her family if not for your academic selfishness."

The granite blocks of the Second Temple crush Rachel again as her shoulders droop.

"What if I could not only offer your safta raba a cure but also one for your friend? What is her name? Massa?" offers the doctor. "That is much more than that dead magnate Murometz would ever have done for you."

Head down, eyes closed, Rachel searches for what she did to get Asherah so mad. The web around her has gotten so tangled, so dense, surely something very bad is about to happen. And then her head nods up and down as her hands clasp each other so tightly they turn white.

"Many great things will happen to you when you confirm your loyalty. When the time comes, the leader of NiQihs will look after those who looked after him. No different from your Yahweh," says the doctor. "Confirm that your Chinese friend's baby is from Gollinger, and you are free from us needing your special bump."

The doctor reaches into her pocket and pulls out a palm-sized black nylon bag. "If not, then in here is a vial surrounded by a cold pack that you activate by squeezing it. You get a live specimen from Gollinger, and we will see who we will impregnate."

"And how do you expect me to do that?" says Rachel, rolling her eyes.

"You have your black cat suit, which I would suggest will be the most enjoyable way for the two of you," says the doctor with a wink. "A hint. Ask him if what he wrote in his book is a reflection of what he's really like inside. Then let him admire your assets in their fullest. Failing that, you kill him to get the live specimen. The prostate will still be functional during the minutes after death."

Holding out a mini surgical kit, the doctor adds, "But then, you will need to extract both his testicles and his God Gene Complex."

Rachel's head nods. This time, not up and down, but side to side.

"So, you don't want to kill him after all," says the doctor. "Then the alternative is much, much more enjoyable. Bed him and get him to impregnate you. Our plans are even better if you bear his child."

A cold glare from Rachel into the doctor's unflinching eyes. Then, placing the specimen pack and the black, tight, hide-nothing outfit into her shoulder bag, Rachel says, "I will kill you the same way I did those three Nazis if you turn on me. Now, go talk with the staff here and get my safta raba and Massa the cure they need."

CHAPTER 34

For out of the heart come evil thoughts, murder, adultery, sexual immorality,
theft, false witness, slander. These are what defile a person.

Matthew 15:19-20, New Testament

Village destined to be Çayönü
9524 BCE

As young children, she and the rest of the great matriarch Nanshe's grandchildren would warm themselves by the bonfire and listen to tales of the other side of the big lake. What sticks in her mind at this very moment as she hides in the dense forest underbrush outside the village where her second daughter, Perima, is being held captive is the story of her grandfather Orzu. To save his sister Illyana from the same horrific enslavement by the reindeer warrior giants, Orzu hid in the forests around the giants' city of the great pyramids, studying every movement, every event's time, every giant, and every building as he devised his plan to save his beloved sister.

And there Tallia lies, skin cut up by the brush, watching the same in this reindeer warrior giant village. She has never been in a reindeer warrior village, but she heard Nanshe's horrifying stories. She thought Nanshe might have exaggerated, as she was only a teen at the time of her captivity. Or maybe the great matriarch told the bonfire tales to scare the children into believing monsters existed. As she lies in the brush, she now knows the truth. Monsters do exist.

But she witnesses the saddened faces of the women in this village. She hears their tears and cries from behind closed doors. Sometimes, you need to understand the exact opposite direction to understand why where you are going is right. She now understands that here lies the exact opposite of what she created in her own village with Nirra. Women are treated worse than domesticated animals. They are traded with other giants. They are offered as gifts to visiting giants. They are no more than objects of pleasure for these beasts. Nanshe had not exaggerated one bit.

Tallia closes her eyes and prays to Nanshe's God to give her the strength to stop this inhumanity forever, that all women could live in equality and safety, as Tallia and Nirra created in their village.

A snap of a twig and Tallia goes entirely still, holding her breath, pressing herself into the ground, hoping to become invisible. But then, she hears three taps followed by two taps and three more. Nirra's signal that it is only him.

For unlike Orzu, she has her Nirra. With him, she knows she will forever be safe. With him, she knows her dreams can be achieved. With him, she knows love, as he is committed to stay by her side. She knows he will be faithful. No matter what.

For two moon cycles, Nirra has stayed as a guest in this village. He found trusted friends from his days as a marauding giant. Ones like him who questioned the ways of the old giants and sought something spiritually greater.

Every night, he sneaks out and brings his beloved wife food and the comfort of his huge hugs. He cries in her arms, as he is horrified at what he now sees in the life of these giants, what he used to be complicit in doing, what is the exact opposite of what he loved about what he and Tallia created. He cries for her forgiveness for what he has had to do to gain acceptance. He is horrified at it all. So horrified, he cannot let Tallia do what she proposes.

"But I want to do this," insists Tallia, as they sit a distance away from the village in a safe clearing. "We will both die anyway, at least inside ourselves, if we do not attempt to stop this insanity, this offense against why God placed us here. How can we remain complicit?"

Shaking his huge head, which rustles the leaves of the adjacent bush as the antlers of a giant deer would, Nirra says, "I have seen what they will do to you if your plan is exposed. Even I could not save you from such a fate."

She pulls down her tunic top to expose the cleavage between her breasts. "Then you would need to spear me or shoot me between my breasts as did my grandfather Orzu to his sister Illyana. The sight of her chest haunts the dreams of the men who have descended from him. Illyana asked Orzu to end her suffering with an arrow through her breast. As a good brother, he finally did. But as she requested, he saved Nanshe, who became his wife, equal in ruling the family since."

"I could not kill you. How could you ask me that?" asks Nirra, shaking.

"Remember what Nanshe said—if you love someone, you will do anything for them," says Tallia.

After more discussion and planning, Tallia rises and takes Nirra's knife. She rips her clothing, exposing what a modest woman should have covered, what a giant insists on seeing of his slave women. Then, to Nirra's surprise, she cuts her hand and smears the redness across Nirra's chest and between his legs. She says this will authenticate that she fought him.

Shaking his head, Nirra binds her hands. Rope around her neck, she follows with her head fully exposed behind Nirra, who drags her behind him like a captured animal.

As they enter the village, the women stare at her. Tallia can sense their pity of what this new woman will suffer. She holds her head down, in part to show submission to her captor giant and in part because she cannot bear witnessing the denigration of the women all around her. How could Nanshe have survived as long as she did under these conditions?

Nirra meets a ruling group of giants. He explains he captured this disobedient animal in the woods spying on the village. She is too old to be of great pleasure for the chief of the giants. He would keep her for domestic help and occasional pleasure if the other women could not please him long enough.

Then, it dawns on Tallia—in order to gain the acceptance of these giants, her Nirra had to participate, to be complicit, in the violation of other women. Where does forgiveness start, and where can it never go?

Her saddened, reddened, teary eyes glance up at him as he ties her to a tree on the outer ring of the village. She listens to these monstrous beasts laugh it up, telling stories of old, of the destruction of men and women alike across the countryside. It has been sixteen cycles since a raid of more than a hundred giants demolished the temple of Ki and An. Men killed, women attacked and enslaved as she had feared Nirra would do to her. Her daughter Perima, what is she like after sixteen sun cycles of depravity?

And then, the father of the village leader excuses himself, going into a hut. And a voice cries out. One that Tallia has not heard for sixteen sun cycles. She pulls on the rope that binds her hands. She pulls on the rope that ties her to the tree until she nearly passes out from choking from the noose around her neck, falling to the ground. The worst of the worst has happened, as she can only cringe with each scream of her daughter. Resigned for the moment, she only has one choice left. She prays.

Did she dream what she had heard? Or did her youngest daughter Perima call out to her as she did in her childhood? Mama. Mama. Please, Mama. End the pain. End the nightmare. Kill me now. Please, Mama.

The sun is gone, and the moon above the trees. She is cold in these torn clothes, which leave her indecently exposed not only to the night but to passersby. What happened to her dearest Nirra? Is he in the throes of torturing some slave woman? Has he reverted to a monstrous giant, having tasted the perversions of his kind?

A warm touch—her beloved has come for her, with warm food. Fed and warmed both in her heart and her stomach, Nirra refuses to allow her to hug him. For he drips with the shame, the ignominy, the inhumanity of what he has had to do.

Wanting his lips upon hers, wanting the assurance of his love, of his security, she is denied all. As the moon shines brighter, she spots the evil glow of their eyes. The giant elders are watching them. Nirra says she must scream, claw, and groan the way she did when he first kidnapped her.

And then his open hand plasters her face. Yes, he pulled his strike. But a giant's pulled punch is like an auroch kicking a man. Crimson flows from her mouth as he acts with the ferocity of someone she has never met before. Her clothes torn off, her body not within her control, she fights back. Discreetly, he cuts himself and spreads his redness all over her inner thighs.

After what seems the whole night, he finishes, leaving her naked, her hands still bound and the noose still around her neck. He spits on her and kicks dust on her. As he approaches the giant elder, who grins in approval, he says she is no good. All dry inside, worse than sex with a dead auroch. She's no better than a dead, smelly fish.

She lies there as if it were real, in horror of what Perima must live through day in, day out, night in, night out. She cannot save Perima, and she may have lost her Nirra. Head to the ground, she prays her choice was the right one.

❧

The light burns her eyes. She is thirsty. Her cold skin welcomes the warmth of the rising sun. Her eyes bleary, she sees a tall figure. Nirra?

No, it is not, and she crawls into a ball and screams.

Then she hears him. Nirra, who says, "See? She is not worth any of your time. She is too old, too tough, too unappealing for our kind."

Hiding in her ball, she cannot tell what hurts her more—the idea that he really believes what he is saying, or what she feels he lives through every day living among humans. God created those who stand upon two feet with the enormous ability to hate, to despise, to denigrate those who are physically different from them.

As the elder giant leaves, Nirra yanks her up by the noose, which burns her neck. He holds her so high she is on her tippy toes, trying not to choke. When the other giant is out of sight, he lets her collapse in his arms. He lightly kisses her ear and whispers, "May your god forgive me. When you escape from here, I will not think untoward if you decide to kill me for what I have done."

He gives her his flask of water and a meager morsel of bread. She first tries to wash the blood off with the water, but he shakes his head no. The whole giant community needs to see how he beat her, how he violently invaded her.

In his sack he has brought a needle and a small amount of thread. She should sew up her clothes enough that it drapes across her body, but not enough to conceal what giants expect to see. He will be back shortly.

She tries to kiss him, saying she loves him no matter what. His head shakes, and he says the worst is yet to come. She must be strong for what they will make her watch.

Her skin dried out from the sun beating on her through the day, that white light of life and death beating down upon her has passed its midpoint in the sky. The water in Nirra's flask is long gone. She sits within her own body waste, no better than a kept goat ready to be killed for dinner.

Nirra arrives with a whip-like stick and another flask. He washes her waste off her and what is left she is given. But only for a few swigs, as he cannot have the others see him treating her as anything but an animal too old to be useful.

He beats her with the stick to guide her through the village. The eyes of all the women follow her. All nodding, knowing exactly what will happen to her. It happened to them.

Her lover, her best friend, her partner of equals, now her tormentor, takes her silently to a place in the center of the village. The giants' eyes are all upon her body. What she would have given for more cloth and thread. Was this what Nanshe suffered through?

They tie her down to a post in a ceremonial area. There, another woman is brought in. Tallia closes her eyes, knowing that what is to happen to this poor woman no human should have to suffer.

Her eyes open to find that woman's eyes fixed onto hers. And that woman's lips silently mouth, "Mama."

Perima is not much more clothed than the day she was born. A human, a man who pretends to be a magical shaman who knows the gods, brings her out to the village center. He gives to Perima a potion. One that turns her eyes into an empty stare. She is to perform a fertility ceremony with several neighboring chiefs, her body only flesh for their consumption. For she is the reindeer warrior giants' goddess of fertility. A gross distortion of the mother goddess concept.

Tallia cannot bear to watch. But that is not to be her decision, as the giant elder shakes his head, staring at her and signaling to Nirra.

Her husband comes to her, but he is not her husband now. He says she must watch, for they want her to know that even though she is too old to offer as a gift, the women she will room with will be gifted in her place if she is ever disobedient and not subservient. And, as directed by the elder, he holds Tallia's eyes open.

For hours she watches with no other choice. Her daughter is resigned to her fate. And the beauty and peace that have come into Tallia's life since meeting Nirra evaporate within minutes of this ordeal.

How could a loving God allow this to happen? She has been so faithful. She is sure her daughter has been so faithful. How could the voice have directed her to come here like this? Is the voice of Nanshe not good? Have they been worshipping the god of the giants all along?

The next morning, Tallia awakens, still tied to the post in the middle of the village. Near her, the body of her daughter lies comatose.

Women of the village arrive as the sun tops the trees on the horizon, the sign they can bring the goddess of fertility back into her hut.

A huge shadow looms over her, and she cringes, trying to curl into a defensive ball. But it is her Nirra, who finally cuts her bindings and the noose around her neck. He lifts her over his shoulder like a dead animal and brings her to Perima's hut.

He cannot enter but says if she still wishes to see him, he will return. She cannot look into his eyes. Her head no longer comprehends the world in the way she once did. She knows she must say something. The life they led together means he deserves an answer. All she can do is lean her head into his abdomen and nod.

Inside, her once-vibrant daughter has a hollow face, eyes gazing into the distance. She barely recognizes her mother. No hug, no kisses, only the plea that her mother kill her, like what her great-grandmother said her husband had done to his enslaved sister. A plea that Tallia heard through the night. Though Perima's eyes are dry, Tallia's are not.

Each morning, Nirra is permitted to get Tallia a moment of time with Perima, who slowly becomes her loving girl for only that moment, only to be dragged back into depravity. Tallia spends her day in the unequal world of women of the giants. She helps care for other women's children and prepares the grain the enslaved men harvest. She quietly talks to women who she thinks she can trust about an entirely different world at her other daughter's temple. Peace and tolerance. The giants' fear of the object protected them.

Two moon cycles pass. Tallia has become as hollow inside as her daughter appears on the outside. But her solace is the time she has each morning with her daughter. Nirra has told the other giants their goddess has taken to his old useless slave like a surrogate mother. And so, Tallia is allowed to spend the mornings with the fertility goddess, helping her recover from the previous night's debaucheries.

Perima lies in Tallia's arms and lap, curled up like she did when she had only ten cycles of the sun. Tallia tries to buoy her daughter's hopes with talk about reuniting with her sister Illyana in the Second Temple with the object of Nanshe. There, they will pray together and hear the voice.

Sixteen sun cycles and so much has changed, says Perima to her mother. She has stopped believing in the voice, who she has not heard since the days before the attack and pillage of their first temple. She can no longer picture what life was like. She knows not what innocence felt like. She knows not what being human feels like. She is only an object to be worshipped by day by the humans for good crops and many children to work the fields. And by night…Perima stops at that thought.

Night is when Nirra is allowed to take his "decrepit" slave to take care of his perversions and pleasures in privacy. They can become husband and wife for a few moments. Tallia cries to Nirra, has she lost her backbone, lost her moxy? She is the niece of the great giant killer Ki. Why can she not save her daughter?

Nirra tries to talk reason to her about the futility of fighting a village of giants in the process of becoming lords of large swaths of farms with human slave labor. And the older giants are still the fierce warriors who ravaged her family and their villages.

∽

Five days later, Perima tries to kill herself, but giants stop her. She is to be offered in a five-day-long depraved ceremony with the three next largest village giant leaders. She cannot do this any longer. In her mother's arms the next morning, she pleads she kills her.

Tallia says to Nirra that it does not matter if she lives anymore. She must stop these giants. The women of this village are ready to flee. The two of them cannot remain complicit. They must both have the backbone to stand up for what is right. He must help them get to Illyana and the Second Temple.

This is a bad, rash idea, he says, but he will garner the support of the few giants who are willing to leave with them.

She gathers the women who live in the hut with her and speaks Nanshe's words. "Everything is a line. It goes forward and backward. As you see backward, you can see forward. By doing so, we see what will save us are the ones we love the most."

Hut to hut she tries to rally the support of the women. At the river, where the women bring the giants' clothing to be washed, she stands up and speaks of the voice and how She wants equality for women. That together, they can elude the giants. With her stands Perima, their fertility god, who speaks of the voice as who she prays to for the benefit of the women in the village.

Tallia is succeeding. A momentum begins among these women. One that says there is hope. Tallia speaks of the Second Temple, where an object from God scares away the giants. There, they will all be safe.

Ten men from the fields arrive. At first, they appear as if they have come to cool down in the river. And then, she spots him, the shaman who stands only half a forehead taller than the rest. The man who has the most to gain by prompting the giants to continue their abuse of Perima.

Silence reigns among the once very vocal women as the shaman circles

Tallia and Perima. He lunges at Perima, only to have Tallia grab him first and throw him to the ground. For she is the well-taught niece of Ki, the giant killer, as she proclaims to the crowd. The giants will run once they know she is Ki's heir apparent.

More men have gathered at the river. These ones have picked up stones from the river, the size of stones the women used to pound the dirt out of the giants' garments. Tallia thinks nothing of this. Finally, the men have come to help the women.

On the horizon are the distinct shadows of giants. At first, Tallia signals Perima that it is time for them to flee. But she sees the distinct silhouette of her giant, and her shoulders relax.

The shaman addresses the two dozen or so men who have gathered at his insistence. They are witness to this false prophet. This woman who would bring the wrath of the giants upon their heads. This woman who would put misleading ideas into their fertility goddess's head. This woman who would seek to steal their fertility goddess so her people will eat and they will starve to death.

This small man will not bully Tallia. Tall he may be next to a human, but he is nothing but small inside. With Nirra now in the group of men, she says the voice says they will have abundance, they will have peace, they can have all of this at the Second Temple. Tallia says the voice, She, will protect them.

That one word gives the shaman the advantage he sought. He says to the men that the great god this woman worships is a woman. They all know the supreme god is a man. Stone this false prophetess before the rest of the lands falsely follow a woman supreme god.

The first stone thrown strikes Tallia's chest, winding her. But she stands straight now, telling the men they should not hide behind the lies of this shaman who would seek to enslave their daughters. The second stone strikes her head, drawing blood. As her vision swirls, Tallia begins to fall, being caught by her giant.

Perima stands to protect her mother and her stepfather. She says that her mother is right. She, Perima, is their fertility goddess, and she talks with the voice herself. And the third, fourth, fifth stones are thrown.

A dozen stones later, Perima's bones are cracked all over as she lays limp over her mother. She touches her mother's cheek and says the voice has answered her prayers. That she will forever love her mother for coming for her. Tallia cries over her daughter, only to have Nirra reach his hand out. For immunity to stones did not confer to giants either. As she checks her poor giant, Perima stares into the sky and says she sees Her. She is waiting for her to ascend into the blue light.

Her daughter dead, her husband dying, Tallia cries to the voice. Is this our reward for spreading your word? We the faithful.

CHAPTER 35

If you're going through hell, keep going.

—Winston Churchill

MoxWorld Asia Headquarters, Shanghai
1:30 p.m. GMT+8, February 10, 2023

"Apparently, our fake black object did not satisfy the Chinese," says Jean-Paul. On the wall screens are live satellite images of the South Pacific. Holograms of Jean-Paul and the Head of MoxWorld Security are with Mei.

"That is, assuming NiQihs did indeed give it to the Chinese for whatever endgame they are planning," says the security head.

"My ruse with the legend of Admiral Zheng He's search in the 1400s for remnants of a great comet in the South Pacific worked too well. At least, too convincing for China to accept a meager black rock from NiQihs," says Mei. "Our president continues to ask me for better triangulation of the splatter zone of that comet's fragments. He's unconvinced the black rock didn't fall on Chinese Taipei, where he's ready to invade."

The Jesuit father's hand is around his chin as he asks, "Mei, now that our Peter has deduced NiQihs is a legacy organization from the first emperor of China, do you think Admiral Zheng He's search was NiQihs-sponsored? That they thought it would have the black stone that could lead to the elixir of life?"

"That might explain why China is so insistent on claiming that comet as its territory. For them, the search for the comet is a more credible legend than our black object," says Mei as she turns to Peter. "That might explain your question about why the NiQihs kidnappers have not provided proof of life. They no longer need him to negotiate with China."

No longer with her disarming, soothing smile, she stares into his eyes and says, "There's no easy way to say this. He's dead."

She waits with her eyes on his.

The silence is as deafening as an exploding comet until Jean-Paul breaks it. "MoxWorld Security confirms that a tactical nuclear missile detonated at the last known location of Alexander's yacht last week. The world's powers have kept this hush-hush so as not to cause a worldwide panic that a global nuclear war has started. That is likely what set off Alexander's INTRBL protocol."

Staring first at Jean-Paul's image, and then at Mei, Peter says, "What if he isn't dead? What if he escaped? What if she escaped?"

Jean-Paul gently says, "Do you know something, Peter? What did the alert he sent to you say?"

"It said, I can't say."

Not as polite, the MoxWorld Security head yells, "Don't play with us, kid. The nuke went off right after you read the alert. Why would he give you heir apparent access to all of MoxWorld's resources, which clearly you have been accessing since?"

Staring right back into the security head's image's eyes, Peter retorts, "Perhaps Mr. Murometz put a read reply trigger to nuke his own yacht. Perhaps the aliens who kidnapped me sent him a nasty gram from on high. Perhaps he only wants her to be saved."

The security head snarls, then addresses Mei and Jean-Paul. "Do we still keep the news embargoed? If MoxWorld's customers find out Mr. Murometz is dead, NiQihs will take over our key clients. Even entire nations may switch their allegiances."

Shaking his head, Jean-Paul says, "The truth we should all honor. But at times, even the Vatican has exercised discretion about how the truth should come forth."

"The truth should come out," asserts Peter. "He would want the world to know right now. Why else would he let someone nuke his yacht?"

The security head says, "Well, Mr. Alien Abductee, perhaps his Russian friends nuked him. He had enough enemies there and everywhere else. The two Russian missile frigates nearby were supposed to protect him from an attack. What if they turned on him?"

Now it's Mei's turn as she glares at Peter. "What do you know? Why would you think NiQihs didn't destroy his yacht, or China, not Russia? Or even your precious US?"

His eyebrows set to a fierce V, he stares into their eyes without blinking. "Because he needed to be a martyr to get to where he needs to go. But a martyr's death is only meaningful if others know about it. Issue the press release, or his death will be in vain."

The contentious meeting over, the two alone, Mei signals Peter to sit on her office divan with her. Patting his knee, she says, "A husband and wife need to share their most intimate secrets for a marriage to work. Even a pretend one. What is really happening? Did he make you interim head of MoxWorld?"

Patting her knee back, he says, "Me? Head of MoxWorld? That really would be the end of the world. You've known Alexander longer than I. His plans always have dozens of layers. I can tell you this. I have to be coupled with a woman of dark hair whose inner self, whose DNA secrets need to return to the cavern of the blue light. That's the only way we'll be able to stop the world's madness. If only Zara were here. She'd know what to do."

Her eyes peering down, her delicate pink tongue wetting her lips, she says, "It must be so hard losing one you truly loved. But you need to let go of her. If Alexander perished in that explosion, it's likely Zara did, too."

Squeezing her knee, he says, "If anyone can survive a tactical nuke, Zara can. Even you said the other day, don't give up on her. Please. Help me learn how to use all the resources of MoxWorld to find her. Maybe even save her."

Squeezing his knee back, she says, "I will. Because I trust your judgment. But why did you need access to the MoxBioRejuvenation pilot program? You're not planning to resurrect Alexander from his tissue samples on file, are you?"

"No," he says. "I'm just following instructions. Perhaps too cold-heartedly, but I promised I would."

Stroking his knee, she says, "But you need to be openhearted. It is possible that who you really need to be with right now is not Zara."

He pats her belly and says, "I thought you were already spoken for."

Her hand atop his atop her child, she says, "No, silly. I mean, there may be another dark-haired woman awaiting you. Someone I know. Someone who we may have seen in the dream of the two women in Mongolian times."

He rises slowly, staring out her window overlooking the skyline of Shanghai. "I thought you needed me to be husband in front of your parents."

Coming by his side, her arm around his shoulder, she says, "I need you to keep peace for me and your sister with my family. Alexander needs you for whatever it is he asked of you. And the world needs you to find the black object and the way to the cavern of the blue light before our countries engage in the insane."

He stares back at her, his hand on the left side of his chest. "And what about my heart?"

Her hand atop his above his heart. "You follow your dreams. And a dark-haired woman has always been in your dreams."

Taking her hand into his, he replies, "Then I will fulfill Pappy's and Alexander's destinies with that woman. Cold-heartedly or not."

Alone in the entrance to the MoxWorld Asia headquarters, he stares at the ten-meter-tall black monolith that dominates the lobby. The same décor as the USA Headquarters in San Francisco when he first met Mei and interviewed for a job with MoxWorld ten months ago. How his life priorities have changed in such a short time.

"I know that look," says a female voice behind him.

"I know that voice," replies Peter. "Have you come to confuse me even more? Little sisters love to play Confuse the Big Brother."

Adorned with her golden-blonde hair up in a high ponytail with face-framing strands interlaced with rose gold threads, Michaela wraps her arm around him. "I heard Mei pushing you to be with someone she knows. I know her heart. She's trying to heal yours in the best way she knows."

Hugging her back, he asks, "And do you think she's right?"

"Follow your heart. Isn't that what you've always told me? Besides, you told me that Pappy insisted you had to bond with a mysterious dark-haired woman, no?" Fingers running through her hair, she says, "Blonde with black hair. Like you and this archeologist friend of Mei. Dogs and cats can love each other like me and Mei."

His knuckles rub her blonde-tressed head. Then, with fingers under her chin, eyes into hers, he says, "Your heart hurts as much as mine."

"What do you mean?" she says with eyes so dour.

"You know," he says as he wipes below her eyes.

A big brother bear hug between the "husband" and "wife" of Mei Tang.

"Don't worry. I'll make it right for you," he says. "I always do."

CHAPTER 36

Myths and beliefs describe the female as the stronger gender,
one endowed with magical powers.
—Marija Gimbutas, archaeologist known for the
Kurgan Hypothesis and author of *The Civilization of the Goddess*

Village outside of Siirt, Anatolian Kurdish State
11:30 a.m. GMT+3, February 25, 2023

The fog. It blinds. The haze. It hurts. The light. It smells. With groggy head and blurry eyes, she tries to focus on what appears to be an angel. Was not the Archangel Jibrīl redheaded? For she hopes she is being escorted to heaven and not the other direction.

"Zara, how are you doing?" asks the angel with a distinctive French accent.

"Will you let me speak with the Prophet, may peace be with him?" asks Zara. "What am I saying? Peace be with me finally."

"Oh, I wish I could be an angel someday. But it is only *petite* me, Magali."

The fuzziness. Hadn't she been stoned to death? She must be in heaven, her mother desperately trying to save her. Or was that another mother? She had Maryam's visage. And her giant husband. With the visage of that evil Sasha. Could one ever forgive what he did? The terrors of what a giant must do? The depravity of it all. The complicity of doing nothing. And should she condemn her mother for consorting with a giant?

Zara blinks several times and then scans around her. Home. Or at least the home of her mother and Roza. She puts her hands around Magali's warm hands, which gently stroke her cold face. "How long?"

"You have been gone for nearly three weeks," answers Magali. "Peter found you three days ago in a hotel of sorts in Karaköy, Turkey, across the bridge from Istanbul."

"He is here?" says Zara as her head throbs from each word she enunciates.

"He's been waiting for you. Every day since they found you, he has been at your side, trying to use your bonding methods to heal you," replies Magali. "He takes your lambs for a walk every day. He's become very popular in your village with the kids."

"And his baby?" asks Zara.

"*Bébé?* I do not know about a child," answers Magali. "He had been in China with Mei for several weeks before you went missing. And he has been here many times since, digging into local lore to find you. Your mother has been teaching him to be Kurdish. He is like her adopted son."

That thought hurt her more than talking. Her mother's son was only her half-brother. "And my mother?"

"She is in the kitchen with Peter, supervising his solo attempt to make us lunch," says Magali, as she strokes Zara's forehead. "Your mother. She seems anxious about your reawakening. And nervous about talking with you. I offered to talk her through her troubles, but she is stoic about her pains."

Zara turns her head to the side. On the dresser is the picture of her family, or who she thought was her family. "And Alexander?"

"No sign of him. Peter only focused on finding you. Mei and Jean-Paul helped, but at your Sasha's last instructions, they focused mostly on finding the object and the blue light cavern."

"Are they here?" asks Zara, as she scans around her room.

"They are in Jerusalem with that all-too-attractive Israeli professor, following a lead that Mei and Peter uncovered in China. Peter is so odd. He seems embarrassed to talk about how they found the lead."

"Who's running MoxWorld?" asks Zara.

"Mei says a virtual avatar with prearranged AI based on Alexander's directions. The Holy Pontiff has temporarily allowed Jean-Paul to command the MoxWorld resources dedicated to finding the black object per Alexander's instructions. Mei has been delegated all responsibility in solving and finding the legends around the blue light. And Peter, he has his own confidential delegations from his giant boss."

"What was I doing in a hotel in Karaköy?" asks Zara, as she tries to sit up. Silence.

"Tell me, what is wrong?" asks Zara, as she pulls her legs over the side of the bed.

Silence as Magali closes her eyes, her lips moving as if she were saying a prayer.

"There is no sin a prayer can protect me from," says Zara. "There is no bad news that I have not already lived through."

The former Sister opens her eyes and explains, "Peter somehow intercepted coded messages he deduced were about their plans for you. He called for me to meet him in Istanbul. Alone. And no word about it to Jean-Paul or Mei. He wanted to protect you. He truly loves you. You should know this. He treasures the Zara who wrote that note from Rome."

Magali places Zara's hand on a laminated note that lies beside her pillow. Zara picks it up. She wrote it for him when he was comatose in the hospital in Rome after their last battle with Alexander nearly nine months ago. She traces her writing.

Am I all that Alexander said?
Did I do to you what he said?
Did I withhold from you what he said?
You did not know for sure.
And yet, you still loved me.

And then, her finger traces the heart she had drawn at the note's bottom. What was she thinking back then? She must have been knocked daft by the explosion of the object. She could not have really been in love. Could she?

Romantic love is a temporary state of psychosis. Perhaps that is what overcame her. Or was psychosis what just happened to her with Zengo and not Peter?

Zara starts to shiver. Magali lays her back down and covers her in blankets. Zara babbles, "I gave my love to him. Twice. I will never do this again."

As Zara's eyes glaze over, Magali says, "I read about your Saint Rab'ia. She suffered, nearly dying during one of her fasts on her own in the desert. She fought the angel of death. She must have had a good angel looking out after her."

Petting Zara's hand, the former Sister says, "You are more like her than you give yourself credit for. You have suffered as she did, only in ways appropriate to your times. Like Rab'ia, a good angel must be looking out after you."

Minutes of silence as the pink returns to Zara's cheeks. Her eyes responsive to the fly buzzing around her ceiling, she says, "My lambs?"

"You mean, your wool-coated dogs?" jests Magali. "Peter has them playing fetch twice a day. They signal their thoughts through the wagging of their tails."

"Mei did something to their mother," says Zara, regaining her strength. "I am their mother now. I have the right to know what she did. Give me my MoxWrap so I can ask her."

"I am not trying to be obstructive," says Magali. "You should come back into this world slowly. Your mind is prone to mix memories as the drugs they used wear off."

"Drugged?" gasps Zara as she sits up. "You said a hotel of sorts. Where did Peter find me?"

"Let us go slowly, Zara. What do you last remember?"

"Other than being stoned? The horrors of what wicked men do to women? The horrors of what the Daesh did to me and my cousins?" ponders Zara.

"Dead fish," blurts the Kurdish woman as she pulls the covers off her legs and places her hands in her lap.

Magali helps clear her brown hair from her face as she says, "Dreaming of dead fish can symbolize the loss of the spiritual, of power, of fertility. You may believe you have suffered all of these."

"No, he called me a dead fish," says Zara, now with feet on the floor as she sits at the edge of the bed, her hands in her lap, flexing her fists.

"And was kissing her behind my back all the time," adds Zara as she puts her hands in front of her chest as if she were squeezing melons. "He dumped me because of the size of her…her…" She slams her fists into the frame of her bed.

She slams her right fist into her left open palm and says, "I dislike being used. He lost his front teeth last time. I should tear off something he said he had lost from his body, but I am a woman of peace."

She stands up, a little wobbly, as Magali lends her a hand. She takes a deep breath. Then another. She stares into Magali's eyes and says, "What are you trying not to tell me? What can be worse than what has already happened to me?"

"Peter has saved you in more than one way," says the former Sister, avoiding eye contact. "He found you in a hotel known as a brothel in the red-light district of Karaköy. He found you passed out on a bed. You know him, he dressed you in a robe to protect your modesty."

Stoic, cold, and expressionless, Zara says, "And what are you still leaving out?"

Magali purses her lips. She blinks several times, then adds, "Around your naked body, he found drug paraphernalia and dozens of condoms, and your body and the sheets were covered in their…their…you know."

"I was violated again! Was I not? You can tell me. Those evil men, under the flag of the Daesh, they used me day and night and passed me around. I hunted them down like the animals they were and killed them all."

As Magali negatively nods, Zara runs her hands down her lower abdomen, adding, "I paid for my sins as they burned me with that electric cattle prod. I cannot ever give to a man the children he may want. They burnt me all the way through my cervix into my uterus because I fought them, I bit them, I clawed them, and when given a chance, I kicked them in their tools of violation. Out of spite, they made sure I could never be a woman again."

Still nodding a negative, Magali grabs her hands and says, "I ran a rape kit on you. No sign they did that to you. As to what happened to you last time, I cannot find evidence of that either."

Head tilted with one eyebrow up, Zara asks, "What do you mean? I have massive scar tissue between my legs, all the way deep into my body."

Magali brings Zara to the mirror on her dresser. As Zara stares at the stranger staring back at her, she runs her hands over her cheek. The one that she ruined with battery acid, trying to make herself too unattractive to be sold as a sex slave. She glances down at her family picture. Her cheeks are as rosy, as smooth, as delicate as they were in her youth.

With a voice less fervent than a moment ago, she says, "They performed plastic surgery on me while I was captive." She turns to Magali, adding, "They were planning on selling me again on the sex slave market."

Magali stands behind Zara and strokes the same cheek. "I am afraid not. That is your skin. Nothing but."

Her eyebrows raised, cheeks drawn in, nostrils widened, Zara turns away from Magali, lifts her nightgown, and runs her fingers in the places they burned away. She gasps.

"I did a full gynecological workup on you," says Magali. "Everything is in working order."

Mouth agape, Zara turns her head to one side, with her eyes glaring out at the far edges of the lids, staring at Magali the nurse. Magali, the never lies, never exaggerates woman of truth, waiting for her next words.

Magali says, "You can have children now."

The voice told her to see Sasha first, not to go to her mother until destiny played itself out with Sasha. And to his yacht she went first. Was it destiny being so cruel, or the voice being so obscuring? What might have happened if she had followed what her heart said? Come home to Mama first.

At the doorway, Maryam peers in, her face tense, her shoulders scrunched together. She had waited until Magali gave the okay signal. The two locked eyes for what felt like an eternity until Zara finally ran forward and embraced her. Together, they collapsed into tears. "Zara, you do not know how difficult it has been not to be able to talk with you, your brother, nor my husband," cries Maryam. "For each day I have been with you, it has been as if a knife stood between us. Something so heinous it would cut us apart."

Zara's first words were four that for forever needed to be said. "I forgive you, Mama." A deep hug, and she adds, "I love you, Mama."

More tears, but these differed from the ones moments earlier as they come from a joy, a release, a longing fulfilled. The knife dissolved. A knife that never really existed.

"He said he was always gentle with you," says Zara, still embracing Maryam.

"For what he had asked, he had been as kind as a man could be who is asking you to betray almost all you believe," Maryam answers. "But he was always there for me. He paid the bribes needed to free your father the second time without asking anything further of me. He absolved me of my guilt of not marrying an afflicted man, because I wanted my choice. You would not be here if not for our one-time act."

She pulls back from her daughter and says, "But above all, he was always there for you, his daughter. All of your education abroad, he sponsored. I knew he must have loved you as a daughter, but to spare our family, he kept his distance, only watching you grow up through all his secret spy networks and devices. He told me through an intermediary that being away from you pained him. But what happened had to happen for the welfare of mankind."

"Do you believe that, Mama?"

She grasps Zara's hands, her warmth on her daughter's cool skin, and says, "I would want nothing other than having you as my daughter. What happened made you. From the moment you first touched me with your tiny pink fingers, I knew I could not wish that it had never happened."

Zara takes her hands and holds them against her cheek, the one that no longer bears the marks of her enslavement.

"The only day he broke his silence was when you left to rescue your cousins from the impending Daesh attack on Sinjar," says Maryam. "His intelligence network found out the Iraqis held up your passage across the Syrian border. He called me and told me I needed to contact you to tell you not to go. But I did not know how."

"It was not your fault, Mama," says Zara. "I made bad choices throughout my life. But if given the choice again, I would always have tried to save my cousins. If only I had arrived a day earlier."

"As soon as he knew of your kidnapping, he began the backroom negotiations and hardball blackmailing to find you. For that year they held you three, he used every resource, friend, favor, to find where they kept you. If not for him, I fear what ultimately would have happened."

Zara squeezes her mother's hand and says, "I would have killed myself like Rona begged me to kill her. Like her sister finally did to herself months later. Hell could not be worse than what we suffered."

Squeezing Zara's hand back, then touching her lower abdomen, Maryam smiles and says, "I understand a miracle has happened. What they took away from you has come back."

A little smile back, and Zara says, "And I thought confessions to a Catholic sister were confidential."

"She did not tell me willingly," says Maryam with a coy wink. "I could see for months now that you have been changing, that the scars were healing."

"I guess I never wanted to look so closely," admits Zara. "I did not want to be reminded of what they took, of what happened because of my poor choices."

Motherly hands again clasp both of Zara's cheeks. "I did not make a bad choice. I had you. Nor did you make bad choices. Everything that has happened has formed who you are and made you ready for that one choice to come. There will be a moment, I am sure, when you make a decision that will forever be the best one. I did."

Another hug. Another set of little tears, but tears of the love that needed to be shed between them for all of Zara's life.

Her hands on her mama's cheeks, then stroking her hair, Zara said, "I dreamt I was a slave again. Held in the depravity that I had been with the Daesh. Only worse. I was their prophetess by day, and by night, the worst of the worst. And I dreamt about a woman who had your face. She came to save me."

Maryam smiles and glances back at Zara's bedroom door. "The one who came to save you, he has been waiting out there for you." Rubbing Zara's hand again, she says, "He has stayed with me when he was not out searching for you. He worried about how Roza and I were doing, asking all sorts of questions about our family. He is a good man. Much like your father."

She brushes Zara's hair away from her face. "You pressure yourself with the notions of destiny. Roza has talked to the world nonstop about your healing people and saving lives. But I believe your destiny is the same as mine, Roza's, and Sara's. A mother of wonderful children."

Maryam gets up to get Zara's brush, and then, as she did for the first fourteen years of her life, the good mother brushes her daughter's hair. "You are free to marry or not marry. A woman should have her choice. You should know he is a very clever man. He turned what might have been a horrible situation into a miraculous one for you. He is an angel, I truly believe. He is your angel. I will let him tell you the story."

❧

His dokliw, a meat and vegetable soup Zara loved as a child, was quite passable. Almost as good as her mother made it. They had nice cordialities to say and discuss with Roza, Maryam, and Magali during lunch. The latter suggested the women take a walk, leaving Zara alone with Peter.

They sat in the mal, the main room of the house where guests entered. Zara's two lambs sat between them as they took turns licking Zara, then Peter, again and again.

Peter says, "They missed you."

"I missed them," says Zara.

"They thought you might have gone to heaven," says Peter, rubbing the black lamb behind its ears.

"I am happy they did not think I went the other way," says Zara. She then scoots her two kids off the sofa. "You and Magali. You both have something you do not want to tell me."

Staring down at his feet, Peter says, "When I thought you might have been killed, I reflected on all the things I should have said to you after our fights at the book signing. I was so consumed with this book thing I acted insensitively with you. I shouldn't have yelled at you during the book signing. Of course, you missed my speech because there are more important things in this world that a woman like you must attend to. And the whole aliens thing. They must have drugged me."

She touches his hand for the first time since she fled San Francisco. "I think I now know something about being drugged. But I do not think the aliens took me like they did you."

"Thank you for humoring me," says Peter, rubbing his thumb along her hand.

"It is I who should be thanking you for bearing with me," says Zara. "A man should be a father to his children. Once, I thought I loved a man so much, I wanted to have a family with him. But I found out he already had a lovely family. So, I left him, and then you. Not because of what you said, but because I cared about you and only wanted you to have the best in life."

Shuffling his feet, Peter says, "There's something you should know about Mei."

"The baby? Nothing has happened to your baby, has it?"

Eyes on his feet. Lower teeth biting his lip. He promised not to tell. Do you break one promise because you want the love of another so much? And he answers that ethical question as he peers into Zara's eyes.

"Oh, the baby is superb. A true Gollinger in the making, to be raised by a Gollinger just as my mother would want," he affirms. "I…I just wanted to say how much I value you. Value your friendship."

She grasps and pulls the Kurdish baggy pants he wears and says, "How can I be a friend to someone who is wearing my brother's pants?" As his face strikes the pose of alarm, she laughs.

"I think dressing you in my brother's clothes was my mother's way of making you feel more Kurdish and for her to grieve my possible death. They look good on you."

She senses the hesitation in Peter even as she tries to comfort him with humor. "Magali tells me you have been my hero once again. I would enjoy hearing your tales of coming to my rescue again."

"That Alexander. It is really his genius and planning that did it all," says Peter, still a little tense. "Must have been during your kidnapping. I received an alert saying I needed to report to a MoxWorld headquarters to receive instructions. So, I flew with Mei to his Asia headquarters, where she taught me how to use the resources of MoxWorld to find you."

"And you know who he is to me?" asks Zara.

"His hologram recording said you had been kidnapped because you were his daughter."

"What else did he say?"

He pauses, gazes into her eyes, then says, "It has been my destiny for thousands of years to save you and stand by your side. And I am not finished yet."

"Do you believe him?" asks Zara.

"It's not whether I believe him. Do you?" answers Peter.

Gazing away from him, she says, "Someone said he would stand by my side. Forever." She looks back at him and says, "And forever lasted but weeks."

Silence as the two watch the lambs chasing each other's tails. In circles they run.

His hand slowly and assuredly circles hers. "You were with him, weren't you? I mean, the very last thing you remember, you were with him."

Her lower teeth dig into her upper lip as she nods.

"His yacht vaporized in a pinpoint nuclear explosion. We announced his death. But I knew you were still alive somewhere. I vowed to find you."

Stoic. Stony-faced. Rigid, but she gives another subtle nod. Death surrounds her. And she has lost yet another father.

Minutes pass before she asks, "How did you find me?"

"He gave me access to all of his tracking programs and surveillance activities, which Mei taught me how to use," says Peter. "I went to a half dozen places, searching for clues. Dead ends. False signals. And so, I came here to stay with your family."

He pops up a recording on his MoxWrap. "Then this came across. It's encoded in Chinese with the Turk's responses. MoxSecurity said it falsely led to the Chinese and Turks, but someone else fabricated it. But it talked of a plan with a woman of your description near Istanbul. So, a MoxWorld Helijet took me straight there."

Peering into her eyes, his hand places a pillow in her lap. She asks, "What is this for?"

"In case you want to punch something. Better this than me."

"I am not amused. Spit it out, Peter," she says, already tapping away at the pillow.

He taps his MoxWrap and up comes a NiQihs News feed. A spy-cam-like through-the-window video, as if a voyeur had been watching her. A half dozen naked men surround her stark-naked body, stroking her, licking her, leaving their fluids all over her. The newscasters talk of the messiah being exposed as a whore, a perverted sex fiend.

Zara twists the pillow until the seams burst. "So now the entire world hates me. Fine. I do not have to live up to a saint's level of reputation."

"Twelve hours after NiQihs News tried to defame you, my newest book launched," says Peter. He plays the video reviews of the book *The Next Prophetess*, a suspense thriller whose heroine is famed as the second coming and is framed with a sordid orgy and labeled a whore. The conspirators are revealed, and she saves the world.

"The business news community has labeled this book launch the world's biggest case of fake news being used to publicize a book. *The Next Prophetess* reached number one within twenty-four hours of its release," explains Peter.

"But how did you write this so fast?" asks Zara in amazement.

"It was your Sasha, your father. He had three dozen versions of books, mostly written, ready for a variety of emergency needs. His AI is so advanced it can create books with certain input from the author. I only had to pick and choose which sections worked well together to tell the story appropriate to your situation and then activate the same editorial group that worked on my first book. Within a day, we had this book ready for release."

Zara stares at the looping video of big butch men getting rough with her body. Just like the giants in her dream. No evidence she took part. For that, she thanks Xwedê.

But is this what that horrible man meant by dead fish? Her mind twists about, trying to piece together who would do this. And why? NiQihs is the logical choice, as they have the most to gain from killing Alexander. But why let her live and frame and defame her?

Then, in the haze of what memory she has of the last moments on Sasha's yacht, Zengo's face when he kissed her and fondled her. That chesty Israeli woman who tried to be her friend but was in the sack with Zengo all the time. Who is she working for? She lied about not working for the Mossad. She must have been. And Zengo? He lied about her being a dead fish in bed. He must have.

She glances over at Peter. On two of his knuckles, the telltale healing scabs. She reaches over and lightly touches them. "You fought with them, did you not? You fought for my honor."

"It is possible I fought for my honor," he says, rubbing her fingers back. "I landed one lucky punch in the shortest one's nose." He points to his MoxWrap. "Then, as the other five pummeled me, Alexander's sonic punches came in handy again."

"Again?" asks Zara.

"Uh, I saved Mei in a cave made by her Goddess Jiang somewhere in Western China. We found out that she took another object out there. We think it now rests in Jerusalem."

"That is wonderful, Peter," she says, trying to cheer him up. "I know how very clever you are. How did you deduce that?"

Silence again. Even her lambs stand still as they stare at the two of them.

Biting his lower lip, he nods his head up and down.

"I never, ever cheated on any of my girlfriends. Ever," he states.

Her head jerks back, her eyebrows raised. She says, "Peter, I left you so you could go back to the mother of your child. I can understand if you two—"

Before she can finish her empathetic statement, Peter blurts, "I cheated on you. I bonded with Mei."

"Bonded?" she says in astonishment.

"Her bump. I mean, her bumps. I mean, she and I are…" stutters Peter.

Just like her mother, she thinks. He needs her in a way she has not been good at in the past. She moves close to him and hugs him from the side. "Peter, whatever it is, I forgive you. Not that you need forgiveness, but know that mine is yours to have."

"So, you know already?" asks Peter as his back bolts straighter with his eyebrows up and his eyes wide open.

She kisses his cheek and says, "I know whatever you did with Mei, you did for me and Sasha. You have our best interests in mind. That is what I love about you."

He kisses her cheek back as his muscles release their tension. "You don't know how much I've fretted about what you would say. Your friendship means so much to me."

"And yours to me," she says with the edges of her lips on the rise.

Squeezing her hand, he replies, "I am so glad I can talk about Mei with you."

At Maryam's suggestion, Peter takes Zara on a short walk with her fluff ball "children," who are delighted to see her again. Almost as much as Peter is.

As they stroll through the village with the two teenaged lambs swirling about their legs, Peter says, "You don't know how much I fretted about what you might think of me bonding with her that way. I mean, it wasn't nearly as clear as when I bond with you."

No response from the newly arisen woman, so Peter says, "We saw a dream about you."

Squeezing his hand back, she says, "And so did I, as you had tried to bond with me to heal me."

Leaning at a tilt, he glances at her from the corner of his eye. "That Mongolian princess. She was so much like you. I'm glad you know already you have to work with Mei's professor friend."

Not fully getting what her quirky Peter is getting at, she asks, "What Mongolian princess? I dreamed of my mother coming to save me from being stoned."

Not picking up on her signals, Peter effusively says, "You and Rachel. Seven hundred years ago, you two paired up to search for the second black object under the Temple Mount."

"That conniving woman!" she exclaims with her irises the size of pinheads. She takes the bottom of her headscarf and wads it up. "His betrayal with that devious Israeli woman. When I see her again, no more nice Zara."

CHAPTER 37

For though we love both the truth and our friends,
piety requires us to honor the truth first

—Aristotle

Jerusalem
10:30 a.m. GMT+3, March 1, 2023

Rachel marvels at the creations within the lobby of the Jerusalem MoxWorld Resort. Different themed areas mimic the three religions that have occupied Jerusalem over the last two thousand years. One area replicates the Court of Women of the Second Temple, another the interior of the Dome of the Rock. The third recreates the Rotunda of the Church of the Holy Sepulchre.

She has heard about these wonders created here, but because Murometz's father was also complicit in her saba raba's death, she has not visited. Even from visiting Massa's family, who are in complimentary economy suites on the east end. But the urgent message from Mei Tang to come meet her here changed Rachel's views of complicity by visiting.

Knowing Mei has its privileges here, as security lets Rachel pass into the ultra-luxury guest lobby. An AI voice named Moxy asks for her identity at the elevator. She is approved for direct access to Ms. Tang's floor.

As the elevator doors close, a hand juts in, triggering them to open again. Her body poised to repel an attack, Rachel takes an offensive stance, ready with an open hand to strike the nose or eyes. But the man who enters is too tall for such a strike from a woman of her more modest size and build.

Before she can ready a groin strike, Lemuel says, "Are you still angry with me? Your files said you were too emotionally labile for critical missions. They sent me to test you."

Hands back at her side, although striking his groin still seems an attractive option, she says, "Well, obviously I failed. Why are you here to bother me? Where's my father?"

He points to the security cams in the elevator. "Not here."

She follows him out of the resort into a grey van. Inside is the normal assortment of surveillance equipment. "You've been tracking me," she protests.

As he shows her a chair to sit in, he says, "For your own security, we excluded your father from these discussions. He is too emotionally involved for what must happen now."

Her eyes narrowed, she pulls the pendant out from her blouse. "Can you handle Asherah around my neck? You are not too emotionally labile to work with a mission-critical asset as myself?" jests Rachel.

He certainly does not appear to be a man of any humor, assesses Rachel as she adds, "And why are you here? Didn't I provide enough intel for you folks?"

Grim lines across his cheeks and mouth, eyes down, he answers, "Things went sideways. It was a real *fashla*. Screw-up."

"Funny, you're the second person in a month to say that to me," says Rachel.

"That Gollinger man is just as devious as his missing master," bemoans Lemuel. "Where did that book launch of his come from? That Kurdish woman is more a messiah today than before she went missing."

He shows her MoxNews coverage of her in Damascus. She, her grandmother, and Peter are leaving a hospital where she cured the wife of the president of the Syrian Province of the Arab Confederation. The crowds are chanting "messiah" while Peter is signing MoxBooks.

Rachel's ears ring with the word *cure*. Is this Kurdish woman another charlatan rallying the Islamic world against the nonbelievers? Or can she really cure? Could Massa be cured by her? Who is the greater demon from hell? Zara Khatum or the agents from NiQihs?

"That Murometz's post-death hologram press release has made him a martyr and her a saint. I cannot tell who is more popular now," says Lemuel. "But what I do know is the Kurd and Gollinger are coming here to meet with your Chinese professor friend. Those of her faith in Jerusalem are organizing a grand welcome for the Kurdish woman. Muslims from Egypt, Lebanon, and the Syrian and Jordanian provinces of the AC have all booked rooms in and around Jerusalem."

Tapping his large fingers on the surveillance panel, he says, "Since she has returned, the MoxWorld Security following her has tripled. And Gollinger, he sleeps in her bedroom. Intel believes there is no sex between them, but I wonder. He tortured and killed a NiQihs agent, so he is more dangerous than our initial assessment suggested."

Shifting in her chair, Rachel again asks, "So why are you here, Lemuel? What do you expect me to do? Ask everyone to join me in prayers to Asherah? Maybe this Kurd is her incarnation."

He stares at the Star of David hanging with the pagan goddess pendant. As his hand reaches out, she reflexively jerks back, but she allows him to pick up her star.

"I know you believe in what I do no matter what you teach," he says. "Israel and Yahweh."

He hands her a palm-sized black pouch. She opens it up and nods.

"It's more discreet than your Jericho and would not appear as if an Israeli agency did the deed," says Lemuel as he puts his index finger against her forehead. "If our going in plan goes sideways again, you neutralize her."

"Come on, Rach, don't be such a baby about this," admonishes Mei as she tries to feather a first layer of makeup on her archaeology colleague's cheek. "This is Rhonda's best ultra-air whip foundation. It's whisked into a lighter-than-air matrix. Even the best makeup artist wouldn't know this isn't your natural skin."

The Israeli woman rotates one cheek, then another, into view in Mei's custom makeup mirrors. Rachel asks, "Your boyfriend, you sure he likes all this stuff on a woman's face?"

"You act as if you've never had a professional work on your face before," says Mei as she continues to feather the edges of Rachel's face.

"I did twice. Three-hour sessions both times," says Rachel.

"And the results, did you catch who you wanted?" asks Mei with eyebrows raised.

"Yes, Mei. I did. I am not homely. At least, you didn't think so," says Rachel.

Mei smiles and kisses the top of her head. "You have a natural kind of beauty. But what I am going to do is make it even more naturally beautiful."

"And the results for you? Do you catch who you want with this stuff?" Rachel teases back.

"I got Peter into my bed, didn't I?" answers Mei.

"And now, you want me to get him into my bed," says Rachel. "I was quite surprised when you told me that was why you wanted me to see you here. I mean, we have searched four different excavations since you arrived and not one peep. Suddenly, you want me to steal your boyfriend."

"You met my mother and father when you visited me in Shanghai," says Mei. "I could not tell them about us any more than I can tell them about Michaela. Besides, you were once in Michaela's situation with me. If you had a brother, what if he had to sleep with me to keep honor in the family? Poor you. So, the most honorable way out for me, for Michaela, is for you to steal my husband. The family will commiserate with a jilted pregnant daughter."

"Why not get that messiah woman to take him away from you?"

"Zara? Oh no, honey. She sleeps next to Peter and nothing happens. She's sworn herself to a life of celibacy following her favorite saint or something like that," affirms Mei. "You know, he has this bonding thing he figured out. He did it to me. I saw the Goddess Jiang dream."

"You mean the one your mother was hounding you about not having?"

"And now, she's happy I am a real woman now," says Mei, her lips beaming ear to ear. "But the real secret is the bonding. It's better than any orgasm. Either from a man or a woman. Once he does it with you, you'll never want another man or woman in your bed."

"Is that what you expect me to do with him once I get him?" asks Rachel.

"You said you swung both ways, like me," says Mei. "I know firsthand you will enjoy what he can do with a woman. Especially her feet. I will miss that part the most after that mind-numbing bonding thing."

Nodding, gauging Mei's eyes, Rachel asks, "But he is the father of your child, isn't he?"

Mei stops feathering her face and turns, stops a second, then gets a concealer as she answers, "Peter is the perfect father. But I am not destined for a husband. Perhaps you are."

Her hands in loose fists on the makeup table countertop, Rachel stares into Mei's eyes in the mirror. "I know you too well, you forget. Honor is the nice story you think would get the honorable side of me to play ball with your predicament. But that's not the real reason. The real Mei is very calculating and deliberate."

Without a blink, Mei's eyes pierce into the image of Rachel's eyes in the mirror. No disarming smile. Just intense eyebrows. "Just how bad do you want to find your Asherah? My due date is within a couple of weeks. Once my water bursts, game over for entering that cavern your Ariella wants us to find. So, the only other super-afflicted eligible bachelorette is you. But you must be carrying his child."

Breaking eye contact, biting her lower lip, Rachel replies, "So, this is for real. Not just another over-the-top favor. It's a high price to pay. Tell me you didn't get pregnant just for some legend."

Her long, thin fingers around Rachel's face bring her eyes up to look into hers, and Mei says, "A nuclear war has already started. Only tactical strikes on limited military targets related to the crazed search for the black object. But an all-out global war is certain to come. Everyone you love will vaporize instantly, or worse, perish from radiation sickness. We are no closer to having a black object in hand after two weeks here in Jerusalem. And you tell me.

Where exactly is that cavern of the blue light?"

Her hands on her abdomen, Rachel's eyes stare at Mei's baby bump, and she says, "Tell me you always wanted to be a mother."

Flashing her disarming smile, Mei says, "Honey, you know me. I'm the perfect tiger mom. My child will rule the fashion world through better genetics."

A burst of air through her nostrils. A laugh suppressed. Then her hands on her cheeks. "What makes you think he will find me attractive in that way?" asks Rachel.

"You doubt the master of making male hormones dance and sing?" says Mei as she gets a dress from the wardrobe. Feeling the fabric, or lack thereof, Rachel can see her fingers through the finely woven tissue. Not that she has not worn provocative clothing before. The time she had to get a man to spill his SS prison guard grandfather's location. Then that one time for the Mossad's archaeology unit. The first and last time for her country. But this lack of opaqueness makes her into anyone's *frecha*.

"And have you ever worn this in public?" Rachel asks.

"Yes, and the crowds loved it," says Mei, taking the dress and tightly wrapping it to Rachel's chest.

As Rachel flinches, transfixed on the fabric's transparency, Mei says, "Seriously, Rachel. This fabric is a lot warmer than if I body-painted you."

"That's no consolation," laments Rachel as she tries not to imagine wearing this in public.

"Afflicted men have a genetic activation when they see an afflicted woman's chest," attests Mei. "As I learned from Peter, it traces to something that happened with the originating husband and some woman. He called out the name Illyana when he reacted to my breasts. Perhaps he will call out Asherah when he sees your perky pair through this dress."

"How do you know he will like a Jewish girl?" says Rachel, flush from imagining parading around in this amount of opacity.

"He told me his college girlfriend was Jewish. He almost converted for her before she broke it off," says Mei. "It's nearing seven p.m. They should arrive shortly. Remember what I said. Let him see that ample perky pair of yours, and his afflicted DNA will take its course. Peter is so predictable. You will love his response."

Rachel pauses, holding the dress up. Her fingers shine through. "If he is really a brainiac, wouldn't he more likely fall in love with one of my dissertations than this lack of a dress of yours?"

Arms akimbo, mouth in a grimace, Mei says, "He's a man. No matter the IQ, testosterone always dumbs them down. Believe me, my way will work. I got him to go on that mission last spring, did I not?"

As Rachel begins to undress so she can wiggle into that dress of Mei's, she asks, "And what about that Kurdish woman? How is she going to react when Peter fawns all over me?"

"Oh, Zara. She doesn't care if Peter is with another woman. Believe me, their relationship is purely platonic."

As Rachel puts on the ultra-clingy, not-even-opaque white dress, she stares at herself in the mirror as every little bump pokes through the delicate tissue. She's not doing this for that Lemuel and his people. But is she doing it for Mei's friendship, for her great-grandmother, or to finally learn the truth?

Taking her own dress out of the closet, Mei says, "You know, you could have been the one that voice talked with. You just had to wear a dress like this for an interview with the big man. He needed to know you would perform that perverse afflicted woman's mating ceremony nude in public. But you flinched at the notion of sex with a stranger in public in the buff."

Seeing Rachel's jaw drop, Mei continues, "Honey, I argued with the big man that you were a better match for Peter than Zara or I for finding the cavern of the blue light. But that giant said Zara and I would be better for finding the black object, which had to happen first."

Her hands on Rachel's, stretching out the translucent dress, Mei says, "If you had just consented back then, it would be you instead of Zara who Peter would be fawning over. You would've been carrying his child right now. We're just doing a little course correction with that dress today."

Blushing as she contemplates the transparency of this lack of cloth hugging her body, Rachel says, "You mean I could have had Asherah talking directly with me if I had worn this? That monstrous man you work for would have picked me over Zara? And I would be the prophetess the world is clamoring to hear?"

With her disarming smile, Mei turns and replies, "Honey, I voted for you. Now's your second chance at redemption. Do your thing in that dress."

As Mei leaves to change into her own dress, Rachel checks her shoulder bag and pulls out that tight black, lack-of-dignity thing from that doctor. Should she or shouldn't she? Not for Ariella. Not for her country. A woman shouldn't be forced into such choices. Certainly archaeology professors shouldn't. But to find Asherah?

How could she bond with this man? One who has hopped from one afflicted woman to another. Worse yet, his DNA is that of a Gollinger. How could she ever think of having a baby with such a man?

Peering back into her shoulder bag, she finds her three other options staring at her: a specimen vial, a surgical kit, and a Ruger silent suppressor .22-caliber palm-sized pistol.

CHAPTER 38

*Life is a series of natural and spontaneous changes. Don't resist them;
that only creates sorrow. Let reality be reality. Let things flow
naturally forward in whatever way they like.*
—Lao Tzu, sixth-century BCE founder of Daoism

Outskirts of Jerusalem
8:30 p.m. GMT+3, March 1, 2023

"No, Moxy, I do not want to talk with the president of Russia. I certainly do not want them to continue bombing NiQihs factories in China. I get it they believe China nuked Alexander's yacht off Russian shores. Let him know that when they wish to come to a peace accord table, we can talk about shipping them the latest MoxDefense technologies," says Zara, quite exasperated at the duties her Sasha tended to on a minute-to-minute basis.

Given the gross security breach on Sasha's yacht, which she caused, she trusts no one now. Except Peter. And Jean-Paul. And of course, Magali. She is not so sure about Mei, whose friend is that cheating Israeli spy. But she needs any friend now more than ever. As such, she rides to Jerusalem in one of Alexander's ultra-high-security Presidential MoxMovers amid a convoy of four other MoxMovers that carry her mother, Roza, Jean-Paul, Magali, a dozen MoxSecurity commandos, and, of course, Peter.

The last several days since she regained consciousness have been quite the whirlpool. Maybe cesspool. Without Zara, and with Zengo being a NiQihs spy who cheated on her with that Israeli seductress, the peace negotiations between the Kurds and Turkey fell apart quickly. China armed Turkey and the Arab Confederation with their latest weapons and aircraft using NiQihs AI. Turkey and the AC have come to terms about which of MoxWorld's factories will go to each country as they lay plans to reabsorb the two Kurdish countries back into theirs.

The same conversation she just had with Moxy she had the day before, as the US president wanted to talk with her. When she refused, messages from Dan came through, followed by more and more desperate ones when they went unanswered.

She is so done with ex-boyfriends. Every time she succumbs to a moment of weakness, look what happens. When she catches up to Zengo and that Israeli woman, they will come to know the voice as She says goodbye to them on their way down to dûjeh, the darkness of hell.

Roza convinced her she had the most powerful alternative to arming the Kurds, the Russians, and the US with more powerful weapons. The messiah has the power of words and vision, which no missile, no tank, no stone could eviscerate. Ironically, while NiQihs methodically created divisions in the Muslim world, her prophethood united the rest.

She wanted to start her peace tour in Ankara, but the Turkish president banned her from entering the country, insisting she is a harlot and an offense to their religion. So they went south.

That posthumous press release from her Sasha decried the treachery of NiQihs, whom he said detonated a nuclear bomb that killed him in their quest for world domination and declared Zara to be the savior of mankind, the inheritor of the divine visions that will lead mankind out of darkness into light. Billions now seek to hear from her. His martyrdom has cemented her messiah status.

Thus, in Damascus, nearly ten thousand gathered to see her talk, with billions more viewing live on MoxWorld Global News. The chants for peace echoed around the world. The leaders of the AC would have to listen to their people and not attack the Kurds. Or anyone else, for that matter.

In no more than a day, her relationship with Peter picked up where they'd left off before his book signing. He hiked with her and her lambs. He stood by her side through Damascus, ever vigilant for anyone who would seek to hurt her.

His dreams are still as vivid as when she first met him. Something about her presence moderates the violence of his nightly visions. After their first night apart in her mother's home, she came to his bed to calm down his dreams, but in the same platonic way of their life before.

Platonic may be what her head says, but her miraculously recovered body says otherwise, something she fights with each night they are together. Those flutters of the stomach, of the heart, have come back, but much stronger than the false ones with Zengo. The last thing the world needs, much less what she needs, is for her to lose focus and be distracted by a romantic, highly physical involvement.

But he gets a spot on her body so heated up. That spot that had been so stone cold since the Daesh ripped her up. She must focus. She must gain people's faith that their voices can avert world war.

He cheated on her. Or so he said. She had to wrestle with that idea. But not in the way Zengo had cheated on her with that shameless, too-busty Israeli woman. In a way, her special bonding with Peter represented something sacrosanct to her, as did the ancient matriarch's with her husband. A sickening, guttural revulsion overcame her when Peter said he bonded with Mei, touching her special bump.

Her rational sense prevailed as she reminded herself he is a platonic friend. And what he did was not for visceral self-pleasure but for the good of all, to find the second object. But it did not help when he sheepishly admitted that Mei became beyond orgasmic at the bonding. She could not suppress fast enough the notion Mei might have been better in bed than she, the dead fish. Messiahs should not succumb to petty jealousies, she told herself.

Once her rational self became the driver of her thoughts, she listened to Peter's recounting of the dream he had with Mei's "assistance." Two women, one Jewish and the other Muslim, on a mission to find the object in the Temple Mount in Jerusalem. How prophetic his dream, but she is not likely to go waltzing hand in hand down any Temple Mount aisle with that temptress Israeli woman. A prophetess for peace she may be, but given ten minutes, she will put peace aside to settle affairs with that woman who plotted and cheated against her with Zengo.

In these moments before the crowds come, before the media cameras, she gazes at Peter, who is napping with his head in her lap. It was the least she could offer to comfort his sleep, as he averaged less than a couple of hours a night for weeks as he searched for her. For a few hours, he dreamed in a bliss cradled by her.

As they roll by the Garden Tomb, believed to be the site of the resurrection of Jesus, he mumbles from another dream. Not one about aliens who bring a new world order edict, hopes Zara. Suddenly, he grabs her, throwing her to the floor of the MoxMover, his body covering hers.

She yells at him as she takes his hands off places off-limits. "What has come over you? You promised. No sex."

In typical Peter manner—aghast, that is—he pulls his hands back and rolls off her. "You were being stoned. I had to protect you. Your daughter, she didn't fare so well."

"My daughter? With whom?" she says. "You? We agreed no such intimacy in our relationship."

As Peter helps her back into the MoxMover seat, he says, "It was that same dream you said you had. A mother and her daughter. I've changed my opinion on matters. We should leave Jerusalem. We should go back to your village and live in peace and equality."

Shaking her head, she says, "First, you say we must come here because of your dream with Mei. Now, you dream with me and we should go back. Perhaps I should allow you to dream with some other woman with an even bigger bump. Perhaps you will say we should go to the North Pole."

Sheepishly, Peter checks his MoxWrap and reviews those last commands Alexander gave him.

The MoxMover caravan arrives at MoxWorld Resorts Jerusalem, situated south of the Old City. Alexander made instant multimillionaires of the several dozen homeowners who had previously inhabited this land overlooking a monastery, with a view of the south wall of the Temple Mount.

MoxSecurity surrounds the pair as they exit their MoxMover while its external nodules rotate barely noticeable blue beams, searching for drone threats. Zara adjusts her light blue headscarf, accenting her off-white, knee-length coat with a gold metallic design. Peter adjusts his light off-white jacket with the same metallic design covering his tan MoxWorld-logoed polo shirt tucked into a pair of khakis.

Masses of women with headscarves chant for Zara, their messiah. Different from Damascus, here, as many other women without headscarves also chant for her. Swamped by a lesser number of women of all races, creed, and religions, but equally vocal, Peter starts signing MoxRead books of both his first and second novels.

In between signings, Peter keeps gazing around. And he spots a woman handing out small packets to the women who have had their MoxReads book signed. She seems so familiar, and she stands next to a man as tall as Alexander but with more white hair, a slivery glint from his teeth, and dark rockstar glasses. Exactly as Alexander's instructions said should happen.

Roza brings Rhonda from MoxWorld Global News, who is dressed in an off-white pantsuit with the same gold metallic design as Zara's—the new acting chairwoman of MoxWorld. Rhonda interviews the crowd first, and then turns over video crew coverage to her uber boss, Zara, and her words for the world.

The people's messiah wishes all the good people of the world who wish only for peace to rise up and tell their governments to lobby the major powers not to irradiate the world with a global nuclear conflict over meteorite rights. She then reminds the crowds that we all should profess we worship the same god, and wars over the interpretations of divine words should be questioned. That same god for all of us would not want us killing each other.

Her words fall on deaf ears among those crowding and bumping each other to get to their favorite author. Most are civil and thankful for his inscriptions, but to his shock, a number want him to autograph intimate clothing they expose, asking if he is like that virile French priest. With eyes closed and desperately trying not to touch the soft tissue covered by what he is autographing, Peter blushes and ultimately declines, thanking them for their fandom.

Watching Peter's dilemma, Zara comes to his rescue with her MoxSecurity team, grabbing the flushing author to enter the exclusive MoxResort VIP lobby. Here the mobs cannot access, but the ultra-rich guests can. Father Jean-Paul brings Zara's family and Magali over to the Dome of the Rock replica area as once again Zara talks with those who believe in her words and visions and VIP women with their MoxRead books out surround Peter.

The fan that catches Peter's eye is the one who looks like she stepped out of a Batman movie set. He turns his head as the décolletage plunges without shame like a streaking high diver.

Oddly enough, she appears somewhat uncomfortable in that tighter than tight, reveal-everything black catsuit. But so is he, as he shivers when she comes up to him, as did the other women who had the erotic romance version, and rubs up next to him, asking if he is as virile as the French priest in his book. As she shows him the passages she would love to relive with the author in more private settings, he says she must be cold as her chest goose bumps are showing. To her surprise, he wraps his jacket around her shoulders, covering that which Zara would never show in public.

Abruptly stopping mid-sentence to her followers, Zara spies the same black-skintight-garment-clad woman with that ample bosom who cheated on her with Zengo now having charmed Peter into wrapping his coat around her. Zara's rage comes not because this woman is trying to steal another boyfriend of hers. Her rage, now fury, comes from the principle of this woman, or lack thereof.

Bolting past her security team and through women in the way, she tackles Rachel, sending both of them sliding across the floor into a potted palm tree. Pinning Rachel's smaller body to the floor, ready to remove her front teeth, Zara halts her strike as her eyes focus on Rachel's eyes. They are no longer the self-assured ones that stared her down on her mountain back in Duhok. Something has happened to her.

As hotel security comes en masse, getting into a scuffle with the corporate MoxSecurity team, Zara sits on Rachel, poking her cleavage with her index finger. "Pretty good for a dead fish you left for shark bait on his yacht before you vaporized it."

Grabbing her finger, Rachel whips back, "I do not know what you're jabbering about, you deranged bully. I'm a land archaeologist, not a marine one. I roll around in the dust, not in the waves. I have never been on a yacht."

Head turned to the side, Zara glares at Rachel out of the corner of her eye with a sneer that could slice through a diamond. Eyeballing those mounds that seduced Zengo and the form of her body, Zara nods. This is the same woman who killed her Sasha.

As Rachel's hands press back on her chest, Zara takes one and examines the wrist. No red marks. Possibly they haven't had bondage sex recently. Peering into her eyes once more, Zara lets go of her wrist.

Tapping Rachel's forehead, Zara says, "I will finish what you started here if you ever touch or entice my Peter again."

Ignoring Peter's fans, who mumble that this altercation is just like Chapter 14 in his book, Rachel digs her elbows into the floor and snatches Zara's finger, saying, "I understood from Jean-Paul that no romantic involvement existed between you two, no physical involvement either. He's man enough to decide when and with whom he should bestow his attentions."

Rolling off the smaller woman, Zara replies, "That does not matter. A woman like you is beneath a man like him."

Rachel fires back, "Israel is a free country. You should let Peter decide if he wishes for a less-than-celibate stay in Jerusalem."

Blushing more at Rachel's comment than he did at the bra signing, Peter stares at the two of them on the floor, unsure of what to do. Only Mei had ever fought over him with Jia, and that was pretend. Now, two women fight over him. What does he do? He offers a hand to each of them.

"Oh my, I missed all the fireworks," says Mei as she enters the lobby, impeccably dressed in a faux Mandarin dress with black princess slippers. "The resort normally waits until the sun sets before entertaining the guests like you two did."

She waves over the resort's VIP hostess, who has been hiding behind the counter, watching the American style big-time wrestling match in horror. She passes out hotel welcome packages to Roza and Maryam, to Zara, to Jean-Paul, and finally, to Magali.

Empty-handed, Peter asks where his welcome packet is. The hostess politely smiles and says those are all MoxWorld headquarters had ordered. Equally polite, Peter smiles and turns to Zara, who shakes her head no—he is not listed in her packet. He turns to Jean-Paul, who says the same. Certainly, they would not put in the same room as Roza, Maryam, or Magali.

Shaking her head at Peter's shenanigans, Mei says as she takes his arm, "Come on, my Peter. My mother is upstairs, awaiting her son-in-law and daughter's reunion."

In a panic, deer in the headlight eyes, he glances back at Zara. At first, her forehead is crinkled down into a V into her nose with nostrils flared. But breaking eye contact with him, she stares at the floor, shaking her head.

"Why haven't you told Zara about Michaela and you?" demands an exasperated Peter. "She insists I be with you as the father of our baby. As your husband. You must understand how difficult this has been for us."

"For you? You have no idea how difficult this is for me, for us. Michaela and I," says Mei. "My mother is expecting us to have our second honeymoon in here after being separated for weeks. You need to get naked and make me sweaty before she comes back."

Still in his MoxWorld polo shirt and khakis, Peter says, "I feel like I'm cheating on Zara. I mean, I felt like I was cheating on you when I was with Zara. I can't keep this charade up."

Hanging up her Mandarin dress, Mei comes back over to Peter, her belly one month larger in clear sight. She rubs her bump and says, "Think about Michaela. My parents find out, or their family finds out about a girl-to-girl relationship, and they break us up. Don't you think that would shatter your sister?"

"What happened to Rachel stealing your boyfriend story?" asks a puzzled

Peter. "That should've been so apparent with that show downstairs."

"Your buddy Zara ruined it. Rachel was supposed to have stolen you from me downstairs and I'd be crying in my mother's arms about having lost my husband to a totally skinny vamp young archeologist."

Staring at the floor, biting his lower lip, his nostrils flaring out and in, Peter says, "I think you misjudge Ming. I think she would love Michaela as your partner as much as you do. And why should you two care what the rest of the family thinks? You two are in love. I can tell from my sister this is a new level of seriousness for her."

He looks up into her fear-ridden eyes and says, "I fretted like you about my first non-Catholic girlfriend and my mother. And when I finally brought Tara home to dinner, my mother loved her. Well, maybe what my mother loved most was the idea that Tara would make little Gollingers for her, but she loved her nonetheless. We are all people. We are all human, no matter our color or faith."

Several deep breaths as Mei stares at the man who just stood up to her and said something awfully sensible, but not doable for her. Head down, she admits, "I guess I don't have your strength. I bow to what my family has asked of me. I bowed to the indignities Alexander asked of me. Even Rachel showed greater strength than me by not wearing my dress but instead that hideous black outfit. Neither here nor there. I cannot disappoint my family with the shame of my relationship with your sister."

"I will stand with you and by you as you talk with Ming," promises Peter.

At first bending toward him as if she would put her head into his shoulder, her body into his assuring hug, she instead shakes her head violently and says, "I need a really long warm shower. When I get back, you better be in the buff under the sheets, waiting for your love-needy wife."

As he hears the water turn on, he reaches to unbutton his pants. But he stops, rubs his foot into the floor, and turns for the door. Outside, in the presidential suite parlor, sits Ming with her motherly smile. She pats the space next to her on the sofa. He tepidly approaches her, thinking she wants a foot massage, so he flexes his fingers.

As he sits, he thinks of what little he can say in Mandarin, but she surprises him by saying, "You, good man."

Peter tries his Mandarin. "*Wǒ hěn róngxìng.* I am very honored. *Xièxiè.*"

Again, surprising him, she answers, "I do speak some English. I appreciate you speaking in Mandarin."

Head tilted forward, gazing at her from the tops of his eyes, he says, "You understood what we have been saying all along?"

She mimics him with her head tilted forward, gazing back from the tops of her eyes. "Most of what you have said. You perfect Daoist. Some see you weak. But you follow path of the way of things. As Lao Tzu said. You honorable man. You should know, your sister is welcome as my daughter-in-law."

Mouth wide open, Peter's vocal cords emit nothing of what his racing mind thinks through.

Ming gives him her version of the disarming smile, patting his knee. "You love Mei too. Or you not pretend to be husband for me. I wait for Mei to trust her mother."

Peter nods. "She expects me back in there to impress you that I am a good husband."

"I see your eyes. You love Kurdish girl. I watch from big staircase your eyes on her," says Ming. "Go to her, mister perfect Daoist. I go tell Mei."

He pauses, thinking through the implications of what is happening. Then he says, "But the baby?"

Disarming smile alit again, Ming says, "Baby with two mothers and a great uncle is as happy as baby with one mother and father."

Standing in front of Zara's suite door, he waits again with trepidation. Ming just liberated him, he thinks. What does he say to Zara?

The door opens an inch. Zara peeks out as she is putting her headscarf back on. Peter moves to come in, but Zara does not open the door further.

Glancing to the side for a second, he explains the conversation he had with Mei's mother, how Mei and his sister are a couple, how Ming said he should come back to Zara because she could see the love in his eyes. Zara opens the door enough to stick her hand through, and she softly touches his cheek.

"That is why I love you so," she says. "You will always do the right thing.

And that you did so tonight once. You went to be with the woman bearing your child. She needs you more than I. Your child needs you. A man should follow his family."

A deep breath and she adds, "I have learned in the most traumatic way what a father is and isn't. And both my fathers are now dead. A woman needs her father. You should be that child's father no matter what."

A kind smile from Zara and the door closes.

Alone in the hallway. Does he go back? Does he camp out on Zara's doorstep, hoping she changes her mind?

He glances at his MoxWrap and taps twice. Michaela is up early. As he walks to the elevator alcove, he taps her face icon. A 3-D image of Michaela appears. Good, her hair is already combed; he didn't wake her up.

"Hey, big bro. Thought you'd call. I have Mei on the other line," says Michaela.

"Are you mad at me?" asks Peter.

"Silly brother. She just told me what you told her mother to do. You did what you said you'd do. Make it all work. You're the best big brother a girl could have."

"Really? It went that well?" says Peter.

"Ming texted her husband, who suspected something was happening as well. He's going to take more time to accept a daughter-in-law. But Ming is already talking about the engagement party they will be throwing back here. That is, if the world powers don't nuke each other and Shanghai in the midst."

"I'm happy for you, sis," he says. "And Ma? When will you tell her?"

"She's the next call." Michaela rubs her eyes, and then asks, "Where are you? It looks like outside the elevators. I thought you'd be bouncing like a rabbit in bed with your Kurdish girlfriend after this news."

"Zara? She is the most thoughtful woman in the world. She couldn't get in between a father and his child. She wished me and Mei all the best."

A long sigh as Michaela brushes aside an errant strand of her blondeness. "Big bro, there's something I've been meaning to tell you, but I couldn't. I mean, you'll be the best uncle a kid ever had. You're the best brother I could ever have."

He gives a half smile and cocks his head to the side.

"You mean you already knew?" she asks.

"I kind of suspected. Mei is discreet. But the way she never answered my questions—and you as well. I could only be happy for the two of you," says the good big brother. "But I have to wonder what's going to happen to the need for men once Mei makes her tech go public."

"You guys just need to be even nicer," jests Michaela. "Hey, I gotta go. Mei is pinging me. Love you. Bye."

Alone again. And nowhere to sleep. He eyes the tiny sofa in the alcove. Maybe if he curls up, he just might fit. And with any luck, it's too late for any more people to come to this floor.

As he just gets his left foot to fit into the curvature of the arm of the sofa, he hears the voice of that other woman again. The one who fought over his attentions with Zara. She must have really wanted his attention, wearing that crazy outfit.

"Need a nicer sofa?" she says, peeking out of her suite door cloaked in a MoxWorld Resort robe.

Rolling off the sofa into a standing position, Peter says, "I locked myself out. No, that makes little sense. Mei locked me out. I've been bad."

"I still have your jacket you kindly covered me with," she says. "Chivalry like yours is out of fashion, but you certainly got my attention. Come with me and we can have a drink in my parlor."

At first pausing and then figuring there's no harm in getting his jacket, Mr. Perfect Taoist follows her. In her parlor, she goes to heat water for the tea he requested. Her resort robe covers her night wear. Her face no longer has that trademark Mei-style makeup, and her hair is devoid of Michaela's metallic strands and pulled back in a simple ponytail. This woman now makes Peter feel more at ease.

Out of Peter's sight, Rachel slips a white powder into Peter's tea. She puts the vial from Dr. Fontaine into her robe pocket. And then she covers her bag with the Ruger, ready to use when all is done. She picks up the tea but then puts it down again. Looking into the mirror, she unbuttons enough of her top that he couldn't miss what she tried to get him to focus on earlier. Now, she is ready.

Sitting down right next to him, close enough he can smell her, close enough he can see her bumps in detail, close enough he can see her other bump under her ponytail in detail, she tells him of her family's history, its oral legends. She touches his bump, at which he flinches, and affirms she knows his family is afflicted. That her great-grandmother told her she must find an afflicted man to be with. And that is how Mei and Jean-Paul found her, because of her oral traditions and bump.

He is so engaged in her conversation he notices not her open robe and open top and does not drink the tea. He tells her the story of his pappy's oral legend and how Mei and Jean-Paul found him as well. He is just about to talk about his pappy's diary from Crimea but stops short, as he has just met her. Instead, he talks of the dream he and Pappy shared about a woman with dark hair and a gun. He pauses, thinking about that woman.

Rachel, constantly glancing at the cup of tea, says he should drink some before it gets too cold. She tries to segue into a more evocative conversation, one that will lead to his pants coming off willingly, as she talks about the eroticism in his book.

"May I ask you a very personal question?" asks Peter.

"Of course. We are in private. Is there something intimately personal you want from me?"

His eyes glance down. A fast breath out through his nose. "Why are you trying so hard to get my attention? It's Mei's coaching, isn't it? She put you up to this."

Her eyes glancing down, she says, "How did you know? Was I that obvious?"

His eyes on the teacup, he says, "We haven't known each other for very long, but I don't think how Mei has dressed you and coached you is a genuine reflection of who you are."

Reaching out to her robe, he covers her up. Her fingers lightly upon his, she says, "Thank you. You are a true gentleman. And, no, I usually have an ugly old but comfy cotton T-shirt and boxer shorts on for bedtime."

He dons a smile, at which she relaxes into the sofa, finally. She says, "You have no idea how many people want you to be in my bed. Do you always have all these women lined up to get you? You're like a chick magnet."

With a blush and a swallow, he replies, "Yeah. A real chick magnet who hasn't had intimate loving sex for weeks on end."

"But all those women in the lobby after you?"

He snorts. "They were paid off. Someone's sending women to get my books signed. The only woman who's ever been all over me is my mother. She so wants to have little Gollingers."

Bolting up straight, Rachel peers into his eyes. "And she should be happy. You made her a little baby with Mei. Your mother's little Gollinger."

Peering right back at her, he asks, "I take it you and Mei have been close. Possibly Michaela and her type close?"

Gazing down, she replies, "Did she tell you that?"

Lips scrunched together, he touches her forehead. "You're kind of like my sister. An aspirational young woman very focused on her end results. She on her metallic designs. You?"

A smile back at him, and she says, "And me on my archaeology. Do you know anything about Asherah?"

"Who? I know about Asefeh."

Touching his forehead back, she says, "Silly. Asherah. God's wife."

A snort, and he says, "A year ago, I would've said that was an oxymoron. But after all we've seen since meeting Alexander, anything is game."

"So, if you are game, will you bond with me the same way you did with Mei?"

Pulling back from her, he stares at her mouth, then eyes. Standing up, he says, "I can't. That would be like cheating on two other women at the same time. I'm already in enough trouble with Zara."

Standing up as well, she says, "I have several confessions to make. I'll be back in a second."

As she is in her bedroom, Peter taps his MoxWrap.

"Here. You know that French priest, Jean-Paul?" she says as she returns, her hair now up in a loose bun. Handing him her gold pendant, she adds, "He says this may come from as far north as Turkey. Possibly 3000 or 4000 BCE. The woman is Asherah."

His fingers tracing Asherah's outline down to her feet, he wastes no time in remarking, "And I'm sure Jean-Paul pointed out the banana slugs at her feet."

Jerking back from him, she says, "He did. How did you know that so fast?"

"Because he has another medallion with the same. That was the one that convinced Zara to finally bond with me."

Pursing her lips, she takes the pendant and his fingers into her hands. "You do not know how many people have asked me to bond with you in that same way. Peter, I know we just met, but I desperately need you to bond with me as well. I need to find Asherah."

He shakes his head. "That's all you afflicted women want from me. Rub your bumps. Make you see things. And in Mei's case, spasm out better than any orgasm she's ever had."

She blushes and says, "She did tell me that. But she also said you two had a vision of two women searching for Asherah. I so desperately need to see them."

Taking his fingers, she places them upon her special bump. "I know my bump isn't as big as the other women in your life. But Jean-Paul said my genetics were the third closest to that ancient matriarch after Mei and your Zara."

Palpitating her God Gene bump, Peter answers, "I'm sure you won't believe a guy when he says that the size of your bump doesn't make up who you are." He places his palm upon her chest and rubs. "It's what's in here." Then he rubs her forehead and says, "And in here."

"The five sense algorithm," she says.

"Well, it started with that, but it's a much more effective variant I found."

Her face softens, as if she became that young girl on the doorstep who is deciding on how to kiss her first date goodnight with her first ever boyfriend. Well, except for the Ruger in her sack and the knockout powder in his drink. He's not at all what she imagined.

Tapping her toes on his, she says, "I'm not the kind of woman who plays around. Far from it. But if I put on my old comfy T-shirt and boxer shorts, will you bond with me?"

He stutters and finally spits out, "I've cheated too much already. I can't be with so many women in the space of so few weeks."

Heading into her bedroom, she turns and says, "It's your decision. I think I know enough about you to say that what you seek is very much what I seek. I'll be waiting for you in my ugly grey boxers."

As he hears her preparing for the night in her bathroom, Peter thumbs through his MoxWrap, reading through her publications on Asherah.

With a deep breath, he looks up and says, "Are you the voice? Are you Asherah? Or just the aliens playing with us little humans?"

Up he stands. A long pause. Then he heads through her bedroom door and gently shuts it.

CHAPTER 39

True devotion is for itself: not to desire heaven nor to fear hell.
—Rabi'a al-Adawiyya, eighth-century Persian philosopher and mystic

Village destined to be Çayönü
9524 BCE

As if death was a miracle, a salvation, a way to a better existence, the women who had gathered at the river return to washing the reindeer giants' clothes, saying nothing of the two murders they have just witnessed.

Crying over Nirra's near-death body, the giant man who said they would die here trying to save her youngest daughter, the giant man who defied his past, his heritage, his lineage, to save her, Tallia silently asks the voice for guidance. Her daughter is no longer breathing. Maybe that is why the voice sent her here, to allow her daughter a quick, albeit painful, exit from an existence devoid of life.

How different the fates of Perima and her sister Illyana have been. Her Aunt Ki could only save one of the two. And Ki chose Illyana, named after Orzu's sister, as she had the strongest link to the voice of all of Nanshe's great-granddaughters. Nearly seventeen sun cycles later, Tallia could not undo that fateful moment of Ki's choice during the demise of the First Temple. For Perima died, as did Orzu's

Illyana, who asked as well to go on to the next existence.

The giant, the husband, the dearest friend left in the lands, Nirra stirs, barely able to breathe, much less talk. He mumbles, at which Tallia puts her ear closer to his mouth. He says slowly, "I will always love you. You must not doubt what happened here. I love you because you are a person of resolve, not just a woman of resolve."

His words only bring forth more rain from Tallia's eyes as her tears soak his blood-caked body. She ignores the pretentious voice of the shaman warning the women that the fate of this false prophetess's family awaits them if they disobey the will of the reindeer warrior giants, if they fail to submit to them.

She cannot save the dead, but she can save the living, she says inside as she stands up. She charges the shaman, who at first has his back to her. The man, who is slightly taller than her, reacts to her charge, striking her face, drawing blood. Undeterred, Tallia charges again, taking him to the ground. As she raises her closed fist, she says, "Make no mistake. It is not the giants you should fear. It is not the giants to whom your subservience should be given. She is the one true god for all of us, whom you should worship. And She would not want me to kill you in vengeance."

The booming hand claps of a few giants take her by surprise as she backs off the shaman, eyeing how she will evade capture by these three monstrous men. But they say they are the friends of Nirra. Two of them carry off the shaman, saying giant-style justice is not for her god to decide but for their fists to.

The remaining giant, Voxen, signals for a woman washing clothes to come over. She introduces herself—Kezina. She shows no sign of abuse, beating, or violation. Voxen is her husband, as Nirra must be Tallia's husband, she says. Tallia now understands what Nirra had tried to explain. More giants like him might wish for a different existence in partnership with a human woman, but they must hide this relationship for fear of hatred, discrimination, and violent retaliation by other intolerant giants—or worse, by other humans. Not all giants are evil.

Kezina touches Nirra and glances back at Voxen, saying he should already be dead from internal damage. She touches the residual drops on Tallia's face.

Kezina says, "Your tears must be magical, as Nirra should be dead from those wounds. My grandmother told me a story of a great woman who escaped the giants from the other side of the lake who also could bring the dead to life through her tears."

Nodding, Tallia replies, "Nanshe, my grandmother."

Smiling back, Kezina says, "My Voxen, his father came from the other side of the lake, just as my family did. He spoke of women of your kind hidden among the great pyramids."

The giant Voxen, gently petting his wife's head, says, "My father escaped the floods as he chased you animals, as he called humans, across the lake in a boat. He taught me our kind, the superior race, the master race who will own all the lands everywhere, have a secret source of power."

"The object of my grandmother? Is that what you speak of?" asks Tallia.

"The other giants fear the object at your temple, as your priestess brought down lightning from the clouds as punishment for giants who attacked your place of worship," replies Voxen. "Your object is just a weak form of this power. According to my father, in our pyramids on the other side of the lake is a source, a blue light that could bring your Nirra back to life. It is possible your tears are healing him enough so he could make the journey."

The reformed giant recalls the lore of his father's race. "The reindeer warriors thought themselves empowered by the great glow coming from the direction of the tail of the bird star. Born into these lands to rule and conquer, or so they thought. In an age longer ago than anyone can recall, man and woman were equal, but after the light from the sky fell, everything changed. Man and woman were no longer equal. Woman became different, possibly stronger inside than man. And the giants became taller and taller. They first tried to dominate women by changing the lore of old. But women kept the old stories alive, talking among themselves in hidden places. The reindeer warrior giants ultimately prevented women from ruling by enslaving them. But those of us who ruled, such as my father, we knew only that the women could access the sacred spots of power. Only the very special women."

Kezina stands up and hugs her giant. She says, "Some women in the past who heard about this blue light made the arduous voyage across the mountains and across the big black lake. We have never heard from them again. Rumor has it they died along the way."

Shaking his huge head, Voxen says, "But be warned, the journey to the light may be deadly for some. For others, a one-way trip. I know stories of two giants who tried to find the lands of our ancestors. One came back burnt all over. His mind had the crazies. But he said no giant should ever try to enter the blue light."

From a pouch, Voxen pulls out two necklaces, each with two halves of a black stone. He says, "These come from the source of power within the pyramid. As you get closer, they will begin to glow. Once you are there, if you are destined, you will know you have arrived. To approach the blue light, put one of these stones inside Nirra."

Tallia remembers the words of Nanshe. You will do anything for the ones you love. Even forgive. She has forgiven Nirra for what he did while acting as a giant in this village. She only hopes he will forgive her for asking him to come here. She will take him to the homeland of the reindeer giant warriors toward the tail of the bird star. The lands of Nanshe and Orzu.

CHAPTER 40

Symbolic violence is violence wielded with tacit complicity between its victims and its agents, insofar as both remain unconscious of submitting to or wielding it.
—Pierre Félix Bourdieu, twentieth-century French sociologist

MoxWorld Resorts Jerusalem
7:30 a.m. GMT+3, March 2, 2023

"Tell me once again, why I should pair bond with Peter?" asks a puzzled Rachel as Mei fusses with how her metallic-design infused blouse lies below her khaki expedition jacket.

"The real question is why are you here bright and early asking for my help," replies Mei.

"I wish I could tell you about how many people are trying to tell me what to do right now," attests Rachel, eking out a little smile at Mei's typical answering but not answering manner.

"Like who, babe? Come on. You know I'm the queen of discretion."

Staring back at her in the mirror, Rachel says, "Well, my safta raba for one. She's putting even more pressure on me to be like you."

"You mean fabulously elegant in my morning maternity wear?" says Mei as she brushes Rachel's hair, getting it ready for metallic strands.

"Maternity, yes. She reminded me that for her to meet Asherah, she carried a child like you. My saba raba had the God Gene bump like her. Like you. Like me."

"Hmm…hence your interest in Peter, eh?"

A pause as Rachel stares at Mei's baby bump. "Peter is the father of your baby, isn't he? I mean, he's committed to raising your child as the father, isn't he?"

Lips pursed, eyes gazing down and then back into Rachel's eyes, Mei says, "Peter knows what his role has been and will be from now on. That is between us and his sister. I no longer need you to steal him to save our family honor. But you need him for you to fulfill your family's quest."

Staring into Mei's eyes in the mirror, she nods her head so slightly. Another nonanswer to her question. But she knows Mei well enough to know what the nonanswer really means and says, "I thought so. Any other available men you know with awesome God Gene bumps?"

"Honey, Peter is as good as they get," says Mei as she intertwines the metallic strands into her hair. "You know I screened them all. And he kept his hands to himself. A proper gentleman."

Leaning forward, her head bent down, Rachel sighs. "I guess I'm clear on what I need to do for that doctor who said she could help Ariella."

"And how is your safta raba? I had gotten her transferred to the MoxWorld Health Center as you had asked," says Mei as she continues to weave in the metallic strands.

"Not good. Her doctors said maybe she has a few weeks unless a miracle occurs. This one doctor said she could provide such a miracle, but for a seriously hefty price. Don't you know someone else in MoxWorld who would cure her instead?"

Pausing a moment, Mei says, "I know a certain Kurdish woman who is known to perform a miracle or two. But she likely will not do any favors for you—the one she tackled in the lobby, and especially after you slept with Peter last night."

Bolting up straight in her chair, Rachel turns and says, "Seriously, Mei. I mean, we bonded like you said to, but he was a complete gentleman."

She stops and peers into Rachel's eyes in the mirror. "You got him into bed in your favorite night clothes and all you can tell me is he was a complete gentleman?"

"I didn't get to see the Mongolian princess you talked about," Rachel laments. "But I saw something even better."

She puts on her necklace with the black stone, the one her safta raba gave her. "I saw your originators. The ancient ones with little black stones just like this. They said they would lead them to the place of the blue light."

The Chinese woman adjusts Rachel's necklace with Michaela's metallic elements connecting to her choker. "You did say you swung both ways, didn't you?"

Rachel shrugs and says, "You look for love where you can find it, right?"

"To find the blue light, you need to get Peter to be much more than a gentleman with you—to want to indulge in you as the most desirable woman he ever met. Apparently, he needs more stimulation than next-to-nothing nighties."

Adjusting Rachel's MoxWrap, Mei adds, "So, I am going to let you into my alpha testing group for a new technology. Michaela's work has been super essential for what will be a thousand-year leap forward for human evolution. Aside from enhancing the aesthetics of hair and dress, these metallic designs have a functional biological role."

Leaning away from Mei and her metallic strands, Rachel asks, "Should I be afraid?"

"My MoxWorld BioGenetics group has developed an algorithm of micro radio frequencies which can activate genes, even dormant ones," explains Mei. "My favorite project is the one you will be able to access. A woman has two forms of pheromones, one that can attract another person and another that can repel another person. Imagine some man is giving you unwanted attention. Press your MoxWrap, and over the course of minutes that man decides you're not his type. Then you find a man whose attentions you would like. Press again and he is progressively all over you."

Scrunching her nose, Rachel says, "I had no idea you were so insidious. What are you going to charge for this service?"

"Hmm. After you try it, you tell me how much it's worth to you," says

Mei with her disarming smile. She weaves the metallic elements into Rachel's hair. "Okay, no showering with these in place."

Lifting her arm, Rachel says, "I thought pheromones were produced down here."

Tickling her armpit, Mei says, "But the impulses to generate them start in your head. Our work suggests an interaction between the pineal and pituitary glands."

Wrinkling her mouth to one side, the professor says, "You're kidding. Aren't you?"

Mei winks at her. "Maybe yes. Maybe no. Besides, I need someone to alpha test this new system on someone who thinks they are deeply in love with someone else. You might have to punch this up to ultra-strong."

Looking at the new app on her MoxWrap, Rachel asks, "Why do I need this? I'm pretty alluring when I need to be."

A kiss on the top of Rachel's head and Mei says, "I know you are, babe. But it's Peter we're talking about. A Frenchwoman who moved from Quebec to British Columbia once remarked to me that microplastics in Pacific fish acted as estrogen mimetics in the men out there. They must have lost their masculinity, as she would get the looks from men in France and Quebec, but not a wink out west. This ultra-strong setting is for that kind of estrogenized Pacific fish-eating man. Like Peter, our cute editor from San Francisco."

As Mei plays with the MoxWrap controls, Rachel says, "Are you sure he won't be too dangerous at that setting?"

"Honey, you will love what he does. I can attest to that. Especially what he will do to your sore feet," says Mei with her disarming smile. "Besides, your old T-shirt and grey boxer shorts routine didn't get you all that far last night, did it?"

Lines running amok across all facets of her visage, Rachel asks, "But what about the Kurdish woman? She'll pulverize me if she thinks I've slept with her Peter."

Patting her hair, now embedded with metallic strands, Mei says, "I called her this morning. I told her to fish or cut bait. She said something hysterical about dead fish. But I made it abundantly clear that the ancient legends insist on Peter being intimate with a woman with the right bump. I assured her I did not need him to be papa to my child. So either do the dirty deed with our editor friend, or let the next 'right' neck bump woman in line have him."

Eyebrows raised with her eyes now more a shade of sky blue than green, Rachel says, "And how did that crazy woman react?"

A laugh and Mei says, "I think I heard something being ripped apart. She certainly was not happy. But after a minute of silence, she came back with that prophetess voice. Something about her destiny is to die. She asked if you were a good woman. Would you be able to take care of him in the way he deserved?"

Shaking her head, Rachel says, "And you said?"

"I promised you would be everything his former girlfriend Tara could be, and much more. Better yet, you believed in aliens."

With a more somber face, Mei stares at the mirror in front of them, directly into Rachel's eyes. "But seriously, my due date is soon upon us. If we can't find your Ariella's cavern soon, we'll need a backup. You and Peter have to make this happen. Hey, no long faces. He'll make a wonderful husband. Just ask my mother."

❧

In the MoxResort VIP circular driveway, the caravan of MoxMovers await. Jean-Paul has his three mini EM detectors and directs the following pairings for exploring the Temple Mount: he with Mei, Peter with Zara, and Magali with Rachel.

Zara nods as she says, "Jean-Paul, count me out today. I wish to visit the Dome of the Rock and Masjid al-Aqsa, the mosque, to pray with my family."

She leans over and whispers into Peter's ear. Something that makes his shoulders slump.

Magali pipes in, saying she will go with Zara and pray at the Church of the Holy Sepulchre.

Staring out the window, Zara studies the Temple Mount, under which lies Mount Moriah, the spot where Xwedê asked the Prophet Ibrāhīm to sacrifice his son. Just as She has asked Zara to sacrifice what she loves.

In Zara's MoxMover, Magali says, "I noticed your signal that you wanted to talk with me. Poor Peter, he looked like the abandoned puppy dog when you said you wanted to go without him."

Crossing her legs and staring out the window, Zara says, "Things are changing too quickly for me to grasp what exactly is going on."

The former Sister adjusts her headscarf, tucking in a wisp of her redness that insists on being free to wave in the winds. "What things specifically? You and Peter?"

"Peter is a different issue. He spent part of the night with that Israeli woman. Or so he said when I found him sleeping at my door this morning. He said he didn't cheat on me. Well, no more than he cheated on me with Mei. They had their clothes on, he insists."

She gazes out the window. "I suppose it is my fault. I turned him out into the cold last night. I shut my door on him. I thought he'd go back to Mei. Not that horrible boyfriend stealing professor."

"I am sure nothing really happened," affirms Magali. "He truly loves you."

"It's not him I worry about. It's her. And her intentions. But Mei says otherwise."

Tightening her crossed legs even tighter together, she puts her hands on her lower abdomen.

"I sense something more is bothering you," says Magali. "You miss Peter. You used to talk these issues out with him as I do with Jean-Paul."

"What bothers me are things I cannot talk about with him," she says. Staring at her with panicked eyes, she adds, "My period is off. I mean, I had a little spotting this morning, but not like my period is about to come," she says.

Turning to gaze into the Catholic nurse's eyes, Zara says, "I smell things I did not smell so much before. And I am still tired, fatigued. Are these the signs of the drugs they used on me?"

With a fleeting smile and inklings of a wink, Magali asks, "You and Peter, you two have been close again after your return. Are you even closer than before? You know, intimately?"

Staring out of the tops of her eyes with her head down, Zara says, "Are you and Jean-Paul closer that way, intimately, since you revoked your vows?"

"I wish," says Magali.

"And so does Peter," replies Zara. "And maybe I just drove him into the clutches of an Israeli conspirator. I guess for the better."

Her fingers drumming along her lips, Magali says, "Perhaps we should stop at a local pharmacy. I think I know just the remedy for your worries."

⇛

As they arrive near the Damascus Gate, Peter watches how Israeli security has controlled the approach to Zedekiah's Cave, a five-acre underground quarry used by Herod the Great to source the stones for the Second Temple. The history professor in Rachel describes how the cave matches descriptions found in ancient texts.

Peter carefully exits the MoxMover with the mini EM detector strategically placed in front of his lower torso. He scans around. A tall man with dark glasses stands twenty meters to the left, surveying them. To the right, a medium-height woman with dark hair wrapped in a red scarf with white polka dots and big movie-star-sized dark glasses stands with a metallic cooler chest. Must be selling cold bottled water, thinks Peter. Something about her is familiar. Certainly they are not there to see him, as neither has rushed forward seeking autographs.

A three-meter-wide rectangle with a rounded top, steel gates, and green siding frames the entrance to the famed cave. Rachel pulls out ten-thousand-lumen, palm-sized lights from her backpack.

As they descend the stone stairs, they pass a sign indicating a winged cherub figure once stood there, now residing in a London museum. The Israeli professor explains the non-canonized Maccabees said this cherub was the marker the Prophet Jeremiah's workers had left to help find this cave. An act which the prophet reprimanded them for. The prophet said the location of the Ark of the Covenant would be unknown "until God finally gathers his people together and shows mercy to them."

More stairs down and through one big grotto, then a second smaller grotto, Rachel points down a path to a third grotto. "Accounts from the Frank crusaders who took Jerusalem in the eleven hundreds say the Ark could be found down that way. Legend has it there is a tunnel at the bottom of the cave leading all the way to Jericho, where the Ark was taken at the time of the Roman destruction of Jerusalem. King Zedekiah was said to have fled the Babylonian destruction of Jerusalem in the sixth century BCE through these tunnels."

His light darting from one wall to another to the ceiling, Peter jests, "Good thing we aren't here to find the Ark. We'd be here for centuries. But maybe we might find the Holy Grail? At least, the Holy Grail of Alexander Murometz, that is."

With a little smile back at him, Rachel points to a series of walls that close off passages, explaining that many were made during the Ottoman rule and others much, much earlier. They pass one of many "do not enter" signs to a chained-off area. Rachel has a key and opens the gate, leading to a narrow passage.

They stand in front of a wall composed of stone bricks a foot wide and half a foot tall. Rachel shows Peter the lack of mortar in the center bricks, which they remove one by one.

As Peter crawls through the hole, he finds a chamber twelve by eight feet that appears recently excavated. Oddly, a green plastic tarp lines the ground. In the far corner are a bottle of bleach and a self-inflating mattress rolled up in a stuff bag. Certainly doesn't look very ancient to Peter as he asks, "Why the tarp? Why would anyone be sleeping in here? And bleach? Alexander had that room where I had to choose between Zara or Mei bleached."

Punching buttons on her MoxWrap, Rachel takes his arm and says, "So, if I were there, you would have picked me to bond with. You still can now."

His breathing follows his rising heart rate, his concentration obscured by his eyes following her every move. Her voice enchants his ears, begging to hear more. He closes his eyes, fighting every molecule of androgen flooding his blood. His nostrils flare with her scent pounding into his mind, his glands, his every thought. All the same signals sleeping on Mei's jet bedroom pillow inspired in him. But these are hyper-amplified. All signs that Mei is behind this.

As she unbuttons her blouse, Peter puts his hand on her fingers and says, "Didn't we talk about this last night? You are trying too hard. I don't think this is the real you. The real Rachel, the archaeologist. And if it makes you feel any better, you're winning at what you're trying too hard to do."

She taps her MoxWrap a couple more times, which puts Peter in a stupor, drooling away. She turns her head and closes her eyes as she imagines her dying Ariella telling of her last wishes. Imagines her father urging her to settle the family debt. Imagines Asherah shaking her head at Rachel for not believing in her enough to get the job done.

Unsure if she should keep unbuttoning, if she should reach into her backpack and pull out the silenced Ruger pistol, follow her father's strict lifelong instructions, and rid the world of one more Gollinger, one more of the offspring of the complicit, or simply scream to the world that she only wants to be an archaeologist, one who gets to decide with whom she becomes intimate, Rachel sighs. She punches the MoxWrap controls to off mode.

Regaining his normal senses, as he had done in the MoxWorld lobby when putting his jacket over her deep plunge outfit, he helps her button up, only stopping to notice not the curvature and softness of her breasts, but her pendant.

Pausing a moment, he asks, "Who put you up to this? Mei? I bet Mei. But Zara just told me before we left the resort I should say yes to your overtures. Did she tell you that too? Everyone is telling me you and I should be together."

Her body goes rigid, her nose flexes up and down with her eyes squeezed shut, and little drops form at the edges of her eyes. She says, "You have no idea what a woman needs to do to get ahead in my field. What she is asked to do that a man would not be asked. You have no idea what my family has done."

Now is the moment she has him helpless and alone. In her head, the image of her saba raba arises. His body lying bloody with his killers laughing as they strip the pendant from his hand. She reaches into her backpack, first feeling the grip of the Ruger, then the surgical kit, and then the cooler pack. Out comes the vial. "They asked me to get you to fill this. I had no choice. I woke up this morning in total fear of failure after forgetting to ask you last night. I thought maybe in total privacy here, you would want to help me out."

"Who asked you such a ridiculous thing? NiQihs?"

She freezes, her lungs paralyzed, her eyes staring at him so very vapid.

And to her relief, he says, "It was the aliens. You saw them too. They took samples from me when they abducted me."

His eyes wide open, he crosses his legs at the thought of what they did to him. He asks, "Did they poke you in places that aren't supposed to be poked and probed?"

Her eyes so wide open the blue around her irises shines, she says, "Yes. Even my ob-gyn would not do that to me. It was simply horrible, Peter. So horrible." More tears and Peter takes her into his arms.

Soaking his MoxWorld-logoed polo shirt, her hands run up under his shirt, feeling his ribs and then up to his chest. Her head tilts up as if to kiss his lips as she lifts his polo over his head. Her lips are just about to kiss his chest when she sees the black stone pendant. Exactly like the one she wears.

Her mind snaps. That question of cohabitation or complicity is answered. He has that black stone only through murder. His genes are not ones she wants melded with hers. A benevolent Asherah would not ask this, wouldn't ask her to have a child with someone with his dark family history. Out of her backpack comes the Ruger, now pointed at his chest. "That belongs to me. Take it off."

Nodding while staring into a pistol for the fourth time in his life, Peter touches his MoxWrap, readying the sonic punch function. "I'd sooner give your aliens their precious sticky sample than give you this pendant. My pappy said that I must find this Crimean man's family here in Jerusalem. That must be your family. Only with both halves of this stone can we find the cavern."

He pulls her gun straight into his chest, ensuring her ability to kill him at any time as he reaches into her blouse and pulls out the pendant he glimpsed. The same as his, but both now emit an aura of blue.

She grabs her pendant back and says, "Your grandfather stole the one you have from my great-grandmother's husband. Your great-grandfather, an SS Nazi, murdered my great-grandfather."

"No, whoever told you that story wasn't there," says Peter, aiming his MoxWrap.

Her hands shake holding that cold steel tool of immediate death, her finger about to pull back on the trigger. But the storm comes back, like it did this morning before she saw Mei. The revulsion. Not psychological revulsion, but purely biological. She lays her Ruger down and heaves into the green tarp.

Third time's the charm again as Peter has taken his T-shirt off to wipe her mouth, his arm around her, comforting her shaking body.

As her throat involuntarily pulses, she says, "Some Mossad agent I would have made."

To her surprise, his foot nudges over her Ruger, which he places back in her hand. Then he takes the pendant stone from his neck and places it around the Ruger. "My pappy wanted you to have this. I gather it wasn't Mei who put you up to this."

She stares at the pendant stone, now emitting a clearly visible blue aura. Putting the Ruger down, she takes her Ariella's pendant and dangles the two in front of her. Both glow with the blue light that she promised to find.

"What was your saba raba called?" asks Peter.

Stunned he knows Hebrew, she pauses, surveying him. Judging him. She sees the faces of the Nazis her father hunted down, her grandmother hunted down. His face does not show the same lack of remorse, the same complicity—only that certain naïveté Mei described.

"My saba raba was named Kemel Ghurdzi. My mother changed her name after she remarried in Turkey."

"Your great-grandfather's real first name was Ya'akov, and he sacrificed himself to get a blue stone from whoever's in that cavern," says Peter. "That larger stone glowed blue like these pendants do when near another similar stone. Alexander Murometz's father kept the blue stone."

Just as her Ariella said would happen. This stranger, this offspring of the complicit, spoke her saba raba's name known only to his parents and Ariella. How could he be her other half?

"Your father's SS genocidal monsters shot my grandfather," mutters Rachel. "His autopsy shows bullets from SS machine guns."

"He was already dying from exposure in that cavern," says Peter. "Whatever's in there kills men and not women. At least, not pregnant women."

"Who told you that? You aren't married with children. My safta raba Ariella says one only tells a man if absolutely needed. Did that slut Zara tell you that?" says Rachel.

"She is not a slut. She was framed."

"Or so says your book," retorts Rachel.

He taps his MoxWrap. "You need to read this. My pappy's diary entry on the last day of your saba raba's life."

She leans away from him, asking, "And why should I do that?"

"Because after that, you can do to me what you have been asked. If you want what the aliens took from me, you can get that from me in any manner you wish."

She nods, and he projects up the diary pages.

July 1945.

He died trying to save us. He died because he sent his wife away to make sure she lived. And because his pregnant wife was not there to go into the cavern of the mysterious woman, he suffered lethal burns without her. He was dead long before the SS bullets hit him. My father told me the SS bullets put him out of the misery he suffered from those burns. What that blue glowing stone was, we will never know. Not in my lifetime. But Dr. Murometz said something about a blue that white light should not touch. The light of the sun. A legend from his mother's mother.

As we hide on the fishing boat taking us to Romania, I live through the guilt of complicity. I could not stop the men who were in the wrong, hurting those whose crime was being born. My father reminds me of the few we could save. We convinced the Nazis that certain men needed to procreate with certain women to create the psychically gifted telepathic children Himmler wanted. More than two hundred men mated with an equal number of women.

I know not if love ever entered into their lives as couples. I know not if their children were as gifted as the eugenics program had envisioned. But I do know they are alive because of the ruse, the partial truth, or the whole truth we created in the minds of those much more evil than us. My father says if the Allies win, he will be tortured and eventually killed for his part in what happened. He only hopes I can live with less guilt knowing we tried to save as many as we could.

Where Ya'akov Ghurdzi met his end was not where the cavern entrance was located. Neither I nor Dr. Murometz knows how to get back to those caverns, much less how to navigate inside them if I were ever to find them again. But that elder woman was very clear. She expected Ghurdzi to help another woman return to her. I suppose this little black stone is the key.

Our world is crumbling around us. The world is insanely angry at that madman who took our Austria into Hell. If I live through this, I will fulfill Ghurdzi's last wish and reunite his stone with the stone of his wife's. And if there is such a thing as magic, maybe it will help that woman who is supposed to return to the cavern. God be with them all, for he has left me and my father. And may they return to Qualqi what she has asked for.

Rachel swallows, glancing down. The pendant stones dangling over the Ruger, she says, "And you expect me to believe this? Your pappy made the story up to make you feel better about your family."

"Perhaps," replies Peter. "But I believe his heart was in the right place whether he wrote this in 1945 or 2015."

She stares into his eyes. Not ones like those her family had hunted. Do eyes lie?

"Do you believe complicity is inherited?" she asks.

"You mean, should you kill me because of what you think my great-grandfather might have done to your family? Our neck bumps link us to an ancient matriarch. In a dream, I saw one of her descendants forgiving a giant who had killed her family and friends. There is much we can learn from our unique dreams of the ancients."

Swallowing hard, in part because of what she must accept in front of her, in part to keep the next round of stomach contents from coming out, she says,

"I am told you have a text from that cavern. One that could threaten Israel and Jewish people worldwide."

A deep breath and Peter says, "Pappy wanted me to trust you. So, here's what Jean-Paul came up with."

She reads the translation. Her stomach settles as the edges of her lips rise. "The last sentence. Man's truth lies toward the tail of the bird star where She first came. It refers to Her. That must be Asherah. I must get to that cavern."

Taking his hand into hers, she hangs the pendant stones around their joined hands. Reunited after more than six decades. A light blue aura surrounding them intensifies, highlighting them as one and not two separated.

"If I can forgive you for something you did not do, could you do the same for me?" she asks.

She brings the pendants and his hand up to her lips, planting a light kiss upon the stones and then upon his fingers.

Peering into his eyes as he gazes into hers, she asks, "I have lived my entire life waiting for the day that I kill a Gollinger, and now all I want to do is kiss you. Which one should I do now?"

Kissing her fingers around the stones, he says, "You have to follow what your heart says is right. That is, unless your soul is telling you something different."

CHAPTER 41

Your vision will become clear only when you can look into your own heart.
Who looks outside, dreams; who looks inside, awakes.

—Carl Jung

Jerusalem
January 17, 1300 CE

Seven days have passed as El had a day and a half to wait for Asefeh to arrive. She refuses her scout escorts' offer of staying at her side as she tours the town, saying they must complete their assignment—to assess the readiness and defenses of Jerusalem. Mongol armies always perform an advance reconnaissance of their targets before they mount an offensive. If Hetoum II did more reconnaissance than touring and his information is correct, the town should be an open door for the next invader, save a few crusaders who would welcome her nephew.

But unlike Hetoum, who visited the Christian sites, she was a devout Muslim and could visit the Noble Sanctuary, also known as the Mount of the House to the Jews. In awe of the Dome of the Rock, she drops to her knees as she stares up at the dome.

Even though she converted to Islam, she felt the awe of her teachers when they told the story of the Prophet Mohammed's single-night journey from the Great Mosque in Mecca to al-Aqsa Mosque, assisted by the Archangel Jibrīl, who then brought the Prophet to the seven stages of heaven to meet the four prophets before him.

For El, growing up a royal horse warrior in the central plains many weeks west, the opportunity to pray at the al-Aqsa Mosque presented the greatest spiritual opportunity she could have short of being granted a pilgrimage to Mecca. She spends most of her day in and around the mosque, in part talking with other Muslims here to worship who seek the same religious moment she seeks, in part surveying the grounds for any sign of where the black stone might be buried. She has heard of a black stone in the Kaaba. Would Allah strike her down if she found the black stone she sought was of the same origin?

The next day, she awaits Asefeh outside the Gate of Eternal Life. She ponders the meaning of this gate's name and the relevance to what they sought. Is not the blue light associated with life and death? Is this gate their sign of where the black stone will be found?

Dressed in a green coat over a light yellow, full-length dress, El adjusts her beige headscarf to appear as proper as possible before entering this famous portal. Asefeh arrives by horse with her husband. Formalities exchanged, her husband takes the horses to a stable.

The two walk hand in hand through the gate. Fine one moment and not so fine an instant later. El's body goes limp. Asefeh's hand helps soften the fall when El's body lands on the ground. A crowd gathers, which Asefeh dispels, saying that standing in the sun has taken its toll on her friend.

Resting in a cool, shaded spot near the gate, Asefeh explains, "Yechezkel chapter forty-four said our messiah will enter Jerusalem through these gates." She chuckles, then says, "The Christians say Jesus did, and he is their messiah. Perhaps you are the Mongol's messiah and that is why you fainted?"

Giving El some more water, Asefeh adds, "When Saladin conquered Jerusalem more than a hundred years ago, he closed these gates. Muslims fear the Jewish messiah will enter through the Gate of Mercy and they will lose their holy sites."

El sits up, feeling stronger, and says, "As a gift to the people of Israel, the Mongols will take these gates away to Damascus. This entrance will remain forever open for your messiah to come."

Asefeh takes El around the perimeter of the Mount of the House, known to the crusaders as the Temple Mount. She points out different places of historical interest and, more importantly, ones germane to their search.

They head toward the Damascus and Herod gates and descend to a cavern entrance. Asefeh explains the cavern's mouth is natural, but everything else is the magic of King Herod, who quarried stone from these rocks to make the Second Temple. The result is a four-hundred-pace-deep system of caverns. Perfect for the priests of the Second Temple to hide their most precious artifacts before the Romans burned down the temple.

Torches in hand, they wander seemingly aimlessly to El for twenty minutes until they reach a spot that appears blocked. Asefeh tries to move a large stone, which El moves instead to spare the smaller pregnant woman undue distress. Through a narrow hole, they come into a small grotto still partially buried.

Asefeh points to the face of a statue half-buried. "Queen Nitzevet's statue of Asherah. It must be. We think this mark on the side is the Royal Queen's seal. What do you think, El?"

"What?"

Asefeh says, "I was asking what you thought."

"No, no. Not you, but Her," answers El. "I did not know. Yes. I am obedient. I am subservient to your will."

As Asefeh stares at her suddenly crazed companion, El says, "You want me to do what?"

Turning to Asefeh, the tall Mongolian princess states, "One of us must die so the other may find the blue light. I am prepared to sacrifice myself so that you, the woman of purity, the woman with child, may fulfill the legends."

CHAPTER 42

For false christs and false prophets will arise and perform great signs and wonders, so as to lead astray, if possible, even the elect.

Matthew 24:24

Jerusalem
12:30 p.m. GMT+3, March 2, 2023

The bliss of sleep after two people share intimacies. They lie asleep on the mattress in a hidden cavern underneath the northern side of the Temple Mount. A buzz in Rachel's backpack wakes them. Rachel tells Peter not to move as she rolls over to get the black triangular device, which buzzes again. Discreetly, she reads the message: "You are needed immediately. Crisis building on Temple Mount. You may need to eliminate the target."

Interrupting her pondering the message, Peter says, "Asefeh and El. They were like what you and Zara need to be. You must work together."

Leaning back over to him, she kisses his forehead and says, "Something bad is happening at the Temple Mount. We need to go." She quickly cleans herself, puts her boxers back on, straightens out her clothes, grabs him and the vial, and runs for the cave entrance.

That woman with the red polka dot scarf still waits at entrance. She looks so familiar to Peter. But Rachel has no time for such nonsense. She throws the empty vial at her. "I'm so done with you," she says.

Peter yells back at the woman, "Tell your alien friends I'm done with them as well."

The tall man with dark glasses watches from afar as Israeli security ushers them into a grey armored SUV and a security forces caravan escorts them around to the western side of the Temple Mount. Peter looks at Rachel, remarking, "They really give you history professors VIP treatment in this country."

Without missing a beat, she replies, "We Israelis take our history very seriously."

Their caravan arrives near the Moroccan Gate next to the Western Wall and the Al-Aqsa Mosque, where Zara has decided to exit the tourist gate for visiting the Temple Mount.

Hundreds of Palestinians chant that her presence is a sign from Allah that Temple Mount should only be for Muslims. Hundreds of Israelis and Muslims counterprotest her visit, but thousands more only chant for the peace of the messiah.

Peter spots the drones overhead. NiQihs News? He knows that MoxWorld News uses MoxWorld satellites to get their overhead shots.

Israeli security gets Rachel and Peter through the crowds up to the MoxSecurity people surrounding Zara and her family. Peter taps his MoxWrap and then gets MoxSecurity to give him access to Zara, who is speaking live on MoxWorld News about how the Temple Mount belongs to all religions as a sign that we all worship the same one God, and She wants us to live in peace and prosperity.

The first rock falls short of Zara as MoxWorld Security closes ranks. Peter grabs her and runs with her under his arm as more rocks fall around them.

The Israeli security, in a show of force, fires their nonlethal beanbag guns, pummeling people in the directions where the rocks are coming from.

As they reach the high-security MoxMover, the blue beams, which the Jerusalem police only allow to be used on close-range targets, shatter the incoming rocks before they arrive, except one that pummels Peter's back as he shoves Zara into MoxMover.

Inside, she rubs his bruised back as he asks, "What were you thinking? Of course, what you did would cause riots."

"She spoke to me," says Zara. "At the Dome of the Rock. We are close. First there will be disarray. Then peace. She wants the world to know that."

In the MoxWorld Health Center outpatient ward, Peter is being treated for severe bruising on his back. Fortunately, no ribs were broken and his spine is intact.

Dismayed at hearing from Peter what he had been doing in Zedekiah's Cave with this irritating woman, Zara had pulled the Israeli professor aside for a woman-to-woman talk.

Toe to toe again. The tall Kurd staring down at the Israeli of lesser stature. Neither with much love in their eyes, at least for each other.

Zara lifts Rachel's wrists. Soft, smooth skin. No discoloration. She says, "Why did you wear that black outfit in the resort's lobby when we arrived here?"

"That is none of your business," says Rachel as she takes her hand back.

"A doctor did. One with your profile. Did she not? One whose wrists show redness."

Rachel's eyes dart aside as she says, "That I can neither confirm nor deny."

"And you did not sleep with that Zengo? Or is that another truth you can neither confirm nor deny?" asks Zara.

"He's not my type," says Rachel, now peering into the Kurd's eyes.

"Peter, he told me you slept with him twice now," says Zara.

"Well, he tells me you keep pushing him away," retorts Rachel. "You shut the door on him last night. Where else was he supposed to go? I took him in like an unwanted, unloved stray cat."

A grimace. A gaze at their feet. A shake of her head. Cats love cats. So Zara says, "I hope you were gentle with him as you bedded him. He deserves respect from the women in his life."

Stepping back, she turns away from Rachel, her eyes uncertain whether to cry for losing a loved one or to beam with joy that Peter will be well taken care of after her death.

"He also talked of the vision you two shared," says Zara. "A woman from Jerusalem and a Mongolian princess. The same he saw with Mei."

Leaning around to make eye contact, Rachel says, "Peter says they were you and me in a different life but with the same common goal. Their story will lead us to the truths we seek. I saw the vision. You and I must work together."

"And that is why you are trying to get close to Peter? You are seeking truth from him?" asks Zara.

"Tell me first, why do you want me to get what I want from him?" asks Rachel. "You pushed him towards me. I thought you two were a couple. Romantically so."

"What I want and what must be have always been very divergent subjects," laments Zara. She touches the notch in between the thumb and index finger of Rachel's gun hand. "You have been asked one thing of Peter and another of me. The legend says two women will enter the cave. Only one will come out. Your destiny is to kill me there. And Peter must be bonded to you before then, or my death will be the emotional end of him as well."

"So, you do love him," says Rachel.

To that comment, Zara remains silent, with only her head ever so slightly shaking back and forth, her fingers rubbing each other. "If that is true, then between you and me, one of us needs to bear his child. Which one of us should it be? Must be you as you are to kill me."

Coming fully around in front of the tall woman, mimicking a gun with her fingers, Rachel takes an imaginary shot at Zara's head. "If I kill you, I martyr you. You will be the messiah for millennia to come. Those of your faith, those of faiths other than mine, will rise and take vengeance on my people. And how will this help your Peter?"

"First, Peter will stand by you forever. He will defend you and your people out of his love for you," replies Zara. "Second, it does not matter that you martyr me. God has decreed our destinies thousands and thousands of years ago. We are only following Her will."

Zara takes off her headscarf, adding, "And third, it is not about my faith, about Islam, or Judaism, or Christianity. It is about the salvation of humanity.

If my wearing this symbol of my mother's, my grandmother's, my great-grandmother's modesty, their respect for themselves, creates doubt about the veracity of the words I pass from the voice to the world, then I will no longer wear this paltry piece of cloth."

Taking the headscarf out of Zara's hand, Rachel runs the length of the cloth through her fingers and then surprises Zara. She delicately wraps the scarf around Zara's head, in the exact style Zara had worn the paltry piece of cloth.

"The Mongolian woman in Peter's dream wore her scarf with the same pride you do," says Rachel. "As I should not compromise what my great-grandmother taught me, neither should you."

"The two women in the dream are symbolic of us. Two women of different faiths, but with the same familial calling, the same destiny to find the cavern of the blue light," says Zara. "These dreams are allegorical, not literal."

A smirk on her face and Rachel says, "Not literal, huh? Like the rumors you can make lightning come down from the sky? Can you bring a plague upon your enemies?"

Lips initially in a frown transform into a smirk back at this Israeli inquisitor, and Zara says, "Perhaps the lightning was coincidental with my prayers. But twice lightning struck when it was needed. The voice has been kind to us."

"And you can teach me to make lightning strike?" asks Rachel.

"That is between you and the voice," replies Zara.

"And when do I hear the voice?" asks Rachel.

"That again is between you and the voice," repeats Zara.

Rachel gets up and walks to the suite window overlooking the south wall of the Temple Mount. "The dream vision was not completely clear on the black stone's location. But I know someone who can help us know where in the Mount of the House we should search." She turns back to Zara and says, "I need your messiah miracles to help her."

Face-to-face with the Israeli professor, Zara says, "What is your interest in what is down there? You are here to secure it for Israel. To preserve the Israeli right to the Mount at all costs. Am I right? Or is it some other, more devious reason for some other, more heinous organization than your Mossad?"

Reaching up, Rachel touches the bump behind Zara's neck and says, "Your skull is as thick as your bump. I am not Mossad. Do you need me to say that another thousand times? Who I work for is simple. I have a legend to fulfill from my great-grandmother, which she inherited from her great-grandmother. The same as do you." She turns away from Zara. "I wish to talk with Her as well."

"Who?" asks Zara. "The voice?"

"To Asherah," replies Rachel.

The Kurdish woman touches the Israeli's neck bump. "You are a woman torn. As am I." Zara squeezes Rachel's upper arm as she adds, "They have asked you to do something, as they did me. Something you would not want to be forced by loyalty or obligation to do. Like mine, your body is for you to do with what you choose."

Rachel turns with a deadpan face and stares into Zara's eyes. "I don't know what you are referring to."

"You know," says Zara without a flinch. "That is why you want to know if I am with Peter. If Peter is free to be with you in the way they want. For me, it was Alexander who insisted, and I resisted. For you, I cannot figure out who you are fighting regarding this matter. Except that Dr. Fontaine texted this morning that you were working with NiQihs."

Looking aside, then moving away from the taller woman, Rachel scoffs and says, "You don't have to believe me about who I serve. All I know is that I must have eaten something this morning that is pressuring me." Holding her lower abdomen, she heads to the bathroom.

⁶⁄ₒ

She has seen women torn up by bullets before. First in Iraq, as she helped the Peshmerga fight Saddam. Then again, in Syria, as she commanded an all-female unit fighting Assad, then the Daesh. She could not cry over these injured women then, and she cannot now over this young Palestinian who cannot talk, who can barely nod in acknowledgment. Not since she heard the news.

The place within her that would lead to tears is one where she wishes not to go. She has killed enough of her loved ones. For Zara bears the guilt of the deaths of her cousins. She killed them. Not the Daesh. But now, she knows she has killed one more.

Moments ago, MoxWorld Security notified her they found parts of Mr. Alexander Murometz's body that had washed ashore from the Black Sea. She killed him as much as she had her cousins. Her blindness to what is important.

In a special ward two wings away from where Peter was treated, Zara looks back up at Rachel, who is still holding her abdomen, and says, "I cannot heal your friend. What is her name? Massa? I am so sorry."

Outside the ward, looking in, Peter holds his hand in front of Roza, who is ready to go to her granddaughter's side. Instead, Peter comes in and kneels next to Zara. He looks up at Rachel and nods for her to give them space.

He takes her head into his shoulder and strokes her through her headscarf. "When my father killed himself, I asked my mother why God couldn't send Christ down to Earth again to resurrect my father. To resurrect everyone who left their children too soon."

Silence. Only Zara shaking her head. "It is not for me to decide who lives and dies. Who suffers and who is healed. All is Xwedê's will."

Continuing to stroke her, but now on her neck and back, he answers, "That is what my mother said to me. The distraught teen who loved his father, who could not understand why he would leave him. And why Xwedê had let him die."

Two meters away, intently listening, Rachel flinches and turns her head away, her head shaking and her hands tightly gripping each other.

"My father left me," says Zara with a quiver in her voice. "Both my fathers left me. Oh, Peter. I worried about the wrong things. Sasha. It was my fault he was captured and is dead. I killed him through my anger over what he did to my mother."

As Zara sniffles, he holds her tight. "I talked with Massa's mother. She feels the same as you and I. If only she had persuaded her Massa not to go chasing after Asherah as their family legend asked of them. If only she hadn't been in that tomb with Rachel, she would be her happy Massa, able to live the rest of her life in health."

The first wet one rolls down her cheek as her throat swims in the flow of fluids. Garbled, she asks, "Who are we to think we can change what is destined?" I could no more have stopped my father from hanging himself than you could have stopped your father from shooting himself."

Now three meters back, lines overwhelm the smoothness of Rachel's face, her body rigid.

As he wipes her tears, she says, "Sasha is dead. I know you wanted him to be your surrogate father. He was my biological father. And we both need to move on without him."

Placing Massa's hand into her wet ones, Peter whispers, "I know you loved him in your own way. And he loved you. As I do."

Standing up, he waves Rachel out of the room and follows her as he closes the ward door.

He glances at Massa's mother and puts his hands together as if in prayer. Rosa hugs him and nods affirmatively.

"May I have a word with you?" whispers Rachel as her rigid arm tugs at his arm taking him to a quiet hallway.

"I am sure Zara will do everything she can for your friend," says Peter.

"It is not that. There is something I must tell you," says Rachel. "It's about your father."

One eye squinted with head turned to the side, he says, "Some secret Mossad intel?"

"No. Of course not," she attests. "Just because I'm Israeli doesn't automatically mean I work for them. Like you don't work for the CIA. Do you?"

"Worse. I worked for the late Mr. Murometz," says a flat-voiced Peter. "Then who are you working for?"

"I am like you. I work for my family's legacy. I have promised my Ariella in the same way you promised your pappy. I need you to be with me so I can fulfill my promise. But there is something I must tell you about your father so it does not become an issue later between us," she says, still rigid, her face so pale.

And before Peter can reply, Roza yells, "Peter, she did it! Another miracle. Bring your Israeli friend. Zara, our messiah, has healed again."

As Peter runs to Massa's room, Rachel spies a familiar figure down another hallway toward her safta raba's ward. She glances down at Massa's room, then at that figure. She has to salvage her rash tossing of that vial at her outside King Zedekiah's cavern.

"You must be thinking that your new Kurdish friend will now help your great-grandmother," says Beverly, tapping her clipboard. "Otherwise, you wouldn't have thrown an empty vial at me."

Unable to say anything, Rachel simply sneers.

Tapping her lower abdomen, Beverly says, "That is, unless you have been getting his genetic material the natural way. We will cure your great-grandmother once you provide proof of your pregnancy."

Taking those hands off her midriff, Rachel stomps one heel and says, "My uterus is mine. Not yours or anyone else's."

"Too bad. Did they tell you your failure to get his genetic material means escalation to more drastic measures?" says Beverly, tugging a sheet on her clipboard. "They can either help or kill the two people you love the most. One is your great-grandmother, whose vitals have deteriorated considerably since the last time we talked. She's on that final leg to death, as she no longer can speak. Perhaps you should run up there now and say goodbye. Unless that Kurdish woman will do you a favor. Heal your loved one or give you that Gollinger man."

Hands shaking, then forming fists, Rachel glares at the doctor. She did not beg them for that agency job, she did not beg them to return the tablet, and she will not bow down to these people. One last eyeball-to-eyeball look and she trots down the hall toward her beloved Ariella's ward.

That doctor did not lie. Her safta raba is on oxygen with a nasal cannula. Next to her bed are vials of an antianxiety drug and morphine. Both signs of impending death.

Rachel places both black stone pendants into her safta raba's blue hands. Her Ariella can only stare at her with empty eyes. She tries to speak, but nothing comes out.

"Oh, Safta Raba. I tried. I did. I got the other stone from him," Rachel says, rubbing the two black stones glowing blue in the aged palm with her tears now dropping down her cheeks, both their hands now soaked as Rachel's soul unleashes the pangs of grief. The impending loss of the woman whom she has followed faithfully ever since she could understand stories.

That aged hand pets Rachel's hair. Looking up, Rachel spies a flash from Ariella's eyes. A pulsating blue glow. In her other hand, the stones emit the same blue pulses.

"Safta Raba, what is happening?" asks Rachel, trying to clear the water from her reddened eyes. "Oh, why am I asking? You cannot talk anymore. I am too late."

"Paper."

Rachel stares in disbelief. Did she just say something without saying it?

Her safta raba's eyes point toward the nightstand, where Rachel spots a piece of paper. She reads it and says, "I do not understand this word. It is not Hebrew. Qualqi. What does that mean?"

"Qualqi. She awaits you."

Eyes wide open, Rachel looks around the room. They are alone. And her Ariella's lips only quiver as if she is trying to talk.

"Safta Raba, I do not understand. I have sought Asherah as you guided me. Who is Qualqi?"

Her Ariella's eyes stare into hers with the look of wanting to connect, the lips mouthing something but nothing.

"Qualqi. Asherah. Gollinger. Baby."

Words again, but not the voice of her safta raba. She needed to have a baby to see Asherah. But why specifically a Gollinger baby?

Qualqi? That was what Peter's grandfather wrote in his diary. Could it be true what was in that diary? The Gollinger family was not complicit in saba raba's death?

Rachel clasps the aged hands and asks, "Safta Raba, if I am to be with Peter, I must know. Did you authorize my father to kill Peter Gollinger's father? Are you asking me to have the child of a man who my father killed?"

And the worst of the worst befalls her. A nod.

CHAPTER 43

*How can we live in harmony? First we need to know
we are all madly in love with the same God.*
—Saint Thomas Aquinas, thirteenth-century theologian

February 3, 1300 CE
Jerusalem

"He came with how many soldiers?" exclaims El Qutlugh Khatun at her scout, who has just returned from Mount Scopus northwest of the city walls. "It is not yet five weeks. He cannot destroy Jerusalem."

His head down in supplication, the scout adds, "He wishes your audience out there on the mount."

Saddling her horse, El leaves the city walls to meet her nephew, the Khan of the Ilkhanate. As her father held that position, she knows full well Ghazan could bring tens of thousands of troops down from Damascus and raze Jerusalem into rubble in ways neither the Romans nor Babylonians could. For the Mongols are the greatest tyranny God has ever unleashed upon mankind.

Dressed in the lightest of armor concealed under clothing befitting not a Khan but ordinary men of the region, Ghazan acknowledges the arrival of his aunt. "Your scout reported the city is undefended. The Mamluks have stayed away for some reason."

"We have been discreet in our surveillance of the city," says El, who scans the men lining the next set of hills to the north. "Why have you come with soldiers?"

"Do I treat you so indifferently you think I do not care about your welfare?" asks the Khan. "I heard nothing from you for two weeks. I feared the worst befalling my headstrong aunt. So, I came with enough soldiers to rescue you."

"Promise me you will kill no one who does not try to kill us first," pleads El.

"Mongols kill as needed. If they need to be massacred to prove our resolve, to prove to others they should surrender as they see the dust of our horses on the horizon, then so be it," says Ghazan, well schooled by four generations of conquerors before him.

"I heard the voice of the ancients, the same as the sorceress woman from Anatolia had described," says El. "I heard the voice twice. We should not harm people here. These are sacred lands. These are sacred people."

"And what did he say, this voice of the Anatolian sorceress?" asked Ghazan.

"She, Ghazan. Why do men assume Allah is a he?"

"I am right. Muslim you dress, but you do still worship the mother earth goddess, Eje," says Ghazan with a wink at his decade-elder aunt.

"I am not amused. Taunting God has led to bad outcomes for those who attack this city," states El. "But if you must know, the second time she talked with me, she said we are close to the black object which we should return to Her. We must follow the star of the ancients. The bright one at the tail of the swan constellation."

Shifting positions in his saddle as his horse also adjusts its stance, he says, "If indeed this magic stone exists, why would we not keep it for our own purposes? And why have you not produced this stone after nearly three weeks here?"

Circling him to face the city walls, she says, "The black stone has been in this city for ages. If you listen to these people, this city has been destroyed time and time again. The black stone is not to be kept by man. Only ill will befall those who try to capture its power. The voice said we must free the black stone."

He waves his hands, signaling with his ten fingers, then an X, and then ten fingers again. One hundred soldiers in plain clothing ride over to their mount. He says they should follow his aunt's instructions on where to search and report back here. In discreet groups of four, the soldiers disperse to enter the city by different gates.

Near the Gate of Eternal Life, or the Gate of Mercy in her religion, Asefeh signals for El, who excuses herself to her nephew. But to El's surprise, the Khan follows her with two escorts.

Arriving at the gate, El asks, "Why did you signal? What is happening?"

"The city elders have become alarmed. People are saying the Mongols have come to plunder the city," says the Jewish woman.

Grimacing, El points to her nephew and says, "Asefeh, meet the Mongol conqueror of Jerusalem, the great Ghazan."

Immediately on the ground in supplication, Asefeh begs forgiveness for her boldness in front of the great ruler.

Ghazan replies, "If this is how the citizens of this city will greet me, they have nothing to fear."

Behind them, the great gates creak as six men try to close them. Ghazan and his two escorts charge the gates scaring the men away. Asefeh begs them not to kill these men, for they only wish to prevent an unwanted messiah from entering the city.

Gate secured, Ghazan sends one escort back to get more soldiers to return. For Jerusalem has no right to keep Mongols out of their city. So, he will remove these gates and bring them back to Damascus.

El asks her nephew to stay outside the gates, as if discovered inside the walls, his presence will cause a defensive reaction by the city. Perhaps a poor decision by the city elders, but surely it will hamper their ability to find the black stone. Ghazan concedes to his aunt's logic as he plans how they will dismantle this offending gate.

Asefeh explains to El that she and her husband bonded in the way of the ancients, something El has only heard of as her husband had been murdered before they could have children. In Asefeh's husband's dream, they saw a priestess of Asherah descend into an entrance to secret tunnels under the Chamber of the Wood in the northeast corner of the Court of Women in Herod's Second Temple closest to the Shushan Gate, the Gate of Mercy.

As they cross under that very gate, El begins to speak but drops to the ground. Asefeh fans her as El says she feels weak of late. Perhaps her late monthlies are finally arriving. As Asefeh helps her up, El questions where they can find this Chamber of the Wood. Asefeh says her husband has heard of an antechamber below the Crusader's Templum Domini, now called the Dome of the Rock under Mamluk rule. The crusaders accessed this antechamber through a passage down to an ancient cistern near the Dome of the Chain between the Dome of the Rock and the Shushan gate. Some say that the Dome of the Chain marks where the Holy of Holies chamber of the Second Temple lay.

That evening, they gather with El's scouts at a predesignated location near the Gate of Damascus. Many of the scouts had been investigating the nearby Caves of Solomon, said to be the quarries of King Herod, which had led only to many literal dead ends. Equipped with picks, ropes, and torches, dressed as Muslims they proceed to the Dome of the Chain. Asefeh counts off the number of steps northeast as she recalled from her dream. Long stone tiles covered the grounds of the Temple Mount up until an area filled with decorative trees. Here they find a small mound, as if someone long ago had buried something.

The covering dirt and cover stone removed, the scouts descend the cistern. Two stay to protect the women as the others investigate the passages below.

Guards pass by, satisfied with the women's explanation of waiting in the woods as their monthlies have come. And the first glimmer appears of a sun trying to rise on the eastern mountains. A scout ascends to the surface with a report to El. Nothing of note in the passages. With but a little Mongol ingenuity, they found hidden chambers.

They found a golden tree-shaped object. No, leave it, says El.

They found a gold inlaid wooden box with a bunch of old clay tablets inside. No, leave it, says El.

They found an ordinary chalice with a golden rim. No, leave it, says El.

Asefeh begs of El that they should save these items from plunder. El says it is not the affairs of the Mongols.

Then another scout arises from the hole. They found a chamber with a black rock. El says this is the affair of the Mongols as she prepares to be lowered down the cistern.

Following the scout, El and Asefeh find the chamber. Both on their knees, they rub the black object. El kisses the surface of this legendary stone. Unsure, Asefeh continues to rub the pocketed black surface, ultimately kissing it as well.

Looking around the chamber, El spies a number of clay tablets with writing in a language she does not understand, and neither does Asefeh. She finds a bronze tablet with the constellations around a goddess. El carefully lines the clay and bronze tablets along a wall under a stout basin for safekeeping, hoping she can return with scholars versed in ancient languages.

El turns to Asefeh, asking how she and her husband bonded to access his dreams. Turning rose flush, Asefeh says what her mother taught her. Did not El's mother teach her? El replies that the stories she heard from her mother and grandmothers described what men would want from their women. The sorceress from Anatolia said otherwise.

Hands over her face, Asefeh cries she has only been with her husband and never intimate with a woman. El touches her tears and then, with wetted fingers, rubs the bump on the back of Asefeh's neck. The pregnant woman calms as she touches the same bump on El. And they follow the rest of what their matriarch lineage had taught.

Minutes pass as they pass through serenity, harmony, peace together. A voice comes to the two of them. A beauty Asefeh has never known. A beauty El has only recently known. The voice tells them the tales of the women of this temple who tried to protect the voice, who tried to let the world know of the voice's wishes for mankind, and who ultimately had their lives sacrificed because mankind was not ready for the voice.

At first afraid, Asefeh asks if She is Asherah. The voice says I am who you wish me to be. I am who your mothers wish you would know. I am all that the men who created their god in their own image would not see in a god.

Not as timid, El asks what the voice wants of them, what She wants of the object. The voice instructs them to remove the object from this place of suffering. To return the object to the lands of the ancient women who protect the cavern of blue light. It is their destiny to follow this path, where they will find welcome and peace among the women of the cavern.

Breaking their touch, Asefeh cries to El that she cannot leave her husband. Her child deserves a father. What this voice asks is not that of a good god as she knows it. How do they know this is not the voice of the adversary of Yahweh, Satan?

Undeterred, El closes her eyes, touching the object. She answers she understands what needs to be done. For if they fail in their quest to find the cavern, she will leave a message for others who search here for the same truth, the same path.

From under her outer coat, El pulls out a small sack. Leather as old as the ages. One that she received from that Anatolian sorceress. She takes a pick from a scout and carves the swan stars into the wall. At the location of the tail of the bird star, she takes blue flakes from the sack and pounds them into the star location. Below she carves in Mongolian the instructions from the voice, which only a woman taught by afflicted grandmothers would understand.

She places the pick against the black object, aiming at a spot to chip a piece off. As her hand guides the pick up and down to fracture a fragment off, she and Asefeh are blown backward against the cavern's back wall.

Checking her belly to ensure her child is unharmed, Asefeh hears Her. She acknowledges she must follow El and the object towards the tail of the swan star.

Placing the object fragment under stones at the back of the chamber, El signals for the scout to get others to take the object. She pauses and says back to the voice she understands and will make sure her nephew knows the same.

The scouts gather, perplexed at how to bring this huge black stone up through the cistern. Asefeh tells of a legendary ancient gateway buried by the Muslims as they built up the Temple Mount hundreds of years ago. The scouts deploy finding a walled in area under large arches.

Calling for reinforcements among the hundred soldiers Ghazan had deployed in the city, a day later they have excavated the gate open, at which there lies an open passage to the east. Supervising the pulling of the black object, El passes under these ancient gates.

On the other side stands Asefeh, who says these are likely the real Shushan Gates. As the two pass back under the gates back towards the west, the dust around El's ancient sack emits a light blue glow. Asefeh says El's eyes have a light blue glow. El says the same about Asefeh's eyes. As Asefeh worries about the effect this may have on her unborn child, El says this is the voice's way of saying they are the saviors of Jerusalem. They are the messiahs of their time.

Circling the black stone, Ghazan says, "All this trouble for this rock." He kicks it. "At best, this might make a good projectile for our catapults to knock down these walls of Jerusalem when I return."

Shaking her head, El says, "She said if you return with an army, you will suffer the greatest defeat of any Mongol in these lands."

Stiffening his back, his hand rocking his sword, Ghazan says, "So says your goddess. My god says we Mongols are destined rulers of all these domains. The Mongols will not be defeated. These people here are weak and destined to be conquered as they have been time and time again."

Still shaking her head, El says, "We have the object of the ancients. Let us leave and find our greater peace."

Mounting his horse, the Khan says, "We have their gate. They cannot keep us out now. And your Jewish woman says you are their messiah now. You have saved them from being conquered this year. But I shall return when our horses have regained their strength in the pastures near the Euphrates. That is unless the Chagatai Khanate does not attack us from the east first."

Helping Asefeh mount her horse and then mounting her own, El says, "You do that. I will follow the words and wishes of the voice. I will not be there to see your defeat."

Toward the tail of the bird star the two women head with an escort of a husband and a horde of Mongols.

CHAPTER 44

A poor girl may have an illusion that a prince will come and fetch her home. It is possible, some such cases have occurred. That the messiah will come and found a golden age is much less probable.

—Sigmund Freud

MoxWorld Resorts Jerusalem
6:30 a.m. GMT+3, March 3, 2023

Peter begins to stir, his night terrors abated by two angels. At his side, Zara strokes his forehead.

A deep breath, an equally deep smile, and Peter utters, "Zzzara. In heaven, you have four hands."

Certainly not the response Zara was expecting as she sits up. But it is a response that touches that place within her that no one has ever touched as has this man lying in front of her.

His hand reaches out to hers as he says, "I had a dream two women were fighting over me. And then they morphed into angels."

She scoffs. "In your dream's dream, Peter. The two women were working together to find the object below the Temple Mount. We saw where it was hidden."

"We?" asks Peter as he sits up. He looks around, scratches his head, and asks, "Why are we sleeping in Rachel's bedroom? Is she sleeping in yours?"

"And how do you know what Rachel's bed looks like?" asks Zara with her head tilted down, eyeing him through the top of her eyes. "You told me you had tea in her parlor. Was there more to that story?"

Grabbing her arm, Peter violently shakes his head. "No, no. I mean we had tea in her parlor. And more in her bedroom. We had our clothes on the whole time."

She pushes on his side at first with her mouth squished down on one side and then a snort. "Your fully clothed Rachel is in the bathroom. I taught her how to bond with you when you are having the night terrors."

Head down, with an upside-down U for a mouth, Peter says, "I thought that the ancient bonding was only between you and me. The ancient matriarch with her husband."

She scruffs up his hair. "But you bonded with Mei. How special can it be between us?"

Still dour, staring down, he replies, "It wasn't the same. The visions were clouded. The touch within each other's soul muted. I am one with you. Only with you. Fully and completely when we bond."

Scuffing his hair more, she says, "You sound like the man who is begging forgiveness for having an affair."

Lifting his head to peer into her eyes, he says, "I thought you understood. Mei's child is from her bond with my sister. She is like my sister-in-law now. Family. Like I want to be your family."

He adds, "If you are so concerned about me bonding with another woman, why were you teaching a strange woman how to bond with me?"

No longer with the face that teased Peter, the somber Zara returns; the woman of a destined soul unto herself takes over. As she rubs his hand, she says, "Part of me wants to be with you in ways I have not let us be together. But the voice is very clear. My fate is to die to save humanity. I love you too much to leave you with the pain of my death, the pain of loneliness. It is best if you learn to bond, to share, with another. Even if she does not know yet how good of a partner you can be."

"That's what you told me last time. That you needed to die on that pier when we gave the first object to your Sasha," exclaims Peter. "And yet, I found a way that neither of us had to die that day. Let me help you. Please."

She rises and walks over to the same window Rachel had stared out earlier after having seen the vision. But she does not stare out the window. Her eyelids shut tightly as if to keep what wells within from spilling out.

He rises and starts toward her, every inclination in his body telling him to comfort her. But suddenly, he stops, those plotting gears turning in his editor brain. Physical comforting is not what will soothe her soul.

He waits until the sound of a stifled sniffle emanates from the tall woman at the window to say, "Jean-Paul told me once of his ancestors."

"Cathars," says Zara. "Magali mentioned them to me."

"They believed in dualism. The good god of light, of the heavens. The bad god of the material, of the earth. They believed the Old Testament, the Torah, spoke of both gods but represented them as one god. One has to ask if the bad god sections misled the believers of these faiths."

He strategically waits again for any sign she is processing what he has planted. A wave of her head and shoulder signals Peter to continue. "Who is the voice? Maybe the object is the ultimate expression of the earthly material. Look what's happened to our world since we found it. They're trying to nuke each other over the possession of a material object they all think could help them rule the world."

Her head bowed, she quietly says, "I am surprised you feel this way about the voice, after all we have experienced together. I guess it is true we are not meant for each other. Perhaps an academic like Mei or the woman in that bathroom would be a better fit for how you think. Cats with cats."

He closes the gap between them, stepping almost to her. "Bev, I mean Dr. Fontaine, said we're both suffering from post-traumatic stress. Our judgment is clouded. We should step back from our instincts, which may be defective, and rethink any rash action."

Stomping her foot, she turns around in scorn and says, "That woman. She is a seductress, not a doctor, not a person who wishes to heal. No more than a *qarînah*, a succubus. An evil one who seeks to deceive us, seeks to take of our body to steal our souls."

Tapping his MoxWrap, Peter reads, then says, "Maybe I am the qarîn in your life. I sleep with you. In my dreams I have relations with you. Very intimate ones. Truth be known, we have sex together in my dreams. Only you wish to suppress those dreams."

She bridges the distance between them, both physically and otherwise, as she touches his arms. "I know you want me in the way a husband wants his wife. I know you want this even more now that you know my body is complete again. You should know I fight the same desires to be with you in that same way. But I was born to fulfill a certain destiny. And in life, one cannot have what one desires, one must follow the will of Xwedê."

Lifting her head so he can make full eye contact, he asks, "And if your voice is not Xwedê?"

She breaks from him, walking toward the bedroom door, then stopping. "That is why you and I are not the best mates. I follow Her with complete subservience. That is why the woman you should seek is the one who will ask the same questions that your soul naturally asks. We are but cats and dogs. You should be with another cat like yourself, like your family."

In the bathroom, Rachel sits on the toilet, head between her knees, stunned by the message.

You gave us no choice. We took both parents. Your rabbi one of them. Get what you were supposed to from Gollinger. In a vial or mated with your ovum. Kill Khatum. One of these must happen today.

As Rachel walks out of the bathroom, Zara points, saying to Peter, "Someone like her. Another cat."

Peter excuses himself to the bathroom, saying, "Possibly could you ladies finish negotiating my rights to my bump. I have urgent affairs to take care of."

Perplexed, Rachel asks, "What was that about?"

Zara walks over to Rachel, stops to glance at her T-shirt top. "So, you are planning to be intimate with him this morning? No bra."

Rachel shakes her chest loose from her top and says, "They are oddly very tender this morning. I would have nothing covering them if no one was in my room."

Zara turns her head aside, saying, "I do not know who is asking you to be with him in this way. The way I have chosen not to. I only ask that you learn to love him. He deserves love. There is only one other man in my life I can say deserved to be loved like Peter. And he is dead."

"He loves you. And you love him," says Rachel. "Even if someone has asked me, perhaps is forcing me, to intercede, to take his love from you, how can I?"

Zara turns and leaves the bedroom, going into her parlor. At the front door, she turns and says, "Because if you wish to talk with Asherah, you have to. Or so says the legend."

Rachel clutches her T-shirt. Sits down on her bed, still warm from his body, and then lets out a long breath through her nostrils. When is the debt too high to pay? When is it time to stop chasing the ring on the merry-go-round?

The door to the bathroom opens too soon for her deliberations. As Peter peeks out to see who is still out there, she pats the bed next to her for him to sit down.

Without a word, he takes the place next to her. She takes a deep breath in and holds her T-shirt tight to her too-tender breasts, asking, "Do you like what you see?"

Not even taking a glance, his hands drop upon hers to loosen up the garment. Another breath out and she says, "They are not good enough for you? Are hers that much better?"

His hands drop off hers and she leans back, awaiting his first move. "Not that you aren't the most attractive woman who lives in Jerusalem. I simply don't admire women that way. Only the color of their hair and if they're holding a gun. Or so the woman of my dreams was. Or so my Pappy had last decreed."

Rachel sits back up straight and says, "That is the oddest way to woo a woman."

He can only stare into her eyes.

And she? A kiss upon his forehead. And then lower. And then again lower.

"Messiahs do not have to die to save us all," says Roza as she combs her granddaughter's hair.

"The voice was very clear on this matter," insists a very stubborn Zara. "Two women must enter the cavern, but only one will return, the other sacrificing her life so the balance of existence can continue."

"Perhaps you misunderstood her," says Roza in the kind tone only a loving grandmother can manage.

Turning around to face Roza, Zara says, "Have you and Peter been talking? She was very clear."

The wise woman puts her hands on her granddaughter's cheeks and asks, "How will the world learn to follow your words, Her words, if you keep saying it is yours to die?"

Turning around facing the mirror again, she quips, "Someone two thousand years ago said the same, and he died here too."

Holding a piece of paper up to the mirror, Roza says, "I want you to see this note asking if the prophetess would come to the hospital."

Zara reads the note, handwritten in Arabic. From the sister of the wife of the president of Turkey. Her granddaughter is terminally ill.

Roza says, "She wishes a blessing from you."

Taking the brush from her grandmother, Zara brushes furiously and says, "I cannot cure people. No more than I can make lightning strike."

Taking the brush back from her granddaughter and more gently stroking through her hair, Zara reflects and then says, "All is up to Xwedê. I can only ask for help in the same way they can ask."

With a smile, the kind a grandparent gives when a child has an epiphany, Roza says, "I saw what you did with Massa. Maybe Xwedê smiles when you smile. Think of what your gesture would mean. The possibility of opening a peace dialogue again between the Kurds and Turkey."

"And if the child dies?"

"It is your gesture that matters. The trueness of your heart," says her grandmother.

Her hand upon her grandmother's, Zara says, "The trueness of my heart is reflected in what I just did for someone I love. Someone who I hope can finally have the love he wants in return."

Roza stares at her granddaughter's eyes in the mirror as if to search for the meaning of what she just said. Pursing her lips, she says, "Maryam told me what happened. Your acceptance of her, your forgiveness of her, is the greatest joy she has had since your father's imprisonments."

"I am happy for the both of us. That wall between us no longer exists. My mother is fully my mother."

"And whatever Peter has done or not done, should you not open your heart to him as well?" asserts Roza.

To which Zara responds, "You want me to be the prophetess. You tell the world that I am here to save us all. Do messiahs have spouses?"

Smiling as a grandmother does with their granddaughters, Roza replies as she wraps a scarf around Zara's head, "Some say the last one in Jerusalem had one. The Cathars believed in her. Mary Magdalene."

Adjusting the scarf, Zara says, "You and Peter have been talking. Both conspiring with Jean-Paul now."

"The Father is a wise man," states Roza. "But he would be happier if his Holy Pontiff allowed him to marry Magali. His angel."

Zara turns to her Roza, stares into her eyes and asks, "If you could only have one wish, my fulfilling your wishes for a messiah or my fulfilling your wishes for family, which would you choose?"

Nodding, Roza says, "Both you and I can have both, can we not? Make sure you are not hiding from your truest deepest destiny. Is the notion you are to die not your way of pushing away someone who might leave you tragically before you are hurt again?"

Looking to the side, Zara says, "I think your question is too late. Peter should have consummated his best destiny by now."

CHAPTER 45

One of his students asked Buddha, "Are you the messiah?" "No," answered Buddha. "Then are you a healer?" "No," Buddha replied. "Then are you a teacher?" the student persisted. "No, I am not a teacher." "Then what are you?" asked the student exasperated. "I am awake," Buddha replied.

—Gautama Buddha

Somewhere below the Temple Mount, Jerusalem
5:10 a.m. GMT+3, March 4, 2023

"Do you intend on shooting me after we find the object?" asks the taller of the two women wearing black headscarves.

"I don't know what you mean," answers the smaller one, dropping to the bottom of the cistern that Massa had described to them.

"Your backpack swings with the weight of your pistol," says Zara as she drops to the bottom of the cistern. "Did you pack the ones with copper hollow tips? I am a large, robust woman. Little solid bullets will not take me down."

Her arms akimbo, hands atop the Kurdish pants adapted from Zara's mother's wardrobe, Rachel stands in front her accuser. She takes her black headscarf off and says, "You keep talking like that and I'm going to shoot you to shut you up."

Staring down the smaller woman, Zara gives her the once-over as she says, "How was he?"

Not engaging the taller woman's stare, Rachel takes the lead through the only passage out of the bottom of the cistern with her MoxWrap providing torch-like lighting. She answers, "He was understandably depressed that you left him. Again."

Keeping close to the Israeli woman, Zara asks, "I meant, how was he in bed?"

Not breaking a step, Rachel says back, "I will not dignify your question with an answer."

"But he fell into your arms and loved you the way you needed him to?" asks Zara, in a much less challenging tone.

Stopping abruptly, practically making Zara stumble over her, Rachel turns around and peers up into Zara's inquiring eyes. "For a prophetess, you are quite conflicted."

"And you are not?" answers Zara, her hands akimbo this time.

With the accusatory finger wagging up at the Kurdish woman, Rachel fires back, "You want him, but you deny yourself your desire by pushing him to other women."

Back stiffened, Zara glances aside, saying, "Rab'ia had many suitors. If she had thought she loved one, then she would be denying Xwedê her love. How better to show her love than finding the best alternative wife for the man she might love."

Running her hands down along her body's curves with a suggestive wiggle, Rachel says, "If I told you he was the best lover I have ever had, that he brought me to ecstasy in ways no woman has ever been brought, that he made me see Asherah in all of her wonders—would you be happier?"

The tall woman's eyes narrow, her pupils so small they are barely visible. Her respiratory rate quickens.

Rachel stands firm and says, "It's the part about seeing Asherah that gets you, not the sex, isn't it?"

Zara's head falls. Her shoulders slump in unison. "Mei said the same thing. He made her see the Goddess Jiang. Peter said she orgasmed in ways she never had before when they bonded."

The Israeli professor turns, heading down the passage as she admonishes

Zara. "This is all your fault. You love him. If you were carrying his love child, I wouldn't be in the situation that's being forced on me."

Pointing down another passageway, Rachel asks, "How do you know Dr. Fontaine?"

"And how do you know her?" asks Zara. "She was with Peter's grandfather in his last months. She knows all about the ancient matriarch legends. She said I should let Peter go. Is she the one saying you need to get Peter to snuggle up with you? Is that your agreement with them? I get kidnapped so you can get Peter?"

Shaking her head, Rachel turns to proceed down the passage. "You are so jealous, lady. You love him. Why don't you drop this prophetess act and just live your life? Live your love."

Right on her tail, Zara says back, "Is that what they want you to do? Stop me by any means? Marry me off or murder me?"

"What makes you think there are outside forces pulling at me?" fires back Rachel.

"Because you are as conflicted as I am," says Zara.

Silence reigns. Two women driven by ancient DNA, ancient callings. Both wishing they could live a different life. Two women verbally hitting each other without mercy on what truly bothers the other. A man's fist-to-fist battle would hurt less than this.

Her eyes now down, Zara says, "A sad pair we are. The modern embodiment of the two in Peter's dream. We cannot fulfill the legend if we continue to bicker. El and Asefeh partnered despite their differences."

Rachel stares at Zara and says, "Détente?"

A nod from Zara to Rachel, who nods back.

Following Massa's instructions, they emerge into a large alcove. Partially open, partially caved in. Rachel drops to her knees and kisses the ground. Zara shines her MoxWrap light around the walls. If there was a roof to this place, it had been collapsed down. She assesses if they are in danger of further collapse.

"Massa's instructions were dead-on correct. This is the Court of Women," says Rachel as her hands run across the floor as if something transcendent would pass between her and the stone. They only let women get this far into the Second Temple. "Women could not proceed further to worship at the Holy of Holies."

Circling the enclosure, Rachel says. "If I am right, there existed another way down beneath the temple where women worshipped in private."

Shining her MoxWrap light against the walls, in between fallen stones, columns, blocks, Rachel searches methodically. "If only I could spend a few years down here, we could rewrite history," the biblical history professor in Rachel muses.

The officer in Zara commands back, "Stay to task, woman. We have one objective. Find where the object has been hidden. Then you can kill me and take my Peter all for yourself."

Her light blinding Zara's eyes, Rachel fires back, "You're just dying to know what happened between us after you abandoned him? You're the one who needs to stay to task."

Rachel flicks her light several paces ahead to the right and says, "There. It looks like an outcropping. One of the side rooms to the Court of Women."

They enter the outcropping. Large stone basins filled with stones and dust line the edges. Rachel says, "They laundered the priests' clothing here. Women's work. They would've hidden the entrance to their secret temple here."

The history professor drops to her knees with her brush. Several minutes later, she says, "Here. These are the lines where the drain would've been." She knocks on the cover stone with her brush. A hollow echo.

Zara helps her clean this section of the floor and then, using Rachel's pickaxe as a lever, they lift the cover stone to find a corroded ladder descending the drain. Rachel throws a couple of glow sticks down. Only four meters deep. Good. She has enough rope in her backpack.

"Here, you hold the rope steady as I go down," says Rachel, handing one end to Zara.

To the former's dismay, Zara ties the rope around her own waist and says, "Not so fast, little woman. I go down first. You will take everything down there in the name of Israel. Or whoever else you are working for."

Arms akimbo one more time, then tugging on the rope, Rachel says, "And who will you claim everything down there for? Your imaginary voice?"

Tugging the rope back from Rachel, Zara says, "So, you *are* working for that seductress doctor. Only she would say that to me." She pauses, remembering Sasha's same conversation with her. Moles. Trust no one.

"Well, that leaves a problem. I am lighter and daintier than you," says Rachel. "I couldn't possibly hold your weight as you descend."

"Are you calling me fat?"

"I'm just an academic calling it as I see it," replies Rachel. "You got a little belly going on since we first met, don't you?"

Searching around, Rachel spies the stout leg of a stone basin. "Come on, fatty. Help me get a rope through here."

Next to Rachel, Zara takes the Israeli's fingers to pinch her side. To Zara's surprise, the pinch test would normally show she is combat lean. But this time, she is carrying a layer of fat. How did that happen?

She sighs and helps cinch the rope.

Acknowledging the Kurdish woman's dismay at her lipid layer, Rachel lets the tall woman go first and then follows, leaving the Court of Women.

In the darkness of the bottom, Rachel stares into Zara's eyes. "They glow. Did you know that? Just around the rim of your irises. A faint blue glow."

Zara's eyes aim down below Rachel's head as she says, "Well, your breasts are glowing blue. Is that from Peter's passionate palpitations? See me. Feel me. Touch me."

"Fish or cut bait, lady," retorts Rachel, echoing Mei as she pulls up the two pendant stones glowing away as one. "If a woman were to reward Peter with her love, it would be for reuniting these stones."

Examining the stones, Zara says, "He gave you one of these?"

"His pappy wanted me to have it," answers Rachel.

"And then he had sex with you?" says Zara, glaring into Rachel's eyes.

"I will not dignify your question with an answer," replies Rachel.

Zara reaches into her tunic and pulls out her circle and crescent pendant. "My mother trusted Peter so much, she gave him this in our search for the first object. I guess he enjoys charming women into his bed using ancient pendants."

"Seriously, drop this jealousy bit," says Rachel as she examines Zara's pendant. "This is identical to the one I found at a dig not far from here. I believe King Solomon's mother wore it."

"Jean-Paul thought it was an emblem from the ancient originator matriarch," says Zara.

"That tall Mongolian woman—remember?" asks Rachel. "Didn't she have one of these too?"

Zara closes her eyes and then nods.

"Perhaps you should give your Peter a little more credit. A little more respect," says Rachel. "Apparently he gives special women ancient pendants not to get into their shorts, but to empower them to find their destinies."

Teeth on her lower lip, Zara nods back.

Zara turns away, shining her MoxWrap light around the drainage shaft. She says, "He could not have made love with you. Crazed sex, maybe. One cannot truly love that very first time. I know."

They search down a series of chambers, unburied and partially buried, until they find one with a loose pile of long-decayed wood. As Rachel brushes away this former fuel for the temple fires, she touches something and lets out a moan. What is better than sex? For an archaeologist, finding what you have long searched for.

She brushes the dust away from the face of Asherah. A statue of the goddess existed below the Second Temple. The stone is identical to the statue fragment Massa first showed her. The women of Israel two thousand years ago worshipped God's wife in secret below the Holy of the Holies.

Zara leans down and runs her fingers along the visage of the ancient goddess. She asks, "Do you believe the Torah represented two different gods? Two different Yahwehs?"

Taken aback by her question, Rachel says, "The scholar in me knows the Torah was written by different generations of authors. Some used the name El, while others used the name Yahweh. Were these two different gods? Or merely different cultures calling the same deity by different names?"

Her fingers running along the stone goddess's lips, Zara asks, "And where does your Asherah fit into all of this?"

Sitting back with a deep breath, Rachel says, "That is the subject of my life studies."

As she did with the Jesuit professors in college, Zara poses a pivotal question. "What if she is one god, and the male is the other? I hear Father Jean-Paul's ancestors believed the Torah represented two different gods. One of the light and one of the dark. Which one is Asherah? Is this question not the one both of us are really down here to find out?"

Her fingers shaking, her breathing more rapid, Rachel stands up, shaking her head back and forth. But nothing comes from her mouth in answer to this Kurdish woman's tough line of questioning. She shines her light all about the chamber and finally says, "This is not the place in the dreams of the two women. We must keep searching."

Zara stands, shaking her head. "We need Peter with us. I can bond with him and we can visualize better where those two women found the object."

For a third time, her arms go akimbo as Rachel protests, "And why is it a man is always needed? That is what the authors of the Torah would want women to believe. Do the authors of your faith say the same?"

Her mouth agape, her eyebrows raised, Zara says, "You mean girl to girl? A woman with a woman bonding?"

Nodding, Rachel says, "Why not? Why is a man needed? You saw those two women bonding. One Jewish, one Muslim."

Shaking her head from side to side, wringing her hands, Zara says, "You have been way too close with Mei. She made her baby without a man."

"I'm not asking you to have sex with me," says Rachel. "I'm asking you to do what is necessary for us to succeed. You and I are alike in this one matter. I'm sure you have done many things you didn't want to in order to get to where you needed to be. I certainly have."

A tightening of her scarf around her face. A pursing of the lips. A shuffle of the feet. And then the headscarf is removed, exposing her special bump, and Zara says, "Okay. But I lead."

Lips pouted out, head shaking side to side, Rachel says back, "That is the problem in your relationship with Peter. You have to lead."

Twisting her black scarf in her hands, Zara fires back, "One, that is not a problem between us. Two, we have no relationship anymore. Three, if you think that he has a problem with the woman leading, then you must have let him lead. Is that how sex was between you two?"

Head leaned in towards the challenging taller woman, Rachel retorts, "Let it go, Zara. You shouldn't have pushed him on me if you didn't want us to bond in all ways."

Zara glances aside, then kneels on the floor. Rachel kneels in front of her, pulling her hair across her shoulder, exposing her neck. Zara takes Rachel's fingers, placing them upon her bump. Rachel does the same with Zara's fingers.

Glaring into the Israeli woman's eyes, Zara says, "If you find things about the Prophet in my mind, in my soul, that you do not agree with, keep that to yourself. Otherwise, I will let the world know how much smaller your bump is than mine."

Chest-bumping her, Rachel retorts, "Peter certainly didn't mind the size of my bumps. Every single one of them."

The two growl at each other. If Asherah were still intact in this chamber, she would have sent these two back to bed without dinner.

One last glare and Zara closes her eyes. Rachel follows. Unlike they did with Peter, they see the lack of clarity. Turbulence, not peace. Swirling disharmonious masses. Not the light and harmony brought forth in their bonding with Peter.

"A fool's errand. It is not working," says Zara as she breaks contact with Rachel.

Wetting her lips with her tongue, Rachel peers into the annoyed Kurdish woman's eyes and says, "We need to kiss."

Pulling back with stiffened back, Zara cries, "You kissed Peter. Was that not enough? Now you need to kiss me?"

"Peter said it was an exchange of hormones through fluid-to-fluid exchange that led to the spiritual bonding," says Rachel.

"I am not kissing you," says Zara as her eyes narrow.

The Israeli woman gets up and says, "Fine. The search for the cavern and the blue light ends here. Because you could not get over ancient morals against women being truly free. I guess your faith's patriarchal underpinnings win and we all lose."

With back now facing her back, Zara says, "Do not make this an issue of Judaism versus Islam. If I were a man, I would not kiss you."

As Rachel begins to leave the chamber, Zara grabs her and forces her down. She kneels in front of Rachel, wetting her finger with her tongue, and touches Rachel's lips.

At first taken aback, Rachel wets her fingers and touches Zara's lips. The Kurdish woman wets her fingers in the Israeli woman's mouth and then rubs her temples. Rachel does the same.

Before she closes her eyes, Zara asks, "Exactly what fluids were exchanged between you and Peter?"

With a coy smile, Rachel says, "You'll just have to make this bonding work and see for yourself inside me."

Eyes closed, a series of deep breaths, and the swirling clouds reappear. Light begins to break through. A warmth, a peace, but not quite harmony appears. Images of two women bonding in the same manner as they come through the clouds.

Through a swirling haze, a fuzzy face of Rachel appears upon that of Asefeh, leading El with the face of Zara down below the chambers of the Second Temple. They descend to a chamber from which passages lead out to beneath the Eastern Gate. And there stands the object. And there El carves her inscription into the walls. As El turns around, Asefeh has a gun pointed at her. The chamber morphs into a cavern lit on one end with a blue light coming from the back. Asefeh fully morphs into Rachel as El morphs into Zara, who is clutching someone, a giant someone, on the ground. Rachel fires several rounds into the giant and laughs. As Zara cries over the giant, Rachel empties the magazine into Zara. Tossing the gun, Rachel walks into the room of the blue light, leaving their bodies to bleed out on the cavern floor.

Her head shakes, her fingers break contact with Rachel's temple, and Zara says, "So that is how it ends. You kill me and Alexander. And you leave Peter with no one to love. No one wins but the Torah scholar."

Grimacing, Rachel retorts, "You said this had nothing to do with our religions. Let's be rational for a minute. Let's find out if the object is still where they found it before you draw any conclusions."

As Zara does nothing but glare at her, Rachel gives Zara her backpack. "It's on the bottom. It's not the Jericho, but something a bit smaller and quieter. You take it, and then I can't kill you with it."

Zara reaches into the pack, pulls out the near-palm-sized Ruger. She aims it at Rachel's lower abdomen and then hands it grip first back to its owner. "If your goddess Asherah wishes you to bring me to my final day, my final hour, then you must follow her with subservience and obedience. The voice asks the same of me. I will follow her words and plan."

Rachel puts the gun back into its case in her backpack. "Then this is all about our faiths. Two gods, or one god directing us to a common end."

"This is about Xwedê, about Yahweh, playing with two women to fulfill his or her wishes. Who are we to disobey?" replies Zara.

Taking out her pickaxe, Rachel taps the floor. "If we are to obey, then we need to find the way below this level."

Another cover stone, this time over a dust-ridden narrow stone staircase, and the two women with colliding destinies descend once again into the darkness. At the bottom, they head east.

Putting her finger in front of her lips, Zara signals silence and points above. She whispers, "Something moved up there."

"I heard nothing," Rachel whispers back.

Sniffing, Zara says, "I smell something."

"I don't smell a thing, but the stale air from two millennia ago," replies Rachel.

"I smell Peter all over you," says Zara as she sniffs Rachel's head.

"You would," replies Rachel. "I smell something too. The jealousy of a crazed Kurd."

"That is not funny," says Zara as she sniffs the direction they came from. "I smell the odor of someone I once knew. But who?"

"Now I smell something," says Rachel as she quickly pulls the two stones up from her chest. "My skin burning from these two." As she holds them up, they glow more intensely.

"Rachel, they are like a divining rod. That is why your great-grandfather wanted you to have them. To find your way back."

As Rachel holds the stones, their intensity varies as she moves them in a one-eighty arc in front of her. Following the variations in intensity as they wander from passageway to passageway, they find the spot. The tail of the bird constellation carved into the wall. The tail star, Deneb, glows in unison with Rachel's stones as if they were long-lost cousins being reunited.

Zara puts her hand on Rachel's cheek. Guiding her head towards her. "Your eyes, Rachel. The irises are glowing. Pulsing in the same rhythm as the star, as your stones."

"Yours too, you crazed Kurd," says Rachel.

Staring into this infuriating Israeli woman's fluctuating eyes, Zara feels what she did once upon a time. She only had a brother. A half-brother, she found out. And they bickered, as she is doing with Rachel.

But she had no sister. Only two cousins who were like her sisters. And Rona asked her to kill her rather than be recaptured by those sex slavers. Is that what bothers her so much about this younger woman? She reminds her of the pain of her cousins. If Sasha's genetic identification program was correct, then Rachel shares as much DNA with her as her cousins did. At least her ancient matriarch DNA.

To Rachel's surprise, Zara ruffles her hair, saying, "You are okay. You and I, we are okay."

At first staring back at Zara, Rachel smiles and turns to the inscriptions next to the glowing constellation. "How is your Mongolian? I bet Mei's is better than yours and mine," she says humorously as she positions her MoxWrap for a photo.

Zara's hand pushes Rachel's wrist down as she takes a photo of the inscriptions with her MoxWrap. "I still do not trust who you really are working for. But I do trust the Jesuits. They have only one allegiance."

As Zara sends the photos to Father Jean-Paul, Rachel searches the edges of the chamber. In the far corner, she finds what El left. An oblong fractured cut of a black stone. She signals Zara, asking, "Is this part of the second object?"

Feeling the length of the fragment with her hands, Zara says, "This appears more than twice the size of the one Peter and Mei found in the cave in China."

Running her hand along the legendary black stone, Rachel asks, "Is this near the size of the ones you united on that pier in Turkey? You know, the two halves that made that EM pulse everyone is so afraid of?"

"This? Oh no. This is but a baby," says Zara as she scans around the chamber. "What is the difference between engraving inscriptions on tablets versus the wall versus in metal?"

"It depends," replies Rachel in her professor voice. "Why?"

"Because I spy something in metal that resembles your pendant," says Zara, pointing under a stout basin to a pile of clay tablets covering one sheet of bronze.

With much care, the archaeologist who carries a mini Ruger with her excavation kit gently surveys and brushes the clay tablets until she gets the bronze one.

"Oh my. The text. It is similar to what I found in Ugarit," says Rachel as she takes her pendant off to place next to the images inscribed in bronze. "Jean-Paul thought my pendant may have come from 3000 BCE and possibly as early as 4000 BCE."

Peering over the ecstatic archaeologist's shoulder, Zara points to the goddess images on both artifacts. "If that is Asherah on your pendant, then this bronze tablet shows where Asherah is found."

Running her brushes lightly over the diagram, Rachel outlines the ancient shoreline. Inland from there are a series of pyramids where a robed female figure stands. On the upper part of the diagram is the tail of the bird constellation, with the tail star at the top. Other constellations line the outer rim.

"The clay tablets are written in the Ugarit alphabet dating back to 1300 to 1500 BCE. They only had about thirty cuneiform letters," she says as she takes photos of some of the tablets. "But this bronze must predate written history."

Lips pursed, her tongue rubbing them, Zara sighs.

"What's wrong, Kurdish lady?" asks Rachel. "I'll send these to Jean-Paul, don't worry."

"That map is not of Crimea, where the pyramids are located according to Peter's grandfather's diaries," says Zara. "The shoreline is all wrong. There are no mountains."

She picks up the blue glowing black stones around Rachel's neck. Brings them up to the Israeli's same blue tinted irises and says, "I've seen this before. I know exactly where we need to go."

Fingers to her chin, Rachel says, "For a non-archaeologist, you are astute. I'll send more photos to Jean-Paul. Maybe he will have some Jesuit-logic-driven wisdom that will decipher this."

After taking only a few photos on her MoxWrap, Zara turns her head, sniffing. "Get your gun out. Quickly," she says.

Not soon enough, as a large man knocks both of them over, grabbing the object fragment. A second bulky man grabs Rachel's backpack and her pendants go flying.

Zara helps Rachel up, saying she knows them, grabbing a rock before she gives chase. The bulkier man is slower than Zara, running with a slight limp. Down the passages, they pass through two arches. Zara tags the back of the bulkier man's head, slowing him down, and then tackles him as Rachel continues after the taller man.

Wrestling for control of the backpack and the weapon contained within, Zara yells out, "Rohan, give it up. You never beat me in a fight."

Rohan. Zara's ultraorthodox cousin. One of the team of assassins who kidnapped Jean-Paul. Part of his ass shot off by Zara's fifty-caliber sniper rifle. Rohan who pulls out the Ruger from the backpack. But not soon enough, as Zara grabs the pickaxe.

He wildly shoots off rounds of .22-caliber bullets, trying to hit his younger cousin. His religiously errant cousin, his sexually immoral cousin according to his reading of their faith, as the maddening Zara has heard too many times. But she was not the weaker sex, ever, as she pins his hand to the floor with the pickaxe. He fires the gun with wild abandon as he howls in pain, Zara once again the victor in their battles as she keeps his gun hand at bay.

Rohan yells in Kurdish that she still is a donkey whore, letting Western kafirs defile her body for pleasure, and then stuns her with a pistol whip to her face. Pulling his hand out of the pickaxe, he flees down the passage, blood flowing out of his wound.

Running blindly down the passage after him, Zara hears more gunshots. More screams, but thank Xwedê, or is it Asherah, that the scream was not Rachel's.

As Zara reaches the end of the passage, she emerges through a monument in a cemetery. Rachel is outside, having grabbed the gun from the bleeding, limping man and emptied the last rounds at a fleeing black van.

Swearing in Hebrew, Rachel sits on the ground. She looks back upon the walls of the Mount of the House, at the modern Golden Gates built by the Ottomans in the 1500s. Sealed, as were the Shushan Gates they passed through.

"They must have found the ancient path down which Jews fled the mount when the Romans attacked," she says to Zara, who ponders why they would want the object fragment and what they could do with it.

"Diversion," yells Zara as she bolts back through the grave monument. "How stupid of us. They wanted us out here."

Still staring at the Golden Gates, Rachel bolts as well. The Torah was clear. The messiah would pass through the open gates. She cannot let that Kurdish woman become the messiah of the Torah. Or worse, the messiah of the Muslims.

What a fool she was, wasting all those bullets on a fleeing van. Now forced to run for her life, for her people's lives, for her great-grandmother, she can barely see the outline of the taller woman down the passageway. She is catching up to her. But will she be in time?

So close, but so far. Rachel makes a flying tackle, just grabbing Zara's ankles as they pass under the arches. No magic sparks. No angels calling from heaven. Just two worn women sprawling on the ground.

"What are you doing?" yells Zara. "Rohan and Zengo were only diversions, so the rest of NiQihs's assassin could get to the engravings and your pendants."

As she tries to get up, Zara's head wobbles about and she faints.

Hearing sounds from down the hallway, Rachel tries to get up. Maybe her crazed Kurd was right. But she wobbles and drops to the ground as well.

≈

Her head hurting, her arms bruised from the battle with Rohan, Zara opens her eyes to the warm and familiar smile of a man who would never let her do wrong. A fatherly smile. That of Jean-Paul.

Next to her, Peter holds Rachel, petting her forehead. Zara closes her eyes in resignation. What she wished for him, what she pushed him for, has happened. Peter is the love of another woman.

CHAPTER 46

MoxWorld Resort Jerusalem
3:30 p.m. GMT+3, March 5, 2023

Neutral territory. Zara had considered Jean-Paul's parlor, but Magali's parlor would allow her a dignified strategic retreat, claiming it is now time for the women to talk. That is if things got weird between her and Peter. Excluding Rachel from this powwow helped on the weirdness front.

But her mother's kidnapping. The package they received. All weirdness needs to be faced head-on. Right now, she needs the most courage she has ever summoned.

"Shouldn't Rachel be here?" asks Peter, his timing so off for Zara's agenda, but so on for everyone else.

The embryonic frown on Zara's face thwarted by a shake of her head and then arrives a peaceful smile. She touches his hand and says, "What I...what we love in you is your fidelity to your family and what you believe is right. And whatever you feel for Rachel I know is because you believe it right."

Eyebrows raised with a neutral line across his lips, Peter peers into Mei's,

Magali's, and then Jean-Paul's eyes for a sign that anyone gets what she is saying.

No help to be found, so Peter says back, "What I feel? I don't feel. I know. As much as you are needed, she too is needed to find the black object and deliver it to the cavern of the blue light. You're just mad she tackled you so you wouldn't become the Messiah of Jerusalem."

That embryonic frown tries to come back, but she flicks it off with a shake of her head. In a higher octave than normal she says, "Is that what she confided in you?"

As he did on the last mission, Jean-Paul steps in as referee in the Peter-Zara sparring match. "You both have valid points of view. But in logical sequence, let us determine what we know collectively and we can bring Rachel in for the sections we deem not as confidential."

He checks in with Zara's eyes, which emote only the slightest quiver at that woman's name. He adds, "As far as the prophets and the Eastern Gate are concerned, only we five know about what happened."

"Six, including Rachel," says Peter, which elicits another quiver out of Zara's eyes.

"We five are who I trust at this time with my mother's life," states Zara. "That includes you, Peter, if you promise not to discuss our meeting with Rachel."

Sitting next to Zara, Magali touches her arm and says, "I think you two need some private time. Perhaps we should adjourn and come back."

Not answering Magali's kind and intuitive offer, Zara plays the ransom request again. Black shaded blurry bodies with digitally encrypted voices created by a random code generator. Likely NiQihs tech avatars if not NiQihs assassins themselves.

Early this morning, Zara received a package containing a headscarf. Her mother's favorite. But it was crusted with bloody hair. Maryam's. MoxWorld Security confirmed the blood's DNA.

The ransom demand? Three women to arrive at a destination to be selected in Crimea. Mei, Zara, and Rachel. The men in black said the MoxWorld team had all the pieces needed to find the cavern that both sides sought. In seventy-two hours, the MoxWorld team should signal where that was and meet there. No MoxWorld Security allowed, or the next piece of Maryam Khatum they will receive will be her head.

Shaking his head, Peter says, "See? Rachel's on our side. They want her as well."

Touching him again, Zara says, "That is so sweet of you. So loyal of you. That is why we all love you." Looking down, she bites her upper lip.

Mei intercedes, saying, "I can understand why they want me there. They need a pregnant woman bearing a child with the ancients' DNA to go in the cave. Why you two?"

Head turned towards Magali, Zara closes her eyes as quivers run down her throat into her chest. The good nurse signals to her faithful Father, Jean-Paul that is, who taps his MoxWrap to bring up the broadcast from an hour ago. The CEO of NiQihs, Mr. Arzu Chagatai, in his first fully visible public appearance. White-haired. Part Asian, part Caucasian. A silvery flash from his teeth. A grey glint from his eyes as he takes his dark glasses off.

"I've seen that man," says Peter, pointing at the man.

"Yes, I have too. He was at your book signing with the doctor," says Zara. "He has been following us."

Mei says, "He was Jia's friend. The owner of the Uyghur guide group."

The sage Father says, "Evidently, he has played us all. He is the head of NiQihs."

The NiQihs CEO Chagatai condemns the Russians for last night's tactical nuclear strikes against a dozen arms factories in China using MoxWorld prototype stealth missiles. His finger wagging at the camera, he challenges the CEO of MoxWorld to show his face. The true Antichrist is this so-called business man who made a puppet of the president of Russia. He has been using the Kurdish woman as his puppet, fostering her prophethood to distract all of us from the true issues they at NiQihs are prepared to help the world solve. If Mr. Murometz does not speak now, NiQihs will fully arm the enemies of worldwide peace with their latest AI technologies. Murometz's so-called surrogate, the woman he passes off as the next messiah, is false, incompetent, and cannot represent Murometz. He gives a seventy-two-hour deadline.

Mei says, "He makes it sound like Alexander didn't get killed."

Zara stares at the ground, her hands shaking. "This is a ruse. They have my mother. How could they think Sasha is still alive?"

Zara rises, goes to the window facing the Mount of Olives. Holding her lower abdomen, she says, "MoxWorld Defense analysts triangulated signals suggesting the Russian and US nuclear submarine fleets are gathering at points ready to launch a full attack on NiQihs-aligned countries. Our analysts give another three days before the assault is ready. The same as the deadline the kidnappers gave for saving my mother. The same as the NiQihs CEO gave for producing Sasha. This debacle has gone far beyond their search for the object."

Her upper body convulses as she puts her hands to her mouth. Magali grabs her, and they run into her bedroom's bathroom.

Zara stands in front of the mirror, staring at a haggard face staring back. She assures Magali she is fine and then dives for the toilet, vomiting once and then again. A warm damp towel in hand, the good nurse cleans up the embattled Kurdish woman.

"I don't know what is wrong with me," says Zara. "I vomited earlier this morning as well."

Flushing the toilet, Magali seats Zara there. She pulls out a white plastic digital device and says for her to urinate on it. A minute later and the nurse nods, showing Zara.

"No. It can't be. These home tests can be wrong," cries Zara.

Brushing her long straight dark hair from Zara's face, Magali says, "It is what I thought. You are four to five weeks pregnant."

"It's only a home test," says Zara, shaking the stick. "Maybe you should run a real lab test."

"No, that would make your results public to anyone who can hack the lab," says Magali. "I assure you this is quite positive, along with the symptoms you have been having. Hypersensitive to smells, fatigue, now morning sickness."

"But you told me I wasn't raped," Zara exclaims, shaking her head.

"I thought perhaps you and Peter had makeup sex after he found you in

Turkey. A much-needed passionate reunion," says Magali.

"No, not with me. But maybe with her," says Zara, staring at her feet. "It must have been those kidnappers. They impregnated me."

Rubbing her crucifix, the former Catholic Sister says, "There may be another answer."

"Maybe you are right," says Zara folded over with her hands around her ankles as she looks up at Magali. "Peter did say he dreamt of sex with me at night. Maybe something did happen between us."

Rubbing Zara's back, Magali says, "I was thinking something more holy. It happened over two thousand years ago to the virgin mother of a woman named Mary."

"Immaculate conception? You must be humoring me."

A sharp exhale through her nose and Magali says, "Mei told me the story of her goddess Jiang. She also had a child from an immaculate conception of sorts."

"Right. Like Mei had an immaculate conception," retorts Zara. "A clean petri dish or however she created a fertilized ovum from herself and Peter's sister."

"I'd like to consult with Jean-Paul about your condition. Your child has profound implications."

"Yes. But not Mei. And certainly not Peter," answers Zara. "And my grandmother. How do I tell her? Pregnant, and I do not know who the father is. I have failed their expectations of me in a bigger way than my last two dozen failures."

Shaking her head, Magali says, "My Church would not condone so, but you have options."

"No, no. I agree with your Church. Human life is sacred. There is a person growing in me. Who is part of me."

Several minutes of on and off crying into the good Sister's blouse and a few towels and Zara finally stands up. She straightens her tunic and re-wraps her headscarf, and they go out to the parlor.

"Where is Peter?" asks Zara.

A pause and Mei answers, "He went to check on Rachel."

"Of course," says Zara, folding her arms in front of her.

Magali signals for Jean-Paul to talk with her in her bedroom. At first, he is reluctant to cross the symbolic threshold only her husband should cross, but ultimately, he does, as her matrimonial hooks in him run deep.

Mei stands up and puts her hands on Zara's upper arms. "It's my fault. I gave Rachel my prototype. Unwanted attention, 'no' button. Wanted attention, 'yes' button. She maxed out on the wanted attention feature with Peter. There's no way he could have resisted the massive onslaught of hormones screaming to mate with Rachel several times over. I thought you didn't want him in that way. If I had known, I wouldn't have given her my alpha test app. I had no idea you were so romantically in love with him."

"Romance has nothing to do with what is happening," says Zara as she goes back to the window to stare upon the Noble Sanctuary, the Temple Mount. She closes her eyes and says, "I was born under a dark cloud. I talk with a dark god. I will die in a dark place."

Nuzzling up to her side and poking her rib, Mei jests, "My, aren't you the bundle of joy? I have a happy app in beta testing. I can do your hair up with the right metallic strands for that app."

Turning for the parlor suite door, Zara says, "No, I must find what's left of my family. My Roza. I need to talk with her."

A knock on the parlor suite door and in comes Peter, whose eyes try to make contact with Zara's. She stops, her lips move as if to say something, but she puts her head down.

"Did I just miss something?" says Peter as he reenters Magali's parlor room. "I just tried to find Rachel, and she's gone."

"Of course," says Zara satirically with her arms folding in front of her. "She is conspiring with that evil doctor friend of yours. Or with the Mossad to protect Jerusalem from the conquering Muslim messiah."

As Peter's eyes simply gaze down at her feet, Zara puts her hands around his arms, saying, "I'm sorry, Peter. I lashed out at you. I should respect you more than that."

Silence.

With the nicest smile she can muster given all that has happened today and last night, she says, "When I am gone, could you find a suitable set of parents to raise my lambs? I don't mind if they live in Jerusalem."

Not smiling back at first, he hesitates, then with his cheeks pulling back on his mouth, he says, "I'm afraid they are not city lambs. They're more and more like dogs who need space to run and play."

Mei perks up the same as a canine would, asking, "Dogs? When did you find these lambs?"

"I have been meaning to talk with you about them," says Zara. "I found them in a crate with your BioGenetics unit logo up in the mountains around Siirt."

Nodding as her eyes circle towards the ceiling and then around, Mei says, "They were a eugenics prototype model that went missing. I had sent them to Jean-Paul, who was exploring an angle in the Crimea."

The mother in Zara emerges as she asks, "What did you do to them? Why do they act like dogs?"

Coming back from Magali's sacred bedroom, Jean-Paul interjects, "That is what I was doing in Çatalhöyük. I found the remains of two foxes there near traces of an object. The oral legends speak of a mother goddess and her two foxes. Mei came up with the idea of hybridizing their DNA with that of an ewe to disguise the project. We thought possibly these lambs could track their master. The mother goddess."

The good Father watches his Chinese protégée punching away on her MoxWrap. He asks, "What do you think, Mei? Can they help us?"

Turning to their foster mother, Mei asks Zara, "Can I send a MoxWorld Security team to get them?"

"Treat them nicely," says Zara.

"I'll need a few days with them to train them for the mother goddess's scent," says Mei.

Now it's Peter's turn to have his ears pop up like a dog's. "You mean you have the scent of a mother goddess?"

The member of the Pontifical Commission for Sacred Archaeology, Jean-Paul, says, "We found the two foxes buried next to a hut and the skeleton of a giant. Likely one of the reindeer giants from your family's oral tradition. In the hut were the remains of women's clothing. From what we could tell from the same woman. We are making a gigantic leap of faith that she was the mother goddess, those were her foxes, and she had left her clothes in that hut."

Smiling away, Peter says, "Like you made a gigantic leap of faith about me several months ago. I know those two frisky lambs pretty well. If Zara is related to the mother goddess, then that's why they adore her so much."

Getting up, Mei says, "Done. I will take a MoxSecurity team and a MoxHeliJet to Siirt, get those frisky lamb dogs, and take them up to Crimea. I will meet you all there."

As Mei leaves the room, Peter approaches Zara. "We need Rachel and her pendants, no matter whom you think she is working for. The lambs play one role, the pendants another."

At first staring beyond him, then at him, Zara says, "Then the end is near. What we both are destined to do is about to come."

With a deadpan expression, he stares into her eyes, shaking his head back and forth. "Don't you go on and on again about dying to save us. I will be there to save you once again from having to die to save everyone else."

Zara touches Peter again. His hands taken in hers, she finally says, "I know these past several months have been hard on you. I have been hard on you. I still care about you. I would be honored if you invite me to your wedding."

"Wow," exclaims Peter, finally cracking a smile. "That must have been some tackle Rachel hit you with. Of course, you're invited to our wedding. Jean-Paul is ready to marry us anytime you say so."

A smile in return, she says, "You are sweet. But another needs you now."

No smile now as Peter says, "You keep pushing me away. Did Mei put her male-zapping app into your MoxWrap? I don't like being made into unwanted attention when it comes to you."

Touching his chest, Zara says, "Wherever Rachel is at this moment, she will need you when she returns."

At the bedside of her safta raba, she rubs her aged bluish hands. Her Ariella is incoherent. Drifting in and out, mumbling with her lips, but nothing is heard.

Her labored breathing barely pulls the oxygen in through her nasal cannula.

If only that Kurdish woman would have come here to cure her Ariella. If only Asherah had granted her the ability to heal the same as she did to the Kurdish woman. If only. If only.

If only she had seen her father before they took him. To tell him how much she loved him once more. He left a 3-D hologram message. One so different from any before. He was to go to see "them" to make amends for his daughter's failures. Whatever happened, he loved her, and she should follow her heart. Not her headstrong head. What her Asherah says, she should follow. If only she knew what he meant.

Her life essence drained by the conflicting interests that have swamped her life, Rachel squats down in a corner of the room, curled head to knees. The same position she assumed when, after her first menses, Ariella first told her about Asherah and the family obligation to find her. And now she must find someone named Qualqi, whom only the son of the man her father killed can help her find.

Now alone with her safta raba and for the third time this morning, her eyes shed their grief in free-flowing droplets down her cheek along her nose. This time all over her safta raba's hands. She leans up to the aged woman's face. Kisses her on her blue lips. Her skin pallid and cold. Holding both the ancient stones to her great-grandmother's lips, Rachel says, "I will not fail you. I have both stones. I will find her."

"I know you will. You must come to me."

Rachel blinks and blinks again. Ariella's lips did not move. Who was talking? It was a woman. She looks around and no one.

Several seconds later, a different female voice from the door behind Rachel says, "We gave her the drugs we promised, but not everyone responds as predicted."

Rachel hides the stones in her blouse, tucking them in her bra to conceal them even more. She turns to see the doctor. "You are not welcome here. She is dying. Have respect for her. Only her family should be here."

Coming into the ward, the doctor says, "Remember, you gave me permission to be her doctor. I mobilized all the medical resources at my disposal. I fulfilled my side of the deal. I expect you to fulfill your side."

Shaking her head, Rachel says, "It was not a good deal. My safta raba is even nearer death. Your drugs hastened her demise."

Pointing to a ward across the hallway, Dr. Fontaine says, "Let's not discuss this here."

Tanned calves up on black stilettoes with rhinestone accents, the not-so-dowdy doctor leads her to an empty room. She closes and locks the door after Rachel enters.

Pulling out a vial from a cold pack, the doctor says, "We secured semen from an afflicted man. His family tree shows a high percentage of affliction. Backside down on the bed and legs up like you do for your ob-gyn."

Rachel surveys the table next to the bed. One of those devices of torture, a speculum. Icy cold for sure. And a syringe with a long Teflon tube attached to painfully poke at the tender cervix, finding the elusive passage into the uterus.

Hold her lower abdomen, Rachel says, "You are too late. Peter made love with me. Several times already. I say love because a man like him does not have sex. Only make love."

A little snort through her nose and Dr. Beverly, the woman who snuggled up to her dear editor for many a late night, says, "That sounds like something that odd man would say to a woman. Then again, you could have read that in his book. It doesn't hurt to have another dose from another man. Females of all species are programmed to seek as many sources of sperm as they can. It enhances the likelihood of the fittest child."

Head shaking, Rachel goes to the door and unlocks it. "I have done my part. I will do no more to my body. You don't own my body, nor my soul."

Beverly puts her hand on the door and with a stern face says, "When the time comes, remember whose side you're on. We sent proof of life to your friends at MoxWorld, and a ransom for the Kurdish woman's precious mother. Your Chinese friend, your Kurdish friend, and you are required to meet us in less than three days. You will know when it's time for you to take the kill shot at Murometz's named successor, Khatum, and even Gollinger, if needed. If you are truly pregnant, as you claim, then you can retrieve what we need from the caverns. But if you aren't, I am told you will have sealed your father's fate. Like the Kurdish woman's mother's fate is in her hands, your father's is in yours."

The Israeli professor pulls the door open and says, "I will do what is needed when the time comes."

Back at her Ariella's side, Rachel spots a little rose showing through the blue of her safta raba's face. To her shock, cold aged hands grab hers. Her eyes still closed, Ariella says, "I saw her. She says you must choose."

Rubbing her great-grandmother's hand, Rachel says, "I know you saw her. But that was decades ago. I will carry out your wishes."

"No, I just saw her."

"I know, Safta Raba. And you will see Saba Raba as well soon," says a humoring Rachel.

"She is waiting for you," says Ariella. "She has waited so long for you."

"Yes. Yes, of course. And she will be with you too."

The nonagenarian says, "She says a moment will come where you need to choose. Who lives in this world. Who must pass on to the next. Murometz must pass on to the next. Until then, you need to live your life for what you want. You will have the moment of choice. Choose wisely. From the heart. Not from the head. Not from pain."

With a labored breath, her eyes still closed, the aged woman says, "I love you, my nina."

"I love you too, Safta Raba."

One last exhale as Rachel cries over her mentor, her inspiration, her reason for being. But the last breath is short. And then nothing.

"No, no. Please do not leave me," cries Rachel.

But her cries are met only by the silence.

"We can make your brother's old room the nursery," says an elated Roza as they sit outside a ward in Jerusalem General Hospital.

But the tears still fall from her granddaughter's eyes, for which this maternity discussion is not a joyful one.

For moments before in that ward room, Zara cried and cried upon the little girl's body and hands. Aysun, the sister of the Turkish president's wife, stood by Zara as she held Aysun's granddaughter's little hand. The tragic victim of a rare orphan disease. The long and enduring economic crisis in Turkey meant even relatives of the president could not access exotic and rare treatment, for the multinational pharmaceutical companies feared the embattled Turkish lira and lines of credit to be worth next to nil.

But Zara did not cry for that little girl. She cried for the thought she carries a human life. Her child. And she is soon to die, and her child will never know the joys of breathing air. The joys of hiking in mountains. The joys of playing with her lambs.

Her grandmother was so understanding of her new condition. If only she could grow to be as understanding as her Maryam has been. If only she could save her mother from NiQihs.

If she were to live, Zara knows she would love her own child, the embryo within, as much as Maryam did her. But fate is so cruel. She will go to her death to save her mother, to save her grandmother, to save the world. But the voice never said, never forewarned, she would take another unborn life to his or her death.

Nurses come out of the little girl's room in a commotion. Doctors come over en masse. They say the little girl's vital signs are on an upward trend. She is miraculously recovering.

Aysun, the joyous grandmother, comes out. Hugs Zara and says, "What you have done is a grand gesture to my family. I hope that my brother-in-law will take your sincerity into account in his plans for our country and your people. I can only help by speaking out about the miracle that has happened here before my eyes."

Turning to Roza, Aysun says, "I will go to speak with the press outside the hospital. You are people of the Prophet, may peace be upon him. I am sure now."

Zara hugs her grandmother, for one thing is going right in her life. Over her shoulder, she spies Peter sitting down in the hallway.

Peeking at what Zara sees, Roza says, "He's been down there all the time you have been with the child. I must say this. He is everything your father, Maryam's Nawdar, was to her. They are alike. Your child will need a father even if he is not your child's biological parent."

Her lips puckered in between her teeth, Zara holds back the welling-up emotions, the welling-up tears. She says, "But I pushed him away into another woman's bed. I am so ashamed. Maybe everyone is right. My mind is still traumatized. I have never been so weak, so feeble, since I came in contact with that object."

Smiling at her daughter's daughter, Roza affirms, "That girl's miraculous recovery is a product of your so-called traumatized mind. I understand from your Chinese friend that those tears from your feebleness may be what is helping these people have miraculous recoveries."

Roza gives her a big grandmotherly hug and adds a more grandmotherly point. "Peter, he does not act like a man who is sleeping in another woman's bed. He is still yours."

"I miss Mama."

"I do too," replies Roza. "What did you always tell your mother when she was blue, depressed?"

Zara pauses and then recites part of Maryam's favorite poem from the Sufi theologian Rūmī.

A moment of happiness,
You and I sitting on the verandah,
Apparently two, but one in soul, you and I.

Hugging her again, Roza says, "You were always there for her, my little Zara."

"As you have been always there for me," says Zara, hugging her grandmother back.

"If she were here, your mother would tell you that one day she will no longer be with her daughter and would hope to be with her Nawdar," says Roza, who pulls back and gazes into her granddaughter's eyes. "But she would lament that you will be alone. You will need your Nawdar."

Zara glances down. And then at Peter.

Before she can go to Peter, Roza points down the hallway, yelling that the press is ready for the prophetess.

As Zara walks down the hallway with her grandmother in hand, Peter does not look up at them. He plays with a virtual 3-D animation of Zara's lambs.

Smiling at what the man is doing—so much like what her little brother would have been doing, so much like Peter—she reaches for his hands and pets them. He rises and walks out with them.

Thousands pack the streets outside the hospital. Those wanting their Islamic prophetess to lead Muslims back to the age of greatness. Those who fear what she means for Israeli rule of Jerusalem. Those who believe she is the savior for all sorts of faiths. And those who most vocally call her a false prophet.

Peter scans the crowds. Israeli security forces are out en masse with nonlethal crowd management tools, and some with lethal weapons. One hopes nothing will happen, Peter wishes.

Oddly enough, there are dozens of people holding a few dozen balloons each. It must be a festival out there, Peter thinks optimistically.

Zara takes her place in front as MoxWorld micro-drone microphones fly in four different positions around her, Roza to one side and to the other, the sister-in-law of the president of Turkey, who has just finished speaking. Turkish security, MoxWorld Security, and Israeli police surround them, with Peter mixed in between.

Adjusting her headscarf, Zara talks of the miracles that everyone can bring into this world by joining together, insisting on peaceful collaboration between nations, people. Islamophobic catcalls come from the crowd. In other countries, Zara would conclude these are signs of bias, of intolerance, but here she realizes they might be authentic voices of fear based on past and future violent attacks.

She pauses and then says, "I hear you. Violence only begets violence."

In a move that takes the cameramen by surprise, she takes off her headscarf and waves it in the air. "I stand here not as a Muslim, not as a Sufi like my grandmother beside me, but as a human being. Judge me not by what I wear, by what I look like, by what faith you believe me to have."

Waving a MoxWorld micro-drone over, she attaches her scarf, and it flies away, waving in the winds above the crowd. She says, "But judge me by what my heart and soul are saying to you. In this world, there is a true evil that is bringing the great nations together in an irrational contest for world domination. They think I am at the center of this. I am not. But the people who support the leaders of these countries are."

Her hands out, palms facing up, gesturing around to the crowds, she adds, "You, every single one of you, have a voice and can speak up. Your numbers will induce your leaders to seek peaceful resolutions. Love the person next to you. Shake their hand. Say something positive about them. Give them a hug."

The crowds begin to jostle. No matter her message, there are those who seek discord in the crowd as small fights break out. Peter scans the motion in the masses. Suddenly, the balloons are released simultaneously. This is not accidental nor coincidental.

As Zara continues to implore the crowds to be peaceful, the chants of false prophet grow louder. Peter moves to Zara's side, but she waves him off. He spots mini-drones behind the balloons. Several dozen with battery packs, unlike the MoxWorld micro-drones, which operate on solar power. Each of the balloons also carries a device of some sort.

He taps the MoxWorld Security chief, pointing out the issues, and his team fires at the drones, but the balloon devices confound their AI tracking systems. As balloons explode and drones flame, falling to earth, the crowd panics, running in all directions, and the false prophet chants continue to get louder. More than a half dozen drones break through.

As if struck by lightning bolt after lightning bolt, Zara's body suddenly jerks backward again and again. Peter has seen this before. She is being bombarded by sonic punches from the mini-drones and she falls down. Roza sees what is happening and puts her body in front of her granddaughter, only to be pulverized by the sonic punches.

Seeing Roza going limp and Zara now exposed, Peter covers her with his body. The pain. He has but micro-moments to do something different or face Roza's fate. He dials his MoxWrap up to maximum and points his sonic punches at the drones.

Luckily, he edited a paper on how to neutralize sonic waves as the pulses against his body are no more dangerous than a mean angry crowd in the NYC subway after the Yankees have lost.

MoxWorld Security neutralizes the remaining mini-drones and begins haggling with the Israeli security team over who's liable for this disaster on worldwide media.

Peter pulls up Roza, whose body is nearly formless, her bones crushed. He tries to assist Zara, but she pushes him away as she cries over Roza.

With her last breath, Roza whispers to Zara, "Save your mother. Marry him. Raise child with him." And her eyes glaze over.

The dark cloud over Zara has just gotten darker.

CHAPTER 47

Walking with a friend in the dark is better than walking alone in the light.
—Helen Keller

Ancient Crimea
9523 BCE

The howling of my beloved foxes outside the cavern entrance belies their fear of being left alone. Of facing the cruelness of the world, which originated from this side of the big black lake.

Comforted only by the warmth emanating into the cavern from the opening of the blue-lit chamber ten paces behind the elder woman who has challenged her, Tallia stares into the hue of the light. A blue of the most serene morning sky mingled with that of the most harmonious evening glow. In the air, the smell of peace. The smell of the silence before dawn. The smell of tens of tens of people in prayer.

At her feet lies the body of her love, her other half, her beloved Nirra, his near-fatal wounds sustained as he tried to save her from being stoned. Her remorse and his salvation are why she has sought this mystical, legendary cavern of the blue light. Her muscles are still taut from a moon cycle of carrying her husband across the mountains to the edge of the big black lake, then another several days paddling across that lake, following the tail of the bird star as described by her grandfather, to reach the lands of her grandmother. Nanshe, the great matriarch of her family and her people.

Days and days ago, Tallia carried her beloved giant to an area a half-day death march away—more like a death climb—from the edge of the big black lake. Here the black stones Voxen gave her glowed with the most intensity. The sands were piled in mountain high mounds all around as if a divine being had scooped up the bottom of the big black lake and dropped it here.

At sunrise this morning, she found one dune had an opening. Tallia tried to bring Nirra in with her, but he experienced such great pains that she left him outside the opening. Holding the blue-aura-surrounded stones in front of her, she followed their flickers as she felt her way down the passageway.

And then she met them. Women. All covered like she, head to ankles. These are the women who were sent into this chamber of the blue light as sacrificial protectors of the giants from those who guarded that caustic light. They found the reindeer giant men could not enter for pain of death. And they have remained in safety ever since.

The giants were afraid of this chamber, so they built this pyramid around the blue stone to protect themselves. But they wanted it preserved. They could tolerate dusty blue bits of the stone, which the leaders would eat to ensure their vitality, their personal strength, their longevity. The ancients said the blue stone would help them rule the world. Thus, as these women explained, they would bring out pinches of dust in a small pouch for a moon cycle's worth of food.

The women told of the Great Flood. The giants sealed the entrance to the pyramid, for this place is sacred to them. For unknown reasons, they did not want it destroyed. After much time passed, the women inside dug their way out to discover that the giants had vanished. God had answered their prayers.

After they quiz Tallia who she is and why she has come, they retreat into the labyrinths of the cavern. Moments later, an older woman appears. Dressed in a long beige robe covering her body, neck to ankles, head covered by a pure white headscarf, the aged woman gazes at Tallia with eyes that bespeak the wisdom of the ancients.

Her name is Qualqi, and she touches her forehead and says that Tallia is the granddaughter of the young one, little Nanshe.

Eyes wide open, mouth too, Tallia is unsure what to say. A bellowing behemoth moan of her beloved giant outside reminds her of her sole mission here, so she explains that her grandmother Nanshe discovered a black object and heard the voice that has guided her grandmother, her aunts, and her ever since.

Smiling as Nanshe would have, Qualqi explains that the blue light is a uniting force, an energizing force. She then asks if the voice is good or bad. Tallia defends the voice and her family, and Qualqi asks, if it is good, why then all the violence that has killed your family?

Tallia is stymied. Says she only knows one thing at the moment. Her love for Nirra. She describes what happened as she tried to save her youngest daughter and how her Nirra, wracked with guilt over his giant past, sacrificed himself to save her. Tallia talks of the voice and forgiveness. Qualqi raises again the issue of the voice as an evil influence.

Tallia says the giant Voxen and his human wife Kezina believed this place could permanently heal Nirra. She would do anything for him. Anything.

In deep reflection, Qualqi peers into the eyes of Tallia. Her fingers probe the front, then the back of Tallia's neck. Then she gives to her a pouch and says sprinkle this on the tongue of the one you love so much. This will help him survive the trip into the caverns.

Outside, next to her ailing Nirra, Tallia looks up to the night sky. To the tail of the bird star, of which her grandfather had spoken so often. Should she run away as his legend had said? Maybe this pouch of dust will heal her beloved. She sprinkles some on his dry tongue and then gives him her water pouch to swallow the glowing blue specks.

Waiting for a sign that the dust provides some curative effect, she only is met with more disillusionment. He is no better. And she cries. And cries until her laments soak his face. His eyes open and he says, it is time. Let us face my end together.

Signaling for her foxes to stay at the entrance, Tallia helps her monstrous man up and with his arm around her shoulders, she walks him into the entrance to the domain of the women of the blue dust.

As a young woman guides her through the multitudes of paths through compacted sand tunnels, they pass through a stone block doorway. The blocks are massive. As large as and larger than those her Aunt Ki and Uncle An erected at the First Temple.

Minutes inside the stone doorway, the young woman brings her to a large, cavernous chamber. At the back is another doorway from which an eerie blue glow emanates and from where Qualqi enters. Tallia gently lowers her giant to the floor, both exhausted from the journey. Not only the one to get to these pyramids, but the one from outside.

"My dear Tallia," the older woman says. "You have two choices. Either your man dies here in your arms or we can heal him. But he must leave you forever to live out his life in the outer world."

Salten drops roll down her cheek, wetting her own weatherworn grey headscarf as Tallia pleads, "But I was only told that my Nirra could be saved if I brought him here. Not that I could never see him again."

The aged woman called Qualqi sighs and places her hand atop Tallia's head. "The blue light transcends us all. It provides the very life we treasure. It provides the life of the giant you so treasure. And yet it requires of us a delicate balance. For only women of great purity can stay near the blue light and fulfill its mission here in this world. If one of us leaves this cavern, another woman of great purity must replace her. In time, if you give your faith, your obedience to the ways of the blue light, you too will be able to heal others. But your giant will have long since died."

Tallia crumples to the floor atop her beloved Nirra. Eyes closed, she begs of the voice to answer her, to answer her questions. *Who are you? Is my god, the voice of Nanshe, the voice of the object, the same as this woman's god? Do I abandon all that I know to be true, all that has guided me to this chamber, to follow a faith, a concept, or perhaps only the mere whim of the aged woman who stands in front of me?*

Raising her head, Tallia's gaze follows the younger woman who guided her here. She reenters the cavernous chamber from the room of the blue light and stands beside the elder Qualqi, who says, "My daughter, Raqli, has been faithful to the light. Since her birth here, her devoted obedience to the light has given her the ability to heal, to bring life to the dead. But for her to heal your husband, she must leave with him to the outside world. It is now her time to spread the wisdom of the light and your time to devote yourself to the light. As I said, once a woman of purity enters these caverns, she can only leave if another woman of purity replaces her. If Raqli leaves to heal your husband, you must stay to replace her."

Nirra's eyes slowly open as he emits a low groan, more akin to a growl. "I live only to be with you, for only you have been family to me. After all that I have done, all my evils I have atoned for, we cannot be separated. You are the only one who loves me for who I am, in spite of being a giant. What is life outside without you? If I live only a day longer, it will be all worthwhile only if I can do so still in your arms. Let us leave here and you can rejoin your daughter Illyana after I die."

Tallia says to Qualqi, "I was told that in the cavern of blue light my husband could be saved. Have I come this far only to be told that to be saved we must never see each other again? That I can never see my family again?"

The elder woman opens up her pure white headscarf to expose her smile and calmly replies, "I did not say never. Time is a fluid thing. Life is not what you think.

"Since the dawn of the age of the reindeer warrior giants, I have guarded this sanctuary," says Qualqi. "A haven for women of purity of the heart, of the soul. Those with the blood, the essence of your Nirra, giant men, can survive but a short time in here, and only with the aid of the blue dust. For them, the blue light shortens their existence here in this time. Their body quickens to death."

Tallia lifts her monstrous man with the strength, both physical and spiritual, that she has gained bringing him here. She says to Nirra, "I will never leave you. Even if we are not of the same blood, we are still family."

Qualqi smiles serenely and asks, "And is that what Illyana told Nanshe to tell you? To leave the light? To leave the force that could bring peace to your lands?"

Eyes open wide as she supports the massive body of her beloved, Tallia utters, "But how? I never told you my great-aunt's name."

"There is someone here who knows your Nanshe," replies Qualqi. "She taught your Nanshe. Taught your grandfather. Who knows of the legend of the tail of the bird star your grandfather taught you. And it is time for you to know what the woman's side of that story is and will be. What would Nanshe tell you to do?"

Tallia pulls her tattered headscarf tighter around her head and neck. "Nanshe taught us to respect the words of the voice. The wisdom she brought to all of her children from the black object. And the voice has guided our family, our people through adversity to find peace."

The elder woman points into the blackness towards the cavern entrance. "You must make a choice. There lies the darkness." She now points into the blue light chamber. "There lies the light. You must follow the light. We will all return one day to the blue light."

"But…but the voice of the black object, the voice of my grandmother's god, said that if I forgive, love would come back into our lives. And now I am to leave that love because I have come here not knowing what the consequences would be? How can the voice not be one of goodness? Not one of a god who cares for us? How could my only choice be to leave my Nirra?"

"My dear Tallia. Your faith has brought you this far. Your openness and tolerance to forgive a giant for all his past aggressions and transgressions. To bring love into his and your hearts shows your soul's purity. But now that you have returned to the blue light that brings us true peace, that promises our future, that illuminates our path forward, you must ask if your Nanshe's voice is not that of darkness. If this voice of the black object you worship is not that of despair. Think about what has happened to your family and around your world since your grandmother found that black object? Death, violence, despair. Am I not correct?"

Qualqi approaches the bewildered Tallia and touches her temple, then her abdomen. "If you will not stay here to fulfill your soul, then do so for your unborn daughter."

Mouth agape, Tallia's head turns upwards towards the eyes of her giant as she shakes her head ever so slightly. "It is not possible for me to bear a child. It has been many sun cycles since I have had the moon cycle bleeds."

The elder hand reaches down to touch the man who this young woman so loves. "Nirra. I sense your love of Tallia. I sense your forgiveness of yourself. You are unlike the giants who chased us into this sanctuary. If you love someone, you will do anything for them. If not for Tallia, then for her new daughter, please go with my daughter Raqli and be healed. Then the two of you must spread the word of the light and heal the world's giants to become like you."

Tallia hugs her giant and says, "That is what Nanshe said. If you love someone, you will do anything for them. As I have done to bring you here to save your life."

A voice comes from the chamber of the blue light, from a woman covered in a royal-blue headscarf over a floor-length black dress, her face not visible through the slit of the headscarf covering her face. "And that is what I taught Nanshe. If you truly love someone, you will do anything to save them."

She glides over to Tallia and rolls down her headscarf to reveal herself.

Tallia gasps. The face. The eyes. Her aunts and uncle have the same. Not that of Nanshe. But of…

"But you are dead," exclaims Tallia.

"What is death but a doorway to what is next? The backdoor is the way to the truth," says the woman, pointing to the blue light behind her. "If I am who you think I am, then would you believe we should be faithful to the blue light?"

Tallia touches this woman's nose, her cheeks, her ears. "It is you," she cries.

She turns to hug her Nirra. "My love, my savior. If you love me, if you love our unborn daughter, you must go and live in the outside world. Do you know who she is? Spread the world about a greater purpose and a greater light. Tell my remaining daughter that she should come and seek out the blue light, for I and her new sister will await her here."

CHAPTER 48

And Abraham stretched forth his hand and took the knife, to slaughter his son.
Tanakh Bereishit—Genesis—22:10

Jerusalem
7:00 p.m. GMT+3, March 5, 2023

Tears over her grandmother's body all the way to the hospital as she refused to be transported in a separate ambulance despite her own wounds—in part because she hoped the miracles that her tears brought for others near death would save her grandmother; in part because, with her mother kidnapped and maybe dead, she realizes how alone she really is. How truly lonely she is. Worse, she shames herself for pretending to be like Rab'ia. A pretense that has led to everyone in her family being dead or about to die. Including the giant biological father in her life.

A tenuous night as the doctors forced her to be treated and recover. Only at Magali's insistence did Zara allow the nurses to insert an IV line into her. Moments after the fluid of artificial peace flowed into her veins, she lost consciousness, her body needing the rest to recover, her mind needing to be sedated before she ripped herself apart from the inside out.

The next day, she refused to follow the doctor's instructions to stay in the recovery ward for more than the morning. For Roza's tradition called for a female family member to wash her body, to wrap her body, to cover her body with her prayer rug. As Maryam remained captive, or worse, dead, Xwedê's will have left no other members of Roza's family who could ensure her passage to the next world according to her traditions. Anatolians buried their loved ones as quickly as possible after their death. So, Zara demanded that they bury Roza in Jerusalem by that evening.

At the burial scheduled late that afternoon, she wanted no one other than herself to be near Roza. Yes, MoxWorld Security came en masse, as did the Israeli police. But no media, no onlookers. Only Magali, Jean-Paul, Mei, and Peter as distant observers.

After thanking Magali, Jean-Paul, and Mei for their kind wishes, Zara, dressed entirely in black from head to toe, walks towards Peter. He had waited quietly and patiently, as always, outside Zara's recovery room. But she wanted to talk to no one and had refused to engage with him.

She stops in front of Peter. There passes a long moment of silence as they both gaze at each other's feet. So little to be said, or so many things left unsaid?

He breaks the silence, saying, "I am so sorry. I…I tried my best."

More silence. Her lips moving. Her lips saying. Her vocal cords ready to say. But nothing. Only her eyes try to emote what her lips will not speak, going from dilated to pinpoint iris to a stormy darkness.

His arms reach out for the hug she always loved. She shakes her head. His fingers wiggle, saying come on. But no. She shakes her head.

Finally, words from her. "She left me. I cannot believe she left me. And it was my vanity that stopped me from seeing what would happen. And my mother is missing. I am alone."

"No, no. You are not alone. Your mother is alive," he says. "You must have faith."

Pulling off her black headscarf, she shakes her head. Her hair free and uncombed, waving about, she says, "Not my mother, but She. Who am I fooling trying to follow Her? I followed the faith of my family and they are nearly all dead." She runs her finger through her freely waving dark hair, bringing it across her shoulder over her chest.

For as she had lain in her recovery bed, she had reflected upon her life.

One of many resolutions she made—she had no more emotional room for anything. Even with this man who fate, who the voice, who someone has left as the only one who tries with his arms, his eyes, to tell her about love.

As Peter patiently waits for her next words, Zara peeks into his eyes for a furtive moment, only to leave to take care of Roza's transport.

Standing at Roza's final destination in a foreign land, she owes him at least an expression of her gratitude for what he did. She kisses his cheek. The last kiss ever. For it is not about him anymore. She knows it is about her. And she leaves him standing there with no other word.

Outside the cemetery, the MoxWorld Security chief standing slightly behind Zara gives her the bad news. They cannot find any evidence of her mother's location. But another proof of life package has arrived—her freshly severed left pinkie.

Her head shaking, her face distorts, her eyes darken, and then she yells, "Do you know who I am? I am not just the boss of all of MoxWorld. I am the daughter of a warrior giant. I am a descendant of the meanest, the most violent, the most violative creatures God put on this earth. You and all those in MoxSecurity should be fearful of your lives, your families' lives, for defying my command to find her at all costs."

That man, a good six foot eight tall, shrank five and a half feet in a matter of a second and a half. As if squeaking like a mouse, he yammers away into his MoxWrap.

Magali offers to head back with Zara in her Presidential Security MoxMover. The good nurse, the good Sister, the good friend, convinces the tall woman she should return to MoxWorld Resorts instead of the hospital. Magali reminds Zara she had only sixteen hours in the recovery ward herself and needed rest. And so, with the help of a little sedation, Magali puts Zara to sleep in her comfortable MoxWorld Resort presidential suite.

Light beams leak through a gap in the curtains, hitting her heavy eyelids. Groggy eyes, groggy head, bloated bladder. She is becoming like her BFF Peri. She rolls back the super-fluffy blankets, rolls out of her super-king-sized bed, and strolls into her super-luxurious bathroom, bumping into at least a half a dozen objects on the way over.

Large enough to host a whole family back in her village the bathroom features a comfy couch after the entrance door, which beckons her to come and visit the world of drug-induced peace. As she washes her hands, gazing at the distraught stranger peering back at her in the mirror, she sees the reflection of a clock. Time for sunrise prayer. The couch will have to wait. As she was raised to do, she dutifully washes each body part thrice.

She exits the bathroom, then turns and eyes the couch again. What did prayers do for her family? What did being obedient and subservient to the voice bring? Was Xwedê angry with her and her family for her subservience to a woman's voice? Could not Peter have saved her Roza instead of her? Could he not see that Roza deserved life more than she?

Stumbling her way back into her bedroom, which itself is the size of an average house in her village, she stops by the dresser, on which her headscarves mysteriously lay in a perfect row for her choosing. She will never wear one again. Ever. Her penance. Her Roza taught her how to wear them for her modesty. Her self-respect. And she has none now. Self-respect, that is. So no more scarves.

Still sleepy-eyed, she turns and steps on her prayer mat. It was not there before. Or was it? She cannot remember for sure. No, it could not have been. She folded it up before she left for the hospital to pray for that little girl. And the mat is already in position, facing towards Mecca. How?

So glad no one gave her this drug Magali had ordered when she was in battle, she debates kneeling on the rug. For every day after she had shot her cousin Rona in the head, she prayed several times a day. In penance? To cleanse her soul?

And suddenly, she senses him. Her head bolts up, and she yells, "What are you doing here? Get out of here. Do you not respect a woman's need to mourn?"

On her bed sits Peter. "And a good morning to you too, Zara. No 'thank you, kind soul' for laying out your prayer mat exactly on time?"

She stands at arm's length, towering over him, and screams, "I have lost my grandmother. I lost both my fathers. I am going to lose my mother. What more has to happen to me so you leave me alone? There is no Shiva in my faith. Only a period of mourning which unmarried non-mahram men should be avoided. And that means you."

Silence as he sits motionless on the edge of her bed, his eyes locked with hers. Pupils dialing down to pinpoints, Zara's head shakes as her nostrils flare. His head is perfectly still, his breath completely measured through his nose.

Then he says, "If you were a widow, then I should not be here. If you were to ask Roza, if you were to ask your mother, I am their family too."

"Go," she demands, pointing to the door.

"No," he replies with a slight twist of his head to one side, still eyeing her back.

Her fists scrunching in front of her, she says, "I will force you out of here. I deserve my time to grieve. You have no place here."

He stands up. In a calm voice, he says, "No."

"Then I will call the MoxWorld Security head and he will get you out," she says.

"He's on my side. He dialed up my MoxWrap's sonic punch with an alpha test module so I could defend you in here."

Her jaw quivering, her head shaking, her irises now blotted out by large black discs, she points again to the door and yells, "Just go. Go ffffu…go stick your… just go back to her. To that Israeli woman. I do not need you."

"No," he says once more, this time a little more forcefully. "You keep trying to drive me away. You keep saying I'm better off with this woman, that woman, any woman other than you."

Turning away from him, she is silent at first and then says, "I cannot love you the way you want me to love you."

"The way you thought Mei would? The way you thought Rachel would?" Peter fires back, not acknowledging her softened tone.

"She said you were the best lover she ever had. She found ecstasy as no other had brought her." She turns fully around with her dark obsidian eyes locked on his and says, "And you made her see Asherah."

Not flinching, not losing contact with her eyes, he says, "And you believe her? What were you two doing? Having the equivalent of boy's locker room boasting?"

"She is probably fuming jealous in her bed right now, wondering why you are not next to her," says Zara with a neutral affect. "She is probably thinking about how you are doing to me what she thought you had committed only for her. She is probably lusting for your…your…"

He turns away from her. Insensitive? Or the plotting editor? He says, "For months now, I thought your rejections came from your disdain of me. That I wasn't good enough for you. That I didn't have prowess, the muscles, the might of your past lovers. That I couldn't protect as well as they would, could, should. And then I remembered how my father felt. He killed himself because he felt the whole world felt the same about him. That he was an abject failure."

His hands now in hard balls, indomitable fists, he says, "I am not a failure." He turns around, eye to eye with her once again, and states, "And if I'm not a failure, then you couldn't be pushing me away because I'm too much of a failure to be with you."

Her eyes break from his as she stares at the prayer mat between them. Her breath quickens as her nostrils remained flared. Her shoulders strain as she flexes her chest muscles.

"Then it dawned on me," he says. "Pushing men away. Pushing me away. Saying you're celibate to emulate your Saint Rab'ia. These actions of self-denial are because you feel you've failed. Because you feel all the tragic events around you, all the deaths all around, are because you haven't lived up to Xwedê's expectations of you. And after you heard the voice, things got worse. You couldn't live up to Her. Pushing me away is only one symptom. The choices you've made haven't been clouded by a dark god, by a dark voice, but by your deepest wish to end it all."

Now it is her turn to say, "No. No." Shaking her finger at him, she says, "Do you not remember what I shared with you when we bonded? You saw my darkest secrets. My deepest pains. Is that not enough for you? Have I not suffered enough for you?"

Taking a wider stance, arms crossed in front of him, he replies, "You showed me what you wanted me to see. Why I should concede to your wishes?

Why I should be conciliatory to your self-deprecation? You think you've recovered from what happened to your cousins. The darkest act in your soul. Your cold-blooded shooting Rona between her eyes to keep her from being captured again. Your vengeance killing for the years before I met you. Assassinating all those who made you kill Rona. Eliminating all those who killed your brother when he was saving a Kurdish village from Turkish attack."

The obsidian disks in her eyes now burn at the edges like a sun spitting out solar flares. She yells back at him, "You know nothing of personal death. You know nothing of what it is like to fight for your life. Do not denigrate me or my loved ones. You are just a little cowardly boy who plays with words."

Arms firmer across his chest, his eyes immune to the solar flares her eyes fire out at him, he says, "Part of what makes this little cowardly boy who plays with words such an outstanding editor, and outstanding writer, is my ability to research what others can't put together. Disparate facts that at first blush, even at second glance, don't relate to anything."

Her eyes drop again to the floor as she reflects, her mouth in a serious downward-bent U.

"Your brother. You sent him into that village. You chose that village. And it was the wrong day. The wrong time," says Peter. "Your father. You couldn't touch something within him. You find out now that it's because he wasn't your father. But you lived with the guilt that he hanged himself even despite your best efforts to get him out of his depression."

"Shut up. Shut up," screams Zara. "You know nothing."

"Your cousin Rona and her sister Diyar. You chose to have them try on the dresses that were the sign of your rebellion against Islamic codes right when the Daesh invaded their house. And then the worst of the worst happens. Their fates your guilt."

Stomping her feet, she yells, "Shut up. Shut up, you kafir."

"Pulling a religious wall between us will not erase your pains," he says as he takes a step towards her. "You hide behind the world's dire need for a new prophetess, pretending you don't want to be her. And yet you carried on with the charade. Your zeal, your self-proclaimed destiny. What did that get you?

Your mother gone. And your Roza, who tried in vain to save you with her body."

"Stop it. Stop it," she cries as she rushes him and throws a mean right hook across his face.

A long stream of saliva arcs from Peter's mouth as his head swivels like a sail arm on a yacht making a turn into the wind. His finger around his jaw, which he flexes around twice, he pushes his feet even firmer into the floor. "Feel better? I'm your punching bag, am I not? You have pushed me. You have abused me. You have used me. Why? Because there's no one left in your life to distract you from your guilt, your pain, your desire to end it all."

The tall woman, the biological descendant of the reindeer warrior giants, the woman who has killed nearly seven dozen, some with her hands, growls.

He turns his face to the side she has not hit and says, "A great man who died here said I should turn this cheek. Give me your best shot. You've been wanting to do this from the day we met."

"No," she says, defiantly stomping her feet.

"Come on, Zara. You know you want it. You've been wanting to beat the crap out of someone for way too long. The real you is a fighter. You're just dying to let it all out. To drop the pretense. You didn't leave your village to elope with a man. You really left to fight a war, because deep down inside you know you're a warrior giant woman destined to terrorize your enemies. This woman of peace thing—it was all a fantasy. A way for you to make peace with your delusions. Isn't that what Dr. Bev told us? We're just two deluded people suffering from our own trauma, and if left untreated, we would hurt many innocent people? And who just died because of your delusions?" He taps his cheek. "Come on. Let it all out."

"No," she says, again folding her arms in front of her. But her hands ball into fists, flexing against her arm muscles.

"Is that what you told Rona when she begged you to shoot her in her head because she broke her ankle as you and her sister tried to escape the Daesh sex slavers?" posits Peter. Flexing his upper chest muscles, he says, "And you blew her brains out. The image haunting you. The image drove you to seek vengeance."

"*Raweste, raweste.* Stop it," cries Zara, as she holds her fists atop her head with her forearms around her cheeks. "Just take that cattle prod and stick it in me and twist it, punch it up as far as you can. You are hurting me more than the Daesh did."

"The Daesh who killed Rona?" says Peter. "You didn't kill her. She pleaded with you. She begged you. Like the sister of the ancient matriarch's husband begged him to kill her so she wouldn't be taken into the most sordid form of slavery. He didn't kill her the first time. And his pain echoed in my DNA. His pain, the source of the afflicted man's dreams. And as much as your fingers tried to pull the trigger, you couldn't kill Rona. Her being left alive, dragged back into that torturous world of violation, is the source of your pain. She died the day after you didn't kill her. A most heinous death because you couldn't pull the trigger."

"No," she screams as she belts him across the other cheek. This time, as his head swivels, the rest of his body goes with it as he spins down atop her bed. "No, no," she screams as she pounds her two fists deep into his back as if he were a bass drum.

She turns him over to bash in his face, only to see blood everywhere. She gasps, her obsidian eyes full of waves of tears, as if the Great Flood washed away her soul. "What have I done? Xwedê, no. No, please no," she cries as she falls atop his body.

Her tears washing his crimson-covered face, his blood mingled with her fluids, she kisses him. At first, a mere mouthy kiss. But the real Great Flood comes. What she truly feels. What she truly wants. And her tongue dances with his, her nose slip-sliding against his. Ecstasy? No. Years of pent-up lust as she pins him down, her lips touching every uncovered bit of his flesh. Her hand reaches down to pull his pants down. What has said hello to her all those nights is saying come and get me now. She pulls up her nightgown and slides his banana slug surrogate between her thighs.

As she begins the final push to give to him what she had withheld, what Sasha said she had to do, what her mother tried in her most discreet way to say she should do, he rolls her on her back. She opens herself to him, ready for all that he would give her.

But he does not. He pulls her nightgown down. Puzzled, she asks, "Why?"

Leaning down to kiss her lightly on her lips, then her forehead, then the tip of her nose, he says, "No. No. No. You are going to make me like one of them. Someone you think only wants you for your body. Someone you can diminish, write off, as another lover."

"Am I that crazy? I cannot even have the love of the man who I truly love?" she asks.

He does his best to pack his engorged member back where it certainly does not want to be packed as he wiggles to get his zipper up. He touches her breasts, caresses her breasts, then puts his head upon them, bloodying her nightgown further. He softly says, "There will be a day not long from now when we will finish what we started here." The day when you choose me freely and wisely as your husband. Not just your lover."

She puts her hands around his shoulders and pulls his head more firmly against her breasts. "Is that what your Catholic mother says? No sex until marriage?"

A little nibble on the protruding nipple closest to his lips and he says, "No, that is what the heart of Zara is saying in my ear. No more lovers. It is time for the matriarch to be with her other half."

"Are you trying to woo me with a twelve-thousand-year-old legend?" she jests as she caresses his head. "Because if you are, it is working."

She rolls him over on his back and strokes something he tried to pack away, saying, "Are you sure your banana slug will be ready for me when the time comes?"

"You're really making it hard on me," he says, taking her hand up and away to kiss it.

"That is clearly my intention," she says, lowering herself onto where he is most heated. "I would not want you to think I am a dead fish in bed."

"I meant difficult," says Peter as he rolls her onto her back and away from her enticements into what his body throbs for, but his head knows it is not time for. "And a dead fish? I wouldn't last the first hour once we consummate our marriage."

"Hour?" she says, feigning alarm.

"Two hours?" replies Peter, unsure if one hour wasn't enough for this daughter of a giant. But he is relieved as she gives him that smile she does when she teases him.

She lifts up her nightgown, not to mount him but to wipe the blood still streaming from his cheek. "Facial cuts bleed like you are about to die. You had me so scared. I did not pull my punches. A lesser man would have been hospitalized after what I hit you with."

He kisses her hand that had wiped his face. "Pretty good for a cowardly milquetoast editor from the City-by-the-Bay."

With both hands around his blood-red cheeks, she asks, "You wanted me to get that angry, did you not? Why? If you pushed me more, I might have actually killed you."

He pulls her up to sit face-to-face with him. As she pulls the sleeve of her gown to press upon the cut, which is clotting, he says, "Believe me, I would never have said what I said if I didn't love you so much."

Glancing away, she replies, "Truth hurts. Nothing you said was anything but the truth. I suppose everything that evil woman said, that qarînah posing as a doctor, may be true. You and I are suffering from delusions. The voice is only what my guilt-ridden head made up to hide my true pains. Your aliens are your way of finding a way to live in peace."

She rubs his side and says, "I shouldn't have pounded you on the back. That is where the sonic attack hit you the hardest. I haven't thanked you enough for saving my life." She leans in, kisses him, and reaches down again for his banana slug.

Taking her feisty feeler hand into his, he says, "How many years of celibacy are you trying to make up for this morning?"

Scooting up closer to him, she hugs him, her hands gently caressing his back. "Too many."

Nibbling on her ear, he whispers, "If you are deluded, I want to be deluded with you. We can happily live our lives out in our own little fantasies. And raise your lovely child with your lambs."

Nibbling his ear back, she asks, "Is that a marriage proposal or a line from one of the romance versions of your book?"

Tip of his nose rubbing the tip of hers, forehead to her forehead, he says, "It is my promise to you."

A little peck on the lips and she says, "I accept your promise. But if you ever feel the need to get me that mad again, I suggest you duck next time."

"Ducking wouldn't have had the right outcome," he says, smiling back at her.

"Well, my friend Peri says makeup sex is worth the fight," she jests. "When are we going to make up?"

"My, have I ever unleashed the sex-starved qarînah in you." Peter jests back. "Seven months of 'I can't touch you there' and now this?"

A look. A continuation of the first look when Zara saw that this man differed from all the rest. His eyes so much like the innocence of her baby lambs. Someone she could trust her life with. Bloodied face and all, that look still remains. She puts her head into his chest, wrapping his arms around her, crimson turning to brown across his chest and her gown. What would someone who walked in right now think?

"That was no accident, was it?" she asks. "You did that on purpose. Every single word specifically chosen. Even the MoxWorld ultra-thin ultra-strong mouth guard."

Pulling the tough-as-steel, gentle-as-cotton-balls mouth guard out from around his teeth, he says, "I like my teeth. And I had an inspirational coach."

"So why did Jean-Paul say you had to get me to beat on you?" she asks as her fingers probe his mouth to see what other surprises might still lurk there.

Putting the mouth guard into her fingers, he says, "What are you thinking you're going to find in there?"

Head up to give another peck on his lips, she says, "Maybe one of those MoxLove tongue vibrators, no?"

"How anyone would know you had to let out your physical desires, your deepest angst, so you could be ready to save your mother is clearly beyond my logic," says Peter. "We have to be ready tomorrow to meet the madmen holding Maryam hostage. I asked the good Father to take my confession after you exploded at that poor MoxWorld Security guy. While you were kidnapped, I ran a thorough research job on you. I should've done that months ago, but I've been so blindly in love with you. But then I didn't know how to handle what I had found. So I confessed. The ex-French army officer in Jean-Paul compromised the good Father's ability to keep my confession confidential. He said that your harboring explosive thoughts about yourself could give NiQihs an edge. If NiQihs had done the homework I did, they could make you derail the ransom delivery."

Her hands, now raging hot, engorged with the heat of her love, stroke his cheeks again. "So, you volunteered to get me to beat you by saying what I wanted no one, even myself, to say to me?"

"If your family cannot tell you the truth, who can?" he replies.

"Family," she says, glancing down. "My mother was always right. You are family. As I am your family too, I need to tell you the truth. You did not bait me into beating you only because of Jean-Paul. Give yourself the credit and respect you deserve. Know that I do."

"You said your Sara told you if you love someone, you will do anything for them," says Peter. "I saw in your house all the pictures of you as a girl growing up. On the surface, a pretty loving girl living for peace. But as I talked to all who knew you as a child, I came to understand that girl was full of precocious, ferocious might and will that guided all of her actions. Not a dark god, but your own inner strength led you. I came to know the Zara trying to be a woman of peace fought every second to contain who she truly was. And if you truly love someone, you will help them be who they really are. Even if it means bruised, bloodied cheeks."

Her hands on those battered cheeks, she plants a gentle kiss followed by a deep throaty one upon his mouth. Letting him have some air, she says, "And I love you for your love of who I am. The daughter of a giant."

Holding her head back against his chest again, she cherishes his arms as they hold her even tighter than before. Why? She pulls back with her irises dilated, her eyebrows up, and says, "It is a vision. Is it not?"

Choking up at first, Zara remembers an image. A woman like her bringing her dying loved one to be cured. Blue dust. Blue light. An aged woman with head covered. She peers into his eyes again. "You bonded with me while I was asleep. Did you not?"

Head turned aside with the face he made when his mother caught him doing something very much not condoned in Catechism class, he says, "Yes.

I wanted to help soothe what hurt so much in you."

She taps his chest. "Is that not like having sex with someone when they are sleeping?"

As the Catholic schoolboy guilt overruns his face, almost hiding his bruised cheeks, she taps him again. "I am only teasing you."

"You didn't seem to like that I bonded with Mei. This afflicted person's bonding is too close to what sex used to mean between two people. What it means to me," he says meekly. He holds her hands, nods his head and says, "You must believe me. I didn't bond with Rachel either in the way I do with you."

Her hands pull his head to hers as she says, "I believe you."

As if his guilt had been relieved, his shoulders relax.

She sucks in her lips and wets them, gazes down, and says, "Fate has given me all of today to figure out how to save the woman who conceived me. Who gave me life."

Rubbing his temples, she says, "Do you remember what I dreamt of? That woman who sought the cavern to save the one she loved the most? I am like her. Now we are ready to go to the Crimea. I know exactly where. Maybe I can save her. My Maryam."

To NiQihs, she taps out a message on her MoxWrap that they will transmit the exact meet spot two hours before the exchange. Both sides need to bring their object fragments.

Back into the warmth and safety of his arms, she says, "If you love someone, you will do anything for them."

CHAPTER 49

*Unexpressed emotions will never die. They are buried alive
and will come forth later in uglier ways.*

—Sigmund Freud

Barrel of Death, South Balaklava, Crimea
9:50 a.m. March 8, 2023

"American, you are not the crazy CIA killer my dearest Zara said you were the last time we met," says Anatoly. "So, if I kill you now, I can have my lovely *solnishko* Zara all to myself."

Adjusting the red sash around his waist, Peter peers at the Russian and points to his deep purple bruised cheeks. "It takes a lot to kill me," he says calmly.

The Russian peeks at both sides, smiles, and says, "Indeed, she must really be smitten with you to have given you such wonderful love taps."

Overlooking the Black Sea, in the lands that caused his nightmares, Peter stands upon the powerful defensive structure of the last world war called "Barrel of Death" by the locals, featuring concrete casemates, platforms for guns, and a whole system of two-to-three-meter ditches. Atop one gun platform thirty meters from the next gun platform, he can see other numerous niches. The perfect place to defend in a battle. But according to her plan, they will not stay here. The meet with NiQihs is deeper into the ancient oak forest.

Next to him, Zara stares out at where Sasha's yacht once floated. Where a tactical nuclear missile vaporized it. The breezes blow her hair, which she has to keep sweeping away from her face. No scarf. No more, she says. For she is the daughter of a man who is far from being from a saint. And so is she.

Looking down at the coastline, she remembers the mysterious effect on her eyes in one tunnel in the old submarine base only a mile or so west under the range they stand upon. The ancient chamber of the blue light lies buried below these hills too, or so she bets.

But she is not a wild gambler. Her dearest Jesuit Father studied the map on the bronze tablet from the First Temple in Zara's photos. She was right that it did not resemble Crimea—Crimea of today.

But the ingenious Jesuit scholar pieced together the ancient map of the major constellations around the edges of the tablet and determined the heavens resembled this pattern over ten thousand years ago. An age before the flood of Zara's Prophet Nuh. The coastline of the Black Sea was vastly different before the post–Ice Age melt inundation.

His other sources with MoxWorld's duodecillion-calculations-per-second computing power, the location of Asherah, the cavern of the blue light, confirmed Zara's bet the cavern is next to the acres upon acres of ancient oak trees below. A feat only MoxWorld could accomplish. Or so hopes Zara, whose plan, made with Peter and Jean-Paul, depends on NiQihs not knowing the precise location of the caverns.

Zara checks the time. They have two hours left before China will launch preemptive nuclear strikes against the United States and Russia, according to NiQihs. They must follow the plan like a script if they are to succeed. She taps her MoxWrap, sending the precise meet location to NiQihs, giving them insufficient time to set up an elaborate trap.

As Peter readies Zara's lambs for their pivotal role in today's plan, Anatoly asks, "What are these beasts? Fluffy, wooly like lambs, but secretly canine inside?"

Eyeing the not amused Peter, the Russian touches his MoxWrap. A copy of Peter's latest book appears and Anatoly asks, "My true solnishko would love it if you could autograph this for her. Your Zara is safe from me, as I am smitten with another."

Her hand on Anatoly's shoulder, Zara says, "And you are safe from me too. I am very pregnant."

"You mean by him?" he asks with eyebrows raised.

Only a smile meets his question as Zara asks, "You have my package?"

He unloads a long case from his truck. More than a meter and a half long and just under a meter wide. She unlocks the case and pulls out a sizeable object fragment. Black with pitting along what had been the outer surface, which braved asteroid belts on its journey to Earth. So large she could only carry it with both arms.

"You never disappoint, Anatoly," she says, giving him a peck on his cheek.

"I hope I can say the same for your plan. Hasty, but as ingenious as the one you outfoxed Murometz with last time," he replies. "I am sorry for your loss. I know you and he had an odd relationship. You were close to him, nonetheless. But I am sure you will save your mother."

"Are you and Peri ready with your part of the plan?" she asks.

"Of course," he says with bravado. "You doubt me?"

Nudging her hip against his, she says, "Let nothing happen to Peri. She is about to pop. If miraculously I live, I want our children to grow up together."

He touches her cheek, to which she says, "You making one last pass at me before we die?"

"Your face. It is different from the last time we gazed upon the sea from up upon these cliffs."

"You mean the scars are gone and I appear more like the minx you seduced anew each time a mission finished."

"No, I am afraid. You scare me," her former Russian lover says. "You are more like the avenging angel that Sasha turned you into. But now, more dark. Maybe even malevolent."

"I am not the same woman I was the last time I was up here. Peace is nonsense. Who was I fooling? The world only responds to a force greater than hell itself. I am the daughter of a warrior giant. I have no morality other than to crush whoever and whatever comes in front of me today. But more important, is your president ready?"

"Why, of course," he says. "We Russians are always ready. But he is expecting you to perform a miracle. Holding our bombing of NiQihs arms factories for even two hours is not a popular decision with our generals." Peering at the old submarine base, he says, "And if you are wrong, the Chinese thirty-gigaton bunker-busting nuke targeted for down there will vaporize us."

Another peck on his cheek and she dials Dan. "And is your president ready?"

Looking a lot more distressed than Anatoly, Dan says, "He's put our ballistic missile submarines on hold for an hour and a half. If you can't resolve this by then, he'll be forced to nuke every factory, every military installation, and every ship in China suspected of harboring NiQihs weapons."

"And we all die in a global nuclear war?" she responds. "I think my solution is healthier. Like gluten-free. Nuke-free."

Grimness written all over his face, he says, "My brother almost died of radiation burns from their attack on our carrier task forces. I'm betting you're right."

"So is everyone with me here," she replies. "Give my regards to your brother."

She walks twenty meters over to Mei, who, with Rachel, is ironically putting coats over her lambs. Woven with Michaela's metallic designs, of course. Zara asks, "They are ready? The training time you had with them worked, right?"

"Honey, don't worry," says Mei as she adjusts her MoxWrap. "They're smarter than some of my college students when I still taught."

The team ready to go, they assemble at a trailhead, Zara dressed in a Kurdish outer coat, yellow with gold trim, and black pants. Her hair blowing in the winds, she says to Jean-Paul, "Father, will you say a prayer for us? Perhaps God will be kinder to you than he has been to me."

Bowing his head, the good Father says, "Lord, let us be instruments of Your peace. Where there is hatred, let us sow love; where there is injury, pardon; where there is doubt, faith; where there is despair, hope; where there is darkness, light; where there is sadness, joy."

Before he can continue, Peter puts his hand in front of him and finishes this prayer, which he too learned in Catholic school. "O Divine Master, grant that we may not so much seek to be consoled as to console; to be understood as to understand; to be loved as to love; For it is in giving that we receive; it is in pardoning that we are pardoned; it is in dying that we are born again to eternal life."

Scuffing up his hair, Zara says, "Peter, I could not have said that any better. Dying and born again. We will see."

As they walk down the trailhead, they meet up with Rachel, who is dressed in a light khaki jacket over a white blouse and olive khaki pants.

The three women walk together as Peter, carrying a rolled mat, leads with the lambs. A strong-backed Jean-Paul carries the object fragment slung over his back and comes beside Peter. "All is ready as by His plan? By His will?" the priest asks.

"Of course," replies the smiling, exuberant Peter. "Despite what you may have thought, I was a very obedient child in Catholic school. I followed the plans in utter detail."

Smiling back, Jean-Paul comes up to Zara and says, "I had spent many months in these lands for Alexander, searching for the buried mythical pyramids. If the legend of Noah, your Prophet Nuh, is to be extrapolated to my tsunami theory, waves from the giant lake that became the Black Sea may have piled debris from the sea floor and beaches upon these hills, making them mountains. But there are thousands of square kilometers where that pyramid might have existed, if at all."

"Then, Father, perhaps your prayers should have been for a miracle," says Zara. "We have but an hour or less to get this one right. I hope you were right about the mother goddess's pet fox genes you put in my lambs. May God's hand guide them to find their master."

As they walk through shrub brush leading towards forests of Crimean oak trees, Mei drifts behind the others next to her Israeli friend and says, "A little puffy today?"

"I don't know. Maybe my period is coming."

"Or missing," replies Mei. "You know Peter and Zara have made up. I mean, if you and he did what we talked about, were you using protection?"

"I'm a big girl," Rachel says. "I knew what I was doing."

"Okay, Ms. Know What You Are Doing, you came unarmed?" asks Mei.

Head tilted and her nose scrunched, Rachel says, "Of course not. It's small enough to fit in my bra."

With a little snicker, Mei says, "I thought your busty perky pair looked even puffier."

Snickering back, Rachel replies, "Nothing a little stuffing couldn't fill out. Or literally, padding around the gun. But my breasts are tender for some reason. And what about you? You carrying?"

"Honey, I'm always armed," Mei says as she runs her hands down her formfitting metallic-threaded coat.

Up ahead, Zara walks with Peter, who is encouraging her lambs in their search for the scent of the mother goddess. "You haven't been saying how you will die today and how I should take care of your lambs," says Peter.

"I do not trust what I see, what I hear, what I feel anymore," she says.

"Actually, I was hoping you would say you want to get this over with so you can plan your wedding."

"Wedding? You are optimistic," she says.

"Positive visioning. See the good outcome and it will happen," he says with his lips rising.

"No, I meant that I would even consider letting you dance with Kurds at a wedding again," she says with a laugh. "At Peri's wedding, we almost had to call several ambulances for all the toes you nearly broke."

"When the time comes, you need to have total trust in me," he says with much flatter lips and tone.

"When the time comes, you and I will be as one," she says in an equally flat tone.

A half hour through the forests, the lambs stop at a clearing near the side of a sandstone hillside. Peter sets the rolled mat down next to the object fragment Jean-Paul puts down.

Her hands around both her lambs' necks, she gives them instructions in Kurdish, not wanting to take the chance that their understanding of Peter's English or Mei's Mandarin is not so good. And off they go, running in different directions along the hillside. "Meh, meh," says the black one. "Meh, meh, meh," says the white one. Like teenage siblings, they have a lamb argument over which one has found what Mama wants.

The black one stops in front of some shrubs and the other one comes running, trying to butt the other away from the spot, both acting as if they want Mama's approval. Her love.

Zara looks up into the sky, then calls Peter over, and they peer into a meter-wide slot in the hillside rocks. She yells, "This is it."

Rachel tries to get her pendant stones out of her blouse, but Mei grabs her hands, saying, "This is no time to be adjusting yourself. I know how tender they can get early on." And she buttons up Rachel's blouse.

Before Rachel can protest and verify this cavern, Zara yells to the skies, "We have delivered what you asked. Three women. Two unborn babies. And our black object."

Out from the oak trees come Zengo and Beverly, both dressed in those tight-fitting black suits, the type street fighters wear so that their opponents have nothing to grab in hand-to-hand combat, his revealing he certainly didn't lose his manhood and hers showing off her ample upper assets. Zengo carries a NiQihs modified QTS-12 Chinese special ops assault rifle with grenade launcher. Beverly has the latest QSW-06 silenced Chinese special ops pistol aimed into Maryam's side. Maryam is gagged, with her hands tied behind his back. Her head shaved, showing the scars of where they tormented her.

"Where is Rohan?" yells Zara.

"He's busy," answers Bev.

Tapping her MoxWrap, Mei announces, "They've neutralized our signals."

With her mouth pouting out, Zara says, "Well, we are even. So are yours."

Zengo tries his NiQband and nods an affirmative.

"Now it is your guns against our pregnant bellies," says Zara, tapping where her bump will one day soon be.

"Don't think we won't kill you, pregnant or not," says Bev.

Glancing to Mei, standing to one side in a voluminous burgundy tent dress, as she is within a week of her due date, then to Rachel, who readies by opening up her top blouse buttons, Zara says, "Why did you ask for three women to be here? Are you taking us hostage in exchange for my mother?"

Her first love pats the doctor's backside and says, "Why would I want you as a hostage? You are such a dead fish. And I have a doctor who knows all the ins and outs of my needs."

"She's not a dead fish," protests Peter.

"Peter, you cannot follow instructions, can you?" says Zara. "I told you not to talk about last night. I mean, do you want Zengo to know that you couldn't handle a third hour of ruckus rolling and rocking around? The bath, the parlor, the balcony, and, well, the elevator?"

"I guess I'm not man enough like he is," says Peter, kicking a stone to Zengo's feet.

Zengo sneers at him, pointing his gun at him.

"Is that supposed to compensate for something?" taunts Peter.

Another sneer and Peter says, "Oh, it's those missing front teeth that are bothering you, isn't it? Zara tried to take my teeth out the other night. MoxWorld sells this nifty mouth guard that you wouldn't even know was there until someone tries to knock all your molars out."

His trigger finger ready to pull, Bev says, "Come on. He's trying to get you into a pissing contest. Don't waste your bullet yet." She pushes Maryam in front of her, kicking her sharply in the buttocks, forcing her down to the ground.

As the battered Maryam rolls a couple of meters in front of Zara, she can see her bruises, her nose crooked from being broken, perhaps an arm broken and reset. They tortured her. She knows the signs all too well. Her eyes are not those of someone long for this earth.

Who are these monsters who would destroy a woman of innocence? Her mother, who must have resisted giving information on their family legend. The only thing that matters now is getting her mother to the cavern of blue light. For only then can she be saved from these mortal wounds. But her mother's eyes signal something to her. Peter.

Picking her up, she takes Maryam and gently sets her mother down near the mat and object fragment. She whispers, "Mama, don't worry. I will make it right. I will get you to the cavern of the blue light. As Sara said, we can heal you in there." As she surveys her arms and legs, her index finger, pointed towards Peter, makes circles.

"I think you forgot about our secret weapon," says Peter, glaring at Zengo.

Zengo glances briefly at Bev, who shrugs and says, "You're so creative. Too bad you won't live through this to write about it."

Putting two fingers in his mouth, Peter lets out a whistle, and from the brush come running two fluff balls who rush Zengo.

"Don't shoot them," yells Bev as Zengo dances around their pass. "They have something to do with finding the elixir."

The lambs continue into the slot in the rocks. Peter says, "You're right, Bev. Your God Gene Complex findings also apply to lambs. They're going to find the people who guard the cavern and bring them back. The last wicked man who tried to play nasty with those people got very crispy."

Bev aims her gun at Maryam and says, "Rachel? You want to end this farce?"

After a pause, then a glance at the MoxWorld team, Rachel comes next to Bev, taking her silenced Ruger out from her bra and pointing it at Zara's head.

"Yes, she has always been working for us," says Bev. "There will be no hostage exchange. We will destroy MoxWorld in a matter of seconds by killing all its key executives right here. Russia will take the blame. The Americans will come on board with NiQihs within days of this momentous moment."

At first, Zara stares at Rachel, who played them again. But then she peers at Peter, nonplussed, saying, "It's all okay. Just like my book says. Trust me."

To Bev, Peter says, "But how does that help you find the source of eternal life, the elixir the First Emperor commissioned your society to find? You kill me and Jean-Paul and all you get is my mother and the Pope mad at you. You kill Mei and Zara, and you have no pregnant women to enter the cave. Or did your intelligence not pick up the part that only women of purity can survive in there?"

Patting her abdomen, Bev says, "I'm surprised at you. I thought you could've thought this out further. There aren't just two pregnant women here. I carry Zengo's love child. Oh, you look so surprised. After you failed to take months and months of my late-night cues that I wanted you in my bed, I had to find someone else willing to make me a 'woman of purity' out of me."

As Peter's jaw drops, the doctor says, "I didn't think you were that stupid. Your master faked your alien abduction, I think to push you into your Kurdish friend's panties. But his team was too cocky and sloppy, and we snatched you away from them. I tried impregnating myself and your former blonde girlfriend with your sperm, but even your gametes are too stupid to know a good egg when they bump into one."

Feeling his crotch, he says, "You didn't have to poke me down there so many times with those needles. If you just asked, I could have given you what you wanted."

The doctor's head tilts to one side as she waves her gun at him. "And don't feign too much stupidity in front of Zengo. He might shoot you first to save our species from your idiot gene. You know all too well that you fathered Rachel's baby. Voluntarily and with pleasure."

Shock. Across each and every MoxWorld person's face. Zara turns her attention to Peter. Mei turns to Jean-Paul. And Rachel's eyes search Peter's, her gun hand quivering.

Not even turning to Zara, Peter looks back into Bev's eyes. "Well, if you really were listening to me all those nights, then you'd know I have this thing for sexy, smart, academic women of the Judaic faith. Rachel reminds me so much of Tara, a sumptuous physics genius who just loved my aliens."

Tapping his chin and gazing up at the sky, he says, "Maybe I just thought her au natural pair were more inducing than the ones your former plastic surgeon boyfriend endowed you with." Eyes back on Bev's, he adds, "Maybe my sperm is allergic to silicon."

Bang. Bev plants a shot between his feet. "Next one is going a little higher," she says.

A smattering of a smile shines upon Zara's game face as she admires her Peter executing his innocent magic, annoying these two with the most random and inane distractions. Both of the black-clad duo are ready to pounce right into something they don't know will hurt them. Just like Peter did to Alexander eight months ago.

Rachel says, "Peter, come over here. I need you alive to help raise our baby together." Her eyes flutter as she waves for him.

His head begins to turn to Zara, who says, "Do not look at me. Keep your eyes on her. We are clearly off script here. You wrote about this in your book. What did the hero say? 'Trust me. You know how this makes me feel. You know what I truly feel.'"

Looking down at his MoxWrap and then at Rachel, he says, "It's three ten, time for Asr prayer. Zara, before I leave you for Rachel, for everything we've been through, we should pray together one last time. You know how I feel about Rachel. She and I will never pray to Mecca."

Bev taps her foot on the ground and says, "How stupid do you think I am? You two are doing exactly what you did to Murometz on that pier when you gave him your half of that oversized black stone. You're stalling while your priest's ex-soldier friends take out our guards. Rohan, come on out."

Rohan and three others have their guns on three men holding sniper rifles above their heads. Three priests, Guillaume, Pedro, and Simon, all like Jean-Paul with their crucifixes hanging out. Rohan's men disarm them and shove them towards Mei and Jean-Paul.

"Once again, the Vatican sends soldiers to take our lands," says the ultraorthodox Rohan. "To Christianize us with high-powered sniper rifles. Russian ones at that."

Bev remarks, "Those are the same priests you had take out Alexander's guards last spring. Don't you two have any imagination? You're doing exactly what you did before. So predictable."

Kneeling on the ground, Peter unties the mat. "Then you would know that last time, we prayed as well. If Zara's going to heaven soon, she should pray first. She's late for Asr prayer."

As he rolls out the mat, Zengo fires a shot, making him stop, and walks over, hitting Peter's head with the butt of his rifle. Rubbing his head, which is bleeding from the butt strike, Peter says, "What do you think I have in here? A gun?"

Zara nods to Peter, who nods back. He slowly unrolls the rest of the mat, revealing Zara's black lamb's wool scarf with the red-and-gold embroidery. Peering up at Zengo, he says, "You must remember this one, her favorite. Oh yes, she lost that before you came along and lied your way into her shorts."

Another rifle butt strike, but Peter rolls, and it glances off his back. "Get on with it," says Zengo.

Placing the scarf in his open palms, he offers the cloth to Zara, who smiles, saying, "No more scarves."

"Trust me, you want to wear a scarf for your last prayer. Maybe tie it looser this time," says Peter as he helps loosely wrap the fabric around her head.

Zara reaches for the object fragment, but Zengo tries to stop her. Peter says, "Oh, come on. You're going to have this fragment along with the one you stole from us in Uyghur after you kill us. Think of this like a death row prisoner's last meal. Our last prayer with a piece of the object."

The two begin their supplication, but Peter scratches his back, then scratches Zara's back, his arm around her, petting her side.

Rohan yells, "Zengo, he is making a mockery of our faith! He offends Allah. He offends us. Rap him on his head again."

Another rifle butt to Peter's head forces him down on Zara's back, his body covering hers, his hands pushing her headscarf off her head and around their object fragment.

With howls that would wake the denizens of the cavern, Peter screams in pain while his hands and Zara's hands fumble around together.

Yelling again, Rohan says, "She is a donkey whore, like I said. She's letting this kafir molest her body in the sacredness of prayer. Hit him again."

As Zengo raises his rifle butt again to finish off this God-offending clown, Peter rolls over with a Russian PP-2000 machine pistol pointed at his gut.

Zara rolls over with her trusty old-school Spetsnaz AK-9 with grenade launcher aimed at Bev and Rachel. The object fragment lies in front of her in broken pieces. One half real black object, the other a hollow fake to hide the guns.

"Drop the rifle," says Peter to Zengo, his barrel aimed at Zengo's crotch.

Rohan waves his hand in the air to rally his soldiers, but Zara says, "Don't try it, Zengo. I'll blow up these two pregnant women and you have nothing."

Kicking Zengo's rifle over to Jean-Paul, Peter gets up and says, "Lucky my head is so stupid and solid. Otherwise, I'd be mad enough about you hitting it so many times that I'd blow off what you lied to Zara about."

With eyes of empathy, eyes of the therapist, eyes of an expert in psychological warfare, Bev takes her warm and welcoming clinical psychiatry professor stance. "My dear. My poor dear Zara. What did we talk about? Your delusions. They aren't your fault. It was those inhumane Islamic State terrorists. What do you call them? The Daesh. It's what they did to you. Your poor mind. It just snapped. Just like your Captain Luciano, who snapped in battle. You liked him. He was your friend. He tried to warn you about your affair with Dan, a married man. But you were too smitten to listen to old Tony."

With wide brown eyes signaling to Zara's narrowed eyes to be open to her therapeutic voice, Bev says, "You should've taken my advice. You could've seen Tony while he still lived. You could've told him how much you appreciated his loyalty to you. Not like that Dan, who took advantage of you. Used you like a piece of meat."

Her nostrils flaring, Zara moves her finger from the grenade launcher trigger to the rifle trigger as she targets between Bev's breasts. The ones that qarînah must have used to seduce Zengo into conning her into reliving first love in their old village.

"Zara, focus. Focus," whispers Peter.

"Yes, Zara. Severe PTSD sufferers like you have a hard time focusing. Listen to your Peter," implores the therapist in wolf's clothing. "Your Tony wandered the halls at the VA and tried to warn everyone that the end was near. Only he knew the solution. Only he talked directly with God. As a group of them beat him for his insolence, he totally lost it. He plotted and planned, and like you, he was exceptional at the military arts. He grabbed the gun belt off a guard and shot up his ward. Cornered, he turned the gun on himself, saying he didn't have the courage to kill his injured female soldier who begged to be shot rather than be tortured and violated by the enemy."

Her head steady, her eyes not flinching, but her trigger finger shaking,

Zara's eyes narrow, moving her aim from the heart between the breasts to the mouth.

"Yes, Zara. Blow out my mouth. The instrument of the truth your mind cannot handle," says Bev. "Tony said the same in his last session with me. His guilt was killing him. His guilt would kill him. Remind you of something you didn't do? Your guilt driving you to play God here? What was her name? Rona? Who killed her? Your Daesh? Or you?"

Her lips pushing against each other so hard that her skin around her mouth wrinkles, her forehead ripples deeper than waves in a tsunami. Her eyes become those obsidian-black, deep-sea-black, evil-black discs. Her mind races from killing Zengo first, then the doctor, the two-faced Rachel, and finally Rohan. "Kill them all" rings in her ears.

But then she hears his voice.

CHAPTER 50

Like the smiting who smote him did He smite him:
like the slaying of his slain ones, was he slain?

Yeshayahu—Isaiah—27:7, Tanakh

South Balaklava, Crimea
12:45 p.m. March 8, 2023

"Trust me" is all he said.

Warmth, love, and a future together is what she knows he meant. In that microsecond in combat, her head moves from racing thoughts of death to keeping on script.

Her finger moves back to the grenade launcher, and she says, "Keep talking, Doctor. Just remember, when Zengo cheats on you, he does not use protection. And you should know, there are some flesh-eating drug-resistant STDs that will rot your womanhood into a cesspool."

Her eyes now narrowed as well, Bev glares at her former editor. "Damn you, Peter. You mentally inoculated her."

"What's a fiancé for if they can't cure you of your pains?" Peter says. Pushing his machine pistol at Zengo's crotch, he asks, "You want me to cleanse him here, so he doesn't spread any more of those womanhood-eating bugs?"

Ignoring Peter, Bev says, "I'll make you a deal, Zara. I spare your mother, Mei and the priest and his friends. You and Peter are too much of a threat to NiQihs to let go."

"I will make you a deal," says Zara, still lying on the ground, making herself a more difficult target. "I don't destroy the remains of the First Emperor. Without them, you cannot resurrect him."

"You are mad. You don't have the military strength to do that much less the ability to use your MoxWrap," says Bev.

"Moxy," Zara calls out. "Dial up the presidents of both Russia and the United States. Use the protocol Alexander used with me."

"Yes, ma'am," says Moxy. "I will need the passcode authorization."

"But how?" exclaims Bev. "You don't have communication access."

"You really think your NiQihs technology is as advanced as the personal system the Mr. Alexander Murometz gave his daughter?" replies Zara.

"Ma'am, awaiting the passcode," says Moxy.

"Peter, I truly love you. With all my heart, I love you."

"Ma'am, voice confirmation of the code and the genuineness of your statement. Dialing the two presidents now."

A pause and both presidents answer, stating they have been waiting for this call.

With her grenade launcher aimed at Bev and Rachel, Zara says, "I want you to execute Plan A. Nuke every pyramid in China. Stand by for Plan B. First strike across all countries affiliated with NiQihs. Destroy all their military weapons, research facilities, and corporate infrastructures."

Rohan raises his hand, signaling his soldiers, but Bev says, "No. No"

"Do you think I signed on for some old emperor?" says Rohan. "I signed on for creating a new world order with a Muslim leader from Central Asia."

"Think, Rohan," says Bev. "Even if they destroy NiQihs, MoxWorld can't rule the world without those three. We can get the elixir and resurrect the true messiah, and he will lead us to a better, unified world."

"Moxy, time to Plan A launch?" asks Zara awfully loud.

"Twelve minutes for all cruise missiles to be readied and confirmed," states Moxy.

Bev hisses. She throws her gun down. Rohan says, "I will not surrender to this bitch. Donkey whore."

"No, cousin, I am a bastard child," states Zara. "The daughter of a giant. Did you not hear?"

Bev signals for the others to drop their weapons as Rohan backs up towards the trees for his escape.

"Let's make a deal," offers the doctor again. "You let me go into the cavern and get some of the elixir. You can have everything else. Peter can even write a book about all this."

Rachel reaches for Bev's gun on the ground, but Zara says, "Hold it right there. Who do you think you are? I knew you were NiQihs."

"Zara, trust me, right?" says Peter. "Let her help us."

Slowly watching Zara's trigger finger, Rachel picks up Bev's gun, pointing it at the doctor. "Zara, you can cover the other NiQihs agents with your grenade."

Retargeting Rohan's companions, Zara says, "Moxy, end attack program."

"What is the passcode?" asks Moxy.

"I promise I will marry Peter. I do. I do."

"Passcode authenticated. The genuineness of the voice authenticated," affirms Moxy.

Backing up toward Zara's side of the invisible line on the ground, still with a diagonal shot on the doctor, Rachel yells, "Lemuel, come on out. They're all yours."

A tall man in green-and-olive combat fatigues emerges from the forest with a dozen armed men, one with a gun on Rohan, who has his hands wrapped around an object fragment. The one he and Zengo stole from the Second Temple ruins.

Lemuel's agents round up Rohan's men. Zengo and Bev stand aside as Rachel drops her hand holding Bev's gun, her other putting the smaller Ruger back into her bra.

"Zara, you have no reason to think poorly of Peter," says Rachel, peering into the Kurdish woman's eyes. "He didn't get me pregnant. To get this far, I had to tell this doctor that I was. NiQihs used any means necessary to persuade me. Unfortunately, that included my late great-grandmother and my father, whom they're holding. They also included my body as theirs. But I'm like you—my body is mine to choose what to do with. I had to be creative."

The Israeli professor adds, "You asked who I work for. My safta raba formed a family syndicate to exact revenge against those who tormented her after her escape from Crimea. I never lied to you. I worked for her and her interests. But her syndicate owed debts to other organizations of power. And so, my family had to pay back those debts. As did I. Your Peter is a good man, a quick thinker. He knew what to say to maintain my cover when Bev's comment surprised you all. I had to tell them I was with child. They would have killed my father if I didn't."

Still keeping their guns in their hands, Zara, then Jean-Paul, then Peter drop their aim on the different NiQihs targets. Peter walks up to Rohan. Gives him the scare stare before taking the object fragment from his arms. "God meant real men to have these." He puts it next to the other fragment.

Lemuel comes and stands by Rachel. "It is time to pay your family's debts. It is finally the moment where you kill all of Murometz's remaining descendants. *Yimach shmam.* May their names be erased."

Down on her knees, Rachel pleads, "Lemuel, please. Let me fulfill what my Ariella asked. I will retract all that I have published. Men will still rule in the Torah, as it has been written. I will say that I was wrong. I will say women like me are weak."

Lemuel kicks Rachel in the head. "You are weak. In the head. The syndicate thought you too stupid to understand where all the funding came from." He signals to his men to give Bev, Zengo, and Rohan their guns back.

On the ground staring at Lemuel, Rachel's mouth mouths "why," at which he kicks her again. "You are such the academic. Nothing happens without funding. Who do you think financed your precious Ariella's revenge? MoxWorld?"

As Rachel stands in abject horror at his revelation, Zara cries out, "Moxy, attack protocol C. Call the Russian president. Nuke Israel. Passcode—Peter, I truly love you. With all my heart, I love you."

Grinning away, Lemuel shakes his head as he says, "You cannot fool me with your fake commands. Our monitoring shows no ship, no sub, no aircraft readied to launch cruise missiles in response to your last attack request."

Lemuel raises his gun in the air and fires two shots, three shots, then two shots.

Pointing her gun at Rachel, who stands forlorn, with vapid eyes, Bev says, "You should have followed my advice. If you had that stupid editor's DNA in a fertilized egg embedded in your uterus, you would be joining me. As we did with Peter, we kidnapped Zara. We tried to impregnate her with the sperm we took from Peter after the faked alien abduction. But that didn't work. So, we let Lemuel execute his organization's mission to defame her. Then I asked you to get fresh sperm. And you failed. I asked you to seduce Peter to get yourself impregnated. You lied and failed. Now you will die with them, never to know if your precious Asherah is in that cave."

Before Bev can pull the trigger on Rachel and Zara, a deep male voice says, "No killings before I say so."

From the woods arrives an older man. Sixties, white hair. Part Asian, part Caucasian face. A silvery glint from his eyes. Chagatai, CEO of NiQihs.

"The ancient trust fund calls for our total obedience, our total subservience to his wishes," says Chagatai. "And in that cave is the answer to his two-thousand-year search. The man whose iron hand unified a great country. The man who made Genghis Khan look like a saint. The man who, when resurrected, will unify the world."

The white-haired man takes Rohan's gun and points it at Rachel. "We have little tolerance for failure. Even less for disloyalty."

He turns. Bang. And down goes Rohan.

Gun trained upon Zara, he says, "You pitiful girl. You preached the people's voice can achieve peace. Peace can only come through war and tyranny. The same in business and in the battlefields. And your master—you led us to him on his private yacht. I thank you for that. The world will remember you after your death as the woman who allowed the First Emperor to return to unite a fractured world."

Gun in hand, he stares down at Maryam. "I recently learned he forced your mother into intimacies with him. And Zara is the accident. Serves you two right."

Zara eyes her trusted old-school Spetsnaz rifle on the ground a meter away but then dives instead to cover her mother.

Bang. Too late as the NiQihs CEO shoots Maryam in the thigh, from which a crimson outflow immediately pools on her pants. Zara grabs her scarf and vainly tries to use it as a tourniquet. But it is too light as it rips.

Kneeling next to her, Peter undoes his red sash, offering it to Zara. She ties it around her mother's upper thigh as Peter manages the bleeding with her torn scarf. "Peter, I cannot pull this tight enough with her so tense from her other injuries. I cannot stop the bleeding enough."

"Zara Khatum. She has at most twenty minutes before she bleeds out. I can save her," says Chagatai. "I need you and your Chinese friend to go into that cave and get the elixir for our emperor."

As Rachel joins Zara and Peter, helping them get the tourniquet tighter, she says to Peter, "I did not know that NiQihs would hurt Zara's mother. You must believe me. They have my father hostage. I don't know what to do anymore."

"No time for not knowing anymore," he says as he reaches into her blouse. "I need both stones."

Both pendants off Rachel's neck and placed around his MoxWrap, a barely visible blue beam fires straight up into the heavens as if to call for the angels to come save them.

Zara says, "It's over. Mei and I will get what they want. I need my mother to live. I don't care about legends or destinies anymore. Family is all that matters. I'll do anything. It is time for me to face my death so others will live."

Tugging on the tourniquet with all her might, she is just about to surrender when Peter gently puts the stones in the bullet wound. A blue glow emanates, cauterizing the tissue. He nods to Zara. "The bleeding has slowed, but she still needs immediate medical attention."

Chagatai nods at Rachel and with a glint of silver says, "Professor Capsali. As Lemuel intimated, we funded your safta raba's efforts. Know we saved her after her escape. The less-than-ethical Tartar fishermen, who transported her to Turkey from Crimea, enslaved then sold her. One of our agents spotted her in the slave market in Iran, her stone necklace glistening blue. We bought her and set her free with the proviso that one day her children would lead us to where she got that stone."

While all eyes focused on the NiQihs magnate, Peter's foot slides over his Russian PP-2000 machine pistol. His fingers rest atop his MoxWrap.

"Professor Capsali. You have failed repeatedly to pay your Ariella's debt," says Chagatai, summoning her. "You have so much potential for our cause. I give you one last reprieve. Your last chance to prove your loyalty to Him, our Lord, the First Emperor." His finger on his NiQband, he adds, "One press and my team will slice your father's carotid artery—his blood spilt because of his disobedient daughter."

Lemuel brings the Israeli professor to the CEO's side. From his gun belt he takes a Jerico 941 pistol, company-issued, and places it into the Israeli professor's hands, aiming it at Zara.

Rachel stares at the gun in her palm. Cold emotionless steel. Just like she needs to be in this moment. Cold like she had to be to fake everyone out, playing them with her fake emotions, just as her father taught her, no? That priest. Mei. Zara. Even Peter. And the moment she has trained all her life for is here. One pull of a little trigger and she has won. She saves her father. She rids her country of a fake prophet. They may even reinstate her academic position. Isn't this what a woman archeologist needs to do to get ahead?

"Prove your worth to NiQihs, young lady," scoffs Chagatai. "It was her father's company's drugs that led to your Ariella's death. His fake medications."

Her eyes stare down the barrel of the instrument of Murometz's precious daughter's demise. Hands shaking. Hands quaking. In the most decisive moment in all her life that will define all time to come. One pull. Just one little pull of the trigger. She needs to be just as cold and emotionless as her Jericho.

But her hands are not cold like steel. Neither is her heart. She really respected that priest. She could have loved Mei and Peter if situations were different.

And Zara, whose eyes are closed. Her lips moving as if in prayer. She's become the strangest of sisters with this crazy Kurd. Fate is all but a single decision at a defining moment of time. If Rachel had agreed to perform that ancient sex ceremony for Mr. Monstrous Murometz, she would have been the prophetess. And would it have been Zara who would be now aiming this cold steel tool of death at her instead? And what would Zara do?

As Rachel's eyes glance up for only a moment, she hears Her. "Is this the way to Asherah?" the voice says. "Is this what She would want in a woman who seeks the light? Who are you really? That is the only question you must know to enter the realm of the blue light."

Her eyes close. She pictures her father's last words to stay true to Asherah. The only time he ever acknowledged the goddess. He meant for her to choose. Him or Her.

Her eyes now move to Peter on the ground with Maryam, who says, "Be the woman who you are. Not who others should say you should be."

Her eyes closed, her nostrils flared, Rachel erupts, "I can't. I can't. I never killed anyone with a gun. Ever. I'm just a history seeking archeologist."

Mouth agape for a moment, Lemuel says, "What about the three Nazis you executed in cold blood? What about that Jericho you hauled around?"

"That was the story that a father who loves his daughter says she should tell, so she is safe in this crazy world," says Rachel, her throat filling with phlegm, her eyes tearing up.

With a tap of his NiQband, Chagatai says, "NiQihs has no use for you or your father." He points his gun at Rachel.

But before a trigger can be pulled, in rapid-fire succession, Peter's sonic punch app knocks Chagatai and Lemuel off-balance long enough for him to get that Russian machine pistol to aim at them. "Drop the guns everyone."

Now, only Peter and Rachel hold guns.

In her soothing therapist persona, Beverly says, "My dear, dear editor. Your pappy told me of your shared dream of a dark-haired woman holding a gun. Didn't that start this whole affair that day in Angel's Rest nursing home?"

Getting into a kneeling position, pistol still aimed at Chagatai, Peter doesn't flinch, his eyes only on the NiQihs CEO.

"Peter, my dear," says Bev. "You're aiming at the wrong person. You should kill the daughter of the man who killed your father. Not the man who will save us all."

"What are you talking about, Bev?" asks Peter, as Rachel's shoulders tense. "My father killed himself."

"Tell him, Professor," says Beverly. "Tell him what your father told you. About how he arranged for depression-causing drugs to be put into Peter's father's coffee at work every day. About how he helped his father get that gun."

Rachel turns around shaking, her eyelids quivering. "Peter, I tried to tell you, but I couldn't. It was the madness of the family syndicate paying back my Ariella's debt."

"Tell him, Professor, about how complicity is an inherited gene," says the doctor. "And how you originally wanted information from me on how to kill Peter because of his inherited complicity."

Her eyes watery, the whites now reddened, looking at her own gun hand shaking as Peter's hands no longer shake, his face reddened like her eyes, his machine pistol aim toggling back and forth between her and the NiQihs CEO, Rachel pleads, "You have to believe me. I don't believe in vengeance or inherited complicity. You taught me that."

As a buzz from the east interrupts, Peter puffs up his cheeks like a puffer fish. His eyes narrowed, his forehead furrowed, he lets out a long breath through his nose as Zara pleads, "No, Peter. Please do not. You will be damned as I am for all the vengeance kills I made. Pulling that trigger is not the man you are. You are greater than that."

"Trust me. Didn't I tell you? Trust me," says Peter, his eyes focused on Rachel's as well his gun at her head. "Bev, tell her how much my pappy suffered from the guilt of my father's death. My mother blamed him, and Pappy suffered so."

"Good, Peter. You're right. You're not delusional. You have a sound mind. Punish the child of the man who killed your father," says Beverly.

Overhead, that buzz becomes visible. Helicopters.

Chagatai grins and says, "Did you think I would not have backup troops? Drop the gun now."

"Peter, please. Don't listen to him. We need to get Zara's mother into the real cavern," pleads Rachel as she drops the Jericho. "I will do anything you ask. Anything."

"Kneel in front of me like you did with Lemuel," says Peter, waving the gun as the helicopters land. "And lick my boots clean."

"Peter?" cries Zara.

"Zara?" Peter mimics. "Didn't I say trust me?"

Kneeling in front of the once-meek editor from California, Rachel looks up at him before putting her head down to his boots, her lips to the dirty, dusty leather. He kicks her head to the black object fragment lying at his feet. Putting the muzzle of the gun atop her head, he says, "Cry for your life. Cry like Zara did."

As Rachel cries over the black fragment, Beverly says, "I didn't think you had it in you to be so mean and despicable. You really have grown."

"Peter," cries out Zara. "You have gone mad. We need to get back on script."

Peter nods as the darkened clouds form above the mountaintop. "Tears from heaven. That's the new script, Zara. Rachel needs you to pray with her. Like Harran. Home of Ibrāhīm. Where you saved Jean-Paul last time. Trust me."

A pause at first, then she nods. Rolling the other black object next to theirs, her tears mingling with Rachel's, she closes her eyes and prays.

The clouds come fast. Not white fluffy happy ones either, but dark ominous angry ones. The air becomes eerily quiet as Rachel and Zara pray with the fragments of the dark, ominous black object.

The heavens spill their tears. For the crimes being committed below. For the invasion of the sanctity of the innocent, of the women who guard the cavern, of the women below whose faiths have been challenged.

As the angry tears from heaven pelt Lemuel's eyes, so brutally, he cannot see anymore. As his men also cover their eyes, Mei and Jean-Paul gather the three priests to huddle with Zara and Peter.

The raindrops as big as bullets begin to beat upon them. Even the first NiQihs commandos reaching the scene to save their CEO scream as the blistering pain of the watery onslaught pummels anywhere not armored on their bodies.

One arm up shielding his eyes, Lemuel grabs one of the commandos' pistols and points it at Zara. Barely able to speak as the rain bullets tear at his lips, he utters, "False prophet, you, the Al-Masih ad-Dajjal, the false messiah, the Antichrist, stand up and face your death."

Her eyes fully dark, Zara the destroyer stands with finger pointed at Lemuel as if to fire a lightning bolt at him.

Rachel screams, "No, Zara. It's not supposed to happen this way."

Undeterred, Zara takes a slow but assured step towards the man with the gun, her finger still pointed at him.

As day has already turned to night, Rachel's eyes, barely open, stare into the sky as the wet bullets fall around her. She screams, "As did plead the high priestess of Asherah of the First Temple, I plead with you, Asherah. Save us from unbelievers. Smote, not smoked."

Lemuel, barely able to see, barely able to hold the pistol aimed in the direction of Zara, says, "Die, ad-Dajjal." His finger pulls the trigger.

"No," screams Peter, as he tries to pull Zara down.

Bang.

And then it comes. Flash. Boom. Over and over again. Smite. Smote. Then smoke.

At Zara's feet lies Peter. She kneels, takes his hand, looks to the heavens, and cries, "It was me you were supposed to take. Not an innocent like him."

PART III

—Rabi'a al-Adawiyya, eighth-century Persian philosopher and mystic

CHAPTER 51

Life and death are one thread, the same line viewed from different sides.
—Lao Tzu, sixth-century founder of Taoism

South Balaklava, Crimea
2:30 p.m. March 8, 2023

And the torrid rain stops as abruptly as it started.

But the skies are now a warm azure blue. The clouds puffy white happy ones. Yet the wet drops still pellet Peter's body. Salten sad ones.

When the booms and flashes stop, only one is left standing. Lemuel. Still holding the pistol that pummeled Peter's poor chest.

As Zara wails with the intensity of an entire city mourning a revered mufti's death, Rachel glares at Lemuel as she covers Zara's body from his next shot. She yells, "Asherah, I asked, I prayed, I begged. Smite all nonbelievers."

"You weak, foolish professor," says Lemuel. "I am as religious as you. Maybe even more. No god of righteousness would smite me."

As Jean-Paul rolls to get a weapon, Lemuel re-aims his pistol at the priest—giving Rachel enough time to grab Peter's machine pistol and do what she prayed she never would have to.

A dozen and a half bangs later, her finger still holds the trigger down. The magazine is empty, but the steel gun hammer keeps clicking away. Her body is in tremors, her teeth chattering as if she were naked in the North Pole. Cold is that steel.

Her dearest priest comes to her to warm her body. She utters, "Oh, Asherah. Please, I beg of you. Please forgive me."

As if rising from the dead, a still-quivering and shivering Rachel is comforted by Jean-Paul's arms. She looks around. Smoke rises from the charred bodies all around. Those sections in the Torah where Yahweh struck down with lightning those of evil have a whole new meaning for her. It was all true. The authors of the Torah did not exaggerate.

Everyone rises but Zara, who holds her mother's cold hand in one and Peter's in another, crying as much as she can, hoping that miracles can happen to her family as much as they have happened to others.

Kneeling with Zara, with head bowed, Rachel says, "Asherah. You are her embodiment. I read about what you did in the scriptures. Forgive me, I lost faith that you were real. As everything went south here, I began to think you were a charade, no more than ancient, disempowered women's myth of hope."

"No, I am not Her, nor do I touch Her," says Zara. "I touch a dark god. One with rage, hate, anger, and the ability to strike down humans. I am the charade. My life has been a charade. I am no more than the daughter of a giant. A monster's daughter. My mother lies here near death, my biological father dead, and now, the only man I truly loved is dead."

Both Zara and Rachel cry over the innocent editor's lifeless body, four hands rubbing their fallen tears in vain into his skin, praying for one more miracle.

Jean-Paul returns, affirming the NiQihs commandos and their leaders are but smoldering ash heaps as he continues to tap on his MoxWrap.

Another buzz in the air gets louder. Zara cringes. For Kurds, that buzz means helicopters coming to kill them.

But helicopters they are not—only a sole MoxHeliJet. And from the nearby clearing where it lands, a booming voice. Only one man—or is that a giant?—could make that sound.

Leading the MoxMedical team is a ghost. Or so Zara, in her depleted condition, surmises. She killed him by strapping him to that chair on his yacht when that traitorous doctor and Zengo took them.

She must be delirious, or this is another hoax. "Please. No more holograms," she cries. "No more games. Nothing will bring the dead back. Nothing will absolve me of their deaths."

But this hologram has warmth as her Sasha puts his arm around her. "You have done as well as I could ever hope a daughter could do."

Her fingers claw into his arm, drawing blood. And her tears come anew into his arm, mixing with his blood. For his blood is her blood.

He wipes her tears as she says, "I thought I lost you. I lost Roza. I lost my mother. I lost Peter."

"Not yet for Maryam and Peter," he says. "But we must get them both to the caverns."

Overhead, a buzz of a different sort. Missiles.

"No. No. They cannot have," utters Zara.

"That bastard Chagatai must have signaled for the Chinese to make first-strike attacks against the Russians and Americans," says Alexander as he hurries his daughter to the MoxHeliJet.

"We have but twenty minutes before a full retaliatory nuclear response occurs," he says, boarding the HeliJet. "Such nonsense, this First Emperor business. That Chagatai only wanted to use NiQih's resources to restore his forefather's Mongol Empire. A completely nuked China is just fine for his plan. Let's hurry before we get nuked."

Jean-Paul gives clean-up instructions to the MoxSecurity team and his fellow priests. He takes both object fragments in a sack and follows Mei, Zara, Rachel, Peri, the lambs, Magali, and the medical team carrying Maryam and Peter into the MoxHeliJet.

Once seated inside, his monstrous arm around her again, Alexander says, "I made a few mistakes I need to be apologetic for. I underestimated the resolve of that doctor to follow a dead emperor. She was my double agent plant in their organization. But she turned on me in the end. Perhaps the promise of eternal life was too much for her to resist," he says. "I had to let you play out your anger and set up NiQihs double agents to expose themselves. The plan worked so well that even their two-faced CEO exposed himself."

He touches Maryam's hand, "But the price for mortally wounding NiQihs was too high. But now I must make amends to you, my daughter."

His massive hand now on Peter's, he says, "And my greatest gratitude to poor Peter. A man worthy enough of being my son. He followed my directions too perfectly. I didn't mean for him to die. In all secrecy, he mobilized my hostage rescue team, helped fake my death, even with those body parts he had my MoxBioRegeneration team create. He was worthy of being your husband."

"Please, Sasha. Let me heal him," gurgles Zara through a drowning throat. "If I can make only one more miracle happen, it would be his resurrection. I would trade my life for his."

The giant man leans over and takes Maryam's hand in his. "Her hand is growing colder, but she is still alive. You must lead us into the cavern of the blue light so we can save her. You must save yourself for the living."

Her eyes clouded, as is her judgment, Zara takes her mother's hand, which is even colder than before. If you could only save one life, would it be your mother or your husband-to-be? Would Xwedê forgive her transgressions and save both in exchange for hers? Oh, how right Peter was. The voice misled her into this valley of death.

The giant arms around her again, Sasha says, "I know you want to save everyone. The entire world if you could. For reasons neither my science nor my tech can explain, you have miraculously healed others. But you must ask yourself if your tears have brought anyone back to return to their life from the realm of death?"

Her eyes close. She squishes them down as hard as she can as her sinuses spill their flood upon her lips. Waiting for a miracle, for words of the voice on what to do, she finally nods and takes Maryam's hand into hers.

The giant man takes the pendant stones out of Maryam's cauterized wound and turns to Rachel. "Place one black stone inside his body. Keep one as you need it to help find the real cavern entrance."

With a quizzical expression, the professor only stares at this monstrous man—the son of the man who killed her safta raba's husband. The man she worked diligently to hunt down, formed an intimate relationship with Mei to get into his inner circle, bonded with Peter to get even closer to. What a turn of events. Here she sits, taking direction from the monster himself. *Oh Asherah. Save our souls.*

At the next landing zone closer to the submarine base, Peri disembarks first with Zara's two lambs. Mei, exiting the HeliJet, pets the two lambs and says, "Go find your other mama."

Holding the two object fragments in a sack over his back, Jean-Paul stands next to Mei scanning the area with his MoxWrap. "God willing, the genetic vaccine from the fox skeletons has endowed them with the DNA memory of their ancestral matriarch."

Alexander stands near and says, "Those damn baby sheep better get it right, or the missiles coming to nuke the submarine base over that hill will irradiate all. Less than fifteen minutes, all. Let's get to it."

MoxMedical staff brings out Maryam on a narrow stretcher with Magali, who says she too may have less than fifteen minutes of life left without the support systems in the MoxHeliJet.

Rachel holds her stone pendant out, which emits a blue glow. She points in the direction the lambs have run to. Thirty meters into the forest, the lambs hover near an outcropping of rocks on the mountainside. Rachel confirms that the pendant stone's increasing glow indicates the cavern is near.

She turns to Zara and says, "Only the purest of women can enter the cavern. Only you, Mei, and Peri. How will you get both your mother and Peter in there? You know you need more help."

Zara says no to Peri going in. She is her BFF about to give birth. And if everything goes south in there, then Peri will live to tell the story. She signals for Mei to come help her carry her mother's stretcher while Sasha carries Peter's limp corpse.

Bending down to get the handles of the stretcher, Mei grabs her lower abdomen and groans. Pop. She yells, "Magali, Magali, I think my water just burst!"

As the medics and the good Sister walk the soon-to-be-in-labor Mei back to the MoxHeliJet's medical unit, Rachel puts her hand on Zara's shoulder and says, "I will help you carry your mother in."

Zara, nearing tears again, says, "No, you can't do this. Peter said you are not pregnant. I believe him that nothing happened between you two."

Grabbing the other end of the stretcher, Rachel says, "I have come this far to find Her. And if I die after I see Her, I touch Her, I hear Her, then it was a life worth living. In death, I join Ariella. Join my father. Let me perform this one last act of nobility by helping you all."

A monstrous grin, Alexander says, "Good. You and I are alike, as I will die after I enter that cavern. We will die together to save the others."

With Alexander carrying the body of his surrogate son over one shoulder and the sack of black object fragments over the other, Zara walks backwards, carrying her end of Maryam's stretcher. As they navigate twist after turn, Rachel calls out the intensity fluxes of the small blue aura stone.

They find the corridor with the giant skeletons and the bull's head carved in the wall, just as Peter's pappy's diary had described. Most important, both Zara and Rachel's eyes emit an aura matching the blue one of the little pendant stones.

Taking a long inhale, then sniffing about, Rachel says, "The air feels fresh, like coastal fog. It smells like spring. Like the onset of life. Just as my safta raba said it would."

In the floor's darkness, something moves ever so slightly. Zara leans over to see better, hoping it is not a disease-infested rat. Oh, how horrible to come this far just to be eaten by rats.

And then, she spies the glistening, the spots. They are banana slugs. Just like the ones her Peter worshipped. Just like the ones on Magali's ancient medallion. Just like the ones at the bottom of Asherah's feet on Rachel's pendant. This must be the place.

Looking at the bones of all the dozens of giants who died trying to invade this cavern, Zara asks Sasha, "How are you doing? Those giants meet their end here. I can take Maryam the rest of the way in."

Snorting with an air of defiance, Alexander asserts, "Not even a singe, so far. Nothing will stop me from getting the two people you love most to their final destination."

"*Ma ani, ez?* What I am? Only a goat? Thanks for asking me too," Rachel says with a touch of sarcasm.

Not sure if Rachel should continue either, Zara leans down to pick up her mother's body. Bad idea as she cannot carry her and the IV bag at the same time. Before she can figure out another solution, a figure comes around the bend. Royal-blue headscarf. Floor-length black dress. Face hidden.

A woman's voice says, "Nanshe. You brought back Orzu."

Turning her head to hear this woman's voice better, Zara wonders. But the robed woman goes to touch Peter's corpse.

"Nanshe, when I said you should marry my brother, I did not intend that you should get him killed," says this woman, unveiling her face and pushing her royal-est of royal-blue scarves back across her cheeks. "A brother should not abandon his sister. You were supposed to take care of him. Protect him. He was so docile he could not even kill a rabbit. But I suppose I should thank you for bringing him back, even in this condition. And how kind of you to bring the three souls who needed to return here."

Puzzled, Zara lifts her eyes to peer into this woman's eyes. Vaguely familiar, but not from this lifetime.

The mysterious woman comes over to Zara, bends down, kisses her forehead, and says, "Nanshe, I knew you would love Orzu. I did not expect you. You must have suffered so. You appear so strained."

As she puts her hands upon Zara's belly, she says, "Let me bear your pains." A blue glow from her hands to her belly and Zara lets out a long, steady sigh. The woman says, "I knew you would love Orzu and bear my niece."

At first staring at this woman, then at Sasha, she says, "But I was told that my child is not from him. He and I, we never…"

"I assure you, you bear my Orzu's child," says the woman, her hand still on Zara's belly. "As I had asked you when we were imprisoned together. I said if my big brother came to save me, you should be his wife. You should take him into your bed. Many times over each day."

Gazing closely at this woman's visage, Zara touches her cheeks. "Illyana?" she asks.

"You know me. The part of you that is Nanshe. You followed my every word, which saved you," she says.

"I'm not sure. In one way it feels so long ago," Zara says. "But your voice is so familiar."

Gently and carefully, she pulls her full-length robe open only enough for Zara to see the scar across the side of her left breast. "Do you remember when Orzu finally speared me through my heart and saved me from the tortures of the giants?"

"His nightmares," says Zara, looking back at Peter's body in Sasha's arms. "They have been all about an arrow pointed there. The one he could not shoot."

She closes her eyes as the pain of Rona's memory sweeps back through her body. "As I could not shoot my dearest cousin to save her from her tormentors."

Her black sleeve hanging from her arm, Illyana puts her hand upon Zara's head. A blue aura emanates from their contact. Illyana says, "Your pain and my brother's pain. You share more than the baby you two have created. Orzu and my mother, Thara, would be so flattered that he found a woman in your times bearing her name."

Her eyes gaze upon Peter's body as Zara reflects upon that comment, remembering Peter's voice saying her name, Illyana, over and over again.

Staring at her pendant stone in full glow, then looking at her MoxWrap, Rachel says, "I hate to break up this family reunion, but the first strike nuclear missiles are within minutes of hitting target. How do we stop the madness?"

Illyana says, "No worries, my child. One does not worry in here. For time does not matter as well here."

Alexander drops the black object fragments out of the sack and says, "I brought these. We need them to stop the war."

The robed woman glides over to Alexander, puts her hand on his arms, which carry the modern embodiment of her brother Orzu. "And Nanshe, you found yourself your own giant. One who has reformed."

She touches Alexander's arm and says, "You know what will happen when black meets its opposite? Do you truly want your black stones to do that?"

He nods.

Her black-robed arm glides over Peter's body, her hand stopping upon the hole in his chest. "Good. You did well placing the small stone into his body. You do retain the knowledge Tallia imparted to you. We must hurry to complete what you started."

Fingers around the bull's head pendant hanging from Alexander's neck, she says, "And you, the love of my great-grandniece Tallia. What did she call you? Nirra? You must return. Is that not what the calling within your soul has hauntingly said to you since your birth?"

Alexander, with the most peaceful look Zara has ever seen, says, "It is you, the sister of the patriarch."

Illyana laughs. "Only a giant would identify me in reference to a patriarch. But I love my brother, so you, giant, you honor me by carrying him. Please come with me."

Glancing down at the giant skeletons all around, Alexander says, "I am to die here, am I not?"

"You will see shortly," she says. Taking a pouch from her belt, she asks Alexander to lean down and put his tongue out. Onto that giant pink organ, she sprinkles blue dust. "Now you too can approach the chamber of the blue light."

Turning back to Zara, Illyana says, "You too had an Orzu moment. You could not kill her, your cousin, like Orzu could not kill me the first time. And as I felt in your Peter, the memory haunts you, pains you, tears you apart. Keeps you from having your own family. Your present self, you wanted to suffer the same tortures that Nanshe did. You unknowingly guided your life into that suffering. Let go of her pain."

"My mother," says Zara. "Heal her. I am not as important."

"Oh, but you are," Illyana says as she leans over to the woman on the ground, stroking Maryam's cheek. "Tallia, I told you what dangers you would re-experience if you went back into the earthly world." She touches Maryam's forehead and the blue aura arises again.

"Rise, Tallia, and be with your Nirra, who waited so patiently for you to return to him," says Illyana, helping Maryam stand up.

The legendary woman of the late Peter's nightmares takes Maryam's hand

and places it into the giant Alexander's hand. Trepidatious, Maryam glances up into Alexander's eyes. Illyana touches the two of them, holding hands, and the three emit a blue aura.

Hugging her giant, Maryam says, "Nirra, I love you. Thank you for finding me. I never thought I would see you again."

"Tallia, you left me with Raqli to heal me," says an enchanted Alexander. "I never thought we would meet again. I tried to keep alive the worship of you, the mother goddess, by the villagers. As I led the other giants who wanted equal relations with human women, the freed villages began to call me El, Baal, or even Elohim and made statues of me. I tried to keep alive your teachings, the teachings of Nanshe."

He lifts her off the ground, hugging her so tightly that Zara thinks her mother will burst. "I lived all this time in angst, not knowing if you would forgive me for the heinous, horrible warrior giant actions I had to take. Not only to save your daughter Perima, but in my life among the humans trying to find you again and return here."

Once her giant puts her feet back on the ground, Maryam waves Zara over to join in a group hug. Maryam, with tears running down her cheek, says, "I would never have had Zara if what happened had not happened. In that, I cannot fault you for following your ancient self to find my ancient self."

Holding the glowing stone in her hands, Rachel comes to Illyana and says, "Are you the one my great-grandmother spoke of? Are you Asherah?"

The ancient woman touches her pendants. "I gave this to your forefather. He asked that we scorch to him to death so the monsters of his day would not try to enter here. He was willing to sacrifice his life to protect ours."

Rachel touches the woman's face in the same way she touched the face of Asherah's statue below the Second Temple. "You are her, aren't you? Asherah. I have sought to be with you all my life."

Illyana touches Rachel's forehead, eliciting the blue aura. Rachel's eyes glow intensely. Not only the edges of her irises, but her whole eyes.

"So much hatred of the man you once nursed back to health," says Illyana touching Rachel's head. "My dear Raqli, you spent your life seeking to kill the man who carries the essence of Nirra, the giant your mother sent you into this existence to heal and help spread the word of peace. How so confused you have become over time. I release you of your pains."

Orzu's sister touches Rachel's abdomen and a blue glow arises. "And you followed your mother Qualqi's instruction. You back came with child."

Rachel's jaw falls straight down, her eyes first looking into Illyana's, then to Zara, whose eyes peer down.

Illyana laughs. "Oh, Nanshe. You worry my brother strayed from your bed. He is true to you. Raqli's child comes from an origin much different from yours."

Rachel stares at Zara's belly, then her own. Her confused eyes looking into Illyana's, she asks, "How many weeks old?"

"Your daughter is four weeks and a few days old," says Illyana.

"But I was with no man then," says a perplexed Rachel, who turns to Zara. "I was up on that mountain with you. I slept with no man that night, and for a long time before."

With her serene smile, Illyana touches Rachel's forehead. "Your friend Zara, my Nanshe, blessed you with a child. Was she not in a sacred spot when you conceived?"

Still perplexed, Rachel's eyes dart from Alexander to Zara and back, seeking some answer they might give. But there is only silence as Zara takes her revived mother's hand into hers.

"Poor Raqli," says Illyana. "Your body has not touched your ancient self. No wonder you are so confused."

Both hands around Rachel's temples, Illyana says, "Close your eyes. Breathe in. And forget about the material. Forget about who you think you are. Feel the light my palms bring to your essence."

Her eyes opening again, Rachel turns to Maryam. "Tallia. I am so, so sorry. Once your Nirra had brought peace to his lands, he wanted to come back here. I tried and tried, but I could not find our way back. Lost to the ages we became."

The Israeli professor takes a moment to sort through her head, then says, "Zara, my great-grandmother told her ancient legend to me. *One day Nearat and her daughter would return. Humanity would wane and wobble, and the woman would save humanity, bringing peace from the blue light. But to return, one must overcome one's fear of death. Two women will fight so that one will die. For only in the death of life as one knows it can one be in the light. Until then, Inanna awaits.* Zara, that is happening to us now."

As Zara stops pondering all that has been happening, the words "one will die" echo as "one must die." Maryam's slumping and groaning in pain interrupts her mortality moment. Zara runs to catch her mother, asking, "But, Illyana, you cured her. Why is this happening?"

"I perform no miracles. I let their essence come forth. But her body is dying, as will Nirra's. We must proceed deeper, to the chamber of the blue light."

They follow Illyana, who has Alexander in one hand and Maryam in the other. As they pass an engraving of the tail of the bird constellation on the wall, Zara pulls up alongside Rachel. "What was that again? Two women will fight so one must die? Only one of us is leaving here is what I saw this other woman tell Tallia in a dream," says Zara. "Remember when we bonded, we were in the exact spot where you shot Alexander, then me."

"Why is it you have such a death wish? Neither of us has a gun here. Those are only aberrations of the perverse the world outside that we have left," says the renewed professor.

"No, that is not what I am saying. It has always been my destiny to come here to die to save the world outside," says Zara.

"Oh, get off that platform, you crazy Kurd," says Rachel. "You heard that wacked-out NiQihs doctor. Forces greater than the two of us have deluded you."

"Who is it I am supposed to be?" asks Zara.

"Nanshe. Someone that woman thinks she trained," says Rachel. "Someone she told to go bed her brother."

"That's my point. My ancient self is the next oldest in here. All of you are younger generations. I will need to stay here so you can leave."

"And what about your father and mother?" asks Rachel.

"You heard what she said. Their bodies are dying," says Zara. "They are not leaving either."

"And Peter?" asks Rachel.

"My point exactly. No matter what I said earlier, if I am to stay, or I am to die, my body is to die, then I want to be with my mother and Peter."

The two women of a destiny to be fulfilled follow Illyana, Maryam, and Alexander, still carrying Peter's body through sandstone tunnels to passageways made of mammoth-sized stones. Certainly made by those giants she has seen in Peter's nightmares, surmises Zara. They finally arrive in a large antechamber. At the rear is a doorway to something glowing very intensely blue.

She turns around to face Zara and Rachel. "It is time. Your Alexander and Maryam must say their goodbyes."

"But where must they go?" asks Zara.

"To where is next," she says.

"To the blue light chamber, Zara," says Rachel.

Alexander tries to peek into the chamber but out walks an elder woman in a beige, floor-length, flowing gown, her head covered with a pure white scarf.

"You remember me?" she asks of Rachel.

Illyana says, "May I introduce you all to Qualqi. She saved me. After Orzu had saved you, Nanshe, the giants let the other women slaves take my body to this sanctuary. She has been here as far back as time is known. At least on this earth."

Rachel interjects, "Are you her? Are you Asherah? You must be."

"She is who you want her to be," says Illyana. "But she is the first mother of us all."

At first, pausing, mouth agape, Rachel's eyes glow more intensely as she slowly approaches the elder woman and hugs her. "Mother. I tried to do as you asked."

Patting Rachel on the back, the woman says, "I know, my child. I am only pleased that you found a way to come home this time."

Pondering, gazing around the cavern, Zara comes up to Qualqi and says, "Then it has been you I have been talking with. You are the voice."

"I am not who has been teaching you throughout time," says Qualqi.

Zara turns to Illyana, her face quizzical, her eyes examining her.

Qualqi smiles and asks, "And my young Zara, do you truly believe that my dear Illyana is your dark god?"

"I do not know. Who is Xwedê? Who is Allah? Who is our God?" asks a bewildered Zara.

Again, Rachel says to the elder woman, "You are Asherah. You must be."

"As Illyana said, I am who you want me to be," says the old Qualqi, touching Rachel's head. A blue aura emanates. She adds, "Your unerring desire to know Asherah is what drove your life's decisions. All so that you would one day return home, my child."

"So, you are the voice," says Zara to Illyana.

"My dearest Nanshe," says Illyana. "As I did when I was assigned to tutor you in the corrupt wanton ways of the giants, I have in my second life tried to tutor you in things much less material, much less earthly corrupt."

"But then I have not been talking with Xwedê. He is a He and not a woman," laments Zara.

"As Qualqi said, I am who you want me to be," says Illyana.

"I do not understand. None of this is in the Torah, the Bible, or the Qur'an," says Zara.

The professor in Rachel comes forth and says, "No male scripture author would want women to know any of this lest they become too powerful."

A smile the only answer to Zara's conundrum, Qualqi's elder hand points to the chamber of the blue light. "It is time for your earthly parents to join with the light. Is that not what your great-grandmother Sara taught you?"

The face of Maryam beckons her to come. Zara hugs her. "We did not have enough time together since the truth between us came out. I feel I truly do not know my mother."

"You know me. You always have," says Maryam. "But as Sara taught me, I have arrived at the blue light. It is my destiny to go into that chamber." She turns to Alexander. "With my ancient husband, I gather."

The monstrous man, the malevolent master, the maker and mentor of the woman whose face connotes loss, Alexander comes to Zara's side. "Do you understand now why I did what I did? That day at Peter's pappy's funeral, he called me evil. The evil villain who should have died. He made sure in his books that the villains had violent, vengeance-filled deaths."

At his monstrous feet lies the sack of black objects. The limp body of his surrogate son draped over his one arm. In the other, he holds Maryam's side and says, "I am to die as I walk into that room. Do you feel rewarded now that the meanest man of your times will be gone?"

Hugging the giant, Zara says, "Thank you for taking care of me. Thank you for bringing me together with Peter for the brief moments we were able to share. I could only wish our child could know their grandparents, know their father."

He lets out a monstrous laugh, then doubles over from the pain. Swallowing and regaining his composure, he says, "If you think your and Peter's genetics are special, wait till you see what your kids will do. Maybe they will come here to know their grandparents.

"Before I leave, I must tell you the final secret," says Alexander as he takes his hallmark bullhead pendant from around his neck and hangs around hers. "You are my heir. You have shown yourself fit to run my entire enterprise. Your Peter once asked me what truly powers all the Mox devices. The clever boy didn't go for the solar-powered story. He read through every file I let him have access to and couldn't see an explanation within the laws of physics that says infinite power is possible. And then the MoxMovers. He said solar-absorbing paint simply couldn't power them as my ads said. Remember, blue light. Not white light."

Watching Zara's eyes, which only well up staring into the chamber of the blue light, then at her mother, he says, "You are the opposite of Peter. You care not for the material."

With that, he wiggles his monstrous fingers at Zara, who comes to hug him. "My little Zara. You fought with me every day you knew me. Or you thought you knew me. But I did not mind. Because you were only being my daughter, only showing my temperament."

Zara reaches out to Maryam to join them. Another family hug and Zara says, "I know now that I am the daughter of a giant. As monstrous at the core as you are. I can only give a giant's most sincere thank you both for creating me, for standing by me, and for bringing me to understand Peter. If only for moments, he was the true humanity in my life."

With salten droplets now dribbling down her cheeks, she touches Peter's body. Her mother kisses her forehead and says, "The time has come. I must go into the blue light with my ancient husband. I leave knowing you have come to finally embrace what love is. And I know how your precious love for Peter has blossomed all these months. I do not know what to tell you except as you see for my ancient self—love will find a way to find you. Give it time."

"Mama, I want to go with you," cries Zara. "I cannot stay here alone. Everyone I love will be gone."

As she cries in her arms, the voice, Her voice, says, "It is not your time. The world needs you."

Zara turns to Illyana, then Rachel, then her parents, and finally Qualqi. But it is the voice of Illyana that speaks. "You are not supposed to be here. And now everyone is dead."

"You finally guided me to know what love truly is, and only for long enough to have it taken away from me," laments Zara. "What is it you want from me? What have I done to deserve such a dûjeh, a hell."

Qualqi puts her hand on her head and says, "Dear child. We are proud that you have finally come to know love. Even of yourself. You have learned to forgive Nirra, your Sasha. You forgave your mother for not telling you. Why do you not forgive the one who you should love the most? Did that one not teach you to forgive yourself?"

Closing her eyes, she remembers the beating. How she almost killed Peter that morning. How he forced her to forgive the one he loved the most. Her eyes open, she says back, "I am ready to forgive. Even myself."

"Good," replies the elder woman. "What we want of you is for you to reflect upon the ultimate question."

"What question?" a teary-eyed Zara asks.

"The one you asked of us, of yourself, moments ago," says Qualqi. "If you could have only one person to share love with, who would it be? Your father? Your other father? Your mother? Your husband-to-be?"

Drying her eyes with the back of her hand, she stares at her mother. She has missed being with Nawdar, her first father. Now her mother. They only had weeks to become truly close after Zara gave her mother the forgiveness she has sought all her life. Her mother was always there when she needed her. And Zara always there for her.

But seeing her hand in his, the giant who she only recently learned truly cared for her as well, Zara says, "I want my mother to be truly happy. In ways I do not fully understand, she is with an ancient husband. A wife should be happy with her husband that she loves."

She comes to hug both Alexander and Maryam one last time. Nirra and Tallia finally coming together forever. She tells them both how much she loves them one last time. A mistake she made with her first father. And with her Peter. What seems too short to say goodbye, she grasps Peter's stone-cold hand, his tissue becoming stiff. She takes his red sash from Maryam and ties it around her waist.

Her eyes closed, she searches within for the love she has missed the most. The love that has pulled her soul out from the darkness. His hugs, which got her through the toughest times. The warmth of the hugs of her true father. Nawdar. The hugs of the man she should have told "I love you" one more time before he died. If there is a heaven, she wants, she needs to be with him again.

"I know," says Zara. "I wish to go to the blue light to be with man I love. The man who truly loved me."

As Qualqi waves Maryam and Alexander to go into the blue light with Peter's body, she says to Zara, "I am happy for you, child. You have shown you are worthy of love."

To her dismay, her mother and father disappear with Peter, Qualqi says as she leaves with them, "In life and in what happens after, what you desire is not what you should expect. True peace comes from within."

Alone again, her fingers playing with Peter's red sash around her face. Alone—well, except for that Israeli woman, who says, "Two women will fight so that one will die. For only in the death of life as one knows it can she be in the light."

Perplexed, Zara stares at her. "How can you be so crass? I have lost everyone. I deserve to die in the light with my family."

Making a headscarf from Peter's red sash, all that is left of her Peter, she heads into the chamber from which emanates the blue light.

"Not so fast, sister," yells Rachel as she pulls Zara back. "I too lost my Ariella and my father. And it is my destiny to die to save you."

"I promised my Sara that I would go to the blue light," says Zara, her hand around Rachel's, ready to put her into a wristlock throw-down.

Swiftly breaking the wristlock, Rachel says, "And Jean-Paul also taught me that one. Besides, I promised my Ariella I would go to the blue light. Do you really want to fight to the death for who has the privilege of dying in that chamber?"

"Then we go together," says Zara, face pointed back into the source of the blue light.

"No. The world needs a leader. That is you, Zara. You are the head of MoxWorld now."

Zara says, "I am but a humble woman who seeks to be with God."

"You cannot fool me. You are the daughter of the great Alexander Murometz," retorts Rachel. "Whatever is still left of our world out there, post-apocalypse Earth needs MoxWorld to heal itself, to be rebuilt into a better place."

Her eyes are wide with irises dark as the black object fragments in the sack on the floor, her fists clenched and hardened. For if it is a fight to the death, she will win. She will die either way.

Before she can throw the first punch, a voice comes from the chamber of the blue light. "No, Nanshe. You still do not understand what I asked. You are not supposed to be here at all."

Out walks Illyana, who stands between them. "Only Raqli was supposed to return. Something became twisted with all those generations mis-repeating what we told Raqli."

She looks at Rachel, then Zara, and says, "Or somewhere, you two changed places?"

A mixed smile from Rachel as she says, "You mean, like Alexander should have picked me and not Zara."

"You mean, I was never destined to come here?" says Zara with a mixed look, not sure whether to be happy or sad.

Her arms around the tall Kurd, Illyana says, "Nanshe, I told you before to make lots and lots of children with Orzu. You are supposed to be in the earthly realm making little Orzus and Nanshes, raising your family, and teaching them to teach the ways of peace. That is your destiny. I thought I was clear in my messages to you, but you must have misunderstood me."

She turns to Rachel and asks, "And you? Why do you think you are ready to enter the blue light? You are too presumptuous."

"I—I thought I was supposed to," says Rachel quietly.

Touching her forehead, Illyana asks, "You once called Zara the Al-Masih ad-Dajjal, the false messiah, the Antichrist. As you two believe these are the end times, tell me that she is, and she will kill you so you can complete your journey."

Shivering, not because of this warm cavern but in the truth's light, the light of her Asherah, she must decide what she truly believes.

Head bowed, Rachel says, "No, she is not."

To Zara's surprise, Rachel gives her a big hug. "No, she is my friend."

"Good, Raqli. You have learned well in the earthly world," says Illyana. "I have waited long for your return. It is time for you to take my place, so I may leave. We console the souls of the lost who cry out to the heavens. In time, you will learn how to save souls like yourself."

As Rachel hesitates, the legendary Illyana takes her hand and says, "Come, child. They are waiting for you."

"They? They who?" asks Rachel.

From under her robe, Illyana puts into Rachel's hands two small black leather boxes with leather straps.

With a quick breath through her nose, Rachel says, "My aba tried to give me these back. Fool that I was, I rejected them. But this time, I accept. I get the meaning."

Opening one box, she pulls out a parchment. "And it has in my writing the original text. For there is only one unifying God."

Illyana says, "Good, child. You are ready to see your aba again."

Head bowed as well, Zara asks, "And I?"

Touching Zara's forehead, Illyana says, "What does your book say of Ibrāhīm? And of what God asked of him?"

"The Great Sacrifice, Zibhin Azeem," she says.

"And have you not done the same? As Ibrāhīm was willing to sacrifice Isaac, you were willing to sacrifice your mother and father, even your Peter, by bringing them here."

The tall Kurdish woman nods.

"These caverns have a delicate balance that we must respect. I must go. And you must leave, for your world needs you," says Illyana.

Before they leave, Zara unwraps Peter's sash from around her head and gives it to Illyana. "It should be with him. If I am to raise our child alone, then so be it."

And alone she is as the two leave, entering the blue light. She glances around, realizing she does not know how to leave. The two pendant stones would be her only guide. One is inside Peter's body, and that Rachel did not even have the courtesy to leave her the other.

She taps her MoxWrap to act as her lantern. The time. The retaliatory strike missiles and planes are only minutes to their targets. What kind of world will she face outside? Alone. That is, what type of world it will be.

As she circles and circles, repeating passageways she has been down many times over, she stops and puts her forehead against the cold sandstone wall. Her irises fully dilate, as dark as these caverns. Her feet hurt. Her head hurts. Her heart too numb to hurt.

She certainly misunderstood. The god of light. The god of dark. Rachel went on to the side of light. And she? Little Zara is left here to be cursed in dûjeh. Hell. Damned to wander aimlessly around and around in circles in the dark while the outside world perishes in radiation.

Slumped on the ground, her cheeks soaked in her dismay, she remembers what her great-grandmother said she should memorize.

Only with child could she have found Her. The blue light. The final point. The only point. The end and the beginning. And she who has been with the light knows that only another like her bearing a child can free her to be with the light. The blue light. The child of her child will one day return with a miraculous child, and the cycle continues. So is the love of our God.

She did all this faithfully. She brought back the daughter to the mother. The husband to the wife. She freed her voice to move on to the light. But where is the love of her God?

Breaking the silence, she hears a voice. But it is not Her.

"You wouldn't believe what is in there," says this fresh voice she hears. That is all she wishes to hear. Her revelation is that it is not only She who she should listen to, but a voice who is a He.

And the warmth comes back. His arms around her, lifting her up, as if heaven had brought back that man who had loved her the most, that man she wished she could have told how much she loved just one more time. She basks in his tenderness. Her eyes shine again with those lighter brown tones with that hint of blue edging.

"I know, I know," he says. "You don't want to hear about extraterrestrials. You know I'm avoiding that A-word you detest me saying."

She rises and gives the source of that voice the grandest hug she ever has given. Kissing his neck, his ears, then his lips, she says, "You can use whatever word you want. A ones, B ones, all the way to Z ones. I will love you the same."

Returning her kisses, he whispers in her ears, "Well, there were all these A ones going up and down from the source of the blue light. Your prophet Jacob dreamed it right. I've only seen one angel before in my life, but I swear those must have been angels going in and out of that chamber."

She kisses his forehead, then the tip of his nose. "You are such a dear. Calling your mother an angel. Your child is so lucky to have you as their father."

Kissing her forehead back, he says, "Zara the humble now. You are and always have been my angel. And now, I am yours."

Her hands around his cheek, then down to his shirt, she opens it up to search for the wound that killed him. Nothing. Nothing but her fully whole Peter.

"How? What happened?" she asks.

"They kicked me out," says Peter with his eyes of innocence, which soothe her heart as she peers into them.

He hugs her and then pets her belly. "What a great sister that Illyana is. Do you know what she told me when she kicked me out?"

Her cheeks soaked with a wholly different kind of tear, she says, "No. And I do not care. I will love you forever."

The kiss. The kiss she never has been open enough to give. Never been fully open to herself to receive. But their lips' embrace is her heaven.

As he gives her a bear hug in the same manner that her father Nawdar had, he says, "Illyana told me I couldn't hang out with them because I had to go hang out with you and make more babies."

Another shorter kiss and he says, "What could heaven be if not a life spent making babies with you?"

She points around. "I do not want to spoil this moment. The one that you have wanted me to have with you since we first met. But we are lost."

His smile. All that she wants for the rest of her life. His smile.

"And where is your voice, dearest Zara?" he says with that smile. "She was your guiding angel. For you, she was the voice of God."

He holds up the two blue glowing stone pendants. "Now, it is my time to guide you. As I will for the rest of your life."

A little laugh because only Peter could make her feel this way. She looks him over again. But this time she notices the black-and-red headscarf, like the one Roza gave her, and the red sash. Both tied not around him, but around a large stone. A glowing blue one.

"Peter, no, dear. Drop it. It will kill you. I cannot lose you again," she cries.

He gives her the stone pendant and says, "Nothing can kill me now. As long as I have your love, I can do anything."

Holding up the stone pendant, she gets a bearing on which way is out. "We must hurry, then. I only hope we are not too late."

"What did I say? Trust me," he says as he pulls on her tunic. "The god of light. The god of dark. Didn't you say? There's a delicate balance."

He takes the blue stone and the sack with the black object fragments. "And these stones. Different colors, but parts of the same. Different but the same. Only together as one can they save our world. Like you and I have always been destined to be."

He puts the blue stone into the sack with the black object fragments. Poofff. Zara feels it. But what?

Her eyes inquisit Peter's, but he only shrugs and says, "Cats and dogs, no?"

She hugs his arm. "Dogs and cats. The same, but different. Dogs can love cats."

Using the pendant stone to navigate their way out of the cavern, they arrive out at the tail of the bird constellation engraving, which Peter traces his finger around. He takes Zara's hand and they both pet the banana slug slithering up the wall next to the ancient symbol that guided them all here. It seems to purr with their touch. Just like the one on Peter's mountain. Smiling at Zara, he leads them into the sunlight. The world of the white light.

Magali has delivered her umpteenth baby. The joyful mother, Mei, rests in the MoxHeliJet with her baby daughter.

Peri comes up to her BFF, saying, "When my water bursts, I want Magali there. Almost painless birth she helped that woman have."

Zara can only smile with the peace of the blue light still glowing within. A face like none other ever having graced her visage for the decade and a half they have known each other.

Jean-Paul walks over with his MoxPad+. "On our last mission, you asked if I believed in miracles."

On his MoxPad+ is a radiation scan of this side of the Earth. Zara recognizes the spots where the first-strike missiles hit military targets in Russia and Europe.

"But what happened to the retaliatory strike against China?" she utters. "And the secondary retaliatory strike by the Chinese?"

"That is your miracle. I can only hope to be graced one day with what you did in that cavern. But an EM-like pulse far greater than the one created from uniting the two halves of the last black object stopped the flight of all nuclear weapons worldwide. From the MoxNews reports, all militarized airborne devices have failed. The world powers are retooling, seeking other means to deliver their nuclear payloads."

She touches him, takes his fingers to form the symbol of the cross across his chest. "I understand God better now. I no longer need to question myself, or Him or Her," she says with the face of the divine.

She turns her head, and a harder visage comes back. Zara tells the head of MoxWorld Security to prep a crate for the now hybridized blue and black stone and gives detailed instructions about what should happen to it over the next twenty-four hours. Then she and Peter visit the new mother.

"How are you doing, Mei?" says Zara as she pets the new baby girl's blanket.

"I'm so glad you and Rach 'smote' all those bad guys when you did," says Mei. "Can you imagine if my water burst when that CEO tried to shoot you?"

Staring at her baby with that look of motherly love, Mei asks, "Where's Rach?"

"She's with Asherah," says Zara. "She sends her love to you."

"So, she was right after all," says Mei. "What did Asherah say to you?"

"To go back into the world and make more babies," says Zara. Not with a frown, but with the first genuine smile in her life.

CHAPTER 52

If I get married, I want to be very married.

—Audrey Hepburn

Siirt, Anatolian Kurdish State
10:00 a.m. March 21, 2023

"Happy Newroz, Zara," exclaims Peri as she kisses her BFF's cheek.

Peri's baby bump gone bye-bye only a week and a half ago, Zara has brought to her friend's home a private celebration of Newroz, Zara's second favorite holiday. Festive blankets for their new son and a surprise package for the new mother who could not go shopping for the Kurdish New Year.

Leaving the two women alone in the bedroom, Petrus goes outside to learn about the latest in MoxSecurity from the chairperson of the board's elite squad and their associated fleet of MoxSecurity vehicles and drones. Peri opens the package to find, on top of the stack of normal-sized dresses, a ravishing royal-blue dress with white embroidery running down the sides. Of course, Michaela's metallic design elements intertwine with the embroidery elements.

"Mei tells me these dresses with her MoxWrap app will help you regain your pre-pregnancy figure," explains Zara with that bullhead pendant prominently hanging from her neck as she holds up the other dresses for her friend's approval. "And not that you need any help keeping your ex-priest's attention, but she programmed your MoxWrap with another special program."

As Peri tries on the Newroz dress, Zara holds her new baby boy as she peruses the titles of Peri's library of what to expect when you are pregnant books.

From the mal of the home, a MoxWorld Security technician calls out that everything is set.

Both Kurdish women, friends through dozens upon dozens of firefights, now prepared for the tougher and rougher job of motherhood, enter the mal, taking a seat on a sofa. Peri undoes the top of her dress, takes her baby back from Zara, and feeds her new son.

Zara says, "Moxy, run the executive team secure line conference program."

Virtual projections of Magali, Michaela, and Mei appear, the latter also breastfeeding her new daughter. After an exchange of Newroz greetings, Zara opens up the meeting. "Ladies, I cannot tell you how busy my Sasha had to be running this MoxWorld Holdings empire. I had thought of him as a perverse playboy type, ravishing women all day long on his private plane, yacht and play dens. As with many things in life, I have found out otherwise. I am not shy or too proud to say I need help. All of your help on the philosophical, ethical, moral direction of this private empire."

The women and their images around the mal all nod in agreement. Zara says, "The first order of business is you all can work from home." She turns to Peri, who is burping her son, and then to Mei, who readjusts her and Michaela's daughter's position on her nipple. "And raising families is a priority for the entire team."

Petting her daughter, Michaela says, "Excuse my naïveté. I'm certainly new at this corporate executive thing. But where are the men?"

A brisk exhale through the nostrils and Zara replies, "Many operating, security, and strategic roles are filled by men." She turns to Magali. "I talked with the Holy Pontiff yesterday. He agrees with my two recommendations. First, the Holy Pontiff appointed Father Jean-Paul as the Vatican's Head of

MoxWorld Relations. And second? Magali, do you care to share with the group?"

A little flush in the face, the former Sister, the good nurse, touches her fingers to her mouth, turns her head aside, and says, "He proposed last night."

A round of applause from her all-feminine executive colleagues, with Peri asking how he could marry given the Catholic policies. Mei gasps and asks if he revoked his vows again.

"Zara convinced the Holy Pontiff that the Cardinals' Council on Marriage had been moving too slowly and agreed a positive test would speed up the process of their policy approval," says Magali with a beaming bright face. She shows a paper band on her finger. "The Holy Pontiff's decision took even him by surprise, and he did not have time to get a ring. So, he made me a makeshift symbolic one. He is such a dear. You are my savior, Zara, my messiah. Thank you."

Nodding her reciprocal appreciation, Zara says, "Magali, I trust your opinion, your judgment. Would you take on the new role of CEO—Chief Ethics Officer of MoxWorld Holdings?"

"I accept," says Magali. "I would kiss your cheeks twice if I could."

"You can do so at the engagement party MoxWorld is hosting for you and Jean-Paul in Rome," says Zara. "Contact the head of special events to set that up at both of your convenience."

Turning to Mei, who has handed their daughter to Michaela to burp, Zara says, "I have read your dossiers, seeking to understand the expansiveness of your genetics programs. Ambitious, brilliant, and mankind-altering. Can I fault your goals? I do not know. Who I have become is in part due to your ancient-dormant-gene-enhancing vaccine program. That is why I want Magali to partner with you to evaluate the ethics of the genetic technologies your team has birthed, who should have access, and under what circumstances."

Stopping a moment to reflect, Zara continues. "Mei and Magali, I would like you two to consider prioritizing other genetic projects ahead of the ones that would alter humankind. The first one is the crop species that could grow in saltwater marshes and mixed-salinity delta waters. If these crops prove safe for human or animal consumption, we could virtually eliminate world hunger. For in abundance, there will be peace, said the great matriarch. Work with candidate nations on appropriately sized tests, with our medical teams constantly monitoring the people and animals who eat these crops. The second is the greenhouse-gas-eating conifer species. Work with candidate nations to test these in the highest-carbon-footprint cities. Perhaps we can slow or reverse global warming."

Zara smiles at Michaela rocking her daughter. "Magali and Michaela, I would like you two to start with a white paper on same-sex conception. While a great leap forward, empowering women with complete choice, what does this mean for the role of men in procreation? Are we saying men are obsolete? In my heart, my soul, I have to think men are still needed. Michaela, did that answer your question about the role of men in MoxWorld?"

Nodding in agreement, Michaela says, "My brother will be relieved that you have not obsolesced him already. What do you have in mind for Peter's role?"

With a warm glow on her face, Zara says with a downward glance, "I want him to keep doing what he has been doing."

"Oh my, the world's in real danger now," says Michaela.

Hand on her BFF's knee, Zara turns and says, "Peri, as you recover, I want you to think about security issues. How do we protect the cavern of the blue light? How do we protect our organization from NiQihs moles? Their threat is far from over, even though we have convinced the world's powers that NiQihs' frozen accounts should pay reparations."

"I can work from home?" jests Peri. "I am in. You know I am always covering your six."

Glancing down for a moment and then around the room into each woman's eyes, Zara says, "With my Peter's superb research help, I have come to understand the power of the blue glowing stones. Last week, I issued an ultimatum to the world's nuclear powers to agree to unilateral disarmament. Not a reduction. Total elimination of nuclear weapons. As you can imagine, they balked. Two days ago, following Sasha's plans, I authorized MoxDefense to activate our defense satellites, newly equipped with upgraded blue stone power systems. Each of the leading nuclear-equipped nations has witnessed examples of the power MoxWorld now yields. Total incineration of two dozen nuclear missiles in each country. Blue-lit lightning from the heavens strikes again."

With a laugh, Mei says, "Oh, Rach would be so happy to know that the bad guys still are getting smote by a woman who is here to save the world from itself."

She turns to Mei and asks, "And your talk with the president of China this morning? How did that go?"

The almond-shape-faced mom chuckles. "Now, knowing what the mission of NiQihs is, he regards any resurrection of the first emperor of China as a threat to the People's Republic. He welcomed my suggestions on how to secure Qin Shi's body in the unopened tomb in Xian."

"We can offer all the resources of MoxWorld to help," says Zara. "Did he say anything else?"

"He certainly was most furious at your demonstration of power," says Mei. "But then again, he recognizes you acted not against China alone, as all his rivals had been treated equally. He fears what the other nations will ask of China because of the first strike they made at NiQihs' persuasion, but he will come to the disarmament summit you have proposed. Ironically, he is more wary of you than he was of Alexander."

"I used to think of my Sasha as a malevolent monster, only to find he was truly benevolent," states Zara. "The world will find I am not so benevolent. Not if they insist on torturing and killing each other. I have no tolerance for political games and lies. If they try to hide their arsenals, their aircraft, their subs, their ships, then they are responsible for the lives connected with those weapons of mass destruction when I have to unleash the power of the blue and black stone."

Zara stands and walks by each woman. "The men who would write our history will speak of me as the most terrifying woman of any recorded era. So be it. Sasha did not seek for my birth to be that of a woman to be liked. If the world hates me, but they all live to have grandchildren and great-grandchildren who are healthy, safe, and fed, then so be it."

Even her BFF stares at her, all the women silent to what she has just proclaimed. Except Mei, who has changed into a formfitting metallic-design-embedded dress. "I wouldn't trade the motherhood experience for anything else, but I did miss my trimmer body dresses. Peri, you will love what these new post-maternity lines will do to restore your pre-pregnancy body tone," she says, running her hands down her recovering figure's sides.

"While you are playing world-altering magnate, don't forget about your personal life, will you?" says Mei. "I programmed your MoxWrap with a maxed-out ultra-powerful version of my 'wanted attention' app. You know, you should keep my new brother-in-law away from those estrogen-mimetic-filled plasticized Pacific fish. That is, if you want more kids like the ancient goddess said. Funny, we go through all that trouble to get you into that mysterious cavern of the blue light, and the deeply profound message you receive is get out of here and have a family."

A laugh through her nose and Zara sits back down next to Peri, her hands out to hold the newborn boy. Rocking the baby, Zara says, "Mei and Michaela, again, I am sorry I missed your engagement party. But I am glad that Peter could come out."

Handing her daughter back to Mei, Michaela laughs and says, "You missed Mei's dad giving Peter the once-over. He's so happy Mei and I have a child, but he is still hoping for a boy in the family. So, he inspected Peter like a horse buyer as his surrogate for what he hoped for new grandson might look like one day. But don't fear, I got my big bro onto the MoxJet on time and he's heading back to celebrate Newroz with you."

Life as the head of MoxWorld Holdings in the age of NiQihs has no element of the discreet. Three MoxHeliJets full of MoxWorld Security flew with her armored MoxHeliJet. She promised the Siirt airport authority she would finance an expansion of their airport.

Landing outside her old village in Duhok Province, a caravan of high-security MoxMovers meets her and the two dozen security guards. Dressed in a simple off-white Kurdish coat made by Michaela's fashion company with her trademark metallic designs intertwined with gold embroidery, a full-length dress of sheer white silk underneath, her hair intertwined with matching Michaela metallic design elements blows freely in the wind. On her ears hang the yellow banana slug earrings Mei had made for her when she first met Peter.

She puts on sunglasses her Peter gave her—oversized retro 1960s glasses exactly like the ones that star of *Breakfast at Tiffany's* wore—and scans the sky. Overhead, a fleet of anti-personnel and anti-drone drones surveys the lands. She is certain that NiQihs did not take her "smiting" their CEO too lightly.

She waves over her two lambs, who chase after her as they deplane the MoxHeliJet. Her two guides to finding the cavern of her Sara's legend. Her first two kids. She tells them to get into her MoxMover.

The caravan of MoxMovers stops a hundred meters from where her old house stood. She commissioned a new estate to be built. The building complex would encompass a recreation of her childhood home. Powered by its own blue stone chip, it would have all the latest and most powerful MoxDefense defense systems. Not even a stealth cruise missile would stand a chance of eliminating her. And Peter.

Her eyes survey the construction, the work parties, the temporary buildings. No banana slug man. She asks the on-site security head about Peter. His MoxHeliJet from Duhok airport arrived thirty minutes ago. She leans down and gives her lambs this very important instruction—in Kurdish, so they do not misunderstand: "Find Papa."

Off the fluff balls go, running up the mountain trail. The one on which her Nawdar, her childhood father, would take her on hikes. Up the mountain where she mistakenly relived first love with that fried dead fish once known as Zengo.

At a fast trot they go until they find Papa on his hands and knees, digging into the earth under the flattop rock that marked where she found the greatest peace of mind. Only several weeks ago, Rachel slept here. Did she conceive her child here? Was it really from Zara's prayers? All river waters well beyond the bridge now.

Rachel is where she was destined to be. For Rachel was the awaited messiah, not her, the new voice for the next millennia of lost souls. She laughs for the moment at her personal missive, her blindness to the situation, interpreting all the divine signs as saying she was the messiah.

Who was she really? This woman Zara has become? And the answer provided by the voice? The partner of that man digging under her rock. The mother of his child as confirmed by Mei's genetics team. Peter is the genetic and biological father of the daughter she carried.

"I assure you that you will not find banana slugs hiding under my rock," scoffs Zara. "And you dare not tell me you are digging for evidence that aliens put my rock there."

"Come over here. I have something to show you."

Her lambs spot his hands signaling to come over, and they trounce upon him with their fluff. Mugging Papa is the newest game these two love. The lambs gaze down the hole along with Zara. A meter and a half down through a layer of copper-laden rocks, the surface black and pitted from having sped through the asteroid belt between Jupiter and Mars to land on Earth.

"It must be the black object that Mongolian woman tried to return to the cavern of the blue light," says Peter. "I bet the copper ore on this mountain shielded it from even Jean-Paul's ultra-sensitive detection systems. Remember the inscriptions written in Mongolian on the wall under the Second Temple, the ones you sent to Jean-Paul?"

Zara nods.

"Mei had them translated. They were addressed to the women of the dreams who would follow her quest. *The black object of the great matriarch we have moved back to Baghdad to await one who could bring us to the cavern of the blue light. May she be with you.*"

More nods from Zara as Peter continues, "I had asked Jean-Paul to research Vatican-Mongol records concerning any female prophets or miracles. One source showed a request from the Mongols around the Black Sea for relief from a drought, which coincidentally started when the two women we saw took the object from Jerusalem. The source said a prophetess with a sacred object had been en route from Baghdad to Anatolia when the two disappeared. Somehow, the object was buried here."

Climbing out of the hole, he pours water from his backpack bottle to clean his hands, arms, and face. All clean, he gives Zara a light kiss. "Isn't this your favorite spot on the entire planet?"

She taps the flattop rock for him to sit next to her. "Yes. This is part of why I want my personal home, our home, and my regional corporate office to be located here. When the world gets too crazy, I can come up here and rediscover my own humanity."

Taking his place next to her, here on this rock as well as in her life, he says, "All your childhood you grew up meditating and praying on top of a black object and didn't know it. How special is that?"

Frowning, she takes his hands in hers and says, "Special might not be the right descriptor. What if the blue objects are the source of what is good? And these black objects are the source of what is bad? The duality of gods that Jean-Paul's ancestors believed. The Cathars? Right?"

Patting her hands and then her barely visible bump of their prune-sized unborn daughter, he says, "I've been giving that a lot of thought since meeting my ancient sister Illyana. The blue objects and these black objects fell to the earth at the same time. From her description, they came from the same falling asteroid, comet, or other extraterrestrial body. Perhaps they are two sides of the same thing? In talking with Ming, Mei's mother, the ancient Chinese religion, Taoism, also talks about the duality of existence. But instead of one being good and the other bad, think about it as Rachel would've. One god male and one god female, both representing one god but two aspects of the same one god. Yin and yang, Western style."

He kisses the bump of their child. Then strokes her rosy cheek. "The Tao of Zaro. Your duality mystified you. One moment the peaceful saint. Next the rampaging daughter of monster. That doesn't make you crazy. You are the same as the blue and black objects. Two sides of the same thing. And I love you for that."

As he uncannily can do, his words put her at peace as she relaxes her shoulders. Her hands wrap around his head to pull him closer. A light kiss on his lips and then a deeper one. "Keep doing that with me. Keeping my mind sane with your words. I love you. I love you for loving me."

Out of her pocket, she pulls out a small black case, four by four centimeters, which she places in his hands. "I had this made especially for you."

He shakes the box and says, "My engagement ring? I didn't have a chance to look for your ring."

She lightly slaps him. "No, silly. Open it up."

Gazing at her Sammy earrings, he says, "You got me a Kurdish version of a banana slug, right?" Opening the box, he says, "Oh my!"

She pulls up the gold chain holding a small piece of the black object. But one with a crucifix carved in it. She drops it over his head and adjusts it center on his chest. "This is the sign of Christ. Like him, you died and were resurrected. Brought back to save me. You are my messiah."

Putting her finger on his lips before he can reply, she says, "I want you to know that I respect your faith. I neither ask nor want you to change your faith, but only to follow what you had been taught. You have been so respectful of my faith, and I realized I had never been respectful of yours."

Pulling his head into hers, she kisses him again. Longer, warmer, and wetter this time. Her lips only a gap away from his, she says, "I respect you, Peter. I want you to know I respect you. I admire you. I love you." And the lips locking together in union continue.

His lips still glued to hers, he feels around in his backpack and out comes a scarf, which he places in her hands. At first, not wanting to break the kiss, she peers down to glance at the scarf with one eye. The most endearing gift he brought back from the chamber of the blue light. Not a replica. But the exact one she lost in London when those Islamophobic boys tried to attack her.

"Oh, that is so kind of you, Peter. I love your thoughtfulness. But I do not want to wear headscarves anymore. That is not who I am anymore. Who I want the world to see."

He starts wrapping the scarf around her head, an action her hands try to stop. "And who is being silly now? In your Siirt home I realized that in all of your pictures, since you turned nine, the age of accountability to Xwedê for your actions, you wore a headscarf. I realized that a scarf around your head is not only symbolic of the Zara I have known, but of who you were. Who you still are."

She pulls the scarf off her head and says, "Who I was. I am not a woman of Xwedê any longer. Not after what we just lived through."

"Nonsense," he says, taking the scarf back. "Just because you couldn't see what I saw in that chamber of the blue light, that shouldn't mean your faith in Xwedê has waned. Maybe after what those two ancient women said, you simply came to understand Xwedê differently than you did before. You will always be a woman of great faith. You are simply maturing in your understanding of the divine. Be it Xwedê, Allah, Yahweh, or God, I will be by your side as you rediscover your relationship with Her or Him."

As he puts the scarf around her shoulders and playfully taps her nose with one end, she says, "What would I do without you? Never stop telling me what you see in me. I am an open scripture to you. And I love that you fear not telling me the truth."

Veiling her lower face with the scarf, he says, "You are a woman of great self-respect. What you learned in that cavern is your self-respect. You are a great matriarch. Then, now, and the future."

He unveils her face and says, "You are the messiah who needs to show the world how much she respects herself and her modesty."

"I am not the messiah," says Zara, tilting her head to the side and gazing away. "Rachel had always been destined to be the messiah. She will find salvation for the world from within the blue light."

"See, that's modesty," says Peter as he wraps the scarf around her head again. "Who left that cave with a blue stone? Who ordered bits of that blue stone deployed in MoxDefense satellites? Who boldly put the ultimatum to the world's greatest powers to immediately disarm? World peace is finally at hand. And Mei showed me the agricultural genetics programs you asked to see. You will fulfill Nanshe's words and provide abundance to the world. Unlimited food and clean energy. If that isn't the work of the messiah, I can't think what would be."

Her hand rests on his, stopping him from wrapping the scarf further. With her other hand, she carefully arranges the scarf in the way Roza taught her on her ninth birthday. "I will be your messiah, Peter, if that pleases you."

He rubs her abdomen and says, "It does please me. You please me. And I will be your angel."

"This better not be something really kinky you are up to. I mean, have you been secretly wanting to do it with a woman in her hijab?" she jests.

Her eyes dilate with huge brown discs surrounded by an aura of blue. "Dogs love cats." She takes his hand and runs it down her silk dress to somewhere lower, moister, and very much warmer.

Eyebrows raised and eyes wide open, he says, "There's something we really should talk about before we get married. You know, setting expectations for a successful partnership."

"Yes, I guess we never really did talk seriously about what marriage meant," she says, rubbing her chin with her other hand. "I expect you to change diapers. Even the poopy ones."

Biting his lip, his eyes assess her eyes. "You were kidding back there in Crimea, right? I mean, about the third hour of ruckus rocking and rolling in bed and all over the place," asks a trepidatious Peter.

Her hand moving down from her chin to right on his visible bulge in his lap, she says, "Back in California, did you eat a lot of fish from the Pacific?"

"What?" says Peter, moving his thighs away from her.

Tapping away at her MoxWrap, she says, "I expect you to stop eating those Pacific fish."

As she madly taps away, Peter's face flushes, his chest too, and something lower down straining to pop out. Rapidly breathing, heart rate maxing out, he puts his hand over his lap and says, "If that's what I think it is, you're tapping it too many times. I'm about to burst."

"Maybe a couple of those taps are to tell the MoxSecurity drones to stop watching this spot," she says, rubbing his chest. "You did want me to respect my modesty, no?"

As he freezes, her hands wander everywhere she never touched him before, and she says, "I am told that this a 'wanted attention' button." She madly taps away again. "And I want no misunderstanding. I really want your attention."

And the woman who has suffered so terribly since she left her childhood mountain has her first truly true love moment with her man from the other side of the world, the other side of everything she once was.

Finally, she is very pleased with who she has become. She saved the world. She gets the guy. She is his Matriarch Messiah.

ACKNOWLEDGMENTS

Thank you for reading *The Matriarch Messiah*.

Please leave a review for this is how others can discover new and intriguing works of fiction.

Follow Maxime at https://www.bookbub.com/authors/maxime-trencavel to learn of upcoming releases.

I wrote *The Matriarch Matrix* with the follow-up story of *The Matriarch Messiah* in mind. Through the editorial process of the first book, I had to balance complete character arcs for Zara and Peter with the rest of their character journey that would happen in the second book. And as of the last chapter here, they have completed their inner and outer journey. For now....

I would like to thank my alpha readers, Elaine, Christine, and Rachel, for their input on The Matriarch Messiah's outline and the early drafts. New to this book is Kisa Whipkey, kisawhipkey.com, who went the extra light year and read *The Matriarch Matrix* before her editorial assessment, her developmental edit, and the final proofing. And coming back to make my words sing and dance in the fashion of Peter is Eliza Dee, clioediting.com, who did the copy/line edit for both books. Both these editors were kind and patient with me as a new author. Finally, I thank Ava Homa, avahoma.com, for her mentorship on Kurdish culture during the creation of *The Matriarch Matrix*. I have grown as a writer from the wisdom of all three editors.

My last book had been dedicated to my daughters, who this time have provided the inspiration for the sisterly spats between Zara and Rachel. Love between sisters is not so obvious on the surface, but is eternal.

Thank you for reading *The Matriarch Messiah*. If you have not read *The Matriarch Matrix*, please take the time to do so—an endeavor that will enrich your understanding of all the MoxWorld characters.

And if you could, please leave a review for this book. Reviews are the primary means in which new authors can be discovered. Thank you.

ABOUT THE AUTHOR

Maxime has been scribbling stories since grade school, from adventure epics to morality plays. Blessed with living in multicultural pluralistic settings and having earned degrees in science and marketing, Maxime has worked in business and sports, traveling to countries across five continents and learning about cultures, traditions, and the importance of tolerance and understanding. Maxime's second novel, *The Matriarch Messiah*, was conceived, outlined, written, and edited in different locations in Belgium, including the Turkish and Kurdish neighborhoods of Brussels, in various islands of the Caribbean, in Colombia, in Madrid, Malaga, Mallorca, Spain, London, UK, and on the two coasts of the United States.

9 780999 335062